W9-BKA-646

seveneves

Also by Neal Stephenson

Some Remarks

Reamde

Anathem

The System of the World

The Confusion

Quicksilver

Cryptonomicon

The Diamond Age

Snow Crash

Zodiac

seveneves

Neal Stephenson

WILLIAM MORROW
An Imprint of HarperCollins*Publishers*

Illustrations by Weta Workshop; copyright © by Neal Stephenson
Lead Illustrator: Christian Pearce
Creative Research: Ben Hawker and Paul Tobin

This book is a work of fiction. The characters, incidents, and dialogue are drawn from the author's imagination and are not to be construed as real. Any resemblance to actual events or persons, living or dead, is entirely coincidental.

Designed by Jamie Lynn Kerner

ISBN 978-0-06-219037-6

TO JAIME, MARIA, MARCO, AND JEFF

seveneves

Part One

The Age of the One Moon

THE MOON BLEW UP WITHOUT WARNING AND FOR NO APPARENT reason. It was waxing, only one day short of full. The time was 05:03:12 UTC. Later it would be designated A+0.0.0, or simply Zero.

An amateur astronomer in Utah was the first person on Earth to realize that something unusual was happening. Moments earlier, he had noticed a blur flourishing in the vicinity of the Reiner Gamma formation, near the moon's equator. He assumed it was a dust cloud thrown up by a meteor strike. He pulled out his phone and blogged the event, moving his stiff thumbs (for he was high on a mountain and the air was as cold as it was clear) as fast as he could to secure the claim to himself. Other astronomers would soon be pointing their telescopes at the same dust cloud—might be doing it already! But—supposing he could move his thumbs fast enough—he would be the first to point it out. The fame would be his; if the meteorite left behind a visible crater, perhaps it would even bear his name.

His name was forgotten. By the time he had gotten his phone out of his pocket, his crater no longer existed. Nor did the moon.

When he pocketed his phone and put his eye back to the eyepiece of his telescope, he let out a curse, since all he saw was a tawny blur. He must have knocked the telescope out of focus. He began to twiddle the focus knob. This didn't help.

Finally he pulled back from the telescope and looked with his naked eyes at the place where the moon was supposed to be. In that moment he ceased to be a scientist, with privileged information, and became no different from millions of other people around the Americas, gaping in awe and astonishment at the most extraordinary thing that humans had ever seen in the sky.

In movies, when a planet blows up, it turns into a fireball and ceases to exist. This is not what happened to the moon. The Agent (as people came to call the mysterious force that did it) released a very large amount of energy, to be sure, but not nearly enough to turn all the moon's substance into fire.

The most generally accepted theory was that the puff of dust observed by the Utah astronomer was caused by an impact. That the Agent, in other words, came from outside the moon, pierced its surface, burrowed deep into its center, and then released its energy. Or that it simply kept on going out the other side, depositing enough energy en route to break up the moon. Another hypothesis stated that the Agent was a device buried in the moon by aliens during primordial times, set to detonate when certain conditions were met.

In any case, the result was that, first, the moon was fractured into seven large pieces, as well as innumerable smaller ones. And second, those pieces spread apart, enough to become observable as separate objects—huge rough boulders—but not enough to continue flying apart from one another. The moon's pieces remained gravitationally bound, a cluster of giant rocks orbiting chaotically about their common center of gravity.

That point—formerly the center of the moon, but now an abstraction in space—continued to revolve around the Earth just as it had done for billions of years. So now, when the people of Earth looked up into the night sky at the place where they ought to have seen the moon, they saw instead this slowly tumbling constellation of white boulders.

Or at least that is what they saw when the dust cleared. For the first few hours, what had been the moon was just a somewhat-greater-than-moon-sized cloud, which reddened before the dawn and set in the west as the Utah astronomer looked on dumbfounded. Asia looked up all night at a moon-colored blur. Within, bright spots began to stand out as dust particles fell into the nearest heavy pieces. Europe and then America were treated to a clear view of the new state of affairs: seven giant rocks where the moon ought to have been.

BEFORE THE LEADERS OF THE SCIENTIFIC, MILITARY, AND POLITICAL worlds began using the word "Agent" to denote whatever had blown up the moon, that word's most common interpretation, at least in the minds of the general public, had been in the pulp-fiction, B-movie sense of a secret agent or an FBI agent. Persons of a more technical mind-set might have used it to mean some sort of chemical, such as a cleaning agent. The closest match for how the word would be used forever after was the sense in which it was used by fencers and martial artists. In a sword-fighting drill, where one participant is going to mount an attack and the other is to respond in some way, the attacker is known as the agent and the respondent is known as the patient. The agent acts. The patient is passive. In this case an unknown Agent acted upon the moon. The moon, along with all the humans living in the sublunary realm, was the passive recipient of that action. Much later, humans might rouse themselves to take action and be agents once again. But now and for long into the future they would be nothing more than patients.

The Seven Sisters

RUFUS MACQUARIE SAW IT ALL HAPPEN ABOVE THE BLACK RIDGELINE OF the Brooks Range in northern Alaska. Rufus operated a mine there. On clear nights he would drive his pickup truck to the top of a mountain that he and his men had spent the day hollowing out. He would take his telescope, a twelve-inch Cassegrain, out of the back of the truck and set it up on the summit and look at the stars. When he got ridiculously cold, he would retreat into the cab of his truck (he kept the engine running) and hold his hands over the heater vents until his fingers regained feeling. Then, as the rest of him warmed up, he would put those fingers to work communicating with friends, family, and strangers all over the world.

And off it.

After the moon blew up, and he convinced himself that what he was seeing was real, he fired up an app that showed the positions of various natural and man-made celestial bodies. He checked the position of the International Space Station. It happened to be swinging across the sky 260 miles above and 2,000 miles south of him.

He pulled a contraption onto his knee. He had made it in his little machine shop. It consisted of a telegraph key that looked to be about 150 years old, mounted on a contoured plastic block that strapped to his knee with hook-and-loop. He began to rattle off dots and dashes. A whip antenna was mounted to the bumper of his pickup truck, reaching for the stars.

Two hundred sixty miles above and two thousand miles south of him, the dots and dashes came out of a pair of cheap speakers zip-tied to a conduit in a crowded, can-shaped module that made up part of the International Space Station.

BOLTED TO ONE END OF THE ISS WAS THE YAM-SHAPED ASTEROID called Amalthea. In the unlikely event that it could have been brought gently to Earth and laid to rest on a soccer field, it would have stretched from one penalty box to the other and completely covered the center circle. It had floated around the sun for four and a half billion years, invisible to the naked eye and to astronomers' telescopes even though its orbit had been similar to that of the Earth. In the classification system used by astronomers, this meant that it was called an Arjuna asteroid. Because of their near-Earth orbits, Arjunas had a high probability of entering the Earth's atmosphere and slamming into inhabited places. But, by the same token, they were also relatively easy to reach and latch on to. For both those reasons, bad and good, they drew the attention of astronomers.

Amalthea had been noticed five years earlier by a swarm of telescope-wielding satellites sent out by Arjuna Expeditions, a Seattle-based company funded by tech billionaires for the express purpose of asteroid mining. It had been identified as dangerous, with a 0.01 percent probability of striking the Earth within the next hundred years, and so another swarm of satellites had been sent up to drop a bag over it and drag it into a geocentric (Earth- rather than sun-centered) orbit, which had then been gradually matched with that of the ISS.

In the meantime, the planned expansion of the ISS had plodded onward. New modules—inflatables and air-filled tin cans sent up on rockets—had been added to the space station at both ends. At the forward end—the space station's nose, if you thought of it as a vaguely bird-shaped object flying around the world—a home was prepared for Amalthea and for the asteroid mining research project that was planned to grow up around it. Meanwhile, at the aft end, a torus—a donut-shaped habitat about forty meters in diameter—was constructed and made to spin like a merry-go-round, creating a small amount of simulated gravity.

At some point during these improvements, people had stopped calling it the International Space Station, or ISS, and begun referring to the old girl as Izzy. Coincidentally or not, this moniker had become popular around the time that each of the station's two ends had come under the management of a woman. Dinah MacQuarie, the fifth child and only daughter of Rufus, was responsible for much of what went on in Izzy's forward end. Ivy Xiao had overall command of ISS and tended to operate out of the torus at its "stern."

During most of Dinah's waking hours, she was at the forward end of Izzy, in a small workspace ("my shop") where she could look out a small quartz window at Amalthea ("my girlfriend"). Amalthea was nickel and iron: heavy elements that had probably sunk to the hot center of an ancient planet long since blown apart by some primordial catastrophe. Other asteroids were made of lighter materials. In the same way that Amalthea's Earth-like orbit had made her both a dire threat and a promising candidate for exploitation, her dense metallic constitution had made her a bitch to move around the solar system, but a rewarding object of study. Some asteroids were made largely of water, which could be hoarded for consumption by humans or split into hydrogen and oxygen to fuel rockets. Others were rich in precious metals that could be returned to Earth and sold.

A lump of nickel and iron like Amalthea could be smelted into structural materials for the construction of orbiting space habitats.

Doing so on anything more than a small pilot scale would require the development of new technology. Using human miners was out of the question, since sending them up to orbit and keeping them alive was expensive. Robots were the obvious solution. Dinah had been sent up to Izzy to lay groundwork for a robot laboratory that would eventually host a staff of six. The budget wars in Washington had reduced that number to one.

Which was how she actually liked it. She had grown up in remote places, following her father, Rufus; her mother, Catherine; and her four brothers to a series of hard rock mines in places like the Brooks Range of Alaska, the Karoo Desert of South Africa, and the Pilbara of western Australia. Her accent betrayed traces of all those places. She'd been home-schooled by her parents and a series of tutors they'd flown in, none of whom had lasted more than a year. Catherine had taught her the finer points of piano playing and napkin folding, and Rufus had taught her mathematics, military history, Morse code, bush piloting, and how to blow things up, all by the age of twelve, when, by family voice vote over dinner, she had been deemed too smart and too much of a handful for life at the minehead. She had been sent off to boarding school on the East Coast of the United States. For her family—though she'd never had an inkling of it until then—was well off.

At school she had developed into a gifted soccer player and parlayed this talent into an athletic scholarship to Penn. During her sophomore year she had blown out her right ACL, terminating her serious athletic career, and turned her attention in a more serious way to the study of geology. That, plus a three-year relationship with a boy who liked to build robots, combined with her background in the mining industry, had made her into a perfect candidate for the job she had now. Working hand in glove with robot geeks on terra firma—a mixture of university researchers, freelance members of the hacker/maker community, and paid Arjuna Expeditions staff—she programmed, tested, and evaluated a menagerie of robots, ranging in size from cockroach to cocker spaniel, all adapted for the task of crawling around on the surface of Amalthea, analyzing its mineral composition, cutting bits off, and taking them to a smelter that, like everything else up here, was specially adapted to work in the environment of space. The ingots of steel that emerged from this device were barely large enough to serve as paperweights, but they were the first such things made off-world, and right now they were weighing down important papers on billionaires' desks all over Silicon Valley, worth far more as conversation pieces and status symbols than as commodities.

Rufus, a die-hard ham radio enthusiast who still communicated in Morse code with a dwindling circle of old friends all over the world, had pointed out that radio transmission between the ground and Izzy was actually rather easy, given that it was line-of-sight (at least when Izzy happened to be passing overhead) and that the distance was nothing by ham radio standards. Since Dinah lived and worked in a robot workshop, surrounded by soldering gear and electronics workbenches, it had been a simple matter for her to assemble a small transceiver following specifications provided by her dad. Zip-tied to a bulkhead, it dangled above her workstation, making a dim static hiss that was easily drowned out by the normal background roar of the space station's ventilation systems. Sometimes it would beep.

A spacewalker gazing at Dinah's end of Izzy, a few minutes after the Agent had fractured the moon, would have seen, first of all, Amalthea: a huge, gnarled twist of metal, still dusty in some places with space debris that had fallen into its evanescent gravitational field over the aeons, gleaming in others where it had been rubbed clean. Scurrying over its surface was a score of different robots, belonging to four distinct "species": one that looked like a snake, one that picked its way along like a crab, one that looked like a sort of rolling geodesic dome, and another that looked like a swarm of insects. These provided sporadic illumination from the blue and white LEDs that Dinah used to track them, from the lasers with which they scanned Amalthea's surface, and from the blinding arcs of purplish light with which they would sometimes slice into it. Izzy was then in Earth's shadow, on the night side of the planet, and so all was dark otherwise, except for white light spilling out from the little quartz window beside Dinah's workstation. This was barely large enough to frame her head. She had straw-colored hair cut short. She had never been especially appearance conscious; back at the minehead her brothers had mocked her to shame whenever she had experimented with clothes or cosmetics. When she'd been described as a tomboy in a school yearbook she had interpreted it as a sort of warning shot and had gone into a somewhat more girly phase that had run its course during her late teens and early twenties and ended when she had started to worry about being taken seriously in engineering meetings. Being on Izzy meant being on the Internet, doing everything from painstakingly scripted NASA PR interviews to candid Facebook shots posted by fellow astronauts. She had grown tired of the pouffy floating hair of zero gravity and, after a few weeks of clamping it down with baseball caps, had figured out how to make this shorter cut work for her. The haircut had spawned terabytes of Internet commentary from men, and a few women, who apparently had nothing else to do with their time.

As usual, she was focused on the screen of her computer, which was covered with lines of code governing the behavior of her robots. Most software developers had to write code, compile it into a program, and then run the program to see whether it was working as intended. Dinah wrote code, beamed it into the robots scurrying around on Amalthea's surface a few meters away, and stared out the window to see whether it was working. The ones closest to the window tended to get most of her attention, and so there was a kind of natural selection at work, in that the robots that huddled closest to their mother's cool blue-eyed gaze acquired the most intelligence, while the ones wandering around loose on the dark side never got any smarter.

At any rate her focus was either on the screen or on the robots, and so it had been for many hours. Until a string of beeps came out of the hissing speaker zip-tied to the bulkhead, and her eyes went momentarily out of focus as her brain decoded the dots and dashes into a string of letters and numbers: her father's call sign. "Not now, Pa," she muttered, with a guilty daughter's glance at the brass-and-oak telegraph key he had given her—a Victorian relic purchased at great price on eBay, during a bidding war that had placed Rufus into pitched battle against a host of science museums and interior decorators.

LOOK AT THE MOON

"Not now, Pa, I know the moon's pretty, I'm right in the middle of debugging this method . . ."

OR WHAT USED TO BE IT

"Huh?"

And then she brought her face close to the window and twisted her neck to find the moon. She saw what used to be it. And the universe changed.

HIS NAME WAS DUBOIS JEROME XAVIER HARRIS, PH.D. THE FRENCH first name came from his Louisiana ancestors on his mother's side. The Harrises were Canadian blacks whose ancestors had come up to Toronto during slavery. Jerome and Xavier were the names of saints—two of them, just to be on the safe side. The family straddled the border in the Detroit-Windsor area. Inevitably, he had been dubbed Doob by his friends at school when they had still been too young to understand that "doobie" was slang for a marijuana cigarette. The overwhelming majority of people called him Doc Dubois now, because he was on TV a lot, and that was how the talk show hosts and the network anchormen introduced him. His job on TV was to explain science to the general public and, as such, to act as a lightning rod for people who could not accept all the things that science implied about their worldview and their way of life, and who showed a kind of harebrained ingenuity in finding ways to refute it.

In academic settings, such as when he was keynoting astronomical meetings and writing papers, he was, of course, Dr. Harris.

The moon blew up while he was attending a fund-raising reception in the courtyard of the Caltech Athenaeum. At the beginning of the evening it was a fiercely cold bluish-white disk rising above the Chino Hills. Lay observers would fancy it a good night for moon watching, at least by Southern California standards, but Dr. Harris's professional eye saw a thin border of fuzz around its rim and knew that aiming a telescope at it would be pointless. At least if the objective were to do science. Public relations was another matter; operating more in his Doc Dubois persona, he occasionally organized star parties where amateur astronomers would set their telescopes up in Eaton Canyon Park and aim them at crowd-pleasing targets such as the moon, the rings of Saturn, and the moons of Jupiter. Tonight would be a fine night for that.

But that wasn't what he was doing. He was drinking good red wine with rich persons, mostly from the tech industry, and being Doc Dubois, the affable science popularizer of television and of four million Twitter followers. Doc Dubois knew how to size up his audience. He knew that self-made tech zillionaires liked to argue, that Pasadena aristocracy didn't, and that society wives liked to be lectured to, as long as the lectures were brief and funny. And he knew that his job was to charm these people, nothing more, so that they could later be handed off to professional fund-raisers.

He was going back to the bar for another glass of the pinot noir, fully in the Doc Dubois persona, slapping shoulders and bumping fists and exchanging grins, when a man gasped. Everyone looked at him. Doob was afraid that the poor guy had been struck by a stray bullet or something. He was frozen, poised on one leg, gazing up. A woman followed his gaze and screamed.

And Doob became one of perhaps a few million people around the dark half of the planet all looking up into the sky, in a state of shock so profound as to shut off the parts of the brain responsible for higher functions like talking. His first thought, given that they were in Greater Los Angeles, was that they were looking at a black projection screen that had been stealthily hoisted into the air above the neighboring property, and were seeing a Hollywood special effect thrown onto it by a concealed projector. No one had informed him that any such stunt was under way, but perhaps it was some incredibly bizarre fund-raising gambit, or part of a movie production.

When he came to his senses, he was aware that a large number of telephones were singing their little electronic songs. Including his. The birth cry of a new age.

IVY XIAO WAS IN OVERALL COMMAND OF IZZY AND SPENT ALMOST all of her time in the torus, partly because her office was there and partly because she was more susceptible to space sickness than she liked to admit. That physical separation—Ivy back in the torus, Dinah up in the forward end, close to Amalthea—was symbolic, in many people's minds, of a difference between them that didn't really exist. Other contrasts were obvious enough, beginning with the physical: Ivy was four inches taller, with long black hair that she kept under control usually by braiding it and trapping the braid under the collar of her jumpsuit. She had the build of a volleyball player. Raised in Los Angeles, the only child of high-strung parents, Ivy had SATed, science faired, and spiked her way to Annapolis, then followed that up with a Ph.D. in applied physics from Princeton. Only then had the navy demanded the years of service that she owed it in return for her tuition. After learning how to pilot helicopters, she had spent most of that time in the astronaut program, in whose ranks she had risen quickly. Unlike most astronauts, who were mission specialists—scientists or engineers carrying out specific tasks after the launch vehicle had reached orbit—Ivy, with her training as a pilot, was a flight specialist as well, meaning that she knew how to fly rockets. The days of the Space Shuttle were long over, so there was no need to joystick a winged vehicle back to a runway. But docking and maneuvering spacecraft in orbit was a good clean match for someone with the motor control of a chopper pilot and the mathematical mind of a physicist.

The pedigree was intimidating, even off-putting to people who were impressed by such things. Dinah, who wasn't, cared little one way or the other. Her informal behavior toward Ivy was interpreted by some observers as disrespectful. Two very different women in conflict with each other made for a more dramatic story than what was actually true. They were continually bemused by the efforts made by Izzy personnel, and their handlers on the ground, to heal the nonexistent rift between them. Or, what was a lot less funny, to exploit it in the pursuit of byzantine political schemes.

Four hours after the moon blew up, Dinah and Ivy and the other ten crew members of the International Space Station had a meeting in the Banana, which was what they called the longest uninterrupted section in the spinning torus. Most of the torus was chopped up into segments short enough that the brain could talk the eye into believing that the floor was flat and that gravity always pointed in the same direction. But the Banana was long enough to make it obvious that the floor was in fact curved through about fifty degrees of arc from one end to the other. "Gravity" at one end of it was aimed in a different direction from that at the other end. Accordingly, the long conference table that ran down its length was curved too. People entering into one end looked "uphill" to the opposite end, but experienced no sensation of climbing as they moved toward it. New arrivals tended to expect that anything placed elsewhere on the table would roll and slide down toward them.

The walls were pale yellow. The usual collection of malfunctioning audiovisual equipment purported to show live video streams of people on the ground, in theory enabling them to teleconference with colleagues in Houston, Baikonur, or Washington.

When the meeting began at A+0.0.4 (zero years, zero days, and four hours since the Agent had acted upon the moon), nothing was working, and so the occupants of Izzy had a few minutes to talk among themselves while Frank Casper and Jibran Haroun wiggled connectors, typed commands into computers, and rebooted everything. Relatively new arrivals to Izzy, Frank and Jibran had made the mistake of letting on that they were good at that sort of thing, so they always got saddled with it. Both of them were more comfortable with it anyway than with making chitchat.

"Primordial singularity" were the first words Dinah heard upon gliding into the room. Gravity here was only one-tenth of that on Earth, and "walking" wasn't the right word for how people moved around—it was halfway between that and flying, a sort of long, bounding gait.

The words had been spoken by Konrad Barth, a German astronomer. It was clear from how the others reacted that Ivy, who was sitting directly across the table from him, was the only other person in the Banana who had the faintest idea what he was talking about.

"And that is?" Dinah asked, since that sort of thing had become her role. Others tended to be so worshipful of Ivy, or so reluctant to show ignorance, that they wouldn't ask.

"A small black hole."

"Why 'primordial'?"

"Most black holes are formed when stars collapse," Ivy said. "But there's a theory that some of them were created shortly after the Big Bang. The universe was lumpy. Some of the lumps might have been dense enough to undergo gravitational collapse. They could form black holes that instead of weighing what a star weighs could be a lot smaller."

"How small?"

"I don't think there's a lower limit. But the point is that one of them could zip through space invisibly and punch all the way through a planet and out the other side. There used to be a theory that the Tunguska event was caused by one, but it's been disproved."

Dinah knew about that, because her dad liked to talk about it: a huge explosion in Siberia, a hundred years ago, that had knocked down millions of trees out in the middle of nowhere.

"That was a big deal," Dinah said, "but not enough to blow up the moon."

"To blow up the moon would take a bigger one, going faster," Ivy said. "Look, it's just a hypothesis."

"But it's gone now?"

"It would be long gone now. Like a bullet through an apple."

It struck Dinah as odd that they were talking about such an event so matter-of-factly. But there was no other way to address it. Emotions were not large enough to encompass such a thing. Besides, it was just a visual effect so far, like something seen in a movie with the sound turned off.

"Is it going to affect the tides?" asked Lina Ferreira. As a marine biologist, Lina would naturally be somewhat concerned about the tides. "Since those are caused by the moon's gravity?"

"And by the sun's," Ivy added with a nod and a little smile. Which was why she was in charge of Izzy and Dinah wasn't. She was willing to correct a Ph.D. marine biologist in front of a roomful of people, but she could carry it off in a way that didn't sting. "But the answer is, probably surprisingly little. The moon's mass is still all there, close to where it was before. It's just spread out a little. But the pieces still have the same collective center of gravity, still in the same orbit as the moon had before. Your tide tables will still pretty much work."

Dinah's facial expression was blank, but she was enjoying Ivy's ability to talk about science with a kind of little-nerd-girl sense of wonder even in spite of the disturbing subject matter. This was why Ivy always got the media interviews, while Dinah had to be dragged out of her den of robots and told, over and over again, to smile. The tone of voice was the giveaway; when Ivy was giving orders or reading PowerPoint slides, she went clipped and military, but when she talked about science her face opened up and her voice went into a vaguely Mandarin singsongy lilt.

"Where are you getting all this?" Dinah asked, drawing startled or disapproving glances from a few who worried that she was being too brusque with the boss. "It's only been, what, four hours?"

"There's a lot of noisy comment thread traffic, as you'd expect, and a few ad hoc email lists sort of congealing out of that," Ivy explained.

A blue screen appeared on the lightweight monitor stretched above one end of the long table, and was replaced by a NASA logo. "Okay, got it," muttered Jibran, who made a sideways bound toward a chair.

Then they were looking at the familiar environs of the ISS Flight Control Room, which was at Johnson Space Center in Houston. The director of mission operations was sitting in front of the camera stroking his iPad. He didn't seem to be aware that the camera was on. A few moments later they heard a door open off camera. The DMO, who was ex-military, stood up out of habit. He reached out and shook hands with a woman who entered from stage right: NASA's deputy administrator, the number two person in the whole org chart and a rare sight at such meetings. She was a retired astronaut named Aurelia Mackey, dressed for business in the environment of D.C., where she spent most of her time.

"Are we on?" she asked someone off camera.

"Yes," said several people in the Banana.

Aurelia looked a little startled by that. Both she and the DMO were looking a little stunned to begin with, of course.

"How are you all today?" Aurelia said, in an absolutely rote, businesslike voice, as if nothing had happened. Running on autopilot while her brain caught up with events.

"Fine," said some people in the Banana, mixed in with a few nervous chuckles.

"I'm sure you are all aware of the event."

"We have a good view of it," Dinah said. Ivy shot her a warning look.

"Of course you do," Aurelia admitted. "I would love to have an extended conversation with you all about what you have seen and what you are experiencing. But this is going to have to be brief. Robert?"

The DMO peeled his eyes off the iPad and sat forward in his chair. "We're expecting an increase in the number of rocks floating around up there." He meant loose chunks of the moon. "Not huge because most will be gravitationally bound. But some may have escaped. So other missions are suspended while you batten down the hatches. Make preparations for impacts."

Everyone in the Banana listened silently, thinking about what that would mean for them. They would tighten precautions, dividing Izzy up into separate compartments so that damage to one wouldn't suck the air from all. They would review procedures. Lina's biology experiments might take a hit. Dinah's robots would enjoy a holiday.

Aurelia spoke into the camera. "All spaceflight operations are suspended until further notice. No one is coming up and no one is going down."

Everyone in the Banana looked at Ivy.

AS SOON AS THEY GOT INTO IVY'S TINY OFFICE, WHERE SHE FELT IT was okay to let tears come into her eyes, they slipped into their Q code.

Q codes were ham radio slang. Dinah had learned them from Rufus. They were three-letter combinations, beginning with Q. To save time in Morse code transmissions, they were substituted for frequently used phrases such as "Would you like me to change to a different frequency?"

Dinah and Ivy's Q codes didn't actually begin with Q. But some of them were three-letter combinations.

Uppity Little Shitkicker was a name that had been hung on Dinah when she had first arrived at private school and, during a soccer scrimmage, intercepted a pass meant for a girl from New York.

Straight Arrow Bitch had been bestowed on Ivy at Annapolis when she had declined to take part in a drinking game during a tailgate party.

The ULS/SAB dynamic was a thing that Dinah and Ivy exploited in meetings, even having meetings-before-meetings to plan how to use it.

Good Looks Wasted had found its way to Dinah in the aftermath of her new haircut, as the result of an improbable chain of "Reply to All" mishaps. She had brought it to Ivy, breathless with excitement, and they had enshrined "GLW" in their private codebook.

"I forgot," when spoken in a breathy, little-girl voice, was a shorthand way of saying "I forgot to put on my makeup," quoted verbatim from a NASA PR flack.

SAR was from a tart exchange between Ivy and a NASA administrator who, upon reading one of her reports, had criticized her for having an "almost pathological predilection for unnecessary abbreviations." This had struck Ivy as a bit odd, given that every other word in NASA prose was an acronym. When Ivy had asked for clarification, she had been told that her abbreviations were "schoolgirlish and recondite."

Space Camp (which both Ivy and Dinah had attended as teens, though at different times) was what they called not just Izzy, but the whole subculture of NASA manned spaceflight.

"What are you going to say to the Maternal Organism?" Dinah asked, as Ivy rummaged in the back of a storage bin for her bottle of tequila.

Ivy stiffened for a moment, then pulled out the bottle and swung it toward Dinah's head like a club. Dinah didn't flinch, just watched it glide to a halt above her head. "What?"

"I can't believe that the Morg has so taken over my wedding that the first thing that comes into your mind is how *she's* going to react."

Dinah looked mildly sick.

"Don't worry about it," Ivy said, "you forgot." *To put on your makeup.*

"Sorry, baby. I was just thinking . . . you and Cal are still going to get married, and have a great life, no matter what."

"But the Morg is going to take the hit," Ivy said, nodding, as she poured tequila into a pair of small plastic cups. "Having to reschedule everything."

"Sounds like she's kind of in her element doing that, though," Dinah said. "Not to minimize it or anything."

"Totally."

"To the Morg."

"The Morg." Dinah and Ivy tapped their plastic cups together and sipped at the tequila. One of the fringe benefits that came of being in the torus was that you could drink normally instead of sucking everything through tubes. The lower gravity took some getting used to, but they were old hands at it by now.

"What's up with your family? Did you hear from Rufus?" Ivy asked.

"My father desires raw data files from Konrad's Wide-Field Infrared Observation Platform, which he has read about on the Internet, so that he can satisfy his personal curiosity about the thing that hit the moon."

"You going to Morse code those down to him?"

"His Internet is working. He has already created an empty Dropbox folder. As soon as I provide him with the files, he'll go back to his usual grousing about how his taxes are too high and the federal government needs to be scaled back to a size where he can personally stomp it to death with steel-toed boots."

• • •

WHAT ASTRONOMERS DIDN'T KNOW OUTWEIGHED, BY AN ALMOST infinite ratio, what they did. And for persons used to a more orderly system of knowledge, with everything on Wikipedia, this created a certain perception of incompetence, or at least failure to perform, on the part of the astronomical profession whenever weird things happened in the sky.

Which was every day, actually. But most of them could be seen only by astronomers and so they were able to keep them a sort of trade secret. Blatantly obvious events such as meteorite strikes caused Doc Dubois's phone to sing. The singing usually portended a series of appearances on talk shows where, among other things, he would be asked to explain why astronomers hadn't predicted this. Why hadn't they seen the meteor coming? Wasn't it just the case that they were a bunch of good-for-nothing propellerheads?

A little bit of humility seemed to go a long way, and if the pundits didn't cut him off too soon he was frequently able to work in a plea for more government support of science. For members of the general public might not care about Wolf-Rayet stars in the Quintuplet Cluster, but they definitely saw why having hot rocks fall on one's head was a good thing to avoid.

He always called it the breakup of the moon. Not the explosion. The term began to gain traction on Twitter, with hashtag #BUM. Whatever you called it, it was an infinitely bigger deal than a single meteor strike. So it seemed to demand more explanation. But there was no way to explain it, yet. Meteors were easy: space was full of rocks too small and dark to be seen through telescopes, and some of them snagged on the atmosphere and fell to ground. But the breakup of the moon could not have been caused by any normal astronomical phenomenon. So Doc Dubois—who spent most of the next week on camera—got out in front of that issue at every chance, always leading with a frank statement that neither he nor any other astronomer knew the cause. That was the pitch, straight down the middle. Then he added the spin: This is absolutely fascinating. It is, as a matter of fact, the most fascinating scientific event in human history. It looks scary and upsetting, but the fact is that no one has been killed by it, save for a few drivers who swerved off roads, or rear-ended stopped traffic, while rubbernecking.

At A+0.4.16 (four days and sixteen hours after the breakup of the moon), he had to amend "no one has been killed" when a meteorite, almost certainly a chunk of moon rock, entered the atmosphere over Peru, shattered windows along a twenty-mile track, and smashed into a farmstead, obliterating a small family.

But the message remained the same: let's look at this as a scientific phenomenon and start with what we know. His friend was a video streaming site called astronomicalbodiesformerlyknownasthemoon .com, which kept a high-resolution feed of the rubble cloud running around the clock. As soon as possible in the interview, Doc Dubois would get that up on the screen and then begin making observations about the cloud. Because making observations calmed people down. The moon had broken up into seven large pieces, which inevitably became known as the Seven Sisters, and an uncountable number of smaller ones. Gradually the big ones acquired names. Doc Dubois was responsible for many of these. He gave them descriptive names that wouldn't scare people. It wouldn't do to call them Nemesis or Thor or Grond. So instead it was Potatohead, Mr. Spinny, Acorn, Peach Pit, Scoop, Big Boy, and Kidney Bean. Doc Dubois would point those out and then draw attention to the way they moved. This was governed entirely by Newtonian mechanics. Each piece of the moon attracted every other piece more or less strongly depending on its mass and its distance. It could be simulated on a computer quite easily. The whole rubble cloud was gravitationally bound. Any shrapnel fast enough to escape had done so already. The rest was drifting around in a loose huddle of rocks. Sometimes they banged into one another. Eventually they would stick together and the moon would begin to re-form.

Or at least that was the theory until the star party that they threw in the middle of the Caltech campus at A+0.7.0, exactly one week after the event.

Normally they held the star parties up in the hills, where the seeing was better, but seeing giant rocks close to the Earth was so easy that there was no need to go to the trouble of driving up into the mountains. It would have undercut the purpose of the event, which was to get as many members of the general public as possible out in a parklike atmosphere to peer through telescopes and make observations. The Beckman Mall was lined with yellow school buses, interspersed here and there with vans from local and network television, their masts deployed so that they could relay live video downtown. Their reporters stood in pools of light, using as backdrop an open green strewn with telescopes of various types and sizes. Little seven-card decks were handed out, each card depicting a different fragment of the moon from various angles and identifying it by its name. Kids were given the assignment to identify each of the rocks through the eyepiece of a telescope, check it off on a homework sheet, and write down an observation about it. Most of the scopes, obviously, were pointed at the Seven Sisters, but one contingent was looking at a darker part of the sky with binoculars or just their naked eyes, expecting to see meteorites. By Day 7, several hundred of these had entered the atmosphere. Or at least, several hundred large enough to be noticed. Most had burned up before hitting the ground. There had been about a score of incidents in which they drew arc-light trails across the sky, illuminating the ground below with freaky bluish radiance and producing huge sonic booms. Half a dozen had struck the ground, doing greater or lesser amounts of damage. The death toll, though, was still far beneath the statistical ground clutter of shark attacks and lightning strikes.

The evening went fine. Doob, who had raised three children to adulthood, had figured out a long time ago that any event largely organized by elementary school teachers was likely to come off extremely well from a logistical and crowd-control standpoint. So he was able to relax and be Doc, autographing Seven Sisters cards for kids and occasionally slipping into Dr. Harris mode for a discussion with a fellow astronomer.

As he wandered about the place, he had three different chance encounters with the same elementary school teacher, one Ms. Hinojosa, and fell in love with her. This was unusual. He had not been in love with anyone in twelve years. He had been divorced for nine. He found it nearly as shocking in its own way as the breakup of the moon. He tried to deal with it in the same way: by making scientific observations of the phenomenon. His working hypothesis was that the breakup of the moon had made Doob young again, exfoliating layers of emotional callus from his soul and leaving a pink shiny impressionable heart just waiting to be colonized by the first appealing woman who came along.

He was talking to Amelia—for that, as it turned out, was her first name—when a buzz moved slowly over the quad, like a gentle breeze, and caused everyone to look up.

Two of the larger pieces—Scoop and Kidney Bean—were headed right for each other. It would not be the first such collision. They happened all the time. But seeing two big chunks heading right for each other with high closing velocity was unusual, and promised a good show. Doob tried to quiet an unsettled feeling in his chest, which might have been caused by what was happening with Amelia, or by the natural trepidation that any sane person would feel upon seeing two enormous pieces of rock getting ready to smash into each other directly overhead. The good news was that people were beginning to treat the evolution of the swarm as a kind of spectator sport, to see it as fascinating and fun, not terrifying.

Scoop's sharper edge slammed into the divot that gave Kidney Bean its name and split it in half. It all happened, of course, in quiet super-slow motion.

"And then there were eight!" Amelia said. Instinctively she had turned away from Doob and toward her brood of twenty-two students. "What just happened to Kidney Bean?" she was asking, in that teacherly way, scanning for upraised hands, looking for a kid to call on. "Can anyone tell me?"

The kids were silent and vaguely sick looking.

Amelia held up her Kidney Bean card and tore it in half.

Dr. Harris was walking toward his car. His phone rang, so startling him that he almost swerved into a school bus. What was wrong with him? His scalp was tingling, and he realized it was his hairs trying to stand up on his head. He checked the screen of the phone and saw that the call was from a colleague in Manchester. He declined to answer it and found himself looking at a new contact that he had been creating for Amelia: a snapshot of her face, just a silhouette in profile against a bank of TV lights, and her phone number. He tapped the Done button.

He had felt that tingling in the scalp once before, on a safari in Tanzania, and had turned around to see that he was being watched, interestedly, by a group of hyenas. The thing that had scared him hadn't been the hyenas themselves. Those, and even more dangerous animals, were all over the place. Rather, it was the sudden awareness that he had let his guard down, that he had been focusing his attention on the wrong thing while the real danger had been circling around behind him.

He had wasted a week on the fascinating scientific puzzle of "What blew up the moon?"

That had been a mistake.

Scouts

"WE NEED TO STOP ASKING OURSELVES WHAT HAPPENED AND START talking about what is going to happen," Dr. Harris said to the president of the United States, her science advisor, the chairman of the Joint Chiefs of Staff, and about half of the Cabinet.

He could see that the president didn't like that. Julia Bliss Flaherty, currently nearing the end of her first year on that job.

The chairman of the JCS was nodding, but President Flaherty was giving him a hard, squinting look, and not just because of the light coming in the window from the skies over Camp David. She thought he was up to something. Trying to shift blame. Trying to push some kind of new agenda. "Go on," she said. Then, remembering her manners, "Dr. Harris."

"Four days ago I watched Kidney Bean break in half," Doob said. "The Seven Sisters became eight. Since then, we've seen a near miss that could have fractured Mr. Spinny."

"I would almost welcome it," said the president, "if we could get rid of those ridiculous names."

"It'll happen," Doob said. "The question is, how long does Mr. Spinny have to live? And what does that tell us?" He clicked a small remote in his hand and brought up a slide on the big screen. Heads turned toward it and he felt a mild sense of relief at not being stared at anymore by the president. The slide was a montage of a snowball rolling down a hill, a fuzzy bacterial culture growing in a petri dish, a mushroom cloud, and other seemingly unrelated phenomena. "What do these all have in common? They are exponential," he said. "The word gets tossed around a lot by people who use it to mean anything that's getting big fast. But it has a specific mathematical meaning. It means any process where the more it happens, the more it happens. The population explosion. A nuclear chain reaction. A snowball rolling down a hill, whose speed of growth is pegged to how much it's grown." He clicked through another slide showing plots of exponential curves on a graph, then to an image of the moon's eight pieces. "When the moon had only one piece, the probability of a collision was zero," he said.

"Because there was nothing to collide with," Pete Starling, the president's science advisor, explained. The president nodded.

"Thank you, Dr. Starling. When you have two pieces, why then, yes, they *can* collide. The more pieces you get, the higher the chances of any two pieces banging into each other. But what happens when they bang into each other?" He clicked the control again and showed a little movie of Kidney Bean's breakup. "Well, sometimes, but not always, they break in half. Which means you have more pieces. Eight instead of seven. Nine instead of eight. And that increase in number means an increase in the odds of further collisions."

"It's an exponential," said the chairman.

"It occurred to me four days ago that it did have all the earmarks of an exponential process," Doob allowed. "And we know what happens to those."

President Flaherty had been watching him intently but she now flicked her eyes over at Pete Starling, who made a dramatic upward zooming gesture with one hand, tracing the profile of a hockey stick.

"When an exponential hits the bend in the hockey stick curve," Doob said, "the result can be indistinguishable from a detonation. Or it can look like a slow, steady increase. It all depends on the time constant, the inherent speed with which the exponential thing happens. And on how we perceive it as humans."

"So it might be nothing," said the chairman.

"It could be that a hundred years will pass before we go from eight chunks to nine chunks," Doob said, nodding at him, "but four days ago I got worried that it might be one of those things that looks more like an explosion. So my grad students and I have been crunching some numbers. Building a mathematical model of the process that we can use to get a handle on the time scale."

"And what are your results, Dr. Harris? I assume you have some, or else you wouldn't be here."

"The good news is that the Earth is one day going to have a beautiful system of rings, just like Saturn. The bad news is that it's going to be messy."

"In other words," said Pete Starling, "the chunks of the moon are going to keep banging into each other indefinitely and breaking up into smaller and smaller pieces, spreading out into a system of rings. But some rocks are going to fall on the ground and break things."

"And can you tell me, Dr. Harris, when this is going to happen? Over what period of time?" the president asked.

"We're still gathering data, tuning the model's parameters," Doob said. "So my estimates could all be off by a factor of two, maybe three. Exponentials are tricky that way. But what it looks like to me is this."

He clicked through to a new graph: a blue curve showing a slow, steady climb over time. "The time scale at the bottom is something like one to three years. During that time, the number of collisions and the number of new fragments are going to grow steadily."

"What is BFR?" asked Pete Starling. For the graph's vertical scale was labeled thus.

"Bolide Fragmentation Rate," Doob said. "The rate at which new rocks are being produced."

"Is that a standard term?" Pete wanted to know. His tone was not so much hostile as unnerved.

"No," Doob said, "I made it up. Yesterday. On the plane." He was tempted to add something like *I am allowed to coin terms* but didn't want things to get snarky this early in the meeting.

Seeing that Pete had been silenced, at least for a moment, Doob tried to get back into his rhythm. "We'll see an increasing number of meteorite impacts. Some will cause great damage. But overall, life is not going to change that much. But then"—he clicked again, and the plot bent sharply upward, turning white—"we are going to witness an event that I am calling the White Sky. It'll happen over hours, or days. The system of discrete planetoids that we can see up there now is going to grind itself up into a vast number of much smaller fragments. They are going to turn into a white cloud in the sky, and that cloud is going to spread out."

Click. The graph continued shooting upward, rocketing up into a new domain and turning red.

"A day or two after the White Sky event will begin a thing I am calling the Hard Rain. Because not all of those rocks are going to stay up there. Some of them are going to fall into the Earth's atmosphere."

He turned the projector off. This was an unusual move, but it snapped them all out of PowerPoint hypnosis and forced them to look at him. The aides in the back of the room were still thumbing their phones, but they didn't matter.

"By 'some,'" Doob said, "I mean trillions."

The room remained silent.

"It is going to be a meteorite bombardment such as the Earth has not seen since the primordial age, when the solar system was formed," Doob said. "Those fiery trails we've been seeing in the sky lately, as the meteorites come in and burn up? There will be so many of those that they will merge into a dome of fire that will set aflame anything that can see it. The entire surface of the Earth is going to be sterilized. Glaciers will boil. The only way to survive is to get away from the atmosphere. Go underground, or go into space."

"Well, obviously that is very hard news if it is true," the president said.

They all sat and thought about it silently for a period of time that might have been one minute or five.

"We will have to do both," the president said. "Go into space, and underground. Obviously the latter is easier."

"Yes."

"We can get to work building underground bunkers for . . ." and she caught herself before saying something impolitic. "For people to take refuge in."

Doob didn't say anything.

The chairman of the Joint Chiefs of Staff said, "Dr. Harris, I'm an old logistics guy. I deal in stuff. How much stuff do we need to get underground? How many sacks of potatoes and rolls of toilet paper per occupant? I guess what I'm asking is, just how long is the Hard Rain going to last?"

Doob said, "My best estimate is that it will last somewhere between five thousand and ten thousand years."

"NONE OF YOU WILL EVER STAND ON TERRA FIRMA, TOUCH YOUR loved ones, or breathe the atmosphere of your mother planet again," the president said. "That is a terrible fate. And yet it is a better fate than seven billion people trapped on the Earth's surface can hope for. The last ship home has sailed. From now on, launch vehicles will rise up into orbit, but they will not go back for ten thousand years."

The twelve men and women in the Banana sat in silence. Like the destruction of the moon itself, it was too big a thing for them to take in, too large for human emotion to get around. Dinah focused on trivia. Such as: just how damned good J.B.F.—the president—was at saying stuff like this.

"Dr. Harris," said Konrad Barth, the astronomer. "I am sorry, Madam President, but is it possible to get Dr. Harris back into the picture?"

"Of course," said Julia Bliss Flaherty, who, with some reluctance, stepped sideways, making room for the larger frame of Dr. Harris. Dinah thought that he looked shrunken and diminished compared to the famous TV scientist. Then she remembered what he had explained to them a few minutes ago, and felt uncharitable for having drawn that comparison. What must it have been like, to be the only man on Earth to know that the Earth was doomed?

"Yes, Konrad," he said.

"Doob, I'm not disagreeing with your calculations. But has this been peer reviewed? Is there a chance that there is some basic error, a misplaced decimal point, something?"

Harris had begun nodding his head halfway through Konrad's question. It was not a happy kind of nod. "Konrad," he said, "it's not just me."

"We have signals intelligence suggesting that the Chinese figured it out a day before we did," the president said, "and the British, the Indians, the French, Germans, Russians, Japanese—all of their scientists are coming to more or less the same conclusions."

"Two years?" Dinah piped up. Her voice was hoarse, broken. Everyone looked at her. "Until the White Sky?"

"People seem to be converging on that figure, yeah," Dr. Harris said. "Twenty-five months, plus or minus two."

"I know that this is a terrible shock for all of you," said the president. "But I wanted the crew of the ISS to be among the first to know about it. Because I need you. We, the people of the United States and of Earth, need you."

"For what?" Dinah asked. In no sense was she the official spokesman for Izzy's crew of twelve. That was Ivy's job. But Dinah could tell, just from looking at her, that Ivy was in no condition to speak.

"We are beginning to talk to our counterparts in other spacefaring nations about creating an ark," the president said. "A repository of the entire genetic heritage of the Earth. We have two years to build it. Two years to get as many people and as much equipment as we can into orbit. The nucleus of that ark is going to be Izzy."

Absurdly, Dinah felt a mild flicker of annoyance that J.B.F. had appropriated their informal term for the ISS. But she knew how it was. She had spent enough time with the NASA PR people to understand. Things had to be humanized, to be given cute names. All the terrified kids down there who knew they were going to die would have to watch upbeat videos about how Izzy was going to carry the legacy of the dead planet through the Hard Rain. They would take out their crayons and draw cartoon pictures of Izzy with a torus halo and a big rock on her ass and a little anthropomorphic smiley face on the side of the Zvezda Service Module.

Ivy spoke up for the first time in a while. A mere two weeks ago, the postponement of her wedding had seemed a big disappointment. But she had just been told that her fiancé—U.S. Navy commander Cal Blankenship—was a dead man walking and that she would never marry him, never touch him, never see him again except through a video link. To say nothing of everyone else she knew. She looked a little spacey. She was talking in her singsongy voice. "Madam President," she said, "I'm sure you know that there isn't much space up here to accommodate new people. I'm sure this must be a topic of discussion."

"Yes, of course," the president said. "Your job is to—"

"Pardon me, Madam President, can I take this?" Dr. Harris asked. Dinah noted the flick of the president's eyes, the look of shock on her face. The president of the United States had just been interrupted.

Shouldered out of the way. As a woman who had made her way up in the world, she probably had some raw nerve endings around that sort of thing.

But this wasn't that. It wasn't J.B.F. asking herself *did he interrupt me because I'm a woman?* They were past all of that now. This was her asking herself *did he interrupt me because the president of the United States doesn't matter anymore?*

"Is Lina there?" Dr. Harris asked. "Pan the camera around please—ah, there you are. Lina, I have read your articles about the swarming behaviors of fish in the Caribbean. Great stuff."

"I didn't know your interests extended to things underwater," said Lina Ferreira. "Thank you."

People were funny, Dinah thought. Talking like this, at a time like this.

"The videos are amazing. They all move in tight formation, until a predator comes through. Then, suddenly, a hole just opens up in the swarm and the predator sails through it and doesn't catch a single fish. A moment later they're back together again. Well, nothing's been decided yet, but—"

"You want to use swarming behavior in the ark?"

"The proposal is called the Cloud Ark," the president cut back in. "And you have it correct. Rather than putting all our eggs in one basket—"

"Eggs . . . *and sperm,*" Jibran muttered, in his Lancashire accent, so low that only Dinah picked it up.

"We will take a distributed architecture," J.B.F. said, with perhaps too careful enunciation, as if she had learned the phrase ten minutes ago. "Each of the ships that will make up the Cloud Ark will be autonomous to an extent. We will mass-produce them, I am told, and send them up just as fast as we can. They will swarm around Izzy. When it is safe to do so, they can dock together, like Tinkertoys, and people can move from one to the other freely. But when a rock approaches, fwoosh!" And she spread her fingers apart, the purple lacquered nails darting away from one another.

But what about Izzy? Dinah wondered. She thought better of asking just now.

"In order to make ready for that, there are tasks for all of you," the president said. "And that is why I asked the director to join us on this call." Meaning Scott Spalding, the director of NASA. "I'm going to turn it over to Sparky, so that he can walk you through the details. As you can imagine, I have some other concerns to look after, and so I am going to bid you goodbye at this point."

The twelve in the Banana mustered a low murmur of thanks to usher the president out of whatever conference room this transmission was coming from. Someone torqued the camera around until it was pointing at Scott Spalding. He had managed to find a blazer but he was tieless, and probably would be for the remainder of his life. As a young astronaut, Sparky had been slated for an Apollo mission that had been canceled during the budget cutbacks of the early 1970s. He had stuck with the program, getting his Ph.D. during the hiatus in manned spaceflight that followed. His run of bad luck had continued when a planned mission on Skylab was scrubbed because of the spacecraft's untimely descent into the atmosphere. His perseverance had paid off in the 1980s with a series of Shuttle missions that had turned him into a past master of the astronaut corps, equally at home fixing busted solar panels and quoting the poetry of Rainer Maria Rilke. After a couple of decades working at tech startups with varying levels of success, he'd been brought back to NASA a few years ago as part of some dimly conceived repurposing of the agency's mission. Most of the people in the Banana found him likable, if somewhat opaque, and had the general feeling that he would back them up in a pinch.

Exactly what Rilke poems Sparky thought could address the world's current predicament, it was impossible to guess. For a moment there, after the camera swung around to autofocus on his sagging and creased face, it almost seemed like some poetry might be on the tip of his tongue. Then he shook it off and found the camera's lens with his pale eyes. "Words fail me," he said, "so I am just going to concentrate on business. Ivy, you remain in charge. There's no one better. Your job is to keep things running up there, communicate with us down here, let us know what you need. If after all of that you find yourself with some free time, let me know and I'll find you a hobby." He winked.

And from there he went down the list.

Frank Casper, a Canadian electrical engineer, and Spencer Grindstaff, an American who specialized in communications and who had been doing mysterious work for intelligence agencies, were going to work on establishing the network infrastructure needed to support the activities of the Cloud Ark. Jibran, an instrumentation specialist who was always getting roped into such problems anyway, would work with them.

Fyodor Panteleimon, their grizzled space walk specialist, and Zeke Petersen, a more boyish-looking American air force pilot who also had many hours of experience in space suits, would begin preparing for the arrival of new modules that, they were assured, were being designed and built with un-NASA-like haste and would begin arriving at Izzy in less than a month. Dinah found that time estimate to be ludicrously optimistic until she remembered that essentially all the world's resources were being thrown at this.

Konrad Barth was simply asked to stay on after the meeting for a talk with Doob. It was obvious enough that he would soon be repurposing every astronomical gadget on the space station to the problem of looking for incoming rocks. This was a topic no one wanted to dwell on. If Izzy got hit by a rock of any size, it was all over. In that sense there really was no point in talking about it.

The life scientists were Lina Ferreira; Margaret Coghlan, an Australian woman studying the effects of spaceflight on the human body;

and Jun Ueda, a Japanese biophysicist running some lab experiments about the effects of cosmic rays on living tissues. Also in that general category was Marco Aldebrandi, an Italian engineer who focused on the more practical matter of running the life support systems that kept the rest of them alive. Of those four, Lina already had a special status in that she had actually done work on swarming. It wasn't that closely related to what she had been doing on the space station, but now she was going to have to dust it off and make it her life's work. Sparky gave her carte blanche to hole up in a quiet place and cram her brain with papers on that topic for a little while, getting back up to speed. Margaret and Jun were told to put their more abstract research work out the airlock and work under Marco on readying Izzy for a large expansion in population.

That covered eleven of the twelve. So far, Sparky hadn't said a word to Dinah.

Meetings had never been her strong suit. She felt like she was playing an away game whenever she sat down in a conference room. Her awareness of this got in the way and turned into a self-fulfilling prophecy. It had always been thus. The fact that the world was ending changed nothing. As Sparky kept ticking down the list, telling each person what they would be doing in the coming weeks, she kept feeling more and more the point of focus precisely because she hadn't been focused on yet. And when it became clear that she was last on Sparky's list, she had a good long while, as he talked to Margaret and Jun and Marco, to wonder what that meant. Being Dinah, her first assumption was that she was considered so important that she was being saved for last. But by the time Sparky finally spoke her name, she had arrived at a different guess as to what was happening. Her heart was already thumping and her pinkies tingling, her tongue bulky in her mouth.

"Dinah," Sparky said, "you're indispensable."

She knew exactly what this meant, in meeting-speak: they would put her out the airlock if they could.

"You have such a wide range of capabilities and we all admire your attitude so much."

Sparky hadn't said a word to anyone else about their attitude.

"Obviously, asteroid mining—which you've devoted so much of your career to—is a project with a long-term payoff. But we are in short-term mode now."

"Of course."

"I am detailing you to assist Ivy and look for ways that you can put your amazing skill set to use in supporting the activities of the others. Fyodor and Zeke can only go on so many space walks. Maybe your robots can be put to use doing things that they can't."

"As long as it involves cutting through iron, they'll be awesome," Dinah said.

"Sounds great," Sparky said, missing the sarcasm entirely. In his own mind he was finished with the conversation, tolerating a few moments' small talk before the after-meeting with Doob and Konrad.

Dinah thought better of herself than this. How could she let herself get into this frame of mind at such a time?

Because maybe there was actually a good reason for how she was feeling.

She was halfway through saying goodbye to Sparky when she pivoted back. "Hang on a sec," she said. "I respect what you said about short-term mode. I get that. But if, or when, this Cloud Ark thing works, you know what's next, right?"

Sparky was in no mood. Not so much annoyed with her as bewildered. "What's next?"

"People need a place to live. And if the surface of the Earth is going to be burned off, we're going to have to make those living places up here, out of stuff we can get our hands on. Asteroids. Of which we have a lot more now, thanks to the Agent."

Sparky put his hands over his face, exhaled, and sat motionless for about a minute. When he took his hands away, she could see he'd been weeping. "I wrote half a dozen goodbye letters to old friends and family before this meeting," he said, "and when it's over I'm going to keep working my way down the list. Maybe I'll write half of all the letters I want before their intended recipients get killed by the Hard Rain. The point being, I guess, that I am thinking like the dead man walking that I truly am. Which is wrong. I should be thinking about what you are thinking about. The future that you and a few others may look forward to if all of this other stuff works."

"You really think we're looking forward to it?"

Sparky winced. "Not in the sense of thinking that that future's going to be great but in the sense of at least thinking about it. I don't disagree with you. But what do you want me to do now?"

"Watch my back," Dinah said. "Don't let them ditch Amalthea. Don't let them cut up all of my robots for spare parts. You want me to work on other stuff for a while, fine. But when the sky turns white and the Hard Rain begins to fall, the Cloud Ark needs to have a viable program for making things out of asteroids or else there is no way people are going to stay alive up here for thousands of years."

"I have your back, Dinah," said Sparky, "for what that is worth." And his eyes strayed in the direction of the door through which the president had exited.

AT A+0, THE TWELVE-PERSON CREW OF THE INTERNATIONAL SPACE Station had included only a single Russian: Lieutenant Colonel Fyodor Antonovich Panteleimon, a fifty-five-year-old veteran of six missions and eighteen space walks, the éminence grise of the cosmonaut corps. This was unusual. In the early years, out of the ISS's usual crew of six, at least two had normally been cosmonauts. The addition of Project Amalthea and of the torus had expanded the station's maximum capacity to fourteen, and the number of Russians had typically varied between two and five.

The moon had disintegrated only two weeks before Ivy, Konrad, and Lina had been scheduled to return home, to be replaced by two more Russians and a British engineer.

Since that rocket and its crew were ready to go anyway, Roskosmos—the Russian space agency—went ahead and launched it from the Baikonur cosmodrome on A+0.17.

The Soyuz spacecraft docked at Izzy's Hub module without incident. Unlike Americans, who liked flying things by hand, the Russians had made docking into an automated process a long time ago.

The Soyuz—the workhorse, for decades, of human space launch—was a stack of three modules. At its aft end was a mechanical section containing engines, propellant tanks, photovoltaic panels, and other equipment that didn't require an atmosphere. Its forward section was a more or less spherical vessel meant to be pressurized with breathable air, and containing enough empty space for cosmonauts to move around, work, and live. In the middle was a smaller bell-shaped section containing three couches where the space-suited occupants would ride into space and later descend back to Earth cloaked in a fiery comet tail. Accommodations in that section were extremely cramped, but it didn't matter since it was only used briefly during launch and reentry; the orbital module, which was the larger sphere on the front, was where the cosmonauts spent most of their time. And on its nose was the mating contraption that enabled it to connect with the space station, or any other object suitably equipped.

Until a couple of years ago the Soyuz capsules had usually docked at the aft end of the Zvezda module, which had been the "tail" of the ISS. More recently a new module called the Hub had been attached to the Zvezda, extending the main axis of the space station "rearward," and providing the axle around which the torus revolved. In order to maintain compatibility with the ubiquitous and time-tested Soyuz, the Hub had been equipped with a suitable port and hatch.

Since the other eleven were busy with the tasks that Sparky had given them, Dinah floated "aft" down the whole length of Izzy—for her shop was attached to its "forward" end—and opened the docking hatch to greet the new arrivals. She was expecting to see a few humans floating free in the orbital module of the newly arrived Soyuz. Instead she saw the head and arm of a single cosmonaut, whom she vaguely recognized as Maxim Koshelev. He was embedded in a nearly solid mass of vitamins.

"Vitamins" was a term of art used by spaceflight geeks to mean any small, lightweight stuff of extraordinary value. Microchips, medicine, spare parts, ukuleles, biological samples, soap, and food all fell under the general heading of "vitamins." Humans, of course, were the most important vitamin of all, unless you were one of those who believed that all space exploration should be conducted by robots. Dinah had sat in many a conference where her colleagues in the asteroid mining industry had argued passionately that rockets, which were so expensive, should *only* be used to transport vitamins. Bulk materials such as metals and water should never be launched from the ground; they ought to be obtained from the billions of rocks that were wandering around in space already.

A sealed box of hypodermic syringes tumbled out and caromed off her forehead, followed by a vac-packed bag of lithium hydroxide gravel, a bottle of morphine, a reel of surface-mount capacitors, and a rubber-banded bundle of number two lead pencils, presharpened. Once Dinah had pawed those out of the way she was able to more fully take in the scene: Maxim, jammed in a narrow human-sized tunnel through a mass of vitamins that had been packed into the Soyuz until it couldn't hold any more.

Someone down in Tyuratam had had the foresight to cram in a few folded-up garbage bags. Taking the hint, Dinah peeled one of them open and used it to corral all the items that had escaped so far and were threatening to go on a random walk around Izzy. Then she began raking out more. Lots of stuff escaped, but most of it went into the bag. Maxim eased himself out into the Hub for a stretch. He'd been crammed into this thing for six hours. Dinah, who was smaller, went into the space he'd vacated and began throwing vitamins out to him; he just held up a garbage bag to catch them.

After a minute she excavated a human thigh in a blue jumpsuit, then a shoulder, then an arm. The arm moved and pushed more vitamins at her, exposing a face that Dinah recognized from having scanned her Wikipedia entry half an hour ago. This was Bolor-Erdene, a woman who had once been rejected from the cosmonaut program because she was too small to fit into any of the standard space suits. She was riding in a couch that had clearly been jury-rigged for the purpose. It was strapped to a part of the orbital module called the Divan with an improvised scheme of cargo webbing that was still dusty from the roads of Kazakhstan. Dinah wondered if it was the last dirt she would ever see, then tried to suppress that thought.

So, both Bolor-Erdene and Maxim had ridden in the orbital module, which was unprecedented; humans were supposed to ride only in the reentry module aft of it.

It would have been indiscreet to point this out, but those two, by riding up front, had signed up for a one-way journey that could have turned into a suicide mission had anything gone wrong. The orbital module was jettisoned during the reentry process, and burned up in the atmosphere. Only the passengers in the reentry module could even theoretically make it back alive.

The vitamin bagging proceeded through the hatch into the reentry module and went viral as faces and arms were freed. In the three couches, where humans were *supposed* to ride, were the two other scheduled cosmonauts, Yuri and Vyacheslav, and the Brit, who was named Rhys.

Bolor-Erdene, Yuri, and Vyacheslav took their first chance to unstrap and move up through the orbital module into the Hub. Rhys requested that he be given a moment.

Dinah went into the Hub to greet the other four. In normal times these moments were at least a little bit ceremonious, with the new arrivals being greeted with hugs, or at least high fives, as they glided through the hatch, and photographs taken. The impending deaths of everyone on Earth cast a bit of a pall over this occasion, but Dinah felt she should at least say a few words to each of them.

Bolor-Erdene urged Dinah to address her as Bo. She was obviously of Far Eastern stock, and yet there was something in her eyes and cheekbones that did not look precisely Chinese. Dinah's preliminary googling had already told her that Bo was Mongolian.

Yuri and Maxim were coming to ISS for their third and fourth times, respectively. Vyacheslav seemed to be a last-minute substitution for a younger cosmonaut who would have been making his first trip to the ISS. Vyacheslav had done two previous stints. So, all the Russians except for Bo were old hands at this, and once they had exchanged brief greetings with Dinah they glided through the middle of the Hub, looking about curiously since some of them hadn't seen it before, and then through the hatch into the Zvezda module, which was like home to them. They exchanged clipped remarks in Russian of which Dinah understood about 50 percent. Everyone who worked on Izzy had to have at least working knowledge of Russian.

Rhys Aitken was an engineer who had made a career of building strange new constructs, usually for wealthy clients. Until seventeen days ago, his mission had been to lay groundwork for the addition of a second, larger torus, built around a newer Hub aft of the existing one and intended for space tourists. This was part of a public-private partnership between NASA and Rhys's employer, a British billionaire who had been one of the early movers in the space tourism industry. Rhys had a new mission now, but he was still a perfect fit for the job.

Dinah went back through the orbital module and peered through the hatch at him, lying there patiently motionless in his couch.

"First time in space?" Dinah asked him, though she already knew the answer.

"Don't you have Google up here?" he responded. From an American it would have been simply obnoxious, but Dinah had spent enough time around Brits to take it as intended.

"You just don't seem very eager to explore your new home."

"I'm stretching it out. The process of discovery. Besides, I was warned not to move my head."

"To avoid nausea. Yeah, that's good advice," Dinah said. "But you have to move it eventually." A loose packet of cucumber seeds, stenciled in Cyrillic, floated past her head. She plucked it carefully out of the air. Finding herself in range, she stuck out her hand. "Dinah," she said.

"Rhys." He extended his hand while gazing rigidly ahead, as he'd been instructed. But in the time-honored manner of most human males, he allowed his eyeballs to swivel her way so that he could check her out, then turned his head so that he could check her out better.

"You're going to regret that," she said.

"Oh, my goodness," he exclaimed.

"You have a few minutes before it all comes up. Come on out, I'll get you a bag."

DURING ONE OF MANY RECENT SLEEPLESS "NIGHTS," DINAH HAD found herself worrying about transistors. Modern semiconductor technology had found a way to make them very small. So small that they could be destroyed by a single hit from a cosmic ray. This didn't much matter down on the ground, because the stakes were lower and cosmic rays were mostly blocked by the atmosphere. But electronics that had to work in space were a different matter. The world's military-industrial complexes had put a lot of money and brainpower into making "rad-hard" electronics, more resistant to cosmic ray strikes. The resulting chips and circuit boards were, by and large, clunkier than the sleek consumer electronics that earthbound customers had come to expect. A lot more expensive too. So much so that Dinah had avoided using them at all in her robots. She used cheap, tiny off-the-shelf electronics in the expectation that a certain number of her robots would be found dead every week. A functional robot could carry a dead one back to the little airlock between Dinah's workshop and the pitted surface of Amalthea, and Dinah could swap its fried circuit board out for a new one. Sometimes the new one would already be dead, struck by a cosmic ray while it was just sitting there in storage. But the vitamins shipped up on the ISS supply missions always had more of them.

The only shielding from cosmic rays was matter. A thick atmosphere such as Earth's would do the trick, or a much thinner bulwark of solid heavy material. Of course, Dinah happened to have one in the form of Amalthea itself. Any object nestled up against Amalthea's surface would be shielded from cosmic rays coming from roughly half of the universe—the half blocked from view by the asteroid. For the same reason, the ISS was always shielded by the Earth from any cosmic rays approaching from that direction. So there was a sweet spot, on the side of Dinah's shop that faced toward Earth but was "under" the bulk of Amalthea, where cosmic rays could only squirt in from a relatively narrow band of space. Dinah stored her spare chips and circuit boards in that general area, just to improve their odds, and she limited the amount of time that her robots spent roaming about on the side of Amalthea that faced deep space.

In clear view of her window was a hollow in Amalthea's side, perhaps an ancient impact crater, big enough to accommodate a watermelon.

On Day 9—five days before the conference in the Banana when Doc Dubois had told them about the Hard Rain and the president had told them that they were never coming home—she had programmed several of her robots—the ones with the most effective cutting heads—to begin making that hollow deeper. Perhaps she'd had a premonition of what was about to happen. Or perhaps she was just doing her job; mining robots would need to have the ability to carry out programmed activities such as boring tunnels into rock, and it was high time she began experimenting with such tasks.

But after that conference in the Banana, she had gone back to her little shop and, as an alternative to crying all night or sticking her head out the airlock, she had altered the program that those little robots were following and told them to begin bending the tunnel, curving it gently as it delved into the asteroid. Until then, the robots had been moving directly away from her and she'd been able to look through her tiny quartz window, into the watermelon-sized hollow, and straight down the tunnel that the robots were cutting. She had to flip a welding glass down over the window when she did this because they were cutting with plasma arcs whose brilliant purple light would burn her eyes. But by the time that the five new arrivals got to Izzy on A+0.17, the robots had disappeared around the bend in the tunnel that they had made. The universe could not see them. Cosmic rays ran in straight lines, like light, and they could not negotiate that bend.

Dinah had them carve a little hollow into the side of that tunnel: a storage niche. She packaged up all of her spare chips and PC boards into a bundle. It was a small one, given how tiny and powerful modern chips were—a cube small enough to hold in one hand. Normally this would have been a bad idea—a single cosmic ray might shoot through the entire stack and kill every board at once. She handed it off to an eight-legged robot and sent that robot through the airlock and down the tunnel. Seeing through the remote eye of its video camera, manipulating a data glove connected to its grappling arms, she maneuvered it into the niche and then made it splay out its arms and go rigid so that it couldn't drift out. Her transistors were now safe.

Rhys watched her do it. He had been on Izzy for five hours. He was too sick to do anything except lie very still. Dinah, whose shop was full of zip ties and clamps and other useful devices, had helped him wedge his head between a couple of pipes, padding them with foam to make it a little more comfortable. She had left him with a supply of barf bags and gone about her work.

"What do you call that type?" he asked.

"A Grabb," she answered. "Short for Grabby Crab."

"Good name, I suppose."

"It's the most obvious body type for something that's meant to pick its way around on a rock. Each leg has an electromagnet on its tip, so it can stick to Amalthea, which is mostly iron. When it wants to pick up that foot, it just switches off the magnet."

"I'm sure you've already thought of this," Rhys said delicately, "but you could hollow out the whole asteroid this way. Create a shielded environment. Maybe even fill it with air."

Dinah nodded. She was busy, placing the Grabb's eight arms one by one, making sure each of them was stuck to a wall of the niche. It would be embarrassing if all of her vitamins floated out and got lost. "We've discussed it. Me and the, like, eight thousand engineers on the ground who are working on this."

"Yes, I didn't suppose it was a solo effort."

"The constraint is working gas. The plasma cutters are very powerful, but they require some gas flow. Almost any gas will do. But industrial gases are rare and valuable up here, and they have this annoying habit of escaping into space."

"But if you were hollowing something out, as opposed to working on its surface—"

"Exactly," Dinah said. "You could seal the exits and recapture the used gas, and recycle it."

"So you're way ahead of me, in other words."

Dinah's upper face was obscured in a VR rig but a smile spread below it. "That's the thing about space," she said. "So many smart people are so interested in it that it's difficult to come up with a really new idea."

There was a pause in the conversation while she switched control to a different robot and got it moving down the tunnel.

"Moving my eyeballs oh so slightly, I see at least three other morphologies in your bestiary."

"The Siwi is adapted from a robot that was made for exploring collapsed buildings. Which in turn was obviously adapted from a snake."

"A sidewinder, presumably, given the name."

"Yeah. The electromagnets are arranged around the Siwi's body in a double helix, so by turning some on and others off, it can sort of roll diagonally along the surface with minimal power usage."

"The thing that looks like a Buckyball seems to be using a similar trick."

"You nailed the name. We do in fact call those Buckies. Technically speaking, it's a thing called a—"

"Tensegrity."

Dinah felt herself blushing. "Of course, you'd know all about those. Anyway, because it's big and roughly spherical, it can roll in any direction by playing tricks with electromagnetics and making its struts get longer or shorter. The brains live in that sort of nucleuslike package suspended in the middle."

"Grabbs, Siwis, and Buckies. What do you call the tiny ones?"

"Nats. Our attempt to build a swarm. Lina's been moonlighting on it."

There was a little gap in the conversation while both of them considered the unfortunate choice of wording.

"It's pretty experimental still," Dinah continued. "But the idea is that they can latch on to each other as needed, like ants making an ant-ball to cross a river. I know this must all seem pretty weird. It's not normal engineering."

"I'm not a normal engineer. I've been doing biomimetics—which is what you are doing—for a while. Except I build things that stand still."

"Okay. You get it then." Dinah peeled off the 3-D goggles she'd been using to see through the eyes of the Grabb. The second robot, the Siwi, had perched itself in the tunnel behind the Grabb and raised its head, cobralike, to shine light on it and shoot video. Gazing at the flat-panel screen, Dinah made the Siwi pan back and forth to inspect the Grabb's position, ensuring there was no way those circuit boards could drift away.

"Yes. I get it," Rhys said. Then he added, "It's not for me to tell you your business. But you know what hermit crabs do, don't you?"

It took Dinah a few moments to access the memory. She had never been a beach kind of person. "They use the discarded shells of other crabs as shelter."

"Not of other crabs, but of mollusks. But yes, you have it."

Dinah thought about it for a moment, then turned to look at him. He seemed slightly less green and sweaty than before. "I think I see where you are going."

"Better yet," Rhys said, "consider the foraminifera."

"What are they?"

"The biggest single-celled organisms in the world. They live beneath the Antarctic ice. And as they grow, they take grains of sand from their environment and glue them together to form hard outer skins."

"Sort of like Ben Grimm?" she asked.

It was a throwaway reference to a comic book character, the armor-plated member of the Fantastic Four. She didn't expect him to pick up on it. But he shot back: "To name another cosmic ray victim, yes. But without the alienation and self-pity."

"I always wanted skin like the Thing."

"It wouldn't suit you nearly as well as the skin God gave you. But as a way for you to protect your robots from cosmic rays, while giving them the freedom to roam around—"

"I think I'm in love," she said.

He clapped a bag over his mouth and threw up.

• • •

HOW DO YOU TELL THE WORLD THAT IT'S GOING TO DIE? DOOB WAS glad he didn't have to say it. Instead he just stood behind the president of the United States. His job was to look serious—which wasn't difficult—as part of a Mount Rushmore of eminent scientists lined up behind a semicircle of world leaders. He stared at the back of J.B.F.'s head as she explained it into a teleprompter. Bracketing her were the Chinese and the Indian presidents, saying the same things at the same time in Mandarin and Hindi. Fanning out into the wings were the prime ministers of Japan, the United Kingdom, France, and (acting as a sort of proxy for most of Latin America, as well as his own country) Spain; the chancellor of Germany; the presidents of Nigeria, Russia, and Egypt; the pope; prominent imams from the main branches of the Islamic faith; a rabbi; and a lama. The announcements were made simultaneously, so that as much of the human race as possible would hear the news at the same instant, and not have to await translations.

If the task had fallen to Dubois Jerome Xavier Harris, Ph.D., he would have said something like this: Look, everybody dies. Of the seven billion people now living on Earth, basically all will be dead a hundred years from now—most a lot sooner. No one wants to die, but most calmly accept that it's going to happen.

A person who died two years from now in the Hard Rain would be no deader than someone who died seventeen years from now in a car crash.

The only thing that had changed now was that everyone knew the approximate time and manner of their death.

And knowing that, they could make preparations. Some of those were internal: making your peace with your God. Others had to do with passing on one's legacy to the next generation.

And that was where things got interesting, because none of the traditional legacy-passing schemes was going to survive the Hard Rain. There was no point in drawing up a last will and testament, because all of your possessions were going to be destroyed along with you, and there would be no survivors to receive them.

The legacy was instead going to consist of whatever the people of the Cloud Ark did in the centuries and millennia to come. The Cloud Ark was the only thing that mattered.

They did it at Crater Lake, Oregon. The State Department had commandeered the rustic lodge perched high above the lake on the crater's rim, flown in the dignitaries, crammed the nearby campgrounds and parking lots with security and media and logistics. At this very moment, marines out on the highway were turning back disappointed holidaymakers, telling them the park was closed, letting them know that they should turn on their radios and listen to the news if they really wanted to understand why. To put the disruption of their vacations into perspective.

The weather was clear, which meant it was cold. The lake down in the crater was the purest blue Doob had ever seen, the sky above it a lighter tint of the same color. He and all the others stood with their backs to it during the announcement. Some political genius on the president's staff had figured out just how the imagery was supposed to work. The cameras were up on a scaffolding so that they could shoot downward, ensuring that the panorama of the crater, Wizard Island with its sparse covering of trees, and the snow-streaked mountain rim were all there in the high-definition backdrop of the shot. The message was there for anyone who wanted to read it. Between six and eight thousand years ago, an unimaginable catastrophe had befallen this place. The surviving humans had kept the story alive in legends of an apocalyptic struggle between the gods of the sky and of the underworld. Now, it was beautiful. The president and some of the other leaders were weaving that story into their announcements. Doob and the scientists around him—professors from great universities all over the world—couldn't hear what was being said. The leaders were projecting their words outward into the world, and the sounds coming out of their mouths were swallowed up in the rushing of the wind over rocks and through trees. Doob, four meters behind the president, watched the wind mess with her hair. J.B.F.'s hair had been much commented on during the days before Zero, when such things had actually seemed important to commentators in the world of fashion and politics. It was dusky blond, streaked with silver. She wore it straight and shoulder-length. She was forty-two years old, which made her the youngest president of the United States, edging out J.F.K. by a year. She had flirted with politics during her student years at Berkeley but then opted for an M.B.A. and a stint with a high-powered business consultancy before taking a job at a clever but struggling Los Angeles tech firm. Under her leadership the company had turned its fortunes around to the point where it had been acquired by Google in a deal that had made her wealthy. She had married an actor turned producer, ten years older, whom she had met at a dinner party in Malibu. He already had dogs in various political fights, since a number of his films had been overtly political documentaries or thrillers with political overtones. Latino, with some family history of persecution under Castro, Roberto was something of a political chameleon, mixing libertarianism and populism in a way that intrigued both sides without repelling anyone save the most hard-core extremists. He got away with it because he was handsome, charming, and, as he freely admitted, not book-smart enough to puzzle out all the issues.

Having thus settled into a family life, and made a much-discussed decision to keep her maiden name, Julia Bliss Flaherty had swung her sights around to politics. She had narrowly lost a senatorial race in California. Visibly pregnant by the time Election Day arrived, she had soon given birth to a baby with Down syndrome and become a human Rorschach blot for all sorts of angst around amniocentesis and selective abortion. Making the rounds of talk shows to discuss those topics, she had drawn the eye of national political campaigns on both sides of the aisle. During the following presidential campaign, she had found herself in the unusual position of being on both parties' vice presidential short lists. She was staunchly middle-of-the-road, with enough ambiguity in her politics to extend the Democrats' reach rightward and the Republicans' leftward. No one had expected her to end up in the Oval Office; that was never seriously expected, nowadays, of vice presidents. But the scandal that had brought down the president in only the tenth month of his inaugural year had elevated her to the presidency and made her hairstyle fair game for dissertation-length treatments in the press. Much of it was about those glints of silver. Were they natural, or artificial? If natural, why didn't she get rid of them? The technology existed. If artificial, then wasn't it really just a sneaky trick to make her look older, more serious? Either way, should a woman in today's society need to make herself look matronly in order to be taken seriously?

Doob was pretty sure that no such articles would ever again be written after the announcement that J.B.F. was making today. And indeed he felt the requisite shame over the fact that he was paying any attention whatever to the president's hair, on this of all days.

But this was how the mind worked. The mind couldn't think about the End of the World all the time. It needed the occasional break, a romp through the trivial. Because it was through trivia that the mind was anchored in reality, as the largest oak tree was rooted, ultimately, in a system of rootlets no larger than the silver hairs on the president's head.

The announcements all started at the same time but some went on longer than others, the imams and the pope segueing into prayers. The president and other secular leaders, having finished their remarks, stood there uncomfortably for a minute or two, then began to shuffle away toward aides who enveloped them in big warm coats. Doob and the other scientists, as much a part of the backdrop as Crater Lake, were obliged to remain in place until the last prayers ended.

He thought he might come up here with Amelia and watch it happen. It would be a fine place to observe the White Sky and the beginning of the Hard Rain. During the announcement, he had seen a single bolide streak across the sky south of them, a trail of white fire bright enough to leave a slow-fading blue streak in his vision, popping apart into two, then five discrete chunks before it all went over the horizon. It was too far away for him to feel its radiant heat on his face. But people who had been closer to recent events reported that the warmth was palpable. It was also fleeting, since the bolides came and went at hypersonic velocities. But when the Hard Rain began in earnest, they'd be coming in thick and fast, their fiery trails crisscrossing the sky and then merging into a continuous sphere of broiling heat. Even those people who were fortunate enough—if that was the right word—not to get hit directly by a rock would be driven beneath cover. And it would have to be something like a sheet of metal that would reflect heat and not catch fire. That would buy them some time, but soon the air itself would become too hot to breathe. He had been wondering at what point during all of that he should just end his own life.

It was three weeks and a day since the disintegration of the moon, and a mere twelve days since he had convinced himself that the Hard Rain was going to happen. He was astonished in a way that the world's leaders had responded so quickly. But they had been driven to it by the spread of rumors. The same calculations had been made by astronomers all over the world. They were accustomed to working in the open, sharing their ideas on email lists. Anyone who really wanted to know, and who had an Internet connection, could have learned about the Hard Rain a week ago. The president and the other leaders, he reckoned, had been impelled to do this sooner rather than later so that they could focus openly on the development of the Cloud Ark.

And also so that they could give the peoples of the world some agency. Not to be confused with the Agent that had torn up the moon. "Agency," in the lingo of the sorts of people who had set up this announcement, meant giving people options, giving them some things that they could do to have an effect—imaginary or not. There was nothing they could do, of course, about the Hard Rain. And very few of them could contribute on a technical level to the Cloud Ark—there were only so many people qualified to go on space walks or assemble rocket engines, and those had already been mobilized.

But there were things that people could do to help the Cloud Ark achieve its mission, and thereby become a part of the legacy that would be carried forward into space.

Once the announcements and the prayers were finished, three people converged on the central lectern where the president had spoken a few minutes earlier. They were going to talk in English and their words would be translated into as many languages as the organizers had been able to find interpreters for. First up on the dais was Mary Bulinski, the United States secretary of the interior, an inveterate hiker and climber, spry at sixty. By training she was a wildlife biologist. Next was Celani Mbangwa, a big South African woman and a well-regarded artist. Last was Clarence Crouch, the Nobel Prize–winning geneticist from Cambridge, moving slowly on a cane because his own genes had played a nasty trick on him and he had come down with colon cancer. He was being assisted over the rocky ground by one of his postdocs, Moira Crewe, who never seemed to leave his side. Clarence's wife had committed suicide ten years ago and King's College was the only thing that was keeping his body and his soul together.

They had all been made aware of what was going to happen several days ago so that they would have some time to recover from the shock and make themselves presentable on television. They had been flown as soon as possible to Oregon and ensconced in rooms at the lodge on the rim. Doob and other scientists, filtering in from all over the world, had set up a kind of war room in a meeting room downstairs, trying to figure out what exactly Mary and Celani and Clarence were going to say. Because that was an essential part of the announcement. No one was really expecting mass panic or chaos. There would be some of that, of course. But billions of people would want to know how they could be useful. And some answers needed to be provided for them.

And so it didn't matter that Mary and Celani and Clarence were standing with their backs to Doob and talking into a cold wind, because he knew what they were going to say, had gone over the text a hundred times.

Mary's piece of it was to talk about how the Cloud Ark was going to preserve the genetic legacy of the Earth's ecosystems, largely in digital form. They couldn't send giraffes into space, or keep them alive once up there, but they could preserve samples of their tissue. Space was a pretty effective refrigerator. Better yet, the genetic sequences could be recorded by feeding samples into machines, taking the DNA strands apart one base pair at a time, and preserving them as strings of data that could easily be archived and replicated. Special machines would be sent up on the Cloud Ark, machines that could take those digital records and turn them back into functioning DNA and embed them in living cells, so that giraffes and sequoias and whales could be reconstituted from raw elements at some point down the road, perhaps thousands of years in the future. How could ordinary people help? By collecting samples of living things in their environment, especially rare or unusual ones, and taking pictures and GPS readings with their smartphones, and sending them to certain addresses, postage free.

In a way Mary had the hardest job, because this part of the plan was utter BS and she had to know it. Biologists had long ago collected all the samples that mattered. All the flowers and raccoon skulls and bird feathers and sticks and snails that got mailed to those addresses by helpful kids would end up being destroyed. All the genetic sequencing machines were already operating full tilt, around the clock, and the machines that made more of those machines were doing likewise. Nevertheless, she managed to sell it, or so Doob guessed from the set of her shoulders and the movements of her head as she spoke into the teleprompter.

Celani's job was to convince the people of the world that they could contribute to a literary, artistic, and spiritual legacy that would outlive them. All the world's books and websites were already being archived. What was wanted now was for people to write stories and poems, draw pictures, or simply aim cameras at themselves and shoot photos or videos that would one day be browsed by the distant descendants of the Cloud Ark pioneers. This was an easier thing to explain convincingly, since it was legitimate, and simple. Archiving lots of digital files and sending them into space was straightforward.

Clarence, the last up, had some explaining to do.

Doob knew the text of his talk by heart. They had discussed various ways of saying this, but Clarence had gravitated toward the High Church phrasings that came naturally to him.

"The time has come for a great Casting of Lots," he announced. "The Lord has seen fit to populate the Earth with people of many colors and kinds. A burden has now been laid on us, as it was once laid on Noah. Like him we must populate our Ark in a manner respectful of the diversity of life around us. Mary Bulinski has already spoken of how we will preserve the legacy of the world's plants, animals, and other life-forms. We will not do this as Noah did, by bringing them aboard the Ark two by two. There is not room for them, and there is no way to keep them alive. We go another way where the plants and the animals are concerned.

"The peoples of the world are a different matter. We will need people in that Ark. It is not an automatic mechanism. It will require the ingenuity and adaptability of human minds. We will populate it. We will begin with astronauts, cosmonauts, military, and scientists whose skills are needed. But there are only so many of those, and they are drawn from only a small portion of the world's peoples."

This question—how many?—had bedeviled them all along. In two years, how many humans could be launched into space, assuming that rocket factories all operated full-time, and we weren't too fussy about safety procedures? Estimates varied through two orders of magnitude, from a few hundred to tens of thousands. They had no idea. And it was one thing to get them up there and another thing to keep them alive. The most solid estimates that Doob had seen were converging on a number somewhere between five hundred and a thousand. But they had carefully scrubbed Clarence's speech of any specific numbers, or even hints.

"We ask every village, town, city, and district to perform a Casting of Lots and to choose two young persons, a boy and a girl, as candidates for training and inclusion in the crew of the Cloud Ark. We do not seek to impose any rules or procedures upon how the selection is made. Our objective is to preserve, as best we can, the genetic and the cultural diversity of the human race. We trust that the candidates selected will exemplify the best features of the communities from which they were chosen."

The statement was subtly self-contradictory. Clarence was saying that they were not going to impose any rules. But they had already done so by insisting that there had to be both a boy and a girl. They knew perfectly well that many cultures would have trouble with that.

"The boys and the girls so chosen," Clarence went on, "will be gathered together in a network of camps and campuses, where they will be trained for the mission they are to undertake, and launched into the Cloud Ark as room is made for them."

Doob, aware that he might be in the background of some camera angle, did his best to maintain a poker face. Clarence wasn't exactly lying. But he was leaving a lot out. How many boys and girls would end up in those camps? More than could be transported to or accommodated in any conceivable space ark. How many of them could really be trained to do anything useful?

In reality it would be much more selective than Clarence made it sound. Only some of those chosen in the Casting of Lots would actually be collected. Those belonging to rare or distinctive ethnic groups probably had a leg up. Once they got to the training center, they would begin to understand that not all of them were actually going to get launched into space before the Hard Rain. It would get competitive. Perhaps brutally so. Doob didn't like to think about it.

For the thousandth time in the last three weeks, he mused about how funny the mind was. It didn't matter that conditions in the training camps might become unpleasant. It was nothing. And yet the thought of young persons being cruel to each other upset him more than the fact that most of them were going to die.

A curtain twitched up in a window of the lodge, and Doob looked to see Amelia, arms crossed, elbows on the windowsill, looking down at him from the room they had shared the last three nights. She had stayed inside so that she could watch it on the TV in the room, let him know how it had looked on video, how the commentators and pundits had framed it.

It was Thanksgiving week. School was out. She'd flown up to Eugene on Wednesday, rented a car, and driven here to be with him.

The staff at the lodge, still unaware of what was about to happen, had served the traditional turkey dinner on Thursday afternoon. The scientists, politicians, and military who had come here from all over the world to contemplate the end of days had tried to see the humor in the holiday. In a way, though, Doob actually *was* thankful. He was thankful that Amelia had come up to spend time with him. He was thankful that she had shown up in his life at exactly the moment when he most needed to have someone around.

On Day 7, when he had met Amelia and fallen for her in the same instant, he'd felt foolish. He'd wondered what was going on in his brain for it to react so. But she'd let him know, in the correct, even steely manner of an elementary school teacher, that the interest was reciprocated. The school where she taught was less than a mile from the Caltech campus and so they would get together for quick early dinners before she went home to grade papers and he went back to his office to check and recheck his calculations about the exponential, the White Sky. The split between the joy of new love and the growing awareness of what was going to happen was almost too wide for his mind to address. He would wake up every morning and enjoy those first few moments of consciousness before his mind swung uncontrollably to one topic or the other.

After he had come back from Camp David and the teleconference where he'd explained matters to the crew of the International Space Station, she had asked him what was troubling him, and he had told her. That night was the first time they had slept together. But they slept together four times before he found himself able to have sex. It wasn't so much the dread of the catastrophe that got in the way. Disasters could be sexy. He'd had some of the best sex of his life while on the road to attend loved ones' funerals. What weighed him down and left him impotent was the stress and distraction of having to communicate what he knew to one person at a time.

Problem solved. Everyone knew now.

Clarence wound up his announcement with some inspiring talk about how the young men and women who ascended to the safety of the Cloud Ark would build a new civilization in space and populate it with the genetic legacy of all mankind. Frozen sperm, eggs, and embryos would be sent up there too, so that even those who were left behind to die on the Earth's surface could enjoy some hope that their offspring would one day grow to maturity in orbiting space colonies, and commune with their departed ancestors through digitally preserved letters, photographs, and videos. To Doob, this part of the talk seemed tacked on, something put in there just to hold out a glimmer of hope. But he knew that it was, in a way, the most important thing that any of the speakers would say today. The rest of the message had been stunningly grim, too shocking for most people to take in. The news anchors covering the announcement had been sworn to secrecy and briefed on it yesterday, just to give them some time to recover emotionally in the hope that they could hold it together on air. The announcement *had* to conclude with some straw for people to grasp at. This kindly, ancient Cambridge professor, hollowed out by cancer, speaking in the cadences of the King James Bible about the new world in the heavens that would be populated by the children of the dead, venerating their ancestors' JPEGs and GIFs, was the closest thing to an uplifting message that anyone was going to see today. He had to sell it, and he did. And Doob and all the other scientists who were now running the Cloud Ark program, along with the world's military and politicians and business leaders, had to follow through.

Moira Crewe, Clarence's postdoc, and Mary Bulinski each got a hand under one of Clarence's arms and helped him down the steps to the rim of the crater, where a few shell-shocked journalists had gathered to ask questions. For the most part, though, the place was dead quiet. None of the usual post-news-conference hubbub. Most of the networks had cut back directly to their headquarters.

Doob looked up at the window. Amelia tucked her hair behind her ear and drew back from the glass. He trudged back to the lodge on legs stiff with cold. He was thinking about those frozen sperm samples and eggs. How long would they last? It was known that such cells could be thawed and used to produce normal babies after as long as twenty years in the freezer. Cosmic rays might complicate things. A single ray passing through a human body might damage a few cells—but bodies had a lot of spare cells. The same ray passing through a single-celled sperm or egg would destroy it.

The bottom line was that every man now on Earth could ejaculate into a test tube, every woman could go in for the much more complicated process of having her eggs harvested, embryos could be gathered and put on ice by the millions, but none of it would make a bit of difference unless there were healthy young women willing to receive those donations into their own wombs and gestate them for nine months. In time the population would grow. A new generation of—to put it bluntly—functional uteruses would come online in fourteen or fifteen years. And a second generation would be available in thirty. But by then, many of the frozen samples that the people of Earth were pinning their hopes on would be past their expiration dates.

Most of the people on the Cloud Ark were going to have to be women.

There were other reasons for it besides just making more babies. Research on the long-term effects of spaceflight suggested that women were less susceptible to radiation damage than men. They were smaller on average, requiring less space, less food, less air. And sociological studies pointed to the idea that they did better when crammed together in tight spaces for long periods of time. This was controversial, as it got into fraught topics of nature vs. nurture and whether gender identity was a social construct or a genetic program. But if you bought into the idea that boys had been programmed by Darwinian selection to run around in the open chucking spears at wild animals—something that every parent who had ever raised a boy had to take seriously—then it was difficult to envision a lot of them spending their lives in tin cans.

The system of camps where the young people chosen in the Casting of Lots would be taken for training and selection was going to be a roach motel for boys. Young men would go in, but they wouldn't come out. Save for a few lucky exceptions.

He had been drifting toward the lodge for a couple of minutes, nagged by the vague sense that there was something he ought to be doing.

Talking to the media. Yes, that was it. Normally, camera crews would be homing in on him. And normally he would be trying to dodge them. But not today. Today he was willing to stand around and talk, to be Doc Dubois for the billions of people out there in TV land. But no one was coming after him. Anchors of many nations were gazing soulfully into their teleprompters, intoning prepared remarks. Journalists of lesser stature—tech bloggers and freelance pundits—were filing their reports. Doob noticed a familiar face,

Tavistock Prowse, off in a corner of the parking lot. He had set up a tablet on a tripod, aimed its camera at himself, and clipped on a wireless mike, and was delivering some kind of a video blog entry, probably for the website of *Turing* magazine, which had employed him lo these many years. Doob had known him for two decades. He looked terrible. Tav had showed up this morning. He didn't have the credentials or the access to get the advance warning, so all of this was news to him. Doob had pinged him a few times last night, on Twitter and Facebook, trying to give him a heads-up so that his old friend wouldn't be wrong-footed by the announcement, but Tav hadn't responded.

It didn't seem like a great moment to be doing an impromptu interview with Tav and so Doob pretended he had not seen him. He flashed his credentials at the Secret Service guys stationed at the lodge's entrance, but this was just to be polite—they knew who he was and had already pulled the door open for him.

He passed the elevators and climbed the stairs to the room, just to get blood moving in his extremities. Amelia had left the door ajar. He hung up the DO NOT DISTURB placard, locked the door behind him, and collapsed into a chair. She was still at the window, leaning back perched on its broad rustic sill. This side of the lodge was facing away from the sun, but the light of the sky came in and illuminated her face, showing the beginnings of lines below her eyes, around her mouth. She was second-generation Honduran American, some kind of complicated African-Indian-Spanish melange, big eyed, wavy haired, alert, birdlike, but with that essentially positive nature that any schoolteacher needed to have. It was a good trait in current circumstances.

"Well, that's over," she said. "It must be a big load off of your mind."

"I have ten interviews in the next two days," he said, "explaining the whys and the wherefores. But you're right. That's easy, compared to breaking the news."

"It's just math," she said.

"It's just math."

"What about after that?" she asked.

"You mean, after the next couple of days?"

"Yeah. Then what?"

"I hadn't really thought about it," he admitted. "But we have to keep gathering data. Refining the forecast. The more we know about when the White Sky is going to happen, the better we can plan the launch schedule, and everything else."

"The Casting of Lots," she said.

"That too."

"You're going, aren't you, Dubois?" She never called him by his nickname.

"Beg pardon?"

Irritation flashed over her face—unusual, that—and then she focused on him, and she gradually became amused. "You don't know."

"Don't know what, Amelia?"

"Obviously, you're going."

"Going where?"

"To the Cloud Ark. They're going to need you. You're one of the few who can be useful up there. Who can actually help its chances of survival. Be a leader."

It really hadn't occurred to him until she said it. But then he saw that it was probably true. "Oh, Jesus Christ," he said, "I think I would rather croak down here. With you. I was thinking we could come up here, camp out on the rim, and watch it. It's going to be the most amazing thing ever."

"A real hot date," Amelia said. "No, I think I'll be spending that day with my family."

"Maybe you and I could be family by then."

Tears gleamed in the pouches beneath her eyes, and she ran a finger under her nose. "That has got to be the strangest proposal ever," she said. "The thing is, Dubois, that my husband is going to be in orbit and I'm going to be in California."

"I could look for a way to—"

She shook her head. "They will never, ever agree to bringing a thirty-five-year-old schoolteacher up to the Cloud Ark."

He knew she was right.

"A frozen embryo, though—that seems like a possibility."

"That has got to be the strangest *proposition* ever," Doob said.

"We live in strange times. I'm fertile right now. I can tell. No more condoms for you, tiger."

So it was that, half an hour after Doc Dubois had listened with high intellectual skepticism to the soothing speech of Clarence Crouch, and picked it apart logically in his mind, proving to himself that it was just a comforting sop for the bereaved billions, a distraction to keep them busy with sex during the two years they had left, he was in Amelia's arms, and she in his, as they got busy making an embryo for him to carry up into space for implantation in some other, unknown woman's womb.

He was already thinking about the videos he was going to make to teach his baby about calculus when he climaxed.

DINAH WAS GLAD NOT TO HAVE BEEN ON THE PLANET WHEN THE Crater Lake announcement was being made. She sat alone in her workshop, peering out her window past the craggy black silhouette of Amalthea at the luminous blue limb of the Earth below. She knew the time of the announcement and she knew how long it was supposed to last. She chose not to watch the video feed. It hit her as strange that the Earth itself did not change its appearance in any way. Down below, seven billion people were hearing the worst news imaginable. They were going through a collective emotional trauma unknown in the history of the human race. Police and military were being deployed in public spaces to "maintain order," whatever that meant. But Earth looked the same.

Her radio started beeping. She looked down, blinked away tears, and saw Alaska, bent over the curve of the world far to the north.

WE ARE PROUD THAT YOU ARE UP THERE

She recognized her father's fist—his touch on the Morse key—as easily as his smell or his voice. She returned:

I WISH THAT I COULD SEE YOU AGAIN

AUNT BEVERLY IS SOWING SOME FLATS OF POTATOES. WE WILL BE FINE.

She cried for a while.

QSL, he signaled, which was a Q code meaning, in this case, "Are you still there?"

She sent QSL back, meaning "Yes."

She knew that the purpose of Q codes was to make communication more efficient, but she understood now that they could serve another purpose. They could enable you to eke out a few scraps of useful information when words were too difficult.

YOU BETTER GET TO WORK KIDDO

AND YOU SHOULD STOP POUNDING THAT KEY AND HELP BEV

LOVE YOU QRT

QRT

"It's still a miracle to me that you can make sense of that."

She turned around to discover Rhys Aitken, poised in the hatchway that connected her shop to the SCRUM: the Space Commercial Resources Utility Module, which was the large can-shaped object that connected Izzy's forward end to Amalthea. Along its sides, the SCRUM sported several docking ports where other modules could be connected. Owing to various delays and budget cutbacks, only one of those ports was currently in use, and Rhys was now hovering in it. Tucked under one of his arms was a bundle, wrapped in a blanket.

She sniffled, suddenly aware that she was a mess. "How long have you been there?"

"Not long."

She turned her back on him, grabbed a towel, and dried her eyes and nose. Rhys filled the time with some gentle patter. "I couldn't stand watching the announcement any longer, so I tried to make myself useful. Discovered something marvelous. Water runs downhill. All right, I already knew that, actually. There's a section of the torus, underneath the deck plates, where condensation tends to collect—it's been a maintenance issue, something we've been keeping an eye on.

"So, I brought you something," he concluded.

She turned and looked at the bundle under his arm. "A dozen roses?"

"Perhaps next week. Until then—" and he held it out.

She took it from him. Like everything else up here it was, of course, weightless, but she could tell by its inertia that it had some heft.

She peeled back the blanket and heard a crinkling, crackling noise, then saw underneath it a layer of the metallized Mylar sheeting that they used all over Izzy as thermal shielding. The object beneath that was lumpy and irregular. And it was cold. She peeled away the Mylar to reveal a slab of ice. It was oval and lens shaped: a frozen puddle.

"Perfect," she said.

A few drops of water spun away from it, gleaming like diamonds in the shaft of sunlight spearing in through her little window. She captured them using the same towel she'd just used to dry her face. But not before pausing, just a moment, to admire their brilliance. Like a little galaxy of new stars.

"You'd said something about a cryptic message from Sean Probst."

"All of his messages are that way," she said, "even after they've been decrypted." Sean Probst was her boss, the founder and chairman of Arjuna Expeditions.

"Something about ice, anyway," Rhys went on.

"Hang on, let's get this in the airlock before it melts any more."

"Right." Rhys pushed himself to the far end of the shop, where a round hatch, about half a meter in diameter, was set into the curved wall. "I see green blinkies all about, so I'll just open this?"

"Fine."

He actuated a lever that released the latching mechanism, then pulled the hatch open to reveal a little space beyond. This was the airlock that Dinah used when she needed to bring one of her robots inside for maintenance, or send one back out onto Amalthea. Human-rated airlocks were big—they had to accommodate at least one person in a bulky space suit—and complicated and expensive, partly because of safety requirements and partly because they were designed by government programs. This one, by contrast, had been prototyped in a few weeks by a small team at Arjuna Expeditions, and was meant for smaller equipment. It was roughly the dimensions of a big garbage can. To save space on the inside, it protruded from the side of the module, jutting into space like a stubby, oversized fire hydrant. At its far end was a dome-shaped hatch that Dinah could open and close from inside her shop using a mechanical linkage of pushrods and levers straight out of a Jules Verne novel. At the moment, of course, that hatch was closed, and the airlock was full of air that had gone chilly, since the sun had not been shining on its outside until a few minutes ago.

Dinah gave the chunk of ice a gentle push and it glided across the shop to Rhys. "Up and under!" he called, and caught it.

"What?"

"Rugby," he explained, and slid the ice into the airlock. "Have you got a Grabb or something that can come round and fetch this?"

"In a minute," she said. "It'll keep in there for now."

"Right." He closed the inner door and dogged it shut. Then he turned back and looked at Dinah, and she looked at him, and they appraised each other for a few moments.

"So water condenses and puddles at this one place in the torus," she said, "which you can reach by pulling up a deck plate?"

"Yes."

"And it freezes?"

"Well, normally, no. I may have helped it freeze by fiddling with certain environmental controls."

"Ah."

"Just trying to save energy."

She was floating in the opposite end of the shop, near the hatch where it connected to the SCRUM. She looked through and verified that no one was around. Some of them, she knew, were in a meeting in the torus, and others were doing a space walk.

"Now, *technically* . . ." she began.

"Technically, this is wrong," he said. She admired the self-aware bluntness. "It is wrong because when you open the outer hatch and put that piece of ice out in space, where your robots can muck about on it, it is going to sublimate."

Sublimation was essentially the same thing as evaporation, skipping the liquid phase; it just meant a process by which a solid, exposed to vacuum, gradually turned into vapor and disappeared. Ice tended to do this pretty quickly unless it was kept extremely cold.

"So Izzy is going to lose water," Dinah said, "which is a scarce and valuable resource."

"It'll never be missed," Rhys said blithely. "This isn't the old days.

Now that those people have made that announcement, rockets will be coming up here thick and fast."

"Still, what Sean wants me to do is an Arjuna Expeditions project. A commercial thing. A private thing. And that water is a shared—"

"Dinah."

"Yes?"

"Snap out of it, love."

A long silence followed, concluded by a big sigh from Dinah. "Okay." Rhys was right. Everything was different now.

"Now, what is it he wants, and how does ice enter into it?"

Her mild annoyance at his curiosity finally gave way. Maybe he could help. She turned her head toward the window and nodded at the familiar bulk of Amalthea, a few meters away. "That's been my career, and my family's career," she said. "Working with minerals. Hard rock. Metallic ore. All of the robots are optimized for crawling around on a big piece of iron. They use magnets to stick to it. Their tools use plasma arcs or abrasive wheels to work it. Now, Sean's basically telling me to shelve all of that. The future is ice, he says. That's all he wants to hear about. All he wants me to work on."

"There's lots of it on Earth," Rhys pointed out, "but you never think of it as a mineral."

She nodded. "It's an annoyance you have to clear out of the way."

"Your colleagues down on the ground? Also working on ice?"

"Judging from email traffic, this is a company-wide directive," she said. "They're buying ice by the truckload, dropping it on the floor of the lab, refrigerating the building—fortunately it's winter in Seattle; they only need to drop the temperature a few degrees. They're all buying long underwear at REI so that they can work in a refrigerator."

"What's it like working for Mr. Freeze?"

"I was going to say the Penguin," Dinah said, "but people in Seattle don't carry umbrellas."

"Nor do they wear top hats, in my experience. No, it's definitely a Mr. Freeze scenario."

"Anyway," Dinah said, "yesterday's shipment of vitamins contained a few of these."

She opened a storage cubby next to her workstation and took out a bag made of the metallic gray plastic used to protect sensitive electronics from static electricity. Taped to it was a NASA business card.

"Nice to have friends in high places," Rhys remarked. He had noticed the name on the card: Scott "Sparky" Spalding, the NASA administrator.

Dinah smiled. "Or low, as the case may be."

It was a weak joke. Rhys didn't respond. Dinah felt her face get a little warm. Not so much because of the failed attempt at humor as out of a kind of political defensiveness. "Scott told me a couple of weeks ago that he wouldn't ditch me out. That he had my back."

"What does that mean exactly?"

"That the robot work would keep going. That I would have a job. I didn't believe him. But I guess he's been talking to Sean Probst. Because Sean FedExed these to Sparky a couple of days ago, and now they're here."

She parted the bag's ziplock closure, inserted her thumb and index finger, and pulled out a contraption about the size of a grain of rice. From a distance it looked like a photovoltaic cell, just a flake of silicon, but with a few tiny appendages.

"What are the dangly bits?" Rhys wanted to know.

"A locomotion system."

"Legs?"

"This one happens to have legs. Others have things like little tank treads, or rolling cylinders, or slammers."

"Slammers? Is that a technical term?"

"A mining thing. A way of moving heavy equipment around on the ground. I'll show you later."

"So," Rhys said, "it would appear that the agenda is to evaluate a number of different ways that robots could crawl around on ice without drifting off and getting lost."

"Yeah. Apparently all of these work, more or less, on the ground in Seattle. I'm supposed to evaluate their performance in space."

"Well!" Rhys said. "How fortunate for you, then, that—"

"That I have my very own chunk of ice. Yeah. Thanks for that."

"All the sweeter for being contraband?" he asked, raising his eyebrows.

The double meaning was clear enough. "Not as romantic as a dozen roses," she countered.

"Still," he said, "what is it that a man is trying to say with a dozen roses? Simply that he is thinking of you."

Shortly after she'd arrived on Izzy she had rigged up a curtain that she could draw across the opening of her shop's hatch. It wasn't much—just a blanket—but it shielded her visually when she wanted to take a nap in her shop, and it sent the message that she was not to be disturbed, at least without knocking first. She reached up now and drew the curtain across the hatchway. Then she turned back toward Rhys, who looked very keen, and very ready.

"How's your space sickness?" she asked. "You seem a little more, uh, sprightly."

"Never better. All bodily fluids fully under control."

"I'll be the judge of that."

THE RUSSIAN INVASION BEGAN A WEEK LATER, WITH A SPATE OF flights producing what NASA described as "mixed results" and Roskosmos termed "an acceptable fatality rate."

Seen from a distance, Izzy consisted almost entirely of solar panels. Structurally, these were to the space station as the wings of a bird were to its body, in the sense that their purpose was to have as much surface area as possible with minimal weight.

Most of the mass, strength, and brains were in the "body"—a stack of can-shaped modules running up the middle between the "wings"—which was tiny by comparison. From many angles you couldn't even see it. The only parts of the stack big enough to be noticed from a distance were the add-ons from recent years: Amalthea at one end and the torus at the other.

The solar panels—as well as some other, vaguely similar-looking structures whose function was to radiate waste heat into space—were held in place by the Integrated Truss Assembly. The word "truss," when used by structural engineers, just meant something that looked like a radio tower or a steel bridge: a network of struts joined into a lattice, giving maximum stiffness with minimum weight. In some parts of Izzy, those struts were visible, but more commonly they were covered up by panels that made them look more solid than they were. Behind those panels resided unfathomably complex wiring, plumbing, batteries, sensors, and mechanisms for deploying and rotating solar panels. With a few minor exceptions, none of the Integrated Truss Assembly was pressurized—none of it was meant to hold air or accommodate human beings. It was like the mechanical works on the roof of a skyscraper, exposed to the elements and rarely visited by humans. Astronauts went there on space walks to mess with the wiring or fix things that weren't working, but most of Izzy's crew spent their whole missions inside the much smaller stack of cans that made up the station's "body."

That was going to have to change.

Izzy herself could only expand so much. This was not a question of stacking on more cans, or adding additional tori. Beyond a certain point you simply couldn't jam more complexity into such a focused volume. Electrical power was needed to run just about everything. Whenever it was used, waste heat was generated. The heat would build up in the space station and cook the occupants unless it was collected by a refrigeration system and piped out to radiators that would "shine" the heat, in the form of infrared light, into space. Jamming more people and systems into the central body of the space station would just require more solar panels, more batteries, more radiators, and more plumbing and wiring to connect them all. And this didn't even address the human factors: how to supply people with food, water, and clean breathable air, and how to recycle carbon dioxide and sewage.

Knowing this, the brain trust behind the Cloud Ark—an ad hoc working group of governmental space agency veterans and commercial space entrepreneurs—had opted for the only strategy that could possibly work, which was decentralized and distributed. Each arklet, as the component ships were being called, would be small enough that it could be heaved into orbit on the top of a single heavy-lift rocket. It would draw power from a small, simple nuclear reactor fueled by isotopes so radioactive that they would throw off heat, and thereby generate electricity, for a few decades. The Soviet Union had used such devices to power isolated lighthouses, and they had been employed in space probes for decades.

Each arklet would accommodate a small number of people. The number kept changing as different designs were drawn up, but it meandered between about five and a dozen. Much depended on how rapidly it would prove feasible to mass-produce inflatable structures; these made it possible to create much more spacious volumes by housing people in what amounted to thick-skinned balloons. But making balloons that could withstand atmospheric pressure indefinitely while also standing up to solar radiation, thermal swings, and micrometeoroids was no small project.

It went without saying that, in the long run, the Cloud Ark as a whole was going to have to be self-sustaining in terms of food production. Water would have to be recycled. Carbon dioxide exhaled by humans would have to be used to sustain plants, which would produce oxygen for the humans to breathe and food for them to eat. All of this had been the subject matter of science fiction stories and practical experiments for decades. Those experiments had produced mixed results that were now getting a lot of attention from people who understood such things a lot better than Dinah. But she gathered that she had better get used to a low-calorie vegetarian diet, and occasional oxygen shortages.

Isolated arklets wouldn't survive for long. It didn't matter how good their internal ecosystems were. Things would go wrong, people would get sick, supplies and nutrients would run low, and people would just plain go crazy from being cooped up with the same few individuals.

The design of the arklets, and of the whole Cloud Ark system, kept changing. One day it was all about being "fully distributed," which meant that in the long run there was no central depot—no Izzy—and that all exchanges of material and "human resources" between arklets would happen through "opportunistic docking," meaning that two arklets would agree to come together and connect nose-to-nose for a time so that food, water, vitamins, or people could be exchanged. This was envisioned as market driven, without any central command and control mechanism.

The next day a new edict would be handed down to the effect that overall coordination would be handled by a command center on Izzy. The space station would also serve as a central depot for anything that could be stockpiled. The torus—or tori, since Rhys was on track to construct a second one—would be available for rest and recreation; arklet dwellers going stir-crazy from living in tin cans and suffering loss of bone density from floating around in microgravity would be rotated through and allowed to vacation there.

The schemes envisioned by the Arkitects, as Dinah and Ivy started calling them, ping-ponged back and forth between those two extremes, and seemed to reflect the existence of at least two factions. The centralizing faction pointed to the dangers of prolonged zero-gee existence as a reason for rotating people through the torus. The decentralizers came back a couple of days later with a sketch of the so-called bolo scheme, wherein a pair of arklets would connect to each other with a long cable and then begin spinning around their common center of mass, creating simulated gravity in each arklet that was stronger and better than what could be achieved in a torus. A couple of days after that, the centralizers posted an animated simulation of what would happen when two bolos ran into each other and got their cables tangled. It was funny in a kind of slapstick-horror way.

None of this really mattered in the short term, because, even on a hysterically accelerated schedule, it was going to take weeks to design and manufacture even a single arklet. And it would take longer to ramp up the production lines for the giant heavy-lift rockets needed to boost them into space. What Izzy's crew would be seeing in the meantime was a hodgepodge of preexisting spacecraft, mostly Soyuz capsules, being sent up using the existing stock of rockets. These would carry "Pioneers" whose job would be to build new extensions onto Izzy's Integrated Truss Assembly: for docking many arklets at a time, for storing material, and for making it all run. The Pioneers would spend most of their time in space suits performing EVAs: extravehicular activities, a.k.a. space walks. There would be something like a hundred Pioneers all told. They were being trained now, and their space suits were being hastily manufactured.

But Izzy in her current form couldn't support anything like a hundred new people. She didn't even have the spacecraft docking ports needed to berth their vehicles when they arrived. So in order to accommodate the Pioneers who would begin arriving in a few weeks, the Arkitects sent up Scouts. The qualifications for being a Scout seemed to be a shocking level of physical endurance, a complete disregard for mortal danger, and some knowledge of how to exist in a space suit. All of them were Russian.

There wasn't room for them on the space station. Actually, to be precise, there was plenty of physical space to accommodate them, but the support systems weren't there. The CO_2 scrubbers could only handle the output of so many lungs. The entire space station had only three toilets, one of which was almost twenty years old.

The Scouts were going to live most of the time in their space suits. This made sense as far as it went, since their mission was to work to exhaustion every day. Sixteen hours in a space suit meant sixteen hours that the Scout was not imposing a direct burden on Izzy's life support systems.

At Zero, the total number of functioning space suits in the known universe had been something like a dozen. Production had been ramped up since then, but they were still a scarce resource. In its most common form, the Orlan space suit used by the Russians could only function independently for a couple of hours, which was fine since normal people were completely exhausted by that point anyway. Beyond that, its internal reserves were used up. So, the Scouts would mostly be working on umbilicals. Their suits would be connected to an external life support system by a bundle of plumbing and cables that would supply air and power while taking away waste and excess heat.

During the few hours they were allowed to rest, the Scouts needed a place to go and to climb out of their space suits.

Whoever was running things at Roskosmos had pulled up an old idea for an emergency crew rescue device and begun actually producing them. It was called Luk. The word meant "onion" in Russian. It was pronounced similarly to "Luke," but English speakers inevitably started calling it "Luck."

In the best traditions of Russian technology, Luk was straightforward. Take a cosmonaut. Enclose him in a large plastic bag full of air.

With any normal plastic bag material, the cosmonaut will suffocate or the bag will pop, because plastic bags aren't strong enough to withstand full atmospheric pressure. So, fill the bag with only as much air as it can handle—some fraction of one atmosphere—and then place another bag inside of it. Inflate that bag with air at slightly higher pressure. That's still not enough air to keep a cosmonaut alive, so put a third bag inside of the second bag and inflate it to higher pressure yet. Keep repeating, like with Russian nesting dolls, until the innermost bag has enough air pressure to keep a human alive—then put the cosmonaut inside of that one. All of those layers of translucent plastic gave it an appearance reminiscent of an onion.

The scheme had many advantages. It was cheap, simple, and lightweight. Deflated, a Luk could be pleated and rolled up for storage in a backpack-sized container.

Of course, the air inside the innermost bag would get fouled with carbon dioxide as the occupant breathed, but this could be handled as it usually was on spaceships and submarines, by passing the air over a chemical such as lithium hydroxide that would absorb the CO_2. As long as a bit of oxygen was bled in to replace what was being used, the occupant would be fine.

Heat produced by the occupant's body would build up in the atmosphere of the innermost bag and become stifling. A cooling system was required.

Getting in and out of the Luk could be problematic. The Russians had somehow determined that just about anyone—or at least anyone capable of meeting the physical standards of the cosmonaut program—could force their body through a hole forty centimeters in diameter. Accordingly, each Luk included a flange—a forty-centimeter ring of fiberglass with bolt holes spaced around its periphery. All the layers of plastic converged on it, further enhancing its onionlike appearance. This became the onion's cut-off stem. To keep the air from rushing out through that forty-centimeter hole, it was equipped with a stout diaphragm of much thicker plastic that could be put into place after the cosmonaut had climbed inside.

So, the general procedure for using the Luk was to unfold the bag and find the flange, then pull it over one's head, squirm through it until the shoulders and pelvis had passed through, draw the feet up inside of it, then find the diaphragm and lock it into place, sealing oneself inside. At this point the Luk was still a giant wrinkled mass of plastic hanging around the occupant like a sleeping bag.

Once the Luk was free in the vacuum of space, it was okay to open the valve that flooded air into its many interstitial layers. Whereupon it would expand to the size of a mobile home, and drift around aimlessly until a rescue vehicle could get to it.

On its outer hatch, the rescue vehicle would need to have an adapter with a bolt pattern made to engage with the holes on the Luk's flange. Once an airtight connection had been made between Luk and vehicle, the hatch could be opened, the diaphragm removed, and the cosmonaut brought in from the cold. Or, given the difficulties of getting rid of excess thermal energy in space, from the heat.

The Orlan suit was built around a hard upper torso, or HUT: a rigid shell for containing the wearer's trunk, with connection points for the arms, legs, and helmet. The back of the HUT was a door with an airtight gasket around its edge. To put the suit on, you opened that door, threaded your feet down the legs, thrust your hands along the arms and into the attached gloves, and ducked into the helmet. The door was then closed behind you. From that point on the suit was an independent system.

Roskosmos had constructed a number of Vestibyul modules, this being a newly invented thing that they had cobbled together from existing parts in about two weeks. Its purpose was to serve as a jury-rigged bridge connecting Luk to Orlan.

The Vestibyul was barely large enough to accommodate a supine human. At one end was a flange that mated with the forty-centimeter ring on a Luk. Having slithered feetfirst from the Luk into the Vestibyul, a cosmonaut had just enough wiggle room to get his feet aimed down the legs of the Orlan suit that was attached to the other end, its door hanging open. Before doing this, however, he would seal off the Luk by manually putting its diaphragm into position and bolting it into place with a ratchet wrench.

Having donned the Orlan, he could then activate a mechanism, built into the Vestibyul, that would close the suit's door behind him. The small amount of residual air in the Vestibyul would hiss out into space and the cosmonaut would be free to depart. At the end of the workday, the whole procedure was reversed. Just like a suburban commuter sleeping in a split-level home with his car parked in the garage, the cosmonaut would enjoy a few hours of rest and relaxation floating around the confines of the Luk with his space suit docked at the end of the adjoining Vestibyul.

There were a number of catches.

- Luk, Vestibyul, and suit formed a closed system. The only way to escape from that system was to successfully don the suit, get the door closed, and spacewalk to an airlock. If anything went wrong that prevented donning the suit and closing the door, rescue was impossible, or at least spectacularly improbable. A perforated Luk, probably caused by a micrometeoroid, caused a fatality on the second day of the Scout program. After that, the Luk/Vestibyul systems were brought forward to huddle in the shelter of Amalthea. The asteroid wouldn't stop all incoming rocks, but it would stop many.
- Since there was no practical way in or out of the system, the Scouts had to fly up from Baikonur in their space suits, pre-attached to their Vestibyuls and Luks. This was necessitated anyway by the fact that none of this equipment could be accommodated inside of a normal space capsule. So they had to fly up crammed, six at a time, into cargo carriers that were not rated for human use and that had no onboard life support. They were, therefore, living off their space suits' internal supplies of air and power from shortly before launch until their arrival at ISS. This journey could not be accomplished in less than six hours and so supplemental air and power had to be delivered to the suits en route. The failure of systems responsible for doing that accounted for two fatalities in the first crew of six Scouts and one fatality in the second crew.
- The capabilities of the suits were being wildly overstretched by these new mission parameters, and of course the Luks didn't

really have significant life support systems of their own, so everything depended on umbilical lines that linked these contraptions to Zavod modules. Zavod was simply the Russian word for "factory." This was another new device that had been cobbled together in two weeks from existing technology. As long as the Zavod was supplied with power, water, and a few consumables, it was supposed to keep a cosmonaut alive by scrubbing CO_2 out of the air, collecting urine, and removing their body heat. The heat was gotten rid of by freezing water on a surface exposed to the vacuum and then letting it sublimate into space. Failures of Zavod modules accounted for four fatalities among the first three crews sent up. Two of these were caused by a bug in the software, subsequently fixed by a patch transmitted up from the ground. One was a leaky hose. The other was never explained, but the fatality was witnessed by Izzy's crew, watching through windows and video feeds, and seemed to match the profile for hyperthermia. The cooling system had failed and the cosmonaut had lost consciousness and succumbed to heatstroke. After that, they had stopped using the jerry-built cooling systems that had shipped up with the Luks and simply used ziplock bags full of ice, delivered daily.

None of this even accounted for mishaps that occurred while the Scouts were actually working. A damaged umbilical nearly killed a Scout on A+0.35, and he was obliged to disconnect himself from his Zavod and execute a heroic and perilous move to the nearest airlock, where they got him inside the space station with less than a minute to spare.

Two days later a Scout simply disappeared without explanation, possibly the victim of a micrometeoroid, or even of suicide.

So, of the first crew of six Scouts, two were dead on arrival and one was killed in the Luk failure the next day. Of the second crew, one was dead on arrival. All six of the third crew made it to Izzy alive. Of the fourteen total survivors, four died from Zavod failures, one disappeared, and one was forced to "retire" from being a Scout and confine his activities to Izzy because of equipment failure.

Ivy, being at the top of the org chart, was responsible for all strange and extraordinary decisions: the problems that no one else knew how, or was willing, to handle. It became her problem to decide what they were going to do with dead people.

Oh, there was a procedure. NASA had a procedure for everything. They had long ago anticipated that an astronaut might die of a heart attack or some mishap during a mission. Since two hundred pounds of rotting flesh could not be accommodated inside of the space station where people lived and worked, the general idea was to let them freeze-dry in space, and then place them aboard the next earthbound Soyuz capsule. Only the middle section of the Soyuz, the reentry module, ever made it back to Earth. The spheroidal orbital module, perched on top of it, was jettisoned before reentry. Eventually it burned up in the Earth's atmosphere. The customary procedure, therefore, was to pack the orbital module with trash so that it would be burned up as well.

Bodies were not trash, of course, but burning them up in the atmosphere seemed as good a way as any to dispose of them—the space-age equivalent of a Viking funeral.

The normal up/down cycle of launch and reentry had, of course, been suspended. Things were supposed to go up, but not come down. Those orbital modules could be preserved and used as habitats, or for storing supplies. The "trash" could be picked over and used again. Bags of fecal material could become fertilizer in hydroponic farms.

Ivy made a unilateral decision that they would carve out an exception to that new policy. The deceased were moved into an empty orbital module docked at the truss. This was left open to space, so that freeze-drying of the bodies could happen out of sight and out of mind. When it filled up with dead people, they would have some kind of ceremony, the thing would be deorbited, and they would watch in silence as it drew a white-hot streak across the atmosphere below.

But it wasn't full quite yet.

They had eight working Scouts until such time as another heavy-lift rocket could be prepared and sent up with a fresh half dozen. These worked in fifteen-, sometimes eighteen-hour shifts divided into three-hour phases. Each of those phases consisted of two hours' actual work followed by an hour of resting in situ, or, using the obvious anagram, in suit.

Dinah, working in her robot shop, didn't have a direct view of what they were doing, since her window faced away from the truss where they spent all of their time. She could watch their activities on video feeds if she wanted, but she had other things she needed to be doing.

After the micrometeoroid/Luk incident, Dinah had scored a small victory for robotdom by putting her flock to work getting the surviving Luks squared away. Amalthea was attached to the forward end of Izzy, which, because of its orbital direction, was most exposed to impacts from space junk. In effect the asteroid had been put there as a sort of battering ram, protecting everything aft of it from collisions. There was enough space on its aft side that several Luks could nestle there, improving their odds of long-term survival as well as cutting down on cosmic ray exposure.

Dinah's crew of iron-mining robots had been made obsolete, at least for the time being, by her boss's pivot toward frozen water. So, when not making tiny critters scurry around on slabs of contraband ice, she had made the older robots useful by getting them to drill holes and anchor some connection points—eye bolts, basically—into Amalthea's back side and then moor the Luks to them using cables. This was not a hard-and-fast mooring system, so at first they tended to drift around and lazily bump into each other like a string of balloons. But after a day or two they settled into a stable configuration that just happened to block Dinah's view out her window. All she could see now was plastic. She didn't mind. After seeing the risks that the Scouts were taking, she didn't mind anything at all.

Individual layers of the Luk were fairly transparent, but the view was gauzy because the layers were so many. She could make out the form of her neighbor's body but not see the face. It was definitely a woman.

The Scouts' shifts overlapped around the clock. The woman outside Dinah's window came back in from her shift every day around what for Dinah was the middle of the morning. Dinah could see her clambering laboriously along the surface of Amalthea, using the mooring points, planning each move, avoiding the cables and the umbilicals. She must have been exhausted beyond words. Dinah had once done a two-hour stint in a space suit and been wiped out for a day. Sometimes Dinah would send a Grabb or a Siwi out to afford the woman an extra handhold when it looked like she needed one. The woman would turn her head and look at Dinah through the glass dome of her helmet and blink her eyes in what Dinah took to be an expression of gratitude. Eventually she would reach the open portal of her Vestibyul and go back into it, whereupon (unseen by Dinah) the automatic mechanism would do its thing, locking her suit into its socket, equalizing the pressure, opening the door, and enabling her to extract her head, arms, and body. Finding the ratchet wrench floating at the end of its chain of plastic zip ties, the woman would reach "above" her head and remove the twenty-four bolts securing the Luk diaphragm onto its flange, carefully rethreading each bolt into its hole so that it wouldn't drift around loose, and then she would finally pull herself through the forty-centimeter portal into the comparatively spacious environment of the Luk. Along the way she would collect her "mail," which was deposited in each Vestibyul during the occupant's shift. This consisted of food; drink; toiletries; a bag of ice that would turn into water, providing a simple temperature-control scheme; bags for disposal of feces; and, in her case, tampons.

Because of the roundabout and improvised manner in which things were working now, Dinah did not have a way to communicate with this woman directly, or even to learn her name. This seemed ridiculous, but it was the same general phenomenon that had made it impossible for the firemen to talk to the police officers on 9/11. The Scouts were just using different radios with different frequencies, and Dinah didn't have one.

By checking biographies on the NASA website, and by the process of elimination, she determined that this was Tekla Alekseyevna Ilyushina. She was a test pilot. She had competed in the most recent Olympics as a heptathlete and taken a bronze medal. As such she might have had glorious career options as a propaganda idol during the old Soviet days. But the recent conservative drift of Russian culture had left few slots available for women in male-dominated professions such as the military or the space program. Consequently much of her work experience had been outside of Russia, working for privately funded aerospace companies. She had returned a few years ago to become one of two active female cosmonauts. Dinah was cynical enough to see politics as the basis of that; in order for Roskosmos to remain on speaking terms with NASA and the European Space Agency, they had to have at least one or two females qualified to go into space.

Tekla was thirty-one. She had been somewhat glammed up for her official cosmonaut photograph, with a stiff, outmoded Princess Di hairdo that didn't suit her at all. During the most recent Olympics she had been rated one of the fifty hottest female athletes by a click-bait website, but she was buried in the back of the rankings. Dinah thought her comely, with the high cheekbones, the green eyes, the blond hair, and all the other attributes one would expect of a Slavic superwoman. But she understood why Tekla had been rated number forty-eight out of fifty, for she had a kind of chilly, strong-jawed look about her that forced the makers of the website to be selective about camera angles, and, Dinah suspected, to make some use of Photoshop. The sort of men who would browse that kind of website would find Tekla off-putting in a way they couldn't quite put their finger on.

They would be intimidated by the taut cords of her deltoids during the shot put competition. Dinah made a point of not reading any of the comment threads. She already knew what those would say.

Tekla had been sent up here to die, and she probably knew it.

At the end of each shift when she squirted through the flange to float free in the milky plastic bubble of the Luk, she would peel off the fluid cooling garment that she wore against her skin all day long. This was made of stretchy blue mesh with plastic tubing stitched between its layers. It had no effect until it was plugged into a pump that circulated cool water through the tubes. Tekla must have hated it after sixteen hours, and so it came off first. Then, peeling her underwear down to her knees, she would deflate and remove the foley catheter that had been draining her bladder while she'd been at work. She would wipe herself down with premoistened towelettes that had been provided in her "mail," and stuff those into a refuse bag. It appeared that she had shaved her head, or simply given herself a buzz cut, prior to leaving Earth, so she didn't have to mess with hair. Only then would Tekla open up her packet of emergency rations and begin to eat. This often led to defecation, which she had to handle in the crudest way possible, with a plastic bag and another series of premoistened towelettes. All of it went into her refuse bag, which she deposited in her Vestibyul for collection during her next shift. Then Tekla would turn off the white LED strip that provided the Luk's only illumination, and sometimes spend a little while gazing at the screen of a tablet computer before sliding a blindfold over her eyes and falling asleep.

Izzy circled the Earth every ninety-two minutes, passing through a complete day/night cycle each time, and so half the time that Tekla was asleep Dinah could look right out her window and see her suspended there, all but naked, floating in the Luk like a fetus in its bubble of amniotic fluid.

Dinah watched Tekla go through this routine for about a week, and found it all inordinately distracting. She brought Ivy, and later Rhys, into the chop shop to behold the sleeping Tekla through the window. They talked of Tekla and emailed each other pictures of Tekla that they had dug up on the Internet.

"That could be you or me, honey," Dinah said to Ivy.

"It is us," Ivy said, "it's just a matter of degree."

"Do you think we're going to end up like that?"

Ivy thought about it, shook her head. "Look, the way she's living isn't sustainable."

"You think it's a suicide mission?"

"I think it's a gulag," Ivy said, "a little gulag right outside your window."

"You think she's in some kind of trouble?"

"I think we're all in some kind of trouble," Ivy reminded her.

"Oh yeah, I forgot."

"She's lucky, remember?" Meaning that Tekla had at least found a way off the planet.

"She doesn't look lucky," Dinah said. "I've never seen anyone so isolated. Does she talk to someone on that tablet? Or is she just surfing?"

"I can ask Spencer, if you want," Ivy said. "I'm sure he's logging all the packets."

Dinah knew that Ivy was only kidding, but she answered, "Nah. She deserves that much privacy at least."

Rhys's reaction was to become aroused. He was reasonably discreet about it. But the elapsed time between his seeing Tekla and having sex with Dinah was, generously estimating, perhaps half an hour. Not that Rhys really needed a lot of help to start his motor. And not that Dinah did either. She had always known they were going to do it.

She had known this based on the way he smelled, at least when he was not in the middle of being sick. In other times and places, the way he smelled would not have been enough. They'd have dated first, or something. There'd have been complications having to do with existing relationships, incompatible lifestyles, fraternization policies. But here it was just automatic. And it was tremendous.

Based on what she was hearing from Internet buzz from the ground, it was also pretty universal. The human race might be about to disappear, but not before putting on a two-year frenzy of recreational sex.

Actually sleeping together was another matter. Rhys didn't seem to mind it in principle. But it was difficult logistically. Astronauts generally slept in bags that kept them from floating about at random while they were unconscious. The bags were designed for one person. NASA hadn't gotten around to manufacturing two-person bags yet, so if they felt drowsy afterward, they would improvise, swaddling themselves together with whatever they could cobble up. But it never lasted more than a few minutes. Then he would go back to his duties, and if she felt like a nap, she would climb into a bag that she kept in her shop, sometimes peeking out the window, guiltily, at poor Tekla.

One day, after Tekla had left for work, Dinah took one of the chocolate bars she had brought up from Earth, wrote her email address on the wrapper, and handed it off to a Grabb, which she then put out the airlock. She piloted the Grabb across Amalthea's surface to the mooring point where Tekla's Vestibyul was cabled in place, then made it climb along the cable (which was easy, it had an algorithm for that) and clamber into the Vestibyul, where it took up position and waited, holding the chocolate bar out in a free claw.

When Tekla came back at the end of her shift, Dinah got the satisfaction of watching her unwrap the bar and eat the chocolate. She held up one hand and sort of waved through the plastic. Dinah couldn't resolve her facial expression.

The Grabb was still in the Vestibyul, and would remain trapped there until Tekla's next departure. Seeing Tekla float over in that direction, Dinah turned to her computer and switched on the video feed from the Grabb. She was fascinated to see Tekla's face, clearly resolved, float into the frame.

She didn't look that bad. Dinah had been expecting someone who looked like a concentration camp survivor. But she appeared to be getting enough food.

Of course, she could not see Dinah. And there was no audio hookup. Since there was no sound in a vacuum, space robots didn't come with microphones or speakers.

Tekla was just staring at the Grabb, impassive, perhaps wondering whether it could see her.

Dinah slipped her hand into the data glove, did the thing that made it connect to the Grabb's free claw, and waved.

Tekla's green eyes flicked down in their sockets as she observed this. Still no emotion.

Dinah was mildly offended. Was the Grabb not adorably cute, in its ugly mechanical way? Was the wave not an amusing gesture?

Tekla held up the candy bar wrapper. On it, beneath Dinah's email address, she had written NO EMAIL.

What did that mean? That she lacked an email address? That her tablet couldn't receive it?

Or was she imploring Dinah not to communicate with her that way?

The Grabb had a headlamp, a high-powered white LED that she could switch on by hitting a key on her keyboard. Dinah turned it on, saw the glow on Tekla's face, the highlights on the lenses of her eyes.

Did the Russians even use the same Morse code as Americans?

Tekla had to know it. She was a pilot.

Dinah made the light flash with the dots and dashes for M O R S E.

Tekla nodded, and Dinah could see her mouth making the word *"Da."*

Dinah signaled:

DO YOU NEED ANYTHING?

The faintest trace of a smile came over Tekla's lips. It was not a warm kind of smile. More bemused.

She held up what was left of the chocolate bar, and pointed to it.

Dinah returned:

TOMORROW

Tekla nodded. Then she turned away, her buzz-cut blond hair glinting in the light of the LEDs, and drifted back into the middle of her onion.

"FIVE PERCENT" WAS HOW IVY BEGAN THE NEXT MEETING IN THE Banana.

It was full to capacity: the original twelve-person crew of Izzy, the five who had come up on the Soyuz on A+0.17, and Igor, the Scout who had come in from the cold when his suit had failed. He, Marco, and Jibran had prepped for the meeting by jury-rigging some fans to blow more air through the space, so it wouldn't fill up with carbon dioxide. This had prompted Dinah to joke that perhaps all meetings should take place in hermetically sealed rooms, so that they could only go on for so long. No one, with the possible exception of Rhys, had seen it as funny. Anyway, the roar of ventilation was even louder than it usually was in space, and so Ivy had to speak up and use her Big Boss Voice.

"This is Day Thirty-Seven," Ivy went on. "That's ten percent of a year. If it's true that we had two years from Zero to the Hard Rain, then we have already burned through five percent of the time during which we can expect to receive any help from Earth. Five percent of the time needed to turn this installation into a society and an ecosystem that is sustainable indefinitely."

Ivy was standing with her back to the big screen, so she couldn't see the reaction of the Arkitects down below, in some conference room at the other end of the video link. For today's meeting, there were three of them: Scott "Sparky" Spalding, who was still the administrator of NASA; Dr. Pete Starling, the president's science advisor; and Ulrika Ek, a Swedish woman who had worked as a project manager for one of the private commercial space startups until recent events had forced a career change: she was now coordinating the activities of several different space agencies and private companies as they worked on the Cloud Ark. Apparently, she had become the Arkitect-in-chief.

"Apparently" being the key word, since every time Dinah had any contact with the ground she was reminded of how little she understood of what was happening there. On one level she was one of the luckiest people in the human race. She was going to get to stay alive. At the same time, she and the others got very little information from the planet, and had to piece things together from a jumble of clues.

She'd compared notes on this with Ivy, who had confirmed that even she had little to go on, and what she did hear contradicted itself from hour to hour.

It had all become Kremlinology. Back in the heyday of the Soviet Union, the only way for Westerners to guess what was going on there was to look at the lineup of dignitaries on Lenin's Tomb in the May Day parade, and riddle it out from the seating chart and who shook hands with whom. Now Dinah was doing the same thing with these three faces on the screen. Sparky was no use. He'd spent so much time in space that he had developed a kind of thousand-light-year stare. He was famous for being oblivious to the political side of things.

His opposite in that respect was Pete Starling. Pete's job was to mutter scientific explanations into the president's ear. He'd been doing rather a lot of it in the last thirty-seven days. He had a background running big science programs at universities, climbing the ladder from Mankato State to Georgia Tech to Columbia to Harvard in a mere ten years. Why was he sitting in on this meeting? There was little he could contribute. He must be here as the eyes and ears of J.B.F.

But why should J.B.F. care? No decisions were going to be made here; it was just a status report, a check-in.

As soon as Ivy finished her sentence, the corners of Pete's mouth turned down. He looked at Ulrika Ek, a somewhat matronly woman in her late forties, extremely good at her job, according to Rhys. On the high-def video feed, Dinah saw the slightest deflection of her eyes, noticing the turn of Pete Starling's head, but not exactly acknowledging it.

Ulrika clearly didn't like him. But there was a reason she was a well-regarded project manager. "Ivy," she said, "just for clarity, when we speak of 'this installation' we're using the term in an elastic sense. Of necessity."

Ivy turned to look at the screen. " 'Installation' probably isn't the right word," she admitted. "Since it's not installed anywhere."

Pete Starling spoke up. "I believe that where Ulrika is going is that the Cloud Ark is a fluid concept that may paradigm-shift beyond recognition as we proceed adaptively through the next ninety-five percent of the timeline."

Ivy's brow furrowed. Something was going on, some kind of political tussle down on the ground. It was important to people like Pete.

"This is not efficient use of time," Fyodor said. "I am working to extend truss to receive Pioneers." Fyodor's English was excellent, but when he was annoyed, as he was now, he dropped his articles. "I have eight suits outside, five inside, for unlucky number of thirteen."

It had become common to use a form of synecdoche in which

"suit" denoted "a person qualified to perform extravehicular activities who is equipped with a space suit that still works."

"Pioneers arrive in two weeks, this is still true? Then I need more Scouts yesterday, as saying goes."

When Fyodor had come up to Izzy six months ago, it had been understood as a valedictory mission before getting shunted to an administrator's job at Roskosmos. Not that he hadn't taken his duties seriously, but he always seemed to be taking the long view, perceiving Izzy through the eyes of a future bureaucrat who would need to make it run smoothly until his retirement. That had all changed on Zero, of course. It had changed even more with the Russian invasion. No new rank or title had been bestowed on Fyodor. None was needed. All the Russians just accepted him, implicitly and without question, as their leader. And his manner had changed accordingly. He was scrupulously respectful of Ivy's authority, but there was no question that he was the boss of all things suit related, and the authority had seemed to make him physically larger and more imposing, his creased face tougher, his voice firmer.

Sparky answered him. "Fyodor, that fuel pump has been fixed. It was just a bad sensor. So the launch is going up as scheduled . . ." He checked his wristwatch, did a mental calculation. "Fourteen hours from now. Six hours after that, you'll have your suits."

"And the Zavods, the Vestibyuls—the things I mentioned."

"We have had teams of engineers working on those fixes around the clock, Fyodor."

"I am very worried about door closing mechanisms."

THE REMAINDER OF THE MEETING HAD TO DO WITH THE PIONEERS who would start coming up in another two weeks, and who would live, for the time being, in rigid or inflatable habitats more accommodating than Luks. These would be docked along a series of pressurized tubes, little different in principle from the big spiral-wound ventilation ducts seen in warehouses, that would ramify outward from attachment points in the truss. Little of it concerned Dinah and so her attention drifted to her laptop. She had other things she could be working on, and Ivy's reminder about the 5 percent had not left her in a mood to woolgather during a long meeting.

Most of her work of late had been on ice crawlers. And, as of the most recent shipment, ice tunnelers. But she had resolved that she would not shut down her progress on the iron-mining robots. Even if she only spent fifteen minutes a day on them, it was better than suspending work altogether. She was afraid that if she ever did that the entire project would disappear.

To that end, she kept a window open in the lower left corner of her screen, showing video from Amalthea, mostly the point-of-view cameras of robots that were actually doing things. It was always there in her peripheral vision as she attended to email and scheduling spreadsheets and Gantt charts.

And at some point she noticed something that wasn't quite right. A few minutes later, she noticed it again and put her other work on hold. She expanded the window and took control of the robot that was transmitting the video. She swiveled its camera around until she had a view of the thing that had been bothering her.

It was Tekla, floating in her Luk. She was bright blue, which meant that she had donned her cooling garment. That was normal. She did it every day as she got ready for her shift. The next step should have been to squirm feetfirst through the Luk's flange into the Vestibyul. But she wasn't doing that. She was going back and forth between the Vestibyul and the middle of the Luk. She would go through the flange headfirst (which was abnormal) and do something for a minute or two, then withdraw into the Luk and thumb away on her tablet for a while.

She was late. Every other day, she'd been in her suit and out on the truss by this time.

Dinah wasn't the only person who had become distracted by her laptop. Fyodor—normally not a fan of email and other such modern diversions—was watching his screen too, occasionally making eye contact with the equally distracted Maxim, who kept making a gesture like tugging at an imaginary beard.

Something was wrong.

What had Fyodor said? *I am very worried about door closing mechanisms.*

He wasn't just saying that in the abstract. He was referring to a specific situation. He was talking about Tekla.

Tekla could clamber from her Luk, through the Vestibyul, and into her suit, but she couldn't close the door behind her back. She needed the mechanism for that. If it didn't work, then she couldn't seal the suit. And if the suit wasn't sealed, she was trapped inside her OVL (as they had taken to calling the combination of the Orlan suit with the Vestibyul and the Luk).

It was not exactly an emergency, but it was bad. In order to get "mail" she had to detach her suit from the Vestibyul, leaving it open for the delivery to be made in her absence. "Mail" included food, water, ice, and fresh CO_2 scrubber canisters.

Dinah didn't know how long Tekla could survive without "mail," but she doubted it was more than a day. The heat would get her first.

They had to figure out some way to get Tekla inside Izzy. And since the OVL was jury-rigged, it didn't have a docking port like a normal spacecraft. There was no hatch, no way of mating to an airlock.

She studied Fyodor's face through the rest of the meeting, which went on for another half hour, and began to understand something: he was getting ready to sacrifice Tekla. "Ready" in the sense of emotionally hardening himself to that reality.

Dinah understood NO EMAIL now. It was simply part of being a Scout that you would probably not survive. And if you knew you were going to be sacrificed, it wouldn't help matters to be spamming the Scout email list with pleas for help and goodbye messages. Tekla could communicate with Fyodor, and Fyodor only, and that was for a reason. It was a reason that the defenders of Leningrad, Stalingrad, and Moscow would have understood and accepted perfectly well. But it was a little bit out of step with the modern ethos.

Correction: with the modern ethos as it had existed during the Age of the One Moon.

It was perfectly in step with how things were now.

Part of her wanted to go and plead with Fyodor to mount a dramatic and heroic rescue mission. There had to be a way to make it happen. They had all seen *Apollo 13,* they quoted lines of dialogue from it all the time.

But she already knew the answer. The Pioneers would begin arriving, shiploads of them, in two weeks. All of them would die on arrival if the correct preparations had not been made. No time could be spared. More Scouts were on the way to replace Tekla.

And for once she was glad that the meeting ran long, that Sparky didn't stick to the agenda, and that Pete Starling exploited it to fill time with more buzzwords. Because an idea was slowly taking shape in her head. She would have to run it by Ivy and Rhys and perhaps Marco, she would want to have Margie Coghlan—the closest thing they had to a doctor—standing by, but she could do it with no help at all from Fyodor or any of the other suits.

Fyodor was typing something with his index fingers. She locked her eyes on his face and kept them there until he was finished. He seemed to have detected her gaze on him, because he then looked up and stared straight into her eyes, maintaining a perfect poker face.

She stared back.

Awareness crept into Fyodor's expression. Awareness that Dinah knew about the problem. Fyodor knew the layout of Izzy better than anyone. He knew where Dinah spent her time, and that Dinah only had to look out her window to see what was going on. She could see him putting this all together in his head.

He was expecting her to make some emotional appeal. So, it was important for her to stay cool. As soon as she turned on the waterworks, she would lose his respect, and his attention, forever.

"Fyodor," she said, "I got this."

He blinked in surprise, then, after some hesitation, made the tiniest of nods.

"Got what?" Pete Starling asked, over the video link. "Am I missing something?"

"No," Dinah said. "We are just proceeding adaptively to leverage our core competencies."

BASED ON STATS FROM THE *50 HOTTEST OLYMPIANS* WEBSITE, IVY WAS a fairly close match for Tekla physically. Tekla was huskier, but Ivy was an inch taller. So, the first thing they did was to stuff Ivy into the small airlock that Dinah used for her robots. With her head tucked and her knees drawn up to her chest, she fit into it with room to spare. Dinah took a picture, then appended it to an email message with detailed instructions.

Spencer Grindstaff, who, as a young CIA contractor, had cut his teeth hacking into email systems operated by foreign governments, figured out a way to send email to Tekla's tablet by wrapping it in an envelope that made it look like it came from Fyodor.

Dinah watched Tekla read that email. She looked up from the tablet toward the window, then turned her gaze toward the airlock. Until then, Dinah had worried that Tekla might be losing consciousness, since she hadn't moved in several hours. She guessed that Tekla was trying to conserve oxygen and reduce thermogenesis by moving as little as possible.

Dinah zip-tied a high-powered LED light to the inner hatch of the airlock, then closed it. She opened the valve that dumped its air into space, allowing it to "fill up" with vacuum, and then actuated the lever—a simple mechanical linkage—that flipped the outer hatch open. She could see the white glow of the LED reflecting against the plastic of Tekla's Luk bubble a few meters away, and she saw Tekla's head turn as the light got her attention.

Several robots had to act in concert to move Tekla's Luk bubble around until it was pressed against the airlock. This was a somewhat maddening process, like trying to grab an inflated balloon with a pair of needle-nosed pliers. Dinah had been trying to do it with Siwis—Sidewinders—of which she now had a dozen in operation. A Siwi could join head-to-tail with another Siwi to double its length, and the process could be repeated indefinitely to construct a sort of smart, instrumented tentacle. By planting the tail of one Siwi against Amalthea, and bolstering the connection by holding it down with a couple of anchored Grabbs, she was able to make another Siwi slither up the first one and connect to its head, which was projecting up into space. A third Siwi climbed up the first two and concatenated itself, and so on and so forth, building a stalk that reached up from the surface of the asteroid and began to curve around the bubble in which Tekla was imprisoned.

So far so good. But the longer the chain grew, the worse it behaved. The Siwis were constructed like caterpillars, consisting of many identical segments connected by flexible joints. The joints were motorized, and the motors were supposed to follow commands embedded in Dinah's code, and it was all supposed to work in a predictable way. The problem was that each joint had a bit of flexibility, which as far as Dinah was concerned was error. Those errors accumulated as the length of the chain grew, so that by the time she had connected three Siwis together, she found it difficult to know, let alone control, the position of the end of the stalk. And when she tried to apply force by making the chain curve around the slippery, bulgy surface of the Luk, matters only got worse.

Rhys showed up a few hours into the project and watched. He'd be silent for hours, then suddenly ask a question that was strangely off-kilter and yet showed he was thinking about the problem.

"What if you turned all the motors off and let the whole thing go slack?" he asked.

"Aren't you supposed to be building a torus?" she demanded, and turned around to give him her best attempt at a killing look.

"First we have to solve this problem," he said gently.

She had more to say, but instead she went silent. Rhys was clowning around with his necklace again. He was in the habit of wearing a chain around his neck—nothing fancy or bulky, just a simple loop of twisted-link jewelry chain in stainless steel, which he used as a way to keep thumb drives and other important small objects from floating away. At the moment, though, he had removed all of that stuff, leaving the chain unencumbered, and he had got it spinning around his neck. It had opened up into a broad, undulating oval that didn't touch his neck or collar anywhere, so it was just orbiting around him in free space. Dinah had seen him do this before, typically while bored in meetings. He had learned a few tricks for speeding it up and coaxing it into different shapes by blowing on it with a drinking straw or flicking it with a fingernail. It didn't form a perfect circle, as one might expect. The moving train of links could be molded into almost any shape, and would stay that way until disturbed. When Dinah turned around and noticed he was doing it again, she was about to roll her eyes and say something like *For fuck's sake can't you do anything useful with that brain,* but the look on Rhys's face suggested that he was up to something more than just playing around.

The chain had been running in an elongated racetrack shape, nearly buzzing his neck on one turn, but he flicked at the straightaways and broadened it into something approaching a circle, then ducked out of it, leaving the loop spinning in midair. "Channeling the wisdom of my ancestors, if you must know," he said.

"You had ancestors in zero gee?"

"Alas, no. My great-great-great-great-uncle John Aitken was an eccentric Victorian meteorologist with an even more eccentric hobby:

studying the physics of moving chains. Unfortunately for him, he had to do it in his drawing room in Falkirk, where there is, I'm sorry to say, gravity. He had to approximate this sort of thing"—Rhys nodded at the whirring loop of chain—"by building exceedingly clever machines."

"Then he must have been a clever man indeed."

"Fellow of the Royal Society and friend of Lord Kelvin, since you mentioned it. Do you see where I'm going?"

"Well, a minute ago you gave me a fat clue by suggesting that I turn off all of the motors in the Siwi train. Were I to do that, it would go completely limp and become, for all practical purposes, a length of chain."

"Yes," Rhys drawled, and poked an index finger up into the chain's path. It caught on his knuckle, hiccupped, and suddenly wrapped around his hand in a chaotic tangle.

"That's confidence-inspiring," Dinah said.

"Hold on, it turns out my uncle John knew a few things. And later on, another chap, name of Kucharski, in Berlin, worked on this stuff too." Rhys was untangling the chain, looking for its clasp. When he found it, he undid it, converting the chain from a loop into a segment about as long as his arm. "Unfortunately there's gravity in Berlin too, so he had to do stuff like this on tables. Hold it right there, would you please?" And he got Dinah to pinch the middle of the chain between her fingers, keeping it fixed in space. From there, he drew the two ends back toward himself, forming the chain into a skinny, elongated U. "You can let go now, gently."

Dinah released the chain and allowed herself to float back from it, since Rhys had taken on something of the air of a magician in performance. He let go of one of the ends, kept the other grasped between his thumb and index finger. "What happens if I pull?" he asked. "Any predictions?"

"The whole thing will move back toward you, I guess."

"Let's try it. Hold your finger up just there."

Dinah pointed "up" and allowed Rhys to reach out with his free hand and grasp her gently by the wrist, arranging her hand so that the finger was several inches away from the vertex of the U-shaped bend in the chain. "Here goes nothing," he said, and began to pull the chain toward him—away from Dinah. Contrary to what she'd expected, the bend started to propagate away from Rhys, and toward Dinah, until finally the free end hurtled around, like a whip cracking, and made several quick turns around her finger, snaring her. "Gotcha," he said, and began pulling her toward him.

"Just like a bullwhip," she observed, unwinding the chain from her finger too late to avoid being drawn into close, cozy contact with Rhys.

"It is exactly the same physics," he confirmed. "Kucharski called that thing—the traveling U-shaped bend—a *Knickstelle*. It means something like 'kink place.' "

"Chains, whips, and now kinks. I'm learning so much about your Victorian ancestors, Rhys."

"You probably thought this was a mere diversion," he said.

"Oh, no. I see your point. Rather than trying to control the Siwi chain, like a tentacle, all clenching muscles, let it relax and whip around the Luk like a smart chain."

This little digression into nineteenth-century physics turned out to be one of those "one step back, five steps forward" sorts of trades. It was the work of a few minutes to concatenate four more Siwis onto the existing chain, then turn off all the motors except a few that she used to fashion a U-shaped bend. Applying tension to one end of it caused the *Knickstelle* to propagate just as in Rhys's demonstration, so that the end of the chain whipped lazily around the entire circumference of the Luk. Several attempts were required before the grappler at the end of the chain was able to snag a handhold on the far side, but then the Luk was securely captured in the chain's embrace. Grabbs could scuttle along it carrying the ends of cables anchored to other parts of Amalthea, or Izzy, and thus the Luk was gradually ensnared in a loose web of hardware that Dinah used to draw it away from the position where it had been anchored, and pull it up snug against the module containing Dinah's shop. As it came closer, the vague nimbus of white light thrown against the Luk by the LED in the airlock narrowed and sharpened, and was finally all but snuffed out as the big balloon enveloped the protruding stub of the airlock chamber. The airlock was now poking into the nested layers of the Luk like a finger prodding a balloon.

Even after the success of the whip-cracking gambit, this took most of a day. Rhys drifted off, as was his habit. Bo, the Mongolian cosmonaut, slipped into Dinah's shop, observed silently for a couple of hours, and then began finding ways to make herself useful. She learned how to use the data glove and the mouse-and-keyboard interface just by watching Dinah, and by the end of the day was piloting Grabbs around, and manipulating Siwis, like an old hand.

Margie Coghlan showed up to watch the final preparations. She was an Australian physiologist who had been sent up to Izzy a few months ago to study the effects of spaceflight on human health. Dinah had always found her a little brusque, but maybe that was just an Australian thing. She brought with her a box of medical supplies and surgical equipment. All the astronauts on the ISS had medical training. Dinah and Ivy had done their time working in Houston emergency rooms stitching up trauma victims and setting bones. But Margie was the best.

"Not exactly what you signed on for," Dinah said.

"None of us is getting what we signed on for," Margie observed.

"With the possible exception of Tekla," said another voice. Ivy's. She was not in Dinah's shop—that was full now with Dinah, Bo, and Margie—but she was in the adjacent SCRUM.

"Ivy, you ready to set another record?" Dinah asked.

"Ready to try," Ivy said.

This was Q code for the number of women on the space station at one time. The old record had been four, set in 2010. They had tied it months ago when Margie and Lina had come up to Izzy, joining Ivy and Dinah. They had broken it when Bo had turned up in the Soyuz launch three weeks ago. Tekla would make six, if they could only get her through the airlock.

Or the number might drop back if this went wrong.

"Bo, thanks for helping. You should probably go out with Ivy."

"Good luck," Bo said, and, pushing off from the inner hatch of the airlock, drifted across Dinah's shop and out through the hatch into the SCRUM, where Ivy hovered, waiting.

"Everything sealed up behind you?" Dinah asked, more out of nervousness than anything else. It was out of the question that Ivy would get that wrong. Since the breakup of the moon, they'd intensified their precautions anyway, keeping the various modules of Izzy separated by airtight hatches wherever possible so that the perforation of one module by a bolide wouldn't lead to the destruction of the whole complex.

Ivy didn't answer.

"You know what to do with that hatch if this all goes sideways," Dinah went on.

"You talk a lot when you're nervous," Ivy said.

"I concur," Margie said. "Are we going to do this or not? That woman might be asphyxiating out there."

"Okay. Giving her the signal now," Dinah said.

In the space program that she had dreamed of when she'd been a little girl with a "Snoopy the Astronaut" poster on the ceiling of her shack in the hinterlands of South Africa, or watching live feeds from the space station on satellite TV in western Australia, the signal would have been a terse utterance into a microphone, or a message struck out on a keyboard. But what she actually did was drift over to her little window and peer through fourteen layers of milky translucent plastic at Tekla, almost close enough to reach out and touch, and give a thumbs-up.

Tekla nodded and held up a small object next to her head. It was a folding knife with a belt clip and a lanyard, which she had prudently wrapped around her wrist. Using one thumb she snapped its serrated blade open.

Dinah nodded.

Tekla nodded back, then drifted out of view, headed toward the airlock.

"Here she comes," Dinah said.

She had already sized Margie up as a woman of some physical strength. She was stocky, but in a powerful rather than a flabby way.

Dinah got a grip on the mechanical linkage that would swing the outer hatch of the airlock closed. "Brace me," she said.

She was worried about all that plastic. Shreds of it were certain to get caught in the hatch's delicate seal.

The principle was simple enough. She'd run through it in her head a hundred times. If Tekla cut a slit, a few inches long, through the innermost layer of the Luk, air would rush out into the space between it and the next layer, which was at a lower pressure. If Tekla put her head and shoulder into that slit, she'd become like a cork in a champagne bottle, and the pressure would try to force her out. If she then cut a slit through the next layer, and the next, and the next, a wave of pressure would build up behind her and spit her out like a watermelon seed. And as long as she kept aiming for the white LED on the airlock's inner hatch, she would be projected into that airlock.

At that point she'd be naked and unprotected in the middle of a jet of air that would be exploding away from her into the vacuum. And at that point—

There was a whoosh and a meaty thunking impact.

"Jesus Christ, I think that was it," Margie said.

"She is out," Bo confirmed. Bo, out in the next compartment, had a tablet on which she was watching a video feed from a nearby Grabb. "I mean she is in the airlock."

Dinah hauled on the handle, swinging the outer hatch closed. Her body, in accordance with Newton's Third Law, moved in the opposite direction, stealing her force, but Margie's arms caught her in a bear hug and pushed back—Margie had found a way to brace herself.

Bo gasped. "You are smashing her foot!"

"Oh, shit."

"Her foot is sticking out."

"Dinah," Ivy said, "you have to open the hatch a little, her foot's caught."

Dinah relaxed her arms. What if Tekla was unconscious? What if she was unable to draw herself up into the fetal position they'd shown her in that photograph?

The change in Bo's and Ivy's tone told her otherwise. "She's in!" Ivy exclaimed.

"Close the hatch, close it!" Bo was shouting.

Dinah swung the handle all the way around and snapped it into its locked position. It didn't feel quite right, but at least it was closed.

Meanwhile Margie was actuating the valve that let air into the airlock. This was supposed to be a gradual process, but she just let it go explosively, with a sudden movement of the air that tugged at their diaphragms and popped their ears.

"Blood is coming out," Bo said dully. "Leaking out of the hatch."

"Fuck!" Dinah said. Because that meant two bad things at once: the outer hatch wasn't really closed, and Tekla was hurt.

"Let's get it open," Margie said.

In the end it took all four of them: Dinah, Margie, Bo, and Ivy, all crammed into the space with their fingers under the rim of the hatch, pushing against the wall with all the strength in their legs and their backs, to break the seal. Whereupon air whooshed out of the compartment and the hatch flew open, like when you finally break the seal on a vacuum-packed jar and the lid flies off.

Tekla was in there, drawn up into the prescribed fetal position, a solid mass of red.

They all stared at her speechless for a moment.

Her head moved. She turned her face up toward them, revealing a huge red smear where an eye ought to have been.

The only thing that kept Dinah from screaming like a little girl was her gorge rising up into her throat. Bo drew in a long breath and began muttering something.

Tekla's hands unfolded and gripped the rim of the chamber. The lanyard of the knife was still wound around her right wrist. The handle of the knife trailed after it. Dinah supposed that its blade had been snapped off until she understood that the whole thing had become embedded in Tekla's forearm.

Tekla pulled herself out a few inches, then stopped. Her head was now projecting into the room.

An eye opened. A bloodshot eye in a bloody face. But a normal, working eye.

Dinah's ears began working again and she realized that she was hearing a loud hissing noise. It was the sound of air escaping from the International Space Station, not through a huge leak but through small gaps in the airlock's outer seal. The air was flowing past Tekla's body, creating a vacuum behind her, a vacuum she had to fight in order to advance into the room.

She felt embarrassed then, in the manner of a hostess who forgets to properly welcome a guest, and she reached down and grabbed one of Tekla's hands. Margie got the other and with a final sucking, squelching noise they dragged Tekla's blood-lubricated form out of the airlock chamber and into the space station.

Dinah half closed the inner hatch of the airlock. The Big Hoover, as old-school astronauts referred to the vacuum of space, took care of the rest, and slammed it closed with frightening violence.

They'd lost a measurable percentage of the atmosphere in this module. Not enough to cause oxygen deprivation but more than enough to set off alarms all over Izzy, and all the way down to Houston.

Maggie got to work on Tekla's arm, which was bleeding quite a lot, while Ivy and Bo, now blue-gloved, cleaned off her face with towelettes. The picture was getting clearer. The basic idea had worked. Tekla's knife work had been true and well aimed, and perhaps more effective than was really good for her. She had been spat out of the Luk's outermost layer, and into the airlock chamber, with great force, slamming her face into a metal fitting along the way and opening up big lacerations above and below the eye. These had bled profusely. In the same moment the blade of her knife had caught on something and turned back on her and been jammed into her forearm. She had lain dazed for a moment, one leg hanging out the open hatch as Dinah had tried to close it on her, then had come to and drawn herself up as planned. For a few moments during all of this she had been exposed to vacuum, which hadn't done her bleeding wounds any favors, but air had rushed into the lock and equalized the pressure before irreparable damage could be inflicted.

As Dinah had worried, scraps of plastic had gotten caught in the outer hatch's gasket, accounting for those hissing air leaks. But most of them drifted off into space when she swung the hatch back open again, and the remaining bits, stuck to the gasket by Tekla's freeze-dried blood, she was able to pick clean using a programmed swarm of Nats. She ended up leaving that project as an exercise for Bo, who was climbing the robot learning curve with remarkable speed.

She drifted down the length of Izzy to the Hub and thence out to the torus, where Maggie, getting advice from trauma surgeons down in Houston, was working on Tekla's arm. This was a lot easier in the weak gravity of the torus—no globules of blood drifting around. Lina Ferreira and Jun Ueda, both also life scientists, were filling in as assistants.

Ivy was in her office fielding a shit storm of angry reaction from people down in Houston.

They were doing the surgery under local anesthesia, so Tekla was awake. They'd cleaned her up, and closed the lacerations around her eye socket with butterfly bandages and Krazy Glue. The silvery-blond stubble that covered her scalp was still darkened with coagulated blood along that side. The whites of her eyes were red, and she had thousands of tiny red marks all over her face. Dinah had been warned to expect those. They were called petechiae: broken capillaries just under the skin, caused by exposure to vacuum. But from the way her eyes moved in their sockets and focused on things, Dinah could see that her vision was basically intact.

"That was uncalled for," Tekla said to her.

"True," Dinah said.

"I shall be in trouble."

"So are we," Dinah said, nodding in the direction of Ivy's office. "We are all in trouble . . . with a bunch of dead people."

Tekla reacted very little, but among Margie and Lina and Jun there was a collective intake of breath, a momentary halt in the proceedings.

"Margie," said a Texan voice from the ground, "this dead surgeon would like you to clamp off that arteriole before it starts bleedin' again."

"Those of us who are going to live," Dinah said, "have to start living by our own lights."

Pioneers and Prospectors

"THE ICEMAN COMETH."

"Ah." Rhys sighed. "I was wondering which of us would be first to go there." He pulled out, drifted away, and did a peel-and-knot on the condom so expertly that it created dark stirrings of jealousy in Dinah's heart. But at least he didn't let anything get loose in Dinah's shop.

"This may have been your last delivery," Dinah said. "Of ice, that is."

"You've got your freezer?"

"Coming up on tomorrow's launch from Kourou."

"Any chance of getting them to send up a martini shaker with it?"

"We use plastic bags for that."

"Well, I hope that my deliveries—of ice, that is—have contributed something to whatever the hell you've been doing."

"Check this out," she said. She'd already wrapped herself in a blanket, but now she prodded the wall with a toe and drifted over to her workstation. With a bit of clicking around she brought up a video. The opening shot was stark: a cube of ice in a black chamber, lit up by bright but cold LEDs.

"From Arjuna HQ, I presume?" Rhys, still naked, came up behind her and wrapped an arm around her waist. She liked to think of it as an affectionate gesture. In part it was. But she'd been in zero gee long enough to understand that he also just didn't want to drift away while watching the movie.

"Yes."

A bearded strawberry-blond man entered the frame carrying a sheet of corrugated cardboard—the lid of a pizza box.

"That's Larz Hoedemaeker, I think—one of the guys I've been working with a lot."

Larz angled the pizza lid slightly toward the camera. It was mostly covered by iridescent fingernail-sized objects, like silicon beetles. Hundreds of them.

"That's a lot of Nats," Rhys remarked.

"Well . . . the whole point is to make a swarm."

"I understand. But it seems they've found a way to ramp up production."

Larz folded the cardboard diagonally to make it into a crude trough and then angled it down toward the block of ice. The Nats avalanched down and tumbled onto it in a heap. Quite a few of them skittered off and tumbled onto the floor. Larz exited the frame for a moment, then returned, pushing a wheeled swivel chair. He arranged this behind the block of ice, then disappeared again, then came back carrying a clock that he had apparently just taken down from the wall of an office. He balanced this on the seat of the swivel chair, leaning back against its lumbar support, so that it was clearly visible in the frame of the video. Then he departed.

A few moments later the lights got much brighter. "Simulating solar radiation," Dinah explained. "The Nats are solar powered, so the only way to test them is to have a light source as bright as the sun."

The clock's minute hand now began to sweep forward. "Time lapse?" Rhys asked.

"Yeah. This stuff happens slowly, as you've seen."

The Nats that had scattered to the floor scurried around aimlessly for a bit, then seemed to find the block of ice, and scaled its vertical sides. "Pretty good adhesion, you'll note," Dinah said.

Meanwhile the heap of Nats on top spread out like a pat of butter softening on a pancake, distributing themselves in a somewhat random but basically even layer atop the ice block. A few of them appeared to sink into the ice. "Melting their way in?" Rhys asked.

"No. Uses too much energy—and wouldn't work in zero gee. They are mechanically tunneling. See the piles forming?" She pointed to the top of the ice block, where mounds of white had begun to form around the exits of the tunnels. "That is spoil being carved out and ejected by the tunneling Nats."

"You can't make mounds in zero gee either," Rhys pointed out.

"One thing at a time!" she said, elbowing him. "The other guys are working on it, see?" She used the cursor to point out another Nat that was making its way along the surface. It seized hold of some little ice grains from a mound, then backed away and headed toward the edge of the ice block.

"How's it doing that?" Rhys asked.

"You know how when your hand is wet and you reach into the freezer and pick up an ice cube, it'll stick to your skin? That's all there is to it," Dinah said. "And that is also how they crawl around on the ice without falling off."

The minute hand on the clock began moving faster, and even the hour hand could be seen sweeping around now. The surface of the ice block became pitted and then began to sink toward the floor as material was removed. But at the same time, one edge of the block developed a bulge that grew into a cantilevered prong, like the horn on an anvil.

"What are they building?" Rhys asked.

"Doesn't matter. This is just a proof of concept."

The growth stopped, the clock dial slowed to normal time, another engineer walked in to snap some pictures of the result. Then the video cut away to a black screen.

"Interesting!" Rhys said.

She grabbed his hand before he could get away. "Hang on. Check out the superfast version."

This started a moment later. It was just the same movie, shown ten times faster. So it only lasted for a few seconds. The Nats were invisible because of the speed of their movement—just a jittery gray fog that came and went in patches. This drew the eye to the block of ice. Shown at this speed, it looked less like a crystalline slab and more like an amoeba, sinking down at one end while smoothly projecting a pseudopod into space.

"One has to assume," Rhys said, "that there's a reason why Sean Probst is so very keen on making ice sit up and do tricks for him."

"Yeah. But he's not sharing it with me."

"Is there any way," he wondered, "of joining those Nats end to end?"

"Into a chain?"

"Yes. The Siwis are serviceable, but much more complicated than they need to be."

"You have got chains on the brain. Yes, there's a way. And you can join them side to side to make a sheet."

"Uncle John is calling to me from beyond the grave, telling me to make something of his hobby."

"Well, stay in my good graces," she said, "and I'll let you play with some."

DAY 56

As of A+0.56, the Hub module around which the torus spun was no longer the aft-most part of Izzy. They called it H1 now. A larger hub, called H2, had been sent up on a heavy-lift booster from Cape Canaveral and mated with it.

H2 had originally been planned as the basis of a large space tourism operation. Rhys's original mission, for which he'd been planning and training for two years, had been to get that up and running. It had a new purpose now, of course, but functionally it would look the same: H2, the big central module, with a new and larger torus rotating around it. That new torus, inevitably called T2, was going to be assembled in space from a kit of rigid and inflatable parts, some of which had been shipped up packed inside of H2, others to follow later on subsequent launches. For the time being, H2 had four fat spokes extending from it to terminate in stubs where other parts, forming the rim of the wheel, would be added later.

The Scouts by then had achieved their basic mission, which had been to employ the Integrated Truss Assembly as a backbone to support a tree of hollow pipes, each about fifty centimeters in diameter, with wide spots every ten meters or so. A human being, provided they were reasonably fit, and did not suffer from claustrophobia, and did not have too much stuff in their pockets, could move through a tube of that diameter, somewhat like a hamster scurrying through a plastic tube in a cage. The wide spots were there so that two people going opposite directions could pass each other. Spherical modules served as connectors and branch points. The tubes terminated in docking locations where spacecraft of various types could lock on to the space station and establish solid, airtight seals.

For it had been obvious from the beginning that docking sites were going to be, in the lingo of Pete Starling, "the scarce resource," "the long pole," "the critical path." Building rockets, spacecraft, and space suits was no easy matter, but at least these things happened on the ground, where colossal resources could be thrown into beefing up production. An armada of space capsules hurled into orbit would have nowhere to go, however, unless they could dock somewhere. And the docking sites had to be built the hard way: on site, in orbit.

Docking was no joke, and required specific technology, but it was thoroughly understood and it had been done many times. The Chinese space program had standardized on the same system used by the Russians, so their spacecraft, like the Russians', could dock at the ISS. So far so good. But the fact remained that every manned spacecraft launched into orbit needed to reach a specific destination within a couple of days' time, before the occupants ran out of air, food, and water. The task of the Scouts, therefore, had been to vastly increase the number of docks in the quickest and cheapest possible way. Docks couldn't be too close together, so the distances between them had to be spanned by hamster tubes. Bracketed to the outside surfaces of those tubes, and still being installed by fresh waves of Scouts, were runs of plumbing and wiring, and structural reinforcements tied into the adjacent trusses.

The initial tube tree, built between about A+0.29 and A+0.50 by Tekla and the other first-wave Scouts, sported half a dozen docking locations. These were spoken for immediately by the first wave of so-called Pioneer launches: three Soyuz spacecraft, two Shenzhous, and a space tourism capsule from the United States.

Encouraged by the success of the launch that had carried Bo and Rhys, the Russians had found ways to cram five or six passengers on each Soyuz.

The Shenzhou spacecraft was based on the Soyuz design, except larger, and updated in various ways. Like the Soyuz, it was meant to carry a crew of three—but this was based on the assumption that those three would want to return to Earth alive. Modified for one-way trips, each Shenzhou carried half a dozen. And the American tourist capsule brought a complement of seven astronauts.

So, all told, the first wave of Pioneers brought three dozen people to Izzy, more than doubling its population. They were obliged to live in their space capsules, which had their own toilets, CO_2 scrubbers, and heat rejection systems. This made for crowded conditions, but it was a step up from the Luks.

On A+0.56, when the H2 module came up on the giant Falcon Heavy rocket, Tekla and the other surviving Scouts spent a day pulling out all that had been stuffed inside of it and anchoring it temporarily to the outside of the module. They then moved into H2, turning it into a Scout dormitory and saying goodbye to their increasingly tatterdemalion Luks, which were deflated, patched, folded up, and stored for later use in emergencies.

About two-thirds of the Pioneers had previous experience doing EVAs or had been hastily trained over the last few weeks. There were not enough space suits to go around—these were being produced as fast as possible on the ground—but the existing ones could be shared. Work shifts were shortened from fifteen to twelve hours, and then to eight, so that fresh bodies could be rotated through the available suits two or three times a day. The spacewalkers divided their time between assembling the T2 torus and extending the tube trees to provide docking space for the next wave of launches.

The remaining Pioneers, the non-spacewalkers, devoted themselves to other activities inside the pressurized parts of the space station. Dinah found herself with two assistants: Bo, who had seemingly assigned herself to the task, and Larz Hoedemaeker—the guy from the video. Larz was a young Dutch man who had been pursuing a graduate degree in robotics at Delft when he had been recruited by Arjuna Expeditions. Dinah knew him as a prolific email correspondent, always willing to answer her questions or supply code patches on short notice. Owing to some lapse in communications, she hadn't even known that he would be one of the passengers on the American tourist capsule that had arrived on Day 52 (for people were now dropping the A+ notation and simply referring to days by their numbers).

All she knew was that a large strawberry-blond man suddenly appeared in her shop, intent on hugging her. This was unusual. To put it mildly, the International Space Station, until now, had never been the kind of place for surprise visits.

Larz had a fistful of chocolate bars in one hand and a camera in the other, and all manner of stuff was spilling out of the pockets of his coverall: vials of morphine, antibiotics, reels of microchips on paper tape, disposable contact lenses, condoms, packets of dehydrated coffee, tubes of exotic lubricants, spare leads for mechanical pencils, bundles of zip ties. The policy now seemed to be that everyone being packed onto a ship first had to be so laden down with vitamins that they could hardly move.

Larz was an enjoyable person, and his first day on Izzy was pure fun for Dinah, who had not been able to have a face-to-face conversation with a colleague in a year. She showed him around the shop, such as it was, and let him drive robots around on the surface of Amalthea, and brought a few of her "Grimmed" robots in so that he could admire them. For, inspired by Rhys's comment of a few weeks ago, Dinah had been putting her otherwise idle robots to work making armor for other robots. The orderly way to do it would have been to bring pieces of the asteroid back to her little zero-gee smelter and produce nice little ingots of pure steel, then weld them onto the frames of the Grabbs. But this was making things too complicated. Amalthea was already made out of perfectly sound material. Maybe it was not structural-grade steel, but it was good enough to serve as radiation shielding. So she had just been slicing pieces of it off, leaving them in their original rough shape, and armoring Grabbs with overlapping plates of the stuff. They looked like walking asteroids now.

"It is an art project," Larz said. For a moment she thought he was trying to insult her. Because she had met a few engineers in her day who never would have combined art and engineering. But his face was happy and guileless, and it was clear that he was paying her a compliment.

Once she'd gotten a bit used to him, she broached the subject that had been on her mind now for several weeks: Why ice? Given that they had direct access to a giant chunk of iron, why was Arjuna now putting all of its efforts into working with a material that for all practical purposes didn't exist on Izzy?

"Some things are not always explained to me," Larz said, "but you know that we have talked for some time about going after a comet core."

"Sure," Dinah said. "We've talked about it. But those things are huge. What are we going to do with a few gigatons of water?"

Larz just blinked and looked mildly uneasy.

"It would take forever to move something that big!" Dinah said. "It is, like, a ten- or twenty-year project! We don't have that much time."

"Under the old conditions, yes."

"What do you mean, the old conditions?"

"Back in the day—before the Agent—when we talked about moving comets, we were talking about sending up a big mirror. Focusing the sun's light on the comet core, boiling off a little water, pushing it slowly to a new trajectory. Yes. That would take a long time. Like pushing a bowling ball with a feather."

"And what about that has changed?" Dinah asked. "Physics is physics."

"Yes," Larz said, "and some physics is *nuclear* physics."

"We're going to use nukes? I thought that was—Jesus. I don't even . . ."

"You don't appreciate how much things have changed down there," Larz said.

"I guess not!"

"The Arkitects came out and said, 'Listen, there is no way of making this work with solar cells. We can't make enough of them, fast enough, for thousands of arklets. They are big and cumbersome.' "

"I'd been wondering about that."

"We have to use nukes, is what they said."

"RTGs?"

Radioisotope thermoelectric generators were the power units used to run most space probes. At the heart of each was a puck of an isotope so radioactive that it remained hot for decades. Energy could be extracted from that heat in various ways.

"Those are not nearly powerful enough," Larz said.

LARZ GOT MESSAGES FROM THE GROUND IN THE FORM OF ENcrypted email, a spate of capital letters in groups of five that looked like something straight out of an Enigma message. In the big nylon wallet that, for Larz, passed as a briefcase was a stack of pages. On each of these was printed a different grid of random capital letters. About half an hour of laborious pencil-and-paper work went into decrypting each message. Dinah couldn't believe her eyes. People used crypto all the time to send email, of course, and it was standard practice for all Arjuna Expeditions email to be enciphered. But apparently that was no longer good enough for Sean Probst. Dinah got used to seeing Larz toiling over these sheets. He wrote a little Python script to make it easier, but he still wrote the messages out by hand.

One day, two weeks after he'd arrived, he decrypted a message with some surprising news. The boss was coming. As in, Sean Probst, the founder and CEO of Arjuna Expeditions.

"How can that even happen?" Dinah asked. "How can anyone just come up to Izzy? Don't you need a launch vehicle? A spacecraft? A place to dock it? *Permission?!*"

These were largely rhetorical questions. Sean had made seven billion dollars from an Internet startup before throwing his energies into asteroid mining. Along the way he'd sunk a billion or two into other private space startups.

"He's coming up alone," Larz said, "in a Drop Top."

It took Dinah a moment, and a quick Google search, to access the memory. Also referred to as "the Convertible," the Drop Top was one of the more creative recent approaches to space tourism. It was based on the idea that what tourists really wanted to experience was the direct view of the Earth, the stars, and (until it had ceased to exist) the moon. Conventional space capsules had tiny windows. What you really wanted to do was stick your head into a transparent bubble so that you could enjoy a clear view out in all directions. In other words, you wanted to be in a space suit, basically floating free in space. The Drop Top was a small, simple capsule, capable of carrying four astronauts, dressed in custom-made space suits with bubble helmets. During the ascent through the atmosphere, and the reentry, they were protected by a sturdy aeroshell. But while they were orbiting the Earth, the shell retracted, like the roof of a convertible, exposing them completely to space, and even giving them some freedom to spacewalk.

"I don't think a Drop Top can reach an orbit this high, can it?" Dinah asked.

"Sean's coming up alone. It is some kind of special one-passenger model—the extra mass is being used for propellant."

"And then what? He just goes to an airlock and knocks on the door?"

"Basically, yes," Larz said. "What will they do? Tell him to go away?"

DAY 68

"This whole thing is bullshit," said Sean Probst as soon as he got his helmet off.

Dinah smiled. It was not that she was happy about the bullshit. When it came to preserving the human race and the genetic heritage of the Earth from destruction, any whiff of bullshit was bad. But she did feel a certain sense of relief. In the back of her mind she had been quietly tallying up the BS for weeks now. No one else here would speak of it, and most of them seemed smarter, better informed than she was.

She knew Sean Probst by his reputation, by his signature on her paychecks, and by the emails he sent her at three o'clock in the morning of whatever time zone his private jet had most recently taken him to. Sean yielded to no one in his knowledge of all things space related. When he walked into a space station and called bullshit, things were about to become entertaining.

One of the few appealing things about him was that he had figured out that his personality was a problem and, in classic "get it done" style, had hired a coach to make him less of an asshole. She could see that working in his face.

"Not your part of it—that's awesome," he admitted.

"I figured you would have said something earlier if that were not the case," Dinah said.

Sean nodded. Done.

His arrival at the space station had been unconventional, and roundabout. There was no docking station to accommodate the Drop Top. There couldn't possibly be, since the Drop Top didn't even have a port or an airlock. So there'd been no way to attach it to Izzy. He had brought the little convertible in under manual control, tapping the thrusters one at a time, spitting bullets of spent propellant into space, then pausing for one, five, or ten minutes to ponder the consequences. Space nerd that he was, he knew perfectly well that orbital mechanics did not obey the rules of earthbound physics. He had enough humility, and enough spare oxygen, to take it slow. Eventually he had drifted close enough to Amalthea that a three-Siwi train with a Grabb on its head had been able to reach out and grapple a fitting on the edge of his cockpit. He had then ejected himself from the vehicle, floating free in space, and gone on a little tour of inspection, firing off occasional messages to Dinah so that she could know where he was. Since there was no direct radio connection, these had to be relayed through a server in Seattle.

He was in a tubesuit: a tourist product that in some ways was less capable, in others more so, than the government-issue ones used by cosmonauts and astronauts. It had no legs at all, since legs were pretty useless in space. It looked like a test tube with a pair of arms and a bubble-shaped dome on the top. The arms had shoulder and elbow joints, but no hands as such. Gloves were notoriously the most troublesome parts of space suits. Instead, the tubesuit's arms terminated in rounded-off stumps. Projecting from each of these was a skeletal hand consisting of a thumb and three fingers, actuated by steel cables that ran through airtight fittings into the arm-stumps. The occupant could slip his hand into a glovelike contraption inside the stump that would pull on the metal tendons as he moved his fingers, thereby actuating the external digits and enabling him to grab things and perform a few simple operations. There was nothing about it that couldn't have been built by a tinkerer in an inventor's lab in 1890, or 1690 for that matter. People who had used them reported that they worked surprisingly well—better in some ways than conventional space suit gloves, which were stiff and fatigued the hands.

There was plenty of extra room inside the stumps, and so when not using the clawlike hands he could pull his fingers free of the internal glove and let them rest on internal touchpads and joysticks where he could type and swipe to his heart's content. The suit had some tiny thrusters that enabled the user to "fly" it around. Sean had put these to work at some length, wandering around the outside of Izzy and inspecting the work of the robots, the modifications made to the truss, and other curiosities.

Finally he had found his way to an airlock at the aft end of H2, where Dinah had let him in, and he had blurted out his opinion.

He looked like any nondescript thirty-eight-year-old nerd at a graduate physics seminar or a sci-fi convention, with stringy dishwater-blond hair stuck to his head by sweat, and a few days' darker stubble. In his official photos he wore contacts, but today he wore thick-lensed eyeglasses. He pulled one arm, then the other, out of the suit and then pushed himself up and out through the big opening at its top where the head-dome had been attached.

"I've been having trouble seeing the long-term sustainability angle," Dinah admitted. For she was not above dangling bait.

"Ya think?!" he shouted. "Has anyone done even the most basic mass balance calculation on this Cloud Ark concept?" Sean was from New Jersey.

She wasn't sure what he meant, so she stalled for time. "People have been pretty distracted. I wouldn't be the first to know."

"They wouldn't tell you!" he shouted. "Because you would see right away that it is bullshit!"

"What is?" Ivy asked, floating toward them with an interested look on her face. "And who the hell are you?"

Before Sean could explain who the hell he was, he was distracted, to put it mildly, by the appearance of a six-foot-tall Amazon with a shaved head and prominent facial scars, headed for him across H2 as if she had been launched out of a cannon. Tekla drove her shoulder into Sean's midsection, slamming him back against a bulkhead. A moment later she was on him. She grabbed an outstretched arm and put Sean into a joint lock that looked pretty much inescapable.

By now Dinah had spent enough time with Tekla to know that she was a practitioner of Sambo, a Soviet combat martial art with many similarities to jujitsu. Out of idle curiosity, Dinah had watched a few YouTube videos featuring Sambo practitioners in action. But she had never imagined, until now, that it could be done in zero gravity.

Sean had made his entry through H2 because it had a useful assortment of airlocks and docking ports on its aft end. But, unbeknownst to him, H2 had been doing double duty as the dormitory where the surviving Scouts lived. His arrival had awoken Tekla, who was off shift at the moment and had been sleeping in her bag.

Dinah tried to imagine what this encounter must have looked like from Tekla's point of view. Sean's arrival was unannounced. Dinah herself hadn't really known when, or whether, he was going to arrive until the Drop Top had swum into view outside her little window.

So, from Tekla's point of view, this guy was an intruder. And when she'd heard Ivy say "Who the hell are you?" she had realized that his presence on Izzy was completely unauthorized.

"Oh, this is awkward," Dinah said.

"Tap! Tap!" Sean kept saying. He was slapping Tekla's leg with his free hand.

"Commander, would you like me to restrain him?" Tekla asked. "What are your orders?"

"He's not dangerous," Dinah put in.

"Let him go, Tekla," Ivy said.

Somewhat reluctantly, Tekla relaxed her grip and allowed Sean to float free. He drifted away from her, sizing her up with a certain degree of bewilderment.

"Sean," Dinah said, "you've already made Tekla's acquaintance. I would like you to meet Ivy Xiao, commander of this installation. Ivy, say hello to Sean Probst."

"Hello, Sean Probst," Ivy said, then turned to look at Dinah. "Did you know he was coming?"

"I had heard rumors," Dinah said. "But I did not think them firm enough to distract you by repeating them. I am sorry."

Ivy looked at Sean long enough to make him uncomfortable. Tekla, hovering almost within reach, did much to help supply the hostile atmosphere that Dinah suspected Ivy was reaching for.

"The closest analogy in the law for what I am here is the captain of a ship," Ivy said. "Do you know the etiquette, Sean, for coming aboard a ship?"

Sean calculated.

"Commander Xiao," he said, "I humbly and respectfully request permission to come aboard your ship."

"Permission granted," she said. "And welcome aboard."

"Thanks."

"But!"

"Yes?"

"If anyone asks, you'll please tell them a little white lie, which is that you requested permission *first,* and *then* came aboard."

"I'm happy to do that," he said.

"Later on we'll evolve some sort of common law, I guess. A constitution for this thing."

"People are working on that, actually," Sean offered.

"That's nice. But right now we have nothing of the sort and so we have to be mindful."

"It is so noted," Sean said.

"Now," Ivy said, "you were saying something about bullshit when I interrupted."

"Commander Xiao," Sean said, "I have the utmost respect for your past accomplishments and for the work you have been doing."

"Do you hear a but coming?" Ivy asked Dinah. "I hear a but coming."

Sean stopped.

"Go on," Ivy said. For at the end of the day, to go on was what Sean wanted, so they might as well get it over with.

HE WORKED IT OUT FROM FIRST PRINCIPLES ON THE WHITEBOARD IN the Banana. Beginning with the Tsiolkovskii equation, a simple exponential, he developed some simple estimates, which he then developed into an ironclad proof, that the Cloud Ark was bullshit.

Or at least that it had been bullshit until he, Sean Probst, had shown up to address the problems he had noticed. Problems that could only be handled by him personally.

It occurred to Dinah to ask herself whether Sean was really rich anymore.

Rich people no longer kept their wealth in gold. Sean's wealth was in stock—mostly stock in his own companies. She hadn't been following the stock market since the Crater Lake announcement, but she'd heard that it had not so much crashed as basically ceased to exist. The whole concept of owning stock didn't really mean much anymore, at least if you thought of it as a store of value.

But legal structures, police, government agencies, and so on still existed and still enforced the law. The law stated that Sean, by virtue of majority ownership of Arjuna Expeditions, still controlled it. And through overlapping relationships with other space entrepreneurs, he still had enough pull to get himself launched to Izzy. So that counted as wealth of a sort.

Having settled that in her mind, she focused her attention back on what Sean was saying.

"Cloud Ark as distributed swarm: fine. I get it. Sign me up. Much safer than putting all our eggs in one basket. What makes it safer? The arklets can maneuver out of the way of incoming rocks. Other advantages? They can pair up to make a bolo, and spin around each other to make simulated gravity. Keeps people healthier and happier. How do they do this? By flying toward each other and grappling their tethers together. What happens when they want to break up the bolo, and go solo? They decouple the tethers and go flying off in opposite directions, unless they use their engines to kill that centripetal motion. What do all of these activities have in common?"

They'd gotten used to Sean's habit of asking, then answering his own questions, so were caught off guard now that he actually seemed to be expecting an answer.

Dinah and Ivy had been joined by Konrad Barth, the astronomer; Larz Hoedemaeker; and Zeke Petersen. The latter finally rose to the bait.

"Use of the thrusters," he said.

Sean nodded. "And what happens when we are using the thrusters?"

Dinah had an advantage, since she already knew that Sean was concerned about mass balance. "We're dumping mass. In the form of used propellant."

"We're dumping mass," Sean said, nodding. "As soon as the Cloud Ark runs out of propellant, it loses the ability to do all of the things that make it a viable architecture for long-term survival. It becomes a big sitting duck."

He let them roll that around in their heads for a bit, then went on: "Mind you, almost everything else that we do up here can be done with minimal effect on mass balance. We can recycle our urine to make drinking water and our poo to make fertilizer. Very few of our activities involve just releasing mass into space in a way that we can't get it back. This is the exception. I have been ranting and raving about this ever since the idea of the Cloud Ark was announced. So far all I get in return, from the powers that be, are vague answers and hand-wavy happy talk."

Ivy and Dinah looked at each other in a way that foretold a one-on-one, after-meeting tequila session.

So, Dinah thought, Ivy had been wondering about this too, in the back of her mind. Worrying about it. Trying to read the tea leaves during those teleconferences down to the ground.

It was something to do with Pete Starling, she now saw. Which meant that it was somehow related to J.B.F.

Zeke was one of those open-faced, basically optimistic team players one saw frequently in the junior officer ranks of the military. "This is so obvious, in a way," he pointed out. "They *have* to have thought of this." Which was Zeke's way of saying *I'm sure that this is all being handled by people above our pay grade.*

"You would think," Sean said, nodding.

Konrad shifted in his chair uneasily and thrust his bearded face into his hand. Unlike Zeke, he was not the sort to place the sunniest interpretation on the problem.

"If the world were run by scientists, engineers," Sean said, "then this would be a no-brainer. We have to go get more mass. Stockpile it so we don't run out."

"It's got to be water. You're talking about a comet core," Dinah said.

"It's got to be water," Sean agreed. "You can't make rocket fuel out of nickel. But with water we can make hydrogen peroxide—a fine thruster propellant—or we can split it into hydrogen and oxygen to run big engines."

"I'm waiting for the other shoe to drop in what you just said," Ivy muttered. Then she spoke up more clearly: "But the world isn't run by scientists and engineers—is that where you're going with this?"

Sean turned his hands palm up and shrugged theatrically. "I'm not a people person. People keep telling me this. Some who *are* people persons might be focusing on that angle."

"The people angle," Konrad said, just clarifying.

"Yeah. The seven billion people angle. Seven billion who need to be kept happy, and docile, until the end. How do you do that? What's the best way to calm down a scared kid, get them to go back to sleep? Tell them a story. Some shit about Jesus or whatever."

Zeke winced. Konrad rolled his eyes, then glanced at the ceiling and pretended he hadn't heard this.

The idea Sean was playing with here was so monstrous in a way that it was almost inconceivable: that everything they were doing up here was a lullaby for the seven billion down below. That it could not actually work. That they were just putting on a show of getting ready. That the people of the Cloud Ark would live only a few weeks longer than the ones left behind.

As such, Ivy and Dinah and Konrad and Zeke ought to have been freaking out at this point.

But none of them—not even Zeke—reacted very much.

"You've all thought it too," Sean said. "Even an Asp-hole like me can see it in your faces."

"Okay, maybe we've all thought it," Dinah admitted. "How could you not think it? But, Sean, what you might not have seen, being based on the ground, is how serious everyone up here is about making this work. If it were just a Potemkin village, we'd be seeing different stuff."

Sean held his hands up, palms out, placating her. "Can we just agree that there might be a range of views down on the ground? And that some people, perhaps highly placed, see its primary function as an opiate of the masses? Like the video you pop into your car's DVD player to keep the kids quiet during a long drive."

"People like that are not going to be our friends when it comes to getting the resources we need," Ivy said.

"Their strategy is always going to seem a little off-kilter, a little beside the point. Opaque. Frustrating."

They were definitely talking about Pete Starling.

Sean continued. "To the extent that such people control launch sites and policy, we have a problem. Fortunately, they don't control everything."

They were now talking about Sean Probst, and his loose circle of billionaire friends who knew how to make rockets.

"There's a lot about this Cloud Ark thing that I, and my associates, don't know yet. We can't sit around waiting for perfect knowledge. We have to act immediately on long-lead-time work that addresses what we do know. And what we do know is that we need to bring water to the Cloud Ark. Physics and politics conspire to make it difficult to bring it up from the ground. Fortunately, I own an asteroid mining company. We have already identified some comet cores in easy-to-reach orbits. We're narrowing down the list. And we're preparing an expedition."

Konrad well understood the timing of such missions. "How long, Sean?"

"Two years," Sean said.

"Well," Ivy said, "I guess you'd better get on it, then. How can we help?"

"Give me all of your robots," Sean said. He turned to look at Dinah.

"SINCE WE HAVE DECLARED OPEN SEASON ON BULLSHIT . . ." DINAH began as soon as she had gotten Sean Probst alone in her shop.

Sean held both of his hands up like a fugitive surrendering to the FBI. "Where would you like to begin?"

"You said that you have identified some comets. That you were narrowing down the list. That's crap. You wouldn't have come up here without a specific plan."

"We're going after Greg's Skeleton."

"What?"

"Comet Grigg-Skjellerup. Sorry. Somebody's offspring called it Greg's Skeleton and the name stuck." Sean always referred to children as offspring.

She'd heard of it. "How big is that?"

"Two and a half, three kilometers."

"That's a lot of arklet fuel."

Sean nodded. He crossed his arms over his body and looked around the shop.

"Hard to move something that big."

Still no answer.

"You're going to jam a nuke into it and turn it into a rocket, aren't you?"

He raised his eyebrows briefly. Since this was the only plausible way of moving something that huge, he didn't consider it worthy of an extended answer.

"We got really lucky on the timing," he remarked.

"You're going to fly a radioactive ice ball the size of the Death Star back here just as the shit is hitting the fan—then what?"

"Dinah, I need to share something with you in confidence."

"Well, it's about fucking time is all I can say."

DAY 73

Doob had almost been to space once, about ten years ago. An acquaintance of his who had made a lot of money in hedge funds had dropped twenty-five million dollars on a twelve-day trip to the International Space Station aboard a Soyuz capsule. It was traditional for the customer to designate a backup—a sort of understudy—who would take his place in the event of some illness or mishap. Since the backup might be swapped in at any time up to shortly before launch, they had to go through all the same training as the customer. And that was really the point, as far as the hedge fund man was concerned. An introvert, he needed someone who could act as a connection to the general public and put an appealing face on the whole thing. So he had selected Doc Dubois as his understudy. They'd set up a website and a blog, and arranged for photographers to follow Doob's progress through the training program, with occasional glimpses of the hedge fund man in the background. In effect, Doob had acted as a publicity decoy. No one made any bones about this. Doob had been more than happy to do it. The training had been great fun, the hedge fund man had been generous in his spending on the website, and Doob had been able to produce a lot of good video explaining fun facts about spaceflight.

And there had even been the small chance that he might go. A week before the scheduled launch, he had flown to Baikonur, bringing his wife and kids with him, video crew in tow. They had watched in a certain amount of amazement as the launch vehicle, a fantailed Soyuz-FG, had been towed horizontally across the steppe on a special train, complete with smoke-belching locomotive, to the launch pad. And this really was little more than a pad, a concrete slab on the almost lunar surface of the Kazakh steppe with a few pieces of apparatus around it to hoist the rocket up off the train and pump fluids into it. The contrast with the NASA way of doing things was stark to the point of being somewhat hilarious. Doob's youngest son, Henry, eleven years old at the time, had failed to pay attention to the elevation of the mighty rocket to its vertical position because he was distracted by the sight of a couple of stray dogs copulating a hundred meters away from ground zero. The launch bunker, shockingly close to the pad, had a little vegetable patch out in front of it where the technicians were growing cucumbers and tomatoes; they explained that the concrete wall soaked up sunlight during the day and helped keep the vegetables warm at night.

Three days before launch, the hedge fund man had been nipped by a stray dog while rehearsing a launch pad escape sequence, and everything had been thrown into disarray as the dog was chased across the steppe by militiamen in wheeled vehicles, locals on horseback, and a helicopter gunship. After they had run it to ground they had shipped it off to a veterinary lab to be checked for rabies. Only three hours before launch, word had come back that the dog was clean. Doob's name had been struck from the manifest and replaced by that of the hedge fund manager. Both relieved and disappointed, Doob had stood on terra firma, very close to the launch pad. Tavistock Prowse had come out to cover the launch. He had come equipped with all kinds of electronic gadgets that had seemed cool at the time. He had stood there on the steppe, facing Doob and the rocket, aiming a video camera at him and catching his narration as the giant vehicle had fired up its engines and hurled itself into the sky.

More than anything else, that image had made Dr. Harris into Doc Dubois and launched his career. It had also led, within days, to divorce proceedings initiated by his wife. She had a number of complaints about his performance as a husband, many of long standing, some that she could barely articulate. But somehow all of them had been summed up and crystallized by the fact that, after largely ignoring his responsibilities as a husband and father for several weeks while training for this launch in Russia, he had spent the actual moment of launch not gathered in a safe place with his children but outside, dangerously close to the rocket, with his bro Tav, ingratiating himself to millions of followers with excited and hilarious commentary.

One way or another, Doob had been paying for it ever since. Partly in the negative sense of suffering just penalties for his sins but partly in the more positive sense of spending time with his kids when he could. And this had become more difficult as they had graduated from school and gone out into the world. He was making a particular effort to do it now that they were all under a death sentence.

On A+0.73, Doob flew into Seattle, rented an SUV, and drove to the campus of the University of Washington. Along the way he stopped at a couple of outdoor stores to pick up some camping equipment. This was now expensive. People had begun hoarding that sort of thing in anticipation of a collapse of civilization. But only a few people. Most understood that there was little point in taking to the hills when the Hard Rain began. Freeze-dried food and backpacking stoves were difficult to come by, but down sleeping bags and fancy tents were still in stock.

Henry was now a junior in the computer science department, living with some of his friends near the campus in a rental house, a classic Seattle down-at-heels Craftsman bungalow half digested by blackberries and English ivy.

In a certain way it made no sense anymore to speak of anyone as being a student at a particular stage in a degree program. And yet people went on thinking this way, kind of in the way that someone who has just been diagnosed with a terminal illness will go on getting up and going to work every morning, not so much out of habit as because the knowledge of impending doom makes them wish to assert an identity.

He was tempted to park the SUV illegally, since, according to his calculations, the authorities were not likely to catch up with him and demand payment of the parking ticket before the end of the world, but it seemed that most of the people of Seattle were still obeying the rules and so he did likewise.

He found Henry, all four of his housemates, and five other students all crammed into the ground floor of the bungalow, keeping it warm in the January chill with their body heat and the warmth emanating from a rat's nest of PCs, laptops, and routers. A quick census of empty pizza boxes suggested that they had been working all night.

"I'll explain it to you while we drive" had been Henry's promise to his dad when Doob had asked him on the phone last night what he was doing. This morning, other than getting up from his La-Z-Boy to give his dad a hug and tell him "I love you," he didn't have much more to say.

Every parent of a teenager gets used to it: the moment in a child's life when he or she decides that certain facts are just too much trouble to explain to Mom or Dad. The parents can't, and needn't, know every last little thing. They just have to accept this, be content with what they can glean on their own, and move on. Henry, of course, had passed through that veil some years ago. Doob had swallowed his pride and accepted it as every parent must. It was part of growing up. But back in those days the subject matter had been fundamentally uninteresting: the size of Henry's collection of Magic: The Gathering cards, the weight lifting program assigned him by his football coach, and who had a crush on whom at school. It was easy for Doob to pretend he didn't care about that stuff.

What he was seeing over the shoulders of the students in this room looked a good deal more interesting. And that, in a way, hurt.

All of them, of course, knew that Henry was the son of the famous Doc Dubois. While trying to play it cool, they all sought a chance to shake his hand and say hi. Doob chewed the fat with them while his eyes strayed to the stuff they had blue-taped to the walls of the bungalow: printouts of CAD drawings, schedule grids, Gantt charts, maps. He was obviously looking at some sort of engineering project in the works, but he couldn't make out what, exactly. On the kitchen table a MakerBot was producing a small plastic part, watched intently by a young woman who was talking on her phone in a mix of English and Mandarin.

Conversation was interrupted by the *beep-beep-beep* of a backup alarm, loud and growing louder. Someone pulled the front door open, letting in a wash of wet, cool Pacific air, to reveal a Ryder box truck backing up onto the lawn, heading straight for the front door. Some unkillable instinct in Doob's head made him glance disapprovingly at the muddy ruts it was leaving in the lawn, made him issue a little *tut-tut-tut* at these irresponsible youth for damaging the grass—grass that in two years would be a thin smear of carbon black over a lifeless cake of hardened clay, presuming it didn't suffer a direct hit and become part of a huge glass-lined crater.

The truck didn't stop soon enough and wrecked a wooden banister beside the front steps.

Everyone laughed. The laughter had a curious tone, a mixture of childish delight with something darker, expectant of much worse to come.

These kids were really adapting better than he was.

He had no idea what was going on, but it seemed to involve throwing everything into the back of the box truck. He stood around for a while with his hands in his pockets, since he didn't know which stuff was going and which was staying. But when they threw in the sofa it became clear they were abandoning the house. He began helping. After a certain point the box truck filled up. Then they began pulling things out of it and putting them back in in a more orderly style. Doob finally hit his stride, stepping into the role of wily old man with excellent packing skills and pointing out ways to use the space more efficiently.

Eventually someone went and got another box truck. Apparently the rental agency was letting them take them for free. Some day laborers wandered down the street from a home improvement center and helped pack. The home improvement market had gone bust. Doob saw traces of Amelia in their faces and wondered how they had first heard the news.

Six of the kids packed themselves and their computers, clothes, and as many tools as they owned or could borrow into the SUV that Doob had rented at the airport. They roped a couple of bicycles and some camping gear to the luggage rack. Doob had no idea where they were going, or why, but they seemed to be planning to construct a new civilization out of blue tarps and zip ties.

They ended up in a caravan of twenty vehicles, headed east out of town at about two in the afternoon. At this time of the year, at Seattle's high latitude, that gave them about two hours of remaining daylight.

Most of the kids fell asleep immediately. Henry, riding shotgun, made a touching effort to stay awake and then fell into slumber. Henry was a sweet kid and Doob knew that when he woke up he would apologize. But Henry wasn't a parent, and he didn't understand that when you were, almost nothing was more satisfying than seeing your kid sleep.

So, feeling as content as it was possible to be under the circumstances, Doob drove into the darkling mountains with his SUV-load of slumbering passengers. The caravan gradually dissolved into the general stream of traffic. Most of the passenger cars peeled off at the suburban exits, before the road began to gain serious altitude. Doob wondered, as he always did, what the hell they were doing: Continuing to go to jobs and school, just to fill the days before the end? But it was none of his business.

Beyond Issaquah, any vehicle still on the interstate was probably headed for the high cold desert on the east side of the mountains. A few people were still interested in skiing—skiing!—but those cars were easily identified. Most of the other vehicles fit the general description of those that had been a part of their original caravan from the university: heavy-laden box trucks, SUVs and pickups with provisions and camping gear.

Doob realized that he had somehow become a sort of Okie.

Except that the Okies had at least known where they were going.

The eternal Seattle drizzle turned into alternating belts of mist and cold rain, forcing him to keep one hand busy on the wiper control. The raindrops became cloudy with ice as he gained altitude, and then turned into snow. The roadway was still clear, but the shoulders became fuzzy with slush that gradually encroached on the traffic lanes. The speed of travel dropped to forty, thirty, twenty miles an hour, and the road ahead congealed into a slurry of taillights as lowering steel-gray clouds clamped down on the remaining traces of daylight.

A few semi-articulated rigs were laboring up the approach to the pass in the slow lane. Some of these were just conventional boxy trucks and so there was no guessing what might be in them, but Doob thought he was picking out an unusual amount of weird industrial traffic: tankers carrying cryogenic liquids, flatbeds with bundles of tubing and structural steel.

The clouds flashed, bright enough to make some of the sleeping students flinch and stir in the backseat. Out of habit, Doob began counting *zero Mississippi one Mississippi two . . .* and when he reached something like nine or ten he felt, as much as heard, the sonic boom. As a child he'd have assumed it was a lightning bolt. Now he interpreted all such events as incoming chunks of moon shrapnel. This one had passed within about three kilometers. A secondary boom, several seconds later, suggested that it had hit the ground, as opposed to just breaking up in the atmosphere as most of them did. So it had been a relatively large piece.

It had been a day or two since Doob had checked the site where his grad students had been tallying observed bolides vs. the predictions of their model. He didn't check it very often because, after some jitter in the first few weeks, the model had been refined to the point where it tracked observations to within a reasonable statistical range. This, of course, was good news for the model and bad news for the human race, since it meant that they were still on track for the White Sky to happen, and the Hard Rain to begin, in another twenty-one or twenty-two months. If memory served, strikes like the one he had just observed were probably happening about twenty times a day worldwide. So it was mildly remarkable that he'd been close to one, but nothing to write home about.

A few minutes later the taillights ahead of him flared as people applied their brakes. After inching along for a short distance traffic came to a complete stop. This woke up some of the students, who remarked on it sleepily. After ten minutes had passed without movement, Henry climbed out, stood up on the SUV's running board, and began loosening ropes holding a bicycle in place on the roof.

Doob sat warm and safe in the driver's seat and watched his son pedal off between the lanes of stopped traffic with precisely the same heartsick feeling as when the boy had gone off on his first solo bicycle ride in the streets of Pasadena.

He was back all of three minutes later. "A rig jackknifed just before the top of the pass," he said. "An oversized load, a piece of a gantry, I think."

Gantry. There was a word that activated deep memories in Doob's brain. Only used in connection with launch pads, only spoken by the likes of Walter Cronkite and Frank Reynolds in the deep nicotine-cured anchorman tonalities of the Apollo days.

Nothing was happening, so they pulled their winter coats out of the back, bundled up, and hiked up the road to see. A lot of people were doing this. This struck Doob as unusual. The normal behavior was to wait in the car, thumb the iPhone, listen to a book on tape, and wait for the authorities to come and deal with it.

The stranded truck was only about half a mile ahead of them. It looked to have gone into a spectacular skid. The colossal weight of the gantry—a welded steel truss looking like a section of a railway trestle—had swung the rear end of the truck forward and sideways, sweeping across all lanes of traffic and finally grinding to a stop by flopping over onto its side and then destroying about a hundred yards of guardrail. Behind it a few cars had spun out as their drivers had stomped the brakes, and a few people were dealing with the aftermath of minor rear-end fender benders, but no one seemed to have gotten seriously injured.

The pedestrian traffic toward the crash had been considerable, and yet Doob saw few of the sorts of people he would classify as gawkers or rubberneckers. Where were they all going? As he and Henry and the other students drew closer he saw cars moving around, headlights sweeping across the wreck to better illuminate it, and then he saw a stream of people squeezing through the gap to the other side, or clambering through the space between the tractor and the trailer. Self-appointed safety wardens had stationed themselves at critical locations to focus the white beams of their LED flashlights on trip hazards and useful handholds. Doob and the others crowded through those gaps and then broke free to the far side of the wreck. The view here was worth a look. The wet interstate, completely empty of traffic, stretched away from them. A ski area, lit up for night use, spread up the mountainside to their right. In the distance maybe ten, twenty miles away, a streaky patch of mountainside was flickering a lambent orange through intervening veils of snow and mist: the impact site of the bolide. Doob saw now how it had all happened. The meteor had passed overhead. To him it had just been a flash above the clouds, but to the people cresting the pass at the same moment it must have been visible as it streaked into the ground and plowed up a mile-long stretch of forest. Cars must have faltered and strayed out of their lanes. The driver of the truck had been forced to apply his brakes and the tires of the trailer had broken loose from the slushy pavement.

The number of people on this side of the wreck must have been well over a hundred.

Twenty minutes later, there were enough of them to flip the rig back up onto its wheels. Like a work crew of Egyptian slaves moving a great block of stone, all of these people in their parkas and their microfiber gloves and snow pants just got under the thing and started lifting it. Towing straps had been fetched from toolboxes and anchored to the other side of it, and run to the trailer hitches and the bumpers of several pickup trucks that had four-wheeled their way to the scene, and they pulled while the humans pushed, and with surprising ease the whole thing came up, balanced for a moment on half of its wheels—the only sound now being the skidding of pickup tires as the drivers burned rubber—and then dropped into place. A huge uproar of people shouted *Whoo!* as much in relief as in exultation. Doob exchanged thumping, mittened high fives with twenty people he'd never met before and would never see again.

Getting the truck pointed in the right direction again, and back on its way down the interstate, was a more tedious operation that would likely span another couple of hours. But within a short time they were at least able to open one lane. By then, people with four-wheel-drive vehicles had already begun to cut across the median strip and claim lanes on the wrong side of the interstate, which was sparsely trafficked by veering cars holding their horn buttons down in long Dopplered howls of protest.

Another slowdown caught them an hour later when they entered a low plume of thick smoke drifting across the highway and bringing visibility down to almost nothing. Galaxies of red and blue flashing lights emerged from the murk and then receded: places where emergency vehicles had clustered to stage firefighting efforts, or to aid locals affected by the strike. At one place, sitting in the middle of the road, festive with road flares, was a rock the size of a car, which had struck the pavement hard enough to pierce it and lever up thick shards bristling with snapped rebar. Not the meteorite itself, but ejecta: shrapnel hurled out from the impact site.

There was another delay, this one purely for gawking, at the place where the interstate crossed the Columbia River, almost a mile wide, at Vantage. Something was going on down below the bridge, on the eastern bank of the river where the low span angled up away from the water to let big barges pass beneath it. Blinding lights had been elevated on poles, creating a mottled spill of daylight where something huge and cylindrical was being winched up off a barge.

With all of those complications it was well after midnight when they reached the town of Moses Lake and turned off the interstate to follow almost all of its traffic in the direction of the Grant County International Airport.

That was its official name. When Doob woke up the next morning, crawled out of the tent he had shared with Henry, and stood up and looked about, he immediately dubbed the place New Baikonur. It was at the same latitude as Baikonur and it was in the same sort of steppe country.

And like the steppe of old it was populated by nomads. Space Okies. At least ten thousand, he guessed.

They seemed orderly enough. Long straight lines had been chalked out on the dry lakebed, apparently with the same equipment used to stripe football fields. These delineated streets and avenues that, for the most part, were being respected by newly arrived tent pitchers. Portable toilets huddled at strict intervals, though Doob's nose told him that some were using pit latrines, or just pissing on the sagebrush.

Henry had filled him in a little during the last hours of the drive. It had been an air force base, part of the northern line of defensive installations from which the U.S. would have defended itself against Communist aggression, had that ever been necessary. Its 13,500-foot runway suggested it might have had offensive purposes as well. It had been an alternate landing site for the Space Shuttle, never used. In any case it was ridiculously oversized for the town of Moses Lake and had tended to be used by the aerospace industry in recent decades for various training and experimental purposes. Blue Origin had used it to test a VTOL craft in 2005, operating from a trailer on the empty lakebed west of the airport where New Baikonur was arising now, and where Doob was walking about trying to track down the scent of frying bacon.

Some giant, windowless aircraft hurtled overhead, deploying a phalanx of tires from its belly, and made a long, slow landing on the big runway, using every one of the 13,500 feet. A cargo carrier.

He came to a broad avenue that led directly into the encampment's center. And there was no mistaking where and what the center was: a concrete pad, still being poured one patch at a time, with a mixed assortment of cranes rising up from what he took to be its center.

They were assembling a rocket there.

It was a big rocket.

It all more or less made sense. There was no cargo too big to be barged up the Columbia River and then trucked the last few miles to Moses Lake. There was no airplane that couldn't be accommodated by that runway. There was no object that the aerospace machine shops of the Seattle area couldn't build. And from this latitude, the same as Baikonur, a well-worn and understood flight plan could take payloads to Izzy.

A mere four days later, Doob stood in the bed of a rusty pickup truck with a random assortment of space rednecks, hoisting a long-necked beer bottle into the sky in emulation of the rocket lifting off from the pad. They all hooted and screamed as they watched it arc gracefully downrange and take off in the general direction of Boise. And the next morning, when they had all sobered up, they got busy building another rocket.

DAY 80

"We talk about sending stuff to orbit as if orbit is a place, like Philadelphia, but it's actually a lot of places, a lot of different ways to be in space. Any two objects in the universe can theoretically be in orbit around each other.

"Most of the orbits that matter to us involve something tiny orbiting around something huge, like a satellite around the Earth, or the Earth around the sun. So, a quick way to label and classify orbits is according to 'What is the huge thing in the middle?'

"If the huge thing in the middle is the Earth, we call it a geocentric orbit. If it's the sun, it's a heliocentric orbit. And so on. Since the moon broke up, we've mostly focused on geocentric orbits. The moon, back when it existed, used to be in such an orbit; it revolved around the Earth. Most of its pieces still remain in geocentric orbits. A small number of those just happen to intersect the Earth's atmosphere. When that happens, we get a meteorite.

"So much for Orbits 101. But keep in mind there can be different levels. So, the old Earth-moon system was, as a whole, revolving around the sun in a heliocentric orbit. And if you zoom way out and look at the entire Milky Way galaxy, you can see that our whole solar system is very slowly revolving around the black hole at its center, in a galactocentric orbit."

The voice was that of famous astronomer and science popularizer Doc Dubois. The images accompanying it were an animation zooming in and out of the solar system. Dinah was getting snatches of it over the shoulder of Luisa Soter, a recent arrival to Izzy and hands-down winner of the "least like a traditional astronaut" competition. Born in New York City to parents who had fled political repression in Chile, she had been raised in a polyglot bohemian household in Harlem, walking through Central Park every day to the Ethical Culture School on West Sixty-Third. She'd followed that up with a succession of degrees in psychology and social work from UCLA, Chicago, and Barcelona. After a few years of work with economic refugees trying to enter Europe on leaky fishing boats, she'd been awarded a genius grant that had given her the freedom to travel the world for a few years doing research on other economic migrants.

Two weeks ago she'd been yanked out of a Fulbright scholarship at the University of St. Andrews in Scotland, given some basic training in how to live in space, strapped into a rocket, and shot up here in a tourist capsule.

Dinah, along with everyone else, made the obvious assumption that Luisa's job was to be the first shrink and social worker in space. Judging from some interactions that had been happening as crowding and stress had gotten more intense, she was going to have her work cut out for her. A bunch of desperate people crowded aboard a pitching and rudderless fishing boat was an uncomfortably close match for the situation up here.

Luisa had a relaxed self-confidence that made it easy for her to admit that she knew absolutely nothing about such topics as orbital mechanics. But it was more than just that; she knew how to use her own ignorance as an icebreaker in conversations. Izzy was full of people who were skewed toward the Asperger's end of the social spectrum, and there was no better way to get them to start talking than to ask them a technical question.

But when everyone else was busy, Luisa was not above googling her question down to Earth and latching on to a YouTube video, as she was doing now.

Dinah, floating behind Luisa's shoulder, watched as the animation was replaced by a live shot of Doc Dubois and a stocky, bald white man standing next to each other on the flat pan of gray-brown dirt that she now recognized as the Moses Lake spaceport. In deep background behind them was another rocket being stacked on the pad, one stage at a time, by a tangled-looking arrangement of cranes, gantries, and cables.

Dinah vaguely recognized the one who wasn't Doc Dubois; he was a tech pundit who popped up frequently on television and YouTube. He turned toward the camera and spoke: "This is Tavistock Prowse, coming to you from the world's newest spaceport here in Grant County, Washington. I'm here with a man who needs no introduction, Doc Dubois, to talk about some of the recent controversial events surrounding the Arjuna Expeditions launches, many of which are originating from the improvised launch complex that you can see directly behind us. Arjuna has prepared an animation that explains what they are all about. So pop some popcorn and pull up a chair."

Their image was replaced by a view of Earth that zoomed back, tilted, and panned to show it in its orbit around the sun. This was helpfully traced out by a thin, curved red line. The animation panned back. The orbits of Venus, Mercury, then Mars and Jupiter came into view. "Traditionally," Doc Dubois said, "when we talk about asteroids, we're talking about the asteroid belt, which is out between Mars and Jupiter."

A ring of dust, with a few larger clumps, was now spattered into the huge gap between those two planets' orbits. "There's a lot of material out there that Our Heritage might one day be able to exploit, but it's too far away to be easily reached by any spacecraft we have now."

So Doc Dubois, in keeping with his rep for staying in touch with the zeitgeist, had adopted the Our Heritage phrasing, a suddenly popular buzzword and hashtag meaning "whatever gets accomplished in the distant future by the descendants of the people who make it onto the Cloud Ark," or, to put it bluntly, "the only reason to go on living for the next twenty-two months."

The animation began zooming back in, to the point where it showed nothing beyond Earth's orbit. "But astronomers have known for a long time that not all of the asteroids are out beyond Mars. There are much smaller—but still significant—populations of asteroids in heliocentric orbits not that different from Earth's."

A finer and sparser dust of particles was now drawn in, forming a sort of fuzzy halo around the red line that represented Earth's orbit.

"And that's where Amalthea came from, is that correct, Doc?"

"Yes, bringing a hunk of metal that big from all the way out between Mars and Jupiter would have taken forever. Because we found it in an Earth-like orbit, it was a little easier."

"And what do you mean by an Earth-like orbit?"

"These rocks all revolve around the sun just like the Earth. Some are a little inside Earth's orbit, some a little outside of it, some cross the Earth's orbit twice every time they go around the sun. We used to worry about those."

"Now, not so much," Tav put in.

Doc paused, and apparently thought better of acknowledging the joke. "Because we *were* worried about them, we made an effort to find them and to know their exact trajectories—their orbital parameters."

Back to Doc and Tav, now walking across the pounded earth of the spaceport with a big truck in the background emblazoned with the Arjuna Expeditions logo.

"In recent years, companies like Arjuna Expeditions have mapped a whole lot more of those asteroids in the hopes of mining them. What we're seeing in the last few weeks is a concerted effort by Arjuna, and an alliance of other private space companies, to throw those efforts into high gear."

"What exactly is Sean Probst thinking, Doc?" Tav asked.

"He's not telling us. But the science of orbital mechanics doesn't leave a whole lot to the imagination. In Part Two of this video, you can learn more about the dance of orbiting bodies in space, and the intricate choreography needed to make an asteroid show up in the right place at the right time."

Luisa's finger hovered over the link that would play the next video, but before tapping it, she turned around to look at Dinah. "Just trying to figure out what you do for a living," she said, in an accent that came from everywhere, but mostly from New York. "You're with Arjuna, right?"

"Shh!" Dinah warned her jokingly. "I'm still trying to stay friends with the Russians."

"What's that about?" Luisa asked.

She was referring to a recent series of testy meetings, and sometimes out-and-out confrontations, between the Russians—still thinking and acting as a bloc under the leadership of Fyodor Antonovich Panteleimon—and the Arjuna contingent, which actually prided itself on being "disruptive." This was a commonplace bit of biz jargon.

But try explaining to a grizzled cosmonaut why being disruptive was a good thing.

Dinah was inclined to say something like "It's cultural," but she felt a little intimidated about using that sort of cocktail-party banter around someone with Luisa's credentials.

"Look, surprises in space are almost always bad," Dinah said. "Traditionally, every mission is planned out to the nth degree, and there's a contingency plan for everything. You don't improvise. You *can't* improvise, because there's nothing to improvise *with*."

"I'm just remembering the duct tape in *Apollo 13*."

"Yeah, that was one of the rare exceptions," Dinah said, "and people are still talking about it decades later. So, to the Russians, the idea that someone can just show up unannounced, and make a claim on our resources—"

"What resources?" Luisa asked.

"They're breathing our air," Dinah said. "Taking up space, using bandwidth, you name it. Larz hitched a ride up here on the assumption he'd stay on Izzy and work for us—instead he's taking off with Sean. And they are taking almost all of my robots."

"But they're sending more, yes?"

"Absolutely. Look, all I'm saying is that it was a surprise. And the sooner Sean and Larz get out of here, and on their way, the less likely it is that Fyodor is going to strangle them with his bare hands."

"On their way to where?" Luisa asked.

"A different orbit."

"Heliocentric or geocentric?" Luisa asked, deadpan, then gave Dinah a wink.

"Geocentric first. Then heliocentric," Dinah answered with a trace of a smile.

"But I thought we were already in a geocentric orbit."

"The wrong one, as far as Sean is concerned. Izzy's orbit is angled with respect to the equator. It has to be that way so Baikonur can launch to it—Baikonur is as far north as Seattle. But when you are doing interplanetary stuff, which is what Sean has in mind—basically, whenever you want to get out of low Earth orbit—you want to be in an orbit that's closer to the equator. Because that's pretty much where the rest of the solar system is—including the big chunk of ice that Sean wants to grab and bring back here."

"Ymir," Luisa said, pronouncing it as she'd heard Sean do: *ee-meer*. A word from Norse mythology referring to primordial ice giants. Sean's code name for a particular hunk of ice that his project had identified, and that he meant to bring back.

"Yeah. Not an official name. Sean doesn't divulge much."

"And how do you get from one to the other?" Luisa asked. "From a geocentric orbit—that's what we're in now, right?"

"Yes."

"To a heliocentric one?"

"Well, first he's going to have to do a plane change—from the angled Izzy orbit we're in now, to one closer to the equator. He'll rendezvous with the rest of his gear."

"Why didn't they just send everything up here?"

"Plane-change maneuvers are expensive. It's not too bad if the only thing plane-changing is Sean and Larz and a Drop Top, but it would be ridiculously wasteful to send the whole expedition package up here only to plane-change later." Dinah didn't mention the other reason, which was that the biggest part of Sean's package was so screamingly radioactive that it couldn't be allowed anywhere near Izzy.

"Okay. But we're still talking geocentric, right?"

"Correct, we're still just a few hundred miles high."

"So, how do they get from the rendezvous point to a heliocentric situation?"

"There's a bunch of different ways to do it," Dinah said, "but if I know Sean he'll go through the L1 gateway."

"I have no idea what that is," Luisa said, then finally lost a fight to suppress a giggle. "But once again I feel that I have been dumped into a sci-fi movie when I hear people around me talking like that."

"Doc Dubois probably covers it in that video," Dinah said, nodding at Luisa's tablet, "but the gist of it is really straightforward." Looking around, she spied a mesh bag stuffed with clothing. She pulled it out of its niche and let it drift in the center of the cabin. "The sun," she said. Now patting herself down, she found in her pocket a small plastic bottle of pills—antinausea medication she had fetched for one of the new arrivals. She opened it up and pulled out the ball of cotton stuffed into its top, then let the cotton drift in the air a little closer to Luisa. "The Earth, in its heliocentric orbit." The sick crew member would have to wait for a few minutes. Dinah carefully tapped a few pills free from the bottle's open neck and let them float for a moment while she pocketed the bottle. Then she began to arrange the pills in the space already staked out by the "sun" and the "Earth."

"Asteroids?" Luisa guessed.

"These are more like abstract mathematical points," Dinah said. "They're called the Lagrange points, or the libration points, and there's five of them around every two-body system. Always in the same basic geometry. Two of them, L4 and L5, are way off to the sides. I'm not going to try to show you those because we don't have room. But the other three are all along the line running between the sun and the Earth." She pushed off and glided to the far side of the "sun" and stationed a pill there, exactly on the opposite side from where the "Earth" was. "This is L3, very far away, invisible to us because the sun's always in the way, not that useful."

Gliding back toward the hovering cotton ball, she stopped herself against a bulkhead and placed a second pill out beyond it. "This is L2, outside of Earth's orbit." Finally, she put a pill in between the "sun" and the "Earth" but much closer to the latter. "And this is—"

"L1, by process of elimination," Luisa said drily, and laughed. "You space people love to count down, I know your ways."

"It's where the gravity of the sun and the Earth balance," Dinah said, "and people sometimes call it a gateway because it's an easy place to effect a switchover between a geocentric and a heliocentric orbit. This even happens naturally sometimes: an asteroid in a heliocentric orbit will wander close to L1 and get captured by the Earth. Or, going the other way, there's a case where an Apollo upper stage orbiting around the Earth passed near L1 and got ejected into a heliocentric orbit for a number of years. Later it came back through the same gateway—only to get ejected again."

Luisa nodded. "Like changing from the D to the A train at Columbus Circle, in New York terms."

"A lot of people have used the analogy of a switching yard or a train station to describe it, yeah," Dinah said.

"So you think Sean and his crew are headed that way."

"Once they get all their—" Dinah paused.

"Their shit together?" Luisa suggested.

"Thank you, yes," Dinah said with a smile. "They need to get to a higher orbit than we are in now if they are going to reach L1. That means burning their engines, expending a lot of fuel in just a few minutes, and then coasting for a few weeks. They'll have to pass through the Van Allen belts and soak up a lot of radiation. No avoiding it, unfortunately. L1 is four times farther away than the moon."

"Or what used to be the moon," Luisa said under her breath.

"Yeah, which means that in a few days Sean and his crew are going to be farther away from Earth than any humans who have ever lived. When they get to L1—which will take five weeks—they'll have to execute another burn that will switch them from the D to the A train—place them into a heliocentric orbit. And from there they can plot whatever course is going to get them to the comet."

Luisa had gotten a bit sidetracked by the first part of what Dinah had said. "Farther away from Earth than anyone in history," she repeated. "I wonder if there might be a certain feeling of jealousy at work in Fyodor's reaction, knowing that after all the time he has spent in space—"

"Some rich whippersnapper is going to show up and make his accomplishments look minor," Dinah said, nodding. "Could be. Fyodor's got the Russian granite face, you can't tell what's going on inside."

"Anyway," Luisa said, "they go and fetch the big ball of ice and then reverse all of those steps to come back to what by that point will hopefully be the Cloud Ark."

"Not exactly," Dinah said. "And that's where things get interesting."

"Oh, I thought they were already pretty interesting!" Luisa said.

Dinah was limited, here, in what she was allowed to say. "Maneuvering a space vehicle—which is designed and engineered to be what it is—around the solar system is one thing. Moving a huge raggedy-ass ball of ice is another."

"It's going to take a long time," Luisa said, nodding. "And it might not work."

"Yeah. Look, I just make robots."

"All of which will be making the trip?"

"Yes," Dinah said. "They'll be needed on the comet's surface, for anchoring cables and netting. It's a big chunk of ice. It's brittle. We don't want it to fall apart like a dry snowball when thrust is applied."

"A dry snowball," Luisa repeated. "Is that a thing, where you come from?"

"The Brooks Range? Yeah. Terrible place to make snowballs."

"Unless you're the kid sister," Luisa said, "and everyone's throwing them at you."

"No comment on that."

"In Central Park," Luisa said, "the snowballs were wet and they were hard."

DAY 90

When Ivy had opened the meeting on Day 37 with the words "five percent," Dinah and most of the others on Izzy had looked around themselves and seen a lack of progress that had troubled them. Which, of course, had been Ivy's point. On that day, twenty-six people had been in space, eight of whom were just barely surviving in temporary Luk shelters. The Banana had, with a bit of crowding, accommodated everyone.

On Day 73, when Ivy had opened another meeting in the Banana with the words "ten percent," the situation had been transformed. There had been no question anymore of fitting Izzy's whole population into the Banana; most of them had had to watch the meeting on video feeds. Thanks to Sean Probst and his Arjuna launches out of Moses Lake, no one quite knew what the total off-Earth population was anymore. Allegedly there was a Google Docs spreadsheet where it was being kept track of, but no one could agree on where it was. The population had certainly gone into the triple digits at least a week before.

In the first two weeks of its operation the new shake-and-bake spaceport at Moses Lake had launched three rockets. One had crashed into a high-end vineyard near Walla Walla, destroying several acres of grapes that would have made excellent wine, had there been enough time left on Earth's clock to age it properly. The others had made it to Izzy.

Most of Arjuna's big payloads, though, were being launched not from Moses Lake but from sites nearer the equator, whence they could get into orbits closer to the plane of the ecliptic. At least two heavy-lift rockets, one from Canaveral and one from Kourou, had effected a rendezvous and docking maneuver in a low orbit above Earth's tropics. Others were said to be in the works. But little was known of this project. Communication wasn't Sean Probst's strong suit, and his career in private enterprise had instilled a habit of playing his cards close to his vest. In this he seemed to be of one mind with the small cohort of people aboard Izzy, like Spencer Grindstaff and Zeke Petersen, who had impressive security clearances. Dinah and Ivy, comparing notes and sharing fragments of circumstantial evidence, had assembled at least a vague theory of what was going on. Ostensibly, Sean Probst was a wild card. But Arjuna had been mailing Nats to Sparky for weeks, and Sparky had been giving them top priority on launches to Izzy. It seemed, therefore, that Dinah's results—the feedback she was sending to Arjuna about which Nats worked in space and which didn't—were of great interest to NASA. And it was significant that at least one of Sean's payloads had been launched from Canaveral—which was, of course, NASA's flagship launch facility. Even more so was a launch out of Vandenberg Air Force Base that added a small additional module to the growing Arjuna complex. They knew it was small because of the size of the rocket used, and they knew it was top secret spook stuff because of the precautions that had been taken on the ground—that much had been reported by ordinary citizens, who had been forced to the shoulder of Highway 101 by a long military convoy, and who had aimed long lenses at the launch pad only to find their view blocked by tarps and camo nets.

The next rocket out of Moses Lake had made an uneventful journey to Izzy. Its upper stage, lacking a place to dock, flew in formation with the space station about a kilometer "aft." Fyodor stared at it balefully out the window and made repeated suggestions that its stores should be confiscated. Its cargo manifest was unusual:

- Spare propellant, and other consumables, that would enable Sean's Drop Top to execute a plane-change maneuver and rendezvous with *Ymir* in equatorial orbit (for the word "Ymir" was now being used to denote both the spaceship that Sean was assembling and its faraway destination)
- Ice

- Fiber for combining with ice to make a stronger material called pykrete
- Several thousand Icenats: tiny robots optimized for crawling around on ice

Fyodor, and perhaps others as well, coveted the ice and the propellant. Pete Starling had begun rattling legal sabers down on the ground, threatening to seize the Moses Lake spaceport—a scheme that vanished overnight after Sean began to rattle sabers of his own, threatening to make a YouTube video exposing the Cloud Ark scheme as a poorly conceived panacea at best. It was strange, to say the least, that such open conflict could exist between the government's left and right hands, but the world had become a strange place. Talking of it over meals or during after-work drinking sessions, Dinah and Ivy and Luisa could only speculate at the shouting matches that must be happening down on the ground between the Oval Office, the military, Arjuna Expeditions, and the Arkitects.

Dinah mostly just kept her head down and worked, programming the robots that Sean was going to take with him on his expedition. A comet core was not a solid piece of ice so much as an aggregation of shards, loosely held together by its own self-gravity—which was extremely weak. Merely touching it could cause big pieces to separate. Arjuna Expeditions had known this for many years and had put millions of dollars into inventing technology for capturing such difficult objects. Though "technology" might be too fancy a word for techniques that would have been recognizable to Stone Age hunter-gatherers: surround it with a net, draw the net closed with a loop of string.

Actually performing that feat in space was what Sean described as "an asymmetrical problem," programmer-speak meaning that there were a lot of contingencies and detail work, so it wasn't amenable to One Big Solution. Robots would probably end up swarming all over the surface of Comet Grigg-Skjellerup, cinching the net down and reinforcing weak spots by melting the ice, mixing the water with fiber, and letting it refreeze into pykrete. Dinah had offered to help out with that, and had been excited by the thought until Sean had brought her down to earth by pointing out some awkward realities. Communication between Izzy and *Ymir* was going to be limited by their one radio. They wouldn't be able to send video. And latency was going to be significant: for a large part of the journey there would be a delay of several minutes as the signals traversed a distance comparable to that between the Earth and the sun. So programming robots on the surface of the comet would be nothing like looking out her window at the ones on Amalthea. Anything Dinah had to contribute, she had to contribute now.

In any case, Izzy's population had dropped by two, and the level of tension and drama had fallen precipitously, when Sean and Larz had departed in the Drop Top on A+0.82. The plane-change maneuver took them to a rendezvous above the equator with *Ymir*. After more rendezvous operations extending over a week, and incorporating yet more payloads launched from Cape Canaveral as well as from private spaceports in New Mexico and West Texas, *Ymir* made a long burn of her main engine that placed her into a transfer orbit bound for L1. A few days after that, she beat the Apollo record for distance traveled from Earth.

Konrad Barth came to Dinah's shop and knocked politely, for she happened to have her curtain drawn, and everyone knew that she and Rhys sometimes had sex on the other side of it. He entered, looked about nervously, and asked her if she knew anything about what *Ymir* was going to do. Before she could answer, he shook her off, took out his tablet, and tapped in his password. Then he spun it around to show her a photograph.

It took her a while to understand what she was seeing. Clearly, it was a picture of a man-made object in space. And it was a good picture, but surrounded by a glamor of pixels that spoke of considerable enhancement. Konrad had taken the picture using one of Izzy's optical telescopes. He had turned it away from its usual objective, which was the system of fragments churning around the former center of the moon, and aimed it at this man-made object. The object was big and complicated, at a guess the largest thing humans had ever assembled in space with the exception of Izzy herself. The picture had been taken from a great distance while both Izzy and the object were moving with respect to each other, and he'd toiled with image processing software to reduce the blur. She could see clearly enough that, like Izzy, it consisted of a stack of modules that had been sent up atop different rockets and plugged together. The one on its tail sported a large nozzle bell, and was obviously its main propulsion unit. Some of the modules just looked like propellant tanks. Others looked like habitations. But far and away the most prominent, and the weirdest, part of this thing was a long spike or probe that extended from its forward end, making it ten times as long as it would have been otherwise. It was a truss, recognizably made in the same way as the new trusses on Izzy.

"Wow," Dinah joked, "a space station with its own radio tower!"

Konrad smiled weakly. "Look at the 'top' of the 'radio tower,' " he suggested. He spread his fingers on the tablet, zooming in on a thick blur of pixels at its tip. This seemed to have a roughly arrowhead-like shape, a small dark tip sitting on a thicker white base, itself resting on a dark base plate.

He was looking at her as if he expected her to understand—or as if she must be privy to secrets.

Which she was. But she couldn't reveal them.

"I'm not a nuclear physicist," she said, "but it's screamingly obvious that the people aboard that ship—it's *Ymir,* isn't it—?"

"Of course."

"—that they want to be as far away as possible from whatever that is, and so they mounted it at the end of the longest stick they could build."

"It is something that makes a lot of neutrons," Konrad said.

"How do you know that?"

"This thing"—he indicated the fat white layer in the middle of the sandwich, like the marshmallow in a s'more—"is probably polyethylene or paraffin, which would be good at absorbing neutrons. Gamma rays might be produced in the process, and so this base plate"—he pointed to the dark graham cracker at the bottom—"is probably lead."

Dinah already knew what it was, because Sean had told her: the core of a large nuclear power plant, rated at a thermal output of four gigawatts, somewhat hastily reengineered for this purpose. But she had been sworn to secrecy, and so all she could do was let Konrad piece it together himself. "Well," she said, "those are impressive precautions on what is probably a suicide mission anyway."

"They want to be alive and capable of doing something when and if they get where they are going," Konrad said.

"Do you suppose anyone has taken pictures like this from Earth?" Dinah asked. "Because I haven't seen anything in the media."

"It was concealed by a fairing until they made their transfer burn," Konrad said. "I took this a couple of hours ago, when I had my one and only clear shot."

They had timed that burn so that they would cross the former moon's orbit at a time when most of the debris cloud was on the opposite side of the Earth, thus minimizing the chance of colliding with a rock.

Nevertheless, a few days after they had passed that distance, and become the longest-range travelers in human history, they stopped communicating.

Until then *Ymir* had been using powerful X-band radios to communicate over the Deep Space Network—a complex of dishes in Spain, Australia, and California that had been used for decades to talk to long-range space probes. Now she had gone silent. She was still out there—Konrad could still pick her up as a white dot on his optical telescope. Since she was merely coasting for thirty-seven days, not firing her engines, there was no way to tell whether the crew was still alive. A perfectly shipshape *Ymir* and a crumpled wad of space junk would have looked and behaved the same.

They drew some hope from the fact that *nothing* came back from her. *Ymir* had automatic systems that were supposed to phone home without human intervention. If those had continued to function while communication from humans had ceased, it would suggest that the crew were all dead or incapacitated. But the fact that all human and robotic signals had been cut off at the same time suggested that it was a radio problem—perhaps damage to the X-band antenna, or to the transmitter itself.

Ymir became tricky, then impossible to see as she approached L1, since that put her squarely between Earth and the sun. She was assumed to have reached that point on Day 126, whereupon she was scheduled to make another burn that would put her into a heliocentric orbit: an ellipse that would intersect with "Greg's Skeleton" over a year later—sometime around A+1.175, or a year and 175 days post-Zero. Once *Ymir* disappeared, from their point of view, into the fires of the sun, there was nothing they could do except wait for her to reach a place where she was observable. If *Ymir* had suffered a catastrophic failure and been turned into a floating piece of space junk, she would probably cycle back on the return leg of the same orbit and pass close to the Earth again—though L1 was such an unstable place from an orbital dynamics standpoint that she could just as easily wander off into a heliocentric orbit, especially if she'd taken a big hit from a rock that had knocked her off course.

As the calendar progressed through the 130s and to Day 140—two weeks after *Ymir* ought to have passed through L1—and she did not appear on that return leg, it became clear that she must have transferred to a heliocentric orbit, whether by accident or because of a controlled burn. Assuming the latter, Sean and the other half-dozen members of the crew would have nothing to do for the next year but float around in zero gee and wait. There was nothing that could be done to speed up the journey; it was a matter of getting two orbits to graze each other.

These events, which would have seemed of world-historical significance a few months ago, now seemed like below-the-fold news compared to all that was happening in what had formerly been the sublunary realm.

The fuss and excitement surrounding Sean and Arjuna, the Moses Lake spaceport, and the voyage of *Ymir* had drawn attention away from the routine, faithful, grind-it-out progress being made the whole time by NASA, the European Space Agency, Roskosmos, China National Space Administration, and the space agencies of Japan and India. These organizations were staffed by conservative old-line engineers, not far removed culturally from the slide-rule-brandishing nerds of Apollo and Soyuz fame. In fact, some of them *were* those nerds, just a lot older and a lot crustier. They were baffled, nay, infuriated by the ease with which a few upstart tech zillionaires could command the world's attention and go rocketing off on ill-advised, hastily planned missions of their own choosing. The departure of Sean and Larz from Izzy had occasioned a big sigh of relief, and a return to the steady and unimaginative work that these people were best at.

And anyone paying attention to the numbing details expressed in the spreadsheets and the flowcharts would see the value of that work on A+0.144, when Ivy opened a meeting in the Banana with the words "twenty percent" (for the latest projections from the astrophysical lab of Dr. Dubois Jerome Xavier Harris at Caltech, and from the other labs doing the same calculations at other universities around the world, were that the White Sky would happen on or about A+1.354, or one year and 354 days after the breakup of the moon; they were one-fifth of the way there).

The purpose of the Scouts—the first wave of what amounted to suicide workers such as Tekla, who had arrived starting on Day 29—had been to build out the improvised network of hamster tubes and docking ports that would make it possible for a much larger population of so-called Pioneers to reach Izzy. The basic distinction between a Scout and a Pioneer was that the Scout went up knowing there was no place to dock, but the Pioneer knew that, at least in theory, there would be an available port for their spacecraft, with pressurized atmosphere on the other side of it. The promise had failed in one case, with the result that half a dozen Pioneers crammed aboard a Soyuz had silently asphyxiated. The problem was traced to a defect in a hastily built docking mechanism. Three Chinese taikonauts lost their lives when the hamster tube in which they were moving was pierced by a micrometeorite and lost pressurization. But from about Day 56 onward, Pioneers were arriving at a rate of between five and twelve per day. There was a lull once all the available docking spaces were occupied, but after that it began to snowball as spacecraft began to dock to other spacecraft, and the hamster tube network was built out, and inflatable structures were deployed.

Izzy, which had been a complicated and hard-to-understand contraption even before all of this had happened, was now an utterly bewildering maze of modules, hamster tubes, trusses, and ships docked to ships docked to ships, "like a freakin' three-dimensional domino game," as Luisa put it. The only way to get one's bearings, looking at a rendering of the complex, was by picking out the rugged and asymmetrical shape of Amalthea at one end and the two tori at the other. Those were "forward" and "aft," respectively, and the axis between them was the basis for the traditional nautical directions of "port" and "starboard" as well as "zenith" and "nadir," which were space lingo for basically "up away from Earth" and "down toward Earth." If you arranged yourself so that your back was to the tori and your face toward Amalthea, with the "port" stuff on your left hand and the "starboard" stuff on your right, then your head would be aimed toward the zenith and your feet toward the nadir and the surface of Earth four hundred kilometers below.

That, however, was the privileged view of people outside the thing in space suits. Inside, it was still easy to get lost in the three-dimensional domino game. Felt-tip markers, always a scarce resource even on Earth, became objects of great value as people used them to mark directions on the walls of hamster tubes and habitat modules.

"IT'S JUST A CHRONOLOGICAL ACCIDENT THAT I'M HERE AT ALL," IVY mused, during one of her and Dinah's increasingly rare drinking sessions. All of their original stashes of booze had long since been consumed, but new arrivals were kind enough to slip them bottles from time to time.

"I disagree," Dinah said. It wasn't exactly a scintillating response. But she'd been caught off guard by the suddenness with which Ivy had dropped her guard.

"If the moon had blown up two weeks later, some Russian sourpuss would be in charge up here and I'd be on the ground, married and pregnant."

"And under the same death sentence as everyone else."

"Yeah, well, there's that."

Dinah reached for the bottle and refilled the shot glasses, trying to stretch out the moment. It had never been easy to get Ivy to open up, even back in the happy days before Zero.

"Look, Ivy, it's *not* an accident that you were in charge of Izzy. They gave you the job for a reason. You're the last girl in the world—or out of it—who should be suffering from impostor syndrome."

Ivy stared at her through a somewhat amused silence. "Go on," she finally said. "What is this impostor syndrome you speak of?" For they'd talked about it before—but usually with Dinah being the one who felt it.

"Don't try to deflect this. What's going on?"

Ivy glanced at the ceiling: a sort of visual signal, borrowed from the Russians, to remind Dinah that you never knew when someone was listening. Then she looked into Dinah's eyes. But only for a moment. She was fundamentally a shy person, who preferred inspecting her shoes while baring her soul.

"You and Sean Probst made great sparring partners," Ivy said.

"He was so fucking obnoxious! He needed someone to—" Dinah cut herself short then, because Ivy had gotten a sort of sad, wry look on her face and held up one hand to stop her.

"Agreed! Yes. Thanks for doing it," Ivy said. "He needed someone like you around. Sometimes it almost looked like a comedy act between you two. And the way that the Russians reacted to him—Tekla first of all, of course, but later Fyodor proposing to place all Arjuna personnel under arrest and confiscate everything they'd brought up with them—that was great drama. Tabloid stories and comment threads galore down on the surface. But I barely survived it."

"What do you mean, you barely survived?"

"You wouldn't believe some of the conferences I had with Baikonur and Houston. People down there wanted me to take a very hard line. To do what Fyodor wanted."

"But you didn't," Dinah pointed out.

Ivy met her gaze again. Then, after a moment, she gave a little nod.

"So you won," Dinah went on.

"I won a Pyrrhic victory," Ivy said. "I negotiated a less draconian solution. The *Ymir* expedition went on its way with no obvious hard feelings."

"And how is that Pyrrhic?"

"I don't want to make my problems yours," Ivy said.

"Who else are you going to talk to?"

"Maybe no one," Ivy returned, showing a flash of something like anger. "Maybe that's what a leader is, Dinah. The one person who can't—who *shouldn't*—share her problems with anyone else. It's sort of an old-fashioned idea. But the human race might need such people going forward."

Dinah just stared back at her. Finally, Ivy relented, and spoke in tones almost devoid of feeling: "My position as the head of the space station came under serious challenge. It made me aware of politics on the ground that have been going on for some time—but that were invisible to me until the Sean Probst controversy surfaced them. Since then, I believe that my authority has been further undermined by people on the ground, leaking things to the press, saying things in meetings."

"Pete Starling."

"No comment. Anyway, I think I am going to be replaced before long."

Ivy's eyes had reddened slightly. She made another glance at the ceiling, but the expression on her face suggested she didn't care who might have heard her. Then she looked at Dinah and smiled. "How have you been doing, sister?" she asked in a weak voice.

"I've been pretty good," Dinah said.

"Really? That's music to my ears."

"Bo, Larz, the others who've come up to work in my crew, they seem to respect what I've done," Dinah said.

"I think it's because of what you did for Tekla," Ivy said.

"Oh really? Not just my amazing natural competence?"

"There are a lot of people on the ground who are competent in the way you mean," Ivy said, "and we are going to be seeing a lot of them up here in the next few weeks. Believe me. I've read their CVs."

"I'm sure you have."

"But everyone kinda senses now that some other qualities are going to be needed besides just pure competence. That's why people are deferring to you."

Another awkward silence. Ivy seemed to be suggesting that she, Ivy, was no longer being given that kind of respect.

"That, and your amazing competence," Ivy added.

Consolidation

EARTH'S ATMOSPHERE DIDN'T JUST STOP. IT PETERED OUT UNTIL IT became indistinguishable, by most measuring devices, from a perfect vacuum. Below about 160 kilometers of altitude, the air was still thick enough to rapidly drag down anything placed in orbit, so those altitudes were used only for short-term satellites like the early space capsules. The higher the altitude, the thinner the air and the more slowly orbits decayed.

Izzy was four hundred kilometers up. Its acres of solar panels and radiators made it extremely draggy in comparison to its mass. Or at least that had been the case until Amalthea had been bolted onto it, suddenly making it far heavier.

Somewhat paradoxically to laypersons, the added mass of the asteroid made Izzy much better at staying aloft. Before Amalthea, the station had lost two kilometers of altitude every month, making it necessary to reboost it by firing a rocket engine on its aft end. In the early days, that engine had been the built-in one mounted on the

Zvezda module. But in general they simply used the engine belonging to whatever spacecraft happened to be docked to Izzy's aft-most module.

In those days Izzy had been like a kite: all surface area, no mass. In technical terms, it had had a low ballistic coefficient: a way of saying that it was strongly affected by what little atmosphere there was. Once Amalthea had been attached, it was like a kite with a big rock strapped to it. It had a high ballistic coefficient. The rock's momentum bulled through the evanescent atmosphere and led to much slower orbital decay. But by the same token, when it came time to reboost Izzy's orbit, a longer burn and a larger amount of propellant were needed in order to accelerate all of that iron and nickel.

Since the Scouts and the Pioneers had begun adding more bits onto Izzy, its ballistic coefficient had been dropping again, and boost burns had come more frequently. And it was always the case that thrusters had to be fired every now and again to correct the station's altitude. All of it grew more problematic as more was added onto the basic structure. Izzy had been an ungainly construct even before all the new pieces had been added onto it. Thrust applied to one part of it would ramify through the other modules as various parts of the truss and other structural members took up the strain and passed it on down the line. To put it in the simplest possible terms, Izzy had gotten all floppy as more stuff was attached to it, and its floppiness made it difficult to reboost the orbit or even to tweak the angle at which it "flew" through space. They had allowed the orbit to decay by a serious amount, over sixteen kilometers, during the busiest part of the Pioneers' efforts, but now reboosting had to become a routine operation. And every firing of the engine on the bottom of H2 revealed structural weaknesses that had to be jury-rigged, sometimes literally with zip ties and duct tape, before it could proceed.

During the span of time from about A+0.144 to 250, the watchword was "consolidation," inevitably trimmed to "consol." It basically meant the retrofitting of new trusswork around the hamster tubes and other sprawling constructs that had been added to the truss during the frantic first couple of months. Other problems were addressed at the same time, most notably the building of more radiators for dumping waste heat into space. These didn't work if they were too closely spaced—they just shone heat on one another. So the heat rejection complex waxed enormous and ended up growing generally aftward, like an empennage—the feathers on the butt of an arrow. It was no mere figure of speech. In the same way that an arrow's heavy head and spreading feathers kept it pointed straight forward, the combination of massive Amalthea at the forward end and the heat radiators trailing away aft helped keep Izzy pointed in the right direction and somewhat reduced the demand for thruster firings. It also protected the radiators from micrometeoroids. Rocks could theoretically come from any direction and strike the space station, but they were most likely to hit its forward end, and so forward-facing surfaces of the space station's modules had generally been equipped with shields. Amalthea, of course, was the biggest and best shield of all.

The number of solar panels might have grown too, had they been doing things the old way. But very early in the Cloud Ark project it had become obvious that, while photovoltaics might be a useful adjunct, the only sure way to keep everything running was with the small nuclear devices called RTGs, or radioisotope thermoelectric generators. These made heat all the time, whether you wanted them to or not, and so created further demand for radiators.

The radiators were, in essence, a gigantic exploit in zero-gravity plumbing. The excess heat had to be collected from where it was produced (mostly, the inhabited and pressurized parts of Izzy) and transported to where it could be gotten rid of (the "empennage" growing to aft). The only plausible way of doing this was by using a fluid, pumping it around a loop, heating it up at one end and cooling it off at the other. At the hot end they used heat exchangers and so-called cold plates that just soaked up heat from wherever it was a problem.

At the cold end the fluid fanned out through networks of thin tubes, like capillaries, sandwiched between flat panels whose sole purpose was to become slightly warm and shine infrared light into deep space, cooling down Izzy by warming up faraway galaxies. Joining the hot and cold ends of the loop was a system of pumps and pipes that got bigger every day and that was prone to many of the same kinds of trouble as bedeviled earthbound plumbing. Making it twice as complicated was that some of the loops used anhydrous ammonia and others used water. Ammonia worked better, but it was dangerous, and you couldn't easily get more of it in space. If the Cloud Ark survived, it would survive on a water-based economy. A hundred years from now everything in space would be cooled by circulating water systems. But for now they had to keep the ammonia-based equipment running as well.

Further complications, as if any were wanted, came from the fact that the systems had to be fault tolerant. If one of them got bashed by a hurtling piece of moon shrapnel and began to leak, it needed to be isolated from the rest of the system before too much of the precious water, or ammonia, leaked into space. So, the system as a whole possessed vast hierarchies of check valves, crossover switches, and redundancies that had saturated even Ivy's brain, normally an infinite sink for detail. She'd had to delegate all cooling-related matters to a working group that was about three-quarters Russian and one-quarter American. The majority of all space walk activity was related to the expansion and maintenance of the cooling system and, uncharacteristically for her, she was content just to get a report on it once a day.

All of that plumbing, and all of those radiators, needed to be supported by Izzy's structure just like anything else—they were especially prone to troubles under the general heading of "too floppy to survive reboost." So, proceeding in the same general putting-out-fires mode, Ivy and the engineers on the ground next had to steer the program in the general direction of "consol," or, as Ivy put it privately, "defloppification," of the space station's overall structure. And since it was out of the question to take apart what the Scouts and Pioneers had put in place, this took the form of building what amounted to external scaffolding around what was there. Viewed from a kilometer away, it looked quite similar to what one saw when some old and treasured building was being renovated: a latticework of structure, ugly but serviceable, grew around the underlying object, enveloping it and strengthening it without actually penetrating it.

In the early going, sections of truss were assembled on the ground, launched up whole, and slammed into place by teams of spacewalkers, buying large increases in structural integrity quickly and expensively. That approach soon fell prey to the law of diminishing returns and it became clear that the Arkers, as they'd started to be known, couldn't be forever dependent on ground-based engineers custom-building structures.

The ground-based engineers didn't even really know what was going on with Izzy anymore. Their CAD models had fallen behind. Dinah knew it because of a sudden surge in messages from exasperated engineers requesting that she send a robot out to such-and-such a place and aim its camera at such-and-such a module so that they could see what was actually there.

The Arkers needed tools and materials for building their own structures in situ. These started to arrive around Day 220. And it was a measure of how much things had changed on the ground that the solutions came in more than one form, from more than one source, often with little to no coordination. In the old days a proposed system would have been given a three-letter acronym and bounced back and forth between different agencies and contractors for fifteen years before being launched into space.

The single most useful structure-building system turned out to be a rough-and-ready implementation of an old but good idea. It was a little bit like the machine used by gutter and downspout contractors, mounted in the back of a truck, fed by a large roll of sheet metal, which would be bent into a gutter shape and extruded in pieces as long as you liked. This machine did much the same thing, except that it bent the sheet metal ribbon into a simple beam with a triangular cross section and then welded the edges together to make it permanent. It had been invented and prototyped long ago in the West, but the Chinese space agency had perfected it in the first couple of hundred days post-Zero and begun to launch the machines up with crews who knew how to use them. As long as they were supplied with electricity and rolls of aluminum they would go on pumping out beams forever. Connecting segments of beam into more complex structures, such as trusses and scaffolding, was a little more difficult. Welding in space, while possible, was complicated, and there wasn't enough equipment. Instead they ended up using Tinkertoy-like connectors, again mass-produced by the Chinese, into which the ends of the triangular beams could be inserted, then tightened down using screws. At first many of these were shipped up in bulk from the ground, but on A+0.247 they took delivery of a 3-D printer that had been optimized to make more of them, with options for modifying the angle at which the beams would be inserted. This gave them the ability to design and build trusses on the fly, which was not possible with the mass-produced connectors. And as a last resort, Fyodor had an electron-beam welding machine that would work in zero gravity and a vacuum, undoubtedly the most expensive welder ever made, a marvel of Russian ingenuity, and he had trained Vyacheslav to use it. Vyacheslav then trained Tekla and two of the other spacewalkers, who set up a job queue and took turns drifting around Izzy's increasingly complex structure tacking down a weld here and a weld there. Thus, constructed largely by the Chinese and the Russians, the scaffolding grew and stiffened. The reboost burns no longer produced alarming pops, bangs, and groaning noises. The hamster tubes gradually disappeared within shrouds of structural reinforcement and shielding. New docking ports began to sprout at Izzy's extremities, like buds on tree branches, in preparation for the next phase: the coming of the first arklets.

Down on the Earth, it was August, the second-to-the-last August that there would ever be. A dozen new or reconditioned spaceports had come into operation. Heavy-lift rockets could now be launched to Izzy from eight different locations around the world. Around those launch pads, rocket stages and three different styles of arklet were beginning to pile up like so much ammunition at a firing range.

DAY 260

"You're going, Dr. Harris," said Julia Bliss Flaherty.

From time to time Doob became distracted by the sheer oddity of the fact that he now met with the president on a regular basis. It was a lot less weird, in the big scheme of things, than the fact that the moon had exploded and that everyone was going to die. But his mind, born and raised in a world free of such prodigies, was more comfortable being freaked out by little things, such as talking to the president. In the Oval Office. With her science advisor Pete Starling on one side and the White House communications director on the other. And a butler pouring ice water into crystal tumblers.

He saw the usefulness of the butler. But what was the point of having the communications director here? Margaret Sloane was good at her job, and the perfection of her grooming was a perpetual source of wonderment, but it had become pretty clear that she was out of her depth in any technical discussion beyond "big rocks from space are dangerous."

They were all looking at him as if he was expected to say something.

What had been the president's words? *You're going.*

Did that mean he was on his way out? Going to be replaced by someone younger and more web-savvy, like Tav Prowse?

Into the awkward silence, Margaret Sloane poured an explanation. "Your skills and your presence have done so much to calm the waters. To give the people of the United States, and of Earth, something to pin their hopes on in the guiding concept of Our Heritage. Your willingness to roll up your sleeves, go to places like Moses Lake, Baikonur, the rocket factories—that has all been so appreciated. But we feel that the time has come—"

"To replace me with a fresh face, I get it," Doob said. "To tell you the truth, that's fine. I would like to spend more time with my kids and my new wife. Tav will do a great job."

For once, the president looked flummoxed. Her eyes flicked toward Margaret.

"That's not where we were going with it at all," said Margaret. "We need you—the people of the world need you—to take the next step—to advance to a higher level."

"We are asking you," said the president, a bit testy with Doob's slowness and with Margaret's breathy and roundabout phrasings, "to travel into space on or about Day 360, and to become part of the population of the Cloud Ark."

"I don't want to go!" Doob blurted out. It was rare for him to forget himself in that way, so he then just sat for a few moments, stunned by his own ineptitude.

"Dr. Harris," said the president after a few moments, "as you probably know from your high school civics class, the person who sits where I'm sitting has a lot of powers. One of them is that I can grant reprieves and pardons for convicted criminals. Every inmate who goes to the execution chamber in Texas goes there in part because I made the decision not to pardon him or to commute his sentence. I have never exercised that power in the case of a death row inmate. In effect, however, I *am* exercising it in your case *now*."

The president paused there for a moment, and Doob became aware that she was waiting for his attention.

He was staring at a flower arrangement on the table in front of him. Wondering how long it would be before anyone cultivated flowers on the Cloud Ark. He reached for his tumbler and took a sip of water.

J.B.F. unnerved him when she was like this. It took a certain conscious and deliberate act of will for him to peel his eyes off the flowers and look up into her eyes. They stared back at him wide and unblinking.

"By virtue of being on the surface of this planet, you are under a death sentence," said the president. "I just pardoned you. You can go into space and live. I cannot. Do you understand that, Dr. Harris? I cannot even pardon myself in this case without flagrantly violating the Crater Lake Accord, which makes national leaders and their families ineligible. Now, what the hell is your problem?"

Doob's honest answer, had he voiced it, would have been most impolitic: *I have become convinced that the Cloud Ark scheme cannot possibly succeed. I have been playing along in public just to keep people happy. I would rather die quickly on the ground with my loved ones than slowly, alone, in space.*

"There are others who deserve it more than I do," he said. And in the same moment he cursed himself for saying something so lame. So easily refuted. Because in all honesty he was a fine choice for inclusion on the Cloud Ark's roster.

"I couldn't disagree more!" exclaimed Pete Starling, with a nervous chuckle. "Doob, you're going to be so useful up there, I'm afraid you'll never get a moment's rest! You have multiple core competencies with surprisingly minimal Venn. You can pivot from working on astrophysics problems, to teaching the young Arkers, to podcasting to folks on the ground, without skipping a beat!"

Doob turned to look into Pete Starling's eyes as he was saying those words and understood, with a shock like diving into cold water, that Pete was lying.

Not about Doob's usefulness. In that he was sincere. He was lying about something more fundamental.

He didn't believe that the Cloud Ark was going to work any more than Doob did.

He needed Doc Dubois to go up there and lie for him.

Now, Doob was a scientist who had spent decades of his life training in a particular discipline, namely, to seek and to speak the truth. Even among hard scientists—a notoriously blunt crowd—he had a reputation for saying what he thought. Never mind whose feelings he wounded, whose careers got damaged as a result. This seemed to come across, somehow, on camera. The very reason that so many people trusted him when he went on TV was that he was a straight shooter, he said things that offended the powerful, he stirred things up, and he didn't care. Certain of those moments had been enshrined forever in YouTube clips and Reddit memes: taking down a Republican senator who didn't believe in evolution, destroying a climate change denier in an impromptu sidewalk confrontation, reducing a movie star to tears on the *Today* show by telling her that her stand against childhood vaccination made her personally responsible for the deaths of thousands of babies.

So, in a way, there were two questions in his head at the same time: whether he *would* lie, and whether he *could* lie.

As to the first question, was it okay for him to lie if it would make billions of people go to their deaths a little happier?

As to the second, would people sense it? Would they detect a shift in the tone of his voice, the set of his face, when he was just standing there in front of the camera talking shit?

That was the real question. Whether he could pull it off. Because if he couldn't pull it off—if he couldn't lie convincingly—then there was no point in even trying.

And he was pretty sure that he couldn't do it.

One of the ice cubes in Doob's glass let out a little pop as it underwent thermal fracturing.

Doob thought of Sean Probst, now half a year into his quest to fetch a big piece of ice. He couldn't believe it had been that long already.

You could get used to anything. You got used to it and then time raced by, and before you knew it, time was up.

He remembered people asking difficult questions around the time of Sean's departure for the L1 gate. What the hell was this crazy billionaire doing? Clearly, it was not part of the official plan. The official plan did not seem to recognize a need for a huge piece of ice. But Sean Probst believed it was so important that he was willing to go up there personally and take care of the problem. There was a good chance he would die in the process, or come back so broken from radiation exposure and long-term weightlessness that his health would never recover. And so people had asked Doob what he thought Sean was thinking. And Doob, who hadn't studied it at the time, had answered vaguely, saying that water was always a good thing to have in space: you could drink it, grow crops with it, use it for radiation shielding, split it into hydrogen and oxygen for rocket fuel, or pipe it through hoses to radiate excess heat into space. All of which was quite true, but sort of begged the question. It was so blindingly obvious that NASA must have thought of it already. What additional demand for water was Sean Probst seeing that NASA had failed to notice, or turned a blind eye to?

Later Doob had figured it out based on background conversations with people at Arjuna and scuttlebutt reaching him through friends working on the planning of the Cloud Ark. It was all about propellant. The Cloud Ark would have to burn a lot of it. Sean didn't think they had enough.

So he had gone up there and done something about it.

Because Sean wasn't a talker. He was a doer. And as such he didn't have to agonize, as Doob was doing now, about what he was going to say. What his public stance was going to be. How he was going to be positioned and perceived.

"That's a hundred days from now," Doob said.

He'd been silent for so long that the other occupants of the Oval Office were a bit startled. J.B.F.'s attention had wandered to a tablet on her desk, and Pete Starling was looking out the window.

"I beg your pardon, Dr. Harris?" said the president, turning that gaze back upon him. But he no longer felt intimidated by it. He was going to go somewhere where she could never look at him again.

"This is 260," Doob said. "You said you wanted me to go up there around 360."

"Yes," said Maggie Sloane, relaxing into an entirely new posture. "That's not the first wave—which is going to be more exploratory, more of a dress rehearsal—but it would be the first *real* wave of Arkers going into space, and our thought was that we would embed you with them. You could partake of their experiences and show the people of Earth what a day in the life of an Arker consists of. Providing a sense of continuity."

Holy shit, Doob thought. Seven years a Ph.D. candidate, two postdocs at major European research institutions, a tenured position at Caltech, shortlisted for a Nobel Prize, and here he was, with the fate of the human race at stake, being positioned as an *observer* to *provide a sense of continuity.*

"I can do that," he said. *And some other things as well, as long as I'm up there.*

What were they going to do, yank him back down to the planet?

The worst they could do was to stop broadcasting his stuff, and that would be fine with him. There had to be something he could do up there that would be more useful than talking into a camera. Sean Probst had identified one problem with the Cloud Ark and taken action to remedy it; in a hundred days, what could Doob learn that might be useful? What actions could he take, once he got up there, to give the whole thing a better chance of success?

"A hundred days," he said. "Three months for me to spend with my wife and my kids and my embryo."

"Embryo?" Pete Starling repeated, not getting it.

Margaret Sloane, mother of three, picked it up instantly. "Amelia's pregnant?" she asked, with the warm smile that, until Zero, had been the normal response to such blessed events. Nowadays, people's reactions were a bit more complicated, of course; but it was hard to shed old habits.

"Not anymore," Doob said. "We froze the embryo. My only condition is that it travel up into space with me."

"Consider it done," said the president, in a tone, and with a look, that told them the meeting was over.

DAY 287

"Got any tater-related humorous items for me?" Ivy asked. " 'Cause oh, man, could I ever use some comic relief."

Dinah wasn't sure how she felt about Ivy looking to her doomed family as a source of casual amusement, but as they were only some 433 days away from the end of the world, she didn't really think there was much point in getting shirty about it.

The situation did breed a kind of coarseness toward those stuck on the ground. It was humanly impossible to extend to seven billion people the full sympathy that each of them deserved. Dinah had begun to hear instances of dark humor over the radio, and had noticed herself being at least a little bit amused by it.

Nor was that dark humor restricted to Arkers, as Dinah's family demonstrated. They were intelligent people—you had to be, to do what they did—but they went in for a certain brand of mining-camp humor, heavy on the practical jokes and novelty items that you'd never see in a boardroom or a faculty lounge. And once they'd latched on to something that they thought was funny, they'd never let go of it. A half-serious Morse code message about planting a flat of potatoes, transmitted by Rufus shortly after the Crater Lake announcement, had sprouted into a whole subgenre of running jokes about the preparations that the MacQuarie clan was making for the Hard Rain. In her occasional care packages from the ground, Dinah was now accustomed to finding fingerling potatoes, still with real dirt on them, or plastic parts for Mr. and Mrs. Potatohead toys. She even had a rusty old Idaho license plate duct-taped to the wall of her shop now, emblazoned with the slogan FAMOUS POTATOES, courtesy of Rufus, who'd gotten it from a mining industry pal in that state's silver-rich panhandle.

"Is that a no?" Ivy asked.

"Oh, I have potato shit all over the place now," Dinah said. "I'm just no longer sure that they're joking."

"What do you mean?"

"At first I thought it was their way of saying, 'We know we are screwed, no point in being babies about it, let's laugh it up until the end.' But now I'm starting to ask myself what it is they're doing. I mean, they're up there in the Brooks Range with all of this equipment. They could drive down to Fairbanks any time they feel like it, and from there go anywhere in the world. Check out the pyramids. See the *Mona Lisa*. Visit old friends and family. Instead they're up in the most godforsaken place I've ever seen, doing what?"

"Prepping?" Ivy said.

"That's the only thing I can think," Dinah said. "Prepping for a five- to ten-thousand-year stay."

"They're not the only ones," Ivy said.

It took Dinah a few moments to catch her friend's meaning. Then it was clear, just from the look on Ivy's face. "Are you shitting me? Cal?"

Ivy made just a suggestion of a nod with her eyes. "Mixed in with the stuff you'd expect from a fiancé—which is *none of your business*—he asks me questions about things like the comparative merits of lithium versus sodium hydroxide scrubbers. He requests copies of Luisa's PDFs about the sociology of persons confined in small places for long periods."

"He can't think you're not going to notice that."

"Sure. I'm going to read between the lines."

"What do you suppose he's thinking?"

"Well," Ivy said, "he does have sole authority over a huge submarine designed to ride out global thermonuclear warfare. And when the United States ceases to exist, I guess there'll be no one above him, chain-of-command-wise. What's a commander to do?"

"But how would it work?"

"I think a lot depends," Ivy said, "on whether the oceans boil dry. If I were him, I'd make for the Marianas Trench and keep my fingers crossed."

"I would think it would be even harder than staying alive in space."

Ivy looked at her friend with dry amusement.

"What?!" Dinah said.

"Staying alive in space is going to be a piece of cake, remember?"

"Oh yeah, sorry. I forgot . . ." *To put on my makeup.* "It would present some fascinating challenges," she corrected herself, switching to her best NASA PR voice.

"I think it's like what we are doing," Ivy said. "You have to break it down into a lot of little things and solve them one at a time, or you get overwhelmed."

"Is that what we're doing?"

"Yeah." Ivy rolled her eyes.

"What's on your mind? Other than the need for comic relief?"

"You. How you're doing. Your health," Ivy said.

"Oh my god, is this an actual meeting? Are we on official business here?"

Ivy ignored her. "You haven't been logging much T2 time."

T2—the second torus, which Rhys had been responsible for

building—had started to spin on Day 140. Its simulated gravity was one-eighth of Earth normal, only a little greater than that on the first torus. It was bigger and spun more slowly, which Rhys hoped would make it a little more comfortable. Simply being in it helped counteract some of the negative effects of living in space for extended periods of time. People who lived without gravity suffered a gradual loss of bone density and muscle mass. Eyes went out of shape and vision deteriorated. Space station crews tried to fight this by using exercise machines that placed stress on the bones, but these were stopgap measures meant for people who were only going to be in space for a few months. Dinah, Ivy, and the other ten members of the original Izzy crew had now been up here for close to a year. During the first few months after Zero, no one had paid much attention to long-term health issues. Everyone was going to die. Scouts were showing up dead on arrival. It had been all emergency, all the time. But during the months of hamster tube building and structural consolidation, the life scientists had been quietly having their say. This wasn't the first time Dinah had been nudged in recent weeks about her failure to spend more time in the simulated gravity field of T2.

"It's just hard to go back and forth between gravity and no gravity," Dinah said. "It makes me barf. And none of my stuff is in T2." She was referring, as Ivy would know, to the shop where she worked on her robots.

"But isn't that mostly remote work? Writing code?"

"Yeah, I just like to be where I can see them out the window."

"Don't they have little cameras on them?"

Dinah had no answer for that.

"Whatever you're doing here," Ivy continued, "you could do from a cabin in T2, where the gravity would build your bones."

"It's also Rhys," Dinah admitted. "Things have been a little weird with him and I just don't want to—"

"Rhys never even goes to T2," Ivy said. "He's been hanging out with the inflatable structures team."

"Okay," Dinah said. "Give me a place to work on T2 and—"

"There's another thing," Ivy said, and let out The Sigh. The Sigh was what Ivy did when the powers that be were making her do something ridiculous. It would never show up in the transcript of a meeting, but it changed everything.

"I don't even want to guess," Dinah said.

"We have all become characters in a reality TV show," Ivy said. "You might not be aware of it."

"Nah, I haven't been watching much TV."

"Well, it's all people have to do anymore, down on the ground. The economy is shutting down, and people are just eating beans and entertaining themselves with screen time."

"Okay."

"I've been asked to pay more attention to message shaping."

"Message shaping? What's that?"

Ivy let out The Sigh.

"Okay, never mind," Dinah said.

"People want to know what became of their Uppity Little Shitkicker."

"Really?"

"Yeah," Ivy said. "People like their ULS. They remember the thing you did with Tekla. Tekla porn is a big thing now too, by the way."

"I don't want to hear about it."

"Anyway, people are asking where is plucky Robot Girl and her mechanical menagerie."

"That explains some weird emails I have gotten."

"From random strangers?"

"No, from my own family! I don't read the ones from random strangers. How about you? What's your role on the reality TV show, Ivy?"

Ivy stared at her coolly. "I'm the uptight bitch who can't handle it."

"Oh."

"To American viewers, I'm not fully American. To Chinese viewers, I'm a banana."

"I'm sorry, Ivy."

"That's the bad news."

"Okay, and what is the good news?"

"All the people saying mean things about me on the Internet are gonna be dead in four hundred and thirty-three days," she said, deadpan.

Okay. It was an example of that dark humor thing.

"After that, none of it matters—except my ability to be of service to Our Heritage."

"Okay, baby, how can I help you?" Dinah asked. "We could take a selfie, you and me, and I could post it on the Uppity Little Shitkicker blog."

"You and I are going to go for a ride on the first operational bolo," Ivy said, "and you are going to be reminded of what one gee feels like."

Casting of Lots

DURING THE FIRST FEW DAYS AFTER THE MOON HAD BLOWN UP, Doob had spent hours gazing up at Potatohead, Mr. Spinny, Acorn, Peach Pit, Scoop, Big Boy, and Kidney Bean. They were visible in the daytime, just as the moon had formerly been, and even on the rare day when it was cloudy in Pasadena, or he was stuck indoors, he could pull up a window on the screen of his computer and watch them on a live video feed.

After he had figured out that they were going to kill everyone on Earth, he had become a lot less interested in staring at them. He had, in fact, sometimes gone for weeks without looking up at the gradually spreading cloud of debris. Sometimes while walking across a dark parking lot or driving down the highway he would catch sight of the moon-chunks in the sky and deliberately turn his gaze away from them. They filled him with horror and even a kind of shame over the fact that he had once found the whole thing such a fascinating science treat. He did not want to be reminded of it. Instead he tracked the slow disintegration of the moon-pieces through spreadsheets and plots shared with him by his graduate students and his colleagues. He did everything he could to reduce the whole state of affairs to two numbers. One of these was the Bolide Fragmentation Rate, or BFR, which was a measure of how frequently big rocks were being made into small rocks. The other was, quite simply, how many days remained before the White Sky.

On Day 7, minutes after they had met, he and Amelia had watched Kidney Bean fracture into two big chunks, later dubbed KB1 and KB2 (though attempts had been made at the time to give them cutesy names of their own). Three weeks later Scoop had collided with Big Boy and broken into three pieces, SC1, SC2, and SC3. Big Boy itself was now BB1, still fairly recognizable, plus a whole family tree of bits that had shrapneled off its smaller piece, BB2. These were given code numbers such as BB2-1-3, meaning the third-biggest fragment of the largest fragment of the second-biggest piece of Big Boy. Beyond about that level it became difficult, and somewhat pointless, to keep track of them all. Mr. Spinny had caused all sorts of havoc before finally breaking in half; its wayward children MS1 and MS2 had gone winging off in opposite directions and ended up in big eccentric orbits around the rubble cloud's shared center of mass, occasionally looping in from a great distance and slamming into one of the slower-moving pieces. MS2 had broken Acorn into three pieces just three days before Doob's memorable Oval Office chat with the president. While he'd been flying back to L.A., a hunk of it the size of an oil tanker had slammed into the Indian Ocean and kicked up a tsunami that had killed forty thousand people on the west coast of India.

After he got home from his trip to D.C., he and Amelia checked into a suite at the Langham, a palatial hotel in Pasadena, so that they could spend a few days together before he went out on a round-the-world journey. All through their romantic dinner on the terrace he made a concerted effort not to look at the remains of the moon. Later they went back to their suite and made love. After twenty minutes' postcoital cuddling, Amelia rolled over on her side and went to sleep, inviting Doob to spoon with her, but Doob, unable to relax, pulled his tablet onto his lap, put on his reading glasses, and started killing time on the Internet. The French doors to the balcony were open, and at some point the breeze coming in through them obliged Amelia to snuggle deeper under the blankets. Doob got up and walked over to close the doors, and was confronted by the sight of the moon-cloud, directly in front of him, hanging over the lights of L.A., and now something like four times the diameter of the original moon. It was arresting, partly because it had been so long since he had looked squarely at it, and so he stood there for a while observing. Peach Pit was still largely in one piece, but other than that the original Seven Sisters were no longer discernible.

Out of curiosity he consulted an app that told him when Izzy would be passing over, and saw that it was going to happen in about ten minutes. So he stood there and waited for it. As he waited, his attention turned again and again to the pieces of the moon. What was their future? He knew that they would shatter into an uncountable number of fragments and become the White Sky and then the Hard Rain. But what was the final *distribution* of sizes going to be, how many big ones and how many small? They had some models based on the simplifying assumption that all moon rock was basically the same, but clearly that wasn't true.

They had done some analysis on the original chunks, trying to figure out why Peach Pit was so resistant to fragmentation, and determined that it was simply the inner core of the old moon. Which was confirmed anyway by an analysis of its mass: Peach Pit was much denser than the other bits, suggesting that it consisted mostly of iron as opposed to rock. The moon had had an iron core, but, relative to overall size, this was much smaller than the Earth's; most of the moon was cold, dead stone.

And yet the core was there, and was thought to consist of a ball of solid iron surrounded by a somewhat hotter jacket of molten iron mixed with various other elements. All of this had been stripped bare and exposed to space by the Agent. For the first few hours, Peach Pit had literally glowed with radiant heat. Or so they guessed, since the dust kicked up by the cataclysm had cloaked it for a while. Some of the core's outer jacket of molten metal must have been torn away, dispersed into the rubble cloud as gobbets and slugs and droplets of melt that soon cooled and hardened. As much was proved by metal-rich bolides that had since plowed into the Earth and been dug up and analyzed. By the time the dust had literally settled to the point where Peach Pit and its siblings were clearly observable, an outer crust had formed over it, consisting of melt that had cooled swiftly as it radiated its heat into space. The cooling had continued ever since. Now, the better part of a year later, Peach Pit, or PP1 as it was now designated, was still warmer than the other parts of the moon. It had shown greater resistance to fragmentation. Other rocks bounced off it, or dashed themselves to pieces on its gleaming surface. A few significant chunks—PP2, PP3, and so on—had been ripped off in the early days when it had still been soft, but now it was clad in a mile-thick armor of solidified iron that was proof against just about any calamity short of a second Agent.

Doob became so absorbed in such thoughts that he almost missed the transit of Izzy across the sky. It angled directly over the rubble cloud, seeming to weave among the giant tumbling boulders, though this was of course an illusion. It had long been the brightest man-made object in the sky, and it was brighter now that so many pieces had been added onto it. The effort had been impressive. Stirring, even. But seeing it against the scale of the disaster behind it forced him to ask himself what was the point. What was the longer-term plan for the Cloud Ark? The swarm concept was a nice architecture, much more survivable than One Big Ship, but where was it going to go?

No one seemed to be talking about that. He understood why. Survival was the first imperative. Long-term strategy came next.

The amount of iron in PP1 was for all practical purposes infinite. It would take humans many thousands of years to find uses for that much metal.

But it was way up high. Hard to reach.

And yet they had to reach it.

And it was closer, easier to reach, than the Arjuna asteroids that Sean Probst was so excited about.

Feeling an idea take shape in his head, like an iron core congealing deep in a moon, he put it on hold and forced himself to turn his attention to more immediate questions. A few days ago in the Oval Office he had formed a resolve to get his ass into space and begin making things happen up there. Which was fine. But he had three months left on terra firma. He couldn't neglect his responsibilities here. Some of which—the most important—were to his kids, to Amelia, and to their frozen embryo. But on top of that he had been given other jobs, and if he screwed them up badly enough, e.g., because he was standing on hotel balconies in the middle of the night thinking about how much iron was in PP1, then they might not send him up to the Cloud Ark at all. He hadn't wanted to go, but once he had assented to the idea, he had begun wanting it more than anything, and he now feared that they would take it away from him. And if they sensed that fear, they could use it to control him. Better to overperform, to exceed expectations, to act like it was nothing at all.

SEVENTY-TWO HOURS LATER HE WAS LOOKING OUT THE WINDOW OF a U.S. Navy helicopter banking through a misty Himalayan valley as it lined up its final approach to a runway in Bhutan. Or perhaps *the* runway in Bhutan was the more correct phrasing.

There were about 750,000 people in this country, which meant that they were entitled to supply two candidates for the Cloud Ark. The arithmetic was a little fuzzy; if the same ratio were applied consistently all over the world, something like twenty thousand candidates would be gathered in. If an arklet could accommodate five people, then four thousand arklets would be needed in the swarm. Each arklet required a heavy-lift rocket to get it into orbit, and some assembly and prep work once it had reached Izzy.

Could it be done? If the entire industrial capacity of the world were thrown into the production of rockets, arklets, space suits, and the other goods needed? Perhaps. But probably not. Doob was privy to some recent estimates that put the numbers at closer to one-quarter of that figure.

And anyway, could the arklets really support five humans each? Without a doubt they were large enough for five people to bang around in, but it was not at all clear that each could be self-sufficient in food production. Building a sustainable ecosystem in a tube the size of a railway tank car was no small task. Biosphere 2, a well-known experiment in the Arizona desert, had attempted to support eight people on an ecosystem the size of a couple of football fields, and been unable to make it work long term. But its mission had been clouded by political strife and odd quasi-spiritual factors. A more down-to-earth project run by the Soviets had determined that eight square meters of algae—an expanse of pond scum about the size of two ping-pong tables—was needed to keep a single human supplied with oxygen. In the space between the hard inner hull and the inflated outer hull of a single arklet there was more than enough room. But much more real estate would be needed if the arklet were also to produce food. And those calculations didn't even begin to address the real complications of keeping thousands of people alive in space for many years. It wasn't enough just not to asphyxiate and not to starve. People would need medicine, micronutrients, recreation, stimulation. Ecosystems would get out of whack and need to be repaired with pesticides, antibiotics, and other hard-to-make chemicals. The thrusters that kept the arklets out of trouble would need to be refueled, and not only that but they would need maintenance and repair. The idea of a completely decentralized Cloud Ark was a chimera; it was not sustainable without a mother ship, a central supply dump and repair depot. The only plausible candidate for that was Izzy. But Izzy wasn't designed for anything like that purpose. They'd been trying to make it over by cramming it with vitamins, but that only delayed the moment when they'd run out of all the goods they didn't know how to produce in space, and people would begin dying in quantity.

From the fact that he had gotten nowhere raising awkward questions about this, Doob inferred that the Arkitects knew about it, and were on it, and just didn't want to talk about it because public doubt and controversy were not going to help. Doob's job, clearly, was to act like everything was okay. Today, that meant scooping up two young people from the Himalayan kingdom of Bhutan.

Did the little performance he was about to put on really mean that twenty thousand people from all over the world were going to end up living happily in the Cloud Ark? He just had to shut down the little Rain Man in his head—"Doob, as in dubious"—and not even think about it.

They had taken off two hours ago from the *George H. W. Bush,* a supercarrier keeping station in the Bay of Bengal. Doob had viewed the ship through the eyes of a man who, in a few months, would be making a permanent move to its orbiting equivalent. She was a completely artificial island, thousands of people densely packed into a wad of pure technology. The professionalism of the crew and the efficiency with which she ran were amazing. Could something like that be duplicated in space, with people chosen by lot from all over the world, and trained in camps over the course of a single year?

He reckoned he would know more in about half an hour.

The navy chopper plunged into a fog-stuffed slot between mountains and knifed through steam and mist for a few minutes. The airport's sole runway came into view, startlingly close to them. The chopper flared to a perfect landing a stone's throw from the terminal building. Doob became aware that his jaw was clenched, and tried to relax it. He had made the mistake of googling this place and learned that it was bracketed by eighteen-thousand-foot mountain peaks, that only eight pilots in the world were certified to land here, and that even they didn't attempt it unless the sun was shining on the runway. Obviously the kinds of guys who flew choppers for the navy operated according to different rules, but it had still been a white-knuckle approach as far as Doob was concerned, and it made him wonder how he was going to react to being hurled into space on top of a hastily constructed tube full of explosive chemicals.

He shifted in his seat and felt a thick manila envelope slide out of his lap and to the deck with a solid *thunk* that almost woke up Tavistock Prowse. Tav had been sitting across from him for the entire duration of the flight, and had been sleeping for the last half hour—prostrate from jet lag. He was a bulky man, not especially tall, but constructed like a wrestler. The bald spot on the back of his head, which had been faintly visible even when he'd been in college, had expanded mercilessly, leaving just a monklike fringe of close-cropped hair around the back of his bullet-shaped head. Perhaps to draw attention away from it, he wore glasses with massive black frames. At one point a serious weight lifter, he had softened and spread in the last decade, and even more so since Zero. It was strange in a way to see him unconscious, for he never seemed to stop moving.

Doob had a pretty good idea why. Tav was hoping he'd get picked. If he worked hard enough, popped up on enough news feeds, garnered enough followers on Twitter, maybe some important person would decide that the Cloud Ark needed a professional communicator—the first, or the last, journalist. To Doob it seemed like long odds. A lot of people with Ph.D.s and even Nobel Prizes were ahead of Tav in line. But you never knew. And he couldn't fault the guy for trying.

He bent forward and retrieved the envelope from the deck. It was a centimeter thick. It was labeled PARO, BHUTAN in neat block letters. The flap had never been opened. He was supposed to have spent the last couple of hours reading its contents, familiarizing himself with the task to be performed. Instead of which he had been looking out the window at the steamy green plains and lazily braided rivers of Bangladesh.

Hoping to make the most of the two or three minutes it would take to get the chopper's door open, he plucked it up off the floor, tore it open, and pulled out a sheaf of pages. This was enough to wake Tav up, but not enough to make him move. He gazed at Doob and watched him read.

"If it's wearing red, yellow, or both, it's a lama," he said. "Bow to it."

"Isn't that a camel from South America?"

"With one L. A holy man. Put the palms of your hands together and make a little bow."

"I don't believe in—"

"It's not gonna kill you, is it? If he's got a big yellow scarf over his left shoulder, he's the king. Bow lower in that case."

"Thanks. Anything else?"

Sitting next to Doob was Mario, their photographer: a man in his thirties with a short, dark mustache, a New York accent, and no expectation whatsoever of being picked for the Cloud Ark. On the flight over he had divided his time between reading his own copy of the same dossier and playing a video game on his phone. He had been on many more of these than Doob or Tav. Getting into the spirit of things, he pocketed his phone and piped up: "People are going to hand you things. Some of them might be really crusty and old and funny smelling. Those things are probably really important. *Really* important."

"Then why are they—"

"Because they believe you are going to take it all up into space and preserve it."

"Oh."

"So if anyone hands you anything, even if you have no idea what on God's green Earth it might be, look impressed, bow, take it carefully, admire it, and then hand it off to the helper kid."

"Helper kid?"

"People have been deputized to follow you around and help you carry all of the priceless national treasures that are going to be bestowed on you. They'll look after the stuff and bring it all back here to the chopper so you can keep your hands free for making those little bows and shaking hands with the king or whatever. As soon as we get back to the aircraft carrier, we'll throw it overboard."

"Done this before, have you?"

"This is my seventy-third abduction run. Let's go." Mario stood up, carefully, letting his cameras and bags swing free, patting each one as it settled into place. Tav and Doob were undoing their seat belts and watching him for cues. Mario took two steps toward the door, which the pilot had just swung open. Cold damp air, scented with pine and coal smoke, was pouring in.

Doob almost rear-ended Mario as he stopped suddenly and turned around to look him in the eye. "One other thing."

"Yes?" Doob said.

"What is about to happen is going to be incredibly fucking sad. Like maybe the saddest thing you have ever seen. Try to hold it together."

Mario held Doob's gaze until Doob nodded and said, "Thanks." Then he turned around and bolted for the door so that he could get some good pictures of Dr. Harris emerging from the chopper.

Dr. Harris paused in the open hatchway. Spread out in front of him were at least two dozen people in red and yellow clothing, drawn up in readiness to extend greetings.

He put his palms together in front of his chest and bowed. In front of him, Mario's shutter began to whirr. Behind him, faint digitized clicks spilled out of Tav's phone as he live-tweeted it.

• • •

THE KING DROVE HIM UP THE MOUNTAIN IN HIS PERSONAL LAND Rover, Doob riding shotgun in the passenger seat on the left—for Bhutan, as it turned out, was a drive-on-the-left country. Mario sat in the back angling to get both of them in the photo, and Tav sat next to Mario muttering voice memos into his phone. The king apologized for today's murky weather, which was blocking potentially spectacular views of high mountains all around.

"But I suppose that is a very small matter in the larger scheme of things," he concluded.

They had stopped at an intersection in the town of Paro to let three boys kick a soccer ball across the road in front of them. Piled up on the road behind them was a small motorcade of lama-packed Toyotas.

"So much joy they take in this simple game," the king mused. "They know, of course. All of them know about the disaster that is to come. When they are thinking of it, it makes them sad. But at other times, they are as you see them—oblivious."

The boys got out of their way and the king eased forward into the intersection. The town had a surprisingly Alpine look to it, with deep brown weather-beaten structures of wood built on stone foundations.

"Until a few days ago," the king went on, "they might have consoled themselves by imagining that they would be the ones chosen."

"In the Casting of Lots," Doob said.

"Yes." The king shot him a keen look. "I was responsible for choosing, you know." He glanced back at Tav. "That is off the record."

"No, Your Highness, I did not know that," Doob said.

"We received guidelines, I suppose you could call them. Saying that it was not a literal casting of lots. The choice is best not left to chance—we must send only the finest candidates. Bhutan has only two places in the Cloud Ark. It would be foolish to waste them on someone unable to represent our people. So, it was a selective process."

"Most people have come to the same conclusion," Doob said. "A pool of promising candidates is identified and then the choice is made from among them by some process which might be random—just so no one person carries the entire responsibility."

"When you are a king you sometimes have such responsibilities whether you want them or not. In this case, though, I was able to involve some of the lamas. There are precedents for such a selection procedure in the way that certain reincarnate lamas are identified—the drawing of lots from an urn is sometimes used."

Tav couldn't resist asking from the backseat: "What does the doctrine of reincarnation have to say about the situation we are faced with now?"

The king smiled. "Mr. Prowse, this is only a journey of ten kilometers. I am taking it slow. If we had a road trip ahead of us of ten thousand kilometers—an enjoyable thought—I might be able to impart enough information to you about what reincarnation means to my people that we would be able to have an intelligent conversation about it."

"Fair enough. Sorry," Tav said, glancing up from the screen of his phone when his brain detected a pause in the king's speech. "You have to understand, my job is to communicate with geeks. People who like math. So I was trying to imagine—"

"When seven billion die, and only some thousands remain, where do the seven billion souls go?"

"Yes."

They turned off what Doob guessed was the main road and onto a fork that wound through a wooded hamlet above the river. This hooked onto a bridge that took them across a fast-running, cold-looking stream, green and milky with rock flour carried down from melting glaciers thousands of meters above their heads. Doob still couldn't get over the fact that in a little more than a year those glaciers would be gone, the rock beneath them exposed for the first time in millions of years, and no scientist would be there to record it.

"We don't believe in anything as simple as metempsychosis—the movement of an individual soul from one body to another. That's not what we mean by reincarnation at all."

"What do you believe in, then?" Doob asked. Tav had lost interest and was belaboring his phone with his thumbs.

"A better analogy might be to a burned-down stump being used to ignite a new candle. But I won't be able to give you a satisfactory answer, Dr. Harris. The teachings are esoteric—deliberately hidden from the uninitiated, specifically to prevent false interpretations. How an enlightened lama would think about the question of the seven billion is as far beyond my comprehension as are the quantum gravity theories that you study in your work."

On this side of the river the ground rose almost vertically. The mountain barrier was cleft by a steep-sided valley that zigzagged up and away from them; the road leaped up into it and switchbacked up a stone cliff, fringed here and there with clusters of hardy evergreens that had found toeholds in crevices. Tendrils and torn veils of mist drifted across the face of the rock, providing occasional glimpses of a white tower, high above them, that had somehow been constructed on the precipice. It was one of those buildings, like some monasteries in Greece and Spain, whose whole point was to proclaim to those below, "This is how far we will go to achieve separation from the world."

They drove up a road between long green terraces until the ground became too steep for wheels, and then the king stopped the Land Rover and set the brake. "How's your cardio?"

"Could be better," Doob said, "but I don't have a heart condition, or anything like that."

"We are at about three thousand meters above sea level. You are welcome to await the chosen ones here in my vehicle, or—"

"I could use a walk, thanks," Doob said, and glanced back at Mario, who shrugged philosophically, and at Tavistock Prowse, who appeared to be biting his tongue.

As they hiked up the trail, followed at a respectful distance by an entourage of lamas, children, photographers, and officers of the Bhutanese military, the king told Doob that the place they were going was called the Tiger's Nest and that it was one of the most sacred sites in their religion, being the spot where Guru Rinpoche, the Second Buddha, had, in the eighth century, flown in from Tibet on the back of a tiger. Later a temple complex had been built around the caves where Padmasambhava (for apparently this was an alternate name for the same personage) had lingered to meditate.

Doob pleased himself by suppressing the urge to point out to the king that tigers were not capable of flight. This was only partly because he was gasping for air. He did not really care about the plausibility of the story, given the astonishing beauty of the place through which they were hiking. It was one thing to be fed a line of religious hokum in a desert hellhole that had nothing to recommend it as a site for tourism. But in order to go for a few hours' walk with a king in Shangri-La, he would put up with any amount of fairy tales and metaphysical ramblings.

Small temples and devotional sites emerged from the mist every few minutes. They stopped part of the way up to enjoy a serving of chai in a little café with a fine view of the Tiger's Nest. Tav, at the end of his rope physically, announced he would go no farther. Doob, Mario, and the king pushed on along the increasingly precarious walkway to the gates of the monastery itself. This, the king had already informed Doob, was off-limits, and in any case would have made a poor showing as a site for a ceremony, being rather cramped, dark, mazy, and ancient. Crag-dwelling hermit monks didn't go in much for grand ceremonial courtyards.

Instead there was a sort of wide spot in the ledge just before the entrance to the white temple. Waiting there were the two Arkers, a boy and a girl, both in their early twenties, clad in what Doob assumed was traditional costume: For the boy, a robe that stopped at his knees, with a large white scarf over his shoulder and crossed to his hip. For the girl, a bolt of colorfully woven cloth, wrapped around her waist and falling to her ankles as a sort of columnar skirt, with a yellow silk jacket above that, draped with many necklaces of turquoise and other colorful stones.

Had she been here, Amelia, in a single glance, would have noticed a hundred details about the weaving, the embroidery, the jewelry, the drape of the fabrics, the choice of colors. She would have charmed the king right out of his saffron scarf. She would have climbed out of the Land Rover back in Paro and made friends with the soccer-playing boys. Amelia, not Doob, was the person who ought to be doing all of this.

But Amelia wasn't going to the Cloud Ark and Doob was.

The boy and the girl—Dorji and Jigme, respectively—were backed up by some leathery oldsters in similar but simpler costumes, presumably their families, and several lamas. Prayer wheels were spinning, bells were chiming back inside the monastery, monks were chanting.

Everyone was crying.

They all bowed to their king.

Doob was glad Tav had not come this far.

Some kind of conversation took place in the local language. Doob didn't even know what the name of that language was. Mario, oblivious to the emotional tenor of the proceedings, darted around snapping photographs, dropping to his knees or even throwing himself flat on the ground so that he could get mountain peaks or temple roofs in the backdrop of shots.

Doob, who had no idea what was going on, couldn't take his eyes off the faces of the elders, who were doing their best to hold it together in the presence of their monarch but clearly suffering through ruinous emotional pain as they prepared to say goodbye to Dorji and Jigme forever. It was almost worse than watching your kid die, Doob thought. Then there was finality, certainty, a grave site to visit. Whereas these two were just going to hike off into the mist. A thunder of helicopter blades would announce their departure, and after that the family members would get vague assurances that Dorji and Jigme were going into space to carry forward the cultural legacy of Bhutan. Assurances that, Doob was pretty sure, were going to be fundamentally dishonest. These people were going to go to their deaths in fifteen months consoling themselves with that belief.

He now understood his job a lot more clearly. Why were the doomed people of Earth not going completely berserk? Oh, there had been some outbreaks of civil disorder, but for the most part people were taking it surprisingly calmly.

It was because events like this were happening in every city and province with more than a few hundred thousand people, and they were being stage-managed well enough to convince people that the system was working.

When he was a kid he had read the Greek myth of Theseus and the minotaur, which hinged on the premise that the people of Athens had somehow been persuaded to select seven maidens and seven boys by lot, every few years, and send them to Crete to serve as monster chow. This had always struck him as the weakest point of what was otherwise a great yarn. Who would do that? Who would choose their kids by lot and send them to such a fate?

The people of Bhutan, that was who. And the people of Seattle and of the Canelones district of southern Uruguay and of the Grand Duchy of Luxembourg and the South Island of New Zealand, all of which Doob was scheduled to visit in the next two weeks to collect the maidens and the boys they had chosen by lot. They would do it if they could be made to believe it would protect them.

As Mario had predicted, Doob was presented with some extremely old-looking artifacts by almost equally old-looking monks who smiled at him through tears and backed away, bowing, once Doob had accepted their prayer wheels and sutras and carvings into his hands.

The king took Dorji and Jigme by the hand, turning his back on the mourners or the well-wishers or whatever they were, and nodded at Doob as if to say "your move."

Doob bowed one last time, then turned around and began leading them down the mountain.

DAY 306

Arklet 1, which had been sent up on Day 285, turned out to have a few teething problems with its maneuvering thrusters, and so the first bolo coupling in the history of the Cloud Ark took place between Arklet 2 and Arklet 3. Those had been launched on Days 296 and 300, respectively. These first three Arklets represented competing designs and so they all looked a little different. No matter; they were destined to be punched out in different factories and launched on different types of heavy-lift rockets from different spaceports, so minor variations in styling were to be expected. They all had the same general shape, though: a cylinder with domed end caps. That was for the ineluctable reason that they had to be pressurized in order to perform their basic function of keeping humans alive, and pressure sooner or later made everything round. Dinah thought that the pressure hulls looked like the big liquid propane tanks seen next to cabins and mobile homes in the rural mining camps where she had grown up. Others likened them to railway tanker cars, or stubby hot dogs.

They were just big aluminum cans with domes welded onto the ends. The walls of the can had a thickness of about a millimeter. The domes were a bit sturdier. The thickest and strongest parts of the hull were in the places where the domes overlapped the ends of the can. The analogy was to a plastic soda bottle, whose thin walls could be crumpled in one hand when the lid was off, but which became amazingly stiff and strong when it was pressurized. Or at least that was what NASA was saying to people who were alarmed by the idea of living one millimeter away from the vacuum of space.

The first three arklets were launched "naked" and smooth, but the hundreds to follow would come up clothed in translucent fabric jackets, pleated and wrinkled during the passage through the atmosphere, protected beneath fiberglass fairings. Once in space the blanket would be inflated to form a flexible outer hull somewhat larger than the inner one. It was in that inter-hull space where food would be grown, making use of sunlight that would diffuse through the fabric. It was not clear yet whether each arklet could be self-sufficient in terms of food production—probably not—but growing some food was better than growing none. Having some green stuff on board helped reduce the load on the CO_2 scrubbers, and having water between humans and space helped stop some incoming radiation.

One of the end caps sported a docking port, designated in NASA public-relations cant as the "front door." It was a bit of a misnomer since it was the *only* door. Once sealed up inside the pressure hull, the occupants could only get out of it by docking the arklet to something with breathable air on the other side of it.

The opposite end of the arklet was called the "boiler room." Mounted outside of it was the trash-can-sized nuclear generator that supplied the arklet with power. Around that were various fittings for connection of plumbing lines, electrical mains, cooling equipment, and the like, none of which would ever be used except in the case when a number of arklets decided to dock themselves together and form a semipermanent cluster.

Those sturdy, thick rings where the domes met the main body served as attachment points for anything of a structural nature—anything that would exert significant forces on the body of the arklet. Radiating from each of those rings were eight stubby, radial spokes, extending outward to halolike rings where thrusters and grappling equipment were attached. Those parts were shipped inside of the arklet, then, once it was in space, extracted through the docking port by spacewalkers and bolted on in zero gee. The halos also served to stiffen and stabilize the inflatable outer hull in arklets so equipped, but in the first three test units they just projected out into space like bicycle rims, studded with small thruster nozzles and laced through with plumbing.

Spanning the distance between the "front door" halo and the "boiler room" halo was a single long spindly member, hinged at the "front" or forward end so that it could, on command, snap up and out, projecting sideways from the arklet for a distance of about ten meters. Mounted to the end of this arm were a camera, a target, and an electromechanical grappling device, collectively known as the Paw. A cable ran from the Paw back down the length of the arm to a reel near the docking port, where 250 meters of it were wound up like thread on a spool. The arm, the Paw, the rope, and the reel were all there to achieve a specific maneuver, never before attempted, denoted in official NASA engineering documents as the Bolo Coupling Operation but referred to everywhere else as the High Five.

On Day 306, after Arklets 2 and 3 had been assembled and checked out, the first Bolo Coupling Operation was initiated. It happened several kilometers away from Izzy. It was done quietly and secretly, in case it failed, but lots of video was taken, in case it succeeded. The operation had many possible failure modes, which was engineering-speak meaning that it could go wrong in so many different ways that trying to think them all through was impossible. So each of the two arklets needed to have a qualified pilot: someone who understood orbital mechanics and spaceship propulsion well enough to bring an errant craft back in hand by manual control. Few such people had ever existed, and only four of them were aboard Izzy. Right now, down on the ground, thousands of young people selected in the Casting of Lots were learning how to do it by piloting virtual arklets in video game simulations, but none of those people was ready, or in orbit, yet. So Ivy ended up at the controls of Arklet 2, with Dinah as passenger and general assistant. Piloting Arklet 3 was a recent arrival, Markus Leuker, a Swiss air force pilot turned astronaut and a veteran of two previous missions to the ISS. His background piloting high-performance fighter jets through Alpine valleys seemed like a reasonable qualification for this job. His assistant was Wang Fuhua, one of the first Chinese taikonauts to have reached Izzy during the Pioneer days of a few months back.

After a good night's sleep and a light breakfast, the four participants met in the Banana to go over the details one last time with engineers on the ground, then ascended a spoke into the weightless environment of H1 and glided up the Stack—the central axis of the space station—snaking through work bays and temporary supply dumps until they reached a docking node that, after a few twists and turns, led them into a hamster tube. One after the other they slithered down it. Dinah, in number three position behind Markus, found it difficult to keep up with him; the soles of his feet kept getting farther and farther away. "Just like scaling the Daubenhorn," he said at one point, "except without the annoyance of gravity!"

"Is that a mountain?" Dinah asked, since the hamster tube was long, and she felt that a bit of light conversation would help ease the lump in her stomach.

"Yes, a famous *Klettersteig* where I grew up—you must come and give it a try one of these days," Markus called back.

A common error in etiquette, among people who had only recently arrived at Izzy, was to talk about Earth as a place that it was possible to go back to. As if this were a temporary mission like all of the previous ones. Dinah said nothing. Markus would realize his mistake, if he hadn't already.

"Oh, well," he added. Yes, he had realized it.

"What's a *Klettersteig*?" Dinah asked, trying to move on.

"It is a mountain climb that is preengineered with cables, ladders, and so on."

"To make it easier," Dinah guessed.

"Oh, no. It is not easy. It is a way to take a climb that would be impossible, and make it merely extremely difficult."

"Okay," Dinah said. "A good metaphor for what we are trying to do up here, then."

"Yes, I suppose so!" Markus said, cheerfully enough.

They came to a junction of hamster tubes, and after scrutinizing the felt-tipped annotations on the walls left by past travelers, they went their separate ways, Dinah leading Ivy to the right while Fuhua and Markus headed straight on. After passing three occupied docking ports, and exchanging perfunctory greetings with the people living in the capsules on the other sides, they came to the end of the hamster tube and passed through a docking port.

They floated into a tubular space four meters in diameter and twelve meters long, illuminated by icy bluish-white LEDs. Its wall was a smooth cylinder of aluminum, striped with bar codes and stippled with batch numbers from the mill that had produced it. A long, straight weld ran up its length. At the far end, the curve of its "boiler room" dome, penetrated by many plumbing and electrical connections, was visible through a flat fiberglass grate—a disk of industrial catwalk material in a bilious shade of green. A ladder, made of the same material, extended "up" from there to the "front door," through which Dinah, and now Ivy, entered. It put Dinah immediately in mind of Markus with his talk of *Klettersteigs*. You didn't need to have a ladder unless you were expecting gravity, or a reasonable facsimile of it. The grate at the far end of the arklet was going to end up serving as the floor.

Or as *a* floor—the lowermost story. The arklet was long enough to divide vertically into as many as five stories by inserting more of those grated disks. Cleats for that purpose were attached to the walls at regular intervals, but the grates hadn't been installed yet.

Dinah pushed off against the top rung of the ladder and flew "down" until she could arrest her momentum against the boiler room grate, then spun herself about so that her feet were touching it and her head was pointed back "up" toward the front door. This brought her eyes level with several flat-panel screens that had been mounted to the walls. They served as status indicators and control panels for the equipment mounted to the outside of the dome. The little nuke was the only thing that mattered to them at the moment. It had a screen all to itself. Dinah woke it up with a tap. It refreshed itself with a graphical display, showing the temperature of the plutonium pellet at its core, its current output level, the RPMs and health metrics of the Stirling engine that converted its heat into electrical power, and the charge level of the batteries and of the supercapacitor that served as a buffer to store energy when it wasn't needed and release it when it was. Everything seemed normal there. Not much could really go wrong with these things. This one was brand new.

She pivoted to another display that gave her information about the array of thrusters mounted to the halo just outside. Arklets were pretty short on windows; the only place you could see out was at the forward end, where a couple of small portholes had been let into the dome adjacent to the docking hardware. Just below one of them was what the engineers called a couch and what the casual observer would be more likely to describe as an expensive lawn chair that had somehow found its way into space. Ivy had already strapped herself into it and was waking up another bank of flat-panel screens there. Dinah could hear her murmuring into the microphone on her headset, which she had jacked into the assortment of plastic boxes that, in this context, passed for a control panel. She was running through a checklist with mission control and talking to Markus, who by now must be strapped in at the controls of Arklet 3.

Gazing around, Dinah saw the gleam of a camera lens, no larger than a raven's eye, set into a tiny plastic pod on the wall in the middle of the arklet.

Then, for no particular reason, she started crying.

There'd been surprisingly little of this. Certain Morse code messages from Rufus were guaranteed to turn on the old waterworks. Ivy and Dinah permitted themselves to shed tears in each other's presence when no one else was around, and a few other people such as Luisa had joined that club more recently. But there was always something to do, some emergency to take care of, always people around watching. No privacy. This empty arklet was the largest volume of uninterrupted, unoccupied space that Dinah had been inside of since boarding the Soyuz capsule at Baikonur a year and a half ago. It seemed vast to her, and she felt alone in it, and she couldn't help herself. She knew that the camera was watching her and that she was being recorded on digital video that was being archived. Psychologists in Houston might be judging her fitness for duty at this very moment. But she didn't care. She'd stopped caring about what the people in Houston thought a long time ago. Once she started crying, it developed a kind of unstoppable momentum and she just had to let it run for a while. Her thoughts had begun to ramble away from her own family and situation and toward the Arkers who would live and die in tin cans like this one. If it didn't work—if the whole Cloud Ark idea was just a panacea, as some people suggested—then the last thoughts and impressions ever recorded by a human soul might take place in an environment exactly like this one. And maybe Dinah would be that soul.

The problem with crying in zero gee was that tears didn't run down your cheeks. They built up in jiggling sacs around your eyes, and you had to shake them off or dab them away. Dinah didn't have anything to dab with—the plastic coveralls they wore were notoriously nonabsorbent—and so she just drifted in the bottom of the arklet, looking at the light from the control screens through bags of warm salt water.

"Some assistant you are!" Ivy called back, after letting her go on for a few minutes.

"Sorry," Dinah blurted out. "That was mission critical."

"Try not to short out any of the equipment. Tears conduct electricity."

"I think they made it all pee-proof. Remember, these things are designed for amateurs."

"Tell me about it," Ivy snorted. "The user interface is so easy to use, I can't do anything."

Something light whacked into Dinah's head. Through the tears she vaguely saw a white object caroming off the nuclear reactor's user-friendly control panel. Pawing it out of the air, her hands recognized it as a packet of tissues. A high-value black market item. She tore it open, pulled out a few sheets, and began the somewhat delicate process of soaking up the tear-globs without smashing them into sprays of equipment-shorting droplets.

"I mean, my God, what would Markus think of you?" Ivy demanded.

It took Dinah a few moments to catch up. "Him and me? You think?"

"It is so obvious."

After a thrilling first few weeks, things had kind of trailed off with Rhys. It was okay. Easy come, easy go. She had never seen him as a stable long-term prospect. The times they'd been living in, and the place they'd been living, weren't really conducive to long-term pair bonding. Luisa, wearing her anthropologist hat, had watched the spontaneous, mostly short-lived couplings of Izzy's inhabitants with a combination of dry amusement, scientific fascination, and frank, hilarious envy.

"I don't know," Dinah said, "I see where you're going, but he seems a little Captain Kirk."

"You need a little Captain Kirk in your . . ."

"In my *what*?"

"In your *life*. Rhys is too introspective."

"Is that a euphemism of some kind?"

"He's depressed."

"Gosh, I wonder why."

"No, not that way. Not about the world ending and everyone

dying. I mean that when he's working on a project he's full of energy but when it's finished he just kind of collapses."

On the tip of Dinah's tongue was a remark about how well that observation aligned with Rhys's lovemaking style, but she held back. "You realize that all of this is being recorded?"

"Get used to it," Ivy said, and Dinah could sense her shrug from twelve meters away. "Hang on, gonna give the forward thrusters a little pop—backing out of our parking space."

She wasn't kidding. The thrusters gave off something very like a bang when they went off. Dinah, who actually wasn't hanging on, felt a few moments of disorientation as the whole arklet moved backward around her while she remained motionless. The green grid dropped away from her and the front door approached—but all so slowly that she needed only to reach out and glide a hand along the ladder to control her relative motion. In a few seconds the forward end of the arklet reached her and she stopped herself against one of the struts of Ivy's couch. Next to it was a knot of straps and pads, like a rock-climbing harness, which Dinah now spent a couple of minutes untangling and climbing into. The bangs of the thrusters, the hisses and clicks of the associated plumbing, and Ivy's murmuring into the microphone served as accompaniment while she got herself strapped in and donned a headset of her own. That enabled her to hear the clipped military-style transmissions among Dinah, Markus, and their controller on Izzy. An engineer in Houston weighed in every few minutes with questions and observations.

Once they had drifted well clear of Izzy, they initiated a programmed burn a few seconds long that took them to a slightly higher orbit. For a while they could see nothing but empty space through the windows. The sun must have risen over the Earth's limb, because bright round spots appeared on the wall.

Ivy said, "I have Three on radar and am engaging MAP." That being the three-letter acronym for Monitored Autonomous Piloting. The operation they were about to perform—the High Five—was deemed way too ticklish to be handled by noob spaceship pilots. It had to be a robotic operation the whole way. But the algorithms, and the sensors that told them what was happening, were all brand new, so experienced pilots had to sit at the controls, watching through the window and taking over if and when the robo-pilot started acting screwy.

The thrusters began to pop in a different rhythm, a patter of tiny firings very different from how a human being would operate them. The star field swung past the windows, the splotches of sunlight veered around the walls, and suddenly Arklet 3 rotated into view, a few hundred meters away. It too was flying under MAP, coming about until its front door was aimed their way. Dinah stifled the impulse to wave at Markus and Fuhua. It was unprofessional, and anyway they wouldn't be able to see her through the tiny porthole.

A spindly white arm swung outward from the side of Arklet 3 and locked into position, extended off to one side. A few moments later they heard and felt their own arm actuating likewise, and watched an animation of it on a flat screen.

"Bringing up the Paw camera," Dinah muttered, and tapped a control that flooded a screen with high-resolution video from a telephoto lens mounted at the end of the arm. This showed nothing, at first, but the blue limb of the Earth's atmosphere down in one corner. Then a targetlike pattern veered across the screen, slowed, and veered back. All of this was accompanied by more fidgety percussion from the thrusters. The feed was remarkably close, and clear. Comparing it to the direct view out the porthole, Dinah could see the target on the end of Arklet 3's extended arm, looking tiny from this distance. But the machine vision system now in control of their little spacecraft had found it, and recognized it, and . . .

"We have a lock," Ivy said. "We see you, Three."

"We see you, Two," Markus answered. "It proceeds."

It proceeded with a longer firing of the aft thrusters that nudged them forward enough that Dinah could feel the pressure on her bottom, sense the straps of the harness tightening. The target flailed around some, but a few moments later, the lock was reestablished. Dinah could see Arklet 3 growing larger. Numbers on a screen, gauging the distance between the ships—or, to be precise, between the two ships' outstretched Paws—were counting down.

"It is all nominal," Ivy said, but the last word was drowned out by a digital voice making an announcement over the arklet's rudimentary PA system: "Bolo Coupling Operation entering its terminal phase. Prepare for acceleration." And then in classic NASA style it counted down: "Five, four, three, two, one, grapple initiated."

At "one" the test pattern on the screen disappeared in shadow, for it was too close now for the camera to even see it. The Paws of Arklet 2 and Arklet 3 slapped together, like runners exchanging a high five as they passed each other going opposite ways. Strange whiny noises propagated down the arm into the hard shell of the arklet.

"Grappling achieved," said the voice.

Dinah's ears finally identified the whiny noise as the sound of cable unwinding from a spool. She felt a lurch in her stomach as the arklet did a half somersault, reversing its direction so that it was pointed back at its bolo partner.

As she knew, having studied this maneuver for weeks, the two arklets were now joined together by a cable. They had flown right past each other, but the tension in that cable had spun them around so that they were pointing toward each other again—she verified this with a glance out the window, which gave her a view of the nose of Arklet 3 slowly receding as it "backed away" from them. The spool of cable mounted next to its docking port was in motion, unwinding as the two craft gained distance from each other. In the exact center, the cables of Arklets 2 and 3 were clasped together by a coupling device that could be remotely disengaged whenever they made the decision to go their separate ways.

"Congratulations, Bolo One," said the engineer down in Houston. "The first autonomously driven coupling of two spacecraft to create a rotating system for production of Earth-normal simulated gravity."

Earth swung past beneath the other half of Bolo One and Dinah felt the awareness of her own throat that would culminate, five minutes from now, in vomiting. The two arklets were already swinging slowly around each other, producing a small amount of simulated gravity—even less than what they experienced in the Banana. But the MAP system wasn't satisfied with that. Once the two arklets were far enough apart not to take damage from each other's thruster exhaust, the system initiated a longer burn that, in combination with the slow unreeling of the cables, put their inner ears through some disturbing changes. The sound of the cable reels changed as automatic brakes engaged to slow their unwinding and avoid a damaging jerk at the end. Then there was silence for a few moments, and then another thruster burn—longer, and directed laterally, to speed up the bolo's rotational velocity.

"Holy shit" was the only thing that Dinah could say for the first minute or two.

They were experiencing one gee—Earth-normal gravity—for the first time in over a year.

Markus, who'd only been in orbit for a few days, sounded great. To judge from what they were hearing in their headsets, he had unstrapped from his pilot's couch and was clambering all over Arklet 3 as if it were the Daubenhorn.

Ivy and Dinah couldn't move for several minutes, and Dinah seriously entertained the possibility that she was dying.

"Can you pass out while you're lying down?" she finally asked.

"Remain in your positions," a voice from Houston was saying, dimly, distantly, as if shouting at them through a bullhorn from four hundred kilometers below. "It is a long fall to the bottom of that arklet."

A long fall. Dinah had ceased to even think in terms of up and down. The concept of falling had become meaningless to her. When you were in orbit, you were always falling. But you never hit anything. She risked turning her head to look at the grate "below," and that was the trigger that forced her to reach for her barf bag.

DAY 333

Doob had known for a while that he was not the easiest guy to be related to. During his last ten weeks on Earth, however, he sometimes feared he was pushing his family's patience beyond human limits with his lust for camping.

Until then, his idea of a satisfying outdoor experience had been to saunter out onto the terrace of a European hotel to smoke cigars and drink brandy. His duties as an astronomer sometimes called him to remote locations such as the summit of Mauna Kea, where he would dutifully go outside, freeze his ass off for a few minutes, remark on the awesomeness of the view and the clarity of the air, and then go back inside to sit behind a workstation and stare at images on a screen. Camping, and the outdoor life in general, simply hadn't been a part of the culture of his family, which tended to look with favor on being under a sound roof, in a heated space, behind locked doors, with plenty of food baking and frying in a modern, fully appointed kitchen. He had always admired his colleagues in the life and earth sciences who could hit the road on short notice with a fully stocked backpack and live rugged adventuresome lives in exotic locales. But he had admired them from a distance.

His sojourn to Moses Lake with Henry had turned him into a late convert to the outdoor life, and left him with a considerable stock of state-of-the-art gear that he was strangely eager to use. The visit to Bhutan had also been a trigger. This had been preceded by a lengthy series of flights across the Pacific and a brief stay on an aircraft carrier: cramped, crowded, artificial environments not unlike where he would be spending the remainder of his days. Then, just for a blessed few hours, he had climbed out of that chopper into the high, cold, piney air of Bhutan, and gone for a ramble in the king's Land Rover, and hiked up a misty mountain that had struck him as being straight from a 1970s album cover. And he had done some introspection about the fact that he couldn't even take such a lovely place at face value but only liken it to such pop culture references. A few hours later he had been back on the aircraft carrier with Dorji and Jigme and about a hundred other Arkers who had been collected in a similar manner from Myanmar, Bangladesh, Nepal, various provinces of India, Sri Lanka, and scattered island groups. He had been struck by the contrast between how centered, how natural, how autochthonous the Bhutanese youths had looked when he had first seen them on the side of the cliff in their home country, and how lost they appeared in the painted steel companionway of an aircraft carrier, mixed up with other South Asians in equally colorful garb, all equally alienated from their native soil, all looking for a place to stow their priceless cultural artifacts.

He had come home with the idea in his head that he needed to get a little bit of native soil on himself before getting shot up to a place where he would be every bit as lost and alienated as Dorji and Jigme had been aboard USS *George H. W. Bush*. Which seemed uncontroversial to him. But when he presented the plan to Tav over a cup of naval coffee in one of the aircraft carrier's eateries, Tav demurred. "You are totally overromanticizing dirt."

Tav liked to play the devil's advocate. He and Doob had had many such conversations. Doob shrugged and said, "Let's say you're right. What's the worst that could happen if I get some dirt on me while I still have access to dirt?"

"Tetanus?"

"Before they started sending me to places like this, they made sure I was up to date on my shots."

"No, seriously, I just don't buy it, Doob."

"Buy what? What is it you think I'm trying to sell you?"

"You're trying to sell me the idea that there is such a thing as a state of nature that humans were designed to live in. It is the 'dirt is good' hypothesis."

"But obviously we evolved in rustic outdoor settings. Those places are, in some sense, natural to us."

"But *we did evolve,* Doob. We're not animals. We evolved into organisms that could make things like this." Tav waved his free hand around at the painted-steel environs of the aircraft carrier. "And this." He raised his cup of coffee and clinked it against Doob's.

"Which is a good thing, you're saying."

"Compared to being torn apart by hyenas? Yeah, obviously it's a good thing."

"Well, I'm not going to get torn apart by hyenas. I'm just going to go camping."

Tav smiled in a way that seemed a little forced. *You don't get what I'm saying, do you?* He said, "Look, you know my views on the Singularity. On uploading."

"I did blurb your book on the topic."

"Yes, thank you for that." Tav was referring to the idea that the human brain could, in principle, be digitized and uploaded into a computer. That this would one day happen on a large scale. That it might actually have happened already—that we might all, in fact, be living in a giant digital simulation.

Something occurred to Doob. "Is that why you were grilling the king about his views on reincarnation?"

"That's part of it," Tav admitted. "Look, all I'm saying is that if you've gone where I've already gone, in terms of thinking about that—"

"If you've drunk the Singularity Kool-Aid, in other words?" Doob said.

"Yeah, Doob, as you know I've already done, then you've already made a fundamental break with trying to be Nature Boy. I am never going to be Nature Boy. I believe that the human mind is almost infinitely malleable and that people are going to adjust, within days or weeks, to life on the Cloud Ark. We will simply turn into a different civilization altogether from the one we grew up in. Our whole idea of nature will be forgotten. And a thousand years from now, people will go on 'camping trips' that will consist of sleeping in arklets, drinking Tang, and peeing into tubes just like their ancestors did."

"To them," Doob said, "that'll be a back-to-nature experience."

"I think that's how we will see it, yes," Tav said.

Doob considered uttering the punch line to the famous joke: *Who's "we," white man?* But he thought better of it.

For the next few weeks his duties had taken him to various other parts of the world, making what Mario the photographer referred to as "abduction runs" and conveying the victims to Arker training camps where they would spend the rest of their time on Earth playing elaborate video games about orbital mechanics. Tavistock Prowse showed up for some of these. When he wasn't doing that, he was making social media posts about the themes he had articulated in his conversation on the aircraft carrier. And when Doob clicked through to those posts he was always impressed by the number of people who were reading them. Tav was developing a following, and a reputation as an important thinker about the sociology of the upcoming space-based civilization.

Whenever Doob got a few days' downtime, he would swoop down on a part of the country where one of his kids was living and grab them and take them camping.

Henry had taken up residence at Moses Lake permanently, or as permanently as anything could be in this world. That was his youngest. Hadley, the girl in the middle, was in Berkeley; she'd been doing volunteer work for an organization in Oakland and had a lot of free time. Doob would drag her away on day hikes to Mount Tam or longer sojourns in the Sierras. Hesper, his oldest, lived outside of D.C. with her boyfriend, a military man stationed at the Pentagon.

The Last Camping Trip happened in early October. Doob still had a few weeks left, but he knew he would spend most of it in training, or talking about training on TV. In the weeks to come he might be able to play hooky and go out on the occasional afternoon hike. But the fact of the matter was that the next time he bedded down in a sleeping bag, it would be in zero gravity, in the cozy environs of a windowless aluminum can.

Perhaps sensing that, Amelia had flown out on the spur of the moment. Normally she'd have been teaching school at this point in the year, but the schedule had become fluid. It was difficult to sustain the illusion that education was of value for kids who would not live long enough to use it. They'd never take the standardized tests that they were prepping for. In a way, Amelia had said, this had led to a kind of renaissance in pedagogy. Free from the constraints of racking up high test scores or getting into colleges, students could learn for learning's sake—which was how it ought to be. The tick-tock curriculum had dissolved and been replaced by activities improvised from day to day by teachers and parents: hiking in the mountains, doing art projects about the Cloud Ark, talking with psychologists about death, reading favorite books. In one sense Amelia and her colleagues had never been more needed, never had such an opportunity to show their quality. At the same time, the routine had loosened up enough for Amelia to take a couple of days off, hop a plane to D.C., surprise Doob, and drive up into the mountains with him and Hesper and Enrique to enjoy the fall foliage.

Doob had never made a real connection to Enrique—a half-black, half–Puerto Rican, all-American army sergeant from the Bronx. But now, sitting on the tailgate of a rented SUV, snuggled under a blanket with Amelia, looking out over a rolling mountain vista gorgeous with fall color, and waiting for some sausages to heat up on the hibachi,

Doob felt as close to the guy as he could to anyone. Enrique seemed to sense the thawing in his mood.

"What are you going to build up there?" he asked.

It said something about how much Doob had changed in the last year that he didn't let out a derisive snort. His face did not even change, or so he told himself. He looked over at Amelia, sitting next to him, for confirmation. She'd been trying to help Doob out. For the kids, she explained. *It doesn't matter what you think, Dubois, or what you feel. It's not about you. It's not even about science. Right now it's about telling the kids in my classroom what it is that they have to hope for. So shut up and get it done.*

These things were important. It wasn't just a matter of hiding what you really felt. If you hid your feelings well enough, it actually changed you. A few months ago Doob *would* have betrayed cynicism, possibly long enough for Enrique to notice it. And a few months before that he might have launched into a detailed explanation of *why* he was cynical, making it clear that the Cloud Ark was going to be an experiment in hastily improvised survival against nearly impossible odds.

None of that happened. He looked at the faces of Enrique and of Hesper, lit on one side by blue twilight and on the other by the glow of the coals, and he answered the question. He answered it as if he were standing in front of a television camera streaming live to the Internet. "The resources up there are basically infinite. That was true even before the moon blew up. Now it has been busted open like a piñata. All it needs is to be shaped into the right architecture—enclosed habitations that we can fill with air and fertilize with the genetic heritage of the Earth. That's going to take a while, and we'll go through some tough times first. It's going to be tough emotionally when the Hard Rain hits and we have to say goodbye to all that was. And it's going to be tough afterward when the Arkers have to learn how to work together and make hard choices. By far the biggest challenge humanity has ever faced. But we'll survive. We'll use what's up there to build incubators for Our Heritage to live in, to grow, and to improve on what we brought with us. And eventually the day will come when we return. The Hard Rain won't last forever. Oh, it'll last for many lifetimes—as long as human civilization has existed until now. And what it is going to leave behind will be a hot and rocky wasteland. But by that point many generations will have devoted all of their hopes and their creative genius to the problem of remaking the world as well as, or better than, what we see here. We will come back. And that's the real answer, Enrique. Will we survive? Yeah. It'll be touch and go, but we will survive. Will we build space habitats? Absolutely. Small ones at first, big ones later. But that's not the real goal. The real goal will take thousands of years. The real goal is to build Earth again, and build it better."

It was the first time he'd said it this way. But it wasn't the last. In the next few weeks—his last weeks on Earth—he'd say it again, to television cameras, to the president, to a stadium full of Arkers in training. All he knew at the time was that Enrique was nodding in a way that said *It's going to be okay, Doob's got this,* and Hesper was snuggling her head against Enrique's powerful shoulder, eyes gleaming, staring into the future that her father was conjuring with those words.

Behind her, a meteor knifed across the twilight sky and exploded out over the Atlantic.

Cloud Ark

Day 365

"TODAY WE'RE GOING TO TALK ABOUT WHAT IT REALLY MEANS TO have a swarm of arklets in orbit," said famous astronomer and science pundit Doc Dubois. He was hovering in the center of Arklet 2, currently docked to Izzy. He was wearing a pressure suit with its helmet detached and slung under his arm. He was talking into one of the arklet's built-in high-def video cameras, trusting that some computer, somewhere, was recording the footage.

"Cut," he said. Then he felt a little sheepish. He was producing and editing his own videos now, so he had just said "cut" to himself. In space, there were no video crews, photographers, production assistants, or makeup artists to follow you around. He rather liked it that way. But there was something to be said for having at least one other human in the room who could react to what you were saying. He needed Amelia there, silently shaking her head or nodding. Instead of which he tried to imagine that he was talking to the kids in her classroom in South Pasadena on a sunny Tuesday morning. He replayed his own dialogue in their ears.

What it really means sounded skeptical. As if everything said on the topic heretofore had been a bunch of BS. And *in orbit* wasn't really necessary. Everyone knew that they were in orbit.

"Today we're going to talk about what it means to have a swarm of arklets," he said. "In normal space, like on Earth, we use three numbers to tell where something is. Left-right, forward-back, up-down. The *x, y,* and *z* axes from your high school geometry class. Turns out that this doesn't work so well in orbit. Up here we need *six* numbers to fully specify what orbit an object, such as an arklet, happens to be in. Three for position. But another three for velocity. If you've got two objects that share the same six numbers, they're in the same place. Right now, my six numbers are the same as those of this arklet that I'm floating in, and so we're moving through space together. But if one or more of my numbers changed, you'd see me drifting."

Doob had brought with him a small can of compressed air—a common convenience used by electronics technicians to blow dust away from things they were working on. He aimed it "down" toward the aft end of the arklet and pressed the button. Air hissed out and he began drifting "up" toward the front door. He raised a hand above his head in time to kill his upward motion against the forward bulkhead, then turned to look into a different camera.

Good. It was the third time he'd attempted this, and he was running out of canned air.

"I can't drift far, confined as I am to the pressure hull. But you can imagine that if I hadn't been able to stop—if I'd been out on a space walk—I might have drifted a long way. And what the science of orbital mechanics tells us is that no two objects in orbit can have the same six numbers, except in the special case I just showed you, where I was inside the hollow arklet so that both of our centers of gravity could coincide. An arklet, or any other object, that is off to the port side of Izzy, or to starboard, or to the zenith or nadir side of it, or forward or aft of it, has different numbers by definition. It's in a different orbit. And so it is going to drift."

He mentally reviewed his notes. Here he had intended to be more specific about the nature of that drift. If it's in a higher orbit, it'll fall behind. If it's in a lower orbit, it'll race ahead. If it's off to one side or the other, it'll converge, then diverge, on a ninety-three-minute cycle. Only if it's directly forward, or directly aft, will it maintain the same relative position. But he thought maybe he could link that out to a different video, one with more graphics. Better to get to the point.

"The moral of the story? In space, there is no such thing as formation flying. Physics will cause two nearby objects to drift closer together or farther away. If you want to preserve a formation, such as a swarm, you have only two options. Physically connect the arklets together, so that they become one object, or else use the thrusters to correct for the drift."

There was another option, which was to put them in single file, like a train in space, but it didn't seem very swarmlike and so he left it out of the reckoning for now. Minutes after the video was posted, outraged YouTube commentators would be all over him, pointing out the error and attributing it to dishonesty, incompetence, and/or a conspiracy.

His last task was to record a voice-over that would be played over footage of young Arkers training in huge industrial video arcades, thrown together for just that purpose in places like Houston and Baikonur. "It's not difficult to learn this stuff—any video gamer can pick it up in a few minutes. Just ask these young Arkers, brought together from all over the world, who've been honing their arklet piloting skills using precision simulators. Most of the time, of course, the arklets will be flying themselves, on autopilot. But if and when it's necessary for a human to take the controls, these young people will be ready for it."

The task complete, he established a link between his tablet and the wireless network of this arklet and spent a few minutes moving video files around so that he could edit them later. Catching sight of himself in freeze-framed thumbnails, he was struck by the roundness of his face—a typical symptom of zero gee as the body retrained itself in how to distribute fluids through its tissues. Up here it was the mark of the newbie. Doob had been in space for six days; this was A+1.0, one year to the day since he had stood in the Athenaeum and watched the moon disintegrate.

Arklet 2, now outmoded by newer models, was docked at the far end of a hamster tube on the port side of the big truss. Sooner or later it would probably be used for overflow storage or sleeping quarters. Doob passed through its docking port and began making his way down the hamster tube. As he'd learned on his way here, this was going to take a while; the tube was barely large enough to accommodate a svelte human in a polyester coverall. A large man in a pressure suit banged and scraped the whole way. And yet it was easier to do it with the suit on than to drag the empty suit behind you, or push it ahead of you, like a zero-gee murderer trying to dispose of a body.

In a few minutes he was able to reach a node, right along Izzy's central axis, where he had more space to move around, and there he began taking the suit off. This was not a full-fledged space suit, which, with its huge backpack life support system, would have been much too bulky for the hamster tube. It was just a helmeted coverall of the type worn by high-altitude pilots. It had a leak, and so was useful only as a costume. Escaping from it developed into a sort of wrestling match, with a lot of cursing and drifting around, banging into walls.

At an opportune moment, he felt a sharp tug on the rear collar of the suit. This pulled it down to the point where he could shrug out of it and get his arms free. "Thanks," he said, and then looked over his shoulder to see a familiar face gazing at him quizzically.

"Aren't you a little short for a storm trooper?"

"Moira?!" Doob said. He grabbed a handle on the wall so that he could spin himself around and get a better look. His glasses had gone askew during the wrestling match, so he poked them back up on his nose. It was her all right, suffering from a clear case of moon face.

He had last seen Dr. Moira Crewe at the Crater Lake announcement, where she had been assisting her mentor, Clarence Crouch, the Nobel Prize–winning geneticist—the poor sod who had been given the job of explaining the Casting of Lots to the world. Since then Clarence had died of cancer in his Cambridge house, surrounded by biological samples and scientific memorabilia that would not long survive the onset of the Hard Rain. No doubt it had been a blessing for him. Doob had lost track of Moira after that, but of all the people on Earth she was one of the most obvious candidates for inclusion on the Cloud Ark. She was of West Indian ancestry, wearing her hair in finger-length dreadlocks that had adapted pretty well to zero gravity—better than white-people hair, for sure. Moon face had added a few years to her apparent age, but Doob knew her to be in her late twenties. Raised in a dodgy part of London, she'd gone to a posh school on scholarship and went on to earn a biology degree at Oxford. She had gone to Harvard for her Ph.D., working with a project there on de-extinction. Her general charisma, and an accent that Americans found charming, had made her into the most well-known spokesperson for that project. She had done TED talks and other public appearances describing her lab's efforts to bring the woolly mammoth back to life. After a brief sojourn in Siberia, working with a Russian oil billionaire who wanted to create a nature preserve stocked with formerly extinct megafauna, she had returned to the UK and begun postdoctoral work with Clarence.

It was not the first time Doob had been pleasantly surprised to bump into a colleague who had, unbeknownst to him, been sent up to Izzy. It always raised an awkward point of etiquette. It was tempting to express delight and give the person a big hug, as you'd naturally do if you encountered them at a party in Cambridge or on the street in New York City. But none of them had come up here on a happy errand. And Moira anyway had a certain owlish way about her, a way of keeping her distance.

And hugging people in zero gee was harder than it sounded. You had to get to them first.

Doob held his arms out to his sides. "Hug," he said.

She did the same. "Is that what one does here?" she asked.

"It is not unheard of. Moira, PCA, it is good to see you up here."

PCA was an abbreviation for "present circumstances aside" and had become a staple of Facebook, Twitter, and the like.

"I had heard you'd come up," Moira said, "but it didn't quite register, as I've been awfully preoccupied."

"I can only imagine," Doob said. "While I've been running around shilling for the Cloud Ark, you've probably been doing actual science, huh?"

"Getting ready to do it might be more precise," she said. Her big brown eyes, behind a geeky but stylish pair of glasses, strayed in a direction. "Is that what they call forward?" she asked.

"Yes."

"Well, the place where I'm working is about as far forward as it's possible to get, because they want my lab to be sheltered by the big rock."

"Amalthea."

"Yes. And if we go there, I can show you a bit of what I've been up to. I feel I should offer you tea as well, but I don't know how to make it here."

Doob smiled at her way of talking. She had been a fiend for theater at Oxford, and might have become an actress. Intensely conscious of the difference between the way her people in London talked and the way people talked at her school and at Oxford, she'd become good at switching between those accents for effect. "I'd be happy to have a look," he said. "I think I know the module you're talking about—I saw it docking a few days ago, and was curious."

HE HOOKED THE UNOCCUPIED PRESSURE SUIT TO THE WALL OF MOIra's lab and it hung there, an inanimate observer, as Moira showed him around. Never one for the life sciences, Doob couldn't understand everything she was saying to him, but he didn't care. Being able to relax and let someone else explain science to him was a welcome turnabout.

"Do you know about the black-footed ferret?" she asked.

"No," Doob said. "I think you can pretty much assume that my answer to all questions about biology and genetics is going to be in the negative."

"Ninety percent of their diet was prairie dogs. Farmers killed almost all of the prairie dogs and so the population of black-footed ferrets crashed to the point where only seven remained. From that breeding stock, it was necessary to bring them back."

"Wow, only seven . . . so inbreeding must have been an issue?"

"We speak of heterozygosity," she said, "which just means the amount of genetic diversity within a species. In general, it's a good thing. If you have too little of it, then you start to see the sorts of problems that we associate with inbreeding."

"But if the breeding stock is reduced to only seven . . . then that's all you have to work with, right?"

"Not quite. Well, technically yes, I suppose. But by manipulating some of the genes, we can create heterozygosity artificially. As well as getting rid of some of the genetic defects that would otherwise propagate through the whole population."

"Anyway," Doob said, "it's obviously of interest to us now."

"If the Cloud Ark's as populous as they claim it's going to be, and if people come up with frozen sperm samples and ova and embryos and all of that, then the human population is probably all right. We'll have enough heterozygosity to make a go of it. My work here is going to be more concerned with nonhuman populations."

"Meaning . . ."

"Well, you've probably heard that we'll be growing algae as a way to generate oxygen. Which is only the start of a simple ecosystem that will have to be developed and grown, and become much *less* simple, over the years to come. Many of the plants and microorganisms that will make up that ecosystem will be cultivated from initially small breeding populations. We don't want to have a repeat of the Irish potato famine, or something analogous, with the plants we rely on to make it possible to breathe."

"So your job will be to do with them what was done in the case of black-footed ferrets."

"Part of my job, yes."

"What's the other part?"

"Being a sort of Victorian museum curator. Did you ever visit Clarence's home in Cambridge?"

"No, I'm sorry to say. But I heard his collection was magnificent."

"It was crammed with all of these stuffed birds and boxed beetles and mounted heads of beasts, gathered by Victorian gentleman-collector types in pith helmets, doing their bit for science on the fringes of the empire. Not scientists as we'd define them today but contributors to the scientific ideal. These things overflowed the museums and Clarence acquired them by the lorry-load, especially after Edwina died and couldn't forbid it. Anyway, I'm that person now, except that the samples are all digital, and they are all on these things." She tapped a thumb drive that was floating around her neck on a chain. "Or their *rad-hard* equivalents." She pronounced the technical term with a dubious and ironic tone of voice, suggesting that she and the International Space Station would take a while getting used to each other. "You know the general story—I've heard you talking about it on YouTube." She switched into a credible imitation of Doob's flat midwestern vowels: " 'We can't send blue whales and sequoias up on the Cloud Ark. And even if we could, we couldn't keep them alive there. But we can send their DNA, encoded as strings of ones and zeroes.' "

"You're going to put me out of a job," Doob said.

"Good. Then I'll put you to work here," Moira said. "This is labor intensive as hell, and they're not sending me enough help."

"I thought it was all automatic."

"If the Agent had given us another couple of decades to improve our gene synthesis technology, it might have become so," Moira said. "As it is, we've been caught in a bit of a gawky adolescent phase. Yes, we can take one of these files"—she tapped the thumb drive around her neck—"and we can create a strand of DNA from it, beginning with a few simple precursor chemicals. But the amount of human intervention is still ridiculous."

"I'm guessing that is some pretty high-level human intervention too."

"My Jamaican grandfather worked in the engine room of a navy ship," Moira said, "which is how our family ended up in England. When I was a little girl, he took me on a tour of one of those ships, and we went down into the engine room, and I saw it, the engine, with all of the bits exposed; the bloody thing was naked and men had to go crawling around on it with oil cans, lubricating the bearings by hand and so on. That's a bit like where we are now with synthesizing whole genomes."

"But for now," Doob said, "that's far in the future, right?"

"Yes, thank God."

"For now you're going to be tinkering with intact organisms."

"Yes. Just so. Still quite difficult, but I think manageable." She looked around. The module in which they floated looked nothing like a lab. Everything was sealed up in plastic or aluminum cases, taped shut and labeled with yellow sticky notes. "Sorry," she said. "Underwhelming. Hardly worth the trip, is it?"

"How can I help?"

"Get me some fucking gravity," Moira said. Then she laughed. "Can you imagine trying to do tricks with liquids in zero gee? Because that's all a lab is."

"It must look frustrating to you now," Doob said. "Everything in boxes, no gravity to make it all work."

"I know, I know," she said. "I'm whingeing. They'll put this thing on a bolo, won't they?"

"Maybe a third torus. Big enough to make something close to Earth-normal gravity. Lots of space to work in. A staff of eager Arkers."

"That's your job now, isn't it?" Moira said. "Cheerleader for the Ark."

"It was my ticket up here," Doob said. He could feel a little warmth creeping into his face, and cautioned himself not to say anything he was going to regret. "We all needed that ticket. Now that we have paid the price of admission, we need to make it work."

Moira, perhaps sensing she'd gone a little too far, kept her silence and would not meet his gaze.

"And as of today," he said, "we have one year."

Part Two

DAY 700

ON DAY 700, ALSO KNOWN AS A+1.335 (ONE YEAR AND 335 DAYS SINCE the destruction of the moon), the Cloud Ark, as seen from the Earth, looked like a bright bead strung on a silver chain. For the reasons that Dr. Dubois Jerome Xavier Harris had tried to articulate during his soliloquy aboard Arklet 2, back on A+1.0, it was expensive, in terms of propellant, to maintain an actual cloud or swarm of arklets around Izzy. Much cheaper and more reliable was to have them precede or follow the space station along the same orbital path, like a queue of ducklings with Mom in the middle. Once an arklet had found its place in that train, changing its position was a maneuver whose complications were a perennial source of surprise and consternation to newly arrived members of the so-called General Population.

Arkies as such—people who had been selected in the Casting of Lots, who had spent up to two years in training for this mission, and who had been sent up here specifically to manage, and live in, arklets—understood it implicitly. As of Day 700, there were 1,276 of those, with about two dozen more coming up each day during the final surge of launches. New arrivals were assigned to empty arklets that awaited them at the head or the tail of the queue. These were launched on separate heavy-lift rockets about four times a day. Since an arklet consisted mostly of empty space, it weighed almost nothing compared to the lift capacity of a big rocket, and so they were always crammed from boiler room to front door with vitamins. These had to be extracted and stowed before the arklet could be occupied. Each arklet had its own unique manifest of stuff. Some of them were just full of compressed gas, such as nitrogen, which would later be used to fertilize crops. Others might be packed with enough diverse and seemingly random goods to open a space bazaar: medicines, cultural artifacts, micronutrients, tools, integrated circuits, spare parts for Stirling engines, Arkies' personal effects, and, in one notable case, a stowaway who was found dead on arrival. With the exception of the stowaway—who was stashed in the morgue with the rest of the deceased—all of these items had to be extracted, cataloged, and stowed appropriately. Each arklet had some onboard storage space, so to some extent the storage was distributed—that being a fundamental tenet of the whole swarm-based Arkitecture. Bulk materials like gases could be pumped into external tanks or bladders: little ones dangling from arklets, big ones distributed around Izzy's periphery where they could serve as extra shielding against radiation and micrometeoroids. So-called dry goods were likewise stashed in mesh bags that lived "outside" until such time as they were needed. Scarce and crowded "inside" space was reserved for organisms and goods that actually needed air and warmth. So, compared to the way it had looked a year ago, Izzy was spare and clean on the inside.

Anyone who had not been chosen in the Casting of Lots and trained as an Arkie was categorized as General Population. There were 172 of those. The number grew only slowly, since most of the people who were qualified, and who were needed, ought to have been sent up a long time ago. Adding new members was attended by much political controversy down on the Earth. The Crater Lake Accord had ratified the general scheme of a Cloud Ark populated by those chosen in the Casting of Lots. It had been obvious, and uncontroversial, that experienced specialists were also needed, and so no one had quibbled over sending up the Scouts and the Pioneers. The concept of the General Population had been written into the Crater Lake Accord precisely to allow for that. People like Rhys Aitken, Luisa Soter, Dubois Harris, Moira Crewe, and Markus Leuker had been sent up under the "GPop clause" because they knew how to do things. For every one of them who got sent up, however, a hundred with similar qualifications were stranded on the ground, where some of them called their congressmen, chancellors, presidents, or dictators. The politics had become so involved as to throttle the incoming flow to a trickle. The remaining available GPop slots were being hoarded by national governments. They were being filled grudgingly and with byzantine premeditation.

For Arkies and members of the GPop alike, it was easy to underestimate the "distance" separating Izzy from an arklet that was only a few kilometers ahead of or behind it in orbit.

The difficulties entailed in moving from one arklet to another could be mitigated by physically docking arklets to a common structure, forcing them to fly in a rigid formation. Or so it might seem to people who had not been steeped in the laws of orbital mechanics. But the fact was that an arklet docked to the end of a truss far off to the port or the starboard wing of Izzy was not in a proper orbit at all. Left to its own devices—free, that is, of the constraints imposed, and the forces exerted, by the truss—it would converge on Izzy, cross through Izzy's orbit, diverge from it, turn around, and converge again, on the same ninety-three-minute cycle that clocked Izzy's orbits around the Earth. An arklet mounted "above" Izzy on the zenith would want to go "slower" and lag behind; one mounted "below" on the nadir would want to race ahead. To the extent that the truss structure prevented those things from happening—to the extent, in other words, that it succeeded in its basic function of holding all the modules and arklets in a fixed configuration—it was undergoing stress, exerting forces on those arklets to prevent them from doing what they wanted to do. Humans in those arklets would notice themselves drifting and bumping into the walls as their natural trajectories, as ordained by Sir Isaac Newton, were perturbed by the structure of Izzy. The larger Izzy grew, and the more arklets and modules were connected to her, the greater those forces became, and the closer she came to breaking.

There was another, even more compelling reason for limiting Izzy's sprawl. She was taking shelter behind Amalthea.

The space station's original orbit had been carefully chosen. Any lower, and the thicker air would make the orbit decay too fast. Any higher, and the danger from micrometeoroids would increase. That was because the rocks zipping around in space were subject to the same slow orbital decay as Izzy herself. Which was a good thing, since it dragged them down into the atmosphere and destroyed them, leaving clear space for Izzy to sail through. Her orbital altitude of four hundred kilometers was a Goldilocks compromise between "too much orbital decay for Izzy" and "enough orbital decay to sweep the sky of dangerous rocks."

The attachment of Amalthea to Izzy's forward end a few years ago had changed all of that for the better. Orbital decay was less of a problem because of the rock's high ballistic coefficient, and micrometeoroids tended to get stopped by the massive nickel-iron cowcatcher.

The White Sky, however, was going to put many more rocks into their path. Big ones could be detected from a distance and avoided, but little ones could do a lot of damage, and so the most important parts of Izzy needed to take shelter in the lee of Amalthea, crowding up against her aft surface. Some rocks might still come in from unexpected directions, but in general there would be a "prevailing wind" in the drift of lunar debris. Amalthea was aimed into it.

But Amalthea couldn't protect any parts of Izzy that projected beyond its silhouette. Dinah and the rest of the Arjuna Expeditions crew had made some progress in "embiggening" the asteroid, carving out slabs of metal and then elevating them like flaps on an airplane wing to extend the sheltered envelope, but it could only get so big. At some point it had been necessary to draw a line under the expansion and "fix the envelope," meaning that Izzy took on a definite shape and size. This had occurred on A+1.233. Since then they had found ways to jam more modules inside that envelope, or, where that wasn't possible, to pack bags and bladders of stored material into gaps. And they had tacked on additional storage in the unprotected volume outside of that envelope. But nothing had been added to her before or since. She couldn't grow in the aft direction because Amalthea's protective shadow only extended back so far—bolides could "wrap around" in any direction, since they weren't in perfectly parallel trajectories. Anyway, boost engines were needed back there, and being in the path of rocket exhaust made standing in hellfire seem like a pleasant summer's day by comparison.

Amalthea was now enveloped in scaffolding, anchored directly into the nickel-iron by connection points welded on, or drilled in, by Dinah's robots. A proboscis extended forward from that cloud of trusswork and supported a little cluster of radar and communication antennas. Forward of that, the closest arklets—seven of them, docked to a hexagonal framework—kept station about a kilometer away, far enough that the firings of their thrusters would not blast those antennas with jets of hot gas. Other heptads, as the seven-arklet clusters were called, were spaced ahead of that one at the same interval. Beyond a certain point these petered out and were replaced by triads—three arklets on a triangular frame—and beyond that were singletons.

A similar tapering could be observed aft of Izzy, though the distance to the first heptad was greater, respecting the danger posed by Izzy's boost engines. These heptads and triads were a bit like Lego or Tinkertoy parts, making it possible to cluster arklets together without much ado; hamster tubes were laced through their trusses so that, once an arklet was docked, persons and material could be easily moved to other arklets on the same frame. Adapters were also floating around that would facilitate nose-to-nose coupling, but these had been found to be not as useful as the hep and tri frames.

Farther out toward the ends of the train, it was not uncommon to see bolos. Each of these spun with its center of gravity—the grapple joining the two cables—tracking along the shared orbital path of Izzy and the other arklets. For now, though, almost all such coupling was for training purposes. Only about three weeks remained before the White Sky. The Arkies could survive that long in zero gravity. Formation of bolos and simulation of Earth-normal gravity was a practice intended for the long haul, when people might live their entire lives in arklets and would need gravity to build and preserve their bones, their eyesight, and other body parts that went bad in its absence.

The Cloud Ark passed through a complete day/night cycle every ninety-three minutes. Time was arbitrary in space, so the ISS had long ago settled on Greenwich time, also known as UTC, as a reasonable compromise between Houston and Baikonur. The Cloud Ark had inherited that system, and Day 700 began at midnight at the Royal Observatory in Greenwich, or A+1.335.0 in ark time. About one-third of the population woke up to begin a sixteen-hour shift. Others would wake up at A+1.335.8, or "dot 8," and at "dot 16." The system ensured that about two-thirds of the population was awake at any given time. Awake people needed more oxygen and generated more heat than sleeping people, so it put less of a strain on life support systems, and enabled the Cloud Ark to support more people, if the waking and sleeping cycles were staggered. A reason for the popularity of triads was that each of the three component arklets could operate on a different shift, observing its own artificially imposed period of darkness and quiet. In a heptad, the same basic scheme could be used, with two of the arklets asleep at any given time and the one in the middle of the hexagonal frame being "always on."

Doob had requested, and been granted, a position in the third shift, meaning that he was basically operating in the same time zone as Amelia, Henry, and Hadley on the West Coast of the United States. He had awakened at dot 16 of the day before, or four in the afternoon in London, which was eight in the morning in Pasadena. So, at the stroke of A+1.335.0, when the first shift of that day began, he had been awake for eight hours and was feeling like a brief nap might do him good. But he knew that this would only make it more difficult to get to sleep at dot 8 and so decided, as usual, to gut it out.

Finding that his brain was too addled to make any sense of the latest figures from Caltech on the continued exponential breakup of moon debris, he went to the "gym," which was a module containing several treadmills. To prevent their users from bouncing off them in zero gravity, these were equipped with waist belts and bungee cords that held the occupants "down," pressing their feet against the belt of the treadmill and forcing the legs to do some real work. Supposedly it was good for the bones and muscles. Amelia kept sending Doob emails asking him whether he'd exercised today, and he liked to make her happy by answering yes.

A few minutes after he began his exercise routine he was joined by Luisa Soter, who had just awakened, as she was on the first shift. She liked to do her "jogging" first thing in the morning, so it was not the first time they had intersected in this way. Six treadmills had been mounted to the walls of this cylindrical module; the users' feet pointed outward and their heads projected in toward the center like spokes converging on a hub, bringing them rather close together and making conversation easy. For extroverted, social people like Doob and Luisa, this was a great setup; more solitary exercisers would don headphones and pointedly focus on a tablet or a book.

"Did you *go* to Venezuela when you were out collecting Arkies?" Luisa asked him.

The way she stressed the word "go" suggested that Venezuela was an obvious topic of conversation—the thing that well-informed persons would naturally begin talking about first thing in the morning. Doob didn't know why. He had heard a few people talking recently about Kourou, which was the place in French Guiana where the Europeans, and sometimes the Russians, launched big rockets into orbit. In the last two years it had become one of the most important launch sites for arklets and supply ships. So he had the vague sense that something was afoot there, something that people were concerned about.

He had been focusing all of his attention in the other direction, on Peach Pit and its iron-rich "children." These were still visible, through increasingly thick clouds of rocky debris. When the White Sky happened they would vanish into a cloud of dirt, and he might not see them for a while. So he had been looking at PP1, PP2, and PP3 while the looking was still good, nailing down their exact orbital parameters, taking high-res photographs. PP3 was especially interesting. It was a congealed glob of mostly iron, similar in composition to Amalthea. It was some fifty kilometers in diameter. And it had a deep cleft on one side, comparable in size to the Grand Canyon, apparently formed by a collision that had rent its outer skin while it was partly congealed. Doob had begun calling PP3 Cleft.

"Doob? You still with me?" Luisa asked. "I was going to say 'Earth to Doob, Earth to Doob,' but it doesn't apply anymore."

"Sorry," he said. He had gone into a reverie thinking about that huge crevice on the side of Cleft, imagining what it must look like from the inside. "What was your question again?"

"Venezuela," she said. "Did you do any of your 'abduction runs' there?"

"No," he said. "Closest I came was Uruguay. Which isn't that close. And by that time I was pretty burned out."

"Why were you burned out?"

Typical Luisa!

"Overscheduling?" she went on. "That is, was it physical burnout? Or more emotional/spiritual?"

"I had just had it," he said. "It's hard. Taking young people—the best and the brightest—away from their families."

"But it was for a good purpose, right?"

"Luisa, where are you going with this?"

"Are you aware of what is going on offshore of Kourou?" she asked in return.

"No," he said flatly.

"You've checked out," she said.

"I talk to my family every day. But other than that? Yes, Luisa, I have checked out of planet Earth. Nice place. Lovely people. But I have to focus on what comes next."

"So say we all," she said. "But one could argue that things happening in Old Earth's final three weeks could have repercussions on New Earth."

"What's going on?" he asked.

"Apparently not a single one of the seventy-five Venezuelans who were picked in the Casting of Lots has actually been sent into space," she said.

"You know that the overall ratio has ended up being something like one in twenty," Doob said. Meaning that for every twenty candidates chosen in the worldwide Casting of Lots and brought to the training centers, only one had found a place up here in the Cloud Ark. Not a figure to be proud of. But it was the best they'd been able to do, and they hoped to bring the number down to more like one in fifteen, or even one in ten, with a last-minute surge of launches.

"Yes. And the Venezuelans know that too. So they're saying that three or four of their seventy-five ought to have made it up here by now."

"Statistically, that is not a valid—"

"These people do not look like statisticians."

"Politics." Doob sighed.

Luisa chuckled. "I hear you, sugar. I'm not gonna say you're wrong. But I have to warn you that this is the word—'politics'—that nerds use whenever they feel impatient about the human realities of an organization."

"And I've been in enough faculty meetings at Caltech to know how right you are," Doob said. "But I meant it in a different way. The way that the Venezuelans ran their selection program was overtly political. In most countries they took the Casting of Lots idea with a grain of salt. There was a random element, yes—but they also filtered for ability. The Venezuelans chose not to do that. So, they ended up sending in kids from the boondocks, truly chosen at random. Many of whom had fine personal qualities. If I had my way, we'd get some of them up here. But I'm not the one who is choosing. The people who *are,* are choosing on the basis of math ability and things like that. So it makes me sad that other people are in line ahead of the Venezuelans, but it doesn't surprise me."

"Three weeks ago, boat people started squatting on Devil's Island," Luisa said, "refusing to move."

"Isn't that a penal colony?" Doob asked. "Why would anyone—"

"It used to be a French prison, yes," Luisa said. "Hasn't been for a long time. Hardly anyone lives there. But it's right under the flight path for launches out of Kourou. So, whenever there's a launch, they evacuate it."

"It must be evacuated all the time then, given the amount of traffic."

"For the last two years, yes. But then a bunch of people showed up there and camped out and refused to move."

"I'm guessing that the French and the Russians went right on launching." In fact, Doob *knew* as much, since he saw arklets and supply ships coming up from Kourou all the time.

"Yes. So the occupation was more of a symbolic gesture at that point."

"These squatters were Venezuelans, I take it."

"Yes. It is a fairly easy cruise along the coast from Venezuela to French Guiana—a few hundred kilometers."

Something was itching in Doob's memory. "Does this have anything to do with the supply vessel that failed to show up yesterday?"

"And the day before. There's been a two-day interruption, going on three, in launches out of Kourou."

"A few squatters on Devil's Island can't explain that," Doob said. Then he added, as a joke, "Unless they have surface-to-air missiles."

Luisa said nothing.

"Are you shitting me?" Doob said.

"It's not so much the ones on Devil's Island as the ones in the blockade," Luisa said. She handed her tablet to Doob. She'd pulled up what looked like an aerial photograph, probably shot out the window of a helicopter. In the foreground was the European Space Agency launch complex, which he'd seen before. It was separated from the Atlantic by a couple of kilometers of flat ground, banded with low, scrubby beach vegetation. In the distance was a trio of small islands, a few miles off the coast; he assumed that Devil's Island was one of them.

The waters between the beach and the islands were choked with vessels: mostly small, but a few rusty freighters as well, a full-sized oil tanker that looked the worse for wear, and some ships that he could have sworn were military.

"When was this taken?" Doob asked.

"A few hours ago," Luisa said.

"Are those naval vessels?"

"The Venezuelan navy is coming out to *maintain order,*" Luisa said.

"And you weren't kidding about the surface-to-air missiles?"

"The pirates who showed up in that oil tanker claimed that they had Stingers, and that they would use them against the next rocket that lifted off from Kourou."

"That is nuts," Doob said.

"Politics," Luisa said. "But we always knew it was going to happen, right?"

"Good morning, Doctors," said a new voice: that of Ivy Xiao, entering the module to begin her own "morning" exercise routine.

"Good morning, Doctor," said Luisa and Doob in unison, though for Doob it was afternoon.

"Did I hear the P-word?"

"Yes," Luisa said. "We were just talking about you, honey."

Doob was appalled. But Ivy laughed delightedly.

Ivy had been replaced, something like eight months ago, by Markus Leuker, the Swiss fighter pilot, mountain climber, and astronaut. Or, to put it more precisely, a new position had been created that made Ivy's post redundant. Izzy was no longer just Izzy; it was the combination of the Cloud Ark fleet plus the vastly enlarged complex that Izzy had turned into. As such, a new leadership structure was required. The person at the top of that structure would shortly become the most powerful leader in human history, in the sense that 100 percent of all people alive would be under his or her authority. It was an altogether different job from being the first among the twelve equals who had been manning the International Space Station of two years ago.

Nevertheless, Ivy could have done it. Everyone who really knew her agreed on that much.

They had replaced her anyway. It was partly a matter of global politics. Placing overall command of the Cloud Ark under a representative of the United States, Russia, or China would have been seen as a provocation by the two countries that had "lost." So it had to be someone from a small country. Preferably one that was seen as politically independent. This narrowed the list of candidates down to basically one: Markus Leuker. The dark horse being Ulrika Ek, the Swedish Arkitect and project manager, who had been launched up to Izzy at the same time as Markus—but on a different vehicle, in case one of them crashed. No one had ever really expected Ulrika to get picked, however. The choice was explained in terms of Markus's dynamic leadership style, his charisma, and other such buzzwords that, as everyone understood, boiled down to the fact that he was a man.

Ivy had failed, in the eyes of the Russians and of many in the NASA hierarchy, by not taking a firmer hand with Sean Probst. That wasn't the only complaint they had about her, but it was the one around which everything else had crystallized. Once everyone had begun to see her as the overly book-smart, well-meaning but week-kneed technocrat, everything she did had been viewed through that lens. Dinah's rescue of Tekla had been examined under what doctors called "the retrospectoscope" and been deemed a failure on Ivy's part to enforce necessary discipline. New arrivals to the Cloud Ark, prepped by Internet comment threads and television pundits to see Ivy as a weak leader, began finding ways to make that into a self-fulfilling prophecy. The success of the Bolo One test, which in other circumstances might have bolstered her, came to be viewed as an almost literal handoff of authority from Ivy to Markus. Presented with some choice opportunities to say supportive things about Ivy, Ulrika had declined to do so, and it wasn't clear whether that was mere absentmindedness or an attempt to cement her position as number two.

In any case it was all squarely in the realm of Politics. Doob had avoided bringing it up around Ivy, not wanting to raise an awkward topic, and so he found it horrifying when Luisa went straight to it, and fascinating when Ivy laughed.

People.

"What is on your docket for today?" Luisa asked.

"Looking at spreadsheets," Ivy said. "Trying to figure out the consequences of losing Kourou."

"That is one monkey wrench we didn't need," Doob said.

"To be sure," Ivy said, "but in a weird way, I'm almost . . ." and she trailed off.

"Glad? Relieved?" Luisa guessed.

"It's like the starting gun finally went off," Ivy said. "We've been prepping for this for almost two years. Awaiting the disaster. Waiting for all hell to break loose. And now it has. Just not in the way we expected."

"What *were* you expecting?" Luisa asked.

"That we'd get hit by a bolide and take a lot of casualties," Ivy said. "Instead something unexpected happened. Which is good training, in a way."

"How's your sweetie?" Luisa asked.

Doob shut off his treadmill and unbuckled the padded belt that connected him to the bungee cords. He was the only man in a room where two women were talking about one of their boyfriends. He knew his cue to make himself scarce.

"He went dark on me two days ago," Ivy said. "Which means he's probably underwater."

"I'm sure he'll pop up for air soon," Luisa said. "Can he send email when the submarine is submerged? I know nothing about it."

"There are ways—" Ivy said, but by that time Doob was floating out of the module.

He made his way aft down the Stack to H2, then clambered down a spoke into the rotating torus T2, which Rhys Aitken had been sent up to build. Gravity in it was one-eighth of Earth-normal. Originally designed as a space hotel for tourists, it had never been quite up to the requirements placed on it by the Cloud Ark project, and so Rhys had been put in charge of building a larger one, concentric with T2, and inevitably called T3. Never one to rest on his laurels, he had invented a completely new system for building it. Unsurprisingly to Dinah, this had consisted of assembling a long loop of high-tech chain and setting it in motion around T2, then adding stuff onto it incrementally. It spun around the same hub at the same RPMs, but because it was bigger, its simulated gravity was a little stronger, about equal to that on the moon. It housed the closest thing the Cloud Ark had to a bridge: a segment of T3 about ten meters long, used by Markus as his headquarters. Attempts had been made to dignify it with names such as "command center," but at the end of the day it was just an upgraded version of the Banana: a conference room with some television screens and power feeds for tablet computers.

Izzy didn't have a helm. It didn't have controls as such. No big wheel to turn for steering it through space, no throttle. Just a bewildering assortment of thrusters controlled through a web interface that could be pulled up on any tablet, provided you had the right password. So, the control room, the bridge, the command center could be anywhere. People had ended up calling the room Markus had chosen the Tank. Adjoining it on one side was a smaller office that served as Markus's sanctum sanctorum. Next to the Tank on the other side was a larger room with a number of cubicles, bizarrely like a suburban office park, where people supporting Markus could sit and work. It had been called the Cube Farm for about ten minutes and was now simply called the Farm. Adjoining the Farm on the other side was a maze of cramped rooms where one could obtain food or use the toilet.

Doob had found that the Farm was frequently the least crowded place on Izzy, just because it didn't occur to people to go there. The gravity was good for his bones and the availability of coffee and toilets were obvious pluses. So he tended to swing by a couple of times a day, get a beverage, see what was happening, and, if things were quiet, grab a vacant carrel and do some work.

He got there at about dot 2. The walls of the Farm, and of the adjoining Tank, were lined with projection screens, known in NASA-speak as Situational Awareness Monitors. They acted as windows onto various parts of the Cloud Ark and its environs. One was showing the Earth below them, another the cloud of debris that had been the moon, another the approach of a supply module from Cape Canaveral getting ready to dock, another the progress of a bolo coupling drill being conducted by some newly arrived Arkies several kilometers aft. Some just displayed statistics and bar charts. The biggest, at the far end of the Farm, was occupied mostly by a grainy video feed from some part of the Earth where it was dark. A label superimposed at the bottom identified it as KOUROU, FRENCH GUIANA. Once Doob had that information to work with, he could make out the general scene: a galaxy of lights from the thousands of boats that had joined the "People's Justice Blockade," and in the background the much more orderly precincts of the spaceport, where an Ariane stood on one pad and a Soyuz on the other, ready to launch, but still unable to do so because of the threat of those Stingers.

The silhouette of a military chopper passed between the camera and the lights of the launch complex.

This was a twenty-four-hour news network. The crawl running across the bottom of the screen was being updated every few minutes by the current BFR, or Bolide Fragmentation Rate, which had started out at zero on A+0 and been climbing ever since then; this was the number that, when it caromed through the bend in its exponential curve, would signal the onset of the White Sky. The networks had been tracking it obsessively. There was an app for it. A bar in Boston had begun offering end-of-the-world drink specials whenever the BFR broke through certain milestones, and the promotion had been copied widely.

Above the crawl was a smaller video inset showing an empty lectern in the White House Briefing Room. Apparently they were expecting some sort of announcement.

Doob sat in one of the carrels, spent a few minutes checking email, and then tried to get back to his main task, which was to write a memo about the distribution of metal-rich moon fragments, how they might be reached and exploited, and why that should be interesting to the management of the Cloud Ark. He was only a few sentences in, however, when movement on the big Situational Awareness Monitor caught his eye, and he looked up into the eyes of the president of the United States.

She was staring into the camera, or rather the teleprompter screen in front of the camera, and delivering some sort of terse announcement. She looked pissed off.

Pinned to her lapel was a loop of ribbon. All the important people had been wearing these for the last few weeks, and they had become popular among the hoi polloi as a gesture of solidarity with the mission of the Cloud Ark. Selecting the color scheme had consumed resources equivalent to the gross domestic product of a medium-sized country. They had settled on a thin red line down the center, symbolizing the bloodline of the human race, flanked by bands of white, symbolizing starlight, flanked by bands of green, symbolizing the ecosystem that would keep the Arkies alive, flanked by bands of blue, symbolizing water, and, finally, edged by bands of black, symbolizing space. The discussion had been as lively as the results were complicated. Black symbolized death to Westerners, white symbolized it to Chinese, and so on. This design offended everybody. It had gotten loose on the Internet as the "official" ribbon design even though the commission charged with designing it had become hopelessly deadlocked and was still evaluating twelve different candidate designs submitted by schoolchildren from around the globe. Factories in Bangladesh had been repurposed to hurl this stuff out by the linear kilometer, they had shown up in kiosks and souvenir shops from Times Square to Tiananmen Square, and the world's leaders had bowed to the verdict and begun wearing them. The president had attached hers using a lapel pin consisting of a simple disk of turquoise rimmed in platinum. The blue disk on the white field was meant to echo Crater Lake amid the snows of November; it was a visual emblem of the Crater Lake Accord, and the closest thing that the Cloud Ark had to a flag.

The sound had been turned down, so Doob couldn't hear what J.B.F. was saying, but he could guess it well enough, and a few seconds later the highlights began to show up in the crawl at the bottom of the screen. The so-called People's Justice Blockade was no grass-roots movement but an operation planned and carried out by the Venezuelan government. It was a reprehensible political stunt that was actively interfering with the all-important building of the Cloud Ark. It was not true, as some had been whispering and the Venezuelan president was now openly saying, that the White Sky was a hoax. The blockade was not, as its sympathizers would have you believe, a peaceful civil disobedience protest; armed intruders had begun landing on the beaches of French Guiana a few hours ago, and were now being held at bay by the French Foreign Legion, bolstered by a multinational force including United States and Russian marines. Doob, doing his best to tune it out, couldn't defeat the irrational feeling that J.B.F. was staring directly at him: a feeling he had come up here partly to get away from.

One of the PR flacks down in Houston reached him over a video chat link that Doob had not had the presence of mind to disable. He talked Doob into spending the next hour writing a little homily about how everyone down on Earth needed to unite behind the all-important mission of the Cloud Ark, and detailing how the Kourou blockade was affecting that. Doob wanted in the worst way to tell this guy to get lost, but he had a soft spot for people who had only three weeks to live.

Doob called Ivy—for Izzy had its own cell-phone system now—and got her to supply a few hard quotable numbers, which he rounded off and typed into his script. He then devoted a minute to psyching himself up to adopt the Doc Dubois persona. Formerly the ruin of his first marriage, the basis of his livelihood, and his ticket to the Cloud Ark, Doc Dubois was a person he rarely had to be anymore. That guy seemed as dated as a character from a 1970s television serial. Getting into the persona was nearly as cumbersome as donning a space suit. It required an extra cup of coffee with sugar. When he felt he was ready, he turned on his tablet's video camera, identified himself as Doc Dubois, greeted the people of Earth, and read his little script.

When he was finished, he emailed the file down to Houston.

Then he tried to go back to his memo, but he became distracted when the Situational Awareness Monitor flashed up a red BREAKING NEWS banner and began to show footage of indistinct flashes against a dark background. Some sort of hostilities had broken out on the ground in French Guiana, between the perimeter of the spaceport and the beach. The French Foreign Legion was participating in what might be the last battle ever fought. But the television news cameras couldn't get anywhere near the action, so the coverage mostly consisted of journalists interviewing each other about how little they knew.

In the middle of all that, the flack in Houston got back to him and asked if he could please relocate to a part of Izzy where zero gravity prevailed, and rerecord the little pep talk. Conspiracy theorists were saying that the Cloud Ark didn't really exist and that it was actually just a bunch of movie sets in the Nevada desert. Whenever they saw video from parts of the space station with simulated gravity, they cited it as evidence, and added millions of friends and followers to their social media profiles.

Doob said he'd see what he could do, and departed from the Farm. Nothing was going on here anyway; Markus wasn't around at the moment. He ascended a spoke to H2 and thus entered zero gravity.

H2 had been the aft-most piece of the Stack—the train of modules that ran up Izzy's central axis—until several weeks ago when the Caboose had been launched up from Kourou and mated to its aft end. The main purpose of the Caboose was to house a large rocket engine, burning hydrogen and oxygen, which would do most of the work of boosting Izzy's orbit. It wasn't possible to extend Izzy any farther back because, beyond that point, anything tacked onto it would no longer reside safely within Amalthea's protective envelope. And indeed there had been long discussions of contingency plans for the case where the Caboose took a hit and its engine was destroyed.

Putting his back to the Caboose, Doob began to drift forward up the Stack. H2 led to H1, which led in turn to the old Zvezda module. This had formerly sported small photovoltaic panels to its port and starboard sides, but these—like most of Izzy's solar panels—had been folded up and removed to make space for other construction. During an intermediate stage of the Arkitects' labors, power had come not from photovoltaics but from little nukes, the same as those on the arklets. These still protruded from attachment points all over the space station, aglow with red LEDs meant as a warning to spacewalkers and pilots. And they still produced a significant amount of power and served as a valuable backup. But most of the station's power now came from a full-fledged nuclear reactor, adapted from those used on submarines, which was mounted on a long stick that projected to nadir from the Caboose. There were a number of reasons why a big power plant might be needed, but the most important of these was to produce rocket propellant by splitting water into hydrogen and oxygen. And this explained why the reactor was where it was. The Caboose housed the big boost engine that was Izzy's largest consumer of propellant. And it was also the central nexus of the Shipyard complex, where smaller vehicles could be assembled from a kit of parts. Once assembled, they too would need propellant.

Zvezda's forward terminus was a docking station with ports to the zenith and nadir sides, where scientific laboratories had been connected back before Zero. This tradition had been preserved, in a way, by turning that docking site into Grand Central station for work related to the Cloud Ark's primary function of preserving the Earth's heritage. If Doob went "up" in the zenith direction, he entered a long module whose main purpose was to support multiple docking ports where other vessels could be, and had been, attached. In general these were crammed with priceless cultural relics, but some of them also supported server farms where digital recordings were stored. Certain relics were easier than others to send into space; the Magna Carta had made it up here, but Michelangelo's *David* was still on the ground. Considerable effort had gone into sealing up heavy relics in "everything-proof vaults" and leaving them on the bottom of the oceans, or in deep mine shafts, but Doob had long since lost track of the progress of that undertaking.

If instead Doob went "down" in the nadir direction, he entered a similar three-dimensional maze of modules. Most of these were devoted to storage of genetic material: seeds, sperm samples, eggs, and embryos. All of these needed to be kept cold, which in space wasn't too difficult; it was primarily a matter of shielding the storage containers from sunlight, which could be done with a featherweight piece of metallized Mylar film, and secondarily a matter of just preventing the warmth of surrounding objects from seeping into the samples. Doob always paused when passing by that hatch. He was not a spiritual man, but he could not humanly ignore the fact that his potential fourth child, the embryo he and Amelia had created, was in there somewhere. Along with tens of thousands of other fertilized embryos waiting to be thawed out and implanted in human wombs.

He passed into Zarya, which was the next module forward in the Stack. Having been mildly spooked by thinking about embryos, he now had a vague intention of going into the Woo-Woo Pod to rerecord his video. This was a spherical inflated structure, ten meters in diameter, with several large domed windows. It was accessed from Zarya via a hamster tube on the nadir side, so it was aimed at the Earth. Ulrika Ek had drawn the ire of every religious group on the planet by refusing to provide separate places of worship for every single one of them in the Cloud Ark. Instead of sending up a church pod, a synagogue pod, a mosque pod, etc., she had provided this one structure, which was something like the interfaith chapel at an airport in that all the different religions had to share it. Internal projectors would display crosses, Stars of David, or what have you on its interior surfaces, depending on what sort of service was happening there at the moment. It had a long, cumbersome, politically correct name, but someone had dubbed it the Woo-Woo Pod and the name had stuck.

That someone paused for a few moments at the entrance to the hamster tube that led to it, and detected the haunting tonalities of the Muslim call to prayer. Too bad. He'd thought that the Pod might actually be a good backdrop for the message he was meant to deliver. But he would have to find another place. Directly across, a hatch led into the rambling group of modules that served as Izzy's sick bay. This had consumed much of the space formerly used by the port-side solar panels. At its farthest extremity, blocked off by an insulated hatch, was the surplus module that had been used as Izzy's morgue and graveyard since the first Scout launch on A+0.29, when two of the cosmonauts had been found dead on arrival. The terrific mortality rate of those first few weeks had half filled this thing with freeze-dried bodies. Since then, fourteen more had died of various causes: one of a subarachnoid hemorrhage that could just as well have happened on the ground, one of a heart attack, two of suicide, two of equipment failure, four just a few days ago in the sudden depressurization of an arklet struck by a bolide. Those, plus the dead stowaway, were all stored in the morgue. The whereabouts of the other four fatalities could only be guessed at. One was a spacewalker who had simply disappeared. The remaining three had been sleeping in a Shenzhou spacecraft docked to the end of a hamster tube, which had been struck by a bolide the size of a coffee table and essentially vaporized. Performing his video surrounded by free-floating, freeze-dried corpses would shut up the "truthers" but otherwise had nothing to recommend it.

On the opposite "wing," where the starboard solar panels had once operated, was a roughly symmetrical arrangement of modules used by the General Population for miscellaneous living and working purposes. These connected to the Stack mostly by way of the old American modules: Unity, Destiny, and Harmony. Consequently, there tended to be a lot of humans flying around in those modules, getting from one part of the space station to another or clustering for the equivalent of watercooler chats.

Beyond Harmony was Node X. NASA liked to give these things names by organizing contests for schoolchildren, which was how Harmony had ended up being called that, but the Node X naming project had been defunded before achieving a result, so Node X it was. It had never really found a purpose, so it had become the place where the life sciences gear was stored—or rather the central connector to which the life sciences modules had docked, one by one, as they had been sent up. This part of the Stack was very close to Amalthea, and accordingly well protected, and so it was a good place to store that irreplaceable equipment during the wait for it to become useful. Doob poked his head into several of those modules, hoping to encounter Moira, then remembered that, London girl that she was, she was on third shift, not due to wake up for another three hours—it was about dot 5, predawn in London.

Beyond Node X was the considerably larger SCRUM, which was literally bolted onto Amalthea at its forward end. So it was the forward-most thing in the Stack. Before Zero it had been nearly deserted. Since then it had grown and developed into the space-based headquarters of Arjuna Expeditions. People called it the Mining Colony. They had plugged in more modules until all of its ports were occupied, and then they had begun to attach scaffolding and additional modules—rigid and inflatable—directly to the aft surface of Amalthea.

It was around now that Doob forgot entirely about the task that the flack in Houston had assigned him, and decided to hang out here for a little while and see what was going on. By all rights this ought to have been his favorite part of the Cloud Ark. Yet he never visited, because coming here put him in mind of politics, which stressed him out and distracted him. His earlier conversation with Luisa had brought home to him, however, that ignoring politics might not be the wisest long-term strategy. He might not care about politics, but politics cared about him. And besides, the people who actually worked here—people like Dinah—were terrific. He had no problem with them personally. He should spend more time with them. Right now he was three hours short of the end of his waking cycle. This was the rough equivalent of mid-evening. Time to kick back and grab a beer. No better people to do that with than miners.

The Mining Colony was political for two reasons. First of all and most obviously, it had originated from a public-private partnership of which the private half was Arjuna Expeditions—Sean Probst's company. Which had been all well and good until he had burst into H2, raised hackles, and ruffled feathers all over the place. Secondly, but much more murkily, there seemed to exist some kind of fundamental disagreement about what the Cloud Ark was supposed to be and how it was expected to develop in the years following the White Sky. Was it going to stay in place, i.e., remain in the same basic orbit? Transition to some other orbit? Would it stay together as a compact swarm or spread out? Or would it split up into two or more distinct swarms that would try different things? Arguments could be made for all of the above scenarios and many more, depending on what actually happened in the Hard Rain.

Since the Earth had never before been bombarded by a vast barrage of lunar fragments, there was no way to predict what it was going to be like. Statistical models had been occupying much of Doob's time because they had a big influence on which scenarios might be most worth preparing for. To take a simplistic example, if the moon could be relied on to disassemble itself into pea-sized rocks, then the best strategy was to remain in place and not worry too much about maneuvering. It was hard to detect a pea-sized bolide until it was pretty close, by which time it was probably too late to take evasive action. A strike from a rock that size would perforate an arklet or a module of Izzy, but not destroy it; people might get hurt and stuff might get broken, but the worst case was that a whole module or arklet would be destroyed with the loss of a few lives. On the other hand, in the more likely scenario where the Hard Rain included rocks the size of cars, houses, and mountains, detection from a distance would be easier. Evasive action would be not only feasible, but obligatory.

Or at least it was obligatory for Izzy. For a single arklet, it didn't matter whether it got struck by a rock the size of a baseball or one the size of a stadium. It was equally dead in either case. Izzy, on the other hand, could survive the first of these with the loss of a few modules, but the second would obliterate the whole space station and probably lead to the slow death of the entire Cloud Ark. Izzy had to be capable of maneuvering out of a large bolide's path.

"Maneuvering" conjured images, in nontechnical minds, of football players weaving among their opponents in an open field. What the Arkitects had in mind was considerably more sedate. Izzy would never be agile. Even if she were, maneuvering in that sense would waste a lot of fuel. If an incoming rock big enough to destroy her were detected long enough in advance, she could get out of its path with a thruster burn so deft that most of her population would not even know it had happened. So, the optimistic view of how this was going to work was that Izzy would remain in something close to her current orbit, with occasional taps on the thrusters that would move her out of the way of any dangerous bolides hours or days in advance of the projected collision. The analogy was made to an ocean liner gliding through a field of icebergs, avoiding them with course changes so subtle that the passengers in the dining room wouldn't even see the wine shifting in their crystal stemware.

There was, inevitably, a more pessimistic vision in which Izzy was more like an ox blundering across an eight-lane highway in heavy traffic. Depending on who was making the analogy, the ox might or might not be blindfolded and/or crippled.

Which of these analogies was closer to the truth boiled down to a statistical argument in which were braided together assumptions about the range and distribution of bolide sizes, the amount of variation in their trajectories, how well the long-range radars worked, and how good the algorithms were at sorting out all the different bogeys and deciding which ones were dangerous.

Somewhere in the middle, between the ocean liner and the blind ox, was the football player pushing the wheelbarrow.

It didn't matter whether "football" for you was soccer or the American sport played by men in helmets. In either case you were meant to envision a player trying to weave a path downfield among defenders. A skilled player could succeed at this when running unencumbered but would fail if obliged to push a wheelbarrow with a boulder in it. The boulder, of course, was Amalthea, and the wheelbarrow was the asteroid mining complex that had been constructed around it. If this analogy were the one closest to the truth, then the wheelbarrow would have to be abandoned.

The image was sufficiently clear, and sufficiently alarming, that some had begun to argue for ditching Amalthea as far back as Day 30. More levelheaded analysts pointed out that if the ocean liner analogy applied, there was no need to take such drastic action, and if Izzy were a blind, crippled ox on a freeway, there was no point anyway.

Doob had his own bias, a bias frankly rooted in a certain frozen embryo, which was that the Mining Colony should be preserved at all costs. When he tried to filter out that bias and to look at the models and the data in a completely objective way, he concluded that the jury was still out. So, technical discussions of the matter tended to be unproductive, except insofar as they revealed the biases that the participants had brought into the room with them. And here was where it started to get difficult for him personally, because he couldn't understand why anyone would harbor a bias different from his own. Why would anyone not want to keep the Mining Colony? What were they thinking? How could the Cloud Ark, and the human race, have a future without those tools and capabilities?

In any case the controversy had ramifications that extended into many seemingly mundane aspects of the Cloud Ark program. If Izzy was going to maneuver with Amalthea attached to it, then the structure holding the rock to the space station needed to be strong. To put it another way, the stronger it was, the more heroic maneuvers could be achieved without breaking it. The ability to perform such maneuvers made the survival of Izzy more likely, and so requests for additional structural work had a kind of self-justifying force. Conversely, a weaker structure limited maneuvering ability and increased the odds that they would have to jettison the Mining Colony in order to survive. And why dump scarce resources into beefing up a subassembly that was going to be abandoned anyway? A similar dynamic obtained in the case of propellant. More of it was needed to maneuver an Izzy with a big rock on it, which meant less of it for the arklets, limiting their autonomy and operating range. Thus physics drove politics to the extremes of "ditch the rock now" or "keep the rock at all costs."

The Mining Colony now comprised eight modules, plus an inflatable dome that was attached directly to the asteroid. The robots had spent several weeks welding a three-meter-diameter ring onto a circular groove that they had prepared on Amalthea's surface. The inflatable had been mated to it about a hundred days ago, and filled with breathable atmosphere. It was not quite a shirtsleeves environment, since the asteroid was cold and chilled the air in the dome. And many of the robots' normal operations produced gases that were toxic, or at least irritating. But that wasn't the point of having a dome. The point was to recapture and reuse the gases used by the robots' plasma torches, making it possible to excavate and reshape the asteroid much faster than had been possible in the early days, when all of those gases had leaked away into space. Since then Dinah's complement of robots had been heavily reinforced by newer and better versions of the same basic models that had been shipped up from Earth. And Dinah herself was now managing a crew of twelve, working in shifts around the clock. They'd been expanding the tunnel she had carved into the asteroid long ago to protect her circuit boards from cosmic rays, making slow progress on hollowing out the asteroid, carrying bits of metal away to a bigger and better smelter that was turning them into steel. Since there was no real place for it in Izzy's master plan, they'd been putting that steel to work in reinforcing Amalthea's structural connection to Izzy, feeding back into the political argument again.

Doob glided through a few of the Mining Colony's modules, asking people where Dinah was, and got noncommittal answers. When he made a move in the direction of her shop, he sensed an uptick in nervous tension, and did not understand why until Markus Leuker emerged, greeted him personally, and engaged him in friendly, inconsequential chitchat. Stalling for time, as Doob understood, so that Dinah could have a few minutes to herself.

It had been known for several months that Dinah had been having sex with Markus, an activity referred to on Izzy as "climbing the Daubenhorn." Two other women were known to have attained that summit, not long after Markus's arrival, but since then Dinah had had him all to herself. By the standards of earthbound organizations, be they corporate or military, it was an eyebrow-raising violation of ethical standards for the boss to be sleeping with a subordinate. But a month from now every living human would technically be one of Markus's subordinates, so he either had to break the rules or be celibate for the rest of his life. No one who knew him very well saw the latter as a realistic option, unless he were to have his testicles surgically removed (a procedure that certain people on Izzy were longing to see performed). That being the case, there was a certain logic in his having settled, quite early, on Dinah. It might be unethical, but at least everyone knew where matters stood. Dinah was no one's idea of a pushover; no sane person could be worried that she was in any way feeling pressured or harassed. And on the other side of that coin, people seemed to feel more comfortable knowing that Dinah was not on the prowl. By the mundane standards of Izzy gossip, her dalliance with Rhys Aitken had been sensational, their eventual breakup a big story, detailed in London tabloids. After that she'd been unable to have coffee with any male crew member without stirring up more whispers. Being unequivocally in the bag with Markus was a lot simpler. And yet it still had to be treated as if it weren't happening, which was why Markus and Doob had to take part in this charade.

"I don't know if you heard," Doob told him, "but fighting has broken out on the ground, between the spaceport and the beach."

It was clear that Markus hadn't heard, which was hardly surprising given that (a) it wasn't his problem and (b) he'd been occupied. He was, understandably, quite relaxed at the moment, and it took a while for him to bring his formidable powers of concentration to bear on the matter at hand.

"I can't believe they will let it go on like that," he said.

"The president made a statement. She looked like she was eating bolts."

"A government run by doomed persons is nothing to trifle with," Markus said, "but I suppose the same could be said of the Venezuelans." He sighed. "I wonder if we should just accommodate some Venezuelan Arkies. There must be a few bright sparks."

"That would have worked a couple of days ago," Doob said, "but now it's turned into one of those 'we don't negotiate with terrorists' things."

A trace of a dry smile came over Markus's lips. He had washed his face with the towelettes they all used; Doob could smell the industrial fragrance with which they were permeated. "Of course," he said, "it wouldn't do to set a precedent that might be abused during the next three weeks."

The joke, such as it was, would have been completely unacceptable when uttered in public, or even in a meeting, and so this was a way of saying to Doob, *You are in my confidence.* Doob wasn't a leader, but he was fascinated by people who were, and how they went about their work.

"Ivy's figuring out the ramifications of not having those arklets, those supplies."

"Thank God for Ivy," Markus said. Since winning command of the Cloud Ark he had never lost an opportunity to praise her—another skill that Doob reckoned must be inculcated into leaders in whatever mysterious Leader Academy churned them out. More likely it was an instinct.

"Well, my day begins," Markus continued. "Thank you for the briefing." Markus, like a lot of the Europeans, ran on third shift, which meant that he was, in fact, beginning his day a couple of hours early.

"Mine is winding down," Doob said. "I thought I would get drunk with some miners."

"No better people for it," Markus said with a wink. "I believe Dinah will be out in a minute. I think she would enjoy seeing you."

With that Markus pulled his phone from the pocket of his coverall and turned his attention to its screen while using the other hand to pull himself out of this module and down the Stack.

Doob was left floating in the middle of the SCRUM. The only thing between him and Dinah was a privacy curtain. He was about to say "Knock knock!" when he heard a string of beeps emerge from a speaker on the other side. An incoming Morse code transmission, which he had not the skill to understand. To that point Dinah had been quiescent, but he now heard her going into movement, peeling herself out of her sleeping bag. He thought better of bothering her just now, and decided to check his own email.

SHE RAN ON FIRST SHIFT, WHICH MEANT THAT THIS WAS MIDAFTERnoon for her: traditionally a time when she began to feel a little drowsy even when Markus had not just been helping her relax. She felt that going fully to sleep would be a bad idea, partly because she had work to do and partly because it would lead to more gossip than was happening already. She could hear Markus chitchatting with Dubois Harris on the other side of the curtain. She knew that he was stalling for her, giving her some time to pull herself together; she was duly appreciative, and she made the most of it, gliding in the liminal zone between dozing and waking until her radio began to beep. She knew immediately that this was not Rufus; she could tell as much by the "fist" of the transmission. It was faint and it was clearly not the work of an experienced ham.

Her eyes opened as a thought came to her: maybe this was the source known as the Space Troll. That term had originated with Rufus, who had first mentioned it several days ago: *Have you heard from the Space Troll yet?* It was his name for a transmitter that he had begun picking up recently, and it matched what Dinah was hearing now.

She ejected herself from the bag, turned up the volume on the receiver, and listened while pulling on a T-shirt and some drawstring pants. The signal sounded as if it was coming in from a home-brew transmitter. The owner had a sketchy understanding of the practices and etiquette of the CW (Morse code–using) radio world. His dots and dashes were perfectly formed, and came rapidly, as much as proving that he was using a computer keyboard and an app that automatically converted keystrokes into Morse. He was sending out a lot of QRKs and QRNs, which were queries about the strength of his own signal and the degree to which it was being interfered with. So, he seemed a little insecure about the quality of his equipment.

According to Rufus, as soon as you started transmitting back to the Space Troll he would shoot back a spate of QRSes, meaning "please transmit more slowly," further proof that he was a novice using a computer keyboard to form the groups, but not very good at deciphering what came back. He transmitted on one frequency only, which was the one that Rufus had, until a year ago, generally used to contact Dinah. This had become known to the Internet in the wake of a human interest story about the MacQuarie family, and so for a few weeks it had been damned near unusable as every CW ham on the planet had tried to use it to contact Dinah. Then word had gotten around that the MacQuaries *père et fille* weren't using it anymore and it had gone pretty silent, except for a few people who apparently hadn't gotten the memo, such as the Space Troll. Anyway, Rufus had gone back to monitoring that frequency again and Dinah was now doing likewise. She had not personally heard any transmissions from the Space Troll. This was not remarkable. Her antenna was nothing compared to the one that Rufus had installed above his mine, and her receiver was something out of a fifth-grade science project. Except when Izzy was passing over his meridian, she and Rufus would naturally "hear" different stations.

According to Rufus, having a conversation with the Space Troll required patience or a sense of humor. The fact that novice hams were screwing around on the radio, which would have driven Rufus into a spasm of righteous fury a few years ago, now just seemed like a sign of the times. Of course people were getting interested in amateur radio; the Internet was expected to go down as soon as the Hard Rain started. And of course many of them were novices.

When they finally did begin an intelligible conversation, Rufus would send QTH, which meant "where are you?" and would get back QET. This was an unofficial Q code, a sort of corny joke meaning "not on planet Earth."

And that was why Rufus called this guy the Space Troll. Because, among other oddities, he didn't have a call sign, or at least didn't use one. The signal she was hearing now was QRA QET, repeated every few seconds; it meant, basically, "Hello, this is E.T., is anyone listening?"

Dinah generally kept the transmit side of her rig turned off when not in use. She turned it on now, but kept her hand well clear of the brass telegraph key. Lurking and listening were harmless, but as soon as she touched that thing, the Space Troll would hear an answering beep, and then she might never be rid of him. More likely, though, was that the Space Troll would give up after a while. Then she could transmit to Rufus, who'd be coming up over the horizon in a few minutes, and let him know that she too had heard from the mysterious "extraterrestrial." It would be good for a laugh, and a few minutes' distraction. Her father sounded like he could use some of both.

It had long since become obvious that he and a number of his mining industry friends had mounted a serious operation to prepare for an extended stay beneath the surface of the Earth. They were hardly the only ones to think that way; people were digging holes in the ground all over the world. Most of them would be dead within hours or days of the beginning of the Hard Rain. Constructing an underground complex that could sustain itself for thousands of years was an operation of which few, if any, organizations were capable. Most of those were governmental or military. But if any private group could do it, it was Rufus and his network. The sorts of questions he had been asking her for the last two years left nothing to the imagination. To the extent that the experts on Izzy knew anything about long-term sustainability of artificial ecosystems, Rufus now knew it too.

Distracted by thinking about Rufus and his mine, Dinah became aware that the Space Troll's transmission had changed. Instead of the familiar QRA QET, it now began with QSO, which in this context meant "can you communicate with . . . ?" This was followed by an unfamiliar call sign, which she didn't recognize as such because it was so long: a string of digits and letters that didn't follow any of the standard conventions for radio call signs.

The third time this transmission was repeated, she wrote it down: twelve characters in all, a basically random assortment of digits and letters. But she did notice that all the letters were in the range A through F. Which was a strong hint that this was a number expressed in hexadecimal notation: a system typically used by computer programmers.

The fact that it had twelve digits was also a clue. The network chips used by almost all computer systems had unique addresses in that format: twelve hexadecimal digits.

And here was where Dinah got a weird feeling on the back of her neck, because the first few digits in that string looked familiar to her. Network interface chips were produced in large batches, with unique addresses assigned to each chip in sequence. So, just as all Fords rolling off the assembly line in a given week might have serial numbers beginning with the same few characters, all the network chips in a given batch would start with the same few hex digits. Some of Dinah's chips were cheap off-the-shelf hardware made for terrestrial use, but she also had some rad-hard ones, which she hoarded in a shielded box in a drawer beneath her workstation.

She opened that drawer, pulled out that box, and took out a little green PC board, about the size of a stick of gum, with an assortment of chips mounted to it. Printed in white capital letters directly on the board was its MAC address. And its first half-dozen digits matched those in the transmission coming from the Space Troll.

She reached for the key and coded in QSO, meaning, in this context, "yes, I can communicate with . . ." and then keyed in the full MAC address of the little board in her hand—different from the one in the original transmission. It was a way of saying, "no, I can't communicate with the one you mentioned, but I can communicate with this other one."

QSB, came the answer back. "Your signals are fading." Then QTX 46, which she guessed meant something like "Will you be available on this frequency forty-six minutes from now?" As anyone on Izzy would understand, this meant "I will call you back when you have orbited around to the other side of the planet."

QTX 46, she answered back. "Yes."

They were passing over the terminator, currently dividing the Pacific into a day side and a night side.

WHO THE HELL ARE YOU TALKING TO?

This was a transmission from Rufus, loud and clear. She looked out the window to see the West Coast of North America creeping over the horizon toward them, identifiable as a pattern of lights delineating the conurbations of the Fraser Delta, Puget Sound, the Columbia River, San Francisco Bay. Which meant that Alaska had line of sight to Izzy.

"Knock knock!" came the voice of Dubois Harris through the curtain. He'd been waiting there a long time.

"Come in," Dinah said, and keyed back a brief transmission to Rufus making a joke about the Space Troll and telling him she would be in touch later. She checked the world clock app on her computer screen. It was shortly before dot 7, therefore 7:00 A.M. in London, therefore ten in the evening for Rufus in Alaska.

A somewhat distracted and scattered conversation followed, Dinah trying to maintain a train of thought with Doob while fielding sporadic, peremptory interruptions from Rufus. "Something kinda weird just happened on the radio," she said. "Do you want a drink? It's evening for you, right?"

"I pretty much always want one," Doob said. "Let's not worry about it. What's up?"

Dinah related the story. Doob looked distracted at first, perhaps because of all the ham radio jargon, but focused when she showed him the MAC addresses.

"The simplest explanation," he pointed out, "is that it's a troll, just messing with you."

"But how would a troll know those MAC addresses? We don't give those out—we don't want our robots getting hacked from the ground."

"The PR people have come through here, haven't they? Taking pictures of you and your robot lab. Mightn't it be the case that a picture got snapped when you had that box open, and some of those PC boards visible?"

"There's no gravity in here, Doob. I can't leave things lying around on my desk."

"Because," Doob said, "obviously what's going on here is that someone wants to talk to you through a private channel—"

"And they are proving their identity by mentioning numbers that could be known only to a few people. I get it."

"And all I'm saying is that a really sophisticated troll would look for some detail like that, in the background of a NASA publicity photo, as a way to fool you."

"Noted," Dinah said. "But I doubt it."

"Who do you think it is, then?"

"Sean Probst," Dinah said. "I think it's the *Ymir* expedition."

Doob got a distracted look. "Man, I haven't thought about those guys in ages."

IT WAS STRANGE THAT A STORY AS EPIC AND AS DRAMATIC AS THE voyage of *Ymir* could go forgotten, but those were the times they lived in.

The ship had stopped communicating and then disappeared against the backdrop of the sun about a month after its departure from low Earth orbit (LEO) around Day 126. A few sightings on optical telescopes had confirmed that it had transitioned into a heliocentric orbit, which might have happened accidentally or as the planned result of a controlled burn. Assuming it was following its original plan, *Ymir* should then have made almost two full loops around the sun. Since its orbit was well inside of Earth's—the perihelion was halfway between the orbits of Venus and Mercury—it would have done this in just a little more than a year, grazing the orbit of Greg's Skeleton—Comet Grigg-Skjellerup—a couple of hundred days ago. But this would have occurred when it was on the far side of the sun from the Earth, making it difficult to observe. The next event would have been a small matter of impregnating the comet's core, or a piece of it, with an exposed nuclear reactor on the end of a stick, and then turning it on to generate thrust by blowing a plume of steam out the entry hole. They would have done a large "burn"—pulling out the reactor's control blades, powering it up, and releasing a plume of steam—that would have altered the comet's trajectory by about one kilometer per second, enough to put it on a collision course with Earth, or at least with L1, a couple of hundred days later. The timing was awkward, and many had griped about it, wondering why Sean hadn't gone after some other comet, or plotted some other course that might have brought it home a little sooner. But people who knew their way around the solar system understood that it was near-miraculous good fortune for *any* comet core to be in a position to be grappled and moved in such a short span of time. The hasty shake-and-bake nature of the *Ymir* expedition, which had stirred up so much controversy, had been forced by the implacable timeline of celestial mechanics. Time, tide, and comets waited for no man. And even if it had been possible to bring a comet back sooner, it would have been reckless, and politically impossible. What if the calculations were wrong and the comet slammed into the Earth? So, the plan of the *Ymir* expedition was the only one that could have worked.

If, indeed, it were working at all. And since much of the action—the rendezvous with the comet and the "burn" of the nuke-powered, steam-fueled engine—had occurred while it was on the far side of the sun, this had been very much in doubt until a couple of months ago, when astronomical observations had proved conclusively that Comet Grigg-Skjellerup had changed its course—something that could only have happened as the result of human intervention. The comet was headed right for them. It would have triggered mass panic on Earth had Earth not already been doomed. Since then they had watched its orbit converging slowly with that of Earth, and plotted the time when it would disappear against the sun once more as it reached L1. The reactor would then have to be powered up again, as a huge "burn" would be needed to synchronize *Ymir*'s orbit with Earth's and pilot it through L1 to a long ellipse that would bring it their way.

"I don't mean that I need you in the same room as I," he said. "I mean that I need your brain here, in space, on the Cloud Ark, not down there. Your family is dead, Dr. Harris."

"Dead. But still talking," Doob said, feeling the start of a slow burn that might lead to him punching Markus in the nose, if only he could get to a place with gravity.

"What is it you think they would most like to hear back from you?" Markus asked. "Lovey-dovey stuff? They know you love them. Were I in their position, you know what I would like to hear? I would like to hear 'Sorry, my darling, but I am very busy just now ensuring the survival of our species.' May I suggest you text something in that vein and then join me in the Tank; we have matters to discuss."

And Markus Leuker, using one of the ropes that were strung across the Woo-Woo Pod as handholds, propelled himself toward the exit. As he passed through into the tube, Doob saw his silhouette against the circle of light, a Da Vinci Man, just for a moment. Then two others swung in behind him and spoiled the effect. That detail caught his attention. Markus now had an entourage. Or perhaps a bodyguard.

• • •

"I THINK ABOUT THEM EVERY DAY," DINAH ANSWERED.

"When are they supposed to hit L1?"

"Any time . . . but it's going to be a long burn, they might sort of grease it in over a period of a few days rather than trying to do one sharp impulse."

"Makes sense," Doob said. "One high-gee maneuver might cause the ice to break apart. When was the last time they communicated?"

"On the X band? The *real* radio? A few weeks after they left. Almost two years ago. But clearly they're still alive. So it must have been radio failure."

"Well, let's go with that theory," Doob suggested. "Jury-rigging a new radio that would transmit over such a distance would be kind of hopeless. The best they could hope for would be to cook something up that might work when they got closer . . . and to settle for lower bandwidth."

"My dad used to talk about spark gap transmitters," Dinah said. "It was a technology they used—"

"Back before transistors and vacuum tubes. Yes!" Doob said.

Dinah telegraphed down:

DOES QET SOUND LIKE AN OLD TIME SPARKY TO YOU?

Rufus returned:

YES COME TO THINK OF IT

"They took some of my robots with them," Dinah said. "All they would have to do is jot down the MAC addresses on those units' interface boards, and they'd have sort of a crude proof of identity. As a matter of fact . . ." and she began to pull up some of the records she had made, almost two years ago, of the robots and part numbers issued to Sean and his crew. Within a few minutes she was able to verify that the MAC address that had come in via Morse code a few minutes ago matched one on a robot that had been taken to *Ymir*.

"Who has access to the file you just consulted?" Doob asked, still in devil's advocate mode.

"Are you kidding? You know how Sean is with the encryption and everything? All of this stuff is locked down. I mean, I'm sure the NSA could get in, but not some random prankster."

"Just checking," Doob said. "It seems awfully roundabout, is all I'm saying. Why doesn't he just broadcast something like 'Hey, Dinah, it's me, Sean, my radio's busted'? That would seem easier."

"You have to know Sean," Dinah said. "Look. Anything he sends out over that channel is getting broadcast to basically the entire Earth. It's going to go up on the Internet . . . everyone's going to know his business. He has no idea what the situation is. There's no Internet up there and his radio's been out for a long time. He doesn't even know if anyone is alive up here. Or if there's been a military coup or something. He doesn't want to come back here if we've turned into the Klingon Empire."

"I think you're right," Doob said. "He's going to ease into it, test the waters."

Forty-five minutes later Dinah was taking down a new message from QET. It started with RTFM5, then the number 00001, and went on as an apparently meaningless series of random letters.

"The only part I understand is 'read the fucking manual,'" Dinah said, "followed by the number five."

"Did he bring any manuals up with him?"

"He brought a bunch of stuff," Dinah said, "from the engineers in Seattle, and left some of it here . . ."

"You have a faraway look in your eye, Dinah . . ."

"I remember asking him, 'Why did you print that stuff out, why not use thumb drives like everyone else,' and he said, 'Owning your own space company brings some perks,'" Dinah said.

She found them after a few minutes' rummaging in storage bins: half a dozen three-ring binders, volumes 1 through 6 of the Arjuna Expeditions Employee Manual. The entire stack was a foot thick.

Doob whistled. "Given the cost per pound of launching stuff into space, this is probably worth more than the Gutenberg Bible that showed up last week."

They went straight to volume 5, which for the most part looked like any other corporate employee manual. But in between the sexual harassment policy and the dress code was a half-inch-thick stack of pages with no readable content at all. Random sequences of capital letters had been printed all over them, in groups of five, column after column, row after row, all the way down each page. Each of these pages had a different number at its top, beginning with 00001.

"This is the boy adventure secret code shit that Larz always used," Dinah said. "But I'll be damned if I know—"

"I'm embarrassed to say that I know exactly what this is," Doob said. "These are one-time pads. It's the simplest code there is—but the most difficult to break, if you do it right. But you have to have this." And he rattled page 00001 in his hand.

Once Doob had explained how it worked, Dinah was able to begin decrypting the message by hand, but in a few minutes Doob had written a Python script that made it easy to finish the job. "I came here thinking I was going to have a drink and a chat about asteroid mining," he said.

"Oh, stop grumbling—this is way more interesting!" Dinah said.

The message read:

TWO ALIVE. THRUSTING AT FULL POWER. SEND SITREP.

"There were six in the original crew, right?" Doob asked.

"Something must have happened," Dinah said. "Maybe they hit a rock or something, damaged the antenna, lost some people. Maybe the radiation got to them."

"Well, it sounds like they are coming back," Doob said.

"Yeah, unless—"

"Unless what?"

"Unless he just wants to hang out at L1. That would be a hell of a lot safer. I don't think any moon shards are going to make it out that far."

Doob reread the message.

"You're right," he said. "All he says is that they're thrusting. Nothing about transferring back to low Earth orbit. Then he asks for a situation report." He put his hands over his face and rubbed it. "I'm fading," he announced. "I should be Skyping my family right now."

"Get outta here," Dinah said. "I can work on the report. And I can encrypt it, now that you showed me how it works."

Doob pushed off and drifted to the exit, then caught himself and turned back. "I could figure this out myself," he said, "but it's late. Maybe you know off the top of your head. If Sean goes into that transfer orbit from L1 to here, how long before he shows up?"

"Thirty-seven days," Dinah said.

"About seventeen days into the Hard Rain," Doob said. "Awkward timing."

Dinah looked back at him. She didn't say a word, but he knew what she was thinking: *If only awkward timing were the worst of our problems.*

"Okay," Doob said. "Thanks, Dinah."

"Next time," she said, and made a drinky-drinky motion with her thumb and pinkie.

"Next time," he agreed, and pushed through the curtain.

Dinah checked the time. Now that she knew roughly where *Ymir* was, she understood the timing of the transmissions. During a certain part of each ninety-three-minute orbit, Izzy was on the wrong side of the Earth, and couldn't receive Sean's signal. Following each blackout period was a window during which they could talk. They had just burned a window taking down his transmission and decrypting it, and were about to go into blackout again. During that span of time Dinah should be able to write a short message and get it encrypted using the next one-time pad.

What to write wasn't entirely clear. She could provide some obvious data like the number of arklets currently in orbit, the number of people, how many robots she had up and running. But she suspected that Sean wanted a different kind of information. He wanted to know what would happen were he to show up, thirty-seven days from now, with a mountain of ice. The Cloud Ark could use it, that was for sure. Likewise, Sean needed the Cloud Ark; two guys on a spaceship pushing a giant ball of ice was not a sustainable civilization. But Sean was going to be cagey. He was going to want something. He would want to make a deal.

He would want to make a deal with Dinah's boyfriend.

One step at a time. Just sending him a few basic stats would occupy the next transmission window. Rather than driving herself crazy worrying about the longer game, Dinah focused on that through the next blackout period, writing up a message as tersely as possible and then encrypting it using Doob's Python script.

The L1 point of the Earth-sun system was located on a straight line between those two bodies. *Ymir,* for all practical purposes, was at L1. So, generally speaking, when Izzy swung around the dark side of the Earth and emerged into the sunlight, it meant that they could "see" L1, and communicate with *Ymir.* This next occurred at about 7:30 A.M. Greenwich time, which happened to be sunrise in London. Dinah, gazing down out her little window, was able to see the terminator—the dividing line between the day and night sides of

Earth—creeping over the Thames estuary down below, and lighting up a few tall spires in the London financial district. Then she turned to her telegraph key, established contact with *Ymir,* and tapped out her message. This ended up consuming the entire transmission window. She had to send the characters very slowly, because Sean wasn't very good at reading Morse code. And because the message was encrypted, he wasn't able to guess missing letters from context, and so every letter had to be read clearly. By the time she was finished, Izzy had swung almost halfway around the world and was about to plunge back into night. She finished her transmission with TBC, which she hoped they would understand as "to be continued," then went right back to work writing and encrypting a supplement.

She was getting ready to open another broadcast window, a little before 9:00 A.M. London time or "dot 9" in Izzy-speak, when Ivy floated in without knocking.

"I want to look out your window," she announced.

"That's fine," Dinah said. "What's up?" Because obviously something was up. Ivy's face looked funny. And she had said "*your* window," not "your *window.*"

"What's so special about *my* window?" Dinah asked.

"It's next to *you,*" Ivy said.

"Is everything okay?" Dinah asked. Because clearly everything wasn't. Her first thought was that the Morse code transmissions had been intercepted and that Dinah was in trouble. But if that were the case, Ivy would not be in here asking to look out her window.

She looked at her friend. Ivy went immediately to the window and then positioned herself to look down at the Earth. By now the terminator had advanced to the point where it had lit up the easternmost bulge of South America. Izzy was about to cross the equator, which was almost directly below them.

"I heard from Cal," Ivy said. She said it without the usual note of pleasure in her voice.

"That's good. I thought his boat was underwater."

"It was until a couple of hours ago."

"They popped up?"

"They popped up."

"Where?"

"Down there," Ivy said.

"How do you know?" Dinah asked. "Surely he's not beaming you his coordinates."

"I can tell," Ivy said. "By putting two and two together."

"What did he say?"

"He said to prepare for some launches out of Kourou."

"They're going to reopen the spaceport?"

Ivy gasped.

Dinah glided over and got right behind Ivy, hugging her and hooking her chin over Ivy's shoulder so that she could share the same viewing angle.

They knew where Kourou was; they looked at it all the time, and sometimes even saw the bright plumes of rocket engines on the launch pads.

What Ivy had reacted to was a little different. Sparks of light were appearing along the coast, spreading, and fading. A barrage of them, peppered across the interval between the beach and Devil's Island.

"What the hell are those?" Dinah asked. "Are those nukes?"

"I don't know," Ivy said.

Then Dinah's question was answered by a much brighter light that flared along the coast to the northwest, fading slightly to a luminescent ball that tumbled upward toward space.

"I think *that* was a nuke," Ivy said.

"We just nuked . . . Venezuela?"

It took a few moments for their eyes to readjust. That was just as well, since their minds had to do some adjusting as well. Once the light had faded, they could see that the mushroom cloud was actually offshore of the Venezuelan landmass, a few miles out to sea.

"A demonstration shot? Visible from Caracas?" Dinah asked.

"Partly that," Ivy said. "But yesterday they were saying that the whole Venezuelan navy was headed for Kourou to restore order. I'll bet that navy no longer exists."

"The smaller fireballs? Near the spaceport?"

"I'm going to guess fuel-air explosives. They would do almost as much damage as tactical nukes without contaminating the launch site."

Ivy had shrugged loose from Dinah's embrace and turned around so that her back was to the window. They were now hovering close to each other.

Dinah finally got it. "You said that Cal's boat had popped up. That it was on the surface. That he knew something. You think—"

"I know," Ivy mouthed.

Cal had received the order, direct from J.B.F., and he had launched the nuke. He'd probably launched cruise missiles with fuel-air devices as well.

People assumed that Ivy and Dinah had grown apart in the last year—but then, people had assumed that they were at odds to begin with. There was no point in trying to keep track of what people imagined. Ivy's loss of her position to Dinah's boyfriend hadn't made matters any simpler. But things had never been bad between them. Just complicated.

Ivy was pretty articulate, but there wasn't a lot about the current situation that could be talked through.

After a few minutes, though, she found a way. "I guess what sucks is that all I'm going to have of him is memories," Ivy said, "and I was trying to cultivate some good ones to carry with me." She wasn't exactly crying, but her voice had gone velvety.

"You know he had no choice," Dinah said. "The chain of command is still in effect."

"Of course I understand that," Ivy said. "Still. It's just not what I wanted."

"We knew it was going to get ugly," Dinah said.

Her radio started beeping.

"Speaking of which . . ."

"Who the hell is that?" Ivy asked.

"Sean Probst," Dinah said. "He's back."

Ivy hung out in Dinah's shop for a while as Dinah laboriously keyed out the second half of her situation report. By the time South America had passed from view, long trails of black smoke were streaking northeast from the burning wreckage of the People's Justice Blockade and casting shadows on the wrinkled skin of the Atlantic. Bright sparks had appeared over Kourou again, but now they were the incandescent plumes of solid boosters chucking heavy-lift vehicles into the sky.

"Back in business," Ivy said. "I guess I better revise those spreadsheets."

"You think Cal is still on the surface? Still reachable?"

"I doubt it," Ivy said, in a tone of voice that suggested she wouldn't know what to say to him. "I don't think it's standard practice to launch a nuclear missile and then just hang out."

CERTAIN ASPECTS OF CLOUD ARK CULTURE WERE MORE OBJECTIONable than others to Dr. Moira Crewe. She just didn't think it decent to live in a place where there were no coffee shops to have breakfast in when she woke up, and no public houses in which to socialize at day's end. This was partly the result of overcrowding; partly because people lived on three different shifts, so there was no unanimity as to when morning and evening fell; and partly because the place had been hastily designed by American and Russian engineers who were blind to the importance of such things. She'd had a number of good chats about it with Luisa, who understood, and they had formed a sort of vague resolution to do something about it once the Hard Rain had begun and the Cloud Ark had settled into some kind of long-term routine. Moira's dream was to be the proprietor of an establishment, perhaps constructed in a single arklet, that would serve that purpose. But she had not yet worked out how to get the timing just right.

Of course, she knew that she had much more important duties: the responsibility of perpetuating the human race, and most other species, was largely on her shoulders. It wouldn't do for her to spend hours every day pulling espresso shots and wiping down counters. They didn't even have the capability, yet, of growing coffee or barley in space, so the supply of consumables was going to run out pretty damned soon and her pub would end up serving Tang. But it was a dream. And in the meantime she could use the coffee room adjacent to the Farm as a sort of R & D laboratory. Arising each day at dot 8, she would make her way back to H2, descend a spoke to the T3 torus, make herself a cup of reprehensible freeze-dried coffee and a little bowl of equally bad freeze-dried oatmeal, and then go to a little conference table in the middle of the Farm and have a sit. As often as not she would be joined by other sleepy-eyed third shifters. Markus Leuker was one of them, and generally too busy to just sit and drink coffee with people, but he would make time for her occasionally. Konrad Barth sometimes joined her, as did Rhys Aitken, and from time to time Tekla would show up. Of these, Tekla was the most curious and interesting case, on more than one level. To put it bluntly, she was of a different social caste. Moira, Doob, Konrad, Rhys, and many of the other members of the General Population were the sorts of people who might once have encountered each other at TED or Davos, or appeared together on panels at think tanks. Not Tekla. Her curious career as one of the rare female members of the Russian military, an Olympic athlete, a test pilot, and a cosmonaut certainly made her *interesting* enough to be invited to a TED-like conference, but her lack of fluency in English and a certain degree of social awkwardness would have ruled her out as a presenter. The lacerations she had suffered during her escape from the crippled Luk had been sewn up by amateurs. On Earth she'd have gone straight into the care of a plastic surgeon, but on Izzy she'd just accepted the results. Moira wished she spoke better Russian so that she could talk to Tekla about her ideas regarding appearance and grooming. The facial scars put her well outside the norms of feminine beauty and she had doubled down by electing to keep the buzz cut. In spite of this, or perhaps because of it, she was, to put it bluntly, kind of hot. Moira hated to say it. But hotness was a part of the human condition and it was pointless to pretend that it did not exist. Moira herself was largely heterosexual. When younger she had slept with two different women, one in the English Cambridge and one in the Massachusetts Cambridge. This had been perfectly all right and she in no way regretted it, but it had required an awful lot of thinking. Way too much cerebration about gender and queer theory had preceded and succeeded those brief moments of passion, and those relationships had faded from her life.

It had occurred to her, in spite of efforts to keep such thoughts at bay, that Tekla would be an altogether different style of partner, and she had to admit that she found this pretty interesting. There was an entire story about Tekla's sexuality that had begun a few weeks after her rescue with some kind of elaborate soap opera, a love triangle or quadrangle involving both men and women, loosely enshrined in the oral history of Izzy but not something Moira had ever cared to learn more about. The gist of it was that after a few months Tekla had begun openly sleeping with other women, eliciting vast amounts of analysis and commentary and drama. The analysis had tended to come from gender theorists talking about the somewhat uncomfortable fact that Tekla was an athlete who had looked kind of butch even when she had been glammed up for the Olympics and looked a hell of a lot more so now. Her coming out (though she had never formally done so) thus tended to reinforce existing stereotypes about female athletes. The commentary came from millions of idiots on the Internet. And the drama occurred in Tekla's relationships with the other Russians, who constituted a powerful bloc on the space station. This had faded as they'd gotten used to it, as more people of various nationalities and sexualities had joined the Cloud Ark, and as everyone had focused their attentions on larger problems. But it had turned Tekla into a curious, solitary creature, socially distant from the only people with whom she could carry on a fluent conversation. The expectation among politically correct academic-leftist observers had been that she would undergo a personal transformation and become like an academic leftist, but she seemed to have retained the same basic attitude about order and discipline that had made her a Scout in the first place and that had led her to putting Sean Probst in an arm lock and offering to choke him out. Sitting across the table from her, drinking her coffee and picking at her oatmeal, Moira idly wondered whether Tekla was aware of the fact that there was a whole genre of Internet fan pornography devoted to imaginary couplings, more or less sadomasochistic, between her and Sean Probst.

In any case Tekla's tendency to occasionally sit with Moira during breakfast seemed like, if not a direct invitation, then at least a preliminary gambit.

Preoccupied with such thoughts, Moira was oblivious at first to the fact that the Farm was suddenly crowded with people looking at the big Situational Awareness Monitor above the end of the table where she and Tekla were having their breakfast. The viewing angle was awkward, and so she had to change her position to get a good look. It was a news channel showing scraps of cell-phone video that had been spliced together to approximate a story. At the beginning of the story the People's Justice Blockade was riding at anchor in the waters between the beach and Devil's Island, just beginning to catch the pink light of dawn. At the end of the story the sun was shining on a churned slurry of crushed hulls and floating corpses visible through gaps between dreadlocks of smoke. In the middle were glimpses of black motes droning in from the sea and fantastic bubbles of flame spreading to envelop vast areas before they burst and disappeared, leaving behind wreckage that looked like it had been beaten with sledgehammers and doused with napalm.

From there the video would loop to sterile three-dimensional renderings of missile submarines and cruise missiles, and footage of the White House Briefing Room, where the president had made a short statement before turning matters over to the chairman of the Joint Chiefs of Staff. Other world leaders were chiming in from Downing Street, the Kremlin, Berlin.

All of which was pretty compelling in and of itself until, just at the moment when Moira was going to look away to her oatmeal, something bright caught her eye on the screen, and she looked back to see video of a mushroom cloud rising over an ocean.

"Did I miss something?" Moira asked. "That didn't look like a meteorite strike."

"Nuke," Tekla said.

Moira looked at her. Tekla's gaze, which some found chilly, was fixed on Moira's face. Moira didn't find it chilly at all. Tekla, for once, glanced away shyly. "Venezuela," she added. "Navy is no longer a problem. Rockets are launched again." She shrugged. She was wearing a tank top. Moira couldn't stop looking at her deltoids. She had to stop doing that. "On the beach it was fuel-air bombs," Tekla continued. "Extrimmly destructive." Tekla leaned back in her chair and draped an arm casually over the back of the empty chair next to her. "What is your opinion, Dr. Crewe?"

"Please, call me Moira."

"Sorry. Russian formality."

Tekla was, maybe, cagier than she looked. She anticipated that someone like Dr. Crewe would be horrified by the fact that we were now nuking people. She wanted to get it out in the open right away, while it was still fresh.

Lost in contemplation of the structure of Tekla's arm, Moira was startled when a large, strongly built man slammed down into the chair next to her. She looked over to see that it was Markus Leuker. He placed a cup of coffee on the table in front of him and contemplated it for a moment, almost pointedly not looking at the video screens with their infinite multiangled replays of mushroom clouds and briefing rooms. Then he turned and looked at Moira, greeting her with raised eyebrows and a nod, and then giving Tekla the same treatment.

So Moira was absolved from having to answer Tekla's question.

Markus answered it, even though no one had asked him. "I know that I am at somewhat of a disadvantage here because I am a speaker of German, and so there is certain baggage. So. Yes. The baggage is acknowledged. I see the awkwardness of it. The delicacy. But—"

"Did you know it was going to happen?" Moira asked him.

"No, it comes as a complete surprise to me."

Moira nodded.

"But, had they asked for my opinion, I would have said yes," Markus said.

"They are all going to die anyway," Tekla said, nodding.

It struck Moira, just then, that Markus and Tekla were quite comfortable with each other. It made sense. Markus would not be the least bit troubled by Tekla's sexuality; on the contrary, it would make things much simpler for a man like him if he knew she were unavailable. He was an ex–military pilot; so was she. Naturally they would tend to view certain things in the same way. For a while, during the Cloud Ark's first year, Tekla had been a sort of itinerant laborer. It might seem strange that a space station could support a person with no particular job. But none of the Scouts had really been expected to survive, so none of them had been sent up with long-term roles in mind. Her alienation from the Russians who took the brunt of the spacewalking work had led her to try her hand at a number of different tasks. She knew the interior of Izzy as well as anyone, but she also knew how to operate the controls of an arklet, and she could put on a space suit and go out and weld things in space. Her period of wandering in the wilderness seemed to have ended when Markus had taken over. Moira was no longer precisely certain what it was that Tekla did for a living. But she now had the clear sense that Tekla was working for Markus directly, that he was trusting her to do something.

"They're all going to die, yes," said another voice. "But we're not." It was Luisa. She came up behind Tekla and wordlessly asked permission to use the chair on which the Russian had draped her arm. Tekla not only gave it but rose to her feet and pulled the chair out as a courtesy.

"We're not all going to die, or at least that's what I'm hoping," Luisa went on, "and we have all just seen this happen. It's in our memories now. And not just that. But in a few hours we'll be taking deliveries from Kourou, reaping the benefits of having used fuel-air explosives and nuclear weapons against people who were basically defenseless. It's in our DNA now." Her eyes flicked toward Moira. "If you'll pardon the poetic imagery, Dr. Crewe."

Moira gave her a little smile and nodded.

Markus said, "So, do you disagree with it?"

"No," Luisa said. "Let's be clear, Markus, I have baggage too. I'm a brown Spanish speaker from South America. I devoted years of my life to hanging out with refugees on boats. And I'm a Jew. That's my baggage, okay?"

"Understood," Markus said.

"I'm not down there, I don't know what advice J.B.F. was getting, what she knew that we don't."

"So what is your point?" Markus asked, crisply but politely.

"We have no laws. No rights. No constitution. No legal system, no police."

Markus and Tekla looked at each other across the table. It was not a sneaky look, or a guilty look, or a conniving look. But it was a significant look.

"It is being worked on," Markus said. He wasn't kidding; ever since the Crater Lake Accord had been signed, a whole think tank full of constitutional scholars had been toiling away on it in The Hague, and one of them was now resident up here.

"I know it is," Luisa answered, "and it is very important to me that atrocities such as what we're seeing on these screens don't somehow infect that process. This cannot be business as usual."

Markus and Tekla, still looking at each other, seemed to arrive at a mutual decision to say nothing.

Moira's phone vibrated. Looking at its screen she saw that she had an appointment in fifteen minutes. She excused herself from what had become a very strange kaffeeklatsch. Oh well, perhaps it had cured her of some sentimental ideas. She had walked in aspiring to somehow re-create the experience of breakfasting in a sidewalk café in Europe and instead been treated to half an hour of nuclear warfare, mass incineration of protesters, and serious ethical discourse, mixed in with a suddenly keen sexual tension between her and Tekla. Like quite a few other people on the Cloud Ark, she hadn't had sex since she had come up here. Many whose consciences were unencumbered by the existence of doomed spouses or fiancés on the ground had figured out a way to make it happen, but many others were not getting any. This couldn't possibly last. A couple of docked capsules had been set aside for conjugal visits, and everyone knew of quiet places around the space station where you could do it. Moira didn't have anyone down on the ground. She had abstained for lack of anyone up here, and just because it was the least sexy place you could possibly imagine. But it was starting to get to her.

One of the items on her long-term to-do list, actually, was to come up with a policy for how to handle pregnancy aboard the Cloud Ark. Since pregnant people weren't fundamentally that different from those who weren't, what that really boiled down to was how to handle babies. The assumption made by the Arkitects was that this was going to be an orderly process, and that anyone who got pregnant would do so with the intent of having the embryo frozen so that it could be implanted later, when conditions were better for raising little ones. Having now spent the better part of a year up here, Moira doubted this. The Arkitects were, she felt, underestimating the cultural difference between the General Population and the Arkies.

Until a few months ago they'd been referred to as Arkers, and, in all official communications, they still were. Then someone had coined the term "Arkies," and, in one of those only-on-the-Internet viral phenomena, it had swept across the planet in about twenty-four hours and become universal. A few sensitive Arkansas historians had registered objections, but they had been steamrolled.

The Arkies were just kids, and they had surprisingly little exposure to the GPop. The arklets they lived in couldn't really change their positions in the swarm. Moving from one arklet to the next was nearly impossible—it was an epic journey in a space suit, requiring some fancy tricks with orbital mechanics. Small utility spacecraft, called Flivvers, were available to squire people around, but there were only so many of them, and qualified pilots were few. Markus, following suggestions from Luisa, had tried to make up for this by "stirring the pot," meaning that about 10 percent of the Arkies at any given time were living and working aboard Izzy. But most of the time, most of them were stranded in individual arks or on triads or heptads, their only connection to the General Population being through videoconferencing ("Scape"), social media ("Spacebook"), and other tech that had been transplanted from the earthbound world. Moira would be astonished if some girls weren't pregnant already, but no one had approached her about getting an embryo frozen.

And any normal person who followed Moira forward through Zvezda and "down" into the cold storage facility would understand why. There was nothing about this place that tickled the nerve endings that mattered to people who wanted to start families. It was clinical/industrial to a degree that was almost laughable.

But by the same token she hoped it would seem impressive to the new arrivals, who showed up right on time for their appointment.

They had arrived several hours ago on a passenger capsule launched from Cape Canaveral: long enough for their antinausea meds to kick in and for them to pull themselves together a little bit. It was a small contingent from the Philippines: a scientist who had been working on genetically modified strains of rice, a sociologist who had been working with Filipino sailors who spent their whole lives on cargo freighters—she'd be working with Luisa, presumably—and a pair of Arkies who, judging from looks, were from ethnic groups as different as Icelanders were from Sicilians. One of them was carrying the inevitable beer cooler. As Moira knew perfectly well—for she did this at least once a day—it contained sperm, ova, and embryos collected from donors scattered around the country of origin—in this case, the Philippines. She accepted it with due ceremony, like a Japanese businessman taking another's business card, and flipped the lid open for inspection. A few chunks of dry ice were still visible on the bottom; good. The finger-sized vials were all contained within a hexagonal cage. She sampled some of them with a pistol-shaped infrared thermometer and verified that none of them had thawed out. Then, after putting on some cotton gloves to protect her skin from the cold, she pulled a few out and spot-checked them just to verify that they had been sealed, labeled, and bar-coded in accordance with the procedures specified in the Third Technical Supplement to the Crater Lake Accord, Volume III, Section 4, Paragraph 11. They had. She'd have expected nothing less from Dr. Miguel Andrada, the geneticist.

She also guessed that Dr. Andrada suspected, at some level, that none of these samples had a snowball's chance in hell of ever developing into sentient life-forms, but this was not a subject to talk about now. For the benefit of the others, Moira gave a little canned speech, trying to make it sound spontaneous, thanking them and, by extension, the people of the Philippines for having entrusted her and the Cloud Ark with these most precious contributions, and hinting, without promising, at a future in which a cornucopia of vibrant humanity would spring forth from each little plastic vial. It was expected that these people would go forth now to their arklets and text or Facebook the news down to their friends and family at home. The promise in those words was meant to keep people on Earth from getting too rambunctious while they waited for the end; and if that failed, as it had in the case of Venezuela, well, J.B.F. could just nuke them.

"May I see how it all works?" Dr. Andrada asked, after the rest of his delegation had been sent on their way. So it was just the two of them now, hovering in a long, slim docking module that projected to the nadir side. "Below" them its far end was sealed off by a hatch with a keypad. Most of Izzy was open to anyone who wanted to wander in and poke around; they didn't get a lot of riffraff. But the HGA, the Human Genetic Archive, had a kind of quasi-sacred status and was kept under the digital equivalent of lock and key.

Dr. Andrada was a small, wiry man with prominent cheekbones. Like some other ag geneticists Moira had known, he had a callused, tanned, leathery look, the result of spending a lot of time in experimental plots, digging in actual dirt. Except for a nice pair of eyeglasses he could have passed for a farmer anywhere in Southeast Asia. But he had a Ph.D. from UC Davis and had been on the fast track for a Nobel Prize before the Agent had intervened.

"Of course," Moira said. "I'd fancy a chat anyway, about how we're going to grow things other than humans up here."

"We need to talk about that," Dr. Andrada agreed.

She drifted down, performing a slow somersault so that she could address the keypad, and punched the button that turned on the iris scanner. After a few moments, the device agreed that she was Dr. Moira Crewe and unlocked the hatch. Bracing herself with a handle on the wall, she pulled it open, then allowed herself to drift through into the docking module beyond. There was barely room in this for both her and Dr. Andrada. White LEDs came on automatically. Clipped to the wall was a simple nylon web belt with a few small electronic gadgets holstered in it. Moira took this and buckled it around her waist.

They had entered through the hatch on the module's zenith side. To port and starboard were openings that had been sealed off by round plastic shields. Each of these had a handle projecting from its center. The closest to Moira was the one on the port side, so she grabbed the handle, squeezed it to release a latch, and then pulled it out of the way.

Dr. Andrada flinched at the frigid air that washed into the space in its wake. They were looking down a straight tube about ten meters long, large enough for one person to work comfortably, or for two to pass each other if they didn't mind bumping bodies. Its walls were studded with long neat rows of smaller hatches about as wide as a splayed human hand, each with its own little handle. Hundreds of them. Closer to the entrance these bore neat machine-printed labels and bar codes; farther away they were blank. Next to each one of them was a blue LED; these provided the space's only illumination.

"Would you like to do the honors?" Moira said.

"If I don't freeze to death first!" Dr. Andrada said.

"Space is cold," Moira said. "We rely on that."

She gave him a minute to put on the cotton gloves, then opened the cooler and held it out. He removed the little rack containing the samples. Moira zapped its bar code with a handheld scanner from her belt. Dr. Andrada pulled himself into the cold storage module and began to drift deeper into it, gingerly prodding the walls in a way that marked him out as a new arrival to zero gravity. "Take the first one that's unlabeled," Moira said. "Leave the door open, please."

Dr. Andrada coughed as the chilly air made his throat spasm. He opened one of the small hatches and slid the sample rack into it. In the meantime Moira was using a handheld printer to generate a sticker identifying the sample in English, in Filipino, and in a machine-readable bar code language. Once Dr. Andrada had returned to the central module, she went up to the open hatch, verified that the sample rack was properly seated in the tubular cavity beyond, then closed the hatch and affixed the sticker to its front. Printed on the hatch was a unique identification number and a bar code conveying the same thing, which she zapped and then double-checked.

The LED next to this hatch had turned red, signaling that the compartment's temperature was too high. While Moira checked her work, it turned yellow, which suggested the cold was "soaking in." Later she'd pull it up on the screen of her tablet and verify that it had gone blue.

She flew back out to the docking module and grabbed the round shield that sealed off the cold store. "Now you know what these are for," she said. "Thermal insulation." She snapped the shield back into place. "I could open the other one," she offered, "but you would see the same thing."

"Thank you anyway," said Dr. Andrada, "but I have never been so cold in my life!"

They went back "up" to Zvezda and then proceeded forward to the complex of modules where most of the genetic engineering gear was stored. There was nothing to see here but boxes. They could just as easily have gone aft to one of the tori, but Moira knew from experience that new arrivals didn't benefit from switching back and forth between zero gee and simulated gravity.

Through the nice eyeglasses, Dr. Andrada was giving Moira a look that she read as polite but skeptical. Fair enough. She decided to broach what was probably on his mind. "Forgive me that bit of ceremony," she said. "I have done it once or twice a day for a year. I'm as much priestess as scientist. You're meant to blog it, of course. To tell the people down below that you personally hand-carried the samples all the way from Manila to a cold storage location on Izzy."

"Yes, I understand that. I will do so." He paused, signaling a change in topic. "It is not exactly decentralized."

Moira nodded. "If that thing gets hit with a rock ten minutes from now, all of the samples are destroyed."

"Yes. That is my concern."

"Mine as well. It all boils down to statistics and mathematics. For now, there aren't that many rocks, and we can see them and avoid them if necessary. Keeping all the eggs in one basket . . ."

"And sperm," Dr. Andrada said, in what had become the oldest joke in Moira's personal universe.

" . . . is actually a safer bet, for the next couple of weeks, than trying to distribute them among all of those arklets. But there is a plan, Dr. Andrada, for so distributing them, which will be triggered when the BFR breaks through a certain threshold."

He nodded. "Please call me Miguel."

"Miguel. Moira, if you would."

"Yes. Now, you know why I was chosen to come up here."

"You figured out a way to make photosynthesis in rice more efficient by transplanting genes from maize. Greenpeace destroyed your research facility in the Philippines but you kept the project alive anyway, in Singapore. Starting shortly after Zero you began developing strains of that rice adapted for cultivation in low-gee hydroponic environments."

"Sprice," Miguel said, with an ever-so-slight roll of the eyes. The term, a contraction of Space Rice, had been coined by an enthusiastic reporter for the *Straits Times* and become an unkillable staple of tabloid headlines and Internet comment threads. "Do you understand, Moira, that it cannot grow without some amount of simulated gravity? There has to be an up and a down or the root system cannot develop. In this it is more difficult than algae, which doesn't care."

"Oh, we're all going to be eating algae for a long time," Moira said. "Sprice will come later, after we have constructed more environments that rotate to make gravity. And then, Miguel, then!"

"Then what?" Miguel asked.

"Sprew."

"Sprew?"

"Space brew," Moira said. "It's not as good as barley, but you can make beer from rice in a pinch."

• • •

"TAP," MARKUS SAID. HE HAD TO SAY IT BECAUSE HE COULDN'T DO IT. The traditional way for a wrestler to tell his training partner that an unbreakable submission hold had been achieved was by tapping him or her on the hand, arm, leg, or whatever could be reached. But Markus couldn't reach anything. Tekla had both of his arms controlled.

She let go of him moments before they drifted into the padded wall of the Circus—a large, mostly empty module reserved for exercise—and they raised their hands to absorb the impact.

Watching interestedly from the far side of the Circus were Jun Ueda, an engineer named Tom Van Meter, Bolor-Erdene, and Vyacheslav Dubsky. The three men were taciturn. Bolor-Erdene, who was nothing if not enthusiastic, permitted herself three claps, then stopped when it became clear that no one else was joining in.

"Okay," Vyacheslav said. "Seeing is believing. It is possible to perform Sambo in zero gravity." His eyes flicked in the direction of the others. "Or jujitsu, or wrestling, or bökh, I presume."

"Obviously there are no throws. None of that shifting of the weight that is so important on the ground," Markus said.

Jun nodded. "It is a subset. A little bit like ground fighting. But without the ground."

Tom Van Meter, who'd been a collegiate wrestler en route to an engineering degree at Iowa, turned himself around to face the padded wall, then tried delivering a punch. In spite of his considerable size and strength, it landed weakly and sent him drifting backward across the module.

"We experimented with that too," Markus said. "Punches are problematic."

Just before striking the opposite wall, Tom flung both arms outward and slapped the mat to absorb energy. "If you're in a torus, or a bolo, all the usual stuff is going to work," he said. "But you're right, martial arts in zero gee is a new frontier."

"Once you have come to grapple," Tekla said, "not so different."

"The Cloud Ark is equipped with a dozen Tasers," Markus said. "I did not request these. They were here when I arrived. No one knows about them. I am not comfortable with having some persons go around with sidearms—even if they are just Tasers—while everyone else is unarmed. And yet. We have a population of two thousand or so. There is no town on Earth of such a population that does not have police. There will be crimes. Disputes."

"What does the Constitution say about police?" Bolor-Erdene asked. "I haven't read it."

All of the others laughed, appreciating her. "No one has read the bloody thing, Bo; it is this thick when you print it out!" Markus said, holding his thumb and index finger two inches apart. "Written by committee, as you would expect."

"To be clear, Markus," said Jun. "You are not suggesting—"

"No, Jun, I am not saying we ignore it. Believe me, I am screaming at these guys every day to make it simpler, to give us the, what do you call it—"

"Cliff's Notes," Tom said.

"Yes. Before we fall off the cliff. A simple owner's manual. But somewhere in there, a police force is mentioned. I grepped it. They will have to be citizen police at first—no professionals. I have studied your personnel records. I know that you are all trained in some sort of wrestling. Wrestling is the only form of organized violence that is actually usable aboard a space station, short of absolutely crazy shit."

"How about stick fighting?" Tom asked.

"I knew you would ask because your CV mentions a little bit of escrima," Markus said. "It is a reasonable idea. I have a question, though."

"Yes?"

"Do you see any sticks?"

"Maybe we could grow some trees," Bo suggested.

"That will take a while," Markus returned. "And so I am simply asking you this, to spend a little bit of time each day getting together in this module to practice wrestling. It might come in handy."

DOOB HAD SLEPT SO POORLY HE SUSPECTED HE HADN'T SLEPT AT ALL. But the clock said it was about dot 15. When he'd climbed into his sack it had said dot 9. He must have dozed off for a while. But he didn't know when.

His nightly videoconference with Amelia hadn't gone well. It hadn't gone *badly*—they hadn't raised their voices, or come to tears—but at first it had been all about what had just happened in Kourou, and after that there'd been a failure to connect. He'd noticed the same thing with Henry.

They were running out of things to say to each other. That was ghastly, but it was true. His family members were all preparing to meet their maker in two or three or four weeks. The government had been handing out free euthanasia pills to anyone who wanted them; thousands had already swallowed them and bodies overflowed the morgues. Mass graves were being dug with end loaders. Meanwhile, Doob was preparing for—to be blunt, to be honest—the greatest adventure of his life.

He wished, at some level, that they were already dead.

He had spoken those seemingly unspeakable words to Luisa several days ago and she had nodded. "Happens all the time," she said, "with caregivers of terminal Alzheimer's patients, or similar cases. An enormous sense of shame and guilt comes with it."

"But Amelia doesn't have Alzheimer's, she's—"

"Doesn't matter. Seeing her, talking to her, makes you feel bad. And at some level, your brain wants the thing that makes you feel bad to go away. Simplest reaction in the world. Doesn't make you a bad person. Doesn't mean you have to give in to it."

Those thoughts had led to more tossing and turning—if those were the right words for not being able to sleep in a loose sack in zero gravity—as he had wrestled with the question of "When?" Predicting it on Day 720, plus or minus a few, had been all well and good back on Day 360. But Day 700 was now approaching its end, and the "plus or minus" thing was seriously bothering him. Lately they'd narrowed it down to "plus or minus three days," but that was in response to political pressure. It wasn't a legit scientific move. And it meant something different to scientists. Laypersons understood it as "certainly between 717 and 723." Scientists would instead say that if you could repeat the experiment of blowing up the moon a large number of times, and keep track of the time-to-White-Sky separately in each case, the numbers would fall into a normal distribution, a bell-shaped curve, with about two-thirds of the instances falling within that range.

Which meant that the remainder would fall *outside* of that range—and some would fall *well* outside of it. It was not out of the question that it could happen *tomorrow*—that it could be happening right now—while Doob floated in a goddamned sack.

So when Dinah came and woke him up just after dot 15, he wasn't angry at her. More relieved.

Basic politeness prevented him from saying so, but she looked a wreck. Not in the sense of being over-the-top emotional. Just drained and beat up.

"You know about Guiana?" she asked him over her shoulder as they wended their way back to the Mining Colony.

"Yeah."

"Okay."

She said nothing further until they were in her shop. Doob could see the wreckage of old-school communication all over the place: many sheets of paper taped to the available surfaces, dull pencils drifting around, loose pages from the "employee manual" with blocks of characters crossed out. "I had to tell Sean to knock it off," she admitted. "I'm used up. Can't do it anymore. Need to get some sleep. This shit is difficult, you have to be precise. Keying slow enough for Sean to copy the transmission is like walking slow."

"Walking slow?"

"You know," Dinah said. "Anyone can walk at a normal pace. That's easy. But when you have to walk at half speed, like because you're accompanying someone who has trouble getting around? It's exhausting."

"Got it."

"When I started to beg off, he changed his topic. To that point it was all, 'Hey, what's going on, how many people are on the Ark?' but when I applied a little time pressure he started talking about sensitivity analysis."

Doob laughed.

"Wow," Dinah said, looking at him keenly. "Not the reaction I expected."

"I've been awake for hours thinking about it," Doob said.

"So you know what he means? Because I'm just a dumb clodhopper, I had to ask him."

"I assume he means, how certain are we really that it's going to happen on Day 720? And just how unstable is the system?"

"Yep, that's what he means."

"The closer we get, the more it's like a nuclear reactor about to go critical, or, well—"

"Pick your metaphor, I get it," Dinah said.

"Anything that's that unstable can be set off by random noise in the system. Things that we inherently cannot predict. Pretty soon it's going to be so on edge that just looking at it funny will set it off. We just don't know which rock is going to trigger the avalanche."

Dinah considered it for a few moments, then broke eye contact and looked at her radio. "Sean does," she said.

"I'm not sure I heard that correctly," Doob said, after a long, groping pause.

"The Eight Ball," she said. "That's what Sean calls it. It's a rock you don't know about. One you can't see coming. It's too dark, too far away."

"Dinah, I'm confused—are we talking about a hypothetical asteroid here, or—"

"No. A specific one. A real one. Look, Doob, you know that Arjuna Expeditions has been putting up cubesats for years. We have hundreds of eyes in the sky, drifting around taking pictures of near-Earth asteroids, cataloging them, recording their orbital parameters with as much precision as we can manage. Well, apparently he's been lying awake at night thinking about the same stuff as you. The extreme instability of the debris cloud. Its sensitivity to any kind of perturbation. And he had the bright idea: Why not search through Arjuna's secret database of asteroids to see whether any bad actors were going to be passing through the middle of the lunar debris cloud during the next couple of weeks, when it's on such a hair trigger?"

"He has that database with him?"

"Sure, whatever, it's just a spreadsheet."

"So he opened that spreadsheet and did that analysis?"

"Yeah. Doob, listen, I'm piecing this together from circumstantial evidence. You've seen how spotty the communication is."

"Understood."

"But I think he did that analysis and found an asteroid, which he is calling the Eight Ball. I assume it's low-albedo."

"Black. As eight balls are," Doob said.

"I don't know anything about its size or its orbital parameters, any of that. But Sean thinks it's going to pass right through the middle of the cloud in about six hours."

"Six hours?!"

"And that it has enough kinetic energy to be, well, interesting."

Doob was thinking about Amelia. About those emotions that had kept him awake earlier. Predictably, everything had now been reversed and he was terrified that she and Henry and Hesper and Hadley were all about to die.

Dinah misinterpreted this as him making astronomical calculations in his head. "I'm going to go and get six hours of sleep," she said. "Good night."

"Good night, Dinah," Doob said.

IT WAS ABOUT DOT 16, SHIFT CHANGE TIME, THE EQUIVALENT OF four in the afternoon for third shifters. So, Markus was approaching the end of what, for any normal earthbound person, would be his workday. Of course, like almost everyone else in the Cloud Ark, he worked the whole time he was awake. Even his recreational activities—such as martial arts practice in the Circus—had a larger purpose. So the "afternoon" shift change and end of his "workday" were purely formal observances. Nevertheless, he was in the habit of using this time of day for dealing with what used to be called paperwork. And as part of that he had invited to his little private office off of the Tank the Only Lawyer in Space, Salvatore Guodian. Son of a Singaporean Chinese father and an Italian countess whose parents had gone to that city-state as tax exiles, he had been educated in a school for mostly British expats, matriculated at Berkeley, dropped out after one and a half years to join a tech startup, lost his shirt, bummed around to various other startups, finally made some money, become interested in the law, essentially bought his way into law school despite not having a bachelor's degree, worked for fifteen years at the Los Angeles, Singapore, Sydney, Beijing, London, and Dubai offices of a white-shoe law firm, been passed over for partnership, resigned, ridden his bicycle across China, moved to San Francisco, and become the general counsel of a digital currency trading firm while in his spare time volunteering for a nonprofit cyber rights organization and going out into the desert to launch very large homebrew rockets to the edge of space. Sal, as he was universally known, had been one of the first people chosen to work on the Constitution of the Cloud Ark, and so had spent a year and a half at The Hague before getting "yanked," as the expression went, and launched up here. He was forty-seven years old but in dim light could have passed for thirty.

As a way to deal with the exigencies of zero-gee life, and a surrender to a receding hairline, he had taken to wearing a short vacubuzz. This was the easiest thing to do with hair in space. The vacubuzzer was a machine that combined the functions of an electric trimmer and an industrial shop vac. Haircuts were self-serve and consumed about thirty seconds if you were unusually fastidious. Earplugs were recommended. In his halcyon days Sal had sported a luxuriant head of long, wavy black hair and a widow's peak that had brought out his Italian heritage, but with a vacubuzz he looked almost purely Chinese. He spoke seven languages, and he came closer than any living human to having the entire Cloud Ark Constitution—or CAC, as he called it—in his brain. If Markus had anything to say about it—which he did—then Sal would very soon combine in one person the functions of attorney general, head prosecutor, justice of the peace, and chief justice of the supreme court.

Sal laughed. He had great teeth. "You realize that those roles are completely incompatible. They are intended to be one another's mutual adversaries in a lot of ways."

"Then you can appoint other people to fill them. Look, Sal, we are talking about a bootstrapping process. We have to start somewhere."

"Let's war-game it," Sal said. "A male Arkie from Outer Bizarristan rapes a female Arkie from Andorra. It happens in a place where we don't have any cameras."

"There are very few such places," Markus pointed out.

"Okay, fine. It happens in an arklet. Or so the victim claims. She goes to sick bay, where medical evidence is gathered."

"Do we even have rape kits?" Markus asked.

"How should I know?" Sal returned. "But we should get some. Anyway, based on that, in some countries a judge might issue a warrant enabling the police to look at the video records from that arklet. Because in some countries, Markus, people have a right to privacy and you can't just be surveilling them all the time."

"And what is the situation here?"

"It's fascinating that you don't even know, but I'll tell you that the CAC recognizes certain rights that, however, may be abrogated or curtailed during periods of simplified administrative procedures and structures."

"PSAPS," Markus said. "That, I know about. It is a euphemism for martial law."

Sal looked somewhere between pained and amused. "May I suggest you stop thinking about it that way—or, failing that, never say it out loud."

"But nevertheless—"

"A better analogy might be the authority a captain wields over a ship at sea. The captain can do things, like preside over marriage ceremonies or order someone confined to quarters, that would not be acceptable if the same ship were tied up to a pier in Manhattan."

"Look, I do not have time now to war-game a whole prosecution of a hypothetical rape," Markus said, glancing at his wristwatch—Swiss, naturally, and made specifically for him by a famous Geneva company, as a sort of legacy, a way of saying *we existed once, and here is what magnificent things we were capable of.* "I want to talk about something very basic, very fundamental, which is: How do I have authority? Or if I am replaced by Ivy or Ulrika, how does she have authority?"

Sal didn't quite see where he was going. "Authority meaning . . ."

When this elicited no response other than impatient muttering, Sal tried: "Authority can mean many different things, Markus."

"In this case I am not speaking of moral authority or leadership qualities or any of that stuff. I do not mean the theoretical loyalty that Arkies have to the so-called captain of the ship. I mean, what happens if we go to arrest the rapist from Outer Bizarristan, and he decides to put up a fight, and his friends decide that they are going to fight with him?"

Sal, to this point, had been viewing the conversation as an enjoyable exercise in legal theory. He now looked more serious. "You're talking about power. What it really means. What it really is."

"Yes."

"It's an old question. A pharaoh, a medieval king, the mayor of New York City, they all have to think about the same thing."

"Yes," Markus said again.

"When you give an order, what assurance do you have that it will be carried out? That is the essential question of power."

"*Jawohl,* counselor!"

"Normally here I would speak to you about moral authority and loyalty and all of that. But you have already ruled this out."

"When push comes to shove, as the English expression has it—"

"The traditional answer has always been that the king has his guard, the mayor his chief of police, the commander his military police, or what have you. And it is their ability to physically coerce others that is the ultimate foundation of the leader's power."

"Now you're talking. And what is that for me, under the CAC?"

"You understand," Sal said, "that the more you actually call upon such persons to coerce, the less power you have, in a way. It is an admission of failure."

"Sal," Markus said, "how long have you been up here?"

"Two hundred and some days."

"How many hours have we spent talking about the CAC?"

"I have no idea, probably a hundred hours over that time."

"And of that, how much time have we spent talking about this one thing?"

Sal checked his own watch. "Maybe fifteen minutes."

"So, based on that allocation of time," Markus said, "maybe you can see that this is not all that important to me in the big scheme of things. But it is important, Sal. When the moment comes when I have to arrest a criminal who is being protected by his comrades, I must have an answer. I must know what to do. I must be prepared. This is what I do. This is why I have this job."

Someone was knocking on the door to Markus's office, which was unusual. Markus ignored it for now.

"Under PSAPS you can deputize specific people to enforce your decisions using appropriate levels of physical coercion. Once we get out of PSAPS . . ."

"How soon do you think that is going to happen?" Markus's tone of voice suggested he had his own opinions on the matter.

"If we are lucky enough to survive? It will be years," Sal said.

"So we must confine ourselves to PSAPS for this discussion," Markus said. Then he hollered at the door, "Just a minute!" Then, back to Sal: "Appropriate levels of physical coercion, what does that mean? Who decides?"

"Well," Sal said, "if you make me attorney general, head prosecutor, justice of the peace, and chief justice of the supreme court, I guess I do."

"If someone gets Tased, and his heart stops, and he dies, is that appropriate?"

"Jesus Christ, Markus, what has gotten into you?"

"I am war-gaming," Markus said. "Trying to be prepared. You should do it too. Not with hypothetical rape cases but with what is likely to start happening soon." He held Sal's gaze until Sal answered with a nod. Then he aimed his voice at the door. "All right! Come in!"

"Door" was a landlubber term for what, on a boat or a spaceship, would be called a hatch. A convention had developed where, in a part of Izzy that had simulated gravity, it was referred to as a door. In the floaty bits, it was called a hatch.

The door opened to reveal Dubois Jerome Xavier Harris. The look on his face, combined with the mere fact that he had interrupted

Markus during a meeting in his private office, suggested that something serious was happening. Markus's mind jumped straight to the most obvious explanation: "Is the president nuking people again?"

Dr. Harris looked startled by the suggestion, then shook it off. No, it wasn't that.

"Does this meeting require privacy?" Markus asked, with a look at Sal. Sal stood up, volunteering to make himself scarce. But Dr. Harris just got a bemused look. "It concerns the least private thing that ever happened, or ever will," he said. "So no thank you. I have reason to believe that the timetable has just been pushed up very significantly. There is a chance that the White Sky could happen as soon as six hours from now." He checked his watch. "Call it five."

Markus's eye flicked to a display on the wall. "I see no uptick in the BFR."

"It will be triggered by the passage of an asteroid through the cloud."

"Does anyone on the ground know?"

"It depends on to what extent this office is under surveillance."

"So, your information does not come from the ground."

"No. It comes from deep space."

"Via encrypted Morse code?" Markus inquired casually. He and Sal exchanged a look. Their conversation had begun, an hour ago, with reading a memo from J.B.F. complaining about such transmissions and demanding that action be taken. It was in discussing *how* to take such action, and whether the White House had any authority in the matter, that Markus and Sal had wandered into their more general discussion of power. Which was how Markus liked it, for now. Because if someone was sending mysterious encrypted Morse code transmissions from Izzy, it had to be his girlfriend. And he wasn't going to arrest *her*. People would howl about conflict of interest: people who would be dead soon, people who had no way to enforce their authority here.

Unless they had planted, among the Arkies or the General Population, fifth columnists with orders to execute a coup d'état if necessary.

"Markus?" Dr. Harris asked. "Are you hearing me? Do you understand what I just said?"

"I beg your pardon, Dr. Harris, I just got distracted thinking about the kind of things that Sal is supposed to think about."

"Feel free to delegate some of that," Sal said. "I know it's not your strong suit, but—"

"Close the door, please," Markus said.

Dr. Harris did.

"I am reasonably sure of no surveillance in here."

"Noted."

"It is Dinah, isn't it, Doob?" Markus asked.

Doob nodded. "She's talking to Sean Probst over an encrypted channel."

Markus shook his head admiringly. "What a girl! My god, she is trouble."

Doob and Sal were silent. During their silence, Markus thumbed out a one-word text message to Tekla.

"Sal," Markus said, "I declare PSAPS."

"I don't think we are yet authorized to—"

"Who is going to stop us?"

Doob and Sal, again, were silent on the matter.

"Is Julia—I do not call her the president anymore—going to nuke us?" He was continuing to thumb out messages as he talked.

"She, or the Russians, or the Chinese, might have other ways of removing you from your position—"

"I have thought about this," Markus said. "About the possibility that there are plants. Military guys with Tasers or whatever. Waiting for such an order. I have talked to Fyodor, to Sheng, to Zeke, trying to sound them out, to get a feel for it."

"Markus," Doob said, "with respect, I don't think that this is what you ought to be focusing on right now."

"Which is why I am delegating the constitutional side of it to Sal and the operational side of it to her." Markus nodded toward the door, which had swung open without a knock. Tekla glided through and closed it behind her. "We don't have to announce to the whole world that we are going to PSAPS. We have five hours in which to begin preparations, quietly. I will contact Moira, and tell her that we must begin preparations to disperse the genetic samples to the arklets. I will tell Ulrika that we must pull the trigger on the Surge." By this, Markus meant a long-planned burst of launches that was supposed to happen in the few days' grace period between the White Sky and the onset of the Hard Rain. "We can be working on these things quietly. Five hours from now, it will happen or it will not. If it does not, we go back to as we were and consider this a dress rehearsal."

The door opened again, this time after a knock, and in came a young man named Steve Lake, preceded by his laptop and followed by his dreadlocks. For Steve, in his year and a half aboard Izzy, had not succumbed to the vacubuzzer's siren song, but he had gotten tired of messing with his long hair and had allowed it to congeal into red ropes. Formerly employed by a consulting firm in northern Virginia that hired hackers to do secret work for intelligence agencies, he had been yanked and sent up to support Spencer Grindstaff, the networks and communications specialist who'd been one of Izzy's original crew on Zero. Spencer was an NSA man through and through, recruited straight out of MIT to work on spooky crypto stuff. Steve seemed to be an altogether different sort of character. He looked a bit mystified just now.

"Steve," Markus said. "It is time for us to have a conversation about power."

Steve's brow furrowed. "You mean, electrical power or—"

"The other kind."

"Okay, and is this going to be, like, an abstract philosophical discussion or—"

"No, it is going to conclude with me telling you, under my PSAPS authority, to change all of the passwords and keys for Izzy's control systems."

"Wow!" Steve said. "Shouldn't you be talking to Spencer then? Because he's above me in the org chart."

"I am familiar with the org chart," Markus said. "Under PSAPS I have the authority to change it."

"What is this PSAPS thing you keep talking about, Markus?"

"Sal will explain it later. For now, we may set it aside. Fundamentally we speak of your loyalty, your allegiance. I think that Spencer is extremely loyal to powers that be on the ground. I do not wish to put him in an impossible bind. He will later come with us, or he will not. You I believe to be a different kind of fellow. I ask you, in effect, to now become loyal to the Cloud Ark and the Cloud Ark alone. Not to Washington. Not to Houston. And to accept the authority of whoever is the boss of the Cloud Ark. Which for now is me."

"Okay."

"You're supposed to think about it first, Steve. Not just say okay."

"I've been thinking about it for a while. But I have to tell you, there might be back doors. I can change all the codes I know about. The ones I don't know about are a different matter."

"Then we shall just have to be vigilant."

White Sky

DOOB COULDN'T GUESS HOW MANY TIMES DURING HIS LIFE HE HAD noted a cottony tuft of cloud in a blue sky, then looked up hours later to discover that it had developed into a bank of clouds that covered the sun and told of a change in the weather. Such phenomena happened too slowly for the mind to discern them as happening at all. During the last hours of A+1.335, something like that occurred in the cloud of lunar debris that had been hanging in the sky for the last seven hundred days. Later they would watch the movies of it in time-lapse, compressing a day's changes into a minute of video, and it would look like an explosion. Or an epidemic of explosions. If you watched the video carefully enough, frame by frame, you could see it progress from one part of the cloud to the next as the Eight Ball shot through. Like a particle lancing through a cloud chamber, it was invisible save for the trail of consequences it left in its wake. A few months earlier it might have passed through without touching anything, but today the density of rocks in the cloud was such that it could not avoid smashing into some of them on its way through. Doob, making a crude statistical calculation, put the likely number of collisions at ten, plus or minus five. Not a large number in a cloud that now contained millions of rocks, but enough to push the system, trembling on the precipice of an exponential explosion, over the edge. Around its unseen track the White Sky took form and fury. The cloud bloomed and evoluted like cream in coffee, spreading and paling, though from place to place one could see fresh bursts as rocks hurled out in earlier collisions found distant targets and touched off smaller chain reactions of their own. In places it took on a cellular structure as curved detonation fronts spread, contacted others, and merged into lacy foams of white arcs. It had an austere, monochromatic beauty about it. There was no fire and no light other than what cold sunlight the rocks bounced back to the eye. Later, when they began to enter the atmosphere, there would be fire and plenty of it. But for now the world was ending in a fractal blooming of dust and gravel, an apocalypse in a gravel quarry.

"You pretty much nailed it," someone told Doob, "when you called it the White Sky."

"Being right does not always bring satisfaction," he said.

The Bolide Fragmentation Rate shot up through all meaningful thresholds within a few hours of the Eight Ball's arrival and Doob stopped paying attention to it. The number was probably wrong now. It was just an estimate, produced by a consortium of observatories based on the amount and distribution of light coming out of the cloud. All the assumptions that went into its calculation had now become obsolete.

He tried aiming his optical telescope at where PP1 and PP2 and Cleft—the large, metal-rich children of Peach Pit—ought to be, but saw nothing except, possibly, some local highlights in the density of the cloud, perhaps caused by rocks dashing themselves to pieces on the steely surfaces of those dark bolides. He wondered if he would ever see them again.

He no longer had an accurate visual memory of the size of the moon in the sky, and so he could not estimate how many times larger the cloud was. Of course, he could look those numbers up and calculate it. But he didn't really care what the numbers said. The full moon had always been the same size, but sometimes it looked huge and sometimes it looked small, depending on how close it was to the horizon, and on factors that were purely psychological or aesthetic. To all but a few of the people on the night side of Earth, looking up at the cloud, those factors were the only ones that mattered. He wanted to know how big it looked to *them;* he wanted to know how it felt. He wanted to see it over the Chino Hills from the courtyard of the Caltech Athenaeum, which was where he had last seen the moon, a few minutes before Zero, and to know how it was to stand there on terra firma and to see it and to know it was death coming.

Like most people, he had drawn up a list of everyone in the world he needed to say goodbye to, then gone through it and ruthlessly weeded out 90 percent of the names, since there wasn't time. And then, during his last few months on Earth, he had sought out and said goodbye to the ones he needed to see in person. From orbit he had said goodbye to others on videoconferencing links or with carefully written email messages. Once he had said goodbye to a given person, he avoided communicating with them again. It was awkward to go out for a last night of drinking with a colleague, reminisce and cry and hug and say farewell, and then find yourself emailing the same person two months later with a question about their latest observations. Consequently, his scope of acquaintances had steadily narrowed as he had worked his way down the list. By this point he was down to his wife and his children. Reaching them became a lot more difficult after the Eight Ball had done its work. The volume of communications between Izzy and the ground was limited by the total bandwidth of the station's antennas and radios. Personal communications had lower priority than operations, and operations were peaking as the final surge of launches was prepared. Or, as Dinah called it, the Splurge. Doob sent text messages to Amelia and the kids all the time; they sat in the delivery queue for minutes or hours, and half of them never got sent at all. Just when he was about to give up hope, he'd get a message back from Henry or Hadley or Hesper. Sending those messages, and seeing the responses, became more important than sleeping, so he "broke shift," as the saying went, and dozed whenever he could, lying on the floor of the Farm or just putting his head down on a table like a kindergarten kid, his phone right next to his face so he'd feel it jump when anything came through.

It finally became clear to him, maybe twenty-four hours after he had given the news about the Eight Ball to Markus, that he was never going to communicate with his loved ones again save through sporadic and unpredictable texts. Anything he needed to say to them directly, he ought to have said before. Which should not have come as news; he had been telling himself for a long time that you had to act as if each conversation might be the last. This did not stop him from reviewing his final video chats with each one of them, on the evening of Day 700, and wishing he'd said certain things.

How does it look from up there? Henry texted him.

Doob checked the time. It was night in Moses Lake. He imagined Henry sitting out on that crappy old couch that they'd moved out of the house in Seattle, drinking a beer between work shifts, watching the White Sky reach out for him like a spectral hand.

Doob didn't know what to say.

I think I am seeing some spread along the orbital axis—the beginnings of rings, he texted back.

I meant Earth, Henry returned.

Doob went looking for a place where he could look down at Earth through a real window—not one of those damned Situational Awareness Monitors. This ended up being the Woo-Woo Pod. It was pretty crowded. Izzy was about to swing over the terminator from day into night. Even over the brightly lit Pacific they could see what looked like hairline scratches in the pellucid shell of the atmosphere: the white trails left by incoming bolides. Above the dark side of the Earth these became arcs of blue fire that sometimes forked, and sometimes ended in red bursts when they made it all the way to the ground. In other words, it looked the way it had looked the day before, and the day before that. This level of meteorite activity would have been the most amazing astronomical event in human history had it happened suddenly, two years ago. But beginning with the first big rock that had plowed into Peru just a few days after Zero, the ambient level of bolide strikes had steadily crept upward. People had adjusted to it. Some had posted red-faced self-portraits after suffering "bolide burn," meaning an acute case of sunburn caused by exposure to the ultraviolet light emitted by meteor trails in the nearby sky.

Looking down at you now, Doob texted. He wanted to add *Wish I was there* but it would have been stupid. *Looks like a big one coming in over southern BC.*

I see it, Henry returned. *Feeling its heat.*

Busy there?

You know it. Racking and stacking the big boys, getting ready for the Surge.

Doob wondered how it worked. What was to prevent desperate people from rushing the launch pads, trying to cram themselves aboard the last of those big boys? Like the last chopper out of Saigon, people dangling from the skids as soldiers punched them in the face. Or was he underestimating human nature? Maybe it was all perfectly orderly down there.

I need you here. That one was from Markus.

Reluctantly, Doob pushed himself away from the window and got turned toward the tube that would conduct him back to the Stack. From there he would make his way back to T3, where Markus was presumably hanging out in the Tank—

Markus Leuker was hovering directly in front of him, face illuminated by the blue light of a phone. He turned it off and slid it into his pocket.

Hard Rain

LIKE ANY GOOD STORM, THE HARD RAIN BEGAN WITH A SUDDEN thunderclap: a kilometer-wide rock that lit up eastern Europe with eerie, silent flashes as it skidded in across the upper atmosphere before digging into thick air somewhere around Odessa. Its trail set fire to dry leaves and combustible litter in the Crimea, then painted a long brushstroke of burning buildings and forests across the northeast rim of the Black Sea, ending with a long elliptical crater in the steppe between Krasnodar and Stavropol. The former city was first set on fire by radiant heat from the sky and then flattened by a blast wave. The latter got only the blast, followed by a rain of ejecta. Both disappeared from human ken.

After a few hours' respite, smaller bolides began to come down. They landed all over the world, but most often in the lower latitudes, close to the equator. Having been told, long in advance, that this would be the case, many people had moved toward the poles in recent months, prompting Rufus MacQuarie and his friends, family, and associates to establish a defensive perimeter around their works in the Brooks Range. That was a terrible place in November. The only refugees likely to make it up that far would be well equipped and well prepared, but those were exactly the kinds of uninvited visitors that Rufus didn't want creeping around. Unencumbered by the limits on bandwidth that applied to all the other radios in the Cloud Ark, Rufus and Dinah had kept up their Morse code correspondence during the three-day "grace period" between the White Sky and the Hard Rain. Rufus was still transmitting from his truck, which he had parked before the entrance to the mine. He had considered erecting a larger antenna on the top of the mountain and hooking it up to an underground transmitter via armored cables, but Dinah, after surveying the predicted effects of the Hard Rain, had told him not to waste his time.

Ivy had said goodbye to the Maternal Organism several days earlier, immediately before the Morg had swallowed her government-issue euthanasia pill. The one person on Earth she was still in touch with was Cal, aboard his submarine, keeping station on the surface offshore of the Norfolk Naval Base, out where the water got blue enough to facilitate a deep dive when the time came. In those days Ivy's main link to her family came through music. For the Morg had given five-year-old Ivy a choice between becoming the best pianist in Southern California or the best violinist in Southern California, and Ivy had opted for the violin. She had never become the best in Southern California, or even close to it, but she had played in various youth orchestras and developed some familiarity with the classical orchestral repertoire. She had a violin aboard Izzy, which she would tune up and play from time to time.

When the Bolide Fragmentation Rate shot up through a certain level on Day 701, marking the formal beginning of the White Sky, a number of cultural organizations launched programs that they had been planning since around the time of the Crater Lake announcement. Many of these were broadcast on shortwave radio, and so Ivy had her pick of programs from Notre Dame, Westminster Abbey, St. Patrick's Cathedral, the Imperial Palace in Tokyo, Tiananmen Square, the Potala Palace, the Great Pyramids, the Wailing Wall. After sampling all of them she locked her radio dial on Notre Dame, where they were holding the Vigil for the End of the World and would continue doing so until the cathedral fell down in ruins upon the performers' heads and extinguished all life in the remains of the building. She couldn't watch it, since video bandwidth was scarce, but she could imagine it well: the Orchestre Philharmonique de Radio France, its ranks swollen by the most prestigious musicians of the Francophone world, all dressed in white tie and tails, ball gowns and tiaras, performing in shifts around the clock, playing a few secular classics but emphasizing the sacred repertoire: masses and requiems. The music was marred by the occasional thud, which she took to be the sonic booms of incoming bolides. In most cases the musicians played right through. Sometimes a singer would skip a beat. An especially big boom produced screams and howls of dismay from the audience, blended with the clank and clatter of shattered stained glass raining to the cathedral's stone floor. But for the most part the music played sweetly, until it didn't. Then there was nothing.

Paris is gone, she texted. Through the military systems, which were patched in with NASA's, she could still communicate with Cal.

Dive bbs, he answered. Which by itself was pretty enigmatic, but she knew its meaning: the submarine had to dive below the surface for a little while, to avoid some danger, but he expected he'd be back soon.

But he might be wrong about that. She might never hear from him again. She decided it was long past time. She texted him a message that he would find waiting when and if his boat returned to the surface: *I release you from your vow.*

Then she felt a strange wave pass through her body, almost as if she were in a submarine in the Atlantic when a pressure wave rolled through from some distant meteor strike. She assumed it was an emotional reaction to what she had just done. But then she noticed that every loose floating object in her workspace was drifting in the same direction, toward the wall against which she had braced her back. Pops and creaks and groans propagated through Izzy. The space station was accelerating gently, at just a fraction of a gee. The thrusters must be firing.

The lights had turned red. The PA speaker in her module emitted a slight pop as it came on. "Alert," said a synthesized voice. "All personnel should now be awake and at stations for urgent swarm maneuver. This is not a drill."

So it had happened. They had been practicing this for months. But this was the first real Streaker Alert. It meant that a bolide had been detected by SI—the Sensor Integration team—on an unusual trajectory that might pose a danger to Izzy unless the course was corrected slightly.

Her first, nervous impulse was to look out the window toward Amalthea. The big rock was still there. The maneuver hadn't caused it to snap off.

But this was Ship thinking: placing top priority on Izzy. She, and everyone else, needed to get in the mental groove of Cloud thinking. The majority of the population lived on arklets. Izzy's purpose was to help the arklets survive.

So she wrenched her gaze away from the window—an antiquated thing, that—and brought up a display on her tablet showing the disposition of every vessel in the Cloud Ark. It was an app called Parambulator. It was not a literal rendering of what the cloud looked like, though you could make it show you that if you clicked the right menus. Parambulator was a tour de force of data visualization that would only make sense to people like Ivy, Doob, and most of the Arkies, who had spent a lot of time learning about orbital mechanics. Starting with empirical observations from Lina Ferreira and other mathematically sophisticated biologists, mathematicians like Zhong Hu had extrapolated swarm algorithms from three to six dimensions and physicists like Ivy had figured out how to make these algorithms work under the special constraints of orbital mechanics. In general, every vessel in the cloud was shown as a dot on a three-dimensional scatter plot showing information about its orbit. Six numbers—the orbital parameters, or, as everyone up here had begun to call them, the params—were required to convey everything about an orbit. Only three could be visualized in any given plot. So that was where the user-interface legerdemain came into play, and where someone like Ivy had to pay attention and engage all available brain cells. But the gist of it was that each arklet was a projectile that could strike Izzy, or another arklet, if its params were wrong. In a hypothetical, extremely simple Cloud Ark consisting of only two arklets, only one calculation needed to be performed: namely, the calculation that answered the question "Will Arklet 1 bang into Arklet 2 if both stay on their current courses?" In a three-arklet cloud, it was also necessary to figure out whether Arklet 1 would collide with Arklet 3, and whether 2 and 3 were going to collide. So, that was a total of three calculations. If the cloud expanded to four arklets, six calculations were needed, and so on. In mathematical terms these were known as triangular numbers, a kind of binomial coefficient, but the bottom line was that the number of calculations went up rapidly with the number of arklets in the cloud. For a hundred-arklet cloud it was 4,950 calculations, for a thousand-arklet cloud, about half a million. It would have flummoxed the simple computers of Apollo days but was nothing by modern standards—provided that accurate information could be had about each arklet's orbit. An old-school, centralized approach would have been for all the arklets to report their params to a computer on Izzy, which would then do all the calculations and report the results. The reliability of that process could be improved if Izzy's radars, observing the arklets and plotting their movements, filled in gaps in the data. And indeed something like that was happening all the time, not just on one computer on Izzy but on several. But this, again, was Ship thinking. Cloud thinking dictated that each arklet make those observations and do those calculations separately. The computer on a single arklet—call it Arklet X— might not have all the information needed to track every single one of the other arklets in the cloud, but it could identify the ones most likely to be a danger and focus on those. Others, as well as the central processors on Izzy, could assist it by sending messages to the effect of "You might not be aware of it, but you are possibly in danger from Arklet Y and might want to move it to the top of your list of things to keep an eye on." To which it might reply "Thank you, but I'm not getting good params for Arklet Y because Izzy is blocking my view on the radar." The cloud would then respond by in some sense becoming aware that Arklets X and Y needed to know more about each other's params and giving a higher priority to making that happen.

The cloud, in other words, became not just a physical cloud of flying objects in space but a computational cloud as well, a free-floating, self-regulating Internet. The function of Parambulator was to give its users an Olympian perspective on all that was happening in that network, and at some level all you really needed to know about it was that scary things were shown in red. Ivy looked at it now, more in curiosity than in alarm, since they had been practicing maneuvers for weeks and she thought she knew what to expect. Whenever Izzy fired her thrusters and changed her params, red propagated through the scatter plots like a drop of blood in a glass of water. All the free arklets, and all the ones connected to bolos or to heptads or triads, now needed to evaluate their params and see whether they were in danger of colliding with Izzy. Or—almost as bad—of drifting away so far that they could never get back to the swarm, a condition shown by a yellow dot in the display. It was a simple matter for any given arklet to plot a new course that would avoid both of those fates. Much more complicated was for three hundred arklets to do it at the same time without banging into each other. So a kind of negotiation had to take place, based not on awaiting commands from Izzy but on observing what "nearby" arklets were doing and coordinating the firing of thrusters with them to minimize the amount of red showing up on the plot.

It was necessary to place the word "nearby" in scare quotes because it had a different meaning in this swarm than it did to a bird in a flock. To a bird, nearby meant just that. To things maneuvering in the six-dimensional parameter space of orbital mechanics, "nearby" meant "any set of params that is potentially interesting to me in the next few minutes," and it could apply to objects that were currently too far away to be noticed. Once that was accounted for, however, the arklets could do as birds did when flying in flocks. In the simulations that they had seen shortly after the concept had been proposed, it had looked astonishingly like the behavior of schooling fish. And the reality of it, which had only been implemented in the last few months of round-the-clock launches from Kourou, Baikonur, Canaveral, et al., answered well to those simulations. It just happened more slowly in real time.

It was happening now, in response to Izzy's course change. The red only spread so far, then began to recede, first fraying around the edges, then dying off in patches. A few dots went yellow, then corrected themselves as they caught up. Ivy's expectation, based on the last few months' tests and exercises, was that the last few red dots would turn white very soon and cease to be a concern. But this didn't happen. Some remained stubbornly red. Spinning the plot around, looking at it in various modes, she zeroed in on those dots and queried them. Almost all of them were cargo modules or passenger capsules that had been launched during the Splurge: the last-minute effort made by all the spacefaring nations of the world to launch every last rocket they had capable of reaching orbit.

Her phone buzzed. A message had come back from Cal; his boat must have resurfaced.

What's that supposed to mean?

He had only just now seen her last text.

It means we are no longer engaged.

That seemed a little blunt, so she added, *You need to find some nice mermaid.*

After a minute he answered *{crying} I was going to do the same. Your odds considerably better.*

She answered *Bullcrap,* which was an old joke between them. When she had first met him at Annapolis, he had been such a straight arrow that he was unable to speak the word "bullshit."

SAB = Straight Arrow Babe came back.

SAB is sad :(Why did you dive?

Big surface wave came through. Bad news for East Coast.

Who tells you? Do you have a chain? Meaning chain of command.

One rung left above me. Then, after a pause, *POTUS has gone dark.*

She typed in *Thank God for that* and hesitated before sending it. But the world was coming to an end; she didn't have to worry about repercussions. She hit Send.

She'd never talked to Cal about what had happened on Day 700: the fuel-air devices, the nuclear warhead. But she was certain it had been his finger on the button.

May God have mercy on her soul, Cal answered, and she knew the subtext: *and may He have mercy on mine.*

This exchange of messages was interrupted by one from Markus: *need u.*

She pocketed the phone to free her hands for movement through Izzy, maneuvered through the maze of habitation modules to the Stack, and headed aft, bound for the Tank. The trip down the Stack took no time at all. A week ago she would have had to maneuver around people clumped in twos and threes for conversation. Since Markus had declared PSAPS, this had changed; one of his edicts had been that the Stack must be kept clear for rapid movement of essential personnel. Right now it was as empty as she'd ever seen it. Down in the Zvezda module she saw some comings and goings, and recognized, for a moment, the spiky profile of Moira's hair. She would be busy making preparations to disperse the Human Genetic Archive to the cloud, a project that in and of itself was at least as complicated as anything happening with swarms and params. Essential personnel indeed.

Luisa popped into view down in H1 and propelled herself up the Stack like she meant business. After nearly colliding with one of Moira's helpers, she let her momentum carry her up into Zarya, then stopped hard at the entrance to the tube that led to the Woo-Woo Pod. She looked into it for a few moments, evaluating, then made a decision and pulled herself into it.

Ivy passed by the same location a few moments later, slowed for a moment, and glanced down the length of the tube. It was possible to see straight down its length, across the spherical Pod, and through its windows to the Earth. Normally this meant the blue light of the oceans and the white light of clouds and ice caps. Sometimes, a lot of green when they were passing over well-watered parts of the world, or some yellow when over the Sahara.

Right now the light was orange because the Earth was on fire.

People were screaming down there in the Pod. Luisa must have been sent there to calm people down. Ivy was almost drawn in by a sort of magnetic power of fascination. Earth looked as if some god had attacked it with a welder's torch, slashing away at it and leaving thin trails of incandescence. Some of these were red and steady: things burning on the ground. Others were blinding bluish-white and evanescent: trails drawn through the atmosphere by meteorites.

She fancied she could almost feel the warmth radiating from the planet.

Markus needed her. She couldn't help the screaming people down in the Pod. She turned her head aft and pushed on.

Hovering in the entrance to the genetic storage modules, Moira was ticking off items on her tablet, listening, dead faced, to something on a large pair of headphones. She noticed Ivy. She peeled a headphone away from one ear and aimed it at her. Ivy recognized a cappella music, medieval polyphony. “King’s College is holding up rather well,” she said. “Do you know the piece?”

“I’m certain I’ve heard it before, but I can’t place it,” Ivy said.

“Allegri’s ‘Miserere mei, Deus,’ ” Moira said. Thanks to the Morg’s insistence that she take Latin, Ivy knew what it meant: Have mercy on me, O God.

“It’s beautiful.”

“They would sing it at Tenebrae, in the wee hours, as they extinguished the candles one by one.”

“Thank you, Moira.”

“Thank you, Ivy.”

A minute later she was in T3. As always, she stood flat-footed for a moment to get the feel of simulated gravity, then headed toward the Farm and the Tank. Passing through the utility section she considered getting herself a cup of coffee. Then she felt shock and shame over the fact that she was thinking about coffee while her planet was being set on fire.

Then she poured herself a cup of coffee anyway and stepped into the Farm. This was crowded. Most of the Situational Awareness Monitors were showing status displays relating to the functions of the Cloud Ark. The big one at the head of the room was just showing a view of Earth through a camera aimed in that direction. But the video image had nothing like the impact of seeing it directly through the windows of the Woo-Woo Pod. The arc-light intensity of the streaking bolides was reduced to a blurry flare of maxed-out pixels. Out of habit she wondered why they didn’t change the channel to CNN, or Al Jazeera, or one of the other full-time news networks. Then she remembered what was happening.

She proceeded to the door that led into the Tank.

Flanking it was a pair of people who were doing nothing—just standing there. Odd.

She noticed that both of them had unfamiliar devices slung from their belts.

She realized that they were Tasers.

Before she could fully adjust to that, one of them—she recognized him now as Tom Van Meter, an engineer and sort of a jock—nodded politely and opened the door for her.

The Tank was a quarter the size of the Farm, just a medium-sized conference room with, at the moment, six people seated around the table working on tablets or laptops. At its far end was the door leading to Markus's office. This was ajar. Ivy went through it, and for the first time since coming to Izzy three years earlier, she felt ill at ease doing so, as if someone might jump out and Tase her. But Markus was sitting there talking to Doob.

"Have you been watching Parambulator?" Markus asked her.

"Yes. After we made that course change, a few minutes ago."

"The performance of the cloud was not everything we could have hoped for."

"There were some stragglers."

"Still are," Doob said, and drew her attention to a projection screen on the wall.

"It looked like they were all new arrivals," Ivy said. "Cargo modules, passenger carriers from the Splurge. I'm assuming they haven't logged on to the cloud yet, are not with the program."

"That is all true but it is dangerous nonetheless," Markus said.

"Of course it is."

"It is distracting me."

"I'll take care of it."

"As far as bolides are concerned, the systems are working okay and Doob is keeping an eye out for anomalies. But I need to delegate to you, Ivy, this problem of the stragglers."

"Consider it done."

"We will destroy them if we have to."

"How would you even do that, Markus? We don't have photon torpedoes."

"We have a module full of freeze-dried dead people," Markus reminded her, "that we need to jettison anyway. And I would be happy to jettison it in the direction of any straggler that is threatening the Cloud Ark."

"I will keep that in mind," Ivy said, "as a bargaining chip."

Luisa entered, looking a little wild, her face wet with tears.

"Luisa?" Markus said politely. "Did you find out what was going on in the Vu-Vu Pod?"

"A few people getting very emotional," Luisa said, "as you would expect. Nothing dangerous. Whoever called that in as a disturbance was being a little paranoid."

"Thank you for investigating it."

"Speaking of which—you have armed guards posted outside the door to the Tank!"

"I will speak briefly to that, because I am busy," Markus said. "My feelings about it are basically the same as yours. But I am not here to express my personal feelings but to carry out certain operations to the best of my ability. I didn't want to be the king of the universe. Nevertheless, now I am. Everything I have ever seen in the history of human civilization, disagreeable as it might seem, says that someone in my position needs to have security."

Luisa's face suggested that she could make all kinds of objections to that. But she got the better of it, and just let out a sigh. "We will talk about it later," she said.

"Good."

"Do you know what is happening down there?"

"I can guess what is happening. It is none of my concern."

"Understood. But I think that the king of the universe needs to make an announcement pretty soon."

"I have one prepared," Markus said.

"Oh, yes, of course you would have one prepared. When were you thinking of delivering it? Because there are a lot of people who need to be calmed down."

"Is one of those people you, Luisa?" Markus asked the question clinically, but not unkindly.

Luisa drew herself up. Ivy braced herself for a sharp reaction, but then a change came over Luisa's face as she saw that Markus was merely asking for information. Not being snide.

"Yes," she answered. "A few minutes ago, Manhattan was struck by a hundred-foot wall of water. I presume that the same is true of most of the East Coast. I was listening to the service from St. Patrick's Cathedral when it went off the air."

Markus nodded and changed the display on the projection screen to a live view of Earth.

Ivy was shocked by how far the fire had spread during the few minutes she'd been in here.

She pulled her phone out of her pocket and discovered a series of messages from Cal, sent during the last several minutes.

Hey

You busy?

OK I guess you got pulled away

In case we get cut off I love you

Will look for a mermaid like you said but no substitute 4 u

Lost contact with Norfolk. No chain above me

Holy crap it is getting hot

Diving

Bye

And the last message in the series was a photograph snapped on his cell phone's camera. It took Ivy a minute of panning and zooming to figure out what she was seeing. Cal had taken the photo while standing in the conning tower of his boat, looking straight up the ladder at the open hatch above him. This provided a tunnel-vision view of a disk of sky.

The sky was on fire.

In his other hand he was holding up his engagement ring—a

simple band of polished titanium. He was holding it between his thumb and index finger, shooting the picture through the ring, making it concentric with the disk of the burning sky.

She looked up. Someone had spoken her name.

"Mine just faded away," Doob told her.

"I beg your pardon, Dr. Harris?" Ivy said, the Morg's manners triumphing over all circumstances.

"I had been gearing up for these final goodbyes with Amelia, with my kids," Doob said. He spoke quietly, without marked emotion, as if relating a mildly surprising anecdote. "But, you know, the communications just broke down slowly over a couple of days, and there was never really a goodbye."

"Very well," Markus said, "I will make the announcement."

HOT ENOUGH TO BAKE TATERS ON HOOD OF THIS TRUCK

GO INSIDE DAD

NOT KIDDING ABOUT THERMAL EFFECTS. PAINT BUBBLING

I AM NOT KIDDING EITHER YOU HAVE TO GET INSIDE

GOT A SPACE BLANKET TO PROTECT ME WHEN I MAKE A RUN FOR IT

THEN FOR GODS SAKE USE IT DAD

AH BUT THEN I CAN'T CHEW THE RAG WITH YOU ANY LONGER DINAH

WHAT IF YOUR GAS TANK EXPLODES

HA HA WE DRAINED IT FOR GENERATOR FUEL. WAY AHEAD OF YOU KID

GOD U R A SMARTASS

Dinah was keying this in, thankful that Morse code still worked when your vision was blurred by tears and your voice choked by sobs, when a voice came out of a speaker. It was Markus's voice: "This is Markus Leuker."

"I know who you are," she answered. But then she understood that Markus was speaking on the all-Ark PA system, which supposedly reached into every corner of Izzy as well as to all of the arklets. They had tested it a few times with prerecorded messages, but never actually used it. Markus considered the thing a relic of the twentieth century, and detested it; communications ought to be targeted, busy people ought not to be interrupted by disembodied voices barking from speakers.

"The Cloud Ark Constitution is now in effect."

Dinah drew breath, knowing what this meant. Markus spelled it out anyway. "This means that all nation-states of Earth, and their governments and constitutions, no longer exist. Their military and civilian chains of command are no more. Oaths you may have taken to them, allegiances you may have held, loyalties you may have felt, citizenships you may have had are now and forever dissolved. The rights granted you by the Cloud Ark Constitution, no more and no less, are your rights. The laws and responsibilities of the Cloud Ark Constitution now bind you. You are citizens of a new nation now, the only nation. Long may it endure."

She keyed:

MARKUS IS CALLING IT

WHO SAID HE WAS BOSS?

Rufus's transmission was getting scratchy. Dinah wiped her eyes and looked out her window to see Earth encircled by a belt of fire. The trails of the incoming meteorites, once a pattern of bright scratches in the air, had merged into a blinding continuum of superheated air that had set fire to anything on the surface capable of burning. Since more of the rocks were coming in around the equator, the belt of radiance and fire was brightest there; but north and south of it, long swaths of the surface were aflame, and the belt was widening to envelop the high latitudes of Canada and South America.

She transmitted:

ABOUT TO LOSE YOU, TELL BOB AND ED AND GT AND REX I LOVE THEM. AND BEV.

ALREADY DID BUT WILL AGAIN. CHRIST IT IS HOT

GET INSIDE DAD

DONT WORRY I AM RIGHT BY THE DOOR. CAN HEAR THEM ALL SINGING BREAD OF HEAVEN.

THEN GO JOIN THE CHORUS DAD

OKAY BOB AND ED ARE COMING OUT TO GRAB ME. BYE HONEY DO US PROUD QRT

QRT QRT QRT QRT

She wasn't sure how many times she keyed that in.

She pulled herself out of her sobs, later, by imagining what had happened: her brothers, Bob and Ed, dressed in silver fireman suits, rushing out of the mine's entrance to haul Dad out of the old pickup truck, wrapping him in the space blanket to keep him from being broiled by the sky, and dragging him inside. An inch-thick steel plate being slammed across the doorway, the welders going to work laying down fat fillets made to last five thousand years. Once that was done, the heavy machinery fired up, shoving tons of rock and gravel up against the steel plate to bolster it against any shock waves powerful enough to punch it out of its frame.

Then silence, save maybe for the distant thuds of meteorite strikes, and sitting around the table to say grace and tuck into the first of fifteen thousand or so meals that the MacQuaries and their descendants would have to prepare and eat if they were ever to escape from that tomb. They had five hundred people down there, and, at least on paper, enough food-growing capacity to keep that many alive. Exactly how you made that a sustainable proposition wasn't clear to Dinah; she hadn't bothered Rufus for every last little detail of his plan.

Markus's announcement was continuing. He was telling everyone what they already knew, which was that Earth was over, and that the great dying that they had been expecting for the last two years was now in the past. Everyone knew it, but someone had to say it.

He asked for 704 seconds of silence: one second for each of the days that had passed since Zero. About twelve minutes. All nonessential duties would be suspended during that time, and it would be the sole responsibility of the survivors to think, and remember, and mourn. After that, they must put Earth in the past, as a thing that had once been, and apply their minds to what was now.

Drawn up into a fetal position, Dinah hovered alone in the middle of her shop, listening to weird squeals and hisses coming out of her radio's speaker. Alone of all the people in the Cloud Ark, she knew that her family was still alive, and might go on being alive for a long time. It was not clear to her whether this was better or worse than simply knowing that they were dead. All she had to go on was

DO US PROUD, her father's final transmission. Morse code didn't leave a paper trail, or an email thread on the screen of your tablet. She would never be able to scroll back and reread the exchange she'd just had with Rufus. She hoped she'd said the right things and that he'd remember it well, and that he would tell the others about it at dinner this evening.

She tried then to mourn for all the others who had died, but it was too big. Emotionally, it was little different from reading about a great war that had happened a hundred years ago. Which maybe was Markus's whole point. Even though the dying was still going on, they had to force themselves to think about it like the Irish potato famine, or like what had happened to the peoples of the New World when Columbus had arrived and infected them with a slew of deadly diseases. Regret, even horror were appropriate. But detachment was necessary. They all had 704 seconds in which to effect that detachment.

So Dinah thought about what exactly would be entailed in doing Rufus MacQuarie proud. There was a simple answer, which had to do with doing the right thing, being honorable, upholding a few rough-and-ready ethical standards. A sort of frontier code of conduct. All of which was easy to understand if not always quite so easy to live up to. But Rufus was not a cowboy, and he certainly wasn't a preacher. He was a miner: a delver, a demolisher, a builder, a businessman. If he lived by a simple code of ethics, it was not an end in itself, but a way to get something done without selling his soul or destroying his reputation. It was a tool to be wielded like a shovel or a stick of dynamite. Tools were for building things; and pride was something you could feel after the fact, when you stood back, looked at what you had built, and passed it on to your children. Dinah could spend the rest of her life living by her word, giving everyone a fair shake, and all of that. Rufus would no doubt approve of all those things. But it was not the charge he had given her. He had told her, though not in so many words, to get busy building a future.

"Are you about finished?"

She turned her head to see Ivy hanging in the SCRUM, looking at Dinah through the hatch.

"We're only, like, two hundred seconds into the—"

"Markus said I could skip it. He sent me on a mission. I need your help," Ivy said.

"Bitch."

"Slut."

"Shall we?"

"REMEMBER WHEN THE INTERNET WAS NEW, AND SOME PEOPLE IN your life just didn't get it?" Ivy asked. She was preceding Dinah through the seemingly endless maze of docked modules and hamster tubes, headed toward the periphery of Izzy.

"People in my world got it pretty fast. You don't know many miners, do you?"

"Not in my world. We had these throwbacks who would do stuff like printing their emails out on paper to read them, or asking you for your goddamn fax number two decades after you had thrown away your fax machine."

They were hurtling through an otherwise perfectly silent space station, still only about five minutes into the twelve minutes of silence. Faces in open hatches would turn to look at them in shock, then recognize them and go back to mourning, praying, meditating, or whatever it was that they were doing.

Dinah understood that this was terribly important but was secretly pleased that Ivy had given her dispensation to get to work.

"How does that apply to—"

"The system works—Parambulator and all of that—as long as every ship in the Cloud Ark is playing by those rules. Logged on to the system, communicating with the agreed-on protocols, obeying the dictates of the swarm. If even one is just hanging out and doing its own thing, well, it might as well be a meteoroid, in terms of its destructive potential."

"We've got one of those?"

"A few of them. But one in particular that is causing havoc."

"Any collisions yet, or—"

"No, but every time it draws near it triggers an explosion of red in Parambulator and a hundred arklets have to burn fuel to alter their courses. It's like the whole Cloud Ark is turning somersaults around the movements of this one ship."

"What is it?"

"Optically it's an X-37."

"Fits," Dinah said.

"Yeah," Ivy said.

Translation: someone had looked at the craft through a telescope and thought it looked like a Boeing X-37 Orbital Test Vehicle, which resembled a miniature Space Shuttle. It was *so* miniature, in fact, that it couldn't carry any crew; it had a cargo bay that accounted for most of its fuselage. It had been developed by DARPA in the late 1990s and early 2000s when it had become obvious that the Space Shuttle was going to be phased out and they needed a small, easily launched vehicle that could go up and, by remote control, perform maintenance tasks on the United States' fleet of military satellites. Since then it had come in for very little actual use, but when it was used, it was for black-budget spook stuff that Dinah and Ivy wouldn't know about. It was a footnote in history, obsolescent, not designed for the requirements of the Cloud Ark. It had probably been launched into orbit by some trigger-happy launch crew that just wanted to send up everything they could. With a sufficient amount of sifting through old emails they might be able to find some record of who had launched it, and what, if any, cargo was aboard; but for now it was easier to just go and look at the damned thing. Nearly all the engineering that had gone into it had been devoted to the problem of reentry. Most of its proudest features were therefore useless to them.

Approaching the end of a side-stack, they were able to see through the round orifice of a port into the vehicle docked to its far side: a Flivver, or Flexible Light Intracloud Vehicle. These had begun showing up a few months ago; they were the jeeps of the Cloud Ark, the small utility vehicles used to move people and valuable stuff from one arklet to another, or between an arklet and Izzy. Because they didn't have to operate in the atmosphere, they had the same general utilitarian look as the arklets. But the pressure hull was smaller in diameter, and instead of an inflatable outer hull the Flivver had more practical stuff: two different styles of docking ports, an airlock big enough to accommodate a human in an Orlan, a robot arm, lights, thrusters. At Dinah's suggestion they had studded the pressure hull with attachment points that a Grabb could latch on to; this made it possible for each Flivver to carry its own complement of Grabbs, Siwis, Buckies, and Nats, which swarmed all over it like crabs, remoras, and sea lice. Instead of being limited by the hard-engineered capabilities of the robot arm, the Flivver was constrained only by the imagination and ingenuity of the programmer inside, telling the robots what to do.

The silvery burr of Tekla's head poked out in front of them; apparently she'd been dispatched to assist with closing the hatch and undocking the Flivver. She'd been waiting in the adjacent DC, or docking compartment, which was just a small side module tacked on to serve as an airlock and provide a little extra space for personnel in cases like this. She drew her head back in to make space as Ivy and then Dinah cruised by her. As soon as those two were inside the Flivver, Tekla emerged and exchanged a nod with Ivy.

"Lamprey is in airlock and is functioning," Tekla said, and closed the hatch. Dinah had some ambivalent feelings about Tekla, but there was no one she'd rather work with in a case like this. She was all business; she got the job done without useless conversation or touch-feely stuff. Dinah closed the Flivver's hatch and began going through the undocking sequence while Ivy, strapped into the vehicle's pilot seat, ran down the preexcursion checklist. Befitting a craft that had been designed in a hurry to be Flexible and Light, this wasn't that lengthy, and so Flivver 3—one of a fleet of eight—was under way before Markus's 704 seconds of silence had quite expired. Dinah strapped into a jump seat beside Ivy's. The Flivver's front end dome consisted largely of windows, bolstered by a sturdy web of curved aluminum struts, so from behind Ivy looked like a bombardier seated in the glass nose of a World War II bomber. She touched the controls and made the craft rotate in a way that caused Earth to pass beneath them, and then the resemblance became stronger. Dinah was reminded of a painting Rufus had shown her, depicting a bomber flying over a burning city, red light flooding into the plane from below. The same effect held now, save that the firestorm covered most of the surface of the Earth.

"I can feel the warmth on my face," Ivy said.

Dinah couldn't think of anything useful to say to that. During their passage from her shop to the Flivver she had forgotten about the fact that the Earth was burning, and she didn't enjoy being reminded of it. Instead she tried to focus on the red light emanating coolly from the screen of her tablet, which was running Parambulator. Flivver 3 had been picked up on the swarm's collective sensorium and identified as a bogey that might potentially collide with as many as a hundred different arklets if it stayed on its current course. Rather than controlling its thrusters directly, which would lead at best to confusion and at worse to a chain-reaction disaster, Ivy was negotiating a solution with the rest of the Cloud Ark, telling it where she wanted to go and finding a way of getting there that would minimize the amount of maneuvering demanded of all the others.

It was not a speedy way of getting around, and indeed ran at right angles to the fighter-jockey ethos of many of the ex-military types who had come up here in the astronaut and cosmonaut corps. But as they got farther away from Izzy they were able to move into orbits that caused minimal consternation to the rest of the cloud, and move in a more direct way to rendezvous with the wayward X-37.

This had been placed, by whoever the hell had launched it, in an orbit with the same period and plane as the Cloud Ark, but with somewhat greater eccentricity. The orbit of Izzy, and hence of the Cloud Ark, was almost perfectly circular. The X-37's was more oval, meaning that about half of the time it was "beneath" the Cloud Ark and the rest of the time it was "above," but twice during each ninety-three-minute orbit it crossed through, each time touching off the havoc that was wasting so much propellant and causing so much annoyance to Markus. Right now it was "above" and due to cross over in another twenty minutes.

"Any bolides we need to worry about before I focus on this?" Ivy asked her.

"Nothing in particular," Dinah said, meaning that there was nothing so big as to force the entire Cloud Ark to make a course change.

"Let's make this fast then," Ivy said, and went over to manual control. For they were now far enough away from the Cloud Ark that she could execute solo maneuvers without making Parambulator screens turn solid red. "Can you scope it?"

Dinah spent a minute refamiliarizing herself with the user interface for the optical telescope mounted to the Flivver's nose; this was an electronic eyeball about the size of an orange. The controls were intuitive, but getting it to aim at a particular bogey took a bit of doing. Soon enough, though, she was able to see something white and bright. She locked on to it and zoomed in.

From longer zoom it was clearly a winged craft with a black nose, like the Shuttle of old, but it seemed to have taken on added parts. Zooming in further she was able to see that the cargo bay doors that constituted most of the X-37's "back" had been opened at some point after it had reached orbit. Its payload had then been lifted out of the bay using the built-in robotic arm, which was still holding it, frozen in position. The payload was almost as big as the X-37 itself; it was yet another dome-ended cylinder. But unlike a Flivver or an arklet, it lacked thrusters or any sort of visible power source. It was just a burnished aluminum capsule, gleaming white on one side from sunshine, red below where it reflected the planetary firestorm.

Ivy was looking at it too, dividing her attention between the Flivver's status displays and the window running this optical feed. "Can you get more detail on the forward end? There's a fitting there that might be a—"

"Yeah," Dinah said, zooming in and panning to center it. "That's a docking port all right."

"Well, I guess we're being invited to dock with it," Ivy said.

"It's weird. I don't like it."

"I agree," Ivy said, "but we can't come back later. That thing is tiny. Less than four feet in diameter. If there's humans in there, they are running out of stuff to breathe."

"Why would they send a human up in something like that?"

"It's some plan that went awry. An email didn't get answered, a transmission got garbled, now these people are marooned and probably waiting to die." Ivy spoke brusquely, a little irked by Dinah's questions.

Dinah heard thrusters pop and felt them nudging her around as Ivy maneuvered. She knew better than to distract her friend when her brain had gone into orbital mechanics mode. She unbuckled herself from the jump seat and moved to the docking port on the Flivver's "top" surface, steadying herself by reaching out to grab the adjacent handles whenever Ivy effected a little course adjustment.

Within a few minutes Ivy had matched orbits, maneuvered the Flivver into the right attitude, and driven it straight onto the capsule's docking port.

"Got a positive mate," Dinah remarked. She activated a valve that flooded the little space between the Flivver's hatch and the capsule's with air. "Here goes nothing."

She opened the Flivver's hatch. She was now looking at the outside of the capsule's hatch, which, until a few seconds earlier, had been exposed to space.

A strange detail: taped to the aluminum hatch was an ordinary sheet of 8½ x 11 inch North American printer paper. On this had been printed a color image: a yellow ring encircling a blue disk lined with stars. Spread-eagled on its center, an eagle with a red-and-white-striped shield. The printer that had spat this thing out had been low on cyan ink and so the image was strangely banded and discolored. Exposure to space hadn't done it any favors either.

Even though the United States had only ceased to exist a few minutes earlier—declared extinct by Markus under the authority granted him by the Cloud Ark Constitution—this image already seemed as old and quaint to Dinah as a pilgrim or a musketeer.

She heard a mechanism activating on the other side of it.

"It's aliiiive!" she called. Then, in spite of this effort at jocularity, she held her breath.

The hatch swung open to reveal a haggard, space-bloated, sickly green face, hair floating around it in disarray. But the eyes in that face were as cold and hard as ever, and they were fixed on Dinah.

"Dinah," the woman said. It was her voice, more than her face, that Dinah recognized. "Even in these tragic circumstances, what a relief to see a familiar face."

"Madam Pres—" Dinah began. Then she caught herself. "Julia."

Julia Bliss Flaherty looked as if she didn't appreciate one bit being addressed that way.

Ivy was using the thrusters quite a bit. Now that the Flivver, the capsule, and the X-37 were all joined together mechanically into a single object, it was possible—though awkward—to maneuver them into sync with the Cloud Ark and clean up all of that Parambulator red. There was some lurching. Julia was getting knocked around a little, learning she had to keep a grip on those handles. Random stuff, including some filled barf bags and a large number of what looked like red marbles, were careering around inside her tiny capsule. Looking through it during a moment when Julia had been flung to one side, Dinah saw a man floating in the far end of the capsule. He was bloody, and he was kind of floppy too. He was dressed in the remains of a navy-blue suit. He was not the ex–First Gentleman.

"I'm sorry for your loss," Dinah said.

"Who the hell is that?" Ivy was shouting. "Markus wants to know if we have survivors."

"My loss?" Julia asked.

"Your husband," Dinah said.

"He took the pill," Julia announced, "in the limo."

"Oh my god."

"I'll need your help getting Mr. Starling squared away. He's too big for me to move."

"No, he isn't," Dinah said.

"I beg your pardon?" Julia said sharply.

"You're in zero gee," Dinah pointed out. "So he's not too big for you to move. But I can still help you if you want."

"If you would be so kind," Julia said. She got a hand over the rim of the hatch while reaching out with the other for a shoulder bag, and looked expectantly at Dinah, who was still blocking her path.

Dinah looked at the back of Ivy's head. "Julia Bliss Flaherty requests permission to come aboard."

Julia let out a hiss of exasperation.

"Granted," Ivy said.

"One casualty on the way too," Dinah said, and cleared out of Julia's way.

Julia launched herself through the hatch too hard, flew across the Flivver, and slammed into the far side of it elbow and shoulder first. "Augh!" she cried. But Dinah didn't think she was hurt, and so she pushed through into the capsule. One of those red marbles was drifting toward her face and she reached out with a hand to brush it away before realizing that it was blood.

Pete Starling was suffering from a number of lacerations, as if he'd been in a stick fight or a car crash. He was groggy, and gagging on blood—probably from a broken nose—which he would cough out explosively when it got in the way of his breathing. Dinah grasped the lapel of his jacket, trying to find a usable handhold. When she pulled on it, the front of the coat came away from Starling's chest for a moment, revealing an empty shoulder holster.

No matter now. She planted her feet, put her back into it, and got him stretched out in the middle of the capsule, head aimed toward the docking port, drifting slowly in that direction. She was looking to Julia to reach through and pull her companion through the hole. But Julia, banged up from her first attempt to move, was still flailing around, learning the basics of zero gee locomotion the hard way.

Dinah was at the back of the capsule, staring at Pete's feet, which were kicking weakly. One of his feet was stocking clad; the other still wore an expensive-looking leather shoe. She grabbed a foot with each hand and tried to push him toward the docking port, but he reacted against it. He had no idea what was going on, didn't understand that he was in space, didn't like having his feet grabbed. She moved forward, got her waist between his knees, hugged him around the thighs, squeezing his legs together to either side of her body, and tried to get him re-aimed toward the port.

She heard a sharp pop and felt warm wet stuff all over her arms. More of it had splashed up her throat, all the way to the point of her chin. She smelled shit and heard a loud hissing noise. Pete Starling jerked once and then went limp.

She looked up toward the source of the hiss and saw starlight through a jagged hole in the skin of the capsule. The hole was about the size of a man's thumb. Triangles of metal were bent back away from it.

On second thought, the hissing was coming from two places at once. Another hole had been punched in the other side of the capsule. Pete Starling's body was between the two holes. The middle of his torso was just a rib-lined crater. Blood was hurtling out of it and accelerating through both holes.

Her ears had popped several times already.

She looked down the length of the capsule at Julia, who had finally gotten herself properly oriented and was looking into the hatch, wild eyed, utterly confused.

"Julia," Dinah said, "we've been struck by a small bolide. We're losing air, but not that fast. Pete's dead. He's in my way. If you could reach through and grab him by the collar and pull him toward you—"

The conversation, and her view of Julia's face, was cut off by the Flivver's hatch swinging shut.

ANY CURVE YOU COULD MAKE BY SLICING A CONE WITH A PLANE—A circle, an ellipse, a parabola, or a hyperbola—could be the shape of an orbit. For practical purposes, though, all orbits were ellipses. And most of the naturally occurring orbits in the solar system—those of the planets around the sun, or of moons around planets—were ellipses so round as to be indistinguishable, by the naked eye, from circles. This was not because nature especially favored circles. It was because highly elongated elliptical orbits tended not to last for very long. As a body in a highly eccentric orbit went rocketing in toward the central body and executed a hairpin turn at the periapsis—the point of closest approach—it was subject to tidal forces that could break it up. It might strike the central body's atmosphere or, in the case of heliocentric orbits, come too close to the sun's heat and suffer thermal damage. If it survived the plunge through periapsis, it would fly out on a long trajectory that would take it across the orbits of other bodies. After rounding the turn at apoapsis—the point of maximum distance—it would cycle back across the same set of orbits on its way back in toward the center. The solar system was sparse, and so the odds that it would strike, or come close to, any given planet or asteroid on any given circuit were small. But over astronomical spans of time, the likelihood of a close encounter or a collision was high. Collision would, of course, result in a meteorite strike on the planet and the destruction of the formerly orbiting body. A mere close encounter would perturb the body's orbit into a new and different ellipse, or possibly into a hyperbola, which would eject it from the solar system altogether. The sun still maintained a stable of comets and asteroids in highly eccentric orbits, but their number dwindled over time, and they were rare events to astronomers. In its early aeons the solar system had been a much more chaotic place, with a wider range of orbits, but the processes mentioned had gradually swept it clean and, by a kind of natural selection, produced a system in which nearly everything was moving in an almost circular orbit.

What was true of the solar system as a whole had also been true of the Earth-moon system. The moon had circled the Earth in a nearly circular orbit. From time to time, a wandering stone from deep space would blunder in through a libration point and get captured into a geocentric orbit, but sooner or later it would hit the moon, hit the Earth, or be ejected by a close encounter with one of those bodies. Thus had the moon swept Earth's skies for billions of years and protected it from most big meteor strikes, making it a suitable place for the development of complex ecosystems and civilizations.

All the rocks that made up the White Sky had once shared the moon's orbit, and most of them, for the time being, remained at a safe distance of about four hundred thousand kilometers. Their orbits, for now, were of low eccentricity, meaning that they were nearly circular. However, the vast number of chaotic interactions within the White Sky had spawned a diversity of orbits. Some of those orbits were highly eccentric, meaning that their apogees might be far away, but their perigees were close to the Earth: close enough to get caught up in its atmosphere or to strike it directly. Any rock whose orbit was eccentric enough to come near the Earth could also come near Izzy. In general, rocks in such orbits were moving at about eleven thousand meters per second when they were that close to Earth. A bolide the size of a peppercorn, moving at that velocity, would have the same kinetic energy as a high-powered rifle bullet.

Of course, high-powered bullets were designed to strike things with great force and do damage in a predictable way, while moon rocks weren't designed at all. So the results of collisions could be unpredictable.

What had probably happened in this case was that a rock closer in size to a chickpea, and packing the energy of several rifle bullets, had punched through the wall of the capsule but, in so doing, fractured into several pieces that had sprayed outward across the capsule's volume in a narrow cone, striking Pete Starling's body something like a shotgun blast but with much more total kinetic energy. Most of that energy had gone into his flesh and caused him to basically explode. The largest single piece of the original rock had kept going through his body, or perhaps missed him entirely, and punched its way out through the opposite side of the capsule.

If the rock had passed a couple of meters to either side, it would have missed them entirely and they wouldn't even have known it was there. In the Earth's atmosphere, of course, it would have been a different story. The rock would have dissolved in a bright streak, turning most of its kinetic energy into heat. The air in its immediate vicinity would have gotten warmer for a bit. Had it happened at night, keen observers might have seen a streak of light. When the same thing happened on a large scale, all over the Earth, the air became so hot that it glowed, as it was doing now.

In any case Dinah now found herself locked into a capsule, lit only by a few strips of white LEDs that were darkened by blood spatter, as the air leaked out of it. She had, of course, been drilling for events such as this one for a significant part of her life. One of the first things they taught you was that the air wasn't really leaking out as quickly as you thought. Only so much air could get through a small hole. Nevertheless, plugging those holes was life-or-death. So Dinah's first move, once she had recovered from surprise, was to shove Pete Starling's remains up toward the larger of the two holes: the one through which the bolide had entered. With a wet sucking sound his bloody flesh sealed that hole. Her ears now enabled her to find the smaller exit hole, which was about the size of her pinkie. She slapped her bloody hand over it. The hiss stopped and she immediately felt a space hickey beginning to form where the Big Hoover was trying to pull her flesh out into the void. It hurt, but not that badly. She listened for a few moments until she was satisfied that there were no other hissing noises—no other leaks.

A bloody bandage floated past. She snatched it out of the air, peeled her hand away from the hole, and stuffed it in there. Some of it got sucked out into space, but then it formed into a wad that moved no further. The hole was still hissing, though, so she grabbed an empty plastic bag and shaped that over the irregular mound of wet gauze. The vacuum sucked it inward and created a nearly airtight seal.

A softer hiss, more of a whooshing noise, emanated from the "back" of the capsule. Dinah's ears felt a change in pressure, but they didn't pop—suggesting that the pressure had just *increased*. She knew nothing about this capsule, but she did know how simple life support systems worked, and she knew that they would likely contain a store of compressed oxygen that would be bled in to compensate for what was being turned into CO_2 in the occupants' bodies and absorbed by the scrubbers. The mechanism was probably trying to compensate for the air that had just been voided into space, bringing the pressure back up to normal.

If that were the case, then it should now be possible to open the hatch on the Flivver. Dinah floated toward it, reached through the capsule's open hatch, and rapped on the metal, leaving bloody knuckle prints.

Nothing happened for a moment, and so she rapped out SOS: three dots, three dashes, three dots.

The hatch opened to reveal Ivy's face. "My. Goodness. Gracious," she said.

"Thanks, sister," Dinah said, and vaulted through as Ivy got out of the way—partly just to be accommodating but largely, Dinah assumed, to avoid getting smeared with the bodily fluids of Julia's late science advisor. Julia herself was strapped into one of the jump seats, buckled over into a fetal position suffering from the dry heaves, and keeping an eye on Dinah out of the corner of her eye.

Welcome to space! was on the tip of Dinah's tongue, but she managed to stifle it.

"While you were, uh, busy, we flew through the Cloud Ark again. We have about forty-five minutes now on its nadir side," Ivy said.

"Should be enough," Dinah said. She strapped herself into the other jump seat, wiped her hands on her thighs, and pulled her laptop close. Holding it down with the heels of her hands so it wouldn't float away, she brought up the set of interface windows that she used to communicate with robots. Over the course of a few seconds, the laptop established communication with all the robots that were within range—which is to say, that were riding along on the outside of this Flivver.

Meanwhile she pulled down a folding arm with a mitten-like contraption on its end. This was the interface for the Flivver's external robot arm.

"Pop the airlock for me, sweetie?" she said.

"Already done, hon," Ivy returned.

In her peripheral vision she could see Julia's eyes swiveling back and forth, reacting to this exchange. She tried to ignore Julia in spite of—perhaps because of—her weird talent for demanding attention, and focused on the video feed from the camera on the end of the robot arm.

The airlock's round orifice grew larger as she reached toward it, revealing the device Tekla had stashed inside.

The Lamprey was a box with a blinking light on it. On the side facing the airlock door it sported a lug, or handle. With the hand on the robot arm, Dinah was able to grapple this easily and pull the device out into the light.

"Any reason not to just 'biner it onto the X-37's arm?" she asked.

"Can't think of any."

"What is it you're doing?" Julia asked.

"Deorbiting that piece of space junk before it kills someone."

"That piece of space junk happens to be carrying the earthly remains of a brave man who gave his life in the name of—"

Dinah said, "Ivy, you want to take this or should I?"

"I'll do it. You're busy," Ivy said. Dinah could hear her twisting around in the pilot's seat to look at Julia. She spoke as follows: "Julia. Shut up. If you say another fucking word I'll stave your fucking head in and put your corpse out the airlock. Nothing about this is acceptable. Starting with the fact that you are flapping your gums, posing a distraction to Dinah while she is carrying out a difficult mission-critical operation to protect the Cloud Ark. You just attempted to countermand a direct order from Markus, who is in charge of everything here under the PSAPS clause of the Cloud Ark Constitution. You are up here illegally. The Crater Lake Accord specifically barred the sending of national leaders to the Cloud Ark. You have violated that commitment and found a way to be launched up here anyhow, and judging from the looks of it there was no end of dirty dealing along the way. Your vehicle approached the Cloud Ark in a manner incompatible with our safety and security procedures, endangering the lives of everyone up here, and forcing arklets and Izzy itself to expend priceless and irreplaceable fuel to perform evasive maneuvers.

We were sent here on an emergency basis, placing ourselves in harm's way and expending more scarce resources to clean up the mess that you created by your cowardly and dishonorable act. For all of these reasons I am commanding you, by my authority as the commander of this vessel, to remain silent until we have docked safely at Izzy."

"Very well," Julia said.

Dinah looked up from her work to see Ivy and Julia glaring at each other.

"I'm sorry," Julia said.

"You really are asking for it," Dinah told her. And then she went back to work.

She had already accomplished much during Ivy's soliloquy. The task at hand was to somehow attach the Lamprey to the X-37. The connection didn't have to look good but it did have to be solid. Back in the days when every maneuver had been planned years in advance by NASA, this would have been a several-hours-long operation making use of custom-designed hardware. But lately the people of the Cloud Ark had been obliged to get good at lassoing random pieces of floating space junk, and so she ended up using a more highly evolved version of the trick that Rhys had come up with for reining in Tekla's Luk. On that occasion, Dinah had fashioned a whip by chaining Siwis together. It had worked, but it was much heavier and more complicated than it needed to be. After the completion of T3 had left Rhys with some free time on his hands, he had begun tinkering with surplus Nats. Being old and obsolete, these were big, clunky, slow, and stupid compared to the new models—which was fine for Rhys's purposes. He had turned them into a new kind of robot that he dubbed the Flynk, for flying link, and taught them to be really good at forming themselves up into chains and then doing the sorts of maneuvers in space that his great-great-great-great-uncle John, and Herr Professor Kucharski of Berlin, could only have dreamed about. There was much room for creativity here, but he had focused most of his efforts on problems that needed to be solved all the time.

Such as precisely the one Dinah needed to solve right now. The robot arm of the X-37 was sticking awkwardly out into space, an obvious target for grappling. A chain with a free end would whip around it easily, just as Rhys had once ensnared Dinah's index finger with his necklace. All Dinah needed was a suitable chain. She happened to have one: a necklace of third-generation Flynks spiraled around the Flivver's hull, ready for use. One end of it was already connected to the Lamprey. By invoking some computer code she was able to set the rest of it into motion, unwinding itself from around the Flivver and snaking out into free space, forming a U-shaped bend, or *Knickstelle,* that was aimed at the X-37's robot arm.

"Ready to undock now," she said.

Ivy had moved back to the port through which their guest had entered. "Undocking," she said, and began running through the checklist that undocked the Flivver from the X-37.

Dinah meanwhile moved up to the pilot's console and punched in a programmed series of thruster burns. As soon as Ivy confirmed separation, Dinah executed the program, effecting a small delta vee that made them back away from the X-37. The *Knickstelle* went into motion, as if the chain were passing around an invisible pulley, and began to propagate away from the Flivver and toward the X-37. Presently the chain's end whipped around the robot arm and spiraled about it several times before grapplers on the Flynks found each other and engaged, lashing the chain into place for good.

Dinah released the Lamprey from the grip of the Flivver's robot arm. The Flynk chain, still following a canned program, pulled the Lamprey in and made it fast to the X-37. The Flynk chain, the X-37, and the Lamprey were now a single object, and would remain thus until they were destroyed.

Dinah brought up the interface that controlled the Lamprey. This was a fire-and-forget device, but someone did have to fire it. She spun a control wheel that adjusted the box's attitude, aiming its business end in a safe direction.

Getting things out of orbit was almost as complicated as launching them. Once a thing was in a legitimate, stable orbit, you couldn't just drop it toward the Earth. It would stay in orbit indefinitely unless you slowed it down. Slowing it down generally meant using thrusters, which meant spending fuel. The Lamprey was a simple alternative.

"We're undocked," Ivy announced, moving back forward to the pilot's chair. "Gonna nudge us free."

A couple of pops from the thrusters signaled that they were gaining some distance from the X-37. Ivy spun the Flivver around so that they could see the X-37 perhaps a hundred meters away, floating upside down above the burning Earth, the elbow of its arm projecting toward the nadir, the Lamprey strapped to it and blinking.

"Okay, the Lamprey is giving me all green thingies. I see no red thingies. So I am activating it in three . . . two . . . one . . . now." Dinah tapped the Deorbit button.

Most of the Lamprey—the entire box—jumped away, headed toward Earth, propelled by white plumes of solid rocket exhaust. After a couple of seconds the motors burned themselves out and the box continued to coast away, unreeling a wire behind it. This came to a stop a minute later, dangling half a kilometer below the X-37, and pulled taut by tidal force.

"We have positive current flow in the tether," Dinah reported. "So it's working." The wire, sweeping through Earth's magnetic field on its orbit, was picking up a weak electrical current, creating a force that would slow the X-37 down. The effect was slight, but within a few hours the X-37's orbit would decay to the point where it no longer posed a danger to the Cloud Ark, and in days or weeks it would descend into the atmosphere and be annihilated.

Twenty minutes remained before the Flivver's orbit would next cross Izzy's. But the physical separation was only a few tens of kilometers and they were still "on swarm," meaning that the Flivver's computer was talking to the Cloud Ark network and searching parameter space for the safest and most efficient way to reintegrate with it and to dock. That, plus the Lamprey's success in moving the X-37 out of the way, ought to have cleared up most of the red that had been maculating Parambulator displays at the time of their departure. But when Dinah and Ivy turned their attention back to those screens, they looked worse than before. It was not immediately clear why. Parambulator was a beautiful thing from the standpoint of mathematics and data visualization, but there were times when you just wanted to know what the hell was happening. You wanted a narrative.

A text came through on Ivy's phone. It was from Markus. She read it out loud. "Approach using visual observation and manual control," it said. "Warning: collision debris."

"Already?!" Dinah exclaimed. It wasn't a good start if they'd already suffered a bolide strike a couple of hours into the Hard Rain.

"It was fratricide," Ivy said, still reading. "Looks like an arklet got cornered."

Getting cornered was a problem that had arisen in simulations. The swarm as a whole would look for solutions that would prevent arklets from banging into each other with minimum expenditure of propellant. In a pinch, of course, it was okay to burn a lot of propellant to avoid a collision. But there were situations where a collision was going to happen no matter what, and there was nothing to do for it but choose the least damaging outcome. Getting cornered wasn't supposed to happen; everything about Parambulator was supposed to prevent it. But the number of possible scenarios was infinite and nothing was ever certain.

"A controlled collision," Ivy said, "no fatalities. But then some follow-on. Still being evaluated. There might be loose debris drifting around. That's why he wants me to fly it in manually."

"What kind of debris?" Dinah asked. "Hard stuff or—"

"Thermal protection, looks like," Ivy said. "So that's good."

Apparently one of the modules, or an arklet, had lost some of the layers of reflective foil and insulation that were used to shield it from the heat of the sun. The stuff was feather light and so probably didn't pose much of a threat to the Flivver. But it would look huge on radar and make Parambulator go crazy.

Ivy, in the pilot's chair, was monopolizing the only window. Dinah didn't like flying blind, so she pulled up the interface for the Flivver's eyeball camera.

Julia began to make a weird repetitive noise, a sort of wet, gurgling drone.

She was snoring.

"Long day for her, I guess," Ivy remarked.

"Yeah." Dinah had no precedents to tell her how she should feel toward the ex-president at a time like this. On the one hand, her behavior had been reprehensible. On the other, she had, within the last few hours, lost her husband, her daughter, her country, and her job.

With a few moments' panning around, Dinah was able to center Izzy in the camera's frame, then zoom in. Izzy was on the night side of the Earth just now. In normal times—or what used to be normal—it would have been dark, but now she was lit up from below by the red glow of the atmosphere, punctuated from time to time by bluish flashes, like lightning strikes, as large bolides plowed into the air three hundred kilometers below. Of course, Dinah had never seen Izzy so illuminated, and it took a bit of getting used to.

From a distance Izzy looked fine, but at higher magnification Dinah began to see visual noise that gradually resolved into drifting bits of debris—the shredded thermal protection that Ivy had mentioned.

Izzy had become unfathomably complicated in the last two years. Dinah rarely saw it from a distance, so she didn't have a strong sense of what was normal. But the more she zoomed in, the more certain she became that something weird had happened on the nadir side, near the junction of Zvezda and Zarya.

Complicated though she might be, Izzy was complicated in a way that was orderly, stiff, and stable. The one exception to that rule was Amalthea, but even that had become more regular as the Mining Colony's robots had reshaped it. What Dinah was zooming in on now was messy, and it was unstable: big expanses of thermal shielding material that had been torn loose and were now stirring randomly in the nearly imperceptible wind. At a glance, it did not look like a serious matter. "Serious" would have meant a hull breach, air erupting from a hole, perhaps dragging debris, or even human bodies, along with it.

"I'm thinking maybe a grazing impact at most," Dinah reported. "A near miss between an arklet, or something, and the nadir side of Zvezda. Destroyed some thermal shielding but caused little if any structural damage."

"They are reporting zero serious casualties," Ivy said. "Some bumps and sprains aboard an arklet. So maybe you're right."

"Maybe," Dinah said. For they had now drawn close enough that the camera could provide more detail. What had been exposed by the damage to the thermal shielding looked unfamiliar to her at first glance: a big T-shaped construct that jutted out to the nadir side of the Stack like a pair of handlebars. It was studded with many long neat rows of small, identical objects, gleaming in the occasional flashes from below.

Finally it all snapped into place in her head: she was looking at Moira's thing. The HGA, the Human Genetic Archive. Moira had given her a tour once, but that had been from the inside, or enclosed and pressurized part of it. Now Dinah was seeing the same thing from the outside. Until now, this had always been concealed from view by the thermal shielding. Once that was torn away, its internal structure could be seen: the rows and rows of hexagonal sample racks, each carrying its load of deep-frozen sperm, ova, or embryos, waiting in the near-absolute-zero cold and dark of space.

"How has Moira been doing with the dispersal project?" Dinah asked, forcing her voice to sound relaxed.

"Well . . . obviously, the schedule got compressed when we learned about the Eight Ball. Just like all of our other preparations did. But I guess my real answer is that I don't know," Ivy said.

Ymir

"... AND THEN THE FORCE OF THE VACUUM CAUGHT HOLD OF THE hatch, and to my horror I saw it slam shut right in front of me! I tried to pull it back open, but the suction was too strong. I cannot tell you, Markus, how helpless and guilty I felt when I realized that Dinah was trapped on the other side."

Markus's eyes went to Ivy. He had been listening to Julia for a long time, and needed a break.

Ivy threw her hands up. "I was trying to fly this ungainly contraption. I didn't really understand what was happening even when Julia tried to explain it to me."

"Yes," Markus said, "I can't believe you were able to fly that thing at all. People will be talking about it a hundred years from now."

Assuming people still exist, Dinah thought.

Ivy was just regarding Markus, blinking slowly, looking for signs that he was being sarcastic. He wasn't. The Markus bluntness worked both ways: he could blurt out astonishingly generous compliments as easily as he could cut and burn you with his words.

"It sure used up all of my brain," Ivy said.

They were sitting around the conference table in the Tank. Markus had not used the term "inquest" to describe this meeting, but that was clearly what it was. Or as close as they would ever get, in any case, to a formal determination of what had happened yesterday. It had gotten off to a reasonably brisk start with a summary from Markus, then gone off the rails as Julia had insisted on telling her story "from the beginning"—which turned out to mean from the moment she had woken up in the White House next to her late husband and gone down to breakfast with her late daughter, straight through to the end of the world, and her hastily arranged launch into orbit, some thirty-six hours later. Along the way had been a sequence of mishaps and coincidences just shaggy enough to be somewhat plausible. No liar could fabricate such a story. The narration had lasted for the better part of an hour despite Markus's increasingly frequent and obvious glances at his Swiss watch, and left all the others in a strange combination of spellbound, bored, horrified, and bemused.

She seemed to believe that they would actually care about all of her interactions with those dead people on that dead planet. It was a common enough mistake among new arrivals. In her case it was magnified considerably by the fact that she was used to being the president. Everyone was always happy to sit and listen to the most powerful person in the world.

"Thank God," Julia said, "that we were able to—"

"Yes," Markus said, cutting her off. Plainly he did not wish to hear any more from Julia. But just as plainly he was a little reluctant to move on to the next part of the story.

Everyone seemed to be pointedly not looking at Moira.

"Thank you, Julia," Markus said, in a tone that made it clear she was free to leave now.

Julia looked a bit startled. "But we haven't heard from Dr. Crewe yet."

"But we *have* heard from *you,*" Markus pointed out.

The point sank in. Julia didn't like it. "Very well," she said, standing up carefully. "As I mentioned before, Markus, I am eager to make myself useful in any way that I can."

"It is so noted," Markus said. He looked across the table, deadpan, at Ivy. Dinah knew what they were both thinking: *You are worse than useless here—which is why you were never invited.* "Thank you, Julia."

The ex-president turned away from the table. She stopped before the door leading into the Farm and turned back toward Markus one last time with a sad-puppy look on her face, perhaps expecting him to just slap his thigh and laugh at the joke and warmly invite her back to her seat. When this failed to happen, a transformation came over her face that Dinah found mildly frightening to watch.

What would it be like, she wondered, to be nuking people one day, and, less than a week later, to be asked to leave a meeting? Evidently it did not put Julia in the best of moods. J.B.F. turned her back on them, as much to hide her face as to find the way out, and opened the door. During the few moments it was open, Dinah caught sight of a young woman in an Islamic-style face veil standing just outside of it, waiting. The bottom half of her face was covered, but her eyes brightened and her body language was warm as she saw Julia emerging. Julia reached out to her affectionately and laid a hand on the small of her back as she turned. The two of them walked away shoulder to shoulder as the door closed.

Remaining in the Tank were Markus, Dinah, Ivy, Moira, Salvatore Guodian, and Zhong Hu, an applied mathematician who was their head theorist when it came to swarm dynamics. Others knew more about orbital mechanics and rocket engines—the old-school techniques for managing individual space vehicles' trajectories—but Hu, a specialist in complex systems, was the main architect of Parambulator, and the only person who could quite understand and explain what went wrong, or right, in a swarm. He'd spent most of his life in Beijing, but with enough time in Western universities to get along fine in English. In response to a nod from Markus, he said, "I have evaluated what happened. As we already know, there was a cornering event leading to a bump." This being the polite term for a mild collision between arklets. "But still, Arklet 214 had enough control authority that it could have avoided the second event."

"Then why didn't it?" Markus asked.

"The algorithm predicted a near miss and so it took no action beyond routine attitude corrections. The human operator was distracted and disoriented and so was reluctant to correct course manually."

"I can't fault the human," Markus said, "since we have warned them so many times about the consequences of flying by hand. But what went wrong with the algorithm?"

"Nothing went wrong with it," Hu said. "It had bad data. I will show you." With a few taps on his tablet he brought up a three-dimensional model of Izzy on the big screen above the conference table. To a first approximation, this seemed reasonably up to date; it depicted modules and space vehicles that had been added to the complex only within the last couple of days. "This is the model that the system was using yesterday for collision avoidance."

Dragging his finger around on his tablet, he rotated the model on the screen so that they were looking at the nadir side. He zoomed in on the distinctive "handlebar" shape of the Human Genetic Archive: the pair of cold storage units projecting to port and starboard below the Zvezda module. The view was much the same as what Dinah had seen from the Flivver the day before.

"Hang on, is this the exact model? Is this everything?" Ivy asked.

"Yes," Hu said.

"This doesn't include the thermal protection," she pointed out. "That adds at least a meter to the collision envelope."

"That is correct," Hu said. "In that sense, this model is obsolete. We have replaced it now with an upgraded version."

As all understood, this was no one's fault. The Arkitects had been struggling for almost two years to keep their three-dimensional model of Izzy up to date and accurate: a nearly impossible task when it changed every day. Soft goods like thermal protection blankets tended to get a lower priority. Humans, looking at the model, would mentally add those. Computers weren't that smart.

"Still," Markus said, "we take the model with a grain of salt. No arklet should ever pass that close."

"Let me show you what happened," Hu said, and brought up a video, shot from an external camera apparently mounted on one of the trusses.

The Human Genetic Archive and its surrounding blanket of thermal protection were not centered in the frame—they were down in the lower right corner. So the camera angle wasn't ideal. But they could see what happened. The arklet approached, creeping in gradually from the port side with closing velocity no greater than a slow walk.

"Is this real time?" Sal asked.

"Yes. Because it was an extremely low-speed approach it was not viewed as terribly dangerous."

"It looks like it's going to be a near miss," Sal said.

"It was—until this," Hu said, and freeze-framed the video. It wasn't easy to make out, but they could see a tiny flash on the forward halo of Arklet 214. "The thruster fires—a small course correction under automatic control." He stepped it forward. The flash faded but expanded into a dim gray cloud. "Exhaust gases. Expanding rapidly but moving quite fast." He stepped it forward several more frames until they could see the thermal protection blanket recoiling from the impact of the gas. A seam parted between two adjoining blankets and one of them flailed out like a rag caught in a wind gust.

Hu let the video run now, and they saw the arklet's rear halo snag on the loose blanket and rip it away, exposing the Human Genetic Archive to the orange radiance of Earth's atmosphere.

Ivy said, "If that thruster hadn't fired at the wrong moment—"

Hu nodded. "Arklet 214 would have passed underneath with two meters to spare. Not a margin to be proud of. But it would have been enough."

After a pause, Hu added, "The HGA's thermal protection system could have been designed better."

Another pause in which everyone else waited to see who would be the first to laugh. If it weren't for dark humor, they'd have no humor at all.

Hu seemed to sense it. "What I mean is that it was engineered for normal thermal loads."

"Meaning sunshine," Dinah said.

"Yes. Not for radiant heat shining up from the atmosphere below it."

"The same thing is true of many parts of Izzy, of course," Markus said. "We are having thermal overloads all over the place now. Moira, what's the damage?"

Dinah had to give Markus credit for a kind of finesse for the off-handed way he dropped the question in. Moira, who had been quiet through the whole meeting, took a moment to snap out of her reverie.

"Well," she finally said, "as Hu said, the thermal protection system—"

"Was bad," Markus said. "We know."

"There was no backup system."

Markus said, "Of course not. The cooling system for the HGA was the rest of the universe. We do not expect to have a backup system for the rest of the universe. We can rely upon it to be cold most of the time."

"Because of the accelerated schedule, caused by the Eight Ball—"

"Stop," Dinah said.

Everyone looked at her.

"Let's get this over with," she said. "Look. When I was fourteen, one of my dad's mines collapsed and killed eleven employees. It was terrible. He never really got better. Of course, he wanted to know what had happened. It turned out to be a long story. One thing led to another, which led to another . . . the individual steps all made sense, but no one could have seen the whole thing coming. Of course, he still felt responsible, but he wasn't, in any normal sense of that word.

"So here's what happened," Dinah went on. "Sean Probst started an asteroid mining company that sent up a bunch of cubesats and gathered a lot of data about near-Earth asteroids, which he kept secret. He took the database with him on his mission to Greg's Skeleton. His radio got hit by a rock and destroyed, so he couldn't communicate. At the last minute, when it was basically too late, he had the idea to look at the database. He learned about the Eight Ball. He alerted me, I alerted Doob, Doob alerted everyone else, and we pushed up the schedule for everything. Moira pulled the trigger on the project, which had been planned for over a year, to disperse the HGA samples to the arklets. Like every other project in the history of the universe, it went slowly at first because all kinds of snags came up. And not only that, but all of the Flivvers were spoken for and all of the space suits were busy, because of the Splurge. So not much got moved. It was obviously safer to keep the samples in cold storage in the HGA while all of these logistical problems got sorted out. The Splurge happened and a lot of random shit got launched in our general direction and made Parambulator light up like crazy. Arklets were getting cornered on a pretty regular basis. We almost lost a couple. Ivy and I took off in the Flivver to fetch Julia and probably added a lot of other noise and chaos to that problem. Then, the thing we just watched happened. Arklet 214 tore most of the badly designed thermal protection system off of the HGA and exposed it to the direct radiance of the Earth's atmosphere. The samples all warmed up before replacement thermal protection could be jury-rigged. All of those samples have been destroyed. Right, Moira?"

Moira, apparently not trusting her ability to speak, nodded.

"Okay," Dinah said. "So I think that what Markus is really asking is how many of the samples in the HGA actually got moved to safe cold storage in other locations before this happened. In other words, how many survived?"

Moira cleared her throat and said, in a faint voice, "About three percent of them."

"Okay. I only have one other question," Markus said. "Have you talked to Doob?"

"I'm sure he suspects," Moira said, "but I have not officially broken the news to him. I wanted to be absolutely sure first."

"Are you sure now?"

"Yes."

Markus nodded and spent a few moments thumbing something into his phone. "I am inviting him to join me and Moira here immediately," he said.

Everyone who was not Markus or Moira stood up to leave. Markus held up his hand to stay them. "Before you go, let me say something about the Human Genetic Archive that was lost."

He then paused for effect, until everyone was looking at him.

"It was always bullshit," he said.

Everyone took a moment to consider it.

"Are you going to tell Doob that?" Ivy asked.

"Of course not," Markus said, "but the real purpose of the HGA was politics on Old Earth."

"Is that what we're calling it now? Old Earth?" Sal asked, fascinated.

"That's what I am calling it," Markus said, "in the increasingly rare moments when I actually think about it."

"Thank you, Markus," Moira said.

HE HAD KNOWN, OF COURSE. IZZY'S COMPLEXITY WAS SO GREAT AS to belie its tiny size: a few hundred people sorted into a volume the size of a few jetliners. News traveled fast. Everyone had known within a few hours that the Human Genetic Archive had been almost completely destroyed.

He was in the Tank with Markus and Moira. They were gazing across the table at him, patiently awaiting some kind of reaction.

"Look," he finally said, "Doc Dubois is no more. That was a persona, you understand? Just an act. I'm a private person. I do not spontaneously emote. Especially when people are watching me and expecting it. A year from now, when I'm alone, when I least expect it, I'll break down in sobs over this. But not now. It's not that I don't feel. But my feelings are my own."

"I am very sorry that it happened," Moira said.

"Thanks," Doob said, "but let me say what all of us are thinking. Seven billion people died yesterday. Compared to that, the loss of some genetic samples is nothing. The embryo that Amelia and I created together, and that I brought up here with me . . . well, that was a special favor that J.B.F. granted me as an incentive to come up here. No one else got that kind of special treatment. It was unfair. I knew it. I accepted it anyway. So here we are."

"Yes," Markus said. "Here we are. Going forward—"

"But I'm not sure I agree with you," Doob said, "that the HGA was so insignificant."

Markus bridled his impatience and raised his eyebrows. Doob looked at Moira. "What was the term you used? Heterozygosity?"

"Yes," Moira said. "The stated purpose of the HGA was to ensure a sufficiently diverse genetic basis for the human race."

"Sounds important to me," Doob said. "What am I missing?"

"We have tens of thousands of human genomes recorded in digital form. From all different parts of the world."

"So there's your heterozygosity. That's what you're saying," Doob prompted her. "That's why"—he glanced at Markus—"the HGA wasn't really needed."

"Yes, but there's a but," Moira said.

"Okay, what's the but?"

"The digitized sequences, as I'm sure you'll understand, are only useful so long as we have the equipment needed to transcribe them into functional chromosomes in viable human cells. By contrast, to make use of a sperm sample, all we need is a turkey baster and some lube. But to make use of a DNA sequence stored on a thumb drive, we need—"

"All of the equipment in your lab," Doob said.

Moira looked a bit impatient. "What you are referring to as my lab bears the same relationship to a proper lab as some ones and zeroes on a thumb drive does to a living human. It is a collection of crated equipment that cannot even be unpacked and used in zero gravity. And even if we set it all up and turned it all on, it would be useless without a staff of Ph.D.-level molecular biologists."

"Really? *Useless?*" Markus asked.

Moira sighed. "For small-scale work, one sample at a time, well, that is easier. But to reconstruct a genetically diverse human population—"

"But, Moira," Markus said, "we cannot do that anyway until so many other things are in place. A large population cannot live in arklets eating algae. We need to establish a viable and safe colony first. Then, we build your lab. Then, we create a more diverse ecosystem: better food, greater stability. Only then do we even begin to worry about the heterozygosity of the human population. Until that time, we have more than enough people to create healthy non-inbred children just by the usual process of fucking each other."

"That is all true," Moira said.

"And that is the basis of my statement that the HGA was bullshit," Markus concluded.

"You're saying," Doob said, "that if we had all of the prerequisites in place—the colony, the ecosystem, the talent—needed to actually exploit the HGA—"

"—we would no longer need it, yes, this is my point!" Markus said. "Can we please stop wasting time on it now?"

"How would you *prefer* to be spending time, Markus?" Moira asked, giving Markus an amused, owlish look through her glasses.

"Talking about how to get there. How to realize that situation we were just talking of."

"And how might I contribute to that, given that the HGA is ninety-seven percent destroyed and none of my equipment will be usable for a long time?"

"I want to talk of preserving that equipment," Markus said, "preserving it against all hazards, and then getting it to a safe situation where we can one day construct this laboratory you speak of."

"It's about as safe as we can make it, isn't that so?" Moira asked. "It was given a sort of privileged position off of Node X—quite close to Amalthea. It's not living dangerously, the way *we* are at the moment."

She was referring to the notion, frequently discussed by Arkitects, of the Cone of Protection that supposedly existed in the lee of Amalthea. To the extent that the paths of incoming bolides were predictable, Amalthea could be pointed into them and used as a sort of battering ram. The forward surface of the asteroid would take a beating—but a solid slug of ancient nickel and iron could survive quite a lot. Anything situated up against its aft surface would be sheltered against virtually all hazards. But the protected zone did not, of course, stretch back infinitely far. The farther you lagged behind Amalthea, the more likely you were to get hit by a bolide coming in from an off angle. The Mining Colony was in the safest position, since, by its nature, it had to be right up against the asteroid. Almost as safe was the cluster of modules connected to Node X, immediately aft of the SCRUM, which was where all of Moira's gear had been stashed. Behind that, the protected zone narrowed, a long acute cone, finally disappearing altogether somewhere aft of the Caboose. When Moira joked about "living dangerously" she referred to the fact that T3, the third torus, in which they were sitting now, was rather wide and rather far aft, placing it close to the limits of that cone. Efforts had been made to beef up its shielding, but it was still at higher risk than many other parts of Izzy.

Markus nodded. "Your stuff is pretty safe. But it would be safer if we moved it inside of Amalthea. I have talked to Dinah about it. She says that they could mine out cavities and store things of great importance there."

A silence while Doob and Moira pondered it.

On one level, Markus's proposal was perfectly obvious. Of course anything would be safer inside of a huge metal asteroid.

On another level, it had ramifications.

As of a few days ago—pre–White Sky, the last time anyone had been able to think straight—the fate of Amalthea and the Mining Colony had still been subject to debate. Was the asteroid the boulder in the wheelbarrow that had to be dumped? Or was it the aegis that would shelter the entire human race? The argument had come down to statistics. They just didn't have enough data to make a decision.

By suggesting that Moira's equipment be moved into the interior of Amalthea, Markus seemed to be committing to a specific course of action.

It was a course that Doob instinctively agreed with. But it was a bit strange for a man like Markus to just decide on a course of action before the numbers were in.

Or did he know something Doob didn't?

Moira, in any case, went first. "What if we Dump and Run?"

She was referring to a gambit, frequently discussed and war-gamed, in which Amalthea would be cut loose and abandoned, and Izzy, lightweight but unprotected, would boost herself to a higher orbit with fewer bolides flying around in it.

"Then we would simply have to move all of that stuff back to Node X first," Markus said. "Or wherever we felt was safest."

This elicited a searching look from Moira. Markus held up his hands. "But I take your point. I am increasingly biased against Dump and Run."

"You know how I feel about the Swarmamentalists," Moira said.

She was referring to another of the basic gambits, Pure Swarm, in which everything—presumably including Moira's lab—would be distributed among arklets, which would then collectively move to higher orbit. People and goods would move among them through a decentralized market-based economy.

"Listen," Markus said, "now that everyone below is dead, and we don't have to put up so much with bullshit, you will find that Hu and the others have a more nuanced view than they were letting on before." He referred to the fact that Zhong Hu, as the foremost swarm theorist and the brains behind Parambulator, was assumed to be a Swarmamentalist.

Doob nodded. It still took some effort to remind himself that the millions of Internet commentators arguing for this or that strategy were all ghosts now.

"You know something," Doob blurted out. Then, as the thought was coming into his head, he added, "From Dinah. The radio."

"Yes," Markus said. "*Ymir* is coming in hot, high, and heavy." He surrounded those three words with air quotes.

"What does that mean?" Moira asked. "She's made of ice, how can she be hot?"

"She is approaching with a high closing velocity. Not unmanageable. But . . . somewhat exciting."

"And 'high'?" Doob prompted him.

"Sean also transmitted his params," Markus said. "It would seem that he did us a large favor. He executed the plane change while it was still easy to do so, way out around L1."

"So when he says he's coming in high," Doob said, "he means that *Ymir* has a high orbital inclination—close to ours?"

"Very close to ours," Markus confirmed. "He is dropping this big chunk of ice into our lap."

"So," Moira said, "on top of everything else, Sean Probst is now preparing to dive-bomb us with a comet?"

"A piece of one."

"A big piece," Doob guessed, "if he specified 'heavy.' "

"The number was impressive." As Markus said this, he shifted toward Doob and looked him in the eye.

"Oh wow," Doob said. "Is it enough for the Big Ride?"

"If we can get *Ymir* to rendezvous with Izzy, then yes," Markus said. "It is more than enough."

The Big Ride was the third of the basic options. It meant to boost Izzy in its entirety—Amalthea and all—to a much higher orbit. It had been considered implausible because of the amount of propellant that would be needed. Not just implausible but—absent the timely return of *Ymir*—physically impossible. Despairing of Sean's chances, its supporters had lately tended to suggest scaled-down variants, such as reshaping a small percentage of Amalthea into bolide deflectors and ditching most of its mass.

"Including the plane change?" Doob asked.

A trace of a smile came onto Markus's face. He knew exactly what Doob was thinking. For, unable to get Cleft out of his head, Doob had shown pictures of his favorite piece of the moon to Markus, to Konrad, to Ulrika and Ivy and some of the others who seemed to make up the informal power structure of the Cloud Ark.

"Let me be clear," Markus said. "When I speak of the Big Ride, I mean it for real. We take all of Amalthea with us. We raise the orbit to the moon's. We change the plane. We circularize. And we end up safe and sound in Cleft."

"And *Ymir* carries enough water for that mission?"

"Yes," Markus said, "if we can control her and bring her in."

"Isn't that Sean Probst's job?" Moira asked.

"Not anymore," Markus said. "The information I just imparted to you was in Sean's final transmission."

Moira and Doob looked at him sharply.

"The health situation has been not so good, for a long time," Markus explained. "Sean was the last member of the expedition to die."

"Are you saying that *Ymir* is a ghost ship?!" Doob asked.

"Yes."

"And there's no way to remote-control her," Moira guessed.

"Unfortunately Dinah's Morse code cannot help us in that regard," Markus agreed.

"So someone has to go and—"

"Someone has to go and land on that fucking big piece of ice," Markus said, "and get inside of *Ymir* and restart the nuclear reactor and commit the final burns that will bring her into sync with Izzy."

"Who the hell—" Doob began, but Markus cut him off by pointing to himself. He did this in a somewhat awkward fashion that, deliberately or not, looked like a pantomime of suicide by handgun. He said, "I am placing Ivy in command of Izzy and the Cloud Ark tomorrow. I am assembling a crew that will depart in a MIV and make a rendezvous with *Ymir*. We will board her and manually execute the procedures needed to bring her under control and get her payload to Izzy. We will then use what is left of the ice to raise Izzy's orbit—and we will bring Amalthea with us on the Big Ride."

"That's . . . major," Moira said. "Who knows? When were you going to announce it?"

"I just decided it now." Markus sighed. "Listen, it is the only way. In my heart I always considered Dump and Run and Pure Swarm both to be too risky. What happened with the HGA just makes this more obvious. The only wise course is the Big Ride. It will take a long time—two years or something. But during all that time the most important resources can be sheltered within Amalthea. And by that I mean you and your equipment, Moira. You can have whatever resources you need from the Mining Colony to create a safe location for the genetics lab."

"Okay," Moira said, "I'll talk to Dinah."

"Talk to whomever she delegates," Markus said. "Dinah is going to have to come with me on the expedition. I need her to deal with all of those *verdammt* robots."

"How can I help?" Doob asked. He wondered if Markus might dragoon him as well, and was torn between being afraid of that and tremendously excited.

"Figure out how we are going to do it," Markus said, after considering it for a few moments. "Lay in a course for Cleft."

"Yes," Doob said. "I'll do that." The little boy in him was crestfallen that he wasn't going on the adventure. Then he reminded himself that he was already part of the biggest adventure ever, and that, so far, it had been altogether miserable.

ALL CONVERSATIONS WORTH HAVING ABOUT SPACE VOYAGES WERE couched in terms of "delta vee," meaning the increase or decrease in velocity that had to be imparted to a vehicle en route. For, in a common bit of mathematical shorthand, the Greek letter delta (Δ) was used to mean "the amount of change in . . ." and V was the obvious abbreviation for velocity. The words "delta vee," then, were what you heard when engineers read those symbols aloud.

Since velocity was measured in meters per second, so was delta vee. The delta vees bandied about in spaceflight discussions tended to be large by the standards of what Markus was now calling Old Earth. The speed of sound, for example—a.k.a. Mach 1—was three hundred and some meters per second, and most earthbound people would consider it awfully damned fast. But it hardly rose to the notice of most people who talked about space missions.

A common delta vee benchmark had been the amount needed to get something from an Old Earth launch pad to an orbit like Izzy's. This was some 7,660 meters per second, or more than twenty-two times the speed of sound: an impossible figure for any object that had to fight its way through an atmosphere. Once a vehicle had reached the vacuum of space, though, things became simpler: rocket engines worked more efficiently, drag and aerodynamic buffeting were absent, and the consequences of failure weren't invariably catastrophic. Getting it from point A to point B was a matter of hitting it with the right delta vee at the right time.

Sean Probst's delta vee history, from his departure from Earth until his departure from life, had gone something like this. The launch from terra firma to Izzy on Day 68 had required a delta vee of 7,660 m/s according to a naive calculation; but as any old space hand would know, losses due to atmospheric friction and the need to push back against gravity would have elevated the practical number to more like 8,500 or 9,000.

Once he had collected Larz and most of Dinah's robots, Sean had needed to execute a plane-change maneuver to get from the Izzy orbit—which was angled at about fifty-six degrees to the equator—to the equatorial orbit in which *Ymir* was being assembled. This was one of those circumstances in which human intuition got it all wrong. The Izzy orbit and the *Ymir* orbit did not seem all that different in most respects. Both of them were a few hundred kilometers above the atmosphere. Both were essentially circular (as opposed to elliptical). And both went in the same direction around the Earth. The only real difference between them was that they were at different angles. And yet the delta vee required to get from one to the other was large enough that it had been necessary to launch a separate rocket, carrying nothing but extra propellant, just to refuel Sean's vehicle in preparation for the plane-change burn.

Once *Ymir* had been assembled, a delta vee of some 3,200 m/s had been needed to place her in a very elongated elliptical orbit that had taken her out to L1. En route, the plane-change problem had once again reared its head. Essentially everything in the solar system, including Comet Grigg-Skjellerup, was confined to a flat disk centered on the sun. The imaginary plane through that disk was called the ecliptic. Conveniently for people who liked seasons, but not so good for interplanetary travelers, Earth's axis and equator were angled with respect to the ecliptic by 23.5 degrees, and so *Ymir*'s initial orbit had been off-kilter by that amount. Fortunately, plane-change maneuvers were much less "expensive" (meaning they required a lot less delta vee) when they were performed far away; and *Ymir* was, of course, going very far away. So, they had done the plane change out at L1 range, as part of the same burn, totaling some 2,000 m/s, that took her out through the L1 gate into heliocentric orbit.

That orbit, more than a year later, had intersected that of Comet Grigg-Skjellerup. As *Ymir* had drawn near to the comet core, she had used another 2,000 m/s of delta vee to sync her orbit with its.

All of these maneuvers, up to the arrival at Grigg-Skjellerup, had been achieved by using *Ymir*'s rocket engines, which were altogether conventional: they burned propellants (fuel and oxidizer) in a chamber, making hot gas, which was vented out of a nozzle to produce thrust. The final burn had emptied her propellant tanks, so this was a one-way journey unless the nuclear propulsion system could then be turned on.

No engine had ever been made that was capable of pushing a comet core around the solar system at any appreciable speed. For that, they had needed to embed the nuke-on-a-stick into the heart of the ice payload, construct an ice nozzle behind it, and then pull out the control blades, causing the reactor's sixteen hundred fuel rods to become very hot. Ice turned to water, then steam, which shot out the nozzle and produced an amount of thrust actually capable of making a difference. So a few months had then been consumed disassembling *Ymir* and integrating its parts into a chunk of ice carved off the three-kilometer ball.

The question might have been asked: Why just a piece of it? Why not bring the *whole* comet core back, if water was so desirable? What was the point of sending a large nuclear reactor into space if you weren't going to use it? And the answer lay in the fact that even a large nuclear reactor did not even come close to having enough power to move such a big piece of ice. The mission would have lasted more than a century, assuming the existence of some kind of a miracle reactor that could operate at full power for that long. In order to get this done in any reasonable amount of time, they could only bring back the bare minimum of ice needed to rendezvous with Izzy and accomplish the Big Ride.

In any case, Sean and his surviving band had used the nuclear engine to impart a delta vee of about 1,000 m/s to the shard they had carved off Greg's Skeleton, thereby placing it into a somewhat different orbit that had, a few months later, glided into L1. Sean had remained alive just long enough to yank out the control blades one last time and execute a delta vee that had basically reversed the maneuver they'd used to leave the L1 gate almost two years earlier. This had simultaneously brought *Ymir* into geocentric orbit while executing, as cheaply as possible, the plane change needed to enable a later rendezvous with Izzy. A couple of days later Sean had tapped out the "coming in hot, high, and heavy" message and dropped dead. Of what, they could only conjecture.

The retrieval team that was now being organized by Markus was going to use a MIV, or Modular Improvised Vehicle, assembled from a kit of parts: a sort of Lego set for the construction of spaceships, neatly sorted on a stack of modules, collectively known as the Shipyard, connected to the Caboose.

The Shipyard was a generally T-shaped contraption. One arm of the T's crossbar, projecting from the port side of the Caboose, was studded with MIV parts. The opposite arm was a cluster of spherical tanks surrounding a collection of splitters. These used electrical power to split water molecules into hydrogen and oxygen, and piped them to chillers, which refrigerated the gases until they became cryogenic liquids that could be stored in the bulging tanks.

So much for the T's crossbar. Its long vertical stroke was a truss terminated by a nuclear reactor: not a small RTG like the ones on the arklets, but a true reactor, originally designed to power a submarine, considerably souped up for this task.

Markus dubbed the Shipyard's first product *New Caird,* after a small boat that had been used in Shackleton's expedition to Antarctica. She was assembled and made ready for use in ten days: about one-third of the time they estimated it would take for *Ymir* to arc in from L1 and make her closest pass to Earth.

To design, assemble, and test such a vehicle so quickly would have been unthinkable two years ago. During the interval between Zero and the White Sky, however, the engineering staffs of several earthbound space agencies and private space companies had foreseen the future need to jury-rig space vehicles from standard parts such as arklet hulls and existing rocket engines, and had provided a kit of parts, lists of procedures, and some basic designs that could be adapted to serve particular needs. In effect, *New Caird* had been designed a year ago by a large team of engineers on the ground, all but three of whom were now dead. Those three had been sent up to join the General Population. Building on their predecessors' work, they were able to produce a general design—enough to begin pulling the bits together, anyway—within a few hours of Markus's decision. Details emerged from their CAD systems as they were needed over the following week and a half, and the necessary parts and modules were shuttled about the Shipyard until the new vehicle was ready.

New Caird would have to execute one burn to reach an orbit that would intersect *Ymir*'s and another to match her velocity, so that the crew could board the ghost ship and take the helm. The total "mission delta vee" for that journey, from its departure from the docking port on Izzy to its arrival at a similar docking port on *Ymir,* was some 8,000 meters per second.

The conversation turned now to mass ratio: a figure second only to delta vee in its importance to space mission planning. It simply meant how much propellant the vehicle needed at the start of the journey in order to effect all the required delta vees.

Laypersons tended to substitute "fuel" or "gas" for "propellant," making the obvious analogy to the stuff that had been burned by the engines of cars and airplanes. It wasn't a bad analogy, but it was incomplete. In addition to fuel, most rocket engines needed some kind of oxygen-rich chemical (ideally, just pure oxygen) with which to burn it. Cars and planes had simply used air. Rockets stored the oxidizer in a separate tank from the fuel until the moment of use. The two chemicals were collectively referred to as "propellant," and their combined weight and volume tended to dominate space vehicle design in a way that hadn't been true of, say, automobiles, whose gas tanks had been small compared to their overall size.

A convenient figure for characterizing that was the mass ratio, which was how much the vehicle weighed at the beginning (including the propellant) divided by how much it weighed at the end, when all the tanks had been emptied. If you knew how good the engine was, and how much delta vee you needed, then the mass ratio could be calculated using a simple formula named after the Russian scientist Tsiolkovskii, who was credited with having worked it out. It was an exponential: a fact that explained almost everything about the economics and technology of spaceflight. For if you found yourself on the wrong side of that exponential equation, you were completely screwed.

When the relevant numbers for the *Ymir* retrieval mission were jacked into the Tsiolkovskii equation, the result was a mass ratio of about seven, meaning that for every kilogram of stuff—Markus, Dinah, other personnel, miscellaneous robots, etc.—that they wanted to arrive safely at the docking port of *Ymir,* they needed to allow for six kilograms of propellant at the moment of departure from Izzy. This wasn't all that difficult to achieve, especially for a vehicle that would never be exposed to the rigors of passage through the atmosphere.

The payload in this case was a single arklet hull that had been augmented with a "side" door: an airlock that could accommodate one person in a space suit. Other than that, it had been stripped to the minimum complement of equipment needed to keep a crew of four alive for a few days. To its mass, of course, needed to be added that of the actual humans and their food and other essentials. The lightness of a bare arklet hull was startling; the newer hulls, made of overwrapped composites, weighed in at eighty kilograms. Stripped of everything that made it comfortable and inhabitable over the long term, and including the "side door," the maneuvering thrusters, and a reasonable supply of thruster propellant, the mass of *New Caird* was about ten times that. The humans weighed three hundred kilograms. The rocket motor that would be doing all the important burns weighed another two thousand. So, in round numbers, the payload mass—the stuff that actually had to get delivered to the docking port of *Ymir*—was some thirty-five hundred kilograms. The mass ratio of seven meant that its propellant load, at the beginning, was going to be some twenty-one thousand kilograms of liquid hydrogen and liquid oxygen.

The Shipyard had been stocked with several cryogenic propellant tanks of various sizes, some designed to hold LH_2 (liquid hydrogen) and others built to the somewhat different specifications needed in the case of LOX (liquid oxygen). The chosen tanks were bolted together in a stack with the rocket engine mounted "below" and thermal protection wrapped all about. *New Caird* proper—the arklet with the humans in it—projected forward on a scrap of scaffolding just long enough that her maneuvering thrusters wouldn't damage any of the other parts when they came on.

While the MIV was being constructed, twenty-one thousand kilograms of water had to be split into hydrogen and oxygen, chilled to cryogenic temperatures, and stored. The Shipyard's port side already had some LH_2 and LOX premade. In general, though, they tended not to keep a lot of them on hand, because they were tiresome substances to work with. The demand was supplied by the naval reactor on the Shipyard's long arm, which was brought up to full power for the first time since it had been launched, piece by heavy piece, from Cape Canaveral on a series of heavy-lift rockets. Pumping juice down heavy cables to the splitters, it was able to turn twenty-one tons of water into gases and chill the gases to cryogenic temperatures while the other preparations were being made.

This was a lot of water—roughly fourteen liters of it for every surviving human. The Cloud Ark recycled water, of course, and was far from running out of the stuff. Nonetheless, the idea of taking that much of it and spewing it into outer space, never to be recovered, gave many people pause: especially the Dump and Run partisans.

There was a strong counterargument, which was that *New Caird*'s objective was to take possession and control over a piece of frozen water that weighed as much as Izzy herself, including the giant piece of iron to which Izzy was attached (and would continue to be, if the Big Ride advocates had their way).

Once *New Caird* had reached her, *Ymir* could presumably be slowed down, and brought to a rendezvous with Izzy, by firing her engine. And that was a primitive beast, but it had a basically infinite supply of energy in the nuclear reactor, and a vast stock of propellant in the form of ice. The "steampunk" propulsion system had much lower efficiency, however, than a properly engineered rocket motor. Consequently, the mass ratio that would be needed to slow *Ymir* down from the high-speed elliptical orbit with which it was falling into Earth's gravity well, to match the much slower, circular orbit of Izzy, was about thirty-four, which meant that 97 percent of the ice currently attached to *Ymir* was going to be melted, turned into steam, and jetted out its makeshift nozzle just to slow it down. The remaining 3 percent, however, would still weigh as much as Izzy and Amalthea put together. Split into hydrogen and oxygen, it would supply the rocket fuel needed to power the Big Ride, all the way up to Cleft.

"I DIDN'T EXPECT IT TO BE BLACK," DINAH SAID. SHE WAS HEARING HER own voice as if down a mile-long sewer pipe. She was pretty sure she had lost consciousness a minute ago. Maybe she wasn't all the way back yet.

Markus was slow in responding. Maybe he had blacked out too. Maybe he was just distracted. "Comet cores are covered in—"

"Stinky black stuff, yeah, I know that, Markus. Remember who I am?"

"Sorry. Not enough blood in brain."

"But this is just a shard that Sean broke off of Grigg-Skjellerup. Why's it all covered?"

"I don't know," Markus said.

They were looking at *Ymir* from a distance of ten kilometers and closing. They were viewing her on their tablets, through a zoomed-in video camera. Vyacheslav Dubsky, floating closest to *New Caird*'s forward end, put his face to the vessel's tiny window and searched the black sky for the black ship, but the squint on his face suggested it was still too far away for naked eyes to be of much use.

"Maybe he was doing us a favor," Dinah said. "The black stuff has all kinds of goodies on it. Carbon, obviously. But also nitrogen, potassium—"

"Micronutrients," Markus said, "that the Cloud Ark will be needing."

"So maybe he used the robots to scrape some of it off Greg's Skeleton, and loaded up on the gunk," Dinah speculated.

"We will know soon," Vyacheslav said. "Presumably he left a document."

"Which we will not be alive to read, unless we stick the landing," Markus pointed out, "so no more chatter from now on, please. Slava—" and he broke into a string of bad Russian meaning something like *I trade places with you now.* Vyacheslav responded in equally bad German. Both men were perfectly fluent in English. But they made a private joke of butchering each other's languages, ostensibly as part of a project to preserve Old Earth's linguistic heritage. Markus then added, "The rest of you, buckle up."

With the deft movements of one who had been in space for two years, Vyacheslav glided aft. He was one of the veteran Russian spacewalkers who had come up to Izzy way back on A+0.17, in the first launch after the moon had blown up. He had been a mainstay of the Scout and Pioneer eras, racking up more time in a suit than anyone, wearing out three Orlans. He was a little worn out too, being sallow and gaunt compared to the strapping hero who had emerged two years ago from the same Soyuz that had carried Rhys and Bolor-Erdene. Markus replaced him at the forward window and buckled himself into the pilot's seat.

Behind that was a row of three acceleration couches, mounted on a frame that spanned a diameter of the arklet's hull. Dinah was loosely belted in on the port side. A few minutes ago she had been tightly belted in. She had not adjusted the straps. The entire couch, and its supporting truss, had been deformed by the same burst of gee forces that had left her so woozy. To starboard was Jiro Suzuki, a nuclear engineer who had been involved with the design of *Ymir*'s nuclear reactor core. It wasn't clear whether he was conscious; but then it never was with Jiro. Vyacheslav, the fourth member of *New Caird*'s complement, settled into the middle position and pulled the top straps of the five-point harness over his shoulders.

A staccato burst sounded from the gamma spectrometer—the modern equivalent of a Geiger counter—floating in front of Jiro's face. Then the Eenspektor, as they called this device in butchered Russian, dropped back into the normal sporadic patter.

Radiation was striking the Eenspektor—and their bodies—all the time, at random moments and in no particular pattern. Sometimes there would be a little burst, and that part of the mind that liked to see meaning in everything would identify it as an event. But then it would die away and be forgotten. That was just the way of the universe, and of the human psyche. There was a lot more radiation in space than there had been down on the ground, but all the survivors had long since come to terms with that, and Jiro had dialed down the sensitivity on his Eenspektor so that it wasn't screaming at them all the time.

If it started screaming in the next few minutes, it wouldn't be because of some faraway cosmic event. It would be because of a radiation leak from *Ymir*.

"Starting to see the exhaust trail," Markus commented. "Can you see it on video? It's faint. The sunlight hits it perfectly a few hundred meters aft of the nozzle bell."

He was referring to a thread of steam that emerged from *Ymir* all the time, even when her engine wasn't powered up. This was how Konrad and Doob and the other astronomers aboard Izzy had been able to track the ship's course using their optical telescopes, and to verify that the params encoded in Sean's last transmission had been accurate. Wispy as it was, the steam trail reflected more light than did the ship itself.

It was created by the slow, steady boiling of ice caused by the latent radioactivity in the ship's fuel rods. When the control blades were pulled out and the reactor operated full blast—which was almost never—it produced four gigawatts of thermal power by splitting uranium and plutonium into smaller nuclei, many of which were themselves unstable isotopes. As these fission fragments decayed into "daughters" and "granddaughters," heat continued to be generated even when the reactor had been shut down. There was nothing that could stop it, so some loss of ice, in the form of this tenuous trail of steam, was unavoidable. It was okay. *Ymir* had plenty more where that came from, and Sean would have allowed for it in his calculations.

Sean, never the most emotionally sharing kind of guy, further throttled by his makeshift radio, had not supplied details as to what had killed him and his crew. Had it been some kind of disastrous problem with the reactor core, he probably would have given them a heads-up. For that matter, *Ymir* wouldn't have made it this far if the system hadn't been basically working. So Jiro was not coming into this thing expecting a total nightmare. But there was no telling.

No one spoke for several minutes as Markus monitored their approach and occasionally touched the controls, spanking *New Caird* into a slightly different course.

They had gotten here by means of two large burns. The first, and smaller, had placed them into an ellipse that had shot beyond the orbit of the former moon. After several days of weightless coasting away from the Earth, they had succumbed to the force of gravity, looped lazily around, and begun to fall back again toward the burning planet. This had been timed in such a way that, about a day later, they would be overtaken by *Ymir,* coming in on a roughly parallel track. But *Ymir* was traveling much faster—coming in hot, as Sean had told them—basically because it had been falling in toward the Earth from an extremely high starting place, gathering speed relentlessly for weeks. Left unmolested, *Ymir* would come screaming in toward Earth with a relative velocity of some twelve thousand meters per second, make a hairpin turn just a few kilometers shy of a catastrophic encounter with the glowing atmosphere, then go hurtling back outward again, not to return for a couple of months. Eventually her orbit would decay to the point where she would get dragged down by the atmosphere and destroyed.

At any rate she would have flashed by *New Caird* too quickly even to be seen, her relative velocity faster than that of a rifle bullet, had *New Caird* not just matched her velocity by making a long, precisely timed burn of her main engine. The four members of the crew were still recovering from this. The vehicle's main engine was oversized—the kit of MIV parts from which she'd been built only had so many options—and so the gee forces had been impressive at the beginning of the burn and brutal toward the end, as the lavish expenditure of propellant had made her lighter and lighter compared to the engine's formidable thrust. If Dinah had blacked out for a few seconds, why, maybe that was just as well, given that they had aimed themselves almost squarely at the Earth and then launched themselves at it as if on a suicide run. This was necessary in order to go where *Ymir* was going, but added up to maybe a little more excitement than she really was in the mood for at this moment in her life.

Earth was, of course, completely unrecognizable. From this distance it was about the size of a tangerine held at arm's length, and about the same color. Formerly a cool blue-and-white lake in the cosmos, it now hung there like a blob of molten steel thrown out by a welder's torch. In the belt between the tropics, where most of the Hard Rain was falling, it glowed orange. The color faded and reddened to a kind of sullen brown around the poles, and the whole planet continually sparkled with the bluish light of vaporizing and exploding bolides. In a few days it would blot out half of the sky for a hectic few minutes while they slingshotted around it. By that time, they needed to have *Ymir*'s main propulsion up and running so that they could execute the huge braking burn that would slow her down to the same velocity as Izzy.

It was crazy. It was a crazy plan. The crushingly high acceleration that they had survived at the end of the big burn a few minutes ago was a physical reminder that they had only taken enough propellant to sync *New Caird* with *Ymir*. If they failed in their basic mission—if they couldn't dock with *Ymir* and get her engine working—they had no way of getting back to Izzy, save perhaps by the utterly insane measure of diving into Earth's atmosphere on their next pass and using the air to slow them down.

Dinah had been a little slow to absorb the full meaning of the little ship's name. The *James Caird* was a small boat that Shackleton had used to make a desperate run for help to save the remnant of his failed South Pole expedition. They had aimed it at South Georgia Island, a speck on the map, in the knowledge that if they didn't hit it spot on, the prevailing winds would never allow them to turn around and make another try.

She wondered if that very craziness wasn't Markus attempting to make a point. The overall situation of the human race was, of course, ludicrously desperate. Doob had been the first to point this fact out in public, two years ago. Planning and preparation had consumed the time since. The work had been hasty, improvised, and politically inflected, but fundamentally it had been a well-ordered and methodical engineering project. As it had to be. But its plodding bureaucratic nature had a kind of lulling effect. How many times in the last two years had Dinah leaned back from a screen full of code and forcibly reminded herself of what was going on, and how bad it was? Unable to keep that squarely in their minds, the fifteen hundred or so survivors tended to live from one day to the next and keep doing what they had done the day before. Of all people, Sean Probst had been the least susceptible to that; he had seen what needed to be done almost immediately, and he had made efforts to do it that had been fantastically strenuous and, in the end, fatal. With his final transmission he had passed that responsibility on to Markus. Dinah suspected that Markus had stepped away from his position at the top of the org chart, and set out on this mission, partly to set an example for everyone else.

And if that was true, bringing Dinah along was to make a point as well. He would spare no one, play no favorites.

Markus broke the silence once during the approach: "Definitely a shard. As you said. Not snowball. Not candle."

"I agree," Dinah said. She could see its shape clearly enough, now, on the screen of her tablet.

Unlike normal ships, which carried their propellant in tanks, *Ymir* was a big chunk of solid propellant—ice—inhabited by a sort of parasitical infestation of equipment whose purpose was to convert that propellant into thrust. Not knowing exactly what he would find on Comet Grigg-Skjellerup, Sean had come equipped with more than one alternative architecture for putting *Ymir* together. If the comet core had turned out to be a loose ball of ice-dust, then he'd have had to scoop out what he needed and pack it into something like a snowball, giving *Ymir* a spherical shape with the reactor embedded in its center. Another option would have been to fashion a long cylinder of ice and plant the reactor in one end of it, then "burn" it forward, consuming the ice en route, like a candle. What they were seeing now looked more like the third architecture, which was the shard. It suggested that, upon his rendezvous with Grigg-Skjellerup, Sean had found it made up of at least one fairly hard and solid crystal that could be relied on to hold itself together structurally during the maneuvers to come. He had split the shard off from the main body of the comet and planted the reactor system somewhere near its middle, then embedded the rest of his ship—the part where the humans lived—in what would become its nose. If the equipment had worked as planned, then executing the "burns"—i.e., pulling out the control blades to place the reactor into operation and make steam—had been a matter of sending signals to actuators embedded in the core: motors that would move the rods, valves that would control the flow of steam and water, and so forth.

Implicit in all of this was a hell of a lot of robot activity, which was why Sean had taken the extraordinary step of traveling personally to Izzy to clean out Dinah's supply of them before proceeding to his rendezvous with *Ymir*. The reactor had to be fed with ice. Because ice was a solid, it couldn't flow through tubes. Robots had to mine ice from the shard and transfer it to a feed system: a set of augers that would move it into the reactor chamber to be melted and vaporized. A Siwi robot could move a lot of material in a hurry by embedding its "tail" in the ice and then using a whirring mill on its "head" to throw off a fountain of fine shavings that could be collected and carried off by Nats. The long intervals of time between burns could be used to store up a supply of shredded ice in hoppers that would feed the augers.

Downstream of the engine, robots were also needed to maintain the shape of the rocket nozzle. This was a long duct with a wide mouth on the aft face of the shard, tapering to a narrow throat near the reactor. The throat had been constructed on Earth and launched up with the reactor. It was made of a corrosion-resistant alloy called Inconel. Any other material would rapidly wear out from the hot steam blasting through it. Conditions in the long spreading bell of the nozzle, however, were more benign, and so it worked fine for that to be sculpted from ice. Nonetheless, it changed its shape as it was used. Deeper in, where the exhaust was hot, it grew wider as its walls were melted by the torrent of steam. Closer to the exit, where the exhaust had cooled to below freezing, it accumulated on the walls and narrowed the passage. So robots had to scuttle around reshaping the nozzle. This was a fine task for the Nats that Larz had experimented with in Seattle.

Finally there was a third "crew" of robots living on the exterior surface of the shard, trying to keep it from falling apart by embedding fibrous reinforcement in the outer layer of ice and wrapping cables and nets around it, somewhat like a butcher tying up a roast to prevent it from collapsing in the oven. This was a good match for the capabilities of the Grimmed (steel-armored) robots, which were mostly Grabbs.

All of these robots needed power, of course. They could store a little of it in batteries, but those had to be recharged. Some of them collected energy from sunlight; others had to converge from time to time on one of *Ymir*'s little nuclear generators to sip electricity.

The general picture was that *Ymir* would not be anything like the traditional idea of a spaceship, in the sense of an orderly, symmetrical piece of architecture. It would be more like a flying robotic anthill, constructed out of a natural found object. The robots crawling around on and in it had general instructions as to what they were supposed to be doing, but could make their own judgments from moment to moment to avoid collision with other robots, or from hour to hour as to when they needed to recharge their batteries.

Or that had been the general scheme, anyway. Since there'd been no guessing what Sean would find, there'd been no way of coming up with any plan worthy of that name. Instead they had sent him up with tools, resources, and ingenuity. Dinah, Markus, Vyacheslav, and Jiro were about to inherit the tools and the resources.

Jiro's Eenspektor made steadily more noise as they approached, but the growth was slow enough that their minds didn't quite register it. Jiro did not seem alarmed by the level of radioactivity, but Dinah didn't know how to interpret that. Earlier in the mission, she had probed him for some general background about what to expect. "If it's very bad, we all just lose consciousness and the mission fails," he'd said. "The flux of radiation just shuts down our nerves, our sphincters open, we never even know it's happening."

"In that case," Markus had pointed out, somewhat testily, "there is little point in discussing that scenario."

"If all four of us throw up," Jiro had continued, "and, say, one or more of us gets diarrhea, then we have hours to live. In that case we should just transmit a warning to Izzy and encourage them to send a second mission. In the meantime, maybe we can transmit some useful information to them. Eenspektor data, pictures, et cetera."

"Noted," Markus had said.

"If, say, one of us throws up, then it means that half of us will probably die, and so we have some chance of accomplishing the mission. If no one is barfing, then none of us is likely to die, at least over a time span of weeks."

"Thanks for that," Dinah had said, and tried to put it out of her mind. Now that they were actually approaching *Ymir,* however, it was coming back to her, and she was trying to convince herself that she wasn't feeling any nausea.

"I am going to traverse the nozzle mouth in about thirty seconds," Markus announced.

"Roger," Jiro said, and then switched off his Eenspektor altogether. He pulled up a window on the screen of his tablet. "Switching to the external gamma spec now."

Suddenly *Ymir* was filling the window. It was dead ahead of them. The glowing Earth, a third of a million kilometers away, "set" below its black horizon as they sidled in behind it. Markus had placed them on a trajectory that would slowly cross that of *Ymir,* bringing them laterally across the ice ship's aft end.

Dinah's older relatives might have described *Ymir* as having a sugarloaf shape, meaning a cone with a blunted tip. If so, this sugarloaf had been splashed with boiling water and attacked with a screwdriver in several places, giving it a scarred, irregular form. But it clearly had a fat end and a narrow end. These were about half a kilometer apart. The fat end, which was beginning to swing across their field of view, was a couple of hundred meters wide. It had a big circular hole in it, which was the outlet of the ice nozzle. *New Caird* could have flown into that hole and followed it almost all the way up to the throat before running out of room. And perhaps they would do so later, if they could find no other way in. But for now they were just going to make a lazy swing across it. The edge of the hole was blurry because of the evanescent steam cloud leaking out of it. This looked not so much like rocket exhaust as like breath emerging from someone's mouth on a cold day. It didn't so much block their view as soften it. But the visual landscape of space was one of intense contrasts, and so it was impossible to see down into the nozzle bell, even when they were squarely in the middle of the cavernous hole. It was just a black disk—like staring into the muzzle of a rifle. Hair-thin needles of frost grew on the window as the steam condensed.

Jiro focused intensely on his tablet until they had drifted past the midway point, then seemed to draw back into himself. He switched his Eenspektor back on. It was making a lot more noise than it had a few minutes ago, but this gradually diminished as they traversed beyond the nozzle exit and across the wide base of the sugarloaf. With a tap on the thrusters Markus got them moving forward with respect to *Ymir.* Earth "rose" on her other side. *New Caird* moved up alongside the shard, headed for her forward end.

"What's the verdict, Jiro?" Markus asked, when he was satisfied with how things were going.

"Based on the gamma spec," Jiro said, "I would say that at least one of the fuel rods ruptured. Not at the beginning, when the rods were new, and not recently, when they were full of fission fragments and daughters, but somewhere in between. Could be worse, could be better."

A memory came back to Dinah. "One of Sean's last messages said he was thrusting at full power."

Jiro shrugged. "This reactor contains sixteen hundred fuel rods, grouped in assemblies of forty, so the failure of a single rod wouldn't measurably affect performance. Even the ruptured rod still makes power, remember. It's just that it would be spewing fuel fleas, fragments, and daughters into the rocket exhaust. We would expect to see a mixture of alpha, beta, and gamma—which is just what the Eenspektor is reporting."

Dinah was no nuclear physicist, but she'd had enough radiation facts drilled into her to get the gist. Gamma was high-energy light. It would pass through just about anything. So, bad news, good news: It was hard to shield against the stuff. But most of it passed right through your body without interacting—that is, without doing damage. It made scary noises on the Eenspektor.

Betas were free-flying electrons. They were easy to shield against. Good news, bad news: You could stop them with a little bit of water or plastic. But by the same token, if they came into contact with your body they were certain to break something inside of you.

Alphas were helium nuclei, four thousand times as massive as betas, moving at relativistic speed. They could not pass quietly through matter any more than cannonballs could, but they did a lot of damage to whatever they hit.

In order to detect anything other than gamma, Jiro had been forced to switch over to equipment mounted on the outside of *New Caird,* since alpha and beta couldn't penetrate the hull. And by looking at the energies of the various particles striking that equipment he had been able to diagnose conditions inside the reactor.

Since she could no longer see *Ymir* out the front window, Dinah focused on the slivers of frost that had grown on the glass. These were rapidly sublimating into space, and would be gone in a few more minutes. She'd found them beautiful until Jiro had made them aware that they were probably contaminated.

"Any residual beta now?" she asked.

"We are well clear of the nozzle and the plume," Jiro said, a little taken aback.

"I mean, did we pick up any contamination on that flyby?"

"It is back down to background levels," Jiro said. "But the detector would only 'see' sources on its side of the hull. We will have to do a more thorough survey later."

"Get a load of this," Markus said, and punched in a maneuver that swung *New Caird* around ninety degrees. They were now flying "sideways," their nose aimed directly at *Ymir,* which was only about a hundred meters away from them. She more than filled the window. Her narrow end—her bow, if you wanted to think of her as a ship—was a hill of dirty ice. A few fine structures suggested that humans had been at work there: some structural netting, some cables, a glinting wire that might have been the radio aerial. But it wasn't obvious, yet, where they were actually going to dock.

"It is really buried," Markus observed. He didn't have to explain that "it" was the command module—the part of *Ymir* that had life support systems. It ought to be reachable through a docking port. But they weren't seeing anything. They had known—because it was part of the plan—that Sean and his crew would have buried it in the ice, to protect them from radiation and from rocks. They looked to have buried it deep.

Dinah's tablet was running a terminal window, a simple programmer's interface that just displayed lines of text. For the last little while, this had shown only a blinking cursor, but now it came alive and began to display cryptic, one-line messages.

"Picking up some new bot sigs," she reported. These were the digital signatures of robots, pinging the universe to find out what, if anything, was listening. *New Caird* had shipped with a complement of robots of various types, but she knew all of their sigs and was filtering them out of this terminal window. Anything that showed up here was, by process of elimination, from *Ymir*'s complement of robots.

Like the clicks on Jiro's Eenspektor, these came up sporadically and in bursts.

"At least twenty . . . so I am going to filter out the Nats," she said, typing in a command. Being so numerous, Nats tended to overload the screen. "Okay, in addition to a pretty well-developed Nat swarm I have half a dozen Grabbs and at least that many Siwis."

"Any clues in their names?" Markus asked. It was possible to give each robot a unique name, which would show up on its sig. By default these were just automatically generated serial numbers, but they could be manually changed.

"Well," Dinah said, "here is a Grimmed Grabb whose name is 'HELLO I AM RIGHT ON TOP OF THE DOCKING PORT,' which seems promising."

"Can you make it flash?"

"Hang on." Dinah established a connection to HELLO I AM RIGHT ON TOP OF THE DOCKING PORT and, after quickly checking its status, told it to blink its LEDs until further notice. Before she even looked up from her screen she could tell, by subvocal exclamations from the others, that it had worked.

"I see it very clearly," Markus said. Some pops and bangs sounded from the thrusters as he adjusted *New Caird*'s attitude. They were now flying in nearly perfect sync with *Ymir,* looking at the flashing Grabb from a distance of maybe five meters. It was anchored into the surface of the shard in an area that was relatively free of the black stuff.

"Aim the light down into the ice, please? And put it on continuously?" Markus requested.

The Grabb's LEDs were mounted on snaky stalks that could be aimed. Dinah made it happen. When next she looked up through the window, she could see the silhouette of the Grabb centered in a nimbus of white light, produced by its aiming its lights directly into the ice. A sharp white disk was visible in the center of that silvery cloud. It was blurred by the ice, but they all recognized it for what it was: a docking port, buried at least a meter deep.

"Did anyone bring an ice pick?" Jiro asked. It was not like him to make a joke, but Dinah was happy to take humor from any quarter at this point.

"Slava," Markus said, "you're up. Dinah, maybe you can help by bringing more of the robots to the area."

By entering a fairly simple command, Dinah was able to summon every Grabb and Siwi in range, telling them, in effect, "Figure out a way to get closer to HELLO I AM RIGHT ON TOP OF THE DOCKING PORT and don't bother me with the details." By the time Vyacheslav was suited up, enough of these had drawn near that she was able to clinch several of them together and form a temporary construct that "reached" up from the surface of the ice to grapple *New Caird,* first in one location and subsequently in two more. So, even though they had not been able to dock yet, they at least had a mechanical link to *Ymir* that would prevent them from drifting away.

Other robots, including HELLO, meanwhile busied themselves carving a hole in the ice "down" toward the buried docking port. Vyacheslav exited through *New Caird*'s airlock, clambered down a stack of robots to the surface, and then made his way toward the site. Since the gravity of *Ymir* was negligible, Vyacheslav's "weight" here was about half a gram, and the faintest contact with the surface would send him rebounding off into space. So instead of walking he had to rely on some sort of anchor fixed into the ice. Dinah was able to send two of *New Caird*'s Grabbs scuttling along ahead of him. These had been engineered for movement on ice, and could rapidly anchor themselves by melting and refreezing it with their footpads. All Slava had to do was follow them and hold on to them. Once he had reached the mouth of the hole he was able to embed anchors and carabiner himself into place. Then he speeded up the work of the robots by scooping out more ice, more quickly, than they were capable of moving with their little claws.

Not knowing what to expect, they had brought with them a small arsenal of improvised ice-mining tools, including a Craftsman garden shovel that had mysteriously made its way up from a Sears, Roebuck in an Old Earth mall. Slava put it to work.

Meanwhile Markus was sending a status report back to the Cloud Ark, and Jiro was doing more typing than seemed necessary just for taking notes. He was communicating with someone, or, more likely, something. Dinah was tempted to ask what, but there was only one plausible answer: he had established contact with the computer that controlled the reactor core.

Markus seemed to have come to the same conclusion. "Jiro?" he asked. "News from the belly of the beast?"

"It's alive," Jiro said, in what might have been either awkward phrasing, or a second consecutive joke. "I am trying to make sense of the logs. There is a lot of repetitive material."

"Error messages?" Markus asked, making the obvious guess.

"Not so much. It is robot stuff. Status reports."

Dinah moved over one seat and had a look. Though she couldn't tell exactly what was going on, her general read tallied with Jiro's. Lots of robots had been working away, executing variations on the same small set of programmed behaviors, pumping out occasional status reports—and, yes, some error messages—that had generated a log too vast for any human to read. They would have to sort it out later by writing a computer script that would crawl through it, accumulating statistics and looking for patterns.

"Could you scroll to the top, please?" she asked. She wanted to know the date and time of the first log entry.

"I checked it," Jiro said. "Right around the time of Sean's last transmission."

So Sean, probably knowing that he was at death's door, had told the robots to do something, and to keep doing it, until they were ordered to stop. Since the outer surface of the shard was pretty quiet, this probably related to some internal work hidden beneath the surface. "Mining fuel, probably," Dinah guessed. Then, before Jiro could object to the incorrect choice of words, "Propellant, that is."

Vyacheslav exposed the docking port. Using a combination of taps on *New Caird*'s thrusters, some pushing and pulling by the robots, and Vyacheslav simply grabbing the spacecraft and nudging it this way and that, they inserted her "front door" docking port into the little crater that Vyacheslav and the robots had excavated, and mated it with that of *Ymir*'s buried command module.

Slava then had to reenter *New Caird* through its side airlock. By sounds conducted through the hull they could track his progress as he climbed into the chamber, closed the outer hatch, and activated the system that would fill the lock with air.

In the meantime, Markus was able to make contact with the computers on the other side of the port, and verify that there was breathable air and other amenities.

It was damned cold, though: about twenty degrees below freezing.

"That was Sean doing us a favor," Markus said. "He turned the thermostat down before he died. His body will be frozen solid." For *Ymir* had no lack of power from its nuclear generators, and its electrical systems were still working.

Markus entered a command that would turn the command module's environmental systems back on and bring the temperature back up. He pressurized the tiny space between *Ymir*'s hatch and *New Caird*'s. Then he opened the latter.

They were all looking now at the slightly domed exterior surface of the hatch that would lead into *Ymir*'s command module.

Someone had written on it with a felt-tipped marker. He had

drawn the trefoil symbol used to warn of radiation hazards and beneath it had written the Greek letters alpha, beta, and gamma. Then, as a darkly humorous doodle, he had added a crude skull and crossbones.

Markus was the first to recover. He spiraled out of the pilot's chair and propelled himself aft to the inner hatch of the airlock. There he punched a virtual button on a screen, which had the effect of locking the inner hatch. He was not letting Vyacheslav come in. He reached up with one hand and adjusted his headset. "Slava," he said, "can you hear me? Good. Listen. We have contamination. You may have picked some of it up on your space suit. Before you come inside, I would like you to go over to Jiro's external radiation detector and see if we pick anything up."

Jiro was already scanning the hatch with his Eenspektor, fortunately without results.

Outside they could hear Vyacheslav cycling the airlock again and clambering back out. Using external handholds on the hull he made his way to the place where the external gamma spec was mounted, and devoted a couple of minutes to turning this way and that, directly in front of them, paying particular attention to his gloves, his knees, his boots—anything that had come into contact with the ice. No bursts of radiation were noticed, and so he was given clearance to go back to the airlock and enter *New Caird.*

They had brought warm clothes, which seemed advisable when going on a journey to a huge piece of ice. Jiro put his on. Dinah reached for the stuff stack in which she had stored hers, but Markus held up a restraining hand. She noticed he was making no effort to dress for the occasion. Jiro was going down there alone.

"I am going to overpressurize us a little bit," Markus said, working with an interface on his pad. Dinah felt pressure building against her eardrums. Markus didn't explain himself, and didn't have to: they wanted clean air from *New Caird* to waft into *Ymir,* as opposed to potentially contaminated air coming in here.

Jiro then pulled a disposable one-piece bunny suit over his cold-weather gear. For they had come prepared to find the ship contaminated. He slung his Eenspektor over the outside of the bunny suit. Dinah handed him a respirator mask, so that he wouldn't breathe radioactive dust into his lungs, and he pulled it on over the bunny suit's hood and checked it for a good seal against his face. He pivoted into the space between the ships, operated the external latch on *Ymir*'s hatch, and jerked forward slightly as the overpressure in *New Caird* pushed it open. He let himself drift into the command module, then got himself turned around so that his feet were oriented toward the "floor." Meanwhile Markus pulled the hatch closed behind him.

Vyacheslav by now had emerged from the airlock. He, Dinah, and Markus were listening to Jiro's breathing on their headsets.

"Sean bled to death," Jiro announced.

YMIR'S COMMAND MODULE WAS ARKLET-SIZED. OF COURSE, THAT went for almost everything now in space, since an arklet was just the biggest object that could be launched into orbit on the top of a heavy-lift booster. Some arklets were "tunnel," meaning that they were laid out in a "horizontal" orientation, meant to lie flat, as it were, like railroad tank cars, with a single long floor running from end to end. This was good if you wanted a large open space, but tended to be a less efficient use of available volume. The command module of *Ymir,* like that of *New Caird,* was "silo," meaning that it was oriented in a "vertical" way, diced into a number of round stories—typically four or five—joined by a ladder. Each story was a fat disk of space about four meters in diameter, big enough for one room that would be considered large by space travel standards, but more often divided into smaller compartments.

Ymir was a five-story silo, meaning that it had low ceilings that must have made it a claustrophobic place in which to spend a two-year journey. The first story Jiro had entered, being closest to the surface with its cosmic ray and bolide hazards, was a single room. On the plans, it was supposed to be used for storage of things like food, scrubber cartridges, robot parts, and tools.

After a few minutes Jiro was able to set up a video link from a camera mounted to his head. They watched it on their tablets.

The frozen body of Sean Probst was floating in a sleep sack that had been zip-tied to the ceiling. The porous fabric was stained dark brown. Very little of it had not been soaked with blood.

Bumping lightly against him was an old-school Geiger counter, tethered by another zip tie. The word BUSTED had been written on it with the same felt-tip pen used to make the sign.

After sweeping Sean's body and the rest of the level with his Eenspektor, Jiro floated down the gangway to the next level "down." The noise of the Eenspektor built steadily.

"Oh, turn the fucking sound off," Markus said, and it went quiet. It would now display the counts per minute on its little screen, which only Jiro could see, but they wouldn't hear the clicks.

The next story was a sort of general meeting, dining, and muster room, mostly open space lined with storage lockers. The third, or middle, story was divided into sleeping compartments, toilets, and showers. The fourth was a laboratory and workshop space. Those functions continued down into the fifth and bottom-most story.

"Cold here," Jiro said, as he reached the bottom level. "Suddenly a lot of beta."

"Okay," Markus muttered, "so the contamination is there. On the fifth level down."

It was cold, as they soon saw, because someone had left the door open: a manhole in the middle of the floor, big enough for a person in a space suit to climb through it and into a round shaft leading straight down into the ice. The entire length of the shaft was illuminated by white LEDs.

"That is remarkable," Markus said.

Jiro descended into the tunnel headfirst and began to propel himself along it by the simple expedient of pulling on a knotted rope that had been fixed into its wall by ice anchors. He moved tentatively at first, then more rapidly. "There is a hatch at the far end—a hundred meters away, maybe," Jiro said.

"Radiation?" Markus asked.

"Not so much," Jiro said. "I do not think this was the route of the contamination."

The hatch at the end was adorned with a more formal rendering of the radiation hazard symbol. They all knew what was on the other side of it: a small pressurized module that was physically connected to the guts of the reactor. Jiro elected not to go through, instead turning around for a return to the command module.

Then he turned back suddenly, and swept the beam of his headlamp across the ice wall of the tunnel. Some long slender object was embedded in the ice.

Two long slender objects.

Two human bodies. Dinah gasped as she recognized Larz's strawberry-blond hair.

Without making any comment, Jiro made his way back "up" the tunnel to the lower level of the command module. He turned his attention to a locker near the hatch. Its door was open. Mining tools and space suit parts were floating around in it. Others had spilled out into the room and were drifting around aimlessly, pushed by currents of air.

"Jiro," Markus said, "talk."

"Strong beta from here," Jiro said. "This is where the contamination came from."

He drifted back up to the common room and found a garbage bag in a cabinet, then returned to the bottom level and went to work sorting through the tools and the clothing, holding each of them in turn up to the Eenspektor as he focused on its screen. From time to time he would grimace at the results and push the item into the garbage bag.

Dinah, Markus, and Vyacheslav waited in *New Caird* for an hour, pretending to pass the time with tasks on the screens of their tablets.

Then they heard Jiro's voice again: "Prepare to put something out the airlock!" he was shouting.

It took them all a few moments to understand Jiro's thinking. *New Caird* and the command module of *Ymir* now formed a closed system. Since the latter was completely embedded in ice, the only way to remove something from that system—to take out the radioactive garbage—was to put it out *New Caird*'s airlock.

There were some distant thuds. Dinah floated forward and opened the hatch to be greeted by a garbage bag, filled to the dimensions of a beach ball, and all wrapped up in duct tape. Propelled by a shove from Jiro, this entered *New Caird*. Dinah pushed it up to Markus, who intercepted it and tapped it sideways into the airlock. Vyacheslav slammed the hatch behind it. Then they heard a hiss, indicating that the lock had cycled. The bundle was now adrift in space.

Jiro's head, then the rest of him came through the port. He had stripped off the bunny suit and the respirator and presumably stuffed them into the garbage bag. He was sweaty and exhausted.

"Just like old times, my friend?" Markus said, referring to Jiro's earlier career running cleanup at Fukushima.

"I don't miss it," Jiro said.

It was warm in the command module now, so they didn't need the parkas. But they all used bunny suits when they went into *Ymir,* and stripped them off before going back into *New Caird*. Contamination was "sneaky," as Jiro put it. The beta emitted by a microscopic speck of fallout could be hidden from the Eenspektor's view by just about any random obstacle—and the command module was cluttered with those. So Jiro's initial sweep was no guarantee that tiny beta-emitting particles weren't still hidden in there. If such particles found their way into a lung, or the digestive tract, fatal radiation damage was likely to result. He had, though, identified a space suit glove on the lower level as being heavily contaminated, and found lower levels of contamination on some other odds and ends that had gone into that garbage bag and out the airlock. With luck all serious sources of contamination had now been removed.

BEFORE IT HAD TIME TO THAW, VYACHESLAV TOOK SEAN'S BODY down from the ceiling. Slava wasn't a life scientist, but he was a jack-of-all-trades. Bundled up in parka and moon suit, he cut the sleep sack open as Jiro stood over him with the Eenspektor. He performed a cursory exam, then wrapped the body back into the sleep sack. He maneuvered it to the lower level, threaded it through the manhole in the middle of the floor, and then pushed it down the tunnel to the end, where Larz and the other crew member had been buried. There, he stashed Sean's body against the ice wall.

Somewhat ruining their appetite, he reported on the findings of this impromptu autopsy as they got ready to eat a meal in the common room.

"Sean bled to death out of his asshole," he reported. "He had an internal rupture of the bowel."

"I picked up some beta through his belly," Jiro added. "He was very emaciated at the end."

"Meaning?" Markus asked.

"He swallowed a particle of fuel. Probably a fuel flea that got loose and somehow was tracked in here."

"Fuel flea?" Jiro had used the term before. No one else knew what it meant. It had gone in one ear and out the other, just another bit of the tech jargon that was so ubiquitous on Izzy. Now that fuel fleas were killing people, it was time to learn about them.

"A tiny piece of uranium or plutonium that has gotten loose from a ruptured rod. As it throws off alpha particles, it zigs and zags around the room—conservation of momentum. So it hops around like a flea. The point is, it is small and it makes a lot of alpha. It lodged in a diverticulum in his bowel. It burned through his bowel wall and started a bleed that could not stop."

Everyone pushed back their food.

"Okay," Markus said. "We eat in *New Caird*."

Once they had finished their meal, Markus told everyone that they needed to sleep, since they had a busy few days ahead of them. Jiro volunteered to take the first watch, and so the rest of them slept while Jiro stayed up going through logs and notebooks, assembling a picture of all that had happened on *Ymir*'s journey.

Suddenly they had a lot of space to spread out in. Dinah was tempted to retreat to the far end of the *New Caird* and get some privacy, but Markus insisted that everyone sleep down in the command module. *New Caird* might be free of radioactive contamination, but it was exposed to the direct hazards of space. A bolide strike would kill anyone in it. Whereas a beta-emitting particle, inhaled into the lung, would take days or weeks to incapacitate the victim—time during which they could do useful work.

So Vyacheslav ended up sleeping in one of the berths on *Ymir*'s crew accommodation level, while Dinah and Markus shared another. Somewhat to her surprise, they actually managed to have sex, a thing that had occurred only once since the White Sky. It was a sly surprise, not the athletic banging around that they had enjoyed the first few times they had done it, back in the good old days when the Hard Rain had seemed far in the future and the Cloud Ark had still felt like an isolated research colony. *Ymir,* now separated from the rest of the human race by millions of kilometers' distance and several thousand meters per second of delta vee, now had some of that old feel to it. And despite the ghoulish scene that had greeted them on arrival, Dinah liked it here—it was the space equivalent of one of Rufus's old mining camps—and didn't really want to go back.

But they were supposed to be saving the human race, not enjoying an exotic holiday, so she tried to get some sleep. When Markus's alarm went off five hours later she peeled out of the bag they'd been sleeping in and did her best to clean up and get into some fresh clothes. *Ymir* had long ago turned into a smelly bachelor pad, short on toiletries, and, as they discovered while rooting around in the common area, on food. Sean had definitely been killed by the fuel flea in his gut, but he had likely been weakened before then by malnutrition, and even by lack of oxygen. For the systems that the crew had been using to replenish *Ymir*'s air supply were not in the best condition. The new arrivals were awakened twice during their sleep cycle by alarms from the life support system, which Jiro silenced and dealt with.

When they were all awake, they ate food from the stores they had brought with them and listened to a briefing from Jiro.

"Let me tell you what happened to this expedition," he said. And then he told them the story as he had pieced it together from the logs left behind by the dead.

The failure of the radio, shortly after the beginning of the mission, had been caused by a defective part for which there was no replacement: a simple, stupid oversight. The longest leg of the trip—the year and a half spent coasting from the L1 gate to Grigg-Skjellerup—had consisted of lengthy stretches of boredom interrupted by occasional panics, most of which had to do with the life support system. This was based on using sunlight to grow algae, a process that worked well in the lab but had turned out to be difficult to sustain on *Ymir*. The newest arklets in the Cloud Ark had benefited, in this respect, from lessons learned operating such systems in the time since Zero, but *Ymir* had been built and launched very early, using systems that now seemed painfully out of date.

Once they had reached "Greg's Skeleton" and thereby gotten access to vast amounts of water, they'd been able to make oxygen by splitting H_2O, and life had improved. Until then, however, they'd been oxygen hungry and tense, trying to keep their consumption of air and food to a minimum by floating listlessly in their sacks watching the same DVDs over and over again. Health, and mental status, had suffered.

They broke the shard from Grigg-Skjellerup using small mining charges planted by hand, or by robots programmed by Larz. Into its nose they embedded the command module, making themselves comparatively safe from cosmic radiation and bolides for the first time since the beginning of the mission. Life began to improve. They started excavating the access tunnel into the core. Into the aft end of the shard they inserted the reactor system, letting it melt its way into the ice. Around it, in the heart of the shard, they began to excavate a cavity and sculpt out hoppers: containers designed to hold broken-up ice produced by the mining robots. Twelve augers—long, spiraling ice movers, like the ones used to transport grain into elevators—were set up to convey that loose ice from the hoppers into the space surrounding the warm reactor vessel, where it would melt and be pumped into the core itself. Meanwhile, a separate corps of robots worked on the outside of the shard, melting the ice a little bit at a time, mixing it with the fibrous material they'd brought with them, and letting it refreeze into the much tougher material known as pykrete.

The "steampunk" propulsion system had basically worked as planned—though not without a lot of tinkering and head scratching—on the first "burn" that had put it on the course back to L1. There had, however, been some problems with the augers that were used to feed ice into the reactor chamber. The augers received their inputs of ice from hoppers that had to be filled up by "mining" solid ice from the inside of the shard, a process for which robots were well suited, and so nothing worked at all without the assistance of a small army of robots conveying flakes of ice from mine head to hopper like ants dismantling a loaf of sugar. This part of it had actually worked. But some of the pieces of ice being mined by the robots had little rocks in them. These jammed the augers. Jams could often be repaired by operating the auger in reverse for a short time, but sometimes a robot, or even a person in a space suit, had to be sent to pry a rock out of the mechanism. An auger accident had led to the death of one member of the crew.

During the months between that first burn and their arrival at L1, Larz did some programming work on the robots, trying to teach them not to collect rocky ice. They conducted a number of system tests intended to make sure that the problems they'd experienced the first time around wouldn't be repeated during the critical second burn. These ranged from small-scale tests on individual robots all the way up to full dress rehearsals where the entire system would be energized and the reactor turned on to generate thrust for a few minutes.

It had been during the first of those dress rehearsals when something had gone wrong in the core, resulting in damage to the jacket of a fuel rod.

Jiro had an idea as to what had gone wrong. *Ymir*'s reactor used water—the melted ice of the comet core—as its moderator. In nuclear engineering, that meant a medium that slowed down the neutrons hurled out by fission reactions, making them more likely to stick around long enough to trigger more such reactions. In the absence of an effective moderator, the neutrons would mostly escape from the system without doing anything useful.

Between being as dead as a doornail and running out of control was a narrow band of normal and healthy power output in which basically all commercial reactor operations happened. The essential problem with *Ymir*'s reactor was that its moderator—being a naturally occurring substance—was impure and unpredictable. The water that flooded into the chamber for the first dress rehearsal had been melted from ice a few months earlier, around the time of the initial "burn," and had been sitting in the plumbing system ever since then. There, it had been in contact with rocks and grit that had made it through the augers. It had leached various minerals out of that rock, and become something other than pure water. When the reactor was started and the pumps turned on, that impure water was drawn through screens and filters intended to exclude all the debris. But it was nonetheless impure water, and when introduced to the core, it failed to perform its function as a moderator. The reactor was sluggish to get going. With the advantage of hindsight, it could be seen that its neutron economy was suppressed, poisoned by the impurities in the water. Overreacting to the slow start, the operators had pulled the control blades out farther than they would have otherwise. But once the first rush of impure water had been flushed through the system and blown out the nozzle, it had been replaced by relatively pure water, only just now melted from the ice. The reactor's power had surged, producing a sudden buildup of fission products inside the fuel rods. Some of those would have been gases such as krypton and argon. The gases would have created pressure. Fuel rods were engineered to withstand it, but one of them had failed and ruptured. Possibly it had left the factory in excellent condition but been damaged en route by a nanometeoroid that had left a microscopic flaw. In any case, for whatever reason, the rod burst open and began to spill out the highly radioactive "daughters" of nuclear fission, which had become mixed with the steam being blasted out the rocket's nozzle.

Most of the fallout had, therefore, dissipated into space. But the whole point of a rocket nozzle was to convert the thermal energy in the gas—its heat—into velocity. The faster the steam went, the colder it got, until the steam near the nozzle exit was so cold that it actually began to condense into snow. Tiny particles of fallout made excellent nuclei around which a snowflake might begin to form. Some of that snow had stuck to the ice walls of the nozzle bell.

The most likely explanation for what had happened next was that one of the robots crawling around in that area maintaining the shape of the nozzle had become contaminated with a mixture of alpha-emitting fuel fleas and beta-emitting daughters, and tracked the material to a location where it had been transferred to the glove of a space suit—possibly by a mechanism as simple as a spacewalker reaching down to brush some ice from the claw of a Grabb, or planting a foot in a location where a contaminated Grabb had stepped. The contamination had then been brought into the command module when the spacewalker came indoors. They might not even have known about the burst fuel rod, so they might not have been checking for contamination. Or, as suggested by Sean's note, their Geiger counters might have broken down, one by one, rendering them blind to the presence of radioactivity in their environment. In any case, the particles had spread around the command module. Some men had inhaled them, some had swallowed them. They hadn't been healthy to begin with.

IN ANY CASE, THE GOOD NEWS, IF IT COULD BE SO CALLED, WAS THAT the reactor and the engine basically worked. The improvements Larz had made to the robots' mining programs had led to fewer rocks in the hoppers, and fewer jammed augers, during the L1 burn. Since then, Nats had been crawling around in the hoppers identifying rocks that had sneaked in anyway, and pushing them away from the augers. The damage to the fuel rod would have been a major catastrophe by Old Earth standards—had it happened on an earthbound reactor. Here, it was messy, and had already been fatal to a few. But everything still worked. Yes, the *New Caird* expedition would be bringing a radioactive disaster right into the middle of the Cloud Ark, but once they drew close enough they would jettison the reactor and let it fall into the atmosphere.

Forty-eight hours, give or take a few minutes, now remained before Earth would loom huge below them, and the nadir surface of the shard would sweat and steam as the radiant heat shining up from the incandescent air softened, melted, and vaporized the ice. It was then that they would have to pull out the control blades and execute *Ymir*'s next big burn. First they would have to spin the whole ship around so that she was flying "backward," her nozzle bell pointed in the direction of movement. For the delta vee they needed was a negative one—a braking, as opposed to accelerating, burn.

For spin moves, all spaceships were equipped with thrusters, not powerful enough to impart big delta vees but capable of rotating the ship as a whole into the desired attitude so that the main engine was pointing in the right direction. As a rule the thrusters were more effective when they were situated out toward the "corners" of the vehicle, where they could exert more leverage and crowbar the thing around with minimal thrust. Not knowing what they were going to find at Grigg-Skjellerup, the mission planners for *Ymir* had packed aboard a collection of modular thruster assemblies that basically consisted of little rocket engines, propellant tanks, wireless control links, and hardware for anchoring them into ice. A cursory survey of *Ymir* and a look at the dead crew's records made it clear that Sean and his crew had embedded those packages into the ice at suitable locations: one complex up at the nose with nozzles aiming in four perpendicular directions, and four more spaced around the fattest part of the shard.

Now that *New Caird* was docked, her engine could also be put to use in getting *Ymir* spun around. But this one maneuver—a 180-degree flip, which would have seemed comparatively simple in a small craft such as an arklet—was fraught with difficulties and complications in something as huge and asymmetrical as *Ymir.* Anticipating a need to use the thrusters, Dinah sent robots out to inspect them during that first "morning," and Vyacheslav suited up and went out to do a bit of troubleshooting on a propellant line that had somehow become kinked. But so ponderous were the shard's movements that the actual rotation, end-over-end, consumed eight hours, and tweaking it into precisely the right orientation then took another six.

Whereupon Markus announced that all of their assumptions were probably wrong anyway.

"The atmosphere is too big," he said. He had been staring pensively, for a long time, at a string of emails from Izzy.

Dinah felt a spear go through her heart. After all that had happened in the last couple of years, it was remarkable that she still had it in her to react in that way to bad news. It seemed to be some kind of built-in psychological program, triggered by phrases like "your mother has cancer," "there's been an explosion in the mine," or what Markus had just said.

They had known, from very early in the planning of the Cloud Ark, that the Hard Rain would heat up the air—*all* of the air, all over the world. When air got hotter, it expanded. The atmosphere had only one direction in which it could expand: out into space. So, whatever drag Izzy felt from the traces of air at its accustomed altitude of some four hundred kilometers was bound to get worse as the atmosphere reached upward. How hot the air would get, how much it would expand, and how heavy the drag would get were questions of colossal import that, however, simply could not be answered until the Hard Rain actually started. As Doob always put it, the experiment of blowing up the moon had never been attempted before. The most they could do was wait and perform observations. Which was exactly what they had been doing ever since the Hard Rain had begun. But Markus had been distracted for most of that time, and was only now absorbing the latest results.

For the Cloud Ark, of course, there were plans to cover various contingencies. In the easy case where the atmosphere didn't expand that much and the drag wasn't too bad, they didn't have to do much. In the more difficult case—which was apparently the way the experiment was now shaping up—they had no choice other than to raise the orbit of every vessel they had—Izzy herself, and each arklet. The delta vees involved were not that large; three hundred meters per second sufficed to nearly double the orbital altitude and get them well clear of the danger zone. Each arklet had its own engine and enough of a propellant supply to accomplish that. For Izzy, matters were a little more complicated. If they were willing to ditch Amalthea they could get three hundred meters per second pretty easily. Bringing

Amalthea along for the ride, however, increased the propellant requirements enormously. All of which had long ago been anticipated by mission planners. This was how the Dump and Run strategy had been dreamed up in the first place.

So it would be easy for the arklets to get clear of the thickening atmosphere by abandoning Izzy, at least for the time being, and jumping to higher orbit. Their drag problems would be solved. But in so doing they would lose the ability to shelter behind Amalthea and begin to take damage from bolides. Exactly how much damage depended on how thick and fast the rocks were coming in, and what the distribution of sizes was—another one of those questions of colossal import that couldn't be answered until the Hard Rain had actually started and data had been gathered.

And, so far, the data were too thin to make any real determination. With a few spectacular exceptions, bolide impacts and casualties had been light. But this didn't mean it would remain thus. The White Sky was an ever-changing phenomenon. The explosive uptick in the Bolide Fragmentation Rate that had signaled its onset was still ongoing. The distribution of rock sizes and orbital parameters would continue changing for thousands of years. Trends could be observed, and predictions could be made, but beyond a certain point it was guesswork.

At any rate, Markus had rolled the dice on the gambit that they were now executing. If it worked, and they could slow *Ymir* down enough to mate her with Izzy, then the Big Ride strategy became possible, and the arklets could climb to higher and safer altitudes behind the shelter of Amalthea's metal and *Ymir*'s ice.

The one part of that plan that Markus apparently had not considered until now was that the atmosphere was too big.

In truth, it wouldn't have made a difference if he *had* considered it. The crucial decision had been made and executed weeks ago by Sean Probst, when he had laid in a course at L1 and executed the burn that had placed *Ymir* on its current trajectory. This was an ellipse with a very low perigee. That was a sound idea from an orbital mechanics point of view in that the steam engine would have maximum leverage at that point—it was the natural place to make a burn and effect a transition to a low circular orbit matching Izzy's. But, sick and exhausted from his two-year odyssey, isolated from the latest scientific discourse by radio failure, Sean might have overlooked the expansion of the atmosphere when making his calculations.

"Are we going in?" Vyacheslav asked. This being a polite euphemism for the scenario where *Ymir* got so deep, and slowed down so much, that it burned up and became just another streak of blue light against the lambent background of the pyrosphere.

"We are more likely to skip, I think," Markus said. Meaning that *Ymir* might bounce off the atmosphere like a flat rock skimming across a pond. "With unpredictable results. But I cannot be sure. All I am saying is that this is not going to be the mission plan that Sean had in his mind. It is going to be something else. Something maybe a little more exciting."

ANTICIPATING THAT CAMILA MIGHT BE ON HER TOES—SHE HAD already survived one attempt—the gunman had crouched behind the rear of her school bus, sawed-off shotgun at the ready, and waited for her to emerge. A narrow stretch of pavement separated the vehicle's side door from the entrance of her school, so he didn't have much margin for error. He jumped the gun, as it were, springing out into the open while Camila was still negotiating the descent to the street; the long hem of her burqa was apt to get caught on her foot as it probed for the running board, so she had to take it slowly. The delay saved her life. Alerted by a schoolteacher standing in the building's doorway, Camila turned back into the bus. Rather than hitting her full in the face, the shotgun blast raked the left side of her jaw, removing eleven teeth, tearing away much of her cheek, and causing massive structural damage to her jaw. Surgeons in Karachi and, later,

London had saved most of the functions of her tongue, rebuilt her mandible from pieces of bone carved from her pelvis, and fitted her with a set of artificial teeth. After a world tour raising money for girls' education in Afghanistan and the tribal regions of Pakistan, Camila had been granted permanent asylum in Holland. Dutch plastic surgeons, funded by charitable donations from all over the world, had gotten to work repairing the cosmetic damage. This was a long-term project that had been interrupted by Camila's selection as one of the Dutch candidates for the Cloud Ark. No one believed that this was a random outcome of the Casting of Lots. Clearly the Dutch authorities had placed their thumb on the scale and seen to it that she was chosen, as a rebuke to some conservative Muslim countries who had refused to nominate female Arkers unless given assurance that arrangements would be made for them to live in orbital purdah. Camila was well suited to serve that symbolic purpose, since she had not adopted Western ways. She dressed conservatively and wore the head scarf and the face veil. She was coy, however, as to whether the purpose of the face veil was submission to the demands of religion or to hide her disfigurement. She had pulled it down several times to display the scars to television cameras, and when she had dined at the White House she had gone uncovered in the dining room, by prearrangement with her hostess, the president of the United States.

Julia's startling arrival in the Cloud Ark had therefore led to a reunion between the forty-four-year-old ex-president and the eighteen-year-old refugee. To call it joyous or even happy would have been wrong given the circumstances. It was a fact of human nature, though, that some people just got on well with each other. This had clearly been the case during that dinner at the White House and was no less true in Camila's abode, Arklet 174, which was where Julia ended up lodging after she had recovered from her eventful flight up and gone through a bit of basic training in how to live in space.

Arklet 174 belonged to a heptad, or a cluster of seven arklets all connected to a hexagonal frame; it and five other arklets surrounded a seventh, which was positioned in the middle of the hexagon, where it served as a twenty-four-hour-a-day common room and working area for the people who lived in the others. Four to five people were assigned to each of those, and two more had been shoehorned into small private cabins at the boiler room end of the central arklet, so the total population of the heptad, including Julia, was twenty-nine. This increased to thirty when Spencer Grindstaff managed to hitch a ride on a Flivver that was bringing a spare part and a technician from Izzy to fix a problem in one of the arklets' thrusters. The technician returned to Izzy when he was finished, but Spencer stayed, and talked his way into a berth on Arklet 215. There was a tendency for arklets within a group to become segregated by sex over time, as the populations sorted themselves out; 215, which was predominantly male, ran on the same shift as 174, which was all-female. They both ran on second shift, which, for reasons that were now purely historical, tended to be culturally American. They slept from dot 8 to dot 16. First shift was Asian and third shift was European. The cultural shadings were perpetuated by food: the warm odors that greeted one's nostrils upon entering the common space first thing in the "morning," the tastes one could expect to savor in the "evening." Since space food was lacking in variety, this was largely a matter of spices. The second shifters had their little bottles of Tabasco, the first shifters had plastic packets of curry powder, and so on.

"Ganging" was the term used by the Arkitects to denote this clustering of arklets into formations of three or seven: triads and heptads. It helped simplify Parambulator's job by reducing the total number of separate objects that needed to be tracked. It gave Arkies more living space to roam around in, and provided some redundancy in the case of a bolide strike. They didn't like to form anything larger than a heptad, though.

"Spencer, I am fully aware that I am out of my depth here," Julia said, "but I don't understand the upper limit of seven. I was assured, during my early briefings, that any number of arklets could in principle be ganged. Limiting it to seven seems arbitrary. Which suggests that some deeper agenda might be behind it."

"One moment please, Madam President," Spencer said. He was doing rather a lot of typing.

"You really shouldn't call me that," Julia returned, though her tone of voice was indulgent.

Spencer smacked his laptop's Enter key, then leaned back slightly and adjusted his glasses. His eyes jumped around to various parts of the screen. Then he looked up, and, in a clearer tone of voice, announced, "It's all shut down."

"The surveillance, you mean."

"Situational Awareness Network," he corrected her, and winked.

"Surveillance to you and me. It's like living in the Nixon White House. Old reference. You wouldn't understand. Now, where was I?"

Camila knew. She hadn't taken her eyes off Julia the whole time; she was on top of it. "The agenda behind the seven-arklet limit?"

"Yes, thank you, Camila. I don't buy their arguments. To me it feels, rather, like a way of atomizing the population. Keeping the Arkies from cohering into their own polity—a polity that might serve as a wholesome and desirable counterweight to the central dominance of the power structure on Izzy. Speaking of which, Spencer, I want to say how much I appreciate the work you have done in . . . *managing* things . . . on the IT front. As just now. Giving us the freedom to talk among ourselves without the SAN recording our every word and gesture."

Spencer nodded as if to say *all in a day's work.*

It was dot 18, the beginning of the workday for second shifters. They were in Arklet 215, home to Spencer, three other men, and a woman. The others had gone to breakfast in the common area, to exercise, or to work. Spencer, Julia, and Camila had been joined by a guest: Zeke Petersen, who had arrived by space suit and was still clad in his thermal coverall. He looked mildly agog. Sensing this,

Julia turned toward him with a smile. "Major Petersen," she said, "it is so good you were able to join us. Though I am new to space, I have some understanding of how difficult it is to simply drop by and say hello, as it were."

"Well, technically I am no longer a major, since that would imply the existence of a military," Zeke said, "but if we are going to use extinct titles as a courtesy, then I'll just thank you for your hospitality, Madam President."

Madam President was a little while parsing that and wasn't sure if she liked it. Nervous at the silence, Zeke went on: "I'll apologize in advance that I can't stay for very long. I'm here with a specific job to do, and once it's done, I need to move on."

"Inspecting Arklet 174 for possible damage from a microbolide strike," Julia said.

"Yes, ma'am."

"I called it in yesterday. I could have sworn I heard a loud banging noise. It scared me to death. But there doesn't seem to be any damage. And the more time goes by the more I wonder if I just imagined it. Space is a noisy environment. I hadn't expected that. The thrusters are so loud when they come on. Maybe it was nothing more than that. I would feel so embarrassed if I summoned you all the way out here to no purpose."

"Summoned me?" Zeke asked, a little bewildered. "The Incident Report System is an automatic queue; the assignments are handed out at random."

Julia exchanged a mischievous look with Spencer. "You and Spencer have been together on Izzy for more than two years," she said. "I'm sure you've come to appreciate his skills—as have I."

Zeke looked just a bit queasy. "So you got in and manipulated the queue?"

"Old habits die hard," Julia said. "I'm accustomed to working with people I know and trust. If an inspection of my arklet is required, and someone has to do it, then why not have that someone be a person I have met before? Since the assignments are handed out at random, as you say, it might as well be you."

"Well," Zeke said, "since you put it that way, I'm glad to be able to catch up with you for a few minutes, Madam President. Just saying that I'll have to complete the full inspection anyway, so we can close the loop on your report."

"Of course, and I'll bet it will go quickly," Julia answered with a wink. "Zeke, you are a member of the General Population, are you not?"

"Of course," Zeke said. "As an original member of the ISS crew, that's naturally . . ." but then his eyes strayed toward Spencer and his voice trailed off.

Julia smiled. "An awkward topic has come up, and it's best to face it with absolute transparency. Despite being a longtime, trusted member of the ISS crew, Spencer here has been removed from the General Population and demoted to the status of an Arkie."

"I wouldn't look at it as a demotion," Zeke began.

Julia silenced him with a dismissive fluttering of the fingers. These were still manicured. Camila had been doing her nails for her. "We all know it was a demotion. Markus sprang it on Spencer when he got news of the Eight Ball and saw what was coming. Oh yes, I've been filled in on all of the carefully laid plans that Markus set into motion when his sweetheart so conveniently gave him the news. Had word of it reached us at the White House, I don't know how I would have reacted—but we were busy protecting Kourou, and supporting Markus as best we knew how. Spencer here, after all those years of patient service, was replaced by that hacker boy—"

"Steve Lake?" Zeke asked.

Julia's eyes darted to Camila, who nodded.

"Yes," Julia said, "Steve Lake. I guess he's quite clever, but obviously no competition for Spencer."

"*Are* they in competition?" Zeke asked.

"In a sense yes, when we Arkies are exposed to the all-seeing eye of SAN, and the GPop is permitted to have some semblance of privacy."

"It depends on where you are in the space station," Zeke began, but then trailed off.

"I wouldn't know, since I've been permitted to spend very little time there. Oh, I know the official justification. I'm not qualified to be a member of the GPop. By process of elimination, that makes me an Arkie. Fine. But that doesn't mean I can't maintain a degree of social connection with old friends who are so privileged." Julia reached out and clasped Zeke's hand briefly.

"To be sure," Zeke said, "and I think that as time goes on those two populations will cease to be thought of as separate groups."

"I know that is the official dogma," Julia said, amused.

"But most of that social interaction is not going to be through face-to-face visits."

"So I'm told. Hard to envision how the populations will merge as long as that is the case."

"Most of it is going to be happening through Spacebook and Scape and whatnot," Zeke went on, referring to the Cloud Ark versions of popular Internet communication apps. "At least until—"

"Until we all ascend into heaven and live happily ever after as one big friendly Ark," Julia said. "Zeke, you know space operations better than anyone. What is your opinion of the strategy that Markus has been foisting on us? The Big Ride? Even the name seems a bit suggestive, doesn't it, of . . . I don't know what." She exchanged a look with Camila, who giggled at the witticism.

Zeke looked around.

"You don't need to worry about that," Julia reassured him.

"About what?"

"Markus's surveillance network."

"SAN? I wasn't worried about it," Zeke protested. "Just thinking."

"About what, pray tell? Major Petersen, all kidding aside, I really am quite keen to hear your opinions as an expert."

"To tell you the truth, I'm thinking about how thin the walls of this pressure hull are," Zeke said. "When you called in that bolide strike yesterday, you sounded pretty alarmed—I heard the message. Well, you had *every reason* to be alarmed. I do this for a living now—I go out and inspect these craters, big and small, that are piling up on our equipment. I patch holes, repair stuff that's broken, and twice now I've had to handle fatalities. It's no joke. If Markus sees an opportunity for us to ascend into heaven, as you put it, behind the shelter of Amalthea, well, I think it's worth a try."

"Is Amalthea going to shelter us from the thickening atmosphere? Camila here has been reading the technical reports for me, which Spencer has been so good as to download from the server. She tells me it's quite serious."

"The expansion of the atmosphere? It's damn serious," Zeke said. "But Izzy's ballistic coefficient, with Amalthea attached, is huge. She can plow through some pretty thick air, and the rock will absorb all the heat. And arklets can ride along in her wake, like bicyclists drafting behind a truck."

"All of the arklets?"

Zeke swallowed. "No. She doesn't make a big enough bow wave to shield all of the arklets. Unless they fly so close together that Parambulator goes nuts."

"This is the part of Markus's plan that I can't understand," Julia said. "What is to happen to all of the arklets that are not afforded the privilege of nestling into Amalthea's wake?"

"I don't know all the details of the plan," Zeke said. "It is fluid."

"Meaning, it's not really a plan," Julia said.

"It depends on when *Ymir* gets back. What kind of condition she's in. How much ice she has. Then we'll make a plan."

"And is that to be a dictatorial process? Under the, whatever it's called—the martial law thing?"

"PSAPS," Camila said.

Zeke shrugged. "I don't think Markus is going to put it up for a vote. He'll get together with his brain trust and they'll decide."

"Why bother consulting the brain trust?" Julia asked, as if the idea were a fascinating novelty.

"To bring in different perspectives . . . make sure they're not missing anything."

"Are there any Arkies in this brain trust, or are we expected to meekly accept its verdict?"

Zeke was flummoxed. Had he been given the ability to rewind and replay the conversation, he would see that he'd been outmaneuvered. Lacking that perspective, he was tongue-tied for now.

Julia wasn't. "I ask only because I've been getting to know a lot of Arkies. I have nothing else to do. No duties. No applicable skills. I find that many of them crave a bit of society. It's a natural human need, just as much as sleep and exercise. So I talk to them—in person here on our little heptad, or through the channels you mentioned, the Spacebook and the Scape. These young people find it at least a novelty to have a conversation with a lonely and bored ex-president. My point being, Major Petersen, that our system worked. The Casting of Lots and the training camps produced the brightest collection of young talent it has ever been my privilege to encounter. They are brimming over with energy and ideas. These are the scarcest resources in our universe right now—scarcer than water, scarcer than living space. And as such I'd consider it a shame if their energy was wasted and their ideas were not taken into account by whatever smoke-filled room Markus assembles to make his plan—assuming he even survives what sounds to me like a somewhat harebrained endeavor."

THE CREW OF THE ORIGINAL *JAMES CAIRD* HAD USED CELESTIAL NAVigation to find their way across hundreds of leagues of stormy seas to the coast of South Georgia Island. The crew of the *New Caird* would have to do something similar. It was easier for them. The navigator on *James Caird* had had no choice but to await breaks in the ever-present cloud cover and snatch observations when he could, comparing them against a mechanical chronometer that he hoped was still telling true time. *New Caird* had better timepieces and a better view of the sky. In place of a sextant, they had a device consisting of a wide-angle lens and a high-resolution image sensor that could tell what direction it was aimed in just by comparing what it saw to an astronomical database stored in its memory. So they knew precisely how they were oriented in space, and how that orientation was shifting as the giant shard of ice to which they were attached progressed through the inexorable mathematics of its long ellipse. That, combined with direct measurements of Earth's position, enabled Markus to calculate the parameters of their orbit and to reckon, with precision that grew each time he rechecked the figures, exactly how low they were going to go. Whenever Izzy was on their side of the planet, which was about half the time, they were able to get the latest figures from Doob concerning the expansion of the atmosphere.

It was in combining those two sets of figures that pure Newtonian mechanics began to break down. For, in a traditional calculation of a space vehicle's trajectory, one assumed no atmosphere and no extraneous forces resulting from it. But there was now no denying that *Ymir* would be going low enough to scrape the air. At a minimum, this meant it would experience some drag that would throw it off the course that Sean Probst had laid in. As these things went, drag wasn't that difficult to calculate. Its effect on their course could be estimated. But because the ice shard wasn't a symmetrical body, coming in straight, it was also going to generate some lift. Not a lot of lift—nothing like an airplane wing—but some. If that lift got aimed in the wrong direction it would make *Ymir* veer downward, like a stricken airplane going into its death spiral. But if they aimed it up, it would ease their passage by pushing them away from the Earth into an altitude where air was thinner. They would lose the benefit of lift then and drift back downward, but as the air got thicker, the lift would resume and push them back up. They might skip off the atmosphere several times during the hectic half hour when they were slingshotting around the world. The results would have been difficult to predict even if *Ymir* had been a traditional vehicle with a fixed and regular shape. But the shard was irregular. They didn't have time to measure it and to feed the data into an aerodynamics simulator, so they could only guess how much lift it was going to produce. And when its leading edge and its underside began to plow through the air—even though the air might be so thin as to be indistinguishable, for most purposes, from a vacuum—it was going to heat up. Steam would rise from it, producing some amount of upward thrust, and its shape would change. So even if they had been able to simulate the shard's aerodynamics, its lift and its drag, those numbers would quickly have become wrong during its first encounter with the upper air.

Compared with all of those complexities, the fact that *Ymir* would be flying backward while operating a damaged, experimental nuclear propulsion system at maximum power seemed like a mere detail.

Faced with so many imponderables, a well-managed aerospace engineering project would have called a halt to all further work and devoted several years to analyzing the problem down to its minutest detail, exposing pieces of ice to the blast of hypersonic wind tunnels, building simulations, and war-gaming possible alternative strategies. But by the time Markus understood the general shape of the problem, they had twenty-four hours remaining to perigee. The tangerine Earth had grown to the size of an orange. No power wielded by humans could prevent *Ymir* from passing around it and scraping the atmosphere. They couldn't even ditch. *New Caird,* detached from *Ymir,* didn't have enough propellant in her tanks to materially change her course and would end up going on the same ride anyway. So Markus made a reasonable guess as to what would be a good angle of attack—the orientation that *Ymir* would adopt vis-à-vis the atmosphere—and initiated a program of thruster firings that, over the course of half a day, swung the ponderous shard around into the position he deemed best.

Ymir's "stern" was now aimed in the direction of movement, the huge mouth of the nozzle aimed forward so that it could make the all-important braking burn. But she was now twisted about her long axis in such a way that *New Caird,* still docked up near the "bow," and projecting from the side of the shard at approximately a right angle, was on the zenith. This meant that during the passage of the high atmosphere her view of the Earth below would be blocked by *Ymir,* the nozzle of her engine pointed "up" toward the stars. Firing that engine would therefore tend to rotate the bow downward and the stern up, an attitude likely to produce more lift and help get *Ymir* out of trouble. Were the shard to tumble the other direction, it could end up in a position that would yield much more drag and much less lift, pulling the whole contraption deep into the atmosphere. In effect *New Caird* had been reduced to the status of a small attitude control thruster. It was a thruster that could only push in one direction, and so Markus had picked out the direction most likely to be useful if things began to go sideways. Vyacheslav would ride it out in *New Caird*'s pilot's seat, from which he would enjoy an arm's length, tunnel-vision view of some dirty, five-billion-year-old ice. He would wait for a verbal command from Markus, ensconced in *Ymir*'s common room, to fire *New Caird*'s main propulsion if needed.

All of this was mere background noise to Dinah, who was entirely consumed with coordinating the efforts of robots. The number of Nats was in the tens of thousands. They could only be talked to collectively, as swarms. Trying to address and control them one by one, while theoretically possible, was a mug's game. Their general task was to morph the shard.

One swarm would be working on the inner surface of the nozzle bell. At the moment, all of those were out on the back end of the shard, sunning themselves to build up their internal reserves of power.

At a signal from Dinah they would all converge on the circular maw of the nozzle, climb down into the bell, and spread out to reshape it as needed during the burn. They'd be running a program that Larz had developed and tweaked. So all Dinah really needed to do was to turn them on.

Likewise, the smallest of the three swarms was down inside the ice hoppers, running Larz's program for keeping rocks away from the augers. Working in the dark, these had to sip power from electrical taps that *Ymir*'s crew had installed for that purpose.

The largest of the three swarms, though, was responsible for sculpting the interior of the big shard as it was hollowed out. By the time the journey to Izzy was finished, most of the ice would have been fed into the hoppers and blown out the nozzle, leaving a hollowed-out shell with just enough internal structure to hold the reactor in place and maintain some semblance of a nozzle bell. This was not as crazy as it sounded, for two reasons. First, it was what miners had done since time immemorial. They didn't just hollow out mountains, since that would lead to collapse. They sculpted the mountains into structurally sound architectural systems, complete with pillars, arches, and vaults. This was just that, except that the material was ice, and the forces in general were not as large. Secondly, most of the shard's interior was of little consequence from a structural engineering standpoint. There was a reason why airplanes and race cars had been hollow shells—all skin and no bones. Most structural forces were naturally transmitted through the outermost layer of the vehicle, so that was the best place to put the strength. Enough strength on the outside made it possible to leave the inside hollow.

Ice, of course, wasn't the best material to work with. It was brittle. But the *Ymir* expedition had shipped out carrying a large supply of high-strength plastic cord, net, fabric, and loose fiber. And during the months that it had been coasting in from Grigg-Skjellerup, Larz's robots had been at work converting ice into pykrete. That outer layer of visually black ice was no longer ice per se, but a synthetic material with much better structural properties. Frozen, it could stop bullets. Melted and strained, it would separate into water, artificial fibers, and black crud from the dawn of the solar system. In any case the larger robots—the Grabbs and the Siwis—responsible for doing most of the heavy material removal on the inside could scrape to within a few meters of that outer skin without compromising *Ymir*'s structure. It was the responsibility of the third Nat swarm to clean up after them and maintain the internal pillars and webs that would keep the reactor and the hoppers suspended in the middle of the hollow shard. This swarm-based ice-sculpting algorithm had been Larz's invention, and he'd had a couple of years in which to perfect it, but Dinah was in charge of it now, and had a lot of learning to do between now and when she became fully responsible for it.

Outnumbered by the Nats, but responsible for moving a much larger tonnage of ice, were the hundred or so Grabbs and Siwis, now mostly stationed at the ready around the shard's interior. Most of these were general-purpose robots with some added-on bits that made them good at moving on ice, but there were also half a dozen Leatherface machines: upsized Grabbs with shovel-studded chain saws for limbs, made to move a lot of ice in a hurry. These were so good at their jobs that they tended to destroy their surroundings, so they had to move frequently. Each one had to be followed around by an entourage of smaller robots cleaning up its mess and getting it anchored to fresh locations.

In theory it was all just a big computer program that, when executed, would smoothly convert the solid hill of ice into something like a walnut with the meat removed: a thick, pockmarked outer shell with an organic internal system of ribs, veins, and webs. As with any other computer program, it might run perfectly when Dinah started it. But it might just as well go sideways, perhaps in a manner that wasn't obvious at first. So situational awareness was going to be a big part of her task. Interesting as it might be to look out the window and watch the Earth screaming by at twenty-four thousand miles per hour, she would need to keep her head down, searching through a roar of weak and ambiguous signals for signs that something was going awry. She liked to imagine that her days as a little girl in a mining camp, sitting in front of a radio console trying to pick out Morse code signals from far away, through static and crosstalk, might have prepared her for it in some way.

A FEW MINUTES INTO HIS SCAPE CONVERSATION WITH J.B.F., DOOB realized that, two years ago, he had done his job too well.

He'd gone into that meeting at Camp David with the mission of getting the president to understand the exponential breakup of the moon that was going to wipe out life on the Earth's surface. Putting on his Doc Dubois hat, he had coined the terms White Sky and Hard Rain as easy-to-grasp handles on phenomena that, truth be told, were much more complicated. Dr. Harris was now wishing that the late Doc Dubois had never opened his big fat mouth.

He was in a corner of the Farm that, since the departure of *New Caird,* had developed into a sort of bullpen where he and Konrad and some of the other orbital mechanics geeks hung out. The Farm had always operated something like a high school cafeteria, with different cliques habitually sitting in certain areas, and now those choices were hardening, becoming a part of Izzy's unwritten procedure manual. Anyway, they had printed out charts and plots representing, in more or less abstract form, everything that they knew about the ongoing development of the lunar debris cloud and what it might mean for the future of the Cloud Ark. The expenditure of paper and printer ink had been somewhat lavish. Two generations from now, if any humans survived, they would look on this heap of documents with some combination of disgust and amazement. Because paper was going to be scarce by then, and they would view its use for such purposes in roughly the same way as Americans of the twenty-first century had viewed the use of sperm whale oil to fuel streetlamps.

But then life would get better, forests of genetically engineered trees would grow in vast rotating space colonies, paper would become plentiful, and these sad yellowed scraps would be displayed in a museum as evidence of the privations suffered by the Arkers.

Assuming they didn't screw it up. Which was really the topic of this Scape call with Julia. She was floating in her arklet. She seemed to have adjusted to zero gee; she'd figured out how to pull her hair close to her head, the moon face had abated, she wasn't visibly nauseated. People were drifting to and fro in the background. The only one Doob recognized was Camila. A couple of other kids were doing what looked like work: prodding and massaging their tablets purposefully, looking up from time to time to engage in brief conversations. A South Asian lad, an African girl, another girl who was probably Chinese.

Girl, kid, lad, girl. His politically correct superego, cultivated during long years of service in academia, was trying to light up his shame neurons. Doob felt no shame—he was way past that—but he was struck by just how young the Arkies were, how different they were demographically from the General Population. It gave him a vaguely troubling sense of being out of touch. It had been decades since he had been young, but he had always been one of the cool kids anyway, with a big following on Facebook and Twitter. Now he was stuck on Izzy and Julia was stuck in an arklet. The two of them were hanging out with completely different populations. GPoppers saw each other all the time and talked face-to-face. Arkies were isolated in their arklets and had to use social media to reach out. Doob hadn't looked at his Spacebook page since the White Sky, and this call with Julia had been delayed for fifteen minutes while he'd tried to figure out the user interface on Scape—something with which Julia was obviously familiar and comfortable. She used it all the time, and if it didn't work, one of those kids in the background would help her with it.

Another straw in the wind: while Doob had been fumbling with Scape, he had overheard a brief snatch of conversation from the other end in which the South Asian kid had addressed Julia as "Madam President." This seemed so odd that he was tempted to bring it up in conversation. But he knew what the answer would be: It was just a courtesy. Former presidents were always addressed thus. It didn't mean anything. Why was he making a big deal about it? He would come off as some combination of uncouth and comically hypersensitive.

"Dr. Harris, as you know, I'm something of a fifth wheel around here, and so I want you to know I appreciate your taking any time at all out of whatever it is you are busy with to touch base," Julia began.

"Not at all, Madam . . . *Julia,*" Doob said, and then, because this was a video connection, resisted the urge to slap himself.

She found that interesting but decided to overlook it. "I feel like a camp counselor here," she said. "Of course, I was on top of every detail of the Arkitects' work during the run-up. But to sit in the White House looking at PowerPoints is one thing. Actually to be here is quite another."

This was quite obviously bait. Fully aware of what a sucker he was being, Doob said, "How so?"

"Well, of course the range of cultural perspectives is vast," Julia said, "but, modulo that, I find a lot of uncertainty. A sense that all of the Arkies' talents and energies are bottled up—like so many genies just waiting for someone to rub the lantern. They all so keenly want to help."

"It is, of course, less than two weeks since the Hard Rain began," Doob pointed out. "We have five thousand or so years left to go."

"The Arkie Community is well aware of those numbers," Julia remarked.

The Arkie Community. Wow. He had to admire the way she'd slipped that in.

"Julia, what's the purpose of this call? Am I to understand that whatever answers I give you will then be somehow disseminated to the Arkie Community? Because we have an email list for such purposes. An email list that includes every living human being."

"That list was most recently used two days ago. An eternity for bottled-up Arkies."

"We have been just a tad busy with the *New Caird* expedition."

"There is a lot of curiosity about that in the Arkie Community."

"There's a lot of curiosity about it *here*."

"I mean about its purpose," Julia said.

"How could its purpose be any clearer?" Doob asked. "Anyone who made it through the screening and the training required to become an Arkie"—*which doesn't include you, Julia*—"will understand exactly what we are trying to do from an orbital mechanics standpoint."

"Obtain the stupendous amount of water that will have to be expended in order to attempt the Big Ride gambit," Julia said. "Yes, Dr. Harris, even I understand that."

"Gambit? Really?"

"Do representatives of the GPop ever make much of an effort to reach out and acquaint themselves with the thoughts and perceptions of the AC?" Julia asked.

"The what?"

"The *Arkie Community,*" Julia explained, with the slightest roll of her eyes.

"At any given time, about ten percent of the Arkies are rotating through Izzy. You know this. It is the largest number we can accommodate."

"I've talked to several who have experienced that rotation. They all report the same thing. As soon as one enters the privileged environment of Izzy, with safer conditions, more room to move about, better food, and greater exposure to senior staff, the GPop worldview seems so sensible. Which only accentuates the reentry shock upon being deposited back into one's arklet."

Doob bit his tongue.

Julia continued. "What about reversing the roles a little—sending members of the GPop on temporary home stays in randomly selected arklets?"

"What about it?" Doob asked. "What purpose would it really serve?"

"From a purely technocratic standpoint, perhaps none whatsoever," Julia said. And left the rest of her thought unsaid.

"If I went on a 'home stay' in a random arklet, what would I learn that I can't learn from Scape or Spacebook?"

"A great deal, since you don't actually use those applications," said Julia, her voice deepening in amusement.

"I'm a little busy trying to get *New Caird* home. Go ahead, tell me. What am I missing?"

Movement caught his eye across the table.

He looked up to see Luisa shaking her head. Then Luisa clamped her face between her palms, closed her eyes for a moment, and opened them again. Doob felt his face warming, and once again resisted the temptation to slap himself.

"There is a lot of ferment in the AC around alternative strategies," Julia said, speaking briskly and authoritatively, as befit a woman who had just been anointed the spokesperson for said Arkie Community. "A fascinating school of thought is developing around the idea of making a passage through clean space to Mars."

"Clean space?"

"Oh, I forget you haven't been following the relevant discussion groups. Clean space is just what Tav has been calling the translunar zone, relatively free of bolides."

"Tav? Tavistock Prowse?"

"Yes, you should have a look at your old friend's blog occasionally."

Tav had been sent up to Izzy a month before the White Sky, when someone on the ground had decided that social media was going to be the glue that would hold the Cloud Ark together and that Tav was just the man for that sort of thing.

"I've been busy," Doob said. "But Tav ought to know that we have simulated and war-gamed the Mars option to within an inch of its life, and it's just not a good idea." He could see Julia formulating an objection that he didn't have the patience to listen to. "Anyone who is seriously advocating we go to Mars is—" He didn't want to say what he was thinking, which was *smoking crack,* and so he settled for "—not taking some of the practical realities into account. One solar flare at the wrong time could kill everyone."

"Only if everyone *goes.*"

"If you're talking about just sending a contingent to Mars, then you have to consider how much of our equipment and supplies they'll be allowed to take with them."

"I think many talented Arkies would volunteer to be part of a small, lean advance party. The lure of clean space is strong."

"Well, we are not in what I guess Tav considers clean space," Doob said. "We are in dirty space, and we have to focus on that reality, rather than woolgathering about trips to the Red Planet."

"You needn't remind me," Julia began.

"Yes. You saw your friend and colleague Pete Starling get chowdered by a bolide. I did actually see your Spacebook post about that, Julia. It was most affecting. I sense a 'but' coming, however."

"As the days go by without a serious incident, people begin to wonder how dirty space really is. Interest grows in the Dump and Run option. The White Sky now feels like ancient history. The Hard Rain is upon us. Every day brings a course correction or two, to avoid a major bolide, and a litany of minor events. But the death toll stands at—"

"Eighteen, as of ten minutes ago," Doob said. "We just lost Arklet 52. See, I am keeping my ear to the ground."

"I am sorry to hear that," Julia said, "and I'll bet the rest of the

AC will feel the same way, once that news has been distributed to them."

"It's on a fucking spreadsheet, Julia. All you have to do is look at it. We don't distribute news. This is not the White House."

"But in many respects it behaves like the White House," Julia said. "An orbiting White House unfettered by constitutional checks and balances. But at least the White House had a briefing room, a way of reaching out. I would be happy to . . ."

"Why are you even talking to me about this?" Doob asked. "I'm a fucking astronomer." Then, a thought. "How many conversations like this one have you been having with other members of the GPop?" He'd been assuming that Julia had singled him out as special, but for all he knew she had a call list as long as her arm, organized by those assiduous youngsters in the background. "Ivy is temporarily in charge."

"I am familiar with the chain of command that has been improvised," Julia returned. "To answer your question, Dr. Harris, I am talking to you precisely because you are an astronomer, and well positioned to answer the questions and concerns among the AC about the exact nature of the dirty space threat. This news from Arklet 52 is going to raise questions about the effectiveness of Ivy's current strategy."

"It is a statistical problem," Doob said. "On about A+0.7 it stopped being a Newtonian mechanics problem and turned into statistics. It has been statistics ever since. And it all boils down to the distribution of bolide sizes, and of the orbits in which they are moving, and how those distributions are changing over time—which we can only know from observation and extrapolation. And you know what, Julia? Even if we had perfect knowledge of every single one of those statistical parameters, we still wouldn't be able to predict the future. Because we have an n of 1. Only one Cloud Ark, only one Izzy to work with. We can't run this experiment a thousand times to see the range of different outcomes. We can only run it once. The human mind has trouble with situations like that. We see patterns where they don't exist, we find meaning in randomness. A minute ago you were casting doubt on whether dirty space was really that dirty at all—obviously arguing in favor of Dump and Run. Then I told you about what just happened to Arklet 52 and now you're swinging around to the other point of view. You are not helping, Julia. You are not helping."

Julia did not look to be accepting Doob's remarks in the spirit intended. Instead she squinted through the screen at him and shook her head slightly. "I don't understand the intensity of your reaction, Dr. Harris."

"This conversation is over," Doob said, and hung up on her. He then fought off a temptation to slam the tablet down on the table. Instead he sat back in his chair and looked Luisa in the eye for the first time in a while. On one level he'd wanted to watch her face the whole time. But Julia would have noticed that, would have figured out that someone else was in the room, silently listening.

Just as someone had probably been doing at Julia's end.

Luisa just sat there in her listening shrink mode.

"It would be easier," Doob said, "if I could figure out what the hell she wanted."

"You're assuming," Luisa said, "that she has a plan. I doubt that she does. She is driven to seek power. She finds some way to do that and then backfills a rationalization for it afterward."

Doob pulled his tablet closer and started trying to find Tav's blog. "To what extent do you imagine she really is reporting facts about the AC? As opposed to creating the reality she describes?" Doob asked.

"What's the difference?" Luisa asked.

DINAH LOOKED UP AND SAW THAT THE EARTH WAS THE SIZE OF A grapefruit. She took a nap, ate some food, and buckled down to work again, then looked up to see that it was the size of a basketball. Still not that big; and yet such was their speed that it was only an hour away.

They had a final briefing session in *Ymir*'s common room, which had become a makeshift bridge for this ungainly ship.

Dinah had scrounged three flat-panel monitors from various parts of the command module and zip-tied them to the common room table. These were covered with overlapping windows of various sizes. Some were terminal windows showing log entries or editors showing code, but most were video feeds showing different robots' points of view on the mining operation. Only one of them looked outward: she'd positioned a redundant Siwi on the stern, toward the nadir, and aimed its camera at Earth. Other than that, her only "situational awareness" would come from a celestial navigation program that would display, in a small window, a three-dimensional rendering of the Earth with *Ymir*'s trajectory superimposed on it as a geometric curve. Along the bottom of that window was a series of graphs plotting velocity and altitude versus time. Their velocity at the moment was some six thousand meters per second, up from four thousand just a couple of hours ago; within the next hour it would double if they took no action, then begin to drop again as they left perigee behind and coasted away into space.

That velocity would take them all the way back out to L1 again unless Jiro succeeded at his task, which was to slow them down. He had satisfied himself with but a single flat-panel screen, which he'd set up directly across the table from Dinah's triptych. From here he would be managing the reactor. He had already begun to pull some of the control blades, just to get a sense of how quickly it would come to full power when he did it for real. A miscalculation on that front had led to the fuel rod breach that had indirectly killed Sean, and Jiro didn't want any surprises this time around.

Some minutes before perigee, if Markus felt that things were otherwise going to plan, Jiro would issue commands that would bring the reactor up to its full thermal power output of about four gigawatts. Ice would melt to superheated water, and steam would howl through the Inconel throat of the nozzle, expanding and cooling in the bell until it turned into a hypersonic blizzard, a white lance of cold fire pushing against the great ship's movement, slowing her down. Not so much as to let her fall into the atmosphere and die, but enough to reduce her orbit to something more like Izzy's. *Ymir* would experience acceleration, which would feel to its inhabitants like gravity. All the stuff that was now floating around loose aboard *Ymir* and *New Caird* would fall "down." Dinah and Jiro would drop into the chairs that they'd positioned in front of their monitors. So would Markus, for he had built his own nest of tablets and monitors at the head of the table, mostly occupied with navigational data. Up in *New Caird,* Slava would find himself pressed into his acceleration couch at an awkward sideways angle. The gee forces would be modest enough—even a four-gigawatt nuclear propulsion system could only exert so much force against the momentum of such a large chunk of ice. If their "weight" remained steady over time, it was a sign that things were going well. If it increased, it probably meant that they were going to die. For the only thing that could slow them down and increase their perceived weight beyond a certain level was contact with the atmosphere. The more they slowed down, the lower they dropped. The lower they dropped, the thicker the air got. The thicker the air got, the more force it exerted on the ship. They would read this as a sense of increased weight. It was an exponential spiral that, beyond a certain point, would lead to the inevitable destruction of *Ymir, New Caird,* and everyone on board. The only real question would be the manner of their death. In a smaller, lighter craft they might be burned alive. Here, being surrounded by ice, it was more likely that they would lose consciousness from the gee forces first—a relatively painless way to go. Dubois Harris and Konrad Barth, gazing down on them from a few hundred kilometers above, would see them go out as a blue streak over the southern hemisphere, and would give the news to Ivy so that she could issue a statement to the Cloud Ark that, if Dinah was any judge of her friend, she had already written, just in case she needed it.

It was strange to be so close to them in distance, but so far away in the nonintuitive space of delta vees. Bandwidth between *New Caird* and Izzy was excellent now, and Dinah had to make a conscious effort not to get distracted by the availability of text messaging and even Spacebook. *See you in a few xoxo,* Ivy had texted her, and Dinah had sent back something in the same vein, then closed the window.

Vyacheslav was donning one of the blue thermal garments worn beneath space suits. This, she knew, was just a precaution, in case he had to "go outside" on short notice for some reason. Slava had stationed his space suit in *New Caird*'s airlock, so that he could exit to the outside of the shard if needed, and Dinah had pre-positioned two Grabbs there, to help him get around.

Markus could be pretty unceremonious about things, which was just his leadership style—his way of implicitly telling people he expected them to do their bloody jobs without pep talks beforehand or congratulations afterward. It didn't work for everyone. Some people liked ceremony. But he hadn't invited any of those along on this expedition. So there was no particular moment when it all started. They just kept getting closer to the Earth. Slava darted up the companionway to the top of the command module, and a minute later announced that he was positioned before the controls of *New Caird*. Jiro called out milestones in the startup of the reactor, occasionally proffering hints as to how the figures should be understood: "That is a little faster than I expected . . . settling down now . . . this is according to plan . . . ready to proceed on your command . . ." and so on. Markus's participation consisted largely of chewing his thumbnail while staring fixedly at his screen. From time to time he would reach out and type something, or swipe and tap on his tablet. Dinah's work was almost entirely abstract, several layers removed from what obviously mattered. She tried to focus on it and to ignore the sounds of a thousand loose objects settling to the "floor" of *Ymir* as gravity "came on" due to a combination of *Ymir*'s increasing thrust and the steady buildup of atmospheric pushback.

"Now," Markus said.

"Acknowledged," Jiro responded. "Control blades are responding to program . . . and . . . we have criticality."

Four gigawatts of thermal power—enough to supply Las Vegas—came online in the next few seconds. Dinah felt it as a massive increase in weight and heard it as a cacophony of creaks, groans, and crashing noises as the command module, and the ice surrounding it, came under structural load. She saw it on her screens as sudden and frantic change in windows that had remained frustratingly static for the last hours. The ice hoppers, which had been brimful for weeks, began to empty at a shocking pace as the augers spun. A couple of her "point of view" robots fell or skidded from their points of anchorage, events that showed up as sudden and unhelpful shifts in camera angle. She hit "go" on a program that tasked every robot in the shard to deliver more ice into the hoppers as fast as possible, and tried to keep one eye on that while monitoring the structural integrity of the shard as a whole. In the traditional scheme of things, miners had done all their work under gravity, so structural mistakes had manifested themselves soon, and dramatically, as cave-ins. *Ymir* was a mine that had been slowly delved under zero gee and only subjected to "gravity" for short periods when the engine came on, and so there was a certain nervous feeling of not knowing whether it might all collapse. So far, it looked fine.

"We are losing velocity nicely," Markus muttered through what was left of his thumbnail, and Dinah permitted herself a glance at the graphs to verify that this was so. Time had gone by faster than she had known; they were just minutes away from perigee. "Nicely" in Markus's phrasing meant "enough to make a difference but not so much as to kill us."

Then Markus said, "Slava. A three-second burn, please."

"Da," answered the Russian. Then, a few second later, he said, "It is beginning."

They wouldn't have known Slava was doing anything, save for an external camera that Dinah had positioned on the surface of the shard at some distance from *New Caird,* looking back at it. This showed a ghostly blue flare emerging from the small ship's nozzle bell, shoving *Ymir*'s nose down and swinging its stern up slightly.

Ymir shuddered faintly. Dinah didn't know what to make of it. She feared it might be a cave-in until she identified it as a sensation she had never expected to feel again: atmospheric buffeting. She had not been this close to the surface of the Earth since she'd been launched into orbit almost a year before Zero. And if the next few minutes went well, she'd never be this close again.

The shuddering didn't last. The graphs on her screen had all picked up little wiggles that were steadily receding into the past. "We skipped," Markus said. "I think we will do it at least one more time."

"Augers four and eleven are down," Jiro announced. "I will try reversing them to clear the jam."

This brought Dinah's attention back. At a glance she checked all of the levels in the hoppers and saw them dropping quickly, as expected, despite the robots' efforts to replenish them. The two that Jiro had identified were overfull, since there was no way to get the ice out of them. Dinah activated a subprogram that would put some Grabbs to work transferring surplus ice from hoppers 4 and 11 to nearby ones that could use it.

"The *Caird* burn worked," Markus said, "but it gave us a little too much rotation. I am counteracting using thrusters—and this will take a little while." He entered some commands that, presumably, turned on those of *Ymir*'s attitude thrusters that pushed in the opposite direction from *New Caird*'s big engine. "By the way, we just passed through perigee—I hope."

Dinah glanced at the plots and saw that they had indeed passed the midway point of the maneuver. Somewhat paradoxically, though, their altitude was dropping—headed for their second, and hopefully their last, "skip" off the atmosphere.

"We're on some weird new course now," she said.

"It is true," Markus said. "If we survive the next few minutes, we can fix it later."

"Auger eleven works again," Jiro reported, "but two and three are down. We may have a critical propellant shortage."

"Damned thrusters are not powerful enough. We have overcorrected," Markus said, "and now we are coming in for another skip. We are flying not only backward but upside down."

So the burn from *New Caird*'s engine had done its job. It had depressed the ship's "nose," which was pointed backward, and prevented the stern, currently pointed forward, from digging in. They'd grazed the atmosphere with the shard's broad side and gotten a nice skip out of it—a bounce that might've saved their lives. But once the shard began to rotate, it was difficult to make it stop, and now it had gone too far. The nose was pointed too steeply downward, the nozzle bell was aimed up toward space.

"So we're thrusting *down* toward the planet now?" Dinah asked.

"Not enough to hurt us. Maintain thrust," Markus ordered.

"I am running out of ice," Jiro said, and glanced over his monitor at Dinah.

Dinah had already warned them that supplying enough propellant to do all of this in one huge burn would be a close-run thing, assuming everything went perfectly. Everything hadn't. She met Jiro's eyes, shook her head, and went back to work.

"Get ready to shut it down, Jiro," Markus said. "We are descending into thick air and I don't know what is going to happen."

Their inner ears told them that *something* was happening. The powerful thrust was still driving them into their seats, but some force had taken *Ymir* by the nose and was torquing it around.

"We hit nose first," Markus said, "and we are spinning back. Main engine shutdown in three. Two. One. Now."

A nuclear steam engine didn't shut off quickly. The thrust faltered and tapered off in response to whatever commands Jiro had entered. It was the better part of a minute, though, before they were back in zero gravity—meaning in a free orbit with no thrust pushing them around.

"I'll give you our new orbital parameters in a minute," Markus said. "It is complicated because we are tumbling."

In the sudden silence that followed the engine's shutoff, Dinah could hear distant, tinny shouting. She realized it was an open audio channel from Izzy, coming from a pair of headphones she had ripped off her head during the maneuver. It was the sound of people in the Tank. When she pulled the phones back onto her head she could tell that they were celebrating.

"THAT WAS A BIG-ASS DELTA VEE YOU GUYS JUST RIPPED OFF!" DOOB said when he heard Dinah's voice on the other end of the link. "You deserve congratulations."

Dinah's response, after a few seconds' delay, was guarded. "But not big-ass enough?"

It was strange hearing the voice of one you knew well modulated through this old-school audio tech. Like hearing Dinah doing a Buzz Aldrin impression at a party. The emotional nuance came through more clearly than the actual words.

"Konrad is still calculating your params," Doob said, "but just on visual inspection we can see how much you slowed down. Fantastic."

"Sounds like we'll be needing another pass then," she said. Meaning that they would have to wait for *Ymir* to loop once more around the Earth, and do another burn at her next perigee, in order to slow down enough to rendezvous with Izzy.

"This time you can work with a higher perigee," he pointed out, "so you don't have to fly that damn piece of ice through the pea soup again."

"Flying this damn piece of ice kind of stresses me out," Dinah allowed.

"The glass is half full, baby," Doob said. "The glass is half full. You *lit* that candle. It worked. You bounced off the atmosphere. You're a hell of a lot closer to us—Konrad is saying your apogee is definitely sublunar." Meaning that *Ymir* would turn around and start falling back toward the Earth before reaching the orbit of the former moon. "This is huge," he added. "It is going to change the picture politically."

After a lengthy pause, Dinah asked, "Politically?" as if she couldn't quite believe what she had heard.

"I'M AWARE OF THE FACT THAT IVY HAS TURNED A DEAF EAR TO ALL of your ideas," Julia began, just as soon as Spencer had typed in the commands that disconnected Arklet 453 from the Situational Awareness Network. "I presume she also went out of her way to place obstacles in the path of your coming here for this meeting."

The Martians—Dr. Katherine Quine, Ravi Kumar, and Li Jianyu—looked somewhat nonplussed. It was *always* difficult to travel between arklets. The waiting time for nonurgent Flivver trips was about two days, and emergencies could rearrange the queue at the last minute. As a member of the General Population, Dr. Quine had the most Olympian perspective on this—she was an urgent care doctor frequently called upon to make excursions to arklets. She was about ten years older than Kumar and Jianyu, who were Arkies chosen in the Casting of Lots from India and China respectively. Those two had ended up together in Arklet 303, which had turned out to be a hotbed of Martian agitation. It was part of a triad with a total population of eighteen, half of whom currently had the flu, and so Katherine Quine had had a legitimate excuse to go there. She'd made the most of the opportunity by scooping up Ravi and Jianyu and coming here with them. Of the people in this conversation, she was probably the least inclined to see dark deeds by Ivy in the slowness of inter-arklet transport. It was a different story with Ravi and with Jianyu, who, for a number of reasons, were receptive to Julia's suggestions on that front. In another time and place, Dr. Quine might have quibbled. But time was short, and trying to raise Julia's opinion of the Cloud Ark's current management did not seem like an efficient way to use it. So she let it go. And by the time she had processed all of that, Julia had moved on anyway.

"Given that, I'm all the more appreciative that you made the arduous and risky journey to meet with me in person," Julia said. "It is my firm conviction that, centuries from now, young Martians sitting in classrooms on the Red Planet will read in their history books—or whatever they have in place of books—about this meeting and what came of it."

Ravi Kumar raised an index finger. "Instead of educating the young in classrooms," he said, "why not do away altogether with the traditional structure of mass education and take a personalized, individualized approach? There's no reason to repeat Earth's mistakes on Mars."

"I could not agree with you more," Julia said, "and these sorts of fresh ideas only make me more eager to find a way of getting as many people there as soon as possible. How do we get started? What would be entailed in sending a forward advance party to Mars?"

For the second time in as many minutes, Dr. Quine looked a bit unsettled. She glanced around Arklet 453. This was the central, common-space arklet of the heptad that included numbers 174—the abode of Julia and Camila—and 215—that of Spencer Grindstaff. Or at least that was what it said on the official records. Some reshuffling had occurred. All the men and women who lived in those two arklets now seemed to conceive of themselves as members of J.B.F.'s personal staff. They had taken over 453 and turned it into a sort of West Wing.

Katherine Quine said, "Presuming we had authorization to send such a mission—"

"Let me just cut you off there, if you would indulge me, Dr. Quine. What you just raised is a matter of politics. I consider that to be my 'superpower' and I would like to place it at the disposal of you and the other members of the Martian Community—the ones you already know of, the ones who sympathize with you in secret, and others who may sign on once it becomes clear to them what a fundamentally sensible idea the Mars trip really is. So I would propose that we assume, for purposes of this little chat, that authorization is not a problem. I would like to see you three using your own 'superpower' of designing this mission in a way that makes sense without letting the political dimension interfere at all. Once we have designed a coherent plan, we can then move on to questions of implementation."

"In a perfect scenario we would dump the rock and simply take everything, all at once," Jianyu said. It was the first time he had spoken, but he seemed to have been emboldened by Julia's talk of superpowers.

"There are powerful forces that would have to be convinced before such a thing could happen," Julia said. "Let's think in terms of an advance party: lean, efficient, smart, but big enough to get the job done. That means landing on Mars and reporting back to the remainder of the Cloud Ark."

"We've been talking about such a mission. We think we could do it with a bolo consisting of a heptad and a triad," Katherine said.

"Ten arklets," Julia said. "That doesn't seem all that many, does it?"

"During the initial delta vee," Ravi Kumar said, "the arklets would be stacked. Once they were on course for Mars they would form a bolo, so that the members of the expedition could experience Earth-normal gravity during the six-month journey."

Jianyu added, "Propulsion and other components could come from the MIV kit. Most of the design work has already been done for us."

Katherine said, "Aerobraking would be needed at the end, to slow it down. Before that, the bolo could be reeled in, the arklets could restack into a unified ship, and there would be time to survey the surface from orbit and decide on a landing place."

Julia nodded. "And if I may put a hard question to you all, what would be the survival time of this isolated colony, once it had landed? How long before it ran out of provisions?"

This caused the three Martians to clam up and look at one another.

"I only ask," Julia said, "because politics—my department—once again rears its ugly head here. Once your heroics have been accomplished, the burden falls to me to seal the deal, as it were. The advance party lands and sends back its joyous message. A ticking-clock element enters the picture. Which I do not mean in a negative way—this can be a powerful incentive to mobilize people's energies, as we saw in the case of the buildup to the Hard Rain. It is at that point when I can address the people of the Cloud Ark and say, 'Here is the opportunity—will we seize it? Or will we shrink away from it and let these brave people slowly expire?' That is a speech that I think I could deliver to great effect. I just need to have some sense of the time element."

"A year for sure," Katherine said. "Beyond that, it becomes a medical question. A statistical question."

"Statistics," Julia repeated, and sighed. "I have been hearing a lot about that from Dr. Harris."

"SO, YOU'RE TELLING ME WE'VE LOST TRACK OF WHO IS EVEN IN J.B.F.'S heptad?" Ivy asked.

There was silence around the big table in the Banana. Ivy had begun to hold important meetings in this old familiar space, closer to the central axis of the Stack and farther forward in Amalthea's cone of shelter. It wouldn't do to have the Cloud Ark's command structure decapitated by a single unlucky bolide strike—a disaster much more likely to happen whenever they met in the big T3 spaces like the Tank and the Farm.

Present for this meeting were Doob, Luisa, Fyodor, and three handpicked members of Markus's staff who had become a sort of executive troika: Sal Guodian, the one-man judicial system. Tekla, the head of security. And Steve Lake, the dreadlocked ginger who was responsible for network and computer matters.

"The default system for keeping track of who is where," Sal began, "is based on the assumption that people will actually cooperate with it."

Ivy held up a hand. "Stop. Before you go into explanations, I need a yes or no."

"Yes," Steve Lake said, "we have lost track of who is in J.B.F.'s heptad."

"Thank you," Ivy said. "And somehow the SAN isn't helping us fill in the gaps?"

Steve said, "One of the people who is definitely in that heptad is Spencer Grindstaff."

Ivy nodded.

Sal said, "Steve, when Markus pulled you into his office, just before the White Sky, and put you in charge of the network—replacing Spencer—you made some remark to the effect that Spencer might know of back doors into Izzy's systems. Back doors that would be impossible for you to know about until he used them."

"Yeah," Steve said. "Almost by definition, we can't find something like that until it's used. Not without manually reading through every line of code."

"You think he has a back door into the SAN?"

"We know he's doing something," Steve said, "because as soon as he turned up there, the arklets in J.B.F.'s heptad began dropping off the network from time to time. Whenever she's having a meeting she doesn't want us to know about, he turns everything off."

Ivy considered this for a moment, then looked across the table at Tekla and nodded. Tekla rose—carefully, for the gravity was quite weak here—and went to the door. She opened it to reveal Zeke Petersen waiting outside, and waved him in.

"Thanks for joining us," Ivy said, breaking a silence during which Zeke took a seat at the foot of the table. Ivy was at the head of it. She was looking "up" a long ski jump ramp at him, and he was doing likewise at her.

"Just like old times, Commander Xiao," Zeke said.

"Well, I appreciate your loyalty," Ivy said. "I know this must be awkward for you."

"Not at all, actually," Zeke said. "The announcement that Markus made, when he called it, at the onset of the Hard Rain—declaring all existing nations to be dissolved—I took that to heart. Julia didn't hear that announcement. She didn't get the memo."

"We've been hearing a little about Spencer's ability to disconnect from SAN."

Zeke nodded. "Confirmed. I was there for one such incident. We had a very strange conversation. I think they were testing the waters to see whether I might be recruited. She spoke to me as if I were already on her side—as if it were unthinkable that I wouldn't be. It's a pretty good persuasive technique—she had me going for a little bit. But once I got out of there and slept on it, I saw how crazy it was."

"Did you have the sense that this was a one-off? Or was she working her way down a list of possible recruits?"

"If I had to guess, I'd say there was a list," Zeke said, "but not a long list."

Ivy nodded. She didn't have to spell it out: J.B.F. might have recruited some others—others they didn't know about yet.

"It tallies with what I saw," Doob said, and glanced at Luisa for a confirming nod. "I think she is just being opportunistic. She reaches out to people, draws them into conversations, drops hints, probes for vulnerabilities."

"Is she nuts?" Ivy asked Luisa.

"In a sense it doesn't matter," Luisa said. "If she's making trouble, she's making trouble. Tracing that to a diagnosable psychiatric condition doesn't really change anything."

"It might change the approach that we take."

"She was narcissistic to begin with," Luisa said. "This isn't a formal diagnosis, mind you. But according to what we heard from you and Dinah, her trip up to Izzy was pretty traumatic. She lost her husband and her child and blood was spilled along the way. It doesn't take a trained professional to guess that she is suffering from some level of PTSD. Connected with that we might expect her to have a dark, paranoid vision of the world. But she may have been that way to begin with."

"She's cagey," Ivy said. "As long as all she's doing is talking to people, there's not much I can or should do."

"Agreed," Luisa said. "She is building a political base among the Arkies. If you take some action against her, with your sole pretext being that she's talking to a lot of people, then you've given her just what she wants. But some outreach on your part to the Arkies might be a good idea."

Ivy sighed. "The only answer to politics is more politics," she said, "and that's where I'm most useless."

"Deeds, not words," Zeke said. "That's what really matters. And when *Ymir* pulls in, you and Markus will have accomplished something that's going to make J.B.F. and her clique look puny."

"I MAY BE OUT OF MY DEPTH HERE," JULIA SAID, AFTER A LONG AND thoughtful pause, "but we seem to have a striking coincidence that is staring us right in the face."

"Go on, Madam President," Camila urged her. "It might be obvious to you, but I for one cannot see it."

Julia looked at Katherine Quine. "As I understand it, the key elements of the proposed Mars ship are a heptad, for the humans to live in during the voyage, and a triad, for bulk storage of propellants and whatnot. And this matches up quite neatly with our strengths." She managed a self-deprecating chuckle. "I say 'our.' What do I mean by that? I suppose I'm going out on a limb by imagining that there might be some sort of a natural alliance between the Arkie Community and the Martians. A sort of ragtag rebel coalition, if you will. Here in this heptad we have rapidly assembled a social hub for advocacy of concerns relevant to the AC. In a sense we have our own heptad now. And in a like sense, you, Ravi and Jianyu, have developed your triad into an intense focus of Martian advocacy. You have your own triad. So the two largest components of the Mars expedition have already been acquired. They just need to be put together."

Ravi was nodding. "Two of the engineers on the MIV team are keen on it. They helped build *New Caird* and are eager to tackle a new problem. Of the two, one might even come with us. Paul Freel. He has been a strong advocate of Mars colonization since long before Zero."

Katherine had been listening intently, and now broke in: "I don't mean to sound a skeptical note, Madam President, but in what sense do you really 'have' this heptad, or do our friends here 'have' the triad where they live? It might be true in the sense of having majority rule. But—"

"But what does ownership really mean in this context? Hmm, yes, it is a very profound question, Dr. Quine, and I'm glad you raised it. So many things we took for granted before, such as property rights and individual liberty, are clouded by Markus's declaration of PSAPS. Or martial law, if we want to call a spade a spade. But as a first step toward answering your question, I would suggest that the ability to come and go at will is inextricable from ownership—that's what it would really mean to 'have' an arklet, or a triad, or a heptad."

"Well, in that sense we're really all subject to the collective dictates of the swarm," Katherine said. "Parambulator is what decides where we go when."

"It truly is one of the most insidious instruments of social control ever devised," Julia said.

Katherine looked mildly aghast. "But without it, we have a disaster."

"That is what makes it so insidious," Julia said. "One can always justify it by making the safety argument. We will all be slaves of Parambulator until and unless someone decides that some things are more important."

Jianyu was looking alert and curious. "If someone did decide that," he said, "it would change nothing unless the arklet in question was switched over to manual control."

"It's my understanding that this can be done at any time," Julia said. "Was I misinformed?"

"No," Jianyu answered, "but it would show up very prominently on Parambulator. It would set off alarms all over the Situational Awareness Network."

"In that case," Julia said, "we shall have to deal with the SAN when and if the time comes to take decisive action."

IVY'S GRANDMOTHER, A GUANGZHOU-BORN, HONG KONG–RAISED woman who spoke only a few words of English, had ruled the family from a mother-in-law apartment over a garage in Reseda. Enthroned on a duct-taped La-Z-Boy and swaddled in crocheted afghans, she had handed down a series of diktats, pronunciamentos, and fatwas that had taken on the force of law within her family of three dozen direct descendants and in-laws scattered across the San Fernando Valley. While not indifferent to money, love, security, and other common psychological drives, she seemed to have been motivated by another need that was obscure and hence mysterious to most of those who paid fealty to her. Anglos might have Orientalized this as "face" or Confucian respect for one's elders.

Ivy came to understand it as a simple need for attention. Anyone who entered or left the house had to check in with Grandmother. And it was not enough just to poke one's head in the door and say hello or goodbye; one had to sit down in the rattan side chair next to the La-Z-Boy and spend a few minutes and say a few words. Grandmother had no power to enforce this regulation other than finding arcane and baroque ways to wreak long-term revenge on those who flouted it.

Julia Bliss Flaherty, as Ivy now realized, was of the same stripe. Pinned down and obliged to justify herself, she would explain her actions in terms of some altruistic plan. And she might even believe it. But it wasn't that at all. She was like Ivy's grandmother. If you paid fealty to her, she would favor you, and your reputation and power would grow among all the others who did likewise. If you sent her off to an arklet and ignored her, you became an enemy of her and of her network. She wielded no power other than that. But, ignored long enough, she could become a mighty foe. Her status as an ex-president—and not just any old ex-president, but the one who had overseen the construction of the Cloud Ark and even used nuclear weapons to protect it—gave her credibility among the Arkies. It had become common to think of those as scattered and demoralized, just waiting for a leader to bring them identity and purpose. Ivy had lost track of whether that was an accurate perception or a self-perpetuating myth spread by J.B.F. In any case, it had taken on the force of reality.

She was sitting across the table from Tekla, wondering whether it would be productive to explain all of these thoughts to her. Would this Russian heptathlete care about, or understand, Ivy's dead Cantonese grandmother in Reseda?

Maybe. But Tekla came from a tradition in which details were hoarded and dispensed on a need-to-know basis. Presented with too much information, she became baffled, bored, and finally irritated. Toward those who talked too freely, she felt the same sort of contempt as a businessman might feel toward a spendthrift. She just wanted to know what her job was.

The same quality made it difficult to get inside Tekla's head. But that was okay. In a big organization with a military-style chain of command, you didn't have to be everyone's friend and treasured colleague. Markus understood as much, which was why he had ended up running the place. More Ivy's speed had been the boutique operation that had been Izzy at Zero. Markus would have been terrible at that.

"This thing with Julia is a distraction. Nothing more," Ivy said. "Much more important things demand my focus. Making a big deal out of it will backfire—give her more power than she deserves. But we can't ignore what she is doing."

Tekla was nodding. Good.

"I want you to go and visit her heptad," Ivy continued. "You will go there in your capacity as Markus's security chief. Do you understand? It is an official visit. You will explain that there have been problems with the Situational Awareness Network that could have dangerous consequences unless they are fixed. Beyond that, I just want you to listen to her. Because I think that she will try to bring you over to her side. It's what she does with everyone. You would be a prize catch."

"If she does as you predict," Tekla said, "what should be my response?"

It was a measure of Ivy's naïveté that she didn't even follow Tekla's question at first. Then she understood that Tekla was suggesting she might pretend to become one of Julia's followers. She was volunteering to become a mole in Julia's network.

Tekla stolidly watched Ivy's face as Ivy figured it out.

"I would suggest taking no immediate action," Ivy said. Which, in truth, was Ivy being not so much cagey as timid.

"Of course," Tekla said, "to show eagerness is poor tactics, it will only arouse her suspicion."

Ivy said nothing. Tekla explained, "I know many people with such minds." *And you obviously don't, honey.*

"My suggestion is that you report to me in person first and then we will come to a decision."

"We?"

"I. I will come to a decision."

"It is good that we meet here. In the Banana," Tekla said.

"You like it?"

Tekla looked nonplussed. "It is not that I like it. The Banana is more secure."

"From bolides, you mean."

Tekla shook her head. "From Grindstaff." Then she stood up—carefully, so as not to fly up and bang her head on the ceiling—and departed, leaving Ivy alone with a head full of questions. Had she really just embarked on the project of setting up an internal espionage network within the Cloud Ark? How was she going to explain that to Markus? Would he be horrified, or impressed? In either case, how would she feel about his reaction? When the hell was Dinah going to get back so that they could discuss this kind of thing over distilled spirits?

And what had Tekla meant by that last comment, that the Banana was more secure from Grindstaff? It was old, pre-Zero, and so its connection to the SAN was retrofitted and kludgy. Tekla seemed to be suggesting that if Spencer could hack the SAN to the extent of disconnecting Julia's arklets from it, then maybe he could also hack it to the extent of placing other parts of the Cloud Ark—including the Farm, the Tank, and Markus's office—under surveillance.

I know many people with such minds, Tekla had said. She was talking about Russian military and intelligence types, accustomed to the byzantine thoughtways of those professions. Perhaps Tekla herself had once been groomed as an intelligence asset. If Tekla really did become a mole in Julia's network, then how could Ivy be sure that she was a straight-up mole, loyal to Ivy, and not a double agent, loyal to Julia?

THE SCRAPE WITH THE ATMOSPHERE HAD LEFT *YMIR* TUMBLING slowly as it hurtled away from the Earth on its new orbit. Calculating exactly what that orbit was took them fifteen or twenty minutes, and told them that they had fewer than four hours in which to take actions needed to save their lives.

If all had gone perfectly, the nuclear burn would have slowed *Ymir* down to the point where a rendezvous with Izzy could then have been achieved with a few small additional delta vees. They had hoped this might happen, but not seriously expected it. The best they could really hope for was to shed some velocity and reduce the height of their apogee.

That figure—the distance separating the Earth and the ship at the top of her orbit—was directly related to how much velocity she had at the bottom. Because *Ymir* had "fallen" in from an extremely high apogee, far beyond the moon's former orbit, she had come in screaming hot for her skip off the atmosphere. Every bit of velocity that was killed by the huge nuclear retro-rocket burn, or by friction with the air, translated into a lower altitude at the succeeding apogee, which—depending on how the numbers had worked out—would occur weeks, days, or hours later.

The answer, once they had run the numbers, turned out to be hours.

In one sense, *Ymir* had missed her target by a mile; the total delta vee she had achieved had been less than a third of what they'd hoped for. And yet this had been enough to bring her apogee down from far beyond the moon's orbit to a figure only about thrice the altitude at which Izzy circled the Earth.

Likewise, the period—the amount of time it took to complete an orbit—had dropped from seventy-five *days* to a mere eight *hours*. The lesson being that huge alterations in those figures could be purchased for comparatively small amounts of delta vee.

Bringing *Ymir* the rest of the way down to Izzy's orbit, on the other hand, would require twice as much delta vee as they'd wrung out of the "burn" just completed.

Long before worrying about that, however, they would have to survive the next eight hours.

Ymir's apogee might have been radically altered, but her perigee altitude was unchanged—meaning that it was still dangerously low. If they took no action, the next go-round would therefore bring them roaring and bouncing across the top of the atmosphere again.

On one level, raising the perigee a bit, so that they'd never have to worry about the atmosphere again, was an easy task. They could do it with a small but precisely calibrated burn at apogee. In a normal space mission, such a thing would have been straightforward. Here, it was complicated by two factors. First of all, their success in lowering the apogee, and shortening the period, had imposed a tight deadline—four hours after perigee—when that burn needed to occur.

The second complication was the ship's slow tumble. This meant that their nuclear rocket engine was never pointed in the right direction, save by lucky accident. During the big burn at perigee, they had wanted the nozzle pointed forward, so that it would serve as a huge retro-rocket. The upcoming burn at apogee was intended to speed her up a bit, and so they needed the nozzle pointed aft. But as long as she tumbled, it was aimed in no particular direction.

So their task now was to stabilize *Ymir*'s attitude by using her thrusters to push back against the unwanted rotation. And, as they had discovered the first time they'd tried it, her thrusters were small and weak compared to the momentum of the big ice shard. In aerospace lingo, they lacked control authority. *Ymir* was like a truck skidding on a patch of oil, responding only faintly to the steering wheel. That problem had been alleviated somewhat by the large expenditure of mass during the burn. Many tons of ice had been hurled out the nozzle in the form of steam. *Ymir* was lighter and more wieldy as a result. Calculating exactly *how much* more wieldy she was, and what it meant for the thrusters' control authority, was, in itself, a significant task that consumed another half an hour just for a rough estimate.

The result was not encouraging. In the three hours remaining, there was simply no way that *Ymir*'s attitude control thrusters—designed for tiny adjustments over long spans of time—could neutralize her tumble. The tumble wasn't especially fast—the crew in the command module could barely sense that they were rotating—but it was enough to make the next rocket burn impossible. And if they couldn't make that burn in three hours, they'd scrape the atmosphere again in an additional four, and again eight hours after that. They might survive one more ride like the first one, but they couldn't survive two.

Once all of this had become clear to Markus, he had divided the crew in half, leaving Dinah and Jiro in the command module's common room to look after the propulsion system and going "above" with Vyacheslav to consider the problem of attitude control.

Dinah's task was, comparatively speaking, routine. During the perigee burn, they had expended most of the ice stored in the hoppers. Some of the augers had jammed, and the whole ice-mining operation had been thrown into general disarray as she had improvised solutions to problems that came at her from every direction. Robots were in the wrong places; some hoppers were overfull while others were empty. New ice needed to be mined and old ice needed to be rearranged. Fixing all of that in time for another burn in three hours was not an insuperable task, but it would require her full attention. Likewise, Jiro had a few reactor issues to think about. Both of them would have to toil diligently between now and the apogee burn in order to be ready.

Assuming, that is, that the other half of the crew had, in the meantime, figured out a way to get *Ymir* aimed in the right direction. Markus had moved that job to another part of the ship where it wouldn't pose a distraction to the propulsion crew. Or such was his intent; but in moments when Dinah lost focus briefly, while compiling some code or foraging for a snack, she found herself wondering what they were doing up there.

By process of elimination, it had to be something involving *New Caird.* They had already demonstrated that *Ymir*'s thrusters weren't up to the task. Only *New Caird*'s main engine had enough thrust to make a difference. The problem was that it was pointed in one fixed direction, which didn't happen to be the one in which they actually needed to push.

Following that chain of reasoning to its logical conclusion made her nervous, to the point where she was almost more distracted than she would have been had Markus and Slava been working in the same room with her.

She held her curiosity and her trepidation at bay until she was certain that the engine would have enough ice to achieve the apogee burn. Her work was finished. Half an hour remained. Jiro seemed to have his side of it under control.

A sharp thud, resounding through the walls of the command module, gave her an excuse to pull up some video and to eavesdrop on the audio channel that Markus and Slava were using. Robots salted all over *Ymir*'s exterior gave her eyes that she could turn in any direction. Even so, it took her a few minutes to obtain a picture of what was going on.

New Caird had undocked from *Ymir* and was nowhere to be seen. Presumably Markus was at her controls.

A man in a space suit was visible on the outside of *Ymir,* "walking" toward the stern by using a pair of Grabbs as mobile anchor points. This had to be Vyacheslav. His feet had sprouted thick white whiskers. It took Dinah a few moments to make sense of the image: he had zip-tied each foot to the back of a Grabb, and the "whiskers" were the protruding ends of the zip ties. It was the kind of improvisation that would have made old-school NASA engineers turn over in their graves, had the Hard Rain not eliminated that possibility. But in the last two years, and particularly the last two weeks, this kind of hillbilly engineering had become routine.

Which only made the question of what the hell Markus was up

to more compelling. If Slava was being that creative with two robots and a sack of zip ties . . .

She finally spotted *New Caird* on a camera belonging to a Bucky that was attached to the stern of the shard, about halfway between its edge and the cavernous maw of the nozzle. The little ship was hanging in space maybe a hundred meters away, white jets erupting from her attitude thrusters every few moments as she tried to keep station behind the slowly rotating shard. Markus was flying her by hand, and it was some fancy flying indeed.

The geometry was difficult to visualize, but Dinah convinced herself that Vyacheslav was "walking" toward the same general location that *New Caird* was aimed at. In their own ways, the two men were focused on the same part of the shard: one of its outermost corners, where the widest part of the sugarloaf terminated and connected to its base, along a sharp but irregular edge. There, embedded in the ice, was a scrap of structural framework about the size of a car. It served as the anchor for a cluster of small conical rocket nozzles: one of those thruster systems that had proven so miserably underpowered for the current job. Aiming another camera at it, Dinah saw a steady jet of blue-white fire emerging from two of the nozzles. They were burning continuously, full blast. They weren't designed to do that. But *Ymir*'s attitude control system had calculated that thrust, and a lot of it needed to be applied in those two directions if its programmed objective—getting the ship's "nose" pointed forward and her nozzle aft—were to be achieved.

Dinah got it. Her thinking was confirmed by the chatter she could now hear, in a mix of English, German, and Russian, between Markus and Vyacheslav. But she could see in her mind's eye what *Ymir* must look like, right now, to Markus, viewing it through the front window of *New Caird:* a huge drifting arrowhead of black ice, generally dark, but decorated at the nose and "corners" by twinkling white lights, and streaks of hot gas: the exhaust from the thrusters, running an automatic program controlled from within. Sometimes they flashed on and off. Occasionally, though, when a lot of thrust was called for in one place, they ran for a long time. Those long steady burns would stand out clearly against the dark of space.

Markus didn't need to calculate *Ymir*'s rotation in his head. He didn't need to know her spin rates about her three axes or the torque needed to counteract them. He didn't even need to pull up the user interface on his tablet. All he had to do was fly around the shard and look for places where thrusters were staying on continuously. Those were the ones that were overloaded and underpowered. Those were, therefore, the ones where *New Caird*'s big engine could be used most effectively.

But how?

Her view of the thruster system was interrupted by a blurry gray form: Vyacheslav moving in front of the camera. He then came back into focus, groping for a carabiner along his waist and snapping it onto a structural member that protruded from the ice. Dinah could hear him breathing. Bracing himself with his left hand, he reached into the network of struts with his right. After a bit of groping he seemed to find something, then worked for a minute, his arm reciprocating slightly.

The thruster jets faltered and winked out.

"Done," Vyacheslav said. "Apologies. Valve was sticking."

"Get clear, *tovarishch,*" Markus said.

"Getting," Slava returned. He unhooked the carabiner and bent away from the framework, trusting himself to the Grabbs zip-tied to his feet, and began to move away with the painfully slow gait of a man walking in hot caramel. "Just do it," he said, then added a phrase in German that Dinah was pretty sure meant *If it doesn't work we are all dead anyway.*

New Caird drifted out of frame. Dinah spent a few moments reacquiring her view. The smaller ship was closing on *Ymir,* headed directly for the thruster system that Slava had just shut down, and coming in on an angle between the two nozzles that had been burning.

The logic was clear; the method was insane. *New Caird* was going to do the job that the tiny thrusters couldn't. Markus had to get her big nozzle aimed in about the right direction, namely, about halfway between the two that had been doing all the work. Fine. But he was also going to have to make a mechanical connection between *New Caird* and the shard, so that the thrust of the big engine could be transmitted into the mass of ice.

And it looked like he was going to achieve this by ramming the little ship into the big one. It was a slow ramming, like a tugboat shoving its nose against the side of an oil tanker to nudge it into a berth. But it was ramming nonetheless: not a thing for which spacecraft were generally designed.

She relaxed her painfully tight grip on the edge of the table just a bit when, moments before the collision, Markus fired the retrothrusters, slowing *New Caird* at the moment of impact. But still she felt and heard the crunch resounding through the walls of the ice palace. She'd heard it before over the last couple of hours and wondered what it was; apparently Markus had done this several times already.

He had aimed for the place where the structural framework emerged from the ice, forming a sort of angle into which *New Caird*'s nose could trap itself, as long as the thrust stayed on. Right now that force was being delivered by her aft thrusters. But Dinah, watching Markus's face through the front window, saw him working at the touch screen that served as *New Caird*'s control panel, and had a pretty good idea of what was coming next.

She pulled up the interface for *Ymir*'s attitude control system and saw craziness: thrusters firing all over the shard, lit up by angry icons warning of too little propellant, not enough time, overheated nozzles. The thing that Markus had just rammed was flashing red, indicating that it wasn't even connected to the system anymore. Graphs at the bottom of the screen, and a three-dimensional rendering of the shard in space, showed just how far off they were from where they wanted to be.

She heard a little symphony of grinding, groaning, and popping, and felt the ship rotating around her.

The video feed showing *New Caird* was awash in white light as her main propulsion came on full blast. A quick glance at the attitude control plots showed good things happening.

"It is good," Jiro said, "but we are going to over-rotate now."

"Not if I got the timing right," Markus said. "We should rotate through the correct attitude just at the time of the apogee burn. Afterward, yes, we'll over-rotate. But we'll have plenty of time to fix it."

Then his transmission was cut off by an exclamation and a thud. He cursed in German, and then the audio went dead.

Dinah looked at the video feed to see *New Caird* canted over at the wrong angle. The flame from the engine flickered out.

The framework against which *New Caird* had been pushing had given way under the thrust of the big engine and crumpled, causing her to slew around. She now lay almost sideways against the ice, the crushed remains of the thruster system sandwiched between her hull and the stern of *Ymir.*

"Some kind of gas escaping," Jiro observed quietly. "Or smoke."

He was right. The eye didn't pick it up right away because smoke behaved differently in space than in an atmosphere, under gravity. But something was burning, or at least smoldering, along the side of *New Caird*'s hull, no more than an arm's length from where Markus sat.

Vyacheslav said, "The hot nozzle of the thruster is melting through the hull."

Markus came back on the air. "Jiro and Dinah, you must be ready to fire the main propulsion at apogee—" The word was cut off by a constriction of his throat, and he coughed several times. When he resumed speaking, his voice had a strangled timbre. "About two minutes from now. Focus on that—initiate the startup procedures. Vyacheslav can help me with this little problem." He was coughing convulsively. "Switching off," he said.

Dinah, against orders, made a last glance at the video feed showing the nose of *New Caird*. Through its front window she could no longer see Markus. She could see only smoke, and the flickering, lambent light of a fire within it.

The realization of what was happening struck her like a two-by-four across the forehead. She grabbed the edge of the table and closed her eyes for a few moments, felt them fill with hot water, felt the snot flooding into her nose.

"Dinah," Jiro said. "The auger startup checklist begins now."

She opened her eyes and saw glowing blurs where user interface widgets ought to have been.

"If it is to mean anything," Jiro said. "Please." Then he reached up to enclose his headset's little microphone with one hand, muffling the sound, and added: "He can probably hear us."

She reached out and typed a command. "Auger one," she said. "Go." And she slapped the Enter key.

And so on down the list. It got easier as she went. Jiro did his part of it delicately, quietly, efficiently. And when the nuke came on to full power, right on schedule, she made sure to mention it. Loudly. In case Markus could hear them.

Only then did she look at the video feed. She was expecting to see Markus's final resting place, a tomb of acrid smoke.

But nothing was there except a crumpled framework and Vyacheslav, standing with one hand braced against it, gazing away aft. In the background, a spreading plume of steam the size of Manhattan as Jiro's engine fired.

"Slava?" she said. "Where is—"

"She fell off," Vyacheslav answered. "When the engine came on, and we began to accelerate. *New Caird* did not come along for the ride."

"Is she—"

"She was entrained in the plume of steam and thrown back. I can hardly even see her now."

"Oh."

"Dinah?"

"Yes, Slava?"

"Markus was already dead."

"IT WOULD READ ALMOST AS SLAPSTICK COMEDY IF IT WERE NOT SO tragic—the consequences so dire," Julia said. She was mesmerized by a video loop, the final transmission from *New Caird* before radio contact had been lost.

The people hovering around her in the White Arklet—as Julia's unofficial base of operations had come to be known—all nodded, or made agreeable-sounding murmurs. They were all reading Tav's blog post about the *Ymir* catastrophe, which had been posted only seconds ago.

The one exception was Tekla, who had become distracted by a detail. Attached to the wall of the arklet with strips of blue masking tape was a sheet of paper on which had been printed the seal of the president of the United States. Only two printers remained in existence, and both of them were on Izzy. So, by process of elimination, this must have been printed on Old Earth, prior to the Hard Rain, by a device that had been running a little low on cyan ink. It had seen hard service: it was torn in two places and repaired with clear tape. It had been creased and crumpled, then smoothed out. Its edges were fuzzy where previous applications of tape had been peeled away. And in the white space below and to the right of the presidential seal there was a brown smudge, oval, the size of the ball of a person's thumb. As a matter of fact, Tekla was certain that it was actually a thumbprint, and the more she looked at it the more certain she became that the brown substance was blood.

She looked Julia in the eye, and became aware that the former president was awaiting some form of reaction from her. Unlike most people, Tekla felt no pressure, no obligation to fulfill any such expectations. Julia, a bit unnerved by that, broke eye contact and continued: "I don't quite understand the story they are telling us anyway!"

"It is pretty convoluted," said one of her aides, a young male Arkie with an American accent. He was one of the MIV engineers. His tone suggested that he was amused by the sheer cheekiness of the powers that be in trying to get people to believe such a yarn, and that he was much too clever to be taken in. "It kind of hinges on the idea that the hull was made out of what amounts to plastic. If it gets too hot, it—"

"It's like plastic on a stove burner, I understand that," Julia said. "It melts and it stinks."

"*New Caird* shifted in a way that caused the hull to come into contact with a nozzle that was extremely hot."

"But according to the story they are putting out, Vyacheslav had shut that nozzle off beforehand."

"They stay hot for a long time. Anyway, the nozzle melted right through the hull. First it would have made a lot of toxic smoke. That would have been enough to kill him. Then, when the melting proceeded to the point where the hull was perforated, all the air would have escaped through the hole."

"Well, that is horrible—if it is true," Julia said, and then swiveled her eyes toward Tekla, looking for some sign in the visitor's face that it might *not* be true. Tekla stared back at her in a manner that betrayed nothing. "What sort of pass have we come to, one wonders, when such crazy improvisations are called for—ramming one ship with another!"

More murmurs of agreement.

Julia was on a roll. "And as far as I can make out, it didn't even solve the problem!"

"Problem is solved," Tekla said. She was fluent in English and was perfectly capable of saying "*The* problem is solved," but sometimes dropped the article for effect. Anglophones found this mysterious and impressive. It was also an implicit statement of Russian pride. The language of the Cloud Ark, by default, was English. That was never going to change. But the dialect was going to evolve over time, and Russians could bend it in their direction by finding ways to inject their grammar and vocabulary into everyday speech. "Burn is complete," she went on.

"But the ship is still tumbling out of control!" said the American boy who so fancied his own intelligence.

"Slow tumble," Tekla said. "Not problem. Plenty of time to fix now that perigee is raised."

"Fix it how?! Markus demolished three of the external thruster packages by *ramming them*! Who does that? Anyway, there are only two of them left. It is a basic reality of physics that you can't control a three-axis tumble using only two thrusters!"

"Thank you for explaining basic reality," Tekla said. "Tumble can be eliminated by making scarfed nozzle."

This silenced them for a few moments. One of Julia's followers—Jianyu, a Chinese Arkie, very passionate about going to Mars—looked like he understood it. Tekla nodded in his direction. "This man will explain later. My time here is limited."

"Yes, Tekla, and we do appreciate that you've been able to make time for us at all," Julia said.

Tekla wanted to slap her so much that her hand actually twitched. The sentence Julia had just spoken, had it been delivered in a different tone, might have actually meant what it said. Instead of which, it meant *I am being callously ignored and it's about time someone important came out to talk to me.* Tekla had an almost physical sense of how that mentality was radiating outward from Julia to infect the other Arkies.

Like almost everyone else in the Cloud Ark, Tekla was wearing a coverall with many pockets, compartments, external holsters, and the like. One of them contained a knife with a four-inch, double-edged blade. Its tip could find J.B.F.'s heart easily. Tekla faded from the conversation briefly as she considered how to manage this. Julia probably wouldn't be expecting a frank assassination attempt—though you never really knew, with people who had such minds.

Tekla said, "Would you like to report any difficulties with the SAN? Repeated outages have been observed."

Julia pressed her lips together in a satisfied way and looked toward Spencer Grindstaff.

"First I've heard of it," Spencer said. The statement was met with perfect, deadpan silence.

Tekla just waited. Soon the temptation to boast would get the better of them. Her training in tradecraft—in how to be a spy—had not been all that extensive. A few basic courses, some assigned reading. The reason was simple: She was too conspicuous to be useful as a spy. Too similar to the Hollywood profile. Real spies went unnoticed. So they had kicked her out of the program and put her to work in roles, such as being an Olympic athlete, where her conspicuousness was an asset. But she had picked up a few general precepts. And she knew that this one thing—the urge to boast of one's accomplishments—had betrayed more secrets and destroyed more careers than anything else.

She looked at Grindstaff. Unlike most people, who soon broke eye contact, he looked right back at her, grinning.

"Unusual," Tekla said, "for one of your background."

"Sources and methods," he said.

"Then I will confine my remarks to what I came here for," Tekla said. This produced an immediate exchange of glances between Julia and Spencer. Tekla ignored it. "For security reasons it is imperative that we have accurate census of which person is in which arklet. Some people like to move around. To trade places. We understand.

Fine. But safety and security problems are created when, for example, arklet is struck by bolide, air is leaking, we do not know how many people are in it, their medical requirements, et cetera. Small person needs less air than big person."

Julia was nodding. "I take your point very clearly, Tekla. Speaking for the Arkie Community, I can confirm that a more informal mind-set prevails out here on the outskirts. The perception of neglect by the powers that be on Izzy leads to a bit of a chip-on-the-shoulder attitude. Reshuffling of people between arklets seems like a harmless form of rebellion. But it's easy to overlook the safety issue that you are pointing out. Which is a mistake. I will say that the confusion as to the *real* threat level we are under, as long as we—"

"As long as we confine ourselves to dirty space," Ravi Kumar threw in.

"Yes, thank you, Ravi. It just seems that one day we hear one thing, the next day we hear another."

"Statistics," Tekla said.

"Yes, that is what we are told again and again, but—"

"I can say no more," Tekla offered, and flicked her eyes at one of the small cameras mounted to the hull of the arklet.

Julia held her gaze this time, and, after a few moments, threw a glance Spencer's way. "Tekla, a minute ago we were dancing around the topic of the Situational Awareness Network and Spencer was being a bit lighthearted—his sense of humor at work. But I feel comfortable telling you that, thanks to Spencer, we do have a way to disconnect from the SAN when we want to just have a normal conversation without wondering who might be listening in. And we have done so now. Anything you say here and now will not leave this arklet."

Tekla favored the circle of hangers-on and admirers with a long, slow panoramic look, then actually rolled her eyes.

"Everyone out!" Julia commanded. "You too, Spencer. Just Tekla and me."

"Your tradecraft is of low quality," Tekla said, when all the others had dispersed through the hamster tubes to the other arklets in Julia's heptad.

"I know," Julia said. "It is so difficult rebuilding an intelligence community from scratch. One must make do with the materials at hand. Their youth, their inexperience, and the openness they've come to expect from living their whole lives on the Internet—all are inimical to doing things as they ought to be done. That is why we need more experienced hands—people who have learned the right instincts."

"It is not just that," Tekla said. "That is obvious."

"Oh?" Julia narrowed her eyes. "What have I missed that is not so obvious?"

"You should not trust Zeke Petersen with further information," Tekla said. "Unless you wish to plant false intelligence, in which case he will be an effective channel."

Ivy and Zeke and Tekla had discussed it beforehand, and Zeke had cheerfully volunteered to be given up by Tekla as a supposed turncoat. It made little difference to him personally. And it would go a long way to cementing the idea, in Julia's mind, of Tekla as a master double agent. By Cold War standards it was an obvious and amateurish gambit, but this was not the Cold War. This was a small town of fifteen hundred people with a former mayor who was trying to stir up trouble.

Julia narrowed her eyes and nodded slowly. She was fascinated. "I had wondered about him," she said. "He seemed like he was just playing along. Just being polite."

"Not a problem with Tekla," Tekla said.

Julia liked that. She had drifted closer, and now reached out to touch Tekla's forearm briefly. "I like that about you, Tekla. What I see is what I get."

"Yes." Then, after a somewhat uneasy silence, Tekla added, "You play long game. Patient."

"To a degree," Julia said, and suddenly her face and attitude had changed, as if her face had been recast in painted steel. "We cannot afford to be patient for very long. Markus's death has changed everything. Until that tragic event, the members of the Arkie Community could look forward to the return of the great leader. Ivy was a mere caretaker. Her shortcomings could be overlooked. Now, awareness is spreading through the swarm that Markus is not coming back. Ivy is back in power. Sal will quote from obscure clauses in the Constitution to legitimize her status. But true legitimacy comes from the support of the governed. She'll be moving now to solidify her hold on the reins. It's at such a time that small, symbolic gestures can have the greatest effect. And that, Tekla, is why the next few days are such a critical time for us. Perhaps *Ymir* will pull through, perhaps not. We can't afford to wait. Preparations are afoot. Three days from now, arklets will begin to break free of the Cloud Ark and begin their epic trek to high orbit. The powers that be might fear to implement the Pure Swarm strategy, for the loss of control it will mean for them. But the Arkie Community, tired of huddling behind an ineffective shield, slowly being decimated by the Hard Rain, knows no such limitations."

"Survival of the breakaway group will demonstrate the falsity of the GPop's predictions of danger," Tekla said, nodding. "The power of the center will be broken."

"For the first time, the Cloud Ark Constitution will truly come into effect," Julia said, "notwithstanding the sophistry of the apologist Sal Guodian. That Constitution, Tekla, as I'm sure you know, calls for the formation of a security force. Not the Praetorian Guard that Markus cobbled together, but something real. I can think of no one better qualified than you to command it."

"HOOK, LINE, AND SINKER," SAID SPENCER GRINDSTAFF AS HE AND Julia watched Tekla's Flivver depart with a staccato series of thruster burns.

"Oh, she definitely bought it," Julia admitted, "but I don't like the note of triumphalism in your voice, Spencer. What we have really learned is that Ivy is a formidable opponent. Somehow she has managed to get people like Tekla on her side. And they have come up with a fairly elaborate strategy for penetrating our organization."

Grindstaff shrugged. "As these things go, it's not that elaborate. Kind of obvious, really."

"Easy to say," Julia said, "given that you have a bug hidden in the Banana, and we knew everything they were going to do. But lacking that information, Spencer, do you really think we'd have seen through it? I thought Tekla did a marvelous job."

"You need to look out for her. She really hates you. And she's carrying at least one weapon."

"Thanks to Pete Starling," Julia said, "so am I." She reached into her bag and drew out a small revolver, just far enough that Spencer could see the butt of its grip, then slid it back in.

"At the risk of insulting your intelligence," Spencer said, "I would like to remind you of the consequences of firing that thing inside of a space vehicle."

"No offense taken. I've actually seen those consequences. And you know what? The air doesn't leak out that fast. Anyway, I'm told that the rounds in this weapon are designed to mushroom on impact, so they are less likely to exit the body."

"That's great," Spencer said, "provided you actually hit a body."

"If it comes down to me and Tekla," Julia said, "I'm not going to miss."

ALL DINAH WANTED TO DO WAS SLEEP. SINCE *NEW CAIRD* HAD DEparted from Izzy she had never gotten more than four consecutive hours, and the numbers for the last day or so were even more dismal. In a weird way, she wanted to sleep so that she would be able to grieve properly. She knew Markus was dead, but it hadn't really sunk in.

Nor would it, as long as she was running from one crisis to the next.

The burn had worked. *Ymir*'s perigee altitude had been raised to the point where it would never again be troubled by the atmosphere. But the ship was still tumbling, albeit slowly. And Vyacheslav was still trudging around on its outer surface with his feet zip-tied to Grabbs.

At the start of this extravehicular activity, Slava had exited through the airlock on the side of *New Caird*—a ship that was no longer with them. His supplies were running low. He had to get inside the command module before he ran out of air. This could be achieved using an airlock built in for that purpose. It was located adjacent to the docking port in the "nose" of the ice-buried command module. Passing through it, he would enter the uppermost level of the module, where he could breathe the same air as everyone else. But he had taken the precaution of checking himself out with an Eenspektor, and found powerful radiation coming from several locations on his suit—basically, wherever he had come into contact with the surface of the shard.

"I was worried about this," Jiro said, "but there was nothing to be done."

"Worried about what?" Dinah asked. "I thought the surface was reasonably clean."

"It was," Jiro said, "until we did the perigee burn. The nozzle was pointed forward. Some of the steam was blown back over us by the wind—by the atmosphere we were passing through. It condensed and stuck to the surface of the shard. So, now there are little pieces of fallout all over the outside of *Ymir*. And some of them have gotten stuck to Slava's space suit."

"He's got to get out of that thing."

Jiro shrugged. "The suit will block most of the beta."

"I mean, he's got to get out of it before he runs out of oxygen."

"That is true."

"Which means he has to come in here."

"Also true."

"He's going to bring that radiation inside with him."

"It will take weeks to kill us. By that time we will have accomplished our mission. Or not."

In the end, though, they came up with a workaround that did not involve dying, which was that they taped some plastic over the companionway that joined the command module's top level to the one below it. Before doing so, they moved a generous supply of food and water to that level, along with toiletries, a sleep sack, and other items Vyacheslav would be needing. Slava passed through the airlock with some minutes to spare, doffed his suit, and closed it up in the chamber of the airlock, which would block most of the beta radiation coming off it. He then stripped off his clothes and went through several repetitions of decontaminating himself with premoistened towelettes, throwing all of it into the airlock chamber before slamming its hatch shut.

Then he threw up.

The upper level of the command module, along with Slava himself, now had to be treated as contaminated, but they didn't need it anymore. Jiro and Dinah would be confined to the lower levels, separated from Vyacheslav and the possible contamination by a sheet of plastic, until they reached Izzy or died. A common air supply circulated through all the levels in ducts, but it had a filter system, which they hoped would catch any floating motes of fallout.

Having seen to all of those matters, they turned out the lights and slept. Dinah slept through her alarm, in fact, and finally woke up to realize she'd been out for twelve hours.

Her next thought was to wonder where Markus was. Then she remembered, with a kind of astonishment, that he was dead. It came as a stinging slap, followed by grief. But on the heels of the grief came a feeling of deep fear that she had rarely experienced in all the time since

Zero. It was not the sharp bracing fear one felt on an adventure, su the ride through perigee, nor the kind of intellectual, abstract fear that had been with them ever since Doob had predicted the Hard Rain. This was a kind of morbid panic that was second cousin to depression. It was how a child might feel upon learning that she had been orphaned. Not a child, rather, but an adolescent, the oldest sibling, on whom responsibility for the family now fell. Markus was gone. He wasn't going to shoulder any more burdens for them. Others would have to take up those burdens. And some of those—the ones, perhaps, most eager to step into Markus's place—would certainly make the wrong decisions. And so, as sad as Dinah felt about the fact that she would never see Markus again or feel his embrace, the thing that really made her want to contract into a fetal position was this knowledge that it was on her now. On her, and Ivy, and Doob, and the others who could be trusted.

She went "up" into the common room and found Jiro, as usual, lost in contemplation of arcane plots on his computer screen, reflected in miniature on the lenses of his bifocals. During the year he had been in space, his prescription had changed, and so he had been the first consumer of the optical lens-grinding machine that had been sent up and installed in Izzy. Without it, much of the Cloud Ark's population would gradually have been rendered nonproductive as their eyeglasses were broken or wore out. It was a military machine capable of making glasses in one style, and one style only. At some point a few years down the road, everyone who needed glasses would be wearing this style. It was interesting to contemplate how many decades or centuries would have to go by before the population had grown, and the economy developed, to the point where it could support an eyewear industry with different styles.

He looked up at her through the milky reflections. "I let you sleep," he said. "Your robots seem to be working fine. There is nothing to do until I finish these calculations."

"And then what?"

"We have to eliminate the last of the tumbling," Jiro said, "before we make the final braking burns."

For Dinah, that was all clear. *Ymir* was in a safe orbit now and would not fall into the atmosphere anytime soon. But she was still going much too fast, and way too high, to rendezvous with Izzy. They needed to finish the execution of the same plan they'd had all along, which was to make one or two more braking burns as *Ymir* passed through her perigee, slowing her down to the point where a rendezvous with Izzy was feasible. This required getting the nozzle pointed forward again, and keeping it that way.

"How much damage was done to the—"

"They were destroyed," Jiro said. "We have two remaining." They were both referring to the thruster packages, embedded in the ice, that would normally have been used to manage the shard's attitude. "It is fine. It was necessary," Jiro added, almost as if worried that Dinah would think poorly of him for criticizing the decisions made by a dead commander.

"Can more be sent out from—"

Jiro nodded. "It is possible to assemble a MIV that could rendezvous with us and assist with the problem. Just in case my idea does not succeed. But since our radio link was lost with *New Caird,* we cannot coordinate this."

"And what is your idea?"

"We can use your robots to alter the shape of the nozzle exit," Jiro said. He held up one hand like a blade, pointed toward the ceiling, and then flexed his knuckles slightly, indicating a shallow bend. "Make it asymmetrical."

"Like a scarfed nozzle?"

"Exactly. When we fire the main propulsion it will give us an off-axis thrust. If the scarf is oriented correctly, it will have tremendous control authority."

"Maybe too much," Dinah said. "We'll end up overcorrecting."

"One thing at a time," Jiro said. "We scarf the nozzle, we do a little correction, we scarf it the other way, we kill the rotation. It might take several repetitions. It can be done. I have been modeling it."

Dinah pulled herself into position before her triptych of flatpanels, and began opening windows, checking on the activities of her menagerie of robots: some sunning themselves on the outside to soak up power, others sipping juice from the reactors, some mining propellant for the next burn, others mending the nozzle. The latter group, mostly Nats, would be responsible for the nozzle-sculpting program. Until now, having an asymmetrical nozzle, delivering thrust at an off angle, had been a problem to be avoided, not a feature to be encouraged. Jiro had emailed her some diagrams of what the nozzle bell would need to look like. The alterations were surprisingly minor. In an engine that produced that much power, a little bit of off-axis thrust went a long way. "When's our next perigee?" she asked.

"We just went through one. So, about eight hours from now."

THE PARAMOUNT DUTY OF THE CLOUD ARK'S COMMANDER—SO IMportant that Markus had broken character and described it to Ivy as "sacred"—was to stay on top of the Bolide Scan, which was a feed of information synthesized out of all of Izzy's long-range radars and optical telescopes. A disproportionate number of GPop members devoted their lives to managing this, or to maintaining the equipment used to produce it. Because the stream of data was continuous, it needed to be broken down, for the consumption of someone like Markus or Ivy, into reports that showed up on their screens at regular intervals. A Triurnal Bolide Scan was issued at the top of each shift: dot 0, dot 8, and dot 16. Ivy read one of them when she woke up, another in the middle of her "afternoon," and the third just before going to sleep. Each of these summarized what was known about bolides that might come near them during the next eight hours, and made recommendations as to what maneuvers the Cloud Ark should execute in order to avoid them. Typically they made small burns several times a day for this purpose. The policy was "default go," which meant that the maneuver would be promulgated to the Cloud Ark via Parambulator, and carried out automatically, unless the commander vetoed it. The only reason this was ever likely to happen was in cases where two dangerous rocks were headed their way at about the same time and they needed to make a decision. Such events had occurred twice during the Hard Rain so far, but they had been simulated and war-gamed hundreds of times before that. The name of the game was to avoid getting cornered.

To be detected eight hours in advance, a bolide had to be pretty big. Smaller ones came along all the time, and weren't picked up on the radars until minutes or even seconds before collision. Accordingly, smaller reports were issued at the top of each hour, listing all noteworthy rocks that had been detected during the last sixty minutes. This covered most of them, so the commander—or whoever covered for her while she was sleeping—could discharge most of her responsibilities in re the Bolide Scan by dropping everything else she was doing at the top of each hour and reading it. From time to time, however, they would become aware of a "hot rock" or "streaker" that had surprised them by coming in from a weird angle, or at unusually high speed, and then the commander would be notified immediately so that an alert could be issued and evasive action could be seen to. The Streaker Alerts combined elements of the small-town midwestern tornado siren with the red alert from *Star Trek*. All sleeping people were awakened, all nonessential personnel were evacuated from the larger tori, which were considered most vulnerable, and hatches were closed between different sections, in case of a breach. Similar precautions were taken by the Arkies. Arklets were, of course, more vulnerable to bolide strikes, but they were also more maneuverable. As the hot rock drew closer and its orbital parameters were determined more precisely, the data would be fed to Parambulator. Any arklets in danger of being hit would be identified, and a collective solution would be calculated that would enable them to move into safer trajectories without banging into anyone else. These events happened, on average, between one and two times a day, but as always the devil was in the statistical details. They had once gone three days without a single streaker. On another occasion they'd had five of them within a twelve-hour period. The first of these events had caused an upwelling of chatter on Spacebook to the effect that the powers that be were overstating the threat in order to cow the Arkies into submission, and the second had generated a hard-hitting blog post from Tav Prowse calling the GPop on the carpet for systematic incompetence.

It was in the wake of such an alert, while cleaning up her desktop of postaction chatter, that Ivy's attention was drawn to a post that had just come up on Tav's blog: an interview with Ulrika Ek.

"Ulrika has a lot to learn about bloggers" was Ivy's verdict, after she'd finished reading it. She shook her head. "You'd think she of all people would know—she's been through PR training."

These remarks were delivered to a Banana that had been slowly repopulating itself, during the last few minutes, with people who had been called away on other duties during the Streaker Alert. Tekla was the last to arrive, bringing Tom Van Meter and other members of Markus's security detail in her wake. Luisa and Sal were already present in the room. Doob had just texted his regrets, explaining that he needed to crunch some numbers about what had just happened.

"She probably dropped her guard," Luisa suggested, "thinking she was just chatting informally."

"You've read it then?"

"I scanned it."

"Referring to what?" Tekla asked.

"Ulrika made a few off-the-cuff remarks about swarm theory, and which strategies we might wish to pursue in the future, and Tav is blowing them up into a cause célèbre," Ivy said.

"What if anything would you like to do about it?" Sal asked.

"Nothing," Ivy said. "Look, the longer this thing with *Ymir* continues, the more anxiety people have about the Big Ride. Every time a hot rock comes in it juices up that anxiety for a little while. Well, either it'll work or it won't. If it doesn't work then we have very little choice anyway—we have to Dump and Run."

Sal nodded. "But if it does work, it'll change everything about the way people think."

Ivy nodded. "Yeah. And I am growingly certain that it will. Even if the scarfed nozzle gambit fails, we still have that MIV we can send out as a backup plan. I think that in a week we'll have a successful rendezvous with *Ymir* and we'll be prepping for the Big Ride."

Ivy made a gesture indicating that the new arrivals should find places for themselves around the table. "Which brings me to the topic of this meeting," she continued. "We know what J.B.F.'s plan is. She's recruiting some number of Arkies willing to strike out on their own. The general scheme seems to be that they'll get a few arklets stocked with provisions for a few weeks' journey. Then, on a signal, they'll break away from Izzy and make burns that will take them to a higher orbit. An orbit that we can't reach without expending a lot of propellant. We don't know what their long-term plan is—or if they even have one—but I think Julia is basically playing the odds that these people will survive long enough to send back messages saying 'Come on in, the water's fine!' and encourage other Arkies to follow suit. They all know that they can't really be pursued once they have departed the swarm. Membership in the Cloud Ark is, under the current state of affairs, voluntary."

"I infer you mean to change that?" Luisa asked drily, casting her gaze over Tekla and the members of the squad.

"They can't make a break for it without hoarding certain critical supplies," Ivy said. "We can't allow people to just ransack our storage facilities for whatever they want. And we have clear evidence that this has been happening. There's traffic on Spacebook about where to look if you want to score a box of fresh batteries or scrubber cartridges. So, our basic approach to this is going to be simple. We've identified the worst offenders, where hoarding is concerned. I'm going to make an announcement in an hour, explaining how the Cloud Ark Constitution works when it comes to theft of public supplies, and I'm going to offer a twenty-four-hour amnesty during which anyone can turn in stuff that they have been hoarding. As soon as that time is up, Tekla and her team are going to move on one arklet that we know is being used as a storage dump for contraband, and they are going to restore order. And then Sal will step in, as prosecutor, and take whatever action he deems justified."

"How can you put people in jail when they are already confined to tin cans?" Luisa asked. "How can you fine them when there is no money?"

"We will have to evolve solutions as we go," Sal said.

Tekla stared him down, then drew her thumb across her throat.

"WELL, THAT SEEMS DEFINITIVE," JULIA SAID.

She and Spencer Grindstaff were hovering in the middle of the White Arklet. Drifting near them was a laptop whose speakers had been playing the audio feed from the Banana. They could hear the sounds of the meeting breaking up, and people separating into smaller conversations as they moved out of the room. Spencer pulled it closer and whacked the volume button a few times to mute the sound.

"As I said before: hook, line, and sinker."

"Unless," Julia said, "they are somehow aware of the fact that we have surveillance on the Banana, and everything we just heard was a sort of radio play staged for our benefit."

Spencer beamed. "Now, *that* is paranoid! I thought I had it bad, but—"

"Just kidding," Julia said, a little too quickly. "This is actionable,

Spencer. I believe we are justified in taking everything we just heard at face value. Which means I am comfortable giving good news to the Martians. Are they ready?"

"Yes, they've been waiting," Spencer said, and thumbed out a text message to summon them.

The Martians all had to come via the same hamster tube, so it took a few moments for the core members of the first human expedition to the Red Planet to filter in: Dr. Katherine Quine, whose professional role was obvious; Ravi Kumar, who would be the expedition's commander; Li Jianyu, who would act as a general science officer; and Paul Freel, an American MIV expert, the head engineer. They, as well as a score of other Arkies waiting in the wings, had sworn an oath that they'd not spend the rest of their lives sealed up in tin cans, but would walk on the surface of Mars or die in the attempt. In their wake came several other members of Julia's "staff."

Julia opened the meeting with a few words of greeting and a solemn announcement to the effect that the Mars mission was a go. Once the ensuing round of zero-gee high fives and embraces had trailed off into an awkward silence, she singled out Paul Freel. "Paul, no doubt you've briefed these others on the very latest while you were so patiently cooling your heels, but might I know what has been going on with the MIV?"

"Of course, Madam President. As you know, they're trying to stabilize *Ymir* with—"

"A Rube Goldberg scheme in the form of an ice sculpture. Yes, I know about that."

Paul chuckled, showing a lot of gum. "Not surprisingly, the powers that be are a little nervous about that and so word came down from on high that we ought to be preparing a backup plan, so we can go pull *Ymir*'s fat from the fire if need be. Well. That couldn't be better, from a Martian point of view! As you know, we have been planning this mission for years. After Zero, I kept it going as a side project all through the development of the MIV program, and we managed to grease it in as one of the use cases."

"Use cases?"

"One of the hypothetical uses to which the MIV kit might eventually be put," Spencer explained.

"Basically it just gave us an excuse to include a few components, like throttleable landing engines and aeroshield material, that might not have made it in otherwise," Paul went on. "So, stabilizing *Red Rover*'s design has been a piece of cake."

"*Red Rover*?"

"Yeah, that's what we're calling her."

"I would like to propose something a little more suggestive of a higher purpose," Julia said. "*Spearhead* or some such thing."

This led to an uneasy silence terminated by Camila, who said, "I'll draw up a list of options and submit it to you right away, Madam President."

"Thank you, Camila. You understand, Paul, that this mission will have symbolic as well as scientific value, and we want to send the right message to the other Arkies so that they will feel inspired to follow in her wake."

"Of course! Consider it a working title only," Paul said. "A code name."

"It's not even good as a code name," Spencer pointed out, "because anyone can—"

"Let's move on," Julia said. "You were talking, Paul, about the design."

"Done. It took, like, a man-day. We just had to make a few tweaks to a preexisting use case to reflect the materials and supplies we actually had on hand."

"Excellent."

"But a design is not a ship, of course," Paul continued, "and until a couple of days ago it would've been pretty darn hard to put the actual propulsion system together without bringing down the wrath of Ivy!"

"That is not a phrase calculated to strike fear into the heart of anyone except those most worshipful of her authority," Julia remarked, speaking with the gravity that could only be summoned by one who had recently used nuclear weapons on live targets.

Paul cackled. "You know what I'm saying, though—everything happens in a fishbowl here! So, you can imagine the grin on my face when we got the order to begin assembling the *Ymir* rescue MIV."

"Are the specifications similar?"

"Similar enough. They can both use the same main engine. The thruster packages, the control systems, life support—all of that stuff is completely standardized; it doesn't change from one use case to another, it's just a matter of punching different parameters into the code. It's just a config file!"

Seeing that Julia didn't necessarily know what a config file was, Spencer put in, "They can essentially download the DNA, if you will, of *Red Rover,* or whatever we end up calling it, into the *Ymir* rescue vehicle with a few keystrokes."

Satisfied with that, Julia asked, "What of the arklets? The heptad and the triad?"

"Well, they're already functional, independent space vehicles. Way more than enough space for twenty-four Martians and their vitamins. Obviously, we've been stocking up," Paul said, waving his hands around at the bags of food and other supplies crowding the White Arklet.

"Yes," Julia said, "but the critical part of the operation is going to be moving them from their default positions in the swarm—which will seem unremarkable as far as Parambulator is concerned—to the propulsion stack that you have been assembling. And that's going to make a hell of a stink, is it not?"

The smile on Paul Freel's face became a bit frozen. "We could just go for it," he said.

"I have a workaround," said Spencer Grindstaff. "I think we can make this happen. A Streaker Alert is all we need. It'll go down tomorrow."

"How do you know there's going to be a Streaker Alert?"

"Such an event is nothing," Spencer said, "other than a particular configuration of bits."

DINAH HAD BEEN DREAMING OF MARS.

As an asteroid miner, she had never been that interested in the distant and inhospitable Red Planet. The politics of the pre-Zero space exploration world had obliged her to show skepticism, even disdain toward those who wanted to go there and to build colonies and terraform the planet. Mars colonists were siphoning attention and resources away from the asteroid miners, who wanted to use easier-to-get resources to make much more human-friendly habitats: space colonies, rotating to provide full gravity, with plenty of water and fresh air.

In any event, it had been a dead issue for two years. But that didn't prevent Mars from showing up in her dreams, and now infiltrating her daydreams. Almost three years had now gone by since she had walked on the surface of a planet, looked up into a sky, seen a horizon. Intellectually she knew that death would take her, sooner or later, before she did any of those things again. She and everyone else in the Cloud Ark would live out their lives in environments resembling bomb shelters, hospital basements, and research labs. The best they could hope for was to look out a small window at the starry sky. The view of the blue, green, and white Earth had once provided fascination and solace. The orange ball of fire they now circled was such a disagreeable sight that most people actively avoided looking at it. No one was ever going back there. For those who still aspired to go for a walk before dying of old age, Mars was the only hope, be it never so impractical. People had been talking about it on Spacebook, and on some of the blogs that had been cropping up on the Cloud Ark's miniature Internet. Before the loss of *New Caird* had severed *Ymir*'s data link to the Cloud Ark, some of it had trickled through to her tablet, and Dinah read it in idle moments.

At least she *had* some idle moments now. Since the decision to try the scarfed-nozzle approach, they had executed two burns, about twenty-four hours apart, each with a slightly different configuration of the ice nozzle: a canted lip, constructed by the Nat swarm, projecting almost imperceptibly above the aft surface of the shard and bending the torrent of steam slightly. The first of those burns had gotten them spinning the way they wanted to go, though "spinning" might be too strong a word for a rotation that took the better part of a day. During that day the Nats had decamped to the other side of the nozzle's rim and built a lip there. The second burn, then, had stopped the rotation that the first one had started, and brought them close enough to their desired attitude that the surviving thrusters could handle the details.

Another perigee was coming up soon. This time the nozzle would be aimed the way they wanted it—forward, once again turning the nuclear engine into a powerful retro-rocket. The robots on the inside of the shard had been at work scooping it out, sculpting the walnut-shell architecture that, according to the structural engineering simulations, would enable the whole thing to hold together during the last round of maneuvers. The hoppers were full of ice, with more on the way, and they'd finally learned how to make the system work consistently. Part of that lesson was not to try to accomplish too much with any one burn. It was better to take it easy, set a reasonable delta vee target, get it done and lock it down, then take stock of the situation and plan the next burn at leisure. Consequently their rendezvous with Izzy looked to be happening much later than they'd first expected, and almost every day brought a further postponement. But at the same time it came to seem more and more of a sure thing, less of a wild chance, and this began to affect Dinah's thinking. Her robots were doing their work almost entirely on autopilot, leaving her somewhat bored. Vyacheslav, sealed up on the other side of a wall of plastic, could be talked to, but preferred keeping to himself. Jiro, on the other hand, had been working almost around the clock and had been showing signs of strain. Dinah would find excuses to float behind him and look over his shoulder at his screen. Was he playing solitaire? Running orbital mechanics simulations? Writing his memoirs? He seemed mostly to be looking at video feeds of machinery. By process of elimination, this had to be near the core of the reactor.

In the floor of the "bottom"-most level, three stories "below" them, was a manhole giving way to a shaft sunk into the ice. At the far end of that shaft was another hatch providing access to what, on an oceangoing ship of Old Earth, would have been called the boiler room. A small pressurized compartment housed control panels and access ports connected to the reactor, which was only a few meters away, on the other side of a heavy wall. The wall was a radiation shield, at least in theory. But sending up a huge piece of lead hadn't been an option for the hastily assembled *Ymir* expedition, and so the "boiler room" got washed with neutrons and gamma rays whenever the reactor was used. The radiation detectors that Sean and company had left behind, the last time they'd closed that hatch, didn't leave much to the imagination. The place was a hellhole now. Fortunately, all the systems connected there had been designed to be operated remotely, from the safety of the command module, so there was no need to go down that ice tunnel and open that hatch.

Their instruments told them they were nearing perigee again. Jiro, assisted by Dinah, executed what they hoped would be the second-to-last burn of the big engine. This went on longer than Jiro had predicted, but it seemed to work. *Ymir* shed most of her excess velocity. Her orbit, at apogee, was now only a few hundred kilometers higher than Izzy's. In spite of attrition suffered by the robots as they wore out, broke, or succumbed to radiation damage, Dinah still had enough of them to restock the hoppers for the final major burn, which they calculated would be happening at a perigee a few hours later.

"If you are satisfied with the disposition of your robots," Jiro said, "I would like to show you how to operate the main propulsion."

She had grown up in mining camps where older men liked to amuse her, and themselves, by teaching her how to operate heavy machinery, blow things up with dynamite, pilot airplanes, and the like. So Jiro's offer didn't seem as unusual to her, at first. Teaching people how to do stuff was, among other things, a way to alleviate boredom. But over the course of the next hour it slowly became clear to her that Jiro really was expecting her to operate the engine during the upcoming burn. It might have been the language barrier; but his English was pretty good, and he was being quite persistent in saying things like "you will keep an eye on this thermocouple" and "you might see some flutter in this valve."

"If you don't hear from me beyond the thirty-second mark," he said at one point, "then you are on your own and you will have to initiate shutdown based on observed delta vee."

"Why would I not hear from you?" Dinah asked. "Where are you going to be?"

"In the boiler room," Jiro said.

"Why would you go there?"

"Some of the control blade actuators have stopped responding," he said. "I think that the electronics have been damaged by radiation. It's okay. We have replacements. But they will have to be installed manually."

"So you're going to go down there?"

"Yes," Jiro said. "And that is where I am going to stay."

"IT IS FOR ALL PURPOSES EMPTY," TEKLA REPORTED OVER AN ENcrypted voice link to Ivy. "Empty of people. Empty of supplies."

She, Tom Van Meter, and Bolor-Erdene had spent the last ten

minutes searching Arklet 98 from front door to boiler room, under the eye of Sal Guodian. They had arrived via Flivver, docked, and entered 98 without incident. Sal had gone through first, carrying a tablet on which was displayed the first search warrant ever issued under the provisions of the Cloud Ark Constitution. He had been ready to show it to the first person who challenged him. But no one was here.

Tekla, Tom, and Bo had then come in, wearing orange vests improvised from survival kits that, since they'd been designed for use on Earth, had no practical utility anymore. These would serve as police uniforms until something else could be stitched together. With any luck, they wouldn't be *needing* a lot of cop gear. But Ivy had been clear, and the others in her ad hoc council had agreed, that if they were executing what amounted to a police action, they couldn't beat around the bush—couldn't try to palm it off as an informal visit. A new constitution had to be exercised, or it was just words.

"Can you get it back on the SAN?" Ivy asked, over the voice link. "I'd like to see what's happening."

"I'll reboot everything," Sal said, pulling himself up into the control couch. "But it depends on what Spencer did—whether he broke it permanently, or just entered a temporary command." He reached around in back of a panel, felt for a connector, pulled it out, and jacked it back in.

"We had estimated that you were going to find ten person-years worth of nonrenewables in that thing," Ivy said. She meant, not bulk food (which could be grown in the outer hull space of an arklet) or air (which was renewed by the life support system), but generally smaller items like toiletries, vitamins, medicine, and specialty food. "That was based on circumstantial evidence—the amount of stuff that's gone missing, the number of Flivver trips and EVAs that have touched that arklet. We always knew it was only a guess. But for it to contain nothing at all is . . . odd."

"More than odd," Tekla said. "Surprise attack."

"You think there's going to be an attack?"

"Maybe not in sense of violent assault," Tekla said, "but something."

"And Arklet 98 was a decoy?"

"Obviously."

A musical tone sounded from the arklet's PA speakers, and the white LEDs changed their hue to red. "Alert," said a synthesized voice. "All personnel should now be awake and at stations for urgent swarm maneuver. This is not a drill."

They'd heard it before. It was a Streaker Alert.

Normally, though, they took it at face value. "Remarkable coincidence," Tekla said.

"I think you guys had better get back in the Flivver," Ivy said. "Follow the usual procedures for one of these, but keep your eyes open."

"STEVE, DO YOU HAVE ANYTHING YET ON THE BOLIDE?" IVY ASKED. They were about five minutes into the alert, which had obliged them to move down into the Banana. As much as Ivy wanted to know what was happening with J.B.F., and what Tekla had characterized as a "surprise attack," her responsibility in a case like this one was clear: all of her attentions had to be focused on the evasive maneuvers being carried out by the Cloud Ark and their possible consequences. Those might include collisions between arklets or the separation of one or more arklets from the swarm. In dire cases it might be necessary to send out rescue teams, which was why her first act had been to get Tekla and the others into their Flivver. For the normal role of that makeshift police service was not to serve warrants on hoarders; it was to respond to emergencies. As keenly as the space geek in Ivy's soul wanted to pay attention to the scientific phenomenon of the incoming rock, it was a task she had to delegate; and she'd delegated it to Steve Lake as soon as the alert had sounded.

Thus far, the alert had been proceeding as most of them did, which meant that most network activity had been shut down to leave open bandwidth for Parambulator. That system swung into action without human intervention, calculating courses, making suggestions, and gathering data about what the motes in the data cloud were doing. The Parambulator screens were looking pretty angry, but that was normal as almost every arklet fired its thrusters and shunted into a new trajectory. In time it would get sorted out. It always did. But part of the sorting-out process was refining what they knew about the trajectory of the incoming streaker. The closer it came, the more precisely they could track it. By the time it passed through, or near, the swarm, they'd have its parameters dialed in to high precision. And once it had flashed by, all Parambulator had to do was clean up the mess.

Ivy had asked Steve about the bolide for a couple of reasons. One was that hot rocks, by definition, tended to come and go rapidly. This one had been approaching for several minutes—a long time to wait. Another was that Parambulator looked more chaotic than usual. Normally there would be a spray of red in the first couple of minutes. Presently it would begin to fade as the arklets reported that they were out of harm's way. But in this case, it never seemed to get any better. "Are we having trouble with bandwidth, or—"

"The rock is weird," Steve said. "Normally I'd expect to see a stream of packets from SI, refining the params as they gathered more data." He meant Sensor Integration: the department that managed the radars and telescopes.

"And you're not?"

"Well, I am—but with different numbers."

"What do you mean, different numbers?"

"It's like we have two different Streaker Alerts happening at once. The packets are stepping on each other. There's some kind of crosstalk going on." Steve sat back from his screen for a moment and tugged his beard. "Just a sec," he said. "I think that these packets are coming from different sources."

"But they should all have the same point of origination," Ivy said. "SI."

"They claim to," Steve said, "but I think that some of them are forgeries."

Feeling his chair shift subtly beneath him, he reached out involuntarily with one hand and held the edge of the table. Izzy was firing her thrusters, coming about to a new orientation, trying to put Amalthea between herself and the bolide—real or imagined.

"You think this whole alert is them spoofing us?"

"It would fit in with Tekla's theory of what's going on," Steve said.

"I'll try to voice with Doob," Ivy said. "Work on that forgery hypothesis."

"MADAM PRESIDENT," CAMILA SAID, PULLING A HEADPHONE AWAY from her ear. "As you requested, I am informing you that Ivy has figured it out."

"She knows?" Julia asked.

"Not quite, but Steve Lake has detected the forged packets and is running further analysis." Camila's eyes were big and her voice—which was always somewhat impaired by her facial injuries—was thick and dry.

Julia threw her a shrewd look, then turned to Spencer Grindstaff, who shrugged. "Sooner or later a man of Steve's talents was bound to—"

"I don't care about that," Julia cut in. "I want to know whether our gambit has bought us enough time."

"There's—" Camila began.

Spencer ran Camila off the road. "It has bought us enough *confusion*. We should be in a position to dock this heptad at the Shipyard in twenty seconds."

"There's another bolide!" Camila squeaked. "I think."

Julia shook her off, keeping her focus on Spencer. "Where is the triad?"

"Already there," Spencer said.

"The spacewalkers?"

"Suited up, out of the airlocks, in position."

"Still. The assembly. The integration. It will take time."

"Madam President, if I may," Paul Freel broke in. "All we need is to slap her together—with zip ties, if that's what it takes—and achieve separation from the Shipyard. A small thruster burn will do it. Izzy doesn't have phasers to blast us out of the sky! They could send a Flivver after us, but what are they going to do? All we need is to get clear. Then we can spend days prepping *Red Hope* before we embark on the mission in earnest."

"I wouldn't put anything past that Tekla."

"Say what you will about her, she'll follow orders," Paul said.

"Well, as a stay-behind supporter of your expedition, I will be happy to run interference for you until you can get cleanly away," Julia said.

Through the heptad's structure, a programmed series of whirrs and clunks resonated as it docked with a port on the long truss projecting to the side of the Caboose: the heart of the Shipyard, rich in airlocks and anchoring points. Docked at the next port along was a glinting, angular framework: the skeleton of *Red Hope,* awaiting its final components. It sported four large propellant tanks clustered around a knot of pumps, valves, actuators, and sensors that fed a rocket engine centered below.

"Madam President?" Ravi asked. "I'm afraid the time is now. Unless you want to go to Mars. Which you would be welcome to do."

Julia snapped to attention. She had been checking herself in the mirror of her compact. Hardly glamorous, but by Cloud Ark standards, her appearance would do.

"It is tempting," Julia said, "but I have responsibilities here, I'm afraid." She snapped the compact shut and glanced over, verifying that Camila was ready to shoot video on her phone. She was, but she still had that rattled look on her face. What had come over her? They'd have to have a heart-to-heart later.

"Very well," Ravi said, with a note of regret that sounded only a little forced. "Perhaps you'll be wanting this."

He held out a sheet of paper. Taking it from him, Julia recognized it as the presidential seal, much the worse for wear. Ravi had carefully peeled it from the wall, bringing most of its rectangle of blue tape with it. Julia smoothed it out and tucked it under one arm.

Slowly drifting away from her, Ravi snapped out a salute.

Julia returned it. "Godspeed, Ravi. I look forward to hearing your first transmission from the surface of Mars."

"And I look forward to sending it, Madam President."

"We shall meet again, I feel. Somehow the intrepid people of the Cloud Ark will find a way, in spite of all opposition, to win through to the realm of clean space and follow *Red Hope* to a better place."

Ravi was one of those who could never quite tell when he was dismissed. He began to mumble out a stirring response, but Julia glanced at Camila to let her know that she could stop recording, then propelled herself toward the nose of the White Arklet. Camila followed in her wake.

After a few moments of squirming through tubes, they emerged from the port into one of the modules that made up the Shipyard. It was something of a madhouse. The total roster of the *Red Hope* expedition was two dozen. Most of those were already aboard the heptad or the triad, waiting to be mated with the vehicle's frame, but a few were "outside" in space suits and several were in here, engaging in hasty conferences or shoving bundles of supplies about.

Adding a bizarre note were four members of the General Population—apparently Shipyard workers—who had been zip-tied, hands behind backs, to convenient attachment points around the inside of the module. Most looked fine, but one man had a stream of small blood globules drifting away from a laceration on his eyebrow. Paul Freel had mentioned in passing that several of the MIV team had become unwitting accomplices, helping to assemble the frame of *Red Hope* on the understanding that it was part of a backup plan to rescue *Ymir*. Apparently they had changed status to witting, and raised objections.

The bleeding man was staring at Julia through the eye that hadn't swollen shut. "Julia!" he called out.

In an odd way Julia had nothing to do. The other Martians were busy shoving their hoarded supplies through the port into the heptad. One by one the Martians were following suit, and so the space was rapidly clearing out. She ignored the bleeding man at first. But it got to the point where only one Martian—Paul Freel himself—was remaining. Lacking Ravi's feel for ceremony, he was checking off items on the screen of his tablet, paying Julia no attention whatsoever.

"Julia!" the zip-tied man said again. He wasn't shouting. His tone was almost conversational.

"Yes," she finally said.

"What's your friend's name?" he asked, nodding toward Camila.

Julia bridled for a moment at the impertinent request, then remembered that it was never too late to turn an enemy into a friend. "Her name is Camila," she said. "And let me say, sir, that I am shocked and dismayed to see what has occurred to you. Let me assure you that—"

"Hey, Camila!" the man said.

"Yes?" Camila answered, sounding very much the scared eighteen-year-old girl.

"Your friend is crazy," the man told her.

"Madam President?" Paul asked, before Julia had time to react.

She turned toward Paul, her face burning.

"If you would do the honors?"

"What honors?" Honestly, these engineers. Was she supposed to break a bottle of champagne over it?

"Close the hatch when I have gone through. Then we can undock."

"Happy to."

"See you on Mars." He stuck his hand out. She grasped it lightly and gave it a little shake. Camila, rattled by the exchange with the bleeding man, had forsaken her duties as camera operator.

Paul Freel reached into the portal joining Earth to Mars, pulled himself through, turned about, and closed the hatch on his side. Julia followed suit on hers. Immediately she felt, as much as heard, the hisses and clunks that signaled the undocking of *Red Hope*. Unfamiliar noises radiated through the module's hull too, very close to her, and she realized that these were the boots of space suits moving around.

"The alert is canceled," announced a synthetic voice. The color of the lights changed.

Camila emitted a short, explosive scream. Then she pointed down the length of the Shipyard, toward where it connected with the Stack.

Down in the Caboose, some thirty meters away, a few people could be seen, dressed in orange vests. One of them looked directly at her.

It was Tekla.

The synthesized voice spoke out again, sounding a second alert.

That wasn't part of the plan.

Tekla must have gathered her legs against something down in the Caboose capable of pushing back, because all of a sudden she was flying toward them like a rocket. Her arms were in motion, reaching this way and that to slap at anything that could help her correct her course, but her eyes were fixed on Julia and she was coming straight for her. Something gleamed in her hand, a thin arc of silver light: the honed edge of a dagger.

A crisp metallic noise resounded through the module as Julia pulled back the hammer on Pete Starling's revolver.

"Gun!" shouted the bleeding man. "Gun! Gun!"

If Tekla heard, she did not care, but only pushed back harder against a strut in the neighboring module and came on faster.

To Julia the weapon's recoil came too soon, as if it had gone off accidentally. She'd been in space long enough to know that it would knock her back, and it did; but she also saw things she could not explain. Camila had entered the picture, flying in from the side with an arm outstretched. The wall of the Shipyard itself reached out to body-check Tekla. A moment later it struck Camila, then Julia. She had expected the high-pitched hiss of a bullet-sized hull puncture; but what followed was more like a roar. Like the crowd in a football stadium when a pass is intercepted. Camila's arm had turned into a wing of fire. Something took Julia from behind and hurled her toward the Caboose. She looked around, thinking, crazily, that the bleeding man had somehow gotten loose and tackled her. But the force pushing her along was no human being. It was a torrent of escaping air.

"JIRO, CAN YOU HEAR ME?" DINAH ASKED FOR THE FOURTH TIME.

She conjectured that he could, but that he was simply too weak to answer. So she went ahead and delivered the good news. "We made it," she said. "I have Izzy on optical. We'll converge with them in about half an hour."

"Good," he said, "good." She was startled to hear anything at all. But the second "good" was a lot fainter than the first one, and she reckoned it was all he could get out.

She decided not to tell him anything further. Entombed in *Ymir*'s boiler room, simultaneously freezing to death while being cooked alive by radiation, he didn't need to hear a description of what Dinah was seeing through the telescope.

They had been calling this the Cloud Ark for two years. The name had been meant somewhat poetically. Today, however, it really did look like a cloud. Her view of Izzy, which usually was so crisp and sharp in the high-contrast light of outer space, was cloaked in a glinting and winking shroud of what might be clinically described as particulate matter.

It went without saying that Izzy had taken a direct hit from a bolide. Beyond that, it was difficult to make out details.

Ymir's final burn—for Jiro, a suicide mission—had settled her in an orbit quite similar to Izzy's: the same plane, the same average altitude. The only difference was that it was a little bit more oval, calculated to cross Izzy's path twice during each revolution around the Earth. They were approaching one of those crossings, and so from Dinah's point of view the space station kept getting closer, filling the window on her computer screen, obliging her to zoom out, giving her a progressively sharper, more detailed picture. As minutes ticked by, she was able to piece together a guess as to what had happened.

The rock must have come in from an angle, missed Amalthea cleanly, and struck somewhere near H2, the hub that anchored Tori 2 and 3. Both of the tori had huge bites taken out of them, and both had stopped rotating. Aft of that point, Izzy's spine—her central Stack—was actually bent. The spreading wings of the Shipyard were still attached to the Caboose, but they were askew, and leaking debris. The original torus—the one that contained the Banana—was still rotating, and looked whole, but as she drew closer she saw it had taken damage, perhaps from shrapnel.

A faint thud resounded through the ice hull. They'd probably struck a piece of jetsam. No matter, it wouldn't be moving very fast. *Ymir* could nuzzle her way through a cloud of that stuff and never feel it.

One of the windows on her screen flashed up a video feed, triggered by the motion detector on a Grabb's camera, and she saw a human body drifting away into space. She swallowed against a sharp contraction of her throat.

Part of her wondered if she would find Izzy a ghost ship—if she were the only human remaining alive. For Vyacheslav had stopped communicating with them yesterday. Before then, he had mentioned that he had been suffering from diarrhea. If this was caused by radiation exposure, it was a death sentence. He might simply have committed suicide rather than wait for the inevitable.

Alone at the controls of *Ymir,* she coasted toward Izzy, silent and adrift in the cosmos, and entertained the thought, just for a while, that she might be the only human being left in the universe.

Then a red light—a laser, aimed right at her—began to flash from the Mining Colony, and her mind began to pick out Morse code.

SENDING FLIVVERS TO EFFECT FINAL
MANEUVERS
DISREGARD STRAY ARKLETS
WELCOME HOME

Lacking any way to respond, she waited, and watched. Shreds of insulation, scraps of structural material, spilled vitamins, and the occasional body tumbled across the window as she panned and zoomed over various details. Everything forward of Zvezda looked pretty good. The Mining Colony and Moira's stash of genetic equipment appeared to be unscathed. Good.

Three Flivvers had separated themselves from the cloud and established trajectories that would bring them to Ymir within a few minutes. She guessed that they would act as tugboats, butting their heads against the shard and using their main engines to effect the final delta vee needed to achieve rendezvous. So, the first part of the transmission made sense. DISREGARD STRAY ARKLETS, however, was something of a mystery. Why would there be such a thing? And what did it mean, anyway, for an arklet to be "stray"? And yet as Dinah panned the telescope across the arc of space forward and aft of Izzy—the realm where most of the arklets normally parked themselves—she found it curiously underpopulated. It was just a general visual impression. She couldn't verify it scientifically without access to a Parambulator screen.

It occurred to her, then, that all she needed to do was switch on her tablet's connection to the mesh network. Shortly after *New Caird*'s departure from Izzy, she had turned it off because, once they got out of range, it was a useless battery drainer. And indeed the tablet soon brought up the little icon announcing it had found a connection, perhaps relayed through one of those Flivvers. A minute or two went by as the device downloaded all of the email and message traffic that had been piling up in her inbox during her "vacation."

She passed the time playing with the telescope. A detail caught her eye as she panned across the scene, and she went back and zoomed in on it for a closer look.

It was a MIV, an unusually big one. Basically a five-layer stack, wasp-waisted. The bottom layer was an engine of the most powerful class in the MIV toolkit. Above that was a fat cluster of propellant tanks. The third layer—the narrow waist—was a single arklet with an airlock on its side—a command module, she guessed, similar to *New Caird*'s. Above that was a triad, and on top, forming the fat head of the vehicle, was a heptad. All of it was shrouded in structural webbing. Snared like little bugs in the edges of that web were small modules that she recognized as attitude control thrusters. The most notable thing about the vehicle was her outsized propellant tanks, hinting at a long journey—to where? The thing was keeping station several kilometers forward of Izzy, in a region that had been largely denuded of arklets.

Her tablet finally finished downloading messages, most of which were long out of date by this point. She sorted them by age, newest first, and scanned the headings. Very few had come through in the last several hours. That stood to reason, given that the Cloud Ark had other things on its mind. But close to the top was one that caught her eye: OPEN COMMUNIQUÉ FROM PRESIDENT JBF TO THE PEOPLE OF THE CLOUD ARK.

Merely seeing those words gave her a feeling as if she'd been socked in the solar plexus. She tapped it anyway, and read it:

> *Today's shocking tragedy has left us all bereaved, and seeking answers. I was in a Shipyard module when it happened, having just bid farewell and godspeed to the brave explorers of the* Red Hope *expedition. Thanks to the automatic closure of a hatch, I experienced only minor injuries and discomfort from partial decompression. As we all know, many members of the General Population were not so lucky. I join with all humanity in mourning their sacrifice. By its nature, the Arkie Community was less affected by this disaster. As I had envisioned from the very beginnings of the Cloud Ark project, the distributed architecture of the swarm prevented serious damage. We did lose three arklets, I am sorry to say, and several more sustained damage from minor collisions or debris impacts. But overall the system worked as we had planned from the beginning. Many members of the AC are now, quite naturally, asking themselves whether it is safe to remain in low Earth orbit, clustered around a heavy, aging space station that lacks the ability to maneuver out of harm's way. The open vista of clean space beckons above us.* Red Hope *will soon fire its main engine and begin its trek across that unexplored frontier to a planet that will one day have room for us all. The Cloud Ark cannot follow her—yet. But as all members of the AC know, having gone through extensive training in space operations and orbital mechanics, it is well within the capability of any arklet to raise its orbit substantially by making use of its engines and its onboard propellant supplies. Alone, a single arklet, triad, or heptad will not long endure. As part of a swarm, however, it has a fighting chance. Many members of the Arkie Community who have been watching the desperate trials and tribulations of the* Ymir *expedition, and who have now witnessed the*

damage inflicted upon Izzy by a single bolide, are now asking themselves whether it is safe to remain, and to trust themselves to the agonizingly slow climb toward clean space envisioned by the partisans of the Big Ride faction. I am a politician, not a scientist, and so I cannot pretend to render a technical opinion. Some may question whether I should be making a public announcement at all. The simple fact of the matter is that my past career as President of the United States has given me prominence in the Arkie Community, whether or not I deserve it. Many have been asking me what I shall do now. Rather than wait for rumor to sow confusion, I am therefore issuing this communiqué. For what it is worth, I have, with the assistance of some loyal friends, escaped from the wreckage of Izzy and found safe haven aboard Arklet 37, currently part of a triad. Shortly after I transmit this message, we will initiate a burn of our main propulsion that will lift us clear of the drifting debris that surrounds what once was the International Space Station, and move us in the direction of clean space. Our orbital parameters will be posted openly on the network so that like-minded members of the AC may join us in creating a swarm-based solution to the acute problems currently imposing themselves on the human race. From a safe position in higher orbit, we will look for ways to extend a helping hand to our surviving friends marooned in the General Population. Working together as a community, we will preserve what we have and build a stable way of life in the sky as we await with breathless anticipation the results of Red Hope*'s inspiring venture to the welcoming surface of Mars.*

"She's right about the 'breathless' part of it," Dinah muttered to herself, closing the window and looking at the time stamp again. It had been transmitted three hours ago. Then, only half an hour ago, Ivy had responded with a counter-communiqué. Dinah didn't read it, but based on the subject heading she knew what it would say: don't listen to J.B.F., stay in formation, we need you and you need us.

But from what Dinah was seeing, both through the optical telescope and on Parambulator, Ivy's message had come too late to forestall the departure of a large number of arklets. Somewhere out there, up above them in higher orbit, a new swarm was taking shape, running its own, independent instance of Parambulator, and looking to J.B.F. for leadership.

Dinah had been through many emotional ups and downs while retrieving *Ymir.* More downs than ups, of course, given the fatality rate. In a strange way, however, the emotional high point was just a few moments ago when she had scanned the word "desperate" in J.B.F.'s communiqué. She rather liked being described as desperate, particularly when she was just on the verge of succeeding.

Parambulator was working on her screen now. She used it to check the status of those three Flivvers. They were still closing. Messages were starting to come in from their pilots, trying to make out whether anyone was still alive in the shard, whether it was safe to approach.

Dinah texted back: *One survivor. Stand clear for a sec while this thing takes a big glow-in-the-dark crap.*

Then she pulled up the window she used to communicate with her network of robots and typed in a single-word command: JETTISON. It was the name of a program that Sean had started, Larz had improved, and Dinah had recently finished. It was a program meant to be run simultaneously by every robot in the shard, as well as some other systems down in the boiler room.

A prompt came back: ARE YOU SURE Y/N

Y, she typed.

CONGRATULATIONS!!! came back. The dead crew of *Ymir* had sent her a message from the void.

She pushed herself over to the companionway, got her head aimed "down" through the hole in the floor, and pulled herself straight to the bottom level of the command module. The hatch in the floor—the one that led to the ice tunnel that terminated in the boiler room—had already been closed, as a basic safety measure. But Dinah verified that one last time and made sure it was sealed. Because in a few seconds, there would be nothing but vacuum on the other side of it.

Ymir had begun grumbling. Dinah felt as if she were trapped inside the belly of a frost giant with indigestion. What she was hearing, she knew, was the collective noise made by thousands of Nats, and hundreds of larger robots, as they moved to safe positions on the inner surface of the hollow shard and gnawed away at the structural webbing that connected it to the reactor core.

She returned to her seat in the command module and pulled up a video feed from the interior of the shard. Its walls were now thin enough to admit some sunlight, and so it had become a sort of vast pellucid amphitheater where all of those robots could look inward to the smooth beryllium pod—a neutron-reflecting shroud—surrounding the reactor core. Formerly this had been buried in ice; the recent excavations made to fuel the big perigee burns had left it exposed, also revealing the smaller pod of the boiler room mounted on its side, and the system of hoppers and augers that fed it. Aft of that was what remained of the ice cavern of the nozzle bell, now mostly melted away to expose the blackness of space beyond. The only thing now holding the reactor chamber in place was the massive central thrust pillar, a tree trunk of ice that grew from its forward end and extended straight up to the solid nose of the shard, where the command module was embedded.

JETTISON did her the courtesy of showing a countdown on the screen, so that she could plug her ears. When it hit zero, a sickening crack resounded through the whole structure. The video feed showed a brilliant spray of ice blown free from the central pillar, just above where it connected to the reactor vessel. Demolition charges, placed there long ago by Sean's crew, had detonated and severed the connection. For a moment she feared nothing further would happen, but then jets of white steam lanced from the reactor vessel's rounded top. JETTISON had opened valves, releasing pressure that had built up in the chamber from the reactor's residual heat, and those valves were now acting as makeshift rocket engines, pushing the whole reactor, and everything attached to it, down toward the vacancy of the nozzle.

The entire reactor chamber dropped out the bottom of the shard and was gone.

If JETTISON continued to do its work, the reactor, now a free-floating vehicle, all brawn and no brains, would execute a few clumsy maneuvers to kill its own orbital velocity and drop itself into the atmosphere.

"Bye, Jiro," Dinah said. "Thank you."

One of the Flivver pilots texted her: *Wow.*

Dinah gave it all one more thorough scan, using several cameras. But there wasn't much to see. *Ymir* was now a hollow, sugarloaf-shaped shell, crawling with robots, and helplessly adrift in space.

She texted, *Did someone place an order for a megaton of propellant?*

INSTINCT HAD HERDED THEM TOGETHER IN THE SCRUM, CLOSE TO Amalthea and far away from the parts of Izzy that had been damaged or destroyed. That was where Dinah found them, after she'd been brought aboard, scrubbed clean, checked and checked again for contamination. Pink and raw, she embraced Ivy first, for a long time, and then made the rounds to Doob, Moira, Rhys, Luisa, Steve Lake, Fyodor, and Bo. Konrad Barth and many others were dead. Tekla was still in surgery. One of her breasts had been damaged by a fragment and was being surgically repaired.

Curled up in very nearly a fetal position at one end of the SCRUM was a woman who was quietly weeping. She hid her face from the room with an arm swathed, from fingertips to shoulder, in white gauze. Dinah recognized her as Camila, Julia's sidekick.

Ivy insisted that they all move back down the Stack and meet in the Banana. It took some gentle persuasion to get Camila to come with them, but eventually Luisa talked her into it. Out of habit she kept reaching for the veil she normally drew across the lower half of her face, but it wasn't there anymore. She was dressed like everyone else, in a shapeless coverall.

"What is Camila doing here?" Dinah asked Moira, as they maneuvered down the Stack.

Moira had obviously been crying and seemed badly shaken up. She and Tekla had become a couple at some point, and Moira was taking the news of her partner's injury hard.

"Tekla came for J.B.F.," Moira said, "and J.B.F. tried to shoot her. Camila reached out and grabbed for the gun, I guess. She was always wearing that gauzy wrap, as a veil. The fabric caught fire from the flash of the gun, and burned her arm before she could get it off."

"But she saved Tekla?"

"Who knows? The bullet struck something else and fragmented, apparently."

The holes where shrapnel had struck T1—the first, oldest, and smallest torus—had been patched, and it had been repressurized. They had always considered it a safe place before; they needed to begin thinking of it in that light again, which was why Ivy had insisted they come here. They took seats in the Banana.

The numbers had come in. Ivy opened the meeting by reciting them.

At the onset of the Hard Rain, the human population—not counting any who might still be alive on Earth—had been 1,551, or 1,553 if you counted the two late arrivals, Julia and Pete Starling. Starling hadn't even made it out of his space capsule, so the initial number had been 1,552.

At the same time there had been 305 occupied, free-flying arklets plus 11 spares that were attached to Izzy but not occupied. The free-flying ones had housed 1,364 people; the remaining 188 humans had lived aboard Izzy as members of the General Population. But at any given time, 10 percent of the Arkies had been rotating through Izzy, bringing its population on a typical day up to 324.

Prior to today's disaster, 26 people had been killed in various mishaps, mostly smaller bolide strikes. Another 24 were now aboard the stolen MIV calling itself *Red Hope,* and if their claims were taken at face value, they would soon be en route to Mars.

Of the persons who had been aboard Izzy at the time of the disaster, 211 had been killed outright and another two dozen or so remained in critical condition. The number of living people aboard Izzy had therefore been reduced to 113. The General Population—the older, more experienced, highly trained specialists—had been reduced from 188 to 106.

At the moment of the disaster, 1,178 persons had been living in arklets. The distributed nature of the swarm, combined with the fact that many arklets had flown the coop with Julia, made it difficult to estimate casualties. The best estimate they currently had was that seventeen arklets had fallen victim, with assumed 100 percent loss of life, reducing that population to about 1,100. If that was correct, then the day's full death toll had been close to 300.

In terms of arklet count, they'd started the day with 299 surviving, occupied arklets, a figure that had been reduced to 282 by the collision. Ten of them—a heptad and a triad—were attached to *Red Hope,* leaving 272. Approximately 200 were missing and presumed to have flown the coop with J.B.F. The remaining 70 or so had elected to stay behind and were still reporting in as members in good standing of the Cloud Ark. The 11 spares were still attached to Izzy and would be inspected for damage later.

The arklets still with them probably had a population of some 300. That plus the survivors aboard Izzy added up to a bit over 400. The population of J.B.F.'s breakaway swarm must then be something like 800 souls. She had taken two-thirds of the human race with her.

"God forgive me," Doob said, "but right now I don't even care about head count. The number I'm after is engines. Arklet engines.

Until Dinah showed up with all of that ice, they were useless. Now, we have a way to fuel them. If we get them all pointed in the same direction, all pushing on Izzy, we can go on the Big Ride." He paused to look at his notes. With his reading glasses down on his nose he suddenly looked a lot older to Dinah. She could only imagine how *she* looked. "Based on what you just told me, am I right in thinking we have—"

"About seventy," Ivy said, "plus the eleven spares. We haven't checked those yet, but on visual inspection they seem undamaged."

"Eighty-one," Doob said. "I like that number. A perfect square."

"A perfect square of perfect squares," Rhys put in.

"If we could come up with a structural system for ganging them in clusters of nine—just a three-by-three grid, with shared propellant feeds—and make nine of those clusters, and integrate them into Izzy's structure somehow—that being the hard part—then we'd have an array of eighty-one engines. If those things all come on at full power when we pass through perigee, it'll give us enough combined thrust to make a difference. I think we can make the Big Ride work with that level of power."

"It's a lot of structure," Fyodor pointed out. "A lot, a lot, a lot."

"We have a lot of raw materials to work with, don't we?" Luisa asked. "I've seen rolls and rolls of that aluminum ribbon for feeding into the extruder machines."

"It is a question of time," Fyodor said. "Yes, we have a lot of material. But to assemble it with so few people is difficult. Atmosphere is growing, drag is increasing, orbit is decaying."

Dinah looked across the table at Rhys. Rhys the biomimetic engineer, the man who had perhaps saved *Ymir* with his idea of turning robots into little, radiation-resistant Ben Grimms.

"We'll build it out of ice," Dinah said.

Rhys looked up at her, pondered it for a second, and nodded.

"Too brittle," Fyodor said.

"I don't think Dinah's speaking of regular ice," Rhys said. "She means the pykrete stuff they used on *Ymir*. Fiber-reinforced ice. It worked to hold the shard together. We can make it work here."

Moira spoke up. "Perhaps I'm missing something, but I was under the impression that the ice was our propellant. Aren't we going to melt it, and consume it, as we go along?"

"Yes," Doob said.

"And doesn't that mean that we'll be consuming the structure that's holding everything together?"

"Yes," Doob repeated, "but it's okay. Because the more of it we use, the lighter we get, and the less thrust we need. So it's okay to sacrifice some structure as we go along."

Sal had been listening intently. "I don't mean to throw cold water on the idea," he said. The pun—assuming he meant it as such—elicited a few groans. "But we've been hearing about radioactive contamination."

"On the outer surface of the shard, yes," Dinah said. "Microscopic motes of stuff that is super radioactive, stuck to the ice. Beta won't penetrate our living spaces. We'll have to be careful, though, not to track it inside. We can program robots to crawl around, look for those hot motes, and get rid of them over time."

Sal looked unconvinced.

"I won't lie to you," Dinah said. "People are going to die of it."

"But the trade is as follows," Rhys said. "Izzy already has a massive battering ram of nickel-iron on her snout. Her flanks are vulnerable, as we learned today. Now we have the ability to shroud everything—the entire space station—in reinforced ice. Oh, it will dwindle over time. But through most of the Big Ride we'll be living deep inside of a gigantic iceberg with a steel nose. I submit that the death toll from possible contamination will be minor compared to what we would experience if we went on the same journey unprotected."

"What do you need to make it happen?" Ivy asked.

"Permission," Dinah said.

"When did you ever ask for that before?"

The joke elicited a high-pitched laugh from the corner of the conference room. Heads turned toward Camila.

"Camila," Ivy said, "we've hardly heard a word from you since we found you in the Shipyard. One of our witnesses there claims you may have saved Tekla's life. You had the opportunity to escape with Julia. Instead you stayed behind to free the bound Shipyard workers. You saved their lives. Now you're here among us. You must know how this looks."

The look on Camila's face made it clear that how it looked had never crossed her mind. She didn't even get what Ivy was saying.

"Dear," Luisa said, "people are going to say you are a spy who volunteered to be left behind."

Camila held up a closed fist and opened it to reveal a small white plastic box, loose tape still dangling from it. "Julia's bug," she announced. "It was here."

No one looked very convinced.

"She invited me to dinner at the White House," Camila said. "She helped me pick out a dress. She introduced me to generals, ambassadors, movie stars. She wrote me letters on White House stationery. I was—I was in love with her. You can call me naive if you want. All right. I was naive. Until this morning. And then all of a sudden I saw. I saw what I was dealing with. I hate her now. And I hate myself for having been in love with her."

"Best remember that, sweetheart," Moira said. "Because she made the wrong choice today. And sooner or later, she'll be coming back."

"I'll be ready," Camila said.

Endurance

SEEN BY HUMAN EYES, THE HOLLOW HULK OF *YMIR*'S ICE SHARD WAS as dead, brittle, and gleaming as the discarded carapace of a beetle. Captured through the electronic eyes of cameras, then speeded up a hundred-thousandfold, so that the events of one day were compressed into one second of video, it looked like an amoeba pursuing, capturing, and swallowing Izzy. A person with no preconceptions of what they were watching would perceive Izzy as a steel-headed insect, all legs and pods and antennas, twitching and kicking in an effort to defend itself from the slow, relentless, liquid onslaught of the ice monster.

In truth, of course, the four hundred survivors, moving at lightning speed compared with the slow evolutions of the ice, were reconfiguring the space station in preparation for the Big Ride. The crippled Caboose was cut free and the components of the Shipyard moved forward. The big power reactor was brought in close to the Stack; from now on they would rely on ice to shield the rest of Izzy from its radiation. The eighty-one arklets arranged themselves into nine groups of nine and were tacked into place at the aft end, nozzles aimed backward. The structural works holding them into place at first were flimsy trellises on which spacewalkers could string cables, propellant lines, and hamster tubes. As soon as those were in place, the ice caught up with them, driven forward by the ceaseless operations of a giant Nat swarm, and the arklets were gradually cemented into place within a solid matrix of the fiber-reinforced ice known as pykrete.

Forward the ice flowed. It was like watching video of a melting iceberg played in reverse. The Nats, blindly following a simple collection of rules, packed it into every vacant space they happened upon. In the few minutes out of each day when the crew could take some rest and eat some rations, they would try to top each other telling funny stories about where they had found a living infestation of ice, and what they had done to beat it back.

Within a month, the remnants of *Ymir* had all been consumed, and Izzy had seemingly ceased to exist. The two of them had merged into an orbiting mountain. Its summit was a battered and scarified lump of nickel-iron, hazy with angular scaffolding where antennas and sensors were mounted. Its slopes were a smooth rampart of black ice, interrupted here and there by outcroppings of thrusters or other equipment, observation domes peeking out like hermits' huts. Its base was a plane decorated with a neat grid of eighty-one small holes from which blue-white fire erupted from time to time as the ship passed through her perigee.

They couldn't make out what to call the thing. People tried and failed to combine the words Izzy and *Ymir*. The closest they came was Izmir, but that had been the name of a city in Turkey. Sentiment was in favor of naming her after the martyrs of the *Ymir* expedition, but there had been several. In honor of Markus it was likened to the Daubenhorn, later shortened to the Horn. Which was not a bad nickname. But the name that stuck was a continuation of the Shackleton theme that Markus had established with *New Caird*. Shackleton's big ship had been called *Endurance,* and was famous for having gotten stuck in the ice. So *Endurance* it was, and Fyodor christened her thus by getting into his battered Orlan, climbing out onto the surface of Amalthea, and dashing a bottle of champagne against the metal.

A more distant camera, looking down on Earth from high above the North Pole and watching the career of *Endurance* over the next years, would have seen a nail-biter of an opening, followed by endless grinding tedium, slowly building to a dramatic final reel.

Prior to *Ymir*'s arrival, the Cloud Ark's pilots had put no small amount of attention into the problem of keeping Izzy out of the expanding atmosphere. This produced greater drag, which Amalthea, with its high ballistic coefficient, was well made to resist. But the decay of her orbit had to be mended from time to time with burns of the big engine that in those days had lived on the aft end of the Caboose, fueled by the Shipyard's reactor-powered splitters.

The Break—as they called the event when the big bolide had smashed into Izzy, and the Swarm and *Red Hope* had gone their separate ways—had put an end to all that. Between then and the day about a month later when *Endurance* was christened, she spiraled gradually downward. Had the featherweight arklets tried to keep formation with her, they'd have been pushed back by the wind. They were forced to creep into the lee of Amalthea and ride along within her bow wave, like bicyclists slipstreaming behind a truck, until they could be integrated into the framework of the ship. Down and down she spiraled, and the SI team had to send Grabbs out onto the forward trusswork and remove the fragile antennas and sensors mounted there, lest they be slowly burned off by a rarefied but white-hot windblast. Fyodor's champagne space walk was a brief one, and when he got back inside he reported that he could see the spraying foam of the champagne being blown backward by the atmosphere.

Their mission was to move their apogee from where it was now—just a few kilometers higher than the altitude of the perigee—all the way out to the altitude of Cleft, some 378,000 kilometers more distant. It was a reversal of the maneuvers that Markus, Dinah, Jiro, and Vyacheslav had executed in order to bring *Ymir* into orbital sync with Izzy. The way to achieve it was to burn the engines for brief intervals as *Endurance* made her regular swings through perigee.

The first of those burns happened about thirty minutes after she was christened, and yielded a delta vee of four meters per second. The acceleration was so mild that most of the crew could not even sense it. For the combined thrust of eighty-one arklet engines was nearly powerless against the bulk of *Endurance,* with her roughly equal masses of iron and ice. Nonetheless it was enough to boost her apogee, which occurred some forty-six minutes later, by 14.18 kilometers. And forty-six minutes after that, another burn during another scrape with the atmosphere gained them another four meters per second that, at the ensuing apogee, added 14.21 kilometers on top of that. The result of *Endurance*'s first day of operations was a boost in apogee altitude of more than one hundred kilometers, enough to get them clear of the expanded atmosphere except during the few minutes each orbit when they swung through perigee.

After that, however, they had to suspend operations, since they'd used up all the propellant stored in the Shipyard's ice-buried tanks. They needed to give the reactor and the splitters some time to catch up. Even a nuclear power plant could split water only so fast.

Not long after, the operation was shut down for a week by problems in feeding clean water to the system. For another month it could only operate at about a quarter of its planned capacity. But over time they worked the bugs out and began to burn the engines more and more at each perigee, gradually extending *Endurance*'s reach toward Cleft.

If they could keep it up, that reach would get less gradual over time. The first delta vee had gained them 14.18 kilometers. The second, equivalent delta vee had reaped 14.21 kilometers—an improvement of about thirty meters. These gains were tiny in comparison to the distances of outer space, but from a mathematical standpoint the trend was extremely significant. It meant that the higher they went—the more elongated the orbit became—the more leverage they could obtain from each one of those tiny delta vees. That difference of thirty meters would grow and grow until it spanned many kilometers, and each of those improvements would feed back into the equations and amplify the next result a little bit more. It was an exponential sort of phenomenon, and this time humanity was on the right side of it.

This didn't even take into account another piece of good mathematical news, which was that *Endurance* grew a little bit lighter with each one of those burns. She had less mass with which to resist the force of the thrusters, and so it gradually became possible to produce more than a piddling four meters per second of delta vee on each turn around the planet.

So everything was going to get better, if they could stay alive and keep *Endurance* working. But these gains accrued painfully slowly at the beginning.

IT ENDED UP TAKING THREE YEARS.

They had planned for one. It took longer because things kept breaking and needed to be fixed. The tools and supplies needed to fix them weren't always available. Sometimes they had to be improvised. Elaborate workarounds had to be devised through the force of human ingenuity, hard work, and, when all else failed, the risking and the sacrifice of lives.

The human capital of *Endurance* dwindled. They were always short on food. Arklets were designed to grow their own food supplies in their translucent outer hulls. But *Endurance*'s arklets were buried in ice to protect them from the Hard Rain. The ones near the outside got enough sunlight to produce some food, but not enough compared to the mouths that had to be fed. She began her journey well stocked with emergency provisions, which were rationed out on a schedule that assumed a mission length of one year. As it became clear that the journey would go on much longer, the rations were cut back. *Endurance* also had abundant stockpiles of vitamins, most of which had survived the Break. These were sought after by the people of the Swarm, who had flown the coop without stockpiling enough of them. Trade began to happen between *Endurance* and the Swarm, but it wasn't the free market that the Swarmamentalists had once envisioned. Deals were negotiated over the radio and consummated by exchanges between MIVs and arklets, difficult to arrange because of the need to match orbits that had now become very different.

As they had done with *Ymir,* they mined ice from the interior volume of *Endurance,* leaving the outer "walnut shell" as a structural support and as a first line of defense against bolides. But as J.B.F. and other Dump and Run partisans had never tired of pointing out, such a heavy craft lacked maneuverability. When a big rock was seen far enough in advance, they could use her engines to make small course changes that would have large outcomes by the time the rock came close. Doing so was the full-time occupation of most of *Endurance*'s complement, which worked at it three shifts a day. But below a certain threshold they could not see rocks soon enough, or maneuver out of their way quickly enough, and then they just had to hope that the bolide would strike Amalthea. Most did, but some hit the icy lower slopes, and of those, some struck with enough power to penetrate and kill.

Suicide took about one in ten over the course of the three-year journey. Sometimes this was for traditional reasons. After a great burst of creative activity during the weeks when *Endurance* was being designed and crafted, Rhys fell into a black depression and took his own life a month into the voyage. In other cases a spacewalker agreed to go on what was clearly a suicide mission, or a patient suffering from cancer decided to end her life rather than create a drain on limited resources of food, air, and medical supplies. And there was quite a bit of cancer, for Dinah's prediction on the day of the Break had been borne out. In spite of all precautions, particles of fallout made their way into the air and the food chain and lodged in lungs and guts. Even without this, the environment of space, with its ambient radiation, lack of exercise, poor diet, and exposure to various chemicals, tended to jack up the cancer rate. *Endurance*'s medical facilities were not up to the job of detecting and treating cancer in the way people had been used to on Earth.

Periodic crises in the supplies of food and air, caused by blights in the greenhouses or breakdowns in equipment, took away people whose strength had been sapped to begin with. The journey entailed thousands of traversals of the Van Allen radiation belts. Rather than passing through these but one or two times, as might have been the case in a more traditional space voyage, they had to do it twice on each orbit; and during the first year they were, for all practical purposes, never out of them. They sheltered as much as they could in shielded parts of the ship. But no shelter was perfect. Some of the crew were obliged by duty or by happenstance to remain in exposed locations. And the mere fact of being crammed together in a confined space for a significant fraction of the time was a drag on health.

The gender ratio began to skew even more toward females. The General Population, whose Break-surviving members had made up roughly a quarter of *Endurance*'s original complement, had been predominantly male. This was a simple consequence of the fact that they had been drawn from traditionally male-dominated professions such as the military, the astronaut corps, and science and engineering. The other three-quarters had been Arkies. The original Arkie population had been 75 percent female and 25 percent male. The ones who had elected to stay with *Endurance* at the time of the Break were more strongly skewed toward women.

The men tended to be older—in many cases two or even three times the age of the Arkies. Compared to the Arkies, who had mostly been sent up at the last minute, they tended to have been in space, and subject to its health effects, for much longer. They had been picked for brains, not for physical fitness. At least at the beginning, while the Arkies were still learning the ropes, they tended to draw the most hazardous duty, such as space walks. And men simply were not as well suited to life in space. They were more biologically vulnerable to radiation. They needed more air and more food. And, whether it was the result of cultural upbringing or genetic programming, they simply were not cut out psychologically for the idea that they were going to spend the rest of their lives in crowded indoor spaces. Many of them felt an urge to go outside and get away from people that manifested itself as a tendency to volunteer for more space walks. People who went on space walks were much more likely to die of radiation exposure, bolide strikes, equipment malfunction, misadventure, or contamination by reactor fallout.

As well, there was an understanding, widely shared but rarely spoken of, that men were not the scarce resource. Women—to be specific, healthy, functional wombs—were. Acting on that belief, or perhaps just electing a more socially constructive form of suicide, men continued volunteering for hazard duty, instinctively herding the women toward the protected interior spaces of the ship; and when the women objected to it, as some did, they were apt to be shut down by the simple, hard-to-argue-with assertion that their lives and health had to be preserved at all costs.

Communication with the Swarm was sporadic and tended to come in bursts, when the Swarm needed something. The groups had separated under conditions that would have been deemed a state of war had the Break not happened in the midst of a catastrophe more deadly than anything that one side could have inflicted upon the other with force of arms. Neither side was likely to begin trusting the other anytime soon. Free, Internet-style communication between them was forbidden on both sides, since it could have been used for purposes that were mischievous or worse. The channel between Swarm and *Endurance* was more akin to a hotline linking two Cold War capitals. It went unused for months at a time. This was not so much a matter of the two sides snubbing each other as it was that they were both fully occupied trying to stay alive. Ivy and J.B.F. were like the captains of two damaged ships, many miles apart in stormy seas, with other things on their minds. When the channel was used, it was to negotiate terms of exchanges between the two groups. Neither side was of a mind to share much information about its status. But much could be inferred from the things that the Swarm urgently asked for: mostly propellant, but also the sort of medicine used to treat radiation sickness, blight-resistant strains of food crops, nutrients, spare parts for CO_2 scrubbers and for the Stirling engines that supplied power to arklets. In exchange they offered mostly food, which was the only thing they could make that *Endurance* didn't already have.

Eleven weeks following the Break, a solar flare had occurred, followed by an event known as a coronal mass ejection: a vast release of charged particles hurled out from the sun into the solar system. With its array of sensors, some of which were always pointed toward the sun for just this reason, *Endurance* had seen the storm coming and had sent a warning message to the Swarm. In those days *Endurance* had been well inside the protection of the Earth's magnetosphere. That plus the shielding provided by iron and ice had enabled her crew to ride out the storm with little exposure to its radiation. They had no way of knowing, though, whether the Swarm had even received or understood the warning. The danger of coronal mass ejections had been well understood by the Arkitects, who had provided "storm shelters" in each arklet: sleeping bags, in effect, made so that water could be pumped into the space between their inner and outer walls, surrounding the occupant with molecules that were good at absorbing high-energy protons. The arklets were also stocked with doses of a drug called amifostine, which protected DNA from damage produced by the free radicals generated in the body by radiation exposure. The scheme was a good one provided the Arkies had at least half an hour's advance warning and enough water in their arklets' tanks to fill up all the shelters. They practiced it every so often, as sailors would perform lifeboat drills. But there was a lot that could go wrong, and it seemed unlikely that all eight hundred Arkies had made it through the storm unscathed.

In the ensuing three years there had been ten more coronal mass ejections big enough to worry about. *Endurance* had transmitted a warning to the Swarm in each of those cases but never received an acknowledgment.

It was worrisome that the Swarm always seemed to want more water. Since the water of an arklet's ecosystem was recycled, the only way the arklet could lose it was by expending it as propellant: splitting it into hydrogen and oxygen and feeding it to a thruster. All the arklets in a swarm would have to do this from time to time, simply in order to remain in formation. That was true even if they never dodged a rock and never changed their orbit around the Earth. But it seemed that they had changed their orbit on several occasions, making it higher and more circular to keep it clear of the Van Allen belts. Presumably they had their reasons for doing so. But if they ran so low on water that they couldn't fill their storm shelters when needed, they were open to a disaster that might kill most or all of them at a stroke. Ivy could only assume that they were still reasonable people and that if things got that bad, they would call for help. In the meantime, she tried to guard against the seductive idea that *Endurance* had all the water it could ever need. There weren't going to be any more *Ymir* expeditions. The water they carried with them might be all that the human race had to live on for hundreds of years.

She had already made up her mind what she would say if J.B.F. ever contacted her with an urgent demand for storm shelter water: nothing doing, come to us, rejoin the crew of *Endurance* and take shelter here. She wondered, sometimes, if J.B.F. had anticipated that

Ivy would make such a demand, and just how far she was willing to go to avoid such an unconditional surrender.

"WELL, THAT WAS HARD," DOOB CROAKED, THEN WETTED HIS WHIStle with a swig of the Ardbeg, mixed with a few drops of five-billion-year-old asteroid water.

He was in the Banana, speaking to an empty room, staring up at a projection screen on the wall. His reading glasses no longer worked; zero gravity had changed the shape of his eyeballs. The people who knew how to operate the lens-grinding machine were all dead or missing, so there was no way to make new eyeglasses until someone figured out where the machine had been squirreled away and read the instruction manual. Since only twenty-eight people remained alive on *Endurance,* this didn't look like it would happen anytime soon. His distance vision was still pretty good, but because of the problem with the glasses he didn't like to use his laptop for long periods of time. Instead he would come here to the Banana, soak up a little gravity, plug the computer into the projector cable, and work at long range.

He had been here for an hour, because he didn't want to miss the big moment. He knew exactly when that moment would occur, plus or minus a few seconds, but in the meantime he couldn't concentrate on anything else. The other twenty-seven were asleep or busy. So he was celebrating alone.

The display in front of him was dominated by a single large window displaying six numbers in fat, easy-to-read block letters. These were the orbital parameters of *Endurance.* They were updated several times a second, the numbers blurring and twitching. The one he was focusing on was labeled R, short for Radius. It was the distance separating *Endurance* from the center of Earth. At the moment, it was the highest it had ever been, at 384,512,933 meters and still climbing, slowly, in the last few digits. *Endurance* was creeping toward apogee, the highest apogee she had ever attained, and the height of that apogee was slightly beyond the distance at which the moon had once orbited Earth. For the first time they were as high in the sky, now, as Cleft.

Loose objects shifted position as *Endurance*'s remaining engines came on. They were down to thirty-seven functioning arklet engines from the original complement of eighty-one. On a good day they could muster thirty-nine. The other half of them had been cannibalized to keep the good ones working. To compensate for the losses, they had jury-rigged all the other engines they could get: the big one from the Caboose, all the propulsion units that had once been part of the Shipyard, and a few spare motors from straggler arklets that had become separated from the Swarm and found a way to rejoin them. Despite the reduction in engine power, *Endurance* was at least as maneuverable now as she had been at the beginning, when she had wallowed at the bottom of Earth's gravity well, burdened with years' worth of propellant. She weighed half as much now as she had in those days.

The burn went on for a while. It concluded with a change in attitude and a burn in another direction. Doob didn't have to read the numbers on the screen to know what they were doing. They'd been planning it for three years.

They were in a highly eccentric orbit now, a pair of hairpin turns welded together by straightaways a third of a million kilometers long. Earth nestled deep in the crook of one of those hairpins. *Endurance*'s perigee hadn't changed in three years; on every one of the thousands of orbits they had made, they had screamed across the top of Earth's atmosphere while running their engines full blast. On the last such pass, which they'd made about five days ago, they'd topped out at more than eleven thousand meters per second of velocity. The visual symmetry of the orbit was deceptive; at their current location, the opposite hairpin, now slightly beyond the old moon's orbit, they were crawling along at a speed that could have been matched, back in the day, by a wheeled vehicle on a salt flat. They were like a car on a roller coaster that had been towed all the way to the top and that was creeping along in that moment before it begins the plunge down to the bottom. The Earth was the size of a ping-pong ball at arm's length. Soon they'd begin falling toward it, building back up toward eleven thousand meters per second during their next perigee pass, five days from now.

In the meantime, though, during these few minutes when they were just inching along, they could work magic. Small changes in velocity out here led to enormous transformations in their orbit down there. *Endurance,* by dint of enduring for three years and persevering in her plan, had reached Cleft's distance from Earth. But she'd always been in the wrong plane: the same plane that Izzy had started out in, the plane that had been chosen, seemingly a million years ago, because it was easily reached from the Baikonur Cosmodrome. Down there, deep in the gravity well, changing that plane would have been catastrophically expensive. If they'd had an Earth to go back to, it would have been cheaper to start from scratch and build a new space station than to move Izzy to the plane where the moon had once orbited. Up here, though, by burning the engines at apogee, they could nudge it closer and closer to the desired plane at much lower cost. So they'd been doing little plane change maneuvers at each apogee. It had been going on for months now. It was a thing that had to happen if they were ever to reach Cleft, but it made Doob's stomach burn, made him wish he hadn't had a couple of slugs of hoarded single-malt.

For the plane of the old moon—the place they had to go to find safe refuge in Cleft—was where all the rocks were. That was where the rocks had started out, at Zero, and for the most part that was where they had stayed. The ones that had fallen to Earth in the Hard Rain were only a tiny fraction of the lunar debris cloud: just a faint dusting compared to what remained up here. During most of *Endurance*'s journey, her pilots had, by choice, kept her in that angled Baikonur-compatible plane, well clear of the moon's debris field. Otherwise they could never have survived for this long.

But the risk that they had to accept, in order to try for Cleft, was to fly through the debris cloud in which Cleft swam. Every time they had reached an apogee in the last few months, and burned their engines to bring their orbit closer to the plane of their destination, they had edged into dirtier and more dangerous space.

Their slowness was part of the problem. If the debris cloud was a fleet of cars roaring around a circular raceway at top speed, then *Endurance* was a child toddling out into traffic. That extreme disparity in speed would remain until the next apogee, ten days from now, when they would make their biggest and longest burn, expending all of *Endurance*'s remaining propellant to accelerate her to the same average speed as the debris cloud. In so doing, they'd convert the dual-hairpin orbit into a nearly perfect circle, remaining 384,512,933 meters from Earth forever. Having merged smoothly with the traffic on the circular raceway, they would go hunting for Cleft. Doob had spied it several times on his optical telescopes, gotten a fix on its params, knew how to find it.

This was his life's work.

If he'd been asked several years ago, before Zero, he'd have said it was something else. But his life until Day 360 had been nothing more than preparation for the mission plan he had laid in and was now executing for *Endurance*. The day of the Break—the arrival of the propellant needed, the death of his friend and colleague Konrad, and the sundering of the Swarm—had made it clear what needed to be done, and who needed to do it. So he'd been doing it.

Ten days remained until they were swimming in the debris cloud. Perhaps a fortnight before they reached Cleft. He wondered if he would live to see it. Quite obviously, he had cancer. Diagnostic facilities were lacking, but the first undeniable symptoms had been in his digestive tract, and since then his liver had become swollen by metastases. Now he was feeling some weird stuff in his lungs. It had grown slowly. It might have been natural causes—something that had been seeded on Old Earth, before he had even come to space—or it might have been a piece of fallout that had made its way into his food and gotten caught in his gut. No matter. The main question on his mind was whether he would live to see Cleft. He actually didn't feel that bad, and so the naive answer would be yes, of course; but cancer growth was something of an exponential phenomenon, and he knew how tricky those could be.

Bolor-Erdene was flying the ship, working in the Hammerhead—the deeply sheltered control room that they had built into the lee side of Amalthea. Or at least she was on the duty roster as the nominal pilot. Distinctions of rank and specialty had ceased to matter much. Everyone who had survived—nine men and nineteen women—knew how to do everything: fly the ship, fix an arklet engine, go on a space walk, program a robot. The Doob of a few years ago would have ridden it out in the Hammerhead with her, looking over her shoulder, checking the params, swapping witty remarks in the occasional moment of downtime. The Doob sitting in the Banana right now had seen it all before, thousands of times, and knew that it was as routine to Bo, or to any of the survivors, as driving to work would have been before Zero. Being there would only have gotten his stomach riled up. He needed to conserve his energy.

He realized that he had dozed off. Opening his eyes and focusing, with some effort, on the screen, he saw that nearly an hour had passed since apogee. They were falling toward Earth for the last time.

His phone rang. Held at arm's length it was blurry, but some vestigial part of his brain could still recognize the smear of pixels as a snapshot of Bo, taken years ago. He swiped it on and answered it.

"We are being contacted by the Swarm," Bo said.

"Are we really?" he answered. Suddenly he was awake. "What does J.B.F. want?"

"It's not J.B.F. It's someone named . . ." Bo paused. "A-ida. Or something. Two dots on the i."

Doob tried to place the name. Aïda. He had a vague memory

of her from his early days on the Cloud Ark. An Italian girl. Young. Arkie, not GPop. Socially a little weird. Hyperacute in a way that could be exhausting.

"It's pronounced 'I-yeeda,'" he told Bo.

"Anyway, they send congratulations on the successful completion of our maneuver, and request a parley. Should I wake up Ivy?"

"I'll be there in a minute," Doob said. "Let her sleep."

He hated to think this way, but the Swarmers well knew what time it was, and which shift Ivy slept on, and that she was sleeping now. Rousting her out of bed would send the wrong message, making the crew of *Endurance* seem overeager.

Which might have been an excess of caution—a J.B.F.-style exercise of byzantine thinking—he reflected, as he pushed himself up the middle of the Stack. This had become a dingy place, sort of yellowed and shiny with human exhalations, condensed on its ice-cold walls and never really scrubbed off. He was glad he couldn't see it very well.

They knew so little about the Swarm. From the straggler arklets they'd picked up over the last three years, they knew that J.B.F. had moved swiftly to consolidate her power, exploiting the crisis of the first coronal mass ejection—which had killed something like 10 percent of the population—to set up her own version of martial law. From there the trains had run more or less on time, albeit with a steadily dwindling population, until about a year ago, when some Arkies had begun to rebel and the Swarm had divided into two Swarms, coexisting with each other—as they had little choice—but not talking.

The people of *Endurance* had paid surprisingly little attention to matters Swarm related, because, in the end, it didn't really matter that much. The die had been cast on the day of the Break. Not so much on the level of politics as on physics. Those who had stayed behind on Izzy had committed themselves to following Doob's plan, his life's work: the Big Ride. You were either aboard *Endurance,* simultaneously trapped and protected by her mass, or you weren't. If you were, there was no getting off. If you weren't, you had to find a way to survive as part of the Swarm, which meant moving to a completely different orbit and following a plan that was incompatible, on an orbital mechanics level, with the Big Ride. Once those orbits had diverged, the only way to reconnect was by effecting a big delta vee. That meant spending a lot of water that you were never going to get back. Less water meant less shielding from coronal mass ejections, limited food production, and hobbled maneuvering when bad rocks came at you. Getting a whole Swarm to agree on that course of action was impossible, and might actually have been a bad idea, since *Endurance* couldn't accommodate a lot of refugees. Her mission plan was predicated on her ability to absorb significant bolide strikes without taking serious damage. A bunch of naked arklets following in her wake would soon get beaten to death. So on a physics level alone, the Break had been irrevocable, even had the two groups badly wanted to get together.

But apparently what was left of the Swarm had been watching *Endurance*. Biding their time, waiting to see whether she would win through.

This Aïda person must understand Doob's plan. She knew what was at stake now. If the remnants of the Swarm could rejoin *Endurance* in the next ten days, before she disappeared into the maelstrom of the debris cloud, they had a hope of reaching the comparative safety of Cleft. Otherwise they were condemned to circle Earth in some relatively clean and safe orbit as their population and their water supply dwindled.

Doob swam into the Hammerhead. Three other people were in here: Bo, Steve Lake, and Michael Park, a former Arkie, a gay Korean-Canadian from Vancouver who had found six different ways to make himself indispensable.

"Aïda Ferrari, according to our records," Bo said, before he asked. "A leader of the anti-J.B.F. faction. Sounds like J.B.F. lost."

Steve seemed busy. It was good to see him active. He had come down with some kind of long-running bowel complaint, an imbalance in the bacteria that lived in his gut. He had kept the dreadlocks, but they were now bigger than he was. He must weigh less than a hundred pounds. But his fingers still flew over the keys of his laptop.

Bo had already turned her attention back to the business of running the ship, but Michael explained, "Steve's getting a video feed going. No one's done it in years."

He meant that no one had recently been doing it over the old-school S-band radios used for long-range communication between space vehicles. Of course, on the short-range mesh network that the Arkitects had set up to knit the Cloud Ark together, people did it all the time using Scape. But depending on where they were in their orbit, the remnants of the Swarm might be hundreds of thousands of kilometers away from *Endurance,* far out of mesh range, and so they had to use the same sort of pre-Internet technology that the Apollo astronauts had used to send television signals back from the moon.

Eventually Steve did get it going, and then they were treated to a full-face image, in blocky pixels, of a dark-eyed woman with a fine-featured head that had been buzz-cut a few weeks ago and little tended since.

Once Steve did him the favor of throwing it up on a big screen where he could actually see it, Doob saw the obvious signs of malnutrition that had been affecting everyone on *Endurance.* He was mildly surprised by that. They had tantalized themselves by imagining the Swarm as a cornucopia of agriculture. But maybe it was low on water. The woman's gaze was downcast, which, as everyone understood, meant that she was focusing on the screen of a tablet below the camera. Once she understood that the link was up and running, she raised her chin and seemed to stare directly into the Hammerhead with a pair of huge dark eyes. The low quality of the video made these seem pitch black, with no distinction between iris and pupil, and starvation had given them a sort of hot gleam.

"Aïda," the woman said, by way of self-introduction. "I see you,

Dr. Harris." She began to smile, offering a glimpse of bad teeth, then thought better of it. Her eyes changed direction momentarily to someone or something off-camera, then came back to them. She raised her tablet up closer to the camera so that she could look at the feed from *Endurance*. Her hand passed briefly in front of the lens and they caught a glimpse of dirty, ragged fingernails, the frayed and shiny cuff of a sleeve. Faint murmurs in the background suggested that other people were in the same arklet with her, off-camera. She was in zero gee, therefore, not part of a bolo. Her eyes were exploring the feed on her tablet, trying to make sense of what she was seeing. The Hammerhead had not existed at the time of the Break, so it was a new thing to her. "Steve Lake," she muttered, as she recognized him.

"Bo," Bo said.

"Michael," Michael said.

"Who is in charge?" Aïda asked. "Is Ivy . . ."

"Ivy's still alive and she is still the commander as per CAC," Doob said. "She's off shift. We can wake her up if you need to speak to her urgently."

"No. Not necessary," Aïda said, recoiling slightly and narrowing the eyes just a bit. The distance between her and *Endurance* introduced a time lag in the video, which made conversation halting and awkward.

"How many do you have?" Doob asked.

"Eleven."

Doob, accustomed to working professionally with extremely large numbers, couldn't quite process one so small. Eleven. One plus ten.

A thought came to him. "Do you mean eleven *arklets*?" That would imply scores, maybe a hundred people.

Aïda looked amused. "Oh no, of arklets we have many more. We have twenty-six."

"Ah. So what is it you have eleven of?"

"People," Aïda said.

"Aïda," Bo said, "just to be clear. So there is no misunderstanding. You are speaking for the entire Swarm. And you are saying that, of the entire Swarm, there are eleven survivors."

"Yes. Plus one . . ."

"One what?"

A look of amusement came over Aïda's face. She broke eye contact. It almost seemed that she rolled her eyes a little. Doob was reminded, hardly for the first time, that the Arkies had been sent up as teenagers. "It is complicated. Let's just say there is one more who might as well be dead."

Those in the Hammerhead still could not quite process it. Something occurred to Michael: "We know that the Swarm broke up into two factions. One led by J.B.F. You were part of the opposing group?"

"Yes." Aïda laughed. Again she reminded Doob of a teenager going through the pretense of talking to a clueless parent about something they would never understand.

Michael, a little wrong-footed, went on haltingly: "And so when you say that there are eleven . . . plus one who is, I take it, in a bad way . . . anyhow, are you referring just to the anti-J.B.F. faction?"

"They were defeated a long time ago. Months."

"When you say that, do you mean that there was some kind of a conflict? A war?" Doob asked.

Aïda shrugged. "There was some fighting." She didn't see it as important. "Call it a war if you wish. More like some brawls. The real battle was, you know, on the Internet. Social media."

Silence ensued. Aïda waited for them to respond. When no one did, she shrugged. "What were we going to do? Smash our arklets into each other? There is no way to have, like, actual violence in this setting! So we just had a war of words." She held her hands up in front of her, making them into little pantomime mouths, aimed at each other, thumb-jaws flapping up and down. "Trying to, you know, persuade others to join our side. Trying to make the other side look bad. Just like the Internet always was." She.chuckled, put one hand to her cheek, rubbed her eye. "Look, it is very complicated and I cannot explain everything right now—how it all came out."

"But you said that J.B.F.'s faction was defeated," Michael said. Of all the people in the Hammerhead, he seemed most committed to the proposition that there was a reasonable and logical explanation for all of this.

"Her and Tav, yes."

"By which you mean, you defeated them with words. Ideas. A social media campaign."

"We were more persuasive," Aïda said. "I was more persuasive. Arklet by arklet, they came over to my side. The White Arklet held out for a while, then they gave up."

"What became of them?"

"J.B.F. is fine. Tav, not so good."

"He's the one you mentioned. The twelfth one who might as well be dead."

"I am afraid so, yes."

"So getting back to the earlier question," Doob said, "the number you quoted is for the entire Swarm. Both factions."

Aïda, finally seeming to understand what they were getting at, sat up straighter and got a more serious look on her face. "Yes. There are no other survivors whatsoever. Of the eight hundred, eleven remain."

There was a long silence as the four in the Hammerhead took this in. They had all harbored fears that the Swarm might go terribly wrong, but this was worse than anything they had imagined.

Finally Doob raised his hands in front of him, palms up, and shrugged. "What happened?"

"Agriculture crashed." Aïda turned her head and stared off-camera for a few moments. "I mean, I could say many things, but that is basically it. Between the CMEs, algae blights, lack of water . . . very few arklets produce food anymore."

"What have you been eating?"

Aïda snapped her head around, as if surprised by the question, and looked quizzically into the camera. "Each other. Dead people, I mean."

There was a long silence during which Doob, Bo, Michael, and Steve all exchanged looks.

The terrible thing was that they had considered doing the same thing, many times. Every freeze-dried corpse that they jettisoned was a big collection of protein and nutrients that, from a certain point of view, could seem mouthwatering.

Seeming to read their minds, Aïda went on: "And you?"

"You mean, have we resorted to eating dead people? No," Doob said.

"Tav started it," Aïda said. "He ate his own leg. Soft cannibalism, he called it. Legs are of no use in space. He blogged it. Then it went viral."

No one had anything to say to that. After a few moments had gone by, Aïda continued. "But *Endurance* is better stocked with MREs and so on. Plenty of water. You would not have gone there."

"No, we did not go there," Doob said. He could tell from the body language of the others in the Hammerhead that they were too shocked to be entrusted with speaking at the moment.

"As for us," Aïda said, "you should also know that supplies were conserved. Even as people died and we lost arklets. We moved what we had into the arklets that survived. Our twenty-six arklets are well stocked."

"With everything except food," Doob said.

"Yes."

"Do you have enough water to match our trajectory?"

"Yes," Aïda said. She was a beautiful young woman, Doob thought, with a fierceness about her that helped explain her success in the social media campaign against Tav and J.B.F. "We have performed all of the calculations. If we jettison mass and pack all we have into a heptad, we can make the rendezvous around the time of your next apogee. But we will need to know your exact params."

"We will discuss your proposal," Doob said, "and make any necessary preparations." He looked over at Steve Lake, who severed the connection just as Aïda was about to say something.

THEY SAT IN THE BANANA AND DISCUSSED IT AS IF THERE WAS ANYthing really to discuss. They all registered their rote shock and disgust at what the Swarm had been reduced to. It all sounded hollow to Luisa. Finally she spoke up. It was what Luisa did. They expected it of her. They relied on it.

"Seven billion died. Next to that, this is small. And God knows we've all thought about eating the dead, so let's not pretend to be shocked that they actually did it. The real reason we're all freaked out by this is that our hopes have been dashed. We thought that the Swarm was going to contain hundreds of healthy people, lots of food, lots of good company. Oh, intellectually we knew it wouldn't be the case, but we were all hoping for it. Now we learn it's eleven carrion eaters. Are we going to leave them to die? No. We're going to make room for them and for their heptad full of scarce vitamins."

"I am terrified of the woman Aïda," Michael Park said.

Luisa sighed. "Let me throw out an idea, which is that you're terrified because you wonder, at some level, whether you could turn into Aïda if you got hungry enough."

"Still—to let her on board *Endurance*—"

"And J.B.F. too," Tekla said. She and Moira were sitting next to each other as they always did, hands clasped, fingers intertwined.

"I hoped I would never see Julia again," Camila put in. "I know it is small and selfish of me, but . . ."

"I understand all of your misgivings," Ivy said, "because I share them. The question, now, is whether those misgivings are going to have any effect on the decision we make. Are we really going to let one-third of the surviving human race die because Aïda's creepy and we hate J.B.F.? Obviously not. So, we transmit our params and our burn plan. And during the remainder of this orbit we make arrangements to accommodate some new arklets."

THE REMAINDER OF THE ORBIT WAS BUSY INDEED, TO THE POINT where they broke out hoarded rations and upped their calorie intake to fuel their brains and their bodies. In the middle of that ten-day stretch, however, was an intermission. Dinah and Ivy had wordlessly agreed to spend it together in what Doob had once called the Woo-Woo Pod, and what they now called the Kupol.

After the Break, when Rhys had reengineered Izzy and *Ymir* into a single moving sculpture of metal and water, he had moved this module to a different location in the Stack and then let the living ice flow around it, completely surrounding its inboard hemisphere and later building up in a protective brow that shielded part of its windowed half. It projected from the side of *Endurance* like an eyeball and gave people a place to go when they wanted to look at the universe. As such it had no legitimate function from an engineering point of view. In fact it was a liability, since it got hit by little rocks from time to time, depressurized, and had to be repaired. Anyone in it was getting directly exposed to cosmic radiation, and so it was a no-go zone when they were passing through the Van Allen belts, which was often. But people loved it anyway, and kept patching it up when it was broken, and went there when they wanted to be alone or when they wanted to share some special time with another person. Putting it there had been one of Rhys's best moves as a designer, and Dinah silently thanked him whenever she used it. Doob's old term for it had begun to seem a little tasteless after the Hard Rain. For a little while, people had instead referred to it as the Dome. But *dom* had a different meaning in Russian, and so they'd settled on Cupola or Kupol, whose meanings in English and Russian respectively were not too far apart. In the latter language it carried a vaguely religious connotation, having to do with cathedral domes.

Ivy and Dinah didn't have to worry too much about cosmic rays during the intermission, because they had so arranged it that the Kupol was on *Endurance*'s nadir side, facing toward Earth. And Earth was close enough to fill their view. Useless as the planet might be for the support of life, it still acted as a very effective cosmic ray absorber. Nothing was getting through that, short of another mysterious Agent that could pass all the way through a planet and keep on going. So, Dinah and Ivy hovered in the middle of the sphere, arms linked so that they wouldn't drift apart, and sucked bourbon from plastic bags, and looked at their old planet for the last time. In their six years of hurtling around this world, they'd grown accustomed to the steep angle that Izzy's orbital plane made with the equator, and the views it afforded them of the high latitudes. Because of the changes they had lately been making to *Endurance*'s plane, however, they were now confined to a belt around the tropics.

Not that it mattered a hell of a lot with Earth in its current state. The sky was still on fire, streaked with the bluish-white incandescence of the Hard Rain. The ground, where they could see it through smoke and steam, was a mottled terrain of dully glowing lava: some of it the hot impact craters of recent big meteorites, some of it spewing up out of the Earth's fractured crust. Oceans were dark at night, hazed with steam in daylight, their coasts difficult to make out, but clearly shallower than they had been. Florida was reaching out toward the Keys but being battered down and chipped away by bolides, and washed away by tsunamis, even as it did so. A year and a half ago, a big rock had torn the lid off the long-dormant Yellowstone supervolcano. That had been cloaking most of North America with ash ever since then; glimmers of yellow light in the northern extreme of their view hinted at a vast outpouring of magma. A long-suppressed habit told Dinah, absurdly, that she should go and turn on her radio in case Rufus was transmitting. This made the tears come, and that in turn made Ivy's tears come, and so they spent the last half of the intermission, from perigee onward, gazing at Earth through water. It didn't really affect the view much. But Dinah tried to register the memories as best she could. Humans would not again look on Earth from such a close vantage point for thousands of years.

The burning planet started to drop away from them. It would only ever get smaller from now. They needed to get back to work. But they found it difficult to let go of each other. Back in the old days, before Zero, they'd had the occasional heart-to-heart about their shared, secret fear that they weren't qualified to carry out the missions for which they'd been sent up, at vast taxpayer expense. That they'd screw it up, fall on their faces, and embarrass a lot of people on the ground. By now, of course, they had long since put those fears to rest, or at least seen them overwhelmed and buried by much greater fears. Ever since the beginning of the Cloud Ark project, however, and especially since they had made the irrevocable decision to build *Endurance* and go on the Big Ride, it had frequently come back to them in a bigger and more dreaded form. What if they were completely getting it wrong? They could scarcely remember, now, the great civilization that had once spread across the planet below them. But the contrast between it and its orbiting residue was painful. The dirty, beat-up kludge that was *Endurance* was an embarrassment to the human race. Could they really have done no better than this? And now, after a voyage of three years—three years that had been an unrelieved spiral of decline, punctuated by catastrophes—they were reduced to a maneuver, coming up in five days' time, that seemed more and more desperate the more they thought about it.

If they screwed it up, it would be their fault, more than anyone else's.

Of course, no one would be left to blame them for it.

They went through these crises of confidence frequently, but usually at different times, so that one could pull the other out of despair.

Right now they were both feeling it together, and so they had to pull themselves out.

Dinah was thinking about Rufus's last transmission:

BYE HONEY DO US PROUD

"Okay," she said. "Come on, sweetie. Let's get to work."

WORK GAVE THEM SOMETHING TO DO DURING THE FINAL ORBIT OF the Big Ride besides worry about what was going to happen at the end of it. The huge burn that they would make at apogee, combining a final plane change with an acceleration into the "fast lane" where Cleft rolled around the world like a ball bearing in a tire, contained so many unfathomable chances that it beggared prediction. The new wrinkle, however, was this: since they would be moving into a stream of rocks moving faster than they were, the rocks would be coming at them *from behind,* where Amalthea had no power to protect them.

Early in the mission Doob had dreamed of reconfiguring *Endurance* at the last minute, moving the vulnerable stuff around to the asteroid's other side. With the manpower they'd had in those days, it might have been possible. As it was, reduced to a crew of twenty-eight starvelings, it was out of the question. It took all the people they had to make accommodations for the Swarm's heptad. They would dock it in the middle of the Stack, lock it in place with a few cables, and hope it stayed attached during the subsequent maneuvers. They would keep the hatch closed. The eleven members of Aïda's group would simply stay in their arklets until it was all over. The justification was that they'd be safer there. The true reason was that no one wanted cannibals in the shared spaces of *Endurance.*

The big project for Dinah, and for the small remnant crew of robot jockeys who tended to work with her, was getting ready to dump Amalthea itself.

On one level the idea seemed nearly unthinkable. They had, however, been planning to do it for a long time. *Endurance*'s final series of maneuvers would have to be accomplished quickly, deftly, in an environment where the rocks tended to be much larger than the ones that made up the Hard Rain. In a sense, the boulders up there were the mothers of the tiny fragments that had destroyed the surface of Earth. Every time two of them collided, a few chips exploded outward from the impact, and a fraction of those ended up falling into Earth's atmosphere. The Hard Rain would continue until all of them had been reduced to sand and organized themselves into a neat system of rings. In any case, Amalthea's ability to protect *Endurance* from the impacts of baseball- or even basketball-sized rocks was of little interest in a place where a rock the size of Ireland would be considered unremarkable. The entire ship, Amalthea and all, would be a bug on the windshield of such a thing. Their only way to stay alive, once they had entered the slipstream of the main debris cloud, was to maneuver around the big rocks and hope that they didn't get hit by too many little ones during their dash to Cleft. And that sort of maneuvering was impossible as long as Amalthea—which weighed a hundred times as much as the rest of *Endurance*—was attached to her.

In addition to Amalthea, *Endurance* was still burdened by a considerable mass of ice, which they had hoarded both as shielding and as propellant. It weighed a significant fraction of what Amalthea weighed. But unlike Amalthea, they could burn it. The basic plan was to split most of that ice into hydrogen and oxygen, then burn it during the final speed-up at apogee. Over the course of a few hectic minutes, *Endurance* would expend most of her water weight by using it as propellant. Between that and the ditching of Amalthea, her total weight would drop by a factor of more than a hundred in the course of an hour. After that, she truly would be like a bug flitting around in heavy traffic, dodging big rocks and taking hits from little ones until she made her way to Cleft.

In any case, they had anticipated all of this long ago. Dinah and the other surviving members of the Mining Colony had had three years in which to reshape Amalthea from the inside. Seen from the forward end, the asteroid looked the same as ever. Internally, however, most of it had systematically been whittled loose. In a sense the process had begun around Day 14, when Dinah had set one of her Grabbs to work carving out a niche in which she could stash her electronic parts. Since then it had proceeded in fits and starts. They'd moved a lot of metal in order to make a storage bay for Moira Crewe's genetic equipment, which in a sense was the raison d'être of everything else they had done in the last three years. Once that was safe they had begun tidying up, enlarging the pockets of protected space, breaking down walls, and joining them together into a cylindrical capsule scooped out of Amalthea's back, called the Hammerhead for the way it lay athwart the top of the Stack.

Thanks to a lot of ticklish work by robots in the last couple of years, the Hammerhead was now separated from the rest of Amalthea—99 percent of the asteroid's bulk and mass—by walls of nickel-iron that were only about as thick as the palm of a person's hand. This still made them extremely massive by the standards of space architecture—more than strong enough to hold in atmospheric pressure and to stop small bolides. But the additional tens of meters' thickness of metal beyond those walls was now physically detached from the hand-thick walls, and could be pushed away by a puff of compressed air.

Or rather, given the disparity in masses, *Endurance* could be pushed away from *it.* Most of Amalthea would stay where it was, and the radically lightened *Endurance* would back away from it like a grasshopper springing off a bowling ball.

When the time came, they would have to shatter the remaining structural links with demolition charges. One of Dinah's duties on the last lap, as they soared back up out of Earth's gravity well toward their rendezvous with Cleft, was to go out in a space suit and inspect those charges, make sure they were packed in where they needed to be and wired up correctly. She was the only person remaining who knew much about explosives, and so she was the only person who could be sure. Just another of those duties that would have left her half paralyzed six years ago and now seemed routine.

"I KNOW THAT WE DON'T NEED ANY MORE BAD NEWS," DOOB ANnounced to the 25 percent of the human race seated around the conference table in the Banana, "but here's some for y'all."

No one said anything. Nothing could make much of an impression on them at this point.

Forty-eight hours remained before apogee, the final burn, the ditching of Amalthea, the dash to Cleft. If Aïda's transmission of half an hour ago was to be believed, the remnants of the Swarm would rendezvous with them shortly before all of those things happened.

"Let's have it," Ivy said.

"I've been keeping an eye on a certain sunspot," Doob said. "Kind of angry looking. Well, about twenty minutes ago it kicked out a huge flare. Not the biggest we've ever seen, but pretty big."

"So, we're expecting a CME?" Ivy asked.

"Yeah. Somewhere between one and three days from now. I'll provide better estimates as soon as I have more data."

They all considered it. Until recently, coronal mass ejections had been of little concern to them except insofar as they made them wonder how the people of the Swarm were getting along. As for the tiny faction that had split away on *Red Hope,* it was assumed that they had long since been wiped out by one or more of the hazards and calamities that had inflicted such a death toll on the Swarm. For the crew of *Endurance,* Amalthea and ice had provided plenty of shielding. Even the comparatively thin walls of the Hammerhead would protect anyone inside of it against the kind of radiation that would envelop them in a CME. But *Endurance*'s flanks were now exposed. Grabbs had been at work carrying away the last of the ice and feeding it to the splitters to be made into rocket fuel. They were storing the cryogenic gases anywhere they could now, pumping them into empty arklet hulls and disused modules. Parts of the Stack were seeing the light of day for the first time since the Break.

"It'll affect our operations," Ivy concluded. "But this is a drill we know pretty well. Take amifostine. Get your space walks finished before it hits. We should make arrangements to accommodate all nonessential personnel in the Hammerhead. Some of us will have to be down farther in the Stack, but we'll have storm shelters ready."

"What about . . . *them*?" Michael Park asked.

"*They* are a problem," Ivy admitted. "They're in plastic arklets. They're gonna get cooked. Even if they have any amifostine left, even if they have enough water to fill their storm shelters, they're going to take damage. Ethically, we need to bring those eleven aboard *Endurance* and get them to safer places."

"The original plan was to send three people out on an EVA to lock down their heptad, make it fast to the stack, so that we could maneuver," said Zeke Petersen. Of all the crew of *Endurance* he looked the most similar to his pre-Break appearance. He was skinnier, of course, with a bit of gray around his temples, but his health was still good, and he'd managed to keep his electric shaver working, so he was beardless. After the deaths of Fyodor, from an accident, and Ulrika, from a stroke, Ivy had designated him *Endurance*'s second in command.

He referred to the fact that *Endurance* was about to shed 99 percent of her mass, which meant that the same complement of engines, producing the same thrust, could make her accelerate a hundred times faster. The gee forces still would not be extreme—well within the range that humans could tolerate—but the maneuver would impose stresses on the ship's frame the likes of which it had never experienced before. This was another of those eventualities that they had foreseen long ago and built into *Endurance* before covering her with ice.

So most of *Endurance* came prerigged for higher acceleration.

Provided that nothing had broken during the last three years, she'd hold together, albeit with a lot of loose junk sliding around her interior spaces the first time they hit the throttle.

They hadn't planned, though, for the last-minute addition of the heptad from the Swarm. This was awkward. It would be connected to the Stack by a docking port, which wasn't designed to take a lot of mechanical strain. It was heavy, because Aïda and her crew had crammed it full of supplies and strapped even more to the outside of it. For the same reason, Ivy didn't want to just ditch it—they could use those supplies. So the plan had been for three spacewalkers to greet the heptad and lash it into place with cables as soon as it arrived.

"We'll just have to see what we can do with robots," Ivy said, looking toward Dinah and Bo. "Just about everything we have out there is Grimmed, correct? So it can operate even in heavy radiation."

"We'll get ready for that," Dinah agreed.

"As soon as the heptad docks, the robots get to work," Ivy said, "locking it down as best we can. We open the hatch and get the eleven down through the hamster tubes as fast as possible—they'll have no protection whatsoever while they're moving through those tubes. We'll have storm shelters waiting for them. They can climb into those and ride out the rest of the journey. The flight crew will operate out of the Hammerhead."

THE NEXT TWO DAYS REMINDED DINAH OF THE *NEW CAIRD* EXPEDItion, in that there was a lot to do but no way to affect the schedule. They were at the mercy of astronomical events. Part of her wanted to pull all-nighters until this thing was finished, but she knew she had to be well rested and fed when it counted, and so she forced herself to eat and sleep on the usual schedule. When awake, she worked on preparations for the arrival of the heptad, pre-positioning Grabbs near the docking port that it would use, connecting cables to suitable anchor points, tuning up the programs that the robots would execute when it came time to snap the other ends of those cables onto the heptad, rehearsing them to check for places where the cables might snag.

The timeline gradually came into clearer focus. Aïda sent out a sharp request for amifostine and water to fill their storm shelters. Of course, it was impossible for *Endurance* to comply. They had plenty of both, but they had long since cannibalized all of their MIV parts and so they had no way to transport them.

Aïda decided to roll the dice by committing all the water she had left to a large burn that would bring them to the rendezvous with *Endurance* a little earlier than they'd originally planned. Meanwhile Doob's space weather forecast was becoming more precise; he had a better idea now of when the radiation storm would break over them and thought that the timing was looking favorable. The heptad might arrive before things got bad. It might be okay after all to have some spacewalkers out there to cooperate with Dinah's robots.

Dinah didn't know how to feel about that. The schedule had been accelerated, and now she had to take into account the vagaries of human spacewalkers. If Aïda's heptad docked soon enough, Doob pointed out, they might be able to transfer many of her heavy supplies through the docking port into the Stack and thereby reduce the awkward strains that all of Dinah's cables were meant to take up.

Meanwhile Ivy and Zeke, the pilots, were addressing similar last-minute convolutions in their mission plan. As they got nearer, they got better information about the part of the debris cloud that they'd be maneuvering through. They could clearly make out Cleft's radar signature, as well as those of many other big rocks that traveled in its vicinity. A clutter of faint noise and clouds on the optical telescope gave them data about the density of objects too small and numerous to resolve. All of it fed into the plan.

Doob looked tired, and nodded off frequently, and hadn't eaten a square meal since the last perigee, but he pulled himself together when he was needed and fed any new information into a statistical model, prepared long in advance, that would enable them to maximize their chances by ditching Amalthea and doing the big final burn at just the right times. But as he kept warning Ivy and Zeke, the time was coming soon when they would become so embroiled in the particulars of which rock was coming from which direction that it wouldn't be a statistical exercise anymore. It would be a video game, and its objective would be to build up speed while merging into a stream of large and small rocks that would be overtaking them with the speed of artillery shells.

The details, the sudden distractions and improvisations, piled up and thickened in a way that made Dinah think of a sonic boom on Old Earth: the onrushing stream of air thickening and solidifying in the path of the airplane, turning into a barrier that must be broken through or succumbed to. They seemed to break through it at the point when Michael and two other spacewalkers pulled on their cooling garments, much patched and mended, and donned their space suits. Doob had the incoming heptad on radar, then on optical, and verified that it was on course to rendezvous with them. This meant, of course, that the heptad was on a collision course with *Endurance;* the difference between a collision and a rendezvous was the final burn of the heptad's thrusters that would slow it down at the last minute and bring its params into nearly perfect synchronization with the larger ship's. *Endurance* herself, still burdened with Amalthea and with many tons of stored propellant, had next to no maneuverability, and so it would all be up to Aïda, or whoever was at the controls of her heptad.

The reunion of *Endurance* and the Swarm began, as it turned out, with a collision. It was not a catastrophic high-speed collision, but it certainly was no orderly and controlled rendezvous. Aïda had the presence of mind to give them about thirty seconds' warning. Until then it had all been going well. The heptad had approached, using its thrusters to kill most of its velocity relative to the larger ship, and executed some little burns intended to bring it home to the docking port. Then Aïda announced, in a barely controlled tone of voice, that one of the thruster modules had run out of propellant and could no longer perform its function.

"It's too heavy," Zeke muttered. "They loaded in too much cargo; the thrusters are eating too much fuel trying to push all of that crap around."

The heptad came in too fast and at the wrong angle and crashed into Caboose 2, which was a module, recycled from the wreckage of the Shipyard three years ago, that they had plugged into the back of H1 to serve as the aft-most thing in the Stack. They saw it happen on their screens, they felt it in their bones, and they heard the three spacewalkers exclaiming and cursing. A little storm of debris emerged from a hole that had evidently been torn in the skin of Caboose 2.

"C2 depressurized," Tekla reported. "Sealed off from Stack."

The debris cloud included one large object that had two arms, two legs, and a head. The limbs were flailing. Everyone watched silently.

"We lost Michael Park," one of the other spacewalkers announced.

"We need more people back there," Ivy announced to the crew in the Hammerhead.

Ivy's message was clear. *Later we will mourn for Michael. Now we have other things to worry about.*

"Moira, you stay," Ivy added.

Moira hadn't even moved. She was accustomed to being treated, against her own will and instincts, like a cherished and fragile child.

"Maybe you could talk to Michael on the radio. He'll be alive for a while."

Moira nodded, swallowed hard, and focused on her laptop, entering the commands needed to establish a private voice link to Michael.

"Dinah, you stay here—run the robots. We are going to have to do some improvising. Bo, go back. Steve too. Luisa, deal with Aïda over voice—for me it's too much stress and distraction. Stay in the

Hammerhead and make that problem go away for me. Doob, stay here. Zeke, go back."

Ivy looked around. "If I haven't mentioned your name yet, go back and see what you can do. Doob, you're the weatherman. Your job is to make announcements about the storm and when it's going to hit."

"Half an hour," Doob said. "But yes. I will do that."

Moira, headphones on, had retreated into the quietest corner of the Hammerhead and was engaging in a murmured conversation with Michael. She was holding a cloth over her eyes to absorb tears before they broke loose in the cabin. Luisa had already gone into her assigned role and had been listening to a voice transmission from Aïda. "She says she is going to try again."

"I thought her thrusters were empty," Ivy said.

"She can transfer propellant from some of the other thruster modules to the empty one. It'll take a few minutes. She requests instructions on where to make the next attempt, since the docking port on Caboose 2 has been rendered unusable."

With a bit of deliberation they agreed that the heptad should make its next attempt on a docking port in the old Zvezda module.

Dinah, who had spent most of the last couple of days preparing for the docking to occur on Caboose 2, sent her robots scrambling forward along the outside of the Stack, bringing their cables with them. That caught her up in a stew of minor complications that more than filled the time it took for the heptad to get its dead thruster up and running again.

They watched the second approach, and the docking, in silence. It took about ten minutes. Doob interrupted once to give an update on the approaching radiation storm.

Unexpectedly, it was Moira who broke the silence. "Don't let them dock," she said.

"What?!" Ivy said.

"It's a trap."

Zeke's voice came over the PA: "Positive docking achieved. Getting ready to open the hatch."

Moira added, "Michael figured it out."

"Fifteen minutes before the storm breaks," Doob announced.

Dinah had entered into a state of intense focus on the problem to be solved, seeing through the eyes of ten different robots performing ten different tasks, occasionally blurting out terse requests to the two surviving spacewalkers, asking them to shake a stuck cable loose or pull a wriggling Grabb out of trouble. She tried to filter out the conversation between Moira and Ivy.

"What do you mean, it's a trap?"

"Aïda's heptad joined the mesh network as soon as it got within range," Moira said. "If you check your email right now, or your Spacebook, you'll see stuff flooding into it. Terabytes of old messages and posts that have been bottled up in the Swarm. Mailing list traffic that's three years old."

"So?" Ivy asked.

"Michael saw some weird stuff just now, and drew my attention to it."

"He's floating in space!"

"He's floating in space and checking his email."

"What weird stuff did he notice?"

"They're cannibals, Ivy."

"We already know that."

"A few hours ago," Moira said, "they slaughtered Tav and ate what was left of him."

Dinah was having difficulty focusing on her work.

"They wanted to be well fed for today."

The time was approaching when the spacewalkers would have to go to their airlocks and get indoors ahead of the storm. Dinah had to focus on them. There was nothing she could do about what Moira was saying. She began speaking to one of them but was interrupted when Zeke came over the PA again: "Ten survivors aboard. Waiting for J.B.F. to emerge from the hatch."

"Zeke, be on your toes," Ivy said. "We have indications they may be up to no good."

"Get inside," Dinah said to the spacewalkers. "Head for the nearest airlock. Stay away from the new people, we don't trust them."

"Ditching the rock," Ivy announced. A sharp hiss came through the walls as compressed air flooded the hair-thin gap between the outer surface of the Hammerhead and the surrounding cavity of Amalthea. "Plug your ears." Then, before anyone could comply, a shattering, sickening bang as Dinah's demolition charges went off, destroying the structural connections that joined Amalthea to *Endurance.* They felt a sharp jostle—more acceleration than they had experienced in three years—as the Hammerhead sprang free, pushing the rest of *Endurance* along with it.

"Three minutes before the storm hits," Doob said.

"J.B.F. is aboard," Luisa announced. She was on voice to Zeke and the rest of the crew aft, relaying what they said to the others in the Hammerhead. Her brow wrinkled. "Something's wrong with her—I don't quite follow."

"Burning hard," Ivy announced. Meaning that they were near their apogee, entering the fringe of the main lunar debris cloud, and that all the surviving engines had just come on full force. She had inaugurated the big burn that would, with a delta vee of some twelve hundred meters per second, inject them into the debris cloud.

Every loose object in the Hammerhead dropped to what was now the floor. At the same time they could hear all manner of percussion, from all over *Endurance.*

Zeke's voice came in over the voice link. "We are in combat," he said.

"Combat?" Ivy asked.

"They shot Steve Lake."

"We are now experiencing very high levels of high-energy proton radiation from the CME," Doob announced. "Everyone who is not in the Hammerhead should be getting into a storm shelter."

"Shot him?" Ivy asked.

"With J.B.F.'s revolver. I suggest you try to lock down the network, they are trying to backdoor it."

After that, communications were hectic and confused for a minute, and seemed to suggest that adversaries in different parts of the ship were all trying to use the same channel.

Then their communications went dead. The equipment still worked; they'd simply been locked out of the network. Ivy could still fly the ship, but none of them could talk to people outside the Hammerhead.

They were startled by a metallic rapping on the hatch that sealed the Hammerhead off from the SCRUM. Dinah's ears soon read it as Morse code.

" 'Chocolate,' " she said. "That's kind of a code word between me and Tekla. I think we should open the hatch."

They did so, not before arming themselves with whatever makeshift weapons they could find, and found Tekla, suffering from a knife wound to the hand; Zeke, looking flustered but unharmed; and a woman, barely recognizable as Julia Bliss Flaherty given that most of her hair was gone and she had both of her hands firmly clamped over her mouth. Tekla vaulted into the Hammerhead and pulled Julia along behind her.

"What is going on?" Ivy demanded.

Zeke held up both hands. "I got this," he said. "We have killed four of them already. Two more are casualties. We have them outnumbered. We just have to keep fighting."

"You need to get into a storm shelter," Ivy said.

Tekla, unaccustomed to working in even weak gravity, had

gotten her footing enough to drag Julia into a corner of the Hammerhead and sit her down on the floor. She then turned back toward the hatch. Dinah had never seen Tekla in this state before, and feared her greatly in that moment. Moira had a different reaction; peeling off her headphones, she lurched across the space and threw her arms around Tekla's neck. It looked like a greeting but soon developed into something else as Tekla began dragging Moira toward the hatch and Moira began trying to prevent her from returning to the fray.

"Sweet one," Tekla was mumbling into Moira's ear, "you want me to use wrestling moves on you? Then you should let me go, because I am going to kill that bitch Aïda."

"Zipping into storm shelters is exactly what they wanted us to do," Zeke explained. "Their plan was to take the ship as soon as we did so. Good thing you warned us."

Tekla by now had peeled herself loose from Moira's grip and advanced toward the hatch with a full stride.

Zeke, waiting for her, reached out with one hand. He was holding a small black plastic box. He pressed it against Tekla's thigh and pulled a little trigger on its side. The device erupted with a sharp ticking, buzzing noise. Tekla's leg collapsed and she floated to the floor, glassy-eyed.

"Sorry, Tekla," Zeke said. "You stay here. Get your hand fixed. Keep Moira company—she needs you. And if you have a little boy, name it Zeke."

Then, before any of them could respond, he slammed the hatch shut.

In the silence that followed, a sharp crack resounded through the structure of *Endurance*. Everyone knew the sound: they'd just taken a hit from a bolide.

"Aren't you supposed to be flying the ship?" Doob shouted to Ivy.

Wordlessly, Ivy went back to her screen.

Dinah rounded on Julia. "What the hell is going on?" she demanded.

Julia's hair had been cropped. In the last three years it had gone silvery. Her hands still obscured the lower half of her face. Her eyes were clearly recognizable, though without benefit of cosmetics they seemed to be staring out of a face two decades older.

Slowly she removed her hands.

She was sticking her tongue out. It looked like a piece of metal was caught in her teeth.

On a closer look, it was clear that J.B.F. now had a pierced tongue. It had been done cleanly and professionally; there was no bleeding, no apparent signs of infection or discomfort. A stainless steel bolt about two inches long had been inserted vertically through the piercing, fixed in place with nuts and washers above and below the tongue. It was too long to fit into Julia's mouth, so it kept her tongue stretched out. Above and below, the rod pressed against her lips.

"Oh Jesus Christ," Dinah said.

Julia tapped at the bolt with one finger, then made screwing and unscrewing gestures with both hands. The nuts had been doubled, and torqued tightly against each other. Dinah took a multitool from a holster on her belt and unfolded its needlenosed pliers, then borrowed Ivy's. By twisting gently in opposite directions she was able to loosen the nuts. Julia pushed her away and unscrewed the nuts with her fingertips, then gently extracted the bolt. Her tongue retracted into her mouth. She put one hand over her lips and leaned back against a bulkhead for a few moments, moving her jaw to work up some saliva and get limbered up.

When she finally spoke, Julia sounded weirdly normal, as if delivering remarks from the White House briefing room. "When we surrendered," she said, "they took my gun, and they tortured Spencer Grindstaff until he spilled everything he knew about the IT systems here. All the passwords, all the back doors, all the details as to how it all works. Exactly what they would need in order to take the place over. Then they killed him, and . . ."

"Ate him?"

Julia nodded. "They have a sort of hacker type among their group.

When he came on board just now, he went to a terminal and began to execute this plan. Steve Lake tried to stop him. One of the others had the gun—shot Steve to death. That was always part of their plan. They knew that only Steve could stop them."

"How many bullets are left in that thing?"

"I'm sure it is empty now. Most of them are using knives and clubs. They didn't expect a real fight, because . . ."

"Because they thought we'd all be zipped up in our storm shelters," Dinah said, "like lambs to the slaughter."

THE BIG BURN LASTED FOR THE BETTER PART OF AN HOUR. BY THE end of it, they'd consumed so much propellant and made *Endurance* so light that acceleration made the blood fall out of their heads and pool in their feet. Ivy piloted the ship lying flat on her back, lest she lose consciousness. The journey was punctuated by a few terrific bangs, and those who could stand to watch *Endurance*'s status readouts could observe various modules turning yellow, then red, then black as they succumbed to damage. Dinah watched through the eyes of several cameras as a ten-mile-long piece of the moon tumbled past them, overtaking them and zooming by just a few hundred meters to their starboard side. Nor was that the last such encounter; but with Doob acting as her wing man, calling out the biggest threats, and with Dinah making such use as she could of Parambulator, Ivy was able to steer them clear of the big stuff.

They had no way of knowing the progress of the combat aft. Zeke had spoken optimistically of their odds, but there was no telling how the damage they'd taken from bolides might have swung the course of the battle to one side or the other. *Endurance*'s automatic sealing off of damaged parts of the ship had now partitioned her into a number of separate zones between which movement was impossible.

Zero gee returned, meaning that the engines had shut off. They were now traveling as fast, on average, as the rest of the debris cloud. Dinah had only just adjusted to the steady acceleration of the big burn and now felt a wave of sickness come over her as the inner ear readjusted. Her eyes closed and she sank into a sort of catnap, floating loosely around the Hammerhead, thudding gently against a wall every so often when Ivy used the thrusters to avoid a rock.

Then she realized she'd been fully asleep for a time.

Part of her wanted to stay that way. But she knew that big things were happening, so she opened her eyes, half expecting to find herself alone, the last person alive.

Ivy was the only person awake, her face lit up by her screen. And for the first time in a long time, it looked the way it had used to when she'd been on the track of some fascinating science problem: alive, intent, fiercely joyful.

"Why's it so quiet?" Dinah asked. For it seemed to her that it had been a long time since she had heard the crack of a bolide or sensed the thrust of one of *Endurance*'s engines.

"We're in the shadow," Ivy said. "A new Cone of Protection. C'mere." She tossed her head.

Dinah came around behind and hooked her chin over her friend's shoulder. The monitor had several windows open. Ivy enlarged one of them to fill most of the screen. A legend superimposed at the bottom identified it as AFT CAMERA.

The field of view was entirely filled by a close-up image of a huge asteroid.

Dinah was an asteroid miner. She had looked at many pictures of asteroids in her day. She had learned to recognize them by their shapes and their textures. She had no difficulty in identifying this one. "Cleft," she said.

Ivy reached out and touched the screen. Red crosshairs appeared beneath her fingertip, which she dragged across the big rock's surface until centered on a vast black crevasse that looked like it nearly split the asteroid in two: the canyon that had given this rock its name. She pulled her finger away, leaving the crosshairs in the middle of the cleft. "I was thinking there," she said.

"How about a little below, where it gets wider?"

"I don't think we want a wide place. Too much exposure."

"Go there, then," Dinah suggested, reaching out and dragging the crosshairs to a slightly different location. "Then we can snuggle into the narrow part once we've gotten inside."

"You ladies enjoying yourselves?" Doob rasped.

"Not as much as you're going to in about an hour," Ivy said.

"I'll try to hold out that long."

THERE WAS NO PROBLEM GETTING INTO IT. IVY FLEW *ENDURANCE* into the great crevasse like a Piper Cub into the Grand Canyon. Within minutes the walls were reaching far above them. The bottom was still lost in shadow.

Following Dinah's general suggestion, Ivy then nudged the ship toward a part of the canyon, several tens of kilometers distant, where the walls converged and the radioactive sky became a narrow, starry slit above. Still she kept pushing onward, occasionally scraping the ship's outlying modules against the walls, until she reached a place where she could go no deeper.

Looking both directions along the crevasse from this place, they could see spots where the sun was shining in. Here, though, they were protected from rocks and radiation alike. Ivy set *Endurance* down on the floor of the canyon. Cleft's gravity was exceedingly faint, but it was enough to give words like that a little meaning, and it was enough to keep the ship lodged in one place until they decided to move it.

Which they never would.

Cleft

ON THE SURFACE OF CLEFT, A HUMAN WEIGHED ABOUT AS MUCH AS three pints of beer would weigh on Earth. *Endurance* weighed about as much as a couple of semi-trailer rigs.

Ivy lit the ship's attitude control thrusters one last time and pivoted her tail up until it was vertical. *Endurance* was standing on her head, the torus aloft, iron Hammerhead nose-down on the iron floor of the crevasse. Dinah sent out some Grabbs to weld the ship to the asteroid. Ivy shut down the thrusters.

Endurance was no longer a ship but a building.

From the Hammerhead, now one piece of metal with Cleft, the Stack ran straight up like the trunk of a tree. Various structures ramified outward from it like boughs. Its widest part was the array of eighty-one arklets that had formerly made up the stern of the ship. These now projected upward like leaves.

Or so they imagined. They couldn't actually go outside and look at it until they got out of the Hammerhead. During the battle, they had sealed the hatch. By the time they had brought her to rest and welded her down, the rest of *Endurance* had been quiet for a long time. Finally they opened the hatch and began to explore it one module at a time. They sent Buckies and Siwis out ahead of them to illuminate dark spaces and aim cameras into hidden corners. Tekla then went in, taking point, with Dinah and Ivy watching her back. They were armed with cudgels made from lengths of pipe. But they never had to use them.

It was some combination of crime scene, battleground, and disaster zone. Only about half of the modules were still pressurized. Some of them had become completely isolated and could only be reached by a person in a space suit. It took days to get to them all.

In one of them they found Aïda, the only other survivor from the heptad. Two days had passed since she had eaten the last of Tavistock Prowse, so she was very hungry, but otherwise in good shape. After becoming trapped by a combination of combat and bolide strikes, she had holed up in a water-filled storm shelter, then begun drinking its contents as she awaited rescue.

The total number of living humans was now sixteen. Several had suffered injuries from combat or from the consequences of bolide strikes. Anyone who had not taken shelter in the Hammerhead, or in a storm shelter, was suffering from radiation sickness. The healthy ones patched holes, repressurized modules, got the torus spinning again, and turned it into a sick bay, which filled up immediately.

Dinah managed to get Doob out for one last space walk. He had been failing for days. Once they got him into the suit, though, his energy flooded back. Dinah took him out on the floor of the crevasse where he could walk, light-footed, with magnetized Grabbs latched onto his boots to keep him from floating away with every step. They rambled for about a kilometer, turning around every so often to look back at humanity's new home. Above the spinning torus, where Moira was even now unpacking her genetics lab, Tekla was inspecting the arklets on the top level, learning which were whole, which were beyond repair, and which could be patched up for future occupancy. On the floor of the crevasse, Grabbs and Siwis were at work, rooting *Endurance* to her final resting place with spreading cables and struts.

Where they walked, it was dark most of the time. That was the price of being sheltered from cosmic rays and coronal mass ejections. Looking up, however, they could see sunlight gilding the edges of the crevasse above them. They talked about how to set up mirrors that would bounce sunlight downward onto the arklets, which could grow food and scrub air in their translucent outer hulls. Doob spoke of Endomement, the idea that, in time, a ceiling could be thrown over the top of the crevasse and walls built to keep in the air, whereupon a whole section of the valley could be given an atmosphere and turned into a place where children could go "outside" without the need for space suits.

Then he walked home and died.

They stored his body with the others, in a damaged arklet that would serve as a mausoleum until such time as they could cut a grave out of Cleft's surface. That would take a long time, but the survivors all shared the conviction that, having sacrificed so much to make it here, they should be interred and not burned. Doob would share a grave with Zeke Petersen, Bolor-Erdene, Steve Lake, and all the others who had died at about the same time.

Some of those remained conscious long enough to relate the stories of what had happened to them during the conflict with the people who had come in from the Swarm, and *Endurance*'s final, hectic passage through storm and stone. Their accounts were recorded and archived. One day some historian would piece the story together, comparing it with data logs to figure out who had slain whom in combat and which module had gone dark when.

Aïda, of course, might have been their best source of information, had she felt like talking. But she didn't. She had sunk into a profound depression, emerging from it at seemingly random moments to chatter about whatever stray thoughts were flitting through her head.

No one wanted to talk to her. When she talked to you, she watched you too carefully with those avid, penetrating eyes, as if she saw, or imagined she saw, too deeply. It was impossible to be the object of that gaze without thinking of what she and the others had done, and without imagining that you were being sized up as food.

An epic tale was told by the three-year backlog of email, Spacebook posts, blog entries, and other ephemera that filled up all of their inboxes as soon as the network of the Swarm recombined with that of *Endurance.* The general arc of the story seemed to be a growing detachment from reality that had afflicted J.B.F. and some of her inner circle. Luisa likened it to the growth of spiritualism after the First World War. During the 1920s, many who had not been able to bring themselves to accept the loss of life in the trenches and the subsequent influenza epidemic had fallen prey to the belief that they could communicate with their lost loved ones from beyond the grave. They had, in effect, sidestepped grief by convincing themselves that nothing had happened.

The analogy was a loose one. The loss of life in the Hard Rain had, of course, been much worse. And few of the Arkies had adopted spiritualist beliefs per se. But after a particularly severe coronal mass ejection had slain nearly a hundred Arkies, Tav had written a blog post about the journey he had made to Bhutan with Doob and the conversation that they'd had en route with the king concerning the mathematics of reincarnation. It was a meditative piece, a secular eulogy for those who had fallen, but in retrospect it seemed to mark an inflection point in the survivors' thinking. The Swarm had always had a sort of quasi-divine status to some, who had perhaps read too much chaos theory too superficially and were prone to believing that its collective decisions, lying beyond human understanding, partook of the supernatural.

The mishmash of techno-mystical ideation that had grown out of that one blog post was unreadable and incomprehensible to Luisa or to anyone else who read it after the fact, with a clear mind, but it seemed to have offered hope and comfort to many terrified young people trapped in arklets. Tav, to his credit, had backed away from any efforts to elevate him to prophetlike status. If anything, though, his modesty might have backfired.

"I have no idea," Luisa said, "how anyone could read these threads and find hope in them. Or even meaning. But they did. Long enough to distract them from the real problems they were facing. And when Aïda and the others finally came to their senses and began to push back against J.B.F. and the others, the reaction was just that much more severe. Because things had gone too far by that point."

The backlash had started in a two-triad bolo where a number of like-minded Arkies, including Aïda, had "called bullshit" on the prevailing tone and substance of official statements emanating from the White Arklet and begun to denounce Tavistock Prowse as a puppet blogger for the regime. Dubbing themselves the "Black Bolo Brigade," they had begun to spread their insurrectionist message to other arklets in the Swarm.

That message—which made perfect sense, as far as it went—was all about the need to face reality and to implement realistic, effective steps to address the Swarm's problems. That included, if need be, throwing themselves on the mercy of *Endurance*. They had demanded that J.B.F. open the books and provide a current and accurate account of all stocks of water, food, and other staples, and how those numbers were changing over time. Julia had resisted those demands until the data had finally been leaked by a turncoat on her staff. The food picture had turned out to be bleak. This had led to a variety of responses that had determined the history and politics of the Swarm ever since: among some, a further retreat into mysticism and wishful thinking, based on a belief that the Agent had been some sort of avenging angel sent by God, or by aliens so powerful that they might as well be God, to bring about the end of days and the merging of all human consciousness into a digital swarm in the sky; among others, a frank embrace of cannibalism—in the sense not of killing people for food but of eating those who had died of natural causes—as a stopgap measure until J.B.F. could be toppled and replaced by people who knew what they were doing. The first group, the mystics, had tended to rally under Julia's banner. The cannibals had ended up under Aïda, who because of her intensity and her charisma had gradually emerged as the leader of the Black Bolo Brigade.

The one Swarm had thus fissioned into two smaller ones, neither of which was as viable, and thereby worsened the same problems that had led to the split in the first place. From there the story had been predictable enough, and had led to the events of the last few days.

Aïda still wasn't talking, but Julia was. According to her, Aïda and the other Black Bolo survivors had calculated, in the last weeks, that their turn to cannibalism would be so repugnant to the survivors of *Endurance* as to render them permanent outcasts. Rather than passively await the judgment—which they foresaw as extremely pious, sanctimonious, and punitive—of Ivy and her claque, they would seize part or all of *Endurance,* beginning with her network, and then negotiate terms from a position of strength.

This explained, at least in a general way, everything that had happened, save possibly for the physical mutilation of both Julia and Tav.

Asked for a theory as to that, Julia shrugged. "We were criminals to them. Criminals need to be punished. It's hard to punish people who are already starving to death in a confined space. What is really left in the executioner's tool kit, other than attacking the body? They wanted to silence me, and so they did. And they wanted to give Tav a taste of his own medicine by uploading his physical body into theirs."

A WEEK LATER, WHEN THE LAST OF THE VICTIMS HAD SUCCUMBED to their wounds or to radiation sickness, eight humans remained alive and healthy.

Ivy called for a twenty-four-hour pause to grieve and to take stock. She then called a meeting of the entire human race: Dinah, Ivy, Moira, Tekla, Julia, Aïda, Camila, and Luisa.

They did not know quite what to do with Julia and Aïda. For years they had dreamed, in idle moments, of one day bringing J.B.F. to justice—whatever that would mean. Then, at the last moment, she had been eclipsed by Aïda. And now it all seemed a moot point anyway. Could six women put two women in jail? What would it mean to be in jail in a place like this? Corporal punishment was at least a theoretical possibility. But Aïda had already gone there, with results that they all found sickening.

J.B.F. was a threat to no one. Aïda still possessed an air of menace. But short of locking her up in an arklet, there was nothing they could do about that save keep an eye on her. And so they did, never letting her out of their sight, never letting her get behind them.

They met in the Banana, sitting around the long conference table. To one side of it was death: the sick bay where Zeke, the last man alive, had given up the ghost a day and a half ago, after making a joke about what a shame it all was: being the only man alive, with eight women to choose from. They had scrubbed the place down with bleach and made the beds with clean sheets in the hopes that none of them would be occupied for a long time. To the other side was life: the series of compartments where Moira had been setting up her genetics lab.

The meeting would later be known as the Council of the Seven Eves. For, though eight women were present, one of them—Luisa—had already gone through menopause. Ivy opened with a report on their general situation. From a certain point of view, this was surprisingly good. They had grown so inured to terrible news that she had to emphasize this more than once. Few places in the solar system were as safe as the one where they had come to rest. No cosmic radiation could touch them here. From coronal mass ejections they were equally immune. Sunlight for energy and agriculture could be had a short distance above them, high on the walls of the crevasse, where the sun shone almost all the time.

In the meantime, their big reactor as well as four dozen arklet reactors were producing far more power than they could ever use, and would continue doing so for decades. Of water they still had a hundred tons left over. While melting and splitting the water they'd used for propellant, they had extracted from it many tons of phosphorus, carbon, ammonia, and other chemicals, left over from the dawn of the solar system, that had once cloaked Greg's Skeleton in a reeking black carapace. That stuff, as Sean Probst had well known, would be priceless as nutrients to support agriculture.

They no longer had to worry, ever again, about the things that had been their obsessive concerns for the last five years: perigees, apogees, burns, propellant, movement of any kind. No bolide could touch them down here. Even if Cleft banged into an equally huge rock at some point, they would probably survive it.

The vitamins that had been packed into every arklet launched up into the Cloud Ark had been intended to support a population of thousands. Even though many of these had been lost, what remained was still more than enough to keep a small colony in aspirin and toothbrushes for a long time.

They were dependent, in many ways, on digital technology. They could not long survive without robots to do work for them and computerized control systems to keep the installation running. They had no ability to fabricate new computer chips to replace the old. But the Arkitects, anticipating this, had stocked them with a large surplus of spare parts that would last for hundreds of years if husbanded carefully. And they had plans for rebooting digital civilization later; they had tools for making tools for making tools, and instructions on how to use them when the time came.

With immediate needs accounted for, the discussion turned toward the obvious problem at hand. All heads turned toward Moira.

"My equipment made it through perfectly unscathed," she said.

"The last three years have been boring for me. I've been treated as a fragile flower. I have spent the time writing up everything I know about how to use that stuff. If I drop dead of something tomorrow, you'll still be able to work it out.

"Obviously, we're all women. Seven of us are still capable of having babies. Or, to be specific, of producing eggs. So, where can we get some sperm? Well, ninety-seven percent of what was sent up from Earth was destroyed in the disaster on the first day of the Hard Rain. What survived, survived because it had already been distributed among ten different arklets. All ten of those later ended up going off with the Swarm. None of that material, however, seems to have made its way here."

Aïda interrupted. Staring across the table at Julia, she announced, "I was in the Swarm, as you know. I can tell you that this fact of the samples in the ten arklets was forgotten. Never discussed. If anyone even knew they were there, they forgot about it soon."

Julia was construing this as an attack on her record. "We had eight hundred healthy young men and women from every ethnic group in the world."

"Had," Aïda repeated. "We had."

"The amount of effort required to keep a few sample containers deep-frozen wasn't worth the—"

"Stop," Ivy said. "If we can start making babies, their great-grandchildren can pore over the records and make judgments and have debates about what should have been done. Now isn't the time for recriminations."

"I was in the meeting where Markus called bullshit on the Human Genetic Archive," Dinah said. She was mildly amazed to hear herself backing Julia's side of the argument.

"We can't make the same mistake again," Aïda said, "of fooling ourselves. Believing in shit that isn't real."

Ivy said, "Had we known that it was going to come down, so suddenly, to seven surviving fertile women, we would have had every healthy male masturbating into test tubes for the last three years. We'd have looked for ways to keep it all frozen. But we never imagined it would come to this."

"It's not clear what the quality of the results would have been," Moira put in. "Given the amount of radiation exposure, I probably would have had to do a lot of manual repair on the genetic material in those samples."

"Manual repair?" Julia asked.

"I should put that in scare quotes," Moira said, reaching up with both hands and crooking her fingers. "Obviously I'm not literally using my hands. But with the equipment in there"—she tossed her head in the direction of the lab—"I can isolate a cell—a sperm or an ovum—and read its genome. I'm skipping over a lot of details, obviously. But the point is that I can get a digital record of its DNA. Once that's in hand, it turns into a software exercise—the data can be evaluated and compared to huge databases that shipped up as part of the lab. It's possible to identify places on a given chromosome where a bit of DNA got damaged by a cosmic ray or radiation from the reactor. It is then possible to repair those breaks by splicing in a reasonable guess as to what was there originally."

"It sounds like a lot of work," Camila said. "If there is anything I can do to ease your burdens and make myself useful, I am at your disposal."

"Thank you. We will all be working at it for months," Moira said, "before anything happens. We have very little else to do."

"Excuse me, but what is the point of discussing this, since we have no sperm to work with?" Aïda asked.

"We don't need sperm," Moira said.

"We don't need sperm to get pregnant! This is news to me," Aïda said, with a sharp laugh.

Moira went on coolly. "There is a process known as parthenogenesis, literally virgin birth, by which a uniparental embryo can be created out of a normal egg. It's been done with animals. The only reason no one ever did it with humans is because it seemed ethically dodgy, as well as completely unnecessary given the willingness of men to impregnate women every chance they got."

"Can you do it here, Moira?" asked Luisa.

"It's not fundamentally more difficult than the sorts of tricks I was just describing in the case of repairing damaged sperm. In some ways, it would actually be easier."

"You can get us pregnant . . . by ourselves," Tekla said.

"Yes. Everyone except Luisa."

"I can have a child of whom I am both the mother and the father," Aïda said. The idea clearly fascinated her. Suddenly she was no longer the prickly, brittle Aïda but the warm and engaged girl who must have charmed the powers that be during the Casting of Lots.

"It will take some tricky work in the lab," Moira said. "But that is the whole point of having brought the lab safely to this place."

They all pondered it for a bit. Julia was the first to speak up. "Stepping into my traditional role as scientific ignoramus: Do you mean to say that you can clone us?"

Moira nodded—not to say *yes,* but to say *I understand your question.* "There are different ways to do it, Julia. One way would indeed produce clones—all offspring genetically identical to the mother. This isn't what we want. For one thing, it would not solve our basic problem—the lack of males."

Camila's hand went up. Moira, clearly annoyed by the interruption, blinked once, then nodded at her. "Is it really a problem?" Camila asked. "As long as we have the lab and can go on making more clones, would it really be such a bad thing to have a society with no males? At least for several generations?"

Moira silenced her with a gentle pushing movement of one hand. "That's a question for later. There is another problem with this version of parthenogenesis, which is, again, that all offspring are the same. Exact copies. To get some genetic diversity, we need to use something called automictic parthenogenesis. Look, it's a long story, but the point is that in normal sexual reproduction there is crossing over of chromosomes during meiosis. It's a form of natural recombination of DNA. It's what causes your children to look *sort of* like you, but not *exactly* like you. In the form of parthenogenesis that I am proposing to use, there would be that crossing over. An element of randomness."

"And both boys and girls?" Dinah asked.

"That's harder," Moira admitted. "Synthesizing a Y chromosome is no joke. My prediction is that the first set of babies—perhaps the first few sets of them—will all be female. Because we simply need to get the population up. During that time I can be working on the Y chromosome problem. Later on, I hope that some little boys will result."

"But these little girls—and later the boys—will still be made out of our own DNA?" Ivy asked.

"Yes."

"So they'll be quite similar to us genetically."

"If I do nothing about it," Moira said, "they'll be like sisters. Perhaps even more similar than that implies. But there are a few tricks that I can use to create a wider range of genotypes out of the same source material. Perhaps they'll be more like cousins. I don't know, it's never been tried."

"Are we talking about the inbreeding problem? It sounds like it," Dinah said.

"Loss of heterozygosity. Yes. I happen to know something about it. It's why I was chosen as a member of the General Population."

"Because of your work on black-footed ferrets and so on," Ivy said.

"Yes. This is a closely analogous problem. But the point I would like you all to keep in mind is that we solved that problem in the case of the black-footed ferrets and we are going to solve it again."

She said it with force and confidence that silenced the others for a few moments and left them looking at her for more.

Moira went on. “I think we all have at least an intuitive understanding of this, yes?”

That one was aimed at Julia, who looked mildly peeved, and bit off the following: “My daughter had Down syndrome. That is all I will say.”

Moira acknowledged it with a nod, then went on: “Everyone has some genetic defects. When you are breeding more or less randomly within a large population, there’s a tendency for those errors to be swamped by the law of averages. Everything sort of works out. But when two people sharing the same defect mate, their offspring is likely to have that defect as well, and over time we see the usual unpleasantness that we all associate in our minds with inbreeding.”

“So,” Luisa said, “if we follow the plan you have laid out, and begin, a few years down the road, with seven groups of what amount to siblings or cousins—”

“It’s not enough heterozygosity, to answer your question,” Moira said. “If you have a genetic predisposition to any disease, for example—”

“Alpha-thalassemia runs in my family,” Ivy said.

“That’s a fine example,” Moira returned. “As it happens, Old Earth compiled vast databases on such things before its destruction. All of which are in there now.” She gestured in the direction of her lab. “We have a very good idea which defects, on which chromosomes, are responsible for alpha-thalassemia. If you supply me with an ovum, I can find those defects and I can fix them before we begin parthenogenesis. Your offspring will be free of that defect. Barring some random future mutation, it’ll never return.”

Dinah raised her hand. “My brother was a carrier of cystic fibrosis. I haven’t been tested.”

Julia raised hers. “Three of my aunts died of the same form of breast cancer. I’ve been tested. I know I carry that defect as well.”

“The same answer applies in all of these cases,” Moira said. “If there's a genetic test for it, then it means, by definition, that we know which defects are responsible for it. And knowing that, we can perform a repair."

A new voice joined the conversation. "How about bipolar disorder?"

Everyone looked at Aïda.

She would live out the rest of her life, and go to meet her maker, without having a friend, or even a friendly conversation. So, no one was in a receptive frame of mind about her question. But the mere fact that she'd asked it suggested a level of introspection they hadn't seen from her before. Moira considered it.

"I would have to do some research. I think that it does run in families to some extent. To the extent that it can be traced to particular locations on particular chromosomes, it can be treated like any other disease," Moira said.

"Do you believe it *should* be?" Aïda asked.

Everyone looked automatically at Luisa, who nodded. "We are long past the point of thinking of mental illnesses as somehow a lesser kind of disease than physical. Such disorders should, in my opinion, be addressed in just the same way."

"Do you believe it *must* be?"

Luisa colored slightly. "What is the point of these questions, Aïda?"

"I have done research on it," Aïda said. "Some say that bipolarity is a useful adaptation. When things are bad, you become depressed, retreat, conserve energy. When things are good, you spring into action with great energy."

"And your point is . . ."

"Will you treat this condition in my offspring *against my will*? What if I *want* to have a lot of little bipolar kids?"

In the flustered silence that followed, Camila spoke. "What about aggression?"

Everyone turned to look at her, as if unsure they had heard her correctly.

"I'm serious," she said. She looked toward Aïda. "I don't mean to trivialize the suffering that your condition causes. But over the course of history, aggression has caused a far larger amount of pain and death than bipolar disorder or whatever. As long as we are fixing those aspects of the human psyche that lead to suffering, should we not eliminate the tendency to aggressive behavior?"

"That's different," Moira began. But she was interrupted by Dinah.

"Hold on a sec," Dinah said. "I'm aggressive. I always have been. I was on track to be an Olympic soccer player! That's the only way I've ever been able to amount to anything—by channeling my aggression into doing things." She nodded across the table at Tekla. "Hell, look at her! How many times has she saved our asses by being aggressive?"

Tekla nodded. "Yes. Dinah saved me by taking aggressive action against rules of space station. Problem is not aggression. It is lack of discipline. A person can be aggressive"—she nodded at Dinah—"and still be constructive in society if she controls her passions." And she threw a significant glare at Aïda, who let out a little snort and looked away.

"So you're suggesting we breed people for discipline and self-control?" Ivy asked. "I'm not sure if I follow."

"I believe that Camila was merely saying that certain personality types, taken to an unhealthy extreme, are as bad as diagnosable mental illnesses per se. If not worse," Julia said.

"I don't want you to speak for me," Camila said. "Please do not speak for me anymore, Julia."

"I am merely trying to be helpful," Julia said. But where the old J.B.F. would have said it reproachfully, the new one merely seemed exhausted.

Dinah broke in. "Well, what I am trying to say is that I don't appreciate being labeled as a genetic freak that needs to be eradicated from the human future."

"No one would say that of you, Dinah," Ivy said. "Camila's talking about the knuckle draggers who tried to kill her for wanting an education."

"And what is *your* opinion?" Tekla asked Ivy.

"Similar to yours. Aggression is fine. It needs to be controlled. Directed. But the way to do that is through intelligence. Rational thought."

That elicited a cackle from Aïda. "Oh, sorry," she said. "I was thinking about the Swarm. Eight hundred people all carefully hand-selected for intelligence and rational thought. In the end, all we could think about was how they tasted."

"None of *us* ate each other," Ivy said.

"But you thought about it," Aïda said with a smile.

Dinah slammed her palm hard on the table. She sat still for a moment with her eyes closed tight, then stood up and walked out of the room.

"I guess she is not disciplined or intelligent enough to control her aggression!" Aïda cracked.

"It is a form of self-discipline," Tekla said. "So that she would not kill you. You see, Aïda, *thinking* about doing such things and *doing* are different. This is why greater discipline is a requirement."

"Sweetie, what do you mean when you speak of discipline?" Moira asked. "I'm just trying to cash that word out in terms of genetics. I can find a genetic marker for cystic fibrosis. I'm not sure if the same is true of discipline."

"Some races are disciplined. Is fact," Tekla said. "Japanese are more disciplined than . . . *Italians*."

She gave Aïda a stare that would have frozen most people to their chairs, but Aïda just threw her head back and laughed exultantly. "You are forgetting the Roman legions, but please go on."

"Men are more disciplined than women. Is just fact. So there must be genes for it."

This produced yet another silence, eventually broken by Luisa: "I'm seeing a side of you I didn't know about, Tekla."

"Call me bad, call me racist if you want. I know what you will say: That it is all training. It is all culture. I disagree. If you do not feel pain, you do not respond to pain. And hormones."

"What about hormones, lover?" Moira asked. Her affection for Tekla was obvious, and took some of the tension out of the room.

"We all know that when hormones are a certain way, emotions have big impact. Other times, not so much. This is genetic."

"Or maybe epigenetic. We really don't know," Moira said.

"Whatever," Tekla said. "My point is that for people to live in tin cans for hundreds of years requires order and discipline. Not from above. From within. If there is a way to make this easier with your genetic lab, then we should do it."

Luisa said, "We never explored Ivy's point that intelligence was key."

"Yes," Ivy said, with a glance at Aïda. "I was interrupted."

Aïda covered her mouth with her hand and sniggered theatrically.

Ivy went on: "If we are really going to open the door to genetic improvement of our offspring, then it seems obvious to me that we should look to the one quality that trumps all others. And that is clearly intelligence."

"What do you mean it trumps all others?" Luisa asked.

"With intelligence, you can see the need to show discipline when the situation calls for it. Or to act aggressively. Or not. I would argue that the human mind is mutable enough that it can *become* all of the different types of people that Camila, Aïda, and Tekla have been describing. But that's all driven by what separates us from the animals. Which is our brains."

"There are many different types of intelligence," Luisa said.

Ivy gave a little shake of her head. "I've seen all of that stuff about emotional intelligence and what have you. Okay. Fine. But you know exactly what I'm talking about. And you know it can be propagated genetically. Just look at the academic records, the test scores of the Ashkenazi Jews."

"Speaking as a Sephardic Jew," Luisa said, "you can imagine my mixed feelings."

"We need brains, is the bottom line," Ivy said. "We're not hunter-gatherers anymore. We're all living like patients in the intensive care unit of a hospital. What keeps us alive isn't bravery, or athleticism, or any of those other skills that were valuable in a caveman society. It's our ability to master complex technological skills. It is our ability to be nerds. We need to breed nerds." She turned to look Aïda full in the face. "You ask for realism. Your complaint about her"—she nodded at Julia—"and the people around her was that they were holding out panaceas. Not facing facts. Fine. I'm giving you facts. We're all nerds now. We might as well get good at it."

Aïda shook her head in derision. "You completely leave out the human component. It's why you are a bad leader. It's why you were replaced by Markus, when wiser people than you were in control. And it's why we are here."

"Here, safe and sound," Ivy said, "unlike the people who followed you. All of whom are dead."

"So they are," Aïda said, "and I am alive, and I can see how it's going to be: you are going to keep me locked up in an arklet making genetic freak babies and taking them away from me." And she broke down weeping.

"She has what I have, except worse," Julia explained. "She sees many outcomes—most of which, given the circumstances, are dark—then acts upon them."

"What an unusual degree of introspection from you, Julia," Moira said.

"You have no concept of my level of introspection," Julia shot back. "I have been clinically depressed for most of my life. I once used drugs to fix it. Then I stopped. I stopped because I decided they were making me stupid, and I'd rather be miserable than stupid. I am what I am."

"Depression is genetically based to some extent. Would you like me to erase it from your children's genomes?" Moira asked.

"You heard what I said," Julia answered. "You know, now, the decision I made. Which was to suffer for the greater good. Because society will go astray if there are not those who, like me, imagine many outcomes. Let those scenarios run rampant in their minds. Anticipate the worst that could happen. Take steps to prevent it. If the price of that—the price of having a head full of dark imaginings—is personal suffering, then so be it."

"But would you wish that on your progeny?"

"Of course not," Julia said. "If there were a way to have one without the other—the foresight without the misery—I would take it in a heartbeat."

"We only need a few people of this mentality," Tekla said. "Too many, and you get the Soviet Union."

"I am forty-seven," Julia said. "I have one baby in me, if I'm lucky. The rest of you can punch them out for twenty years. Do the math."

"It amazes me that we have already gone over to the competitive angle!" Camila wailed. "I am so sorry that I brought this topic up."

A sharp rapping noise brought the room to attention.

Heads turned toward the Banana's window. It was not large—about the size of a dinner plate. For three years it had been buried in ice and forgotten about. But now it afforded a clear if somewhat dizzying view of their surroundings.

Outside of it, carabinered to the spinning torus, was Dinah. She had put on a space suit and gone out through an airlock.

Seeing she had their attention, she reached up and slapped a small object onto the glass. It was a lump of clay, some wires, and an electronic gadget. She depressed a button on the gadget and it began to count down from ten minutes.

Aïda screamed with laughter and clapped her hands.

"What on earth is she doing?" Julia asked.

"That's a demolition charge," Ivy said. "It's going to kill us all ten minutes from now if she doesn't take it off the window." She turned to survey the room.

"Well, what is her point?" Julia demanded.

"I think my friend is trying to tell us that if we can't settle this in ten minutes, the human race doesn't deserve to go on existing," Ivy said.

They all sat silently for perhaps half a minute before Moira said: "How's this: every woman decides what is going to be done with her eggs."

Hearing no objection, she continued: "Oh, let me be clear. If it's a real disease—something on the books, defined in the medical literature as such—then I will fix it. With no distinctions made between physical and mental disorders. No matter how many of those conditions each of you may be suffering from, I will fix them all before taking any other action. However." And she smiled, and held up an index finger. "Once all that is done, each of us gets a free one."

"Free what?" Tekla asked.

"One alteration—one improvement—of your choice, applied to the genome of the fertilized ovum that will grow into your child. And your child *only*. You cannot force it on any of the others. So, Camila, if you think it would improve the human race to get rid of its aggression, why then, I will search through the scientific literature for a way to reach toward your goal genetically. And likewise for the rest of you, and whatever changes you happen to think will improve the human condition. Your child, your choice."

They all considered it, glancing at one another from time to time, each trying to gauge the others' reactions.

Ivy glanced at the timer outside. "Are there any questions? We have eight minutes remaining."

Luisa said, "I don't think we need eight minutes."

Ivy looked each of them in the eye, then turned toward the window and gave a thumbs-up.

Dinah's eyes, seen through the glass of the window and the dome of her space suit's helmet, pivoted to focus on that. She nodded.

Moira smiled and put her thumb up. This too was noted by Dinah.

Then Tekla. Then Luisa, Camila, Julia.

All eyes were on Aïda. She would not look back at them. She was, at bottom, very shy. "Whatever," she mumbled.

"She needs to see your vote," Ivy said.

"Really? You mean that I could single-handedly destroy the entire human race, simply by not putting my thumb up in the next seven minutes?"

Tekla pulled a folding knife from a pocket on her coverall and flicked the blade open. She kept it low, down in her lap, and pretended to clean a fingernail with it. "Either that," Tekla said, "or population of human race suddenly goes from eight to seven, and we have unanimous decision."

Smiling, Aïda thrust her hand out, thumb down.

"I pronounce a curse," she said.

Luisa let out an exasperated sigh.

"This is not a curse that *I* create. It is not a curse on *your* children. No. I have never been as bad as you all think that I am. This is a curse that *you* have created, by doing this thing that you are about to do. And it is a curse upon *my* children. Because I know. I see how it is to be. I am the evil one. The cannibal. The one who would not go along. My children, no matter what decision I make, will forever be different from your children. Because make no mistake. What you have decided to do is to create new races. Seven new races. They will be separate and distinct forever, as much as you, Moira, are from Ivy. They will never merge into a single human race again, because that is not the way of humanity. Thousands of years from now, the descendants of you six will look at my descendants and say, 'Ah, look, there is a child of Aïda, the cannibal, the evil one, the cursed one.' They will cross the street to avoid my children; they will spit on the ground. This is the thing that you have done by making this decision. I will shape my child—my children, for I shall have many—to bear up under this curse. To survive it. And to prevail."

Aïda swept her gaze around the room, staring with her deep black eyes into the face of each of the other women in turn, then looked into the window and locked eyes with Dinah.

"I pronounce it," she said, then slowly rotated her hand until her thumb was pointed up.

DINAH PEELED THE DEMOLITION CHARGE AWAY FROM THE WINDOW. She had no idea what Aïda had just said. Nor did she especially care. It would be the usual histrionic Aïda stuff.

Several minutes remained on the countdown timer. She could have simply turned it off. But she felt like going for a walk. Whatever had just happened in the Banana looked unpleasant. She was tired of being cooped up with these people—even the ones she loved. She felt no great compulsion to rejoin them.

She unclipped the carabiner and let go of the lazily spinning torus. Her momentum carried her toward the wall of the crevasse. Long accustomed to movement in zero gee, she timed a slow somersault and planted her feet on the wall to kill her speed, then turned on the magnets in her boots and began hiking up the crevasse wall. The weak gravity made directions arbitrary. Walking "vertically up" a cliff was little different from walking "horizontally along" the canyon floor.

A tone sounded from the speakers in her helmet, alerting her that a voice connection had been made.

It was Ivy. "Going for a stroll?"

"Yeah."

"Look, we just realized something."

"Oh?"

"We all voted—except for you."

"Mmm, good point." Dinah glanced down at the countdown timer. The screen was getting more difficult to read, since she was nearing the terminator—the knife-sharp line between sunlight and shadow—and the bright canyon wall above her was reflecting from the screen. Tilting it for a better view, she saw that it was just about to drop through the sixty-second mark. "It's okay, I still have a minute to make my decision."

"Well, do you want to know what the rest of us agreed on?"

"I trust you. But sure."

"We're all going to try to have babies just like you, Dinah."

"Very funny." Dinah crossed over the terminator, and the sun rose. She raised her free hand and flipped down the sun visor on her helmet.

"Moira's working on it now."

"Is that why Aïda was being such a drama queen about it?"

"Exactly."

Thirty-five seconds.

"What did you really decide?"

"One free gene change for each mommy."

"Oh yeah? So what are you going to do? Make really smart little straight arrow bitches?"

"How'd you guess?"

"Just an intuition."

"What about you, Dinah?" Dinah could hear the beginnings of anxiety in her friend's voice. She looked down into the crevasse, saw humanity's cradle welded helplessly into place, imagined for a moment throwing the demolition charge down on it, like a vindictive goddess hurling a lightning bolt.

She was thinking of Markus. Of the kids she should have had with him. What would they have been like?

Markus had been kind of a jerk in some ways, but he knew how to control it.

Really—she now understood—what had prompted her to slam the table and get up and storm out of the Banana a few minutes ago had not been Aïda at all. Aïda was provocative, yes. But more infuriating had been a slow burn that had started with Camila, and her remarks about aggression. Remarks that Dinah now saw as aimed not so much at Dinah as at Markus. She wished she could grab Camila by the scruff of the neck and sit her down in front of a display and make her watch the way Markus had spent the last minutes of his life.

Markus was a hero. It seemed to Dinah that Camila wanted to strip humanity of its heroes. She'd couched what she'd said in terms of aggression. But by doing so, Camila was just being aggressive in a different way—a passive-aggressive way that Dinah, raised as she'd been raised, couldn't help seeing as sneaky. More destructive, in the end, than the overt kind of aggression.

It was this that had made her so flustered that she'd had to leave the meeting.

"Dinah?" Ivy said.

"I'm going to breed a race of heroes," Dinah said. "Fuck Camila."

"It's going to be . . . interesting . . . sharing confined spaces with a race of heroes for hundreds of years."

"Markus knew how to do it," Dinah said. "He was a jerk, but he had a code. It's called chivalry."

She gave the demolition charge a toss straight up.

"Did you just vote yes?"

"Oh yeah," she said, watching it dwindle against the stars. The red lights of the LED timer glittered like rubies.

"We're unanimous," Ivy said. Dinah understood that Ivy was announcing it to the other women in the Banana.

For the first and last time, Dinah thought.

The red light had shrunk to a pinprick. Like the planet Mars, she thought, except sharper and more brilliant. Then, silently, it turned into a ball of yellow light that darkened as it spread.

Part Three

FIVE THOUSAND YEARS LATER

KATH TWO WAS STARTLED AWAKE BY PATCHES OF ORANGE-PINK light cavorting across the taut fabric above her. A very old instinct, born on the savannahs of Old Earth, read it as danger: the flitting shadows, perhaps, of predators circling her tent. During the five thousand years of the Hard Rain, that instinct had lain dormant and useless. Here on the surface of New Earth, just beginning to support animals big and smart enough to be dangerous, it was once again troubling her sleep. Her shoulder twitched, in the way that it did sometimes when you were half awake, and not sure whether you were really moving or dreaming of it. She had thought of reaching under her pillow for the weapon. But coming fully to, she found that her arm had not really moved, other than the twitch. Through the thin padding beneath her head she could still feel the hard shape of the katapult.

By then it had become obvious that the moving light on the tent had nothing to do with large predators. It was too dappled and volatile. Not even birds could move so. Its twinkling and swirling were mysterious, but its hue told her it was the first light of the day. This meant that she had slept a little too long and was in danger of missing the dawn breezes that she had hoped would bear her into the sky.

She stumbled out of her little tent, feeling yesterday's hike in the muscles of her legs. That was surprising. She thought she had trained well. But even in the largest space habitat, you couldn't go downhill for all that long. On an actual planet, you could go on losing altitude for days. And, as it turned out, those long downhill runs were what really killed your legs. Yesterday she had shed almost two thousand meters, descending from a range of hills toward a blue, water-filled crater thirty kilometers across. She had stopped a few clicks short of its rim, where the ground dropped away toward a swath of grassland between her and the shore. The break in the slope had been subtle, but Kath Two's throbbing knees had made it obvious enough. She had taken a dozen or so strides down it, gauging its angle in her blistered soles, sensing the air's currents with her lips, her hair, and the palms of her hands. Then she had turned around and trudged back up to an inflection point that would have been invisible had the low evening sun not been grazing it, casting a sharp terminator on the ground.

Where wind streamed over bent ground, it stretched. The stretching had been faint in the dying wind of yestereve, but she had known that it would become more pronounced in the morning, as the sun rose and the air fled from its warmth. So she had dropped her pack and made her camp.

The source of the dappled light, as she now saw, was sunlight sparkling from waves on the lake below, shooting rays through the branches of trees, perhaps a hundred meters down the slope from her, that were beginning to stir in the morning breeze, making soft noises, as when a sleeping lover exhales.

She bent down, pulled the katapult out from under the sack of laundry she'd been using as a pillow, felt it thrum as it recognized her fingerprint. After a short walk and a careful look around—for she did not actually wish to use the katapult—she squatted and urinated in the largest open space that was handy. Only in the last few decades had the ecosystem here matured to the point where TerReForm—her employer—could seed it with predators. And that was always somewhat hit-or-miss. On the mature ecosystems of Old Earth, predators and prey had, according to the histories, evolved to some kind of equilibrium. On the remade ones of New Earth, you never knew. You couldn't assume that all the predators around here were getting enough to eat; and even if they were, they might view Kath Two as a bit of tempting variety to add to their diet.

Kath Two was Survey. Whether or not this made her military was a topic of almost theological complexity. But regardless of whether you considered Survey to be a purely scientific corps with ad hoc liaisons to the military—merely for logistical convenience and situational awareness—or viewed it as an elite scout unit working hand-in-glove with Snake Eaters, its stated mission was to observe and report on the growth of New Earth's ecosystem. Not to kill the animals that the human races had gone to so much trouble to invent and import. During her two-week stint on the surface, she had grown used to the katapult and stopped seeing it as remarkable that she was carrying a weapon. But the awareness that she was going home today made her see all of this through the eyes of the sophisticated urbanites she might be mingling with tomorrow: habitat ring dwellers who would never believe that only a short time earlier Kath Two had been in a place where one did not pee without carefully looking around first, did not venture into the open without a weapon in hand.

During the minutes since she had awakened, the sparkling light had warmed to brassy gold. Everything in the scene was a combination of exceptionally complex and unpredictable phenomena: the wavelets on the lake, the shapes into which the branches of the trees had grown during the century or so since this ground had been seeded by pods hurtling down out of space, tumbling like dice on jumbled ejecta from the myriad bolide strikes of the Hard Rain, finding purchase in crevices prepped by rock-munching microbes. The branches and the leaves responded to the currents of the wind, which were themselves random and turbulent in a way that surpassed human calculation. She thought about the fact that the brains of humans—or of any large animals, really—had evolved to live in environments like this, and to be nourished by such complex stimuli. For five thousand years the people of the human races had been living without that kind of nourishment. They had tried to simulate it with computers. They had built habitats large enough to support lakes and forests. But nature simulated was not nature. She wondered if humans' brains had changed during that time, and if they were now ready for what they had set in motion on New Earth.

And then, because she was a Moiran, she wondered if all that had to do with the fact that she had overslept. Her previous Survey missions had been quick insertions lasting a few days. And they had typically sent her to less developed biomes: the fringes of the TerReForm process, where the seeding of the ground had occurred more recently, and less complexity struck the eye, nose, and ear. This mission, however, had lasted long enough that she could feel it changing her.

Eve Moira had been a child of London, fascinated by the natural world, but drawn to the city. So, Kath Two looked to the bright lights of the big city. Here that meant gazing up into the sky.

Yesterday had been overcast, with little movement in the air. She might have been hard-pressed to find and organize the energy she would need to get home. But matters had changed during the night. The air was moving. Not strongly enough, yet, that she could feel it on her face, but enough to stir the leaves at the tops of the trees and to wobble the heavy heads of the tall grass. Above, it must be moving more strongly, for yesterday's sheet of clouds had been shredded to tufts and tissues, purplish-gray on the bottom and pink-orange on their eastern faces. The sky between them, however, was perfectly clear, and still dark enough that she could see a few bright stars and planets. And, to the south—for she was in the northern hemisphere—an orderly ring of brilliant points erupting from the eastern horizon and arching across the vault of the sky until it plunged into the shadow of the world, off to the west. From here she could see nearly half of the ten thousand or so habitats in the ring. Far to the east, just above the horizon, was an especially big dot of light, like the clasp on a necklace. That would be the colossal structure of the Eye, currently stationed above the Atlantic.

It was time to go there.

She had pitched her little shelter on a flat lozenge of soft grass some distance back from the brow of the hill where the wind would soon be bending. She struck her camp, shouldered her pack one last time, and carried it a short distance to the break in the slope she had noticed yesterday. She popped the clasp on the hip belt and let it drop to the ground.

Unrolling the deflated wings and the tail structure was as easy as giving each a swift kick. Smaller bundles had been stuffed between them: a foot-operated pump and a hard sphere, somewhat larger than Kath Two's head.

She devoted a few minutes to stomping the pump. The wrinkles began to disappear from the splayed runs of fabric, and it began to look like a glider.

The sun had cleared the opposite rim of the crater. The tops of the wings began gathering its energy and feeding it to built-in air pumps that would pressurize the wing and tail tubes beyond what could be achieved with muscle power.

She got dressed. Which began with getting naked, and cold. She was glad she had worked up a sweat operating the pump.

The hard sphere was a glass bubble with an opening at the bottom large enough to admit Kath Two's head. At the moment, though, it was stuffed with a roll of gray fabric. She withdrew this and kicked it out on the ground. It was as long as she was tall. Rolled up in it had been a semirigid funnel with straps dangling from its edge. Stuffed into the funnel were two packets. One of the packets was tiny, just a pill that would stop up her bowels for a day. She swallowed it. The other was a heavy and distressingly cold sac of gel. Kath Two bit off one corner and then smeared the gel all over herself, wincing at its chilly touch. It was an emollient, rumored to be very complicated, and it had an official name. But everyone called it Space Grease. The stuff would never be sold as a cosmetic; it lay heavy on her skin, and she could practically feel her pores clogging.

The funnel-and-strap contraption was for collecting urine. She stepped into it, pulled it up over her pubic mound, and cinched the straps high over her pelvic crest. A short tube dangled from it, tickling her inner thigh.

She then picked up the gray fabric thing. This was a one-piece bodysuit whose only opening was at the neck. It was a mesh of nearly microscopic nats—simple three-legged robots that knew how to do very little other than hold hands with their neighbors. It would have been impossible to put on were it not for the fact that the nats, talking to each other in a simple language, could stretch and shrink those connections according to a shared program. She got both of her hands into the neck hole and pulled opposite ways. Recognizing the gesture, the nats relaxed, and the opening widened to the point where she could insert one foot, then the other. This required good balance, which Kath Two was fortunate enough to have. She was standing on a towel that she had spread out on the ground. The classic error was to lose one's balance and plant a foot in the dirt, or even fall down, and get covered with dirt and rocks and twigs that would stick to the Space Grease. But Kath Two got her feet into the suit without incident. Finding the leg holes, and then the individual toe holes, was, as usual, slapstick comedy. Once she got the suit pulled up over her buttocks she was able to sit down and manage this one digit at a time. Then she reached down inside the still-baggy thighs and connected the urine tube to a fitting on the inside of her right thigh. Recognizing as much, the fabric drew tight, nearly trapping her hands inside. The tightness moved up in a wave from toes to knees to thighs to buttocks, pausing once it had noticed her waist. She shrugged the suit's upper half on over her shoulders and got her fingers sorted into the gloves that terminated its arms. The suit, sensing what she was up to, grew tighter as she went, save at the neck.

From the helmet's orifice she detached a rigid collar with a hinge on one side and a latch on the other. She snapped it into place around her neck, then pulled the loose fabric of the suit up over it and held it in place as it shrank, forming a tight connection to the collar.

From the hard collar down to her toes, she was now clad in gray material that fit her so closely she could see tendons in the backs of her hands, nipples reacting to the early morning chill, and the little valleys where her nails erupted from their beds.

She hesitated to lower the helmet over her face. This would be her last opportunity for a while to breathe the fresh air of New Earth. The scientist in her was at odds with a deeper layer, common to all human races, that wanted to see beauty and purpose in the "natural" world. She knew perfectly well what Doc—or just about any other Ivyn—would say to her, if he could read her mind. The water in that lake below you is there because we crashed comet cores into the dead Earth until it stayed wet. The air you're breathing was manufactured by organisms we genetically engineered and sprayed all over the wet planet, then killed once they had accomplished their task. And the sharp scent you like so much comes from vegetation that, for many years, existed only as a string of binary digits stored on a thumb drive on a string around the neck of your Eve.

None of which changed the fact that she liked it. But the breeze was building, making the craft jostle and fidget. It was trimmed for minimum lift and unlikely to go anywhere, but a sudden gust might still carry it away.

Unnerved by a sudden movement, Kath Two reached out and

slapped the upper surface of the right wing, about an arm's length in from the tip.

Kath Two felt her own touch. A patch of skin on the back of her right forearm, a finger's length in from the wrist, thrilled as the suit's fabric contracted over it: a configuration of puckers no larger than a fingerprint. But shaped, unmistakably, like a miniature hand—Moira's hand. Her skin and that of the glider had become joined in a common sensorium, mediated by the smart fabric of the suit.

It never got old. She slid her hand out toward the tip of the wing and watched with a little grin as the hand-shaped disturbance in her suit moved out toward her wrist. She lifted her hand from the wing and the pucker vanished.

She dropped the helmet over her head and got it seated in the collar. Other than a padded brow band to support the weight of her head, and a sparse geodesic array of miniature speakers, the helmet was just a transparent bubble, mercifully free of heads-up displays and other clutter.

In the fuselage that joined the wings was a nest barely large enough to accommodate her. She straddled the nose, lifted one knee, and nestled it into a padded and insulated gutter that would support it and her shin. Then she followed suit with the other leg. She was kneeling in the cockpit now. Resting loose on the belly pad in front of her was a parachute folded up into a slim backpack. She picked this up, slung it over her back, and tightened the straps around her waist and thighs. She leaned forward and took her weight on her arms, then did a reverse push-up, settling onto her belly.

Then she made connections: the pee tube to a system that would drain it. Drinking water at her collar. She didn't yet need the tubes for incoming and outgoing atmosphere, but she connected them anyway, as well as a power cable.

Then she reached back behind her, all the way down to her ankles, and found the handle for the zipper. She had no idea why it was called that. It was a linear closure, consisting of more dumb, specialized nats, that sealed her body inside the fuselage, snug under many layers of crinkly insulation. As she pulled it up she felt the glider's flexible top clamp around her buttocks and cleave together up the length of her spine until it had closed around the collar of her suit. Only her head-bubble was now exposed. It had become the glider's nose cone.

She extended her arms then to the sides like a bird spreading its wings, sliding them into insulated tunnels where they rested comfortably on inflated supports. For a moment she thought that some little stones had somehow made their way onboard and gotten trapped under her arms. Then one of them shifted a little, and she realized that this was the suit again, sensing the pressure of a rock on the underside of the wing and mirroring it.

The insulation also helped to deaden sound, and so she could now hear almost nothing from outside.

Which didn't mean she couldn't hear anything. She could hear the wind. A phrase that didn't really do justice to the soundscape now being rendered by the array of miniature speakers. "The canid smelled the forest" was a completely different sentence from "The man smelled the forest," not because the words had different meanings, but because the canid's olfactory apparatus was infinitely superior to that of the man. In a loosely analogous way, the real-time, three-dimensional sonic portrait of the wind generated by the glider's onboard systems and rendered by the helmet's speakers was as far beyond what she could sense with unaided ears as the canid's scenting of the forest was beyond the man's. For the vehicle had lidars pointed in all directions, looking out into the air to a range of several hundred meters and seeing its myriad currents, shears, and vortices. To convey all of that information in sound was impossible, but what came through was more than enough to tell Kath Two where she wanted to go: namely, where the energy was. And right now the symphony of tones, whooshes, crackles, and rustlings told her that her intuition yestereve had been more or less correct. The wind climbed the slope from the lake in a fairly continuous sheet, but as it molded itself over the brow of the hill, the wind higher up, on the outside track, had to go faster in order to keep up with the ground layer. There was a gradient in speed between the wind aloft and that at the ground. She could use it.

Her eyes were busy too, tracking a pair of birds flying parallel to the slope, dipping in and out of the shear in the wind, sipping power. Far above them, the clouds were telling her a story about the conditions she'd be facing in a few minutes' time, but this was no concern of hers now.

The wind gusted. The feeling of pressure beneath her arms increased and at the same time she felt the entire craft rising. She moved her feet and her hands in a way that the suit recognized and transmitted to the glider's control surfaces. Just that quickly, it was configured for lift. Biting suddenly into the wind coming up the hill, the craft sprang into the air; she could feel the knots of pressure vanish as the ground lost contact with the wings. Then the only sensations on the skin of her arms were caused by the wings reading the currents of air flowing over them. She let herself rise high enough to buy some margin of error, then dropped the nose and glided down the hill, trading altitude for velocity. The game she'd be playing for the rest of the day was to build up a fund of energy by stealing it from the atmosphere. At the end she would trade it all for altitude, and spiral up to a place where the atmosphere failed.

Closer to the shore of the lake, the meadow gave way to trees. This was one of the more mature forests on New Earth. It had been seeded only a few years after the First Treaty, about a hundred years ago. She pulled the nose up, skimmed over the highest branches, then dropped again until she was gliding over the blue water of the lake: the melted core of a comet, still coming alive with seeded algae and fish. With a voice command she caused the glider to drop a tube, no thicker than her finger, into the water skimming by a few meters below. On her first pass across the lake's diameter she collected twenty kilograms of water, which slowed the glider down somewhat. She found a thermal on the other side and rode it up a few hundred meters before rolling over and diving down for another, faster pass over the lake, and another long drink of water. This part of the journey was the most ticklish, so it was good that it came first, when she was still fresh. A glider that was light enough to carry around on her back was, by the same token, too light to store very much kinetic energy. Its lack of momentum placed limits on the maneuvers Kath Two could perform in the higher atmosphere; small twitches in the flow of air would bat it around like a feather. It needed to get a lot heavier. The way to do that was to scoop water out of a lake, as she was doing now. But it all happened at low altitude and low speed, where the margin for error was slender. The first few passes, when the glider weighed practically nothing, were the most delicate. So she took her time at each side of the lake to find good thermals and harvest their force. After an hour of that, however, she was dive-bombing her way across the crater with terrific authority, carrying hundreds of kilograms of ballast in the belly and the wings. By then she had learned where to hunt for thermals that, as the morning wore on, bloomed with increasing vigor from the open meadows in the shoulders of the great crater.

It was on her last pass, just as she was getting ready to pull up and skim over the tops of the trees that grew from the onrushing shore, that she saw the human.

The human was not exposed on the shore, but standing back among the first line of trees, apparently watching her. He or she—the distance was too great to read gender—was dressed in clothing that blended in with the surroundings. Not the bright coveralls of Survey. But neither did it look military. Perhaps sensing that he or she had been spotted, the human immediately stepped back into the young forest. At the same moment, Kath Two was obliged to pull her nose up, lest she collide with the trees. So great had been her surprise that she almost did it too late, and felt a few thin branches whipping against the belly of the fuselage as she put the lake behind her for good.

Directly ahead was a broad meadow, angled toward the sun, that she knew to be an excellent source of power. As she drew close enough for the lidars to read the air, and for her eyes to pick out the movements of the birds, she banked into the thermal. Her first approach was a crude guess based on what she was hearing, but as soon as she got into it and felt the fine-grained currents of the air in her arms and her fingertips, she was able to use it as birds did.

Half an hour's climbing left the lake a blue disk far below and put her in sight of open country to the southeast, dotted with mushroom-cap clouds that were a dead giveaway. Trading altitude for distance, she glided in a nearly straight line until she could pick up those thermals and recharge her store of energy. She had her eye on a range of mountains several hundred kilometers distant, rising up above the eastern shore of the Pacific Ocean. Above them, clouds were arranged in long folds, running parallel to the crest of the range.

The photocells in the wings had stored up enough power now that she was able to send a burst of data up into space. Packets coming back a few seconds later told her when and where she could expect hangers along her projected route. It was too early to lock in on a specific plan, but useful to get a general picture. And it was good practice to let people know where she was and when to expect her.

It looked like about twenty other surveyors were operating in the same general zone. She considered the number astonishingly high, and double-checked it. While she was waiting for confirmation to come back, she scanned the skies around her and spotted two of them.

After some thought, she sent a voice message to Doc. "I want to talk to you when I get back. Not urgent. But important."

Then she put such distractions out of her mind and attended to the problem at hand, which was stringing together enough thermals to get her into the mountain wave that awaited her downrange. Once she had stored enough energy in her glider—mostly in the form of altitude—the thermal-riding part of it became nearly automatic and she was able to doze off for stretches of twenty minutes at a time.

In truth, there was no aspect of this flight that could not have been managed by a robot. Robot gliders were at this moment operating all over New Earth. But she was leery of letting her own powers dwindle by delegating them to machines, and so she liked to fly the glider at least part of the time. The algorithms worked, but they wouldn't get better unless humans gardened them; and to do that, you had to fly.

A surge of acceleration awakened her from an early afternoon nap and she looked down to see the snow-covered peaks of the mountains a thousand meters below her. She had found the mountain wave, a source of sustained atmospheric power that dwarfed anything that could be obtained from thermals. It was a ridge of rising air running from north to south. If she turned north from here, she could probably ride it all the way to the polar vortex, and take that up to where the atmosphere failed. But she had farther to go than wings could take her, so she banked south and trimmed the glider to slip sideways along the wave, skimming enough power from it to gain altitude even while screaming southward at three hundred kilometers an hour. She was a fly hitching a ride on a hurricane.

Knots in the tapestry of sound told her of other solid objects above and below, left and right. She was able to pick them out visually as the setting sun lit up their fuselages and wingtips against the deep purple of the sky.

Higher yet—unfathomably far above, and yet only in "low" Earth orbit—were larger structures, moving more slowly, like the minute hands of great clocks. Linear constellations with fatter, brighter lights on their ends. One of them was sweeping across the sky directly south of her, and she knew she was already too late to catch it. But looking off to the west she saw another approaching, like a giant leg striding across the sky, its foot swinging downward, not yet planted. She didn't even need to check the params to know that this was the hanger for her. But she ran the calculation anyway, partly to confirm her guess and partly as a courtesy to other aircraft in this crowded space that might be aiming for the same one.

Darkness fell before she reached it. The hanger—it was a pun on "hangar," a term from Old Earth aviation—was a big hollow pod hanging on the end of a tether that, just now, extended far up into space. At its opposite end, thousands of kilometers above, was another hanger just like it, serving as a counterweight. The two hangers formed a bolo, rotating around each other to keep the tether stretched tight between them. The bolo orbited the Earth just like any other satellite, the difference being that the height of that orbit, and the length of the tether, had been tuned so that on every rotation—or, as it appeared from Kath Two's point of view, each long stride across the heavens—the hanger on the low end would swing down into the uppermost reaches of the atmosphere and seem to hover, almost still, for a minute. Somewhat analogous to the way that a runner's foot will remain planted on the ground, unmoving, for an instant during each stride, even though the runner is traveling swiftly. In any case it came low enough and went slowly enough that a glider, pumped to great velocity and brought high into the atmosphere by the power of the mountain wave, could catch it and match it.

Kath Two's eyes and ears told her of other vehicles converging on the same target. A few minutes prior to rendezvous, it became obligatory to hand control of the craft over to a version of the ancient program Parambulator, which managed the final approach. Kath Two could have stuck the landing without assistance, had she been alone. But coordinating her approach with the other vehicles was the sort of task best left up to a five-thousand-year-old algorithm.

At the time she ceded control, the hanger still seemed impossibly far away, but over the next few minutes it loomed out of the sky like a slow-motion meteorite, studded with red running lights. It was shaped like a rugby ball, streamlined fore and aft, with stubby winglets that were finding traction in the thin air, adjusting their angles of attack to stabilize its flight. Kath Two and the other aircraft were converging on it from behind, overtaking it rapidly as it slowed almost to a stop.

Most of the hanger's aft end was a broad aperture that now irised open to reveal a spacious deck, brightly illuminated, like a magic doorway hanging in the sky. In front of her she could see the lights of other vehicles sidling into the queue ahead of her.

The hanger's bright orifice grew huge, like a chilly sun falling out of the sky. One by one the vehicles slipped into its lee and bounced and skidded to a stop on its deck. From a distance this appeared level. In fact it was angled slightly upward, so that the aircraft climbed a gentle ramp as they rolled into it. This helped them kill their excess velocity. Her glider bounced twice before the ramp took its weight. Then gravity—real and simulated—came down like a fat hand on her back, and she felt a rush of blood to the head as the glider slowed sharply.

Visually, she was at rest now. In truth, she was contained in a revolving object: one extremity of a bolo four thousand kilometers long. Even though its revolution, seen from a distance, had looked ponderous, the bolo as a whole was wheeling fast enough to produce two gees of simulated gravity. That plus the one gee of real gravity she was feeling from New Earth added up to a massive amount of down force pressing her into the water-filled ballast sacs that made up the glider's belly.

A human-sized grabb, untroubled by the weight, dragged her glider off to the side, making way for other aircraft coming in for a landing behind. All told, the hanger collected eight aircraft during this pass. Besides Kath Two's, two others were piloted by humans. Each was of a different design; both were powered. The other five were robot gliders, looking similar to Kath Two's, but solid rather than inflatable. As soon as the last of these was stowed, the hanger's tailgate constricted and closed behind them. Its stride complete, the hanger was already swinging back, gaining altitude "heel" first, rising back up toward space.

It was much too large a volume to be pressurized. What little air it had scooped up during its dip into the atmosphere rapidly leaked out. So Kath Two was effectively in outer space now. Knowing this, the fabric of the suit had contracted against her skin to supply the back pressure that was no longer provided by the atmosphere. It was porous, and so the only thing really between her skin and the void was Space Grease. The combined effects of that and the nat mesh fooled her skin and muscles into believing that they were under a nice thick blanket of air—the way humans were meant to live. The only part of the outfit that was pressurized like an old-fashioned space suit was the helmet.

Dangling above the middle of the hanger's landing deck were four flivvers of various sizes and designs—the latest iterations of a vehicle type that had been in existence since before the onset of the Hard Rain. During the series of landings just completed, these had been kept up and out of the way. As soon as the door of the hanger closed, one of them—a medium-sized, four-passenger model—was lowered to the ramp by winches. It came to rest about ten meters away. Incongruously for a space vehicle, it seemed to have wheels. It was, in fact, resting on a low, wheeled sled that was designed to roll up and down the ramp.

Green lights beside the flivver's airlock door told her that all was well on the other side. Kath Two had about ten minutes to reach it. That would be plenty of time if she didn't pass out. She issued a command that allowed the glider's body to deflate. She felt rather than heard the air escaping and the water draining. The soft top of the fuselage parted over her shoulders, back, butt, and thighs. Meanwhile she was wriggling her arms in from the insulated sleeves where they had been spread like a pair of wings. This was good exercise, given that they weighed three times as much as normal.

By the time that was all done, the glider was just a wrinkled cross of fabric, flat on the deck. Kath Two disconnected herself from its air scrubber and its urine collection system, then unplugged the power and data from her collar. She gathered her arms under her and began to belly-crawl toward the flivver, sliding one knee, then the other forward along the deck plates, like a lizard. A big siwi corkscrewed out and kept pace with her, tracking her vital signs, ready to supply extra air or other forms of assistance if needed. But Kath Two made adequate progress. She probably could have crawled on hands and knees, as one of the other human pilots was doing, but she saw no need.

Something strange caught her eye, and she went to the effort of rotating her head slightly just to verify it was real: the third pilot was actually walking upright. He was trudging along with short deliberate strides, carefully judging his balance and the loads he was placing on his joints, while somehow managing to keep enough blood in his brain to remain conscious.

Kath Two could never have stood up, let alone walked, under three gees. The same was true of most of her race. This man, however, was a Teklan. That was obvious from his size, as well as his coloration and the shape of his head, which were visible through his helmet. It was hinted at by his musculature and by the style of the suit he was wearing—heavier, partly armored, slung about with load-bearing straps made to support various burdens. His scabbards, holsters, and bandoliers were vacant. Even without any of those clues, however, she could have guessed his race from the fact that he had chosen to perform the feat of walking when he could have more safely and more easily crawled.

Had it not been for the racial bond that joined Moirans and Teklans, Kath Two might have rolled her eyes and muttered a joke about it. Teklans didn't need blood in their brains to keep dutifully trudging forward. Something along those lines. But that kind of stereotyping could just as well have been turned back on her. The Teklan had piloted his vehicle into the hanger under power. The thing had engines. Why *not* use engines if you belonged to a civilization that knew how to make them? Kath Two, on the other hand, had reached the same destination in an unpowered glider, using skill and wit to draw energy from the atmosphere. She could have turned pilot's duties over to an algorithm anytime she wanted. Instead, she had chosen to do most of it herself. In its own way, this was no less an act of pointless bravado than what the Teklan pilot was doing right now. She had been testing and sharpening a set of skills that was important to her. Mutatis mutandis, this Teklan was doing the same.

Kath Two got to the airlock with time to spare. Its floor was padded as a courtesy to people who, like her, were experiencing it through all the body's boniest parts. She rolled heavily onto her back, slightly bumping the pilot who had reached it on hands and knees, and connected her air tube to a socket on the airlock wall. New air flooded her helmet. The Teklan entered and allowed himself to collapse onto a bench. The outer hatch closed and locked. The air pressure rose and the nat mesh reduced its fierce clutch on her body. It became no tighter than an athletic jersey as the pressure approached one standard habitat atmosphere—a thinnish concoction of gases similar to what humans of Old Earth had breathed in places like Aspen, Colorado.

The inner hatch opened. Crawling now on hands and knees, Kath Two followed the others into the main cabin, where four acceleration couches were waiting. They climbed into three of them, strapped in, and made themselves comfortable. They were now lying on their backs, legs elevated. At some point their suits' systems had found their way onto the flivver's voice network—she knew as much from the fact that she could hear the other two breathing as heavily as she was. But no one said anything. Talking would become a lot easier in a few minutes. True to form, the Teklan, with a controlled exhalation, heaved his meaty arms up off the rests, grabbed his helmet, and pulled it off. He let its weight rest on his stomach and allowed his arms to thud back onto the couch. Kath Two got a vague peripheral glimpse of platinum hair and cheekbones, as expected, but didn't feel like turning her head. Instead she looked at a display screen mounted above her face, focusing as well as she could with her eyeballs flattened into their sockets by gees.

They had entered the hanger in level flight, traveling at a hundred kilometers per hour. In the minutes since then, the centripetal force that had obliged her to crawl on the floor like a lizard had been accelerating them upward and forward, steadily pumping kinetic energy into them and everything around them, whirling them up to the immense velocities more typical of space travel. Compared to the baroque, fire-breathing systems that their ancestors had used to the same purpose, there was nothing to it. The bolo was mechanically identical to the sling used by David to slay Goliath. The flivver was the stone nestled in its pocket.

The bolo had made about a quarter of a revolution, so they were now traveling directly away from the surface of the Earth—aimed toward the distant ring of habitats that they and the three billion other members of the human races called home.

Seen on a video window in the display above, the hanger's tailgate dilated, showing a disk of black sky. A tattoo of metallic clunks let them know that the brakes on the sled had been released. Driven down the ramp by centripetal force, it built speed all the way to the lip of the hanger deck and then stopped short with a sneeze from its shock absorbers. The flivver jerked free of the sled. From its occupants' point of view, it seemed to fall off the edge of the deck and into space. En route it picked up a bit of a tumble, which was killed by quick firings of its thrusters.

They became weightless. Kath Two took her helmet off but kept her head nestled in the couch's rest for a minute while her inner ear adjusted. Meanwhile she was groping in a compartment in her armrest for a varp, which was what people normally used in place of flat-panel display screens when they wanted to interact with some kind of app. It was an old enough word that most people had forgotten it was an acronym for something like Vision Augmentation Retro-Projector. Styles varied, but the baseline model looked like a heavy-framed pair of glasses. Mounted in that frame were cameras that could see the way her hands were moving, a microphone that could hear her speech, and other cameras that could track her gaze. A number of glowing figments appeared in her peripheral vision as she slipped them on, and she was able to reach out and activate one of them to launch Parambulator. This gave her a schema of the flivver's situation in the universe: in the center, a blue disk representing New Earth, under a gray film of atmosphere. Well outside of that, the orbital track of the bolo's center, the twin trajectories of its two hangers snaking around it. This was what they had just left behind. A blinking green dot showed their current location on their new orbit, a fat ellipse whose apogee coincided with the circle of habitats that hung above the planet at geosynchronous altitude. Over the next twelve hours they would coast up to that height, then strap back into the couches and use other means to effect a delta vee that would sync them up with whichever habitat they decided upon.

The world in which essentially all three billion humans lived, as depicted from "above" (high over the North Pole, looking "down" on the whole system) was a hair-thin ring some eighty-four thousand kilometers across—roughly seven times the diameter of the blue-and-white planet in its center. The objects that made up the ring, though they seemed big to the humans who lived in them, were evanescent particles compared to the ring's overall scale. Imagine the thinnest possible jewelry chain, a nearly invisible trace of platinum around a woman's neck. Make a perfect circle of that same chain ten meters in diameter, and that gives a picture of the ring's thinness in comparison to its overall size. It was more easily viewed in artificial renderings like the one on Kath Two's varp, where the points that made up the ring—the individual habitats—were drawn as unrealistically large, color-coded pips.

Seen that way, the circle was chopped into eight arcs of roughly equal size, each subtending about forty-five degrees. At long zoom, these were glinting and luminously iridescent, with much shorter gray arcs—the boneyards, they were called—sticking them together.

At a closer zoom, the pointillistic nature of the image became obvious, and the system began helpfully to superimpose labels and numbered meridians. There were more than nine thousand active habitats distributed among those eight segments. The boneyards contained another several hundred—mostly obsolete ones being cut up for scrap—as well as unused fragments of the moon and the odd captured asteroid, there to serve as raw material for new construction.

Any object that was not inhabited—because it wasn't finished yet, because it was abandoned, or because it was just a rock—was rendered as a gray dot. This accounted for the dull appearance of the eight boneyards.

Sparkling with pure colors were the eight much longer arcs between them. Seen from a distance, each arc had a predominant color. Encoded in those colors was the history of their building, and in turn that of the human races during the last thousand years—the Fifth Millennium, the Millennium of the Ring. Prior to that—during the first four thousand years of the Hard Rain—space had been so dirty that the human races had been obliged to hunker down in the shelter of massive nickel-iron bodies such as Cleft, whose orbits were, of course, similar to that of the moon whose core had once comprised them—nine times farther away from Earth than the habitat ring was now. As Dubois Harris had foreseen, the orbit of the former moon had been a fine place—the only place, really—to restart a civilization, as long as hellfire was raining down on Earth. But to the extent that the human race, as a whole, was capable of having a plan, it was to return to Earth eventually. The Hard Rain diminished, gradually at first, and then, during the Fourth Millennium, more steeply as fleets of robots, issuing from their nickel-iron fastnesses like bats from caverns, began to sweep the skies clean, policing the rubble cloud, herding specks and pebbles together, and spiraling them down into disciplined orbits at geosynchronous altitude. Most of the work was accomplished using the pressure of sunlight, a weak form of propulsion that took hundreds of years to have its effect.

At the dawn of the Fifth Millennium, about a thousand years ago, the first new habitat in geosynchronous orbit had been constructed. It was called Greenwich because it was positioned above Old Earth's prime meridian. In the way of neighbors, it at first had nothing but rubble and worn-out robots. As soon as Greenwich was complete, however, construction of more habitats had spread outward from it. The human races and their robots had begun burning their way through the ring of raw material in both directions, consuming it like fire on a fuse.

Greenwich had been a joint project of all seven human races. The same was true of its first neighbors: Volta, then Banu Qasim to the east, Atlas and Roland to the west, later more in both directions. All of these were, therefore, colored white in the display that Kath Two was seeing in her varp.

Greenwich was one of eight equidistant points plotted around the ring. The other seven, proceeding west, acquired the names Rio, Memphis, Pitcairn, Tokomaru, Kyoto, Dhaka, and Baghdad. In due course, each of them was seeded with a new habitat as well as the production capabilities needed to manufacture more yet. As the centuries went by, their inhabitants likewise burned their way through the raw materials lying to their western and eastern sides, building new habitats at a pace to match the growth of their populations.

It was self-evident that if that process went on long enough, the arc of habitats reaching west from, say, Greenwich would make contact with that growing east from Rio. The increasingly narrow bands of unused material and recyclable junk between segments became the boneyards, and might have disappeared altogether had they not been so useful—in the early going, as materials depots, later as political buffers and as liminal zones, akin to frontiers, to which people could escape when they had learned that the close-packed life of space habitats was not for them. The one halfway between Greenwich and Rio was called Cape Verde. Other boneyards, proceeding westward from Cape Verde, were Titicaca, Grand Canyon, Hawaii, Kamchatka, Guangzhou, and Indus. Completing the circle, the one between Baghdad and Greenwich was called Balkans. Some were bigger than others. Guangzhou, which formerly had separated the Aïdan and Camite segments, had been used up entirely as the populations to either side had grown.

When pronouncing her Curse, Eve Aïda had said much that was true. It had become clear within the first few generations after the Council of the Seven Eves that the seven races were going to be around forever. They were as permanent in the human picture as toenails and spleens. Though no official policy had ever been proclaimed to that effect, they had tended to vote with their feet. Rio had become predominantly Ivyn. Moirans had flocked to Memphis, and Teklans to the next one around the arc in that direction, which was Pitcairn.

Baghdad, flanking Greenwich on the other side, had been settled by Dinans. Proceeding east from Baghdad, Dhaka had filled up with Camites. Aïdans and Julians had found a way of expressing their perpetual sense of alienation from the other races by opting for the Antipodean habitats of Kyoto and Tokomaru respectively; closing the ring, this brought the Julians, on their eastern end, up against the Teklans' western extremity, separated only by the Hawaii boneyard, which was relatively large, if only because the Julian race was not numerous enough to make much headway in using its resources.

The levels of racial purity varied. Greenwich had been founded by all of them together, and so it would forever be the most diverse part of the ring. Baghdad and Rio, flanking it, also tended to have a lot of residents who were not, respectively, Dinans or Ivyns. That three-segment arc was, therefore, fairly cosmopolitan. The other races, in general, tended to be more inward looking, so their segments were not as thoroughly mixed. Anomalous outposts speckled the ring: a habitat containing fifty thousand Julians located spang in the middle of the Dinan segment, for example.

Eve Moira had employed a color-coding scheme to keep track of the lab samples from which all the races had spawned. It was purely the result of what she'd had lying around in the way of office supplies: an assortment of colored test-tube stickers and felt-tipped pens. Nevertheless, it had become a universal convention.

Blue: Dinah
Yellow: Camila
Red: Aïda
Orange: Julia
Cyan: Tekla
Purple: Moira herself
Green: Ivy
White: no particular race

The same code was used to render the dots that made up the ring. So, a predominantly Dinan habitat would be colored blue, and so on. Because they were so tiny and so numerous, the dots all merged into an iridescent, sparkling arc on the screen. But general trends could be seen. Whether or not it had been a deliberate choice on Eve Moira's part, colors in the cool part of the palette—blue, green, purple, cyan—were linked to the four Eves she was personally closest to, while warm colors—red, yellow, orange—were saved for the others.

When the entire ring was plotted according to this scheme, and the plot was viewed as a whole, with Greenwich at twelve o'clock and Tokomaru at six, one therefore saw a great arc of cool colors starting at about ten o'clock (the western end of the Indus boneyard) and sweeping around to about five o'clock (the eastern end of the Hawaii boneyard). A shorter arc of warm colors ran from a little before six o'clock to a little after nine. The ring's "top"-most segment, centered on Greenwich, was frosty white, like a polar icecap flanked by purple mountains, green hills, and blue water. But on its bottom left side, the ring looked as if it were being heated by a blowtorch, glowing in the warm tones that spoke of predominantly Camite, Aïdan, and Julian populations.

That segment was marked off, on the plot, by two red lines drawn athwart the ring. One was located at the longitude of 166 degrees, 30 minutes west, above the former Pacific island of Kiribati. This placed it near the eastern end of the Julian segment. The other was at precisely 90 degrees east, running through the habitat called Dhaka, in the exact center of the Camites' arc. The lines were borders: not just imaginary frontiers but literal barriers that had been constructed, like turnpikes, across the ring. The warm-colored arc of habitats stretching between them, incorporating most of the Julian segment, all of the Aïdan segment, and exactly half of the Camite segment, was, to Kath Two and the others aboard this flivver, another country. The relationship between it and the larger, cool-colored segment where they lived could be described in many possible ways, of which the most succinct was war.

THE TEKLAN, SEEING THAT KATH TWO HAD LIFTED HER HEAD FROM the rest and thereby joined the temporary society of the flivver, turned toward her. He stuck his right elbow out to the side, made a blade of his hand, palm down, and snapped it in until his thumbnail was touching the point of his chin, then, after a moment's pause, elevated it to the level of his forehead. "Beled Tomov," he said. But Kath Two had already known this, since it was stenciled on the outside of his suit.

Kath Two made a similar gesture, though in the style of her race she used her left hand and kept the palm toward her, fingers curled into a loose fist. "Kath Amalthova, Two."

Both of them looked toward the Dinan. During the previous moments he had kept his gaze averted in a way that, as everyone understood, meant that he had been taking a leak into his suit's urine collection system and wanted privacy. But now he looked up and performed the gesture, also left-armed, with a slight variation in the attitude of the hand, beginning with his palm toward him but flipping it over to face outward as he brought it to his forehead. "Rhys Alaskov."

This style of greeting was a throwback to the early days of the Cloud Ark and the first generations spawned on Cleft by the Seven Eves. People then had spent a lot of time in space suits equipped with outer visors that could be flipped up or down to compensate for sunlight. When the visor was pulled down, it concealed the wearer's face behind a reflective metallized screen. When it was pushed up, the face could be seen. In the crowded environments of those days, the upward movement of the hand had become a signal meaning "Hello, I am available for social interaction," and its reverse had come to mean "Goodbye" or "I wish for privacy now." These gestures' practical necessity had withered away as the human races had spread out into habitats where they could get privacy whenever they desired it. They lived on, however, as salutes. Beled Tomov had opted for a military style, using the right hand, the subtext being "I am not going to kill you with a concealed weapon." In gravity, the next move might then have been to reach out for a handshake. In zero gee this usually wasn't practical and so was rarely done. The left-handed version suggested a nonmilitary vocation, implying that the saluter's right hand was busy doing something useful. The variations in hand position were racial and their origins were the subject of folkloric research. All agreed, however, that they were useful for signaling one's race when far away, or when obscured in a space suit. The cues in size, shape, posture, and bearing that distinguished the races could be subtle, particularly when it was not possible to see facial features and hair color. Rhys Alaskov had the honey hair and freckled skin typical of a Dinan. Teklans too were fair. But where Rhys had an open, appealing face and an engaging manner, Beled was all cheek- and jawbones, sleek and bony at the same time, eyes so blue they were nearly white, hair like fiber-optic glass, cropped close to his skull. His affect matched his look. Kath Two was dark brown, with green eyes and woolly black hair. Close, in other words, to the way Eve Moira had looked. Among the three in this flivver, the largest contrast was therefore between her and Beled. And yet five thousand years of acculturation shaped the way they would interact. If some crisis were to arise, Kath Two and Beled would likely find themselves back to back, each instinctively seeking qualities wanted in the other. And in the absence of a crisis, they might find themselves front to front. A similar complementary relationship obtained between Dinans and Ivyns, but as it happened Rhys Alaskov was without an opposite number at the moment—that empty fourth couch.

All of which, and more, was just subtext, passed over in a fraction of a second. Rhys pushed off gently and floated toward the nest of displays that served as the flivver's control panel. The same functions, of course, might have been served within his varp, but it was considered desirable to make the ship's status clearly visible to everyone in the cabin, and so that kind of information tended to be splashed up on large screens.

Rhys was going to establish contact with whatever habitat was at their apogee, chat up whoever was "answering the phone" on the other end, and smooth the way in general. While he was floating slowly across the cabin, he said, "I trust you both had good surveys?"

"Nominal," Beled announced.

Kath Two was about to make a remark in the same vein when she remembered the Indigen, or whoever it was, watching her glider from the shelter of the trees by the lake. The impression had been so fleeting. Had she imagined it? She was certain she hadn't. But memory could play funny tricks.

"Mine was fascinating," Rhys said, when Kath Two failed to take the bait for a while.

"Any irregularities?" asked Beled, just as Kath Two was saying, "What was so interesting?"

Sensing Beled's gaze on her, Kath Two turned his way and understood that his question had been aimed as much at her as at Rhys.

It was in Rhys's nature as a Dinan, however, to assume that the question was all for him. His eyes flicked between Kath Two and Beled. Knowing he was the odd man out here, he responded with a grin that was, of course, charming. "I think I can answer both questions at once." He had reached the chair centered in the cockpit. "The canids are going epi in a huge way. They've become nearly unrecognizable." He brought the controls to life with a few sweeps of his fingers, and the screens lit up all around him.

A canid was a thing like a dog, wolf, or coyote. Rather than trying to bring back individual species, Doc—Dr. Hu Noah—had drawn inspiration from research that had emerged in Old Earth scientific journals shortly before Zero, suggesting that the boundaries among those commonly recognized species were so muddy as to be meaningless. They all could and did mate with each other and produce hybrid offspring. For various reasons these tended to group by size and shape in a way that human observers saw as being distinct species. But when humans weren't looking, or when the environment shifted, all manner of coy-dogs and coy-wolves and wolf-dogs appeared. Coyotes began hunting in packs like wolves, or wolves went solo like coyotes. Creatures that had avoided, or eaten, humans struck up partnerships with them; family pets went feral.

Hu Noah was 120 years old. As a young man he had been one of many scientists who had rebelled against a tradition of TerReForm thought that had passed as gospel for hundreds of years previously.

Thanks in part to the young Turks' propagandizing, this older approach had become hidebound and stereotyped as the TOT, or Take Our Time, school. The premise of TOT was that ecosystems—which on Old Earth had evolved over hundreds of millions of years—would have to be rebuilt slowly, through a sort of handcrafting process. Which was fine, since living in habitats was safer and more comfortable anyway than the unpredictable surface of a planet. The human races could enjoy thousands of years of safe, secure habitat life while slowly re-creating ecosystems down below that would resemble those of Old Earth. The planet would become a sort of ecological preserve. Africa, whose outlines were still vaguely recognizable, though heavily reshaped by the Hard Rain, would have giraffes and lions sequenced from the ones and zeroes dating all the way back to the thumb drive around Eve Moira's neck. Likewise with the other battered and reforged continents.

Doc was the last surviving member of the young Turk faction that had named, then rubbished, "the TOT lot." They were called the GID, or Get It Done, school. Their leader had been Leuk Markov, who himself had been over a hundred years old when he had become Doc's teacher. Obviously from his name (which was taken from the surname of Eve Dinah's boyfriend Markus), Leuk had been a Dinan, but Doc and most of his followers were Ivyns, which gave them an air of seriousness and credibility that had proved useful in pressing their agenda. They had formed a partnership with mostly Moiran philosophers who had begun questioning the TOT lot's premises, pointing out that re-creating simulacra of Old Earth biomes, in addition to taking an unreasonably long time, reflected a basically sentimental way of thinking about nature. It was an expression of a sort of post-traumatic stress disorder that the human races had carried on their backs ever since the Hard Rain. It was time to discard that. The old ecosystems would never return. Even if it were possible to bring them back, it would take so long as to not be worth it. In any event—and this was the nail in the coffin, supplied personally by Doc—it would fail anyway because the forces of natural selection were unpredictable and uncontrollable.

The most powerful weapon in the GID school's arsenal, however, was not philosophy. It was impatience, a failing shared to a greater or lesser degree by all the races. Second only to that was competitiveness, a quality absent in Camites but present in the other six. Anyone so motivated would of course want to Get It Done, to make the TerReForm happen in centuries rather than millennia.

Their rise to power had, however, produced political consequences they had never imagined by giving the races something to compete for—namely, territory on the surface of New Earth.

In the early 4820s, Leuk Markov had published papers speculating that the surface of New Earth could be made ready for permanent human habitations as early as 5050. While that was startlingly soon by the standards of the Take Our Time school, it had seemed far in the future to the average person, and so the council of scientists responsible for planning the TerReForm had seen no problem with enshrining it in the schedule, and later even moving it up to 5005—the anniversary of the landing on Cleft. But the shift in thinking had unleashed long-pent-up political forces that had led to the formation of what amounted to two different countries in the year 4830. The Aïdans, who dominated one of them, bringing many Camites and Julians under their sway, had built the turnpikes at Kiribati and Dhaka in 4855, cleaving the ring. They eventually came up with a formal name for their country, obliging the rest of the ring to come up with a name for theirs, but everyone simply called them Red and Blue.

TerReForm had continued anyway, through ad hoc cooperation between scientists and labs straddling the Red/Blue borders. Twenty-three years later, however—practically as soon as New Earth's atmosphere had become breathable without artificial aids—had begun the War on the Rocks, a struggle carried out partly in space but mostly on the still-nude surface of New Earth. This had been terminated in

4895 by what was now called First Treaty, which stipulated among other things how subsequent TerReForm activity was going to proceed. It had thus paved the way for the Great Seeding, which was responsible for the trees that Kath Two had been flying over this morning. In subsequent decades, larger and larger animals had been set loose on the surface as part of a planned program to jump-start whole ecosystems.

Some of those—the ones Kath Two had been worried about this morning—were canids. When Rhys said that they were "going epi," he meant that they were passing through some kind of epigenetic shift.

If the Agent had blown up the moon a couple of decades earlier, Eve Moira wouldn't have known about epigenetics. It was still a new science at the time she was sent up to the Cloud Ark. During her first years in space, when she and her equipment had been coddled in the most protected zones of Izzy and *Endurance,* she'd had plenty of time to bone up on the topic. Like most children of her era, she'd been taught to believe that the genome—the sequence of base pairs expressed in the chromosomes in every nucleus of the body—said everything there was to say about the genetic destiny of an organism. A small minority of those DNA sequences had clearly defined functions. The remainder seemed to do nothing, and so were dismissed as "junk DNA." But that picture had changed during the first part of the twenty-first century, as more sophisticated analysis had revealed that much of that so-called junk actually performed important roles in the functioning of cells by regulating the expression of genes. Even simple organisms, it turned out, possessed many genes that were suppressed, or silenced altogether, by such mechanisms. The central promise of genomics—that by knowing an organism's genome, scientists could know the organism—had fallen far short as it had become obvious that the phenotype (the actual creature that met the biologist's eye, with all of its observable traits and behaviors) was a function not only of its genotype (its DNA sequences) but also of countless nanodecisions being made from moment to moment within the organism's cells by the regulatory mechanisms that determined which genes to express and which to silence. Those regulatory mechanisms were of several types, and many were unfathomably complex.

Had it not been for the sudden intervention of the Agent, the biologists of Old Earth would have devoted at least the remaining decades of the century to cataloging these mechanisms and understanding their effects—a then-new science called epigenetics. Instead of which, on Cleft, in the hands of Eve Moira and the generations of biologists she reared, it became a tool. They had needed all the tools they could get, and they had wielded them pragmatically, bordering on ruthlessly, to ensure the survival of the human races. When creating the children of the other six Eves, Moira had avoided using epigenetic techniques. She had felt at liberty, however, to perform some experiments on her own genome. It had gone poorly at first, and her first eight pregnancies had been failures. But her last, the only daughter of Moira to survive, had flourished. Cantabrigia, as Moira had named her after the university of Cambridge, had founded the race of which Kath Two was a member.

By the time the Great Seeding was in the works, thousands of years later, epigenetics was sufficiently well understood to be programmed into the DNA of some of the newly created species that would be let loose on the surface of New Earth. And one of the planks in the Get It Done platform was to use epigenetics for all it was worth. So rather than trying to sequence and breed a new subspecies of coyote that was optimized for, and that would breed true in, a particular environment, as the TOT school would have had it, the GID approach was to produce a race of canines that would, over the course of only a few generations, become coyotes or wolves or dogs—or something that didn't fit into any of those categories—depending on what happened to work best. They would all start with a similar genetic code, but different parts of it would end up being expressed or suppressed depending on circumstances.

And no particular effort would be made by humans to choose and plan those outcomes. They would seed New Earth and see what happened. If an ecosystem failed to "take" in a particular area, they would just try something else.

In the decades since such species had been seeded onto New Earth, this had been going on all the time. Epigenetic transformation had been rampant—and, since Survey was thin on the ground, largely unobserved by humans. Still, when it led to results that humans saw, and happened to find surprising, it was known as "going epi." Use of the phrase was discouraged for being unscientific, but Rhys Alaskov knew how to get away with it.

Rhys brought up a rendering of the habitat ring and zoomed in on the whitish segment at its top. Their projected route was superimposed as a crisp green arc that curled through apogee near a succession of relatively small habitats just to the east of Greenwich. For the first habitats constructed in each segment—close to the seeds of Greenwich, Rio, et al.—had naturally tended to be smaller than the ones that came along later, when the construction process had hit its stride. The closer to a boneyard you got, the larger the habitats generally became. As Rhys panned and zoomed around, habitat names came and went on the screen: Hannibal, Brussels, Oyo, Auvergne, Vercingetorix, Steve Lake. The latter aroused a flicker of interest. Kath One had had an old friend living there. But the friendship wouldn't likely have survived the transition to Kath Two.

She brought the same thing up on her varp and zoomed out to remind herself of the current location of the Eye.

If the habitat ring as a whole was like the dial of a clock, then the Eye, with its inner and outer tethers—one depending toward Earth, the other reaching out beyond the habitat ring—was a hand.

Any description of the Eye had to begin by mentioning that it was the largest object ever made. Most of its material had come from Cleft. It was, in a sense, the thing Cleft had ultimately shape-shifted into. Its innermost piece was a spinning, ring-shaped city of sufficient diameter—some fifty kilometers—that even the largest space habitats could pass through its center with plenty of room to spare. This made the Eye capable of sweeping all the way around the ring, encompassing in turn each of the ten thousand separate habitats.

Or at least that had been the original plan. In practice, its sweep was limited to the Blue part of the ring that began at Dhaka and ran westward about two-thirds of the way around the ring to the fringe of the Julian segment. At both of those locations, barriers—literal turnpikes, consisting of long splinters of nickel-iron laid directly across the ring—had been constructed by Red to physically block movement of the Eye into "their" segment. So instead of sweeping around like the hand of a clock, it bounced back and forth between the turnpikes, confining itself to Blue habitats. During the ensuing century and a half, Red had been at work on something huge that appeared to be an anti-Eye in the making, and that would presumably sweep back and forth, in like manner, over their segment. But it had never budged from its geostationary orbit above the Makassar Strait, and no one in Blue really knew how soon it might become operational.

The Great Chain, as the rotating city was called, lined a circular opening, like an iris, in the middle of the Eye. To either side of it, the Eye tapered to a point. One of those points was always aimed toward the center of Earth and the other was always aimed away from it. A cable, or rather a redundant, self-healing network of them, emerged from each of those two points. The inner one hung almost all the way down to the Earth's surface, where a thing called Cradle dangled from it. The outer cable stretched for some distance beyond the habitat ring and terminated in the Big Rock, which served as a counterweight. By adjusting the length of the latter cable it was possible to move the whole construct's center of gravity closer to or farther away from Earth, causing it to speed up or slow down in its orbit relative to the habitats in the ring. Thus it could sweep around like the hand of a clock, passing around each habitat along the way, or pausing for a time as needed. And when it was encircling a particular habitat it could easily exchange people and goods with it, via flivvers, or cargo shuttles, or swarms of nats, or mechanical contraptions that could snake out like tentacles.

To be in a habitat—even a quite large and cosmopolitan one—when the Eye came around was, in pre-Zero terms, a little bit like being in a small town on the prairie and having a mobile Manhattan suddenly roll over the horizon, surround you, have a hundred kinds of intercourse with you, and then move on. Among its many other functions, it was a passenger ferry: the most straightforward way of moving among habitats. This was why Kath Two needed to remind herself of where it was at the moment and which direction it was moving.

The answer was that it was about twenty degrees west of their projected apogee, encircling a large new habitat called Akureyri, and heading generally in the direction of the Cape Verde boneyard that separated the Greenwich segment from the Rio segment. Which meant that it would soon be in the predominantly Ivyn part of the ring.

"Whip over high and catch the Eye?" she asked.

This amounted to a proposal that they should avail themselves of a kind of huge aluminum bullwhip—a very common device on the ring—to project their flivver into a higher orbit. As they curved slowly through apogee out beyond the ring, everything below them—the entire contents of the habitat ring, including the Eye—would speed past them on the inside track, so that by the time they looped back to it, the Eye would have caught up with them. They could dock their flivver to any of its hundreds of available ports, pass through Quarantine in relative comfort, and go their separate ways, using the Eye as a ferry to take them wherever they wanted to go, or as a transit hub where they could change to passenger flivvers or liners that might transport them more directly to other places in the system. Or they could ride the elevator down to Cradle. Or they could just remain on the Eye, a habitat in its own right where many people lived their entire lives. When possible, "catching the Eye" was almost always preferable to ending up on some random habitat whence it might take days or even weeks to get transit onward, and so proposals like this one were rarely controversial.

"Works for me," Rhys said immediately.

Kath Two glanced toward Beled and saw him looking back at her. She understood that the Teklan had, in a manner unchanged through thousands of years of racial subspeciation and acculturation to the social and cultural environment of space, been checking her out.

She raised an eyebrow at him, just slightly.

"Of course," said Beled.

"Unanimous. I'll punch it in," Rhys announced, and went to work at the interface panel.

Kath Two had felt a mildly embarrassing faint tingle between her legs, a sort of blush, accompanied by a bit of warmth in the face. She expected that Beled was reciprocating at some level. But Teklans were trained not to show their feelings, out of a belief, supposedly traceable all the way back to the ancient Spartans, that emotions such as fear resulted from their visible expression, rather than the other way around.

Perhaps sensing what was going on between Kath Two and Beled, Rhys focused on his task somewhat more intently than was really needed. The complications, as always, had to do with avoiding collisions and respecting what was still called "air space" around habitats, even though it had no air in it and might more properly have been called "space space." Kath Two, keeping half an eye on the brief and businesslike conversation between Rhys and Parambulator (which, to her eyes, had nothing whatsoever in common with whatever was meant by "punching it in"—but this was just how Dinans liked to express themselves), saw that they would pass through the twenty-kilometer-wide gap between habitats named Saint-Exupéry and Knutholmen. Midway between them was a whip station. Almost every habitat of significance was bracketed between two of these installations. The whip stations were small habitats, crewed by half a dozen or so humans who got rotated out every few months so they would not go crazy from boredom. Their job was to look after thousands of flynks: the latest generation of a lineage of robots that went all the way back to Rhys Aitken's work aboard Izzy. He had been working with fingernail-sized nats. The ones on whip stations performed the same functions, but they were much bigger. The chains that they formed had the mass and momentum of pre-Zero freight trains, capable of undulating and cracking like a whip, or reaching out at distant targets like the fly on the end of a fishing line. Some wear and tear was involved. Flynks could have been inspected and repaired by other robots, but Blue's overall cultural bias in favor of having humans in the loop had led to much of the work being done by flesh-and-blood crew members. In any case, supposing those people had been doing their job, keeping their fleet of flynks ready for use, and assuming that no other space travelers had already reserved that time slot on that whip station, the flivver carrying Kath Two, Rhys, and Beled would, in something like twelve hours' time, rendezvous with the tip of an aluminum bullwhip that would then snap it into a circular orbit with a slightly higher radius than that of the ring. A few hours later, they would dock at Port 65 in the Quarantine Section of the outer limb of the Eye.

The Eye observed whatever time was local on the part of Earth lying directly below it. Currently, it was about eight in the morning there. She could look forward to some serious jet lag—another term from the pre-Zero era that had become embedded in the language despite the obsolescence of its literal meaning. According to one convention, they should switch over to Eye time now, so that they could begin adjusting. But they had all finished long days on New Earth and were too exhausted at this moment to maintain the pretense that it was first thing in the morning for them. They would have plenty of time to adjust in Quarantine. Kath Two reserved a Moiran-friendly bed and meal plan at Port 65, then plummeted into sleep.

THE IRIS OF THE EYE WAS TOO BIG TO HAVE BEEN FABRICATED AS A single rigid object. It had been built, beginning about nine hundred years ago, out of links that had been joined together into a chain; the two ends of the chain then connected to form a loop. The method would have seemed familiar to Rhys Aitken, who had used something like it to construct Izzy's T3 torus. For him, or anyone else versed in the technological history of Old Earth, an equally useful metaphor would have been that it was a train, 157 kilometers long, made of 720 giant cars, with the nose of the locomotive joined to the tail of the caboose so that it formed a circular construct 50 kilometers in diameter.

An even better analogy would have been to a roller coaster, since its purpose was to run loop-the-loops forever.

The "track" on which the "train" ran was a circular groove in the iron frame of the Eye, lined with the sensors and magnets needed to supply electrodynamic suspension, so that the whole thing could spin without actually touching the Eye's stationary frame. This was an essential design requirement given that the Great Chain had to move with a velocity of about five hundred meters per second in order to supply Earth-normal gravity to its inhabitants.

Each of the links had approximately the footprint of a Manhattan city block on Old Earth. And their total number of 720 was loosely comparable to the number of such blocks that had once existed in the gridded part of Manhattan, depending on where you drew the boundaries—it was bigger than Midtown but smaller than Manhattan as a whole. Residents of the Great Chain were acutely aware of the comparison, to the point where they were mocked for having a "Manhattan complex" by residents of other habitats. They were forever freeze-framing Old Earth movies or zooming around in virtual-reality simulations of pre-Zero New York for clues as to how street and apartment living had worked in those days. They had taken as their patron saint Luisa, the eighth survivor on Cleft, a Manhattanite who had been too old to found her own race. Implicit in that was that the Great Chain—the GC, Chaintown, Chainhattan—was a place that people might move to when they wanted to separate themselves from the social environments of their home habitats, or indeed of their own races. Mixed-race people were more common there than anywhere else.

As in Manhattan, the discretization of the space imposed form on how it had developed, with each link of the chain—each city block—acquiring its own skyline and identity. Groups of consecutive blocks had long since coalesced into neighborhoods. Each block was, in effect, a fully independent space vehicle with its own system for keeping the air from leaking out. But each was connected to its two neighbors by a bundle of passageways routed through its foundation slab, which made it possible to move easily from one to the next in the same way that the Londoners of Old Earth had used underground passages—"subways" in the London sense of that word—to cut beneath crowded intersections. Some of the subways were sized for human pedestrians. Four of them carried trains: locals and express service running both directions around the full circuit of the Great Chain. Still others were reserved for robotic vehicles programmed to carry cargo. Beyond that was a wide range of smaller conduits carrying air, water, power, and information. All of them went by the name of subways—this was a conflation of the old London and New York senses of the word. At each end of each block was a system of airlocks; these would seal themselves off in the event that a block were to depressurize. People ran marathons through them—four consecutive marathons made up about one circuit around the entire Chain.

Every fifth link in the Chain was public property. These tended to be parks, though some served as cultural facilities. So you were never more than two links away from green, or at least open, space. The other 576 links were privately owned, and constituted a commercial and residential real estate market that would have been easily recognizable to any pre-Zero property magnate. The Great Chain had been likened more than once to the ancient board game of Monopoly. Some stretches of the loop were more high-rent, others less so. The pattern was interrupted in several places by special links, or short series of links, placed there to serve industrial and civic requirements, such as making the transit system work.

One of those was the Ramp Link, whose purpose was to make connections, every five minutes, with the On Ramp and the Off Ramp. Since the Great Chain was moving at about five hundred meters per second with respect to the nonrotating frame of the Eye, persons wishing to get from the latter to the former needed to be accelerated to a fairly spectacular velocity—almost Mach 1.5—before they could set foot on the Ramp, or any other, Link. And those wishing to dechain, as the expression had it, needed to be decelerated by the same amount. The acceleration and the deceleration were handled by machines built into a place on the rim of the "iris" of the Eye. Though some efforts had been made to camouflage their essential nature, they were really just guns for shooting humans, albeit humans strapped into comfortable, pressurized bullets.

Outside of the Great Chain, the rest of the Eye was lightly infested with human beings, heavily so with robots. Most of it existed in microgravity, since the entire contraption—Great Chain, tethers, and all—was in geosynchronous orbit, hence free fall, around Earth. As you moved away from its center, toward the two extremities of the Eye where the tethers emerged, you might begin to notice tidal forces, which would show up as very mild gravity-like tugs. These shifted whenever the Eye adjusted its orbit to move around the habitat ring, and people who spent a lot of time there could always feel in their bones when a move was under way, like Old Earthers predicting the weather in their knees.

The skeleton of the Eye was a simple space frame built in the Amalthean style, which was to say that it had been carved and shaped from existing material (Cleft) as opposed to fabricated from scratch. Aesthetically, it meant that the big structural elements had a rough-hewn, space-battered look about them, a bit like a log cabin with all the knots and bark still visible. Vacancies between the big structural elements had been filled in with giant machines, most notably several immense rotating masses whose purpose was to stabilize the whole Eye gyroscopically. The nooks and crannies between the machines had been caulked with pressurized spaces where humans could move about. Some of those rotated to produce simulated gravity; they were like miniature, torus-shaped space colonies pinned to a much bigger structure. Docking ports tended to cluster near those.

As Kath Two's eyes closed into sleep, she was gazing at the usual ring-shaped formation of iridescent sparkles, so densely packed that they blended into each other on the varp. The Eye was a slightly larger white dot between twelve and one o'clock; it would have been difficult to see were it not for the long white line representing its tether system, which ran from just above Earth's surface all the way through the big white dot and beyond to the Big Rock.

Their flivver's trajectory, a sharp green ellipse, projected from where they were now (near Earth) all the way out to slightly beyond the ring before curving back in to intersect the Eye.

Through her eyelids she could see indistinct patterns, reminding her a little of the first thing she'd seen this morning: the flickering lights on the walls of her tent. But then the varp figured out that her eyes were closed and shut off the display.

When she opened her eyes, the varp noticed it and came back to life, rendering the display again. Generally it looked the same, but the Eye had moved a little bit, and the dot representing the flivver had covered most of the distance to the habitat ring. Zooming in, she could see the two habitats between which they were going to pass, and the much smaller rendering of the whip station between them, exercising its long hair-thin flagellum in preparation for their arrival. She must have slept for something like ten hours. Moirans were notorious for it. Remembering the looks she had exchanged earlier with Beled, she felt, then stifled, mild embarrassment over the fact that she had spent most of the journey snoring away.

She unstrapped and floated over to the zero-gee toilet at the end of the flivver's cabin. When she emerged a few minutes later, she saw that Rhys was asleep, loosely strapped in before the control panel. Beled was still in his acceleration couch. He too had slipped on a varp, and she guessed from the way he was moving his hands and wiggling his fingers that he was working, as opposed to playing. He was probably filling out his Survey report. Which was what Kath Two ought to be doing.

They represented a civilization that had, during the Fourth Millennium, executed a plan to undo the damage caused by the Agent by identifying, cataloging, reaching, corralling, and revectoring millions of rocks in orbit around Earth, while also reaching as far as the Kuiper Belt to acquire chunks of frozen water and methane and ammonia and bring them home and smash them into the ruined planet. Essentially all of this work had been accomplished by robots. So much metal had gone into their construction that millions of humans now lived in space habitats whose steel hulls consisted entirely of melted down and reforged robot carcasses. It would have been easy for them to blanket the surface of New Earth with robots and, without ever sending down a single human being, perform a kind of survey: one that was heavy on data and light on judgment. In that version of the world, Kath Two and the others would have spent their lives in habitats, working at varps and mining data. All sorts of interesting philosophical arguments could have been framed as to whether that approach was better or worse than what they were in fact doing. But philosophy didn't really enter into it. The decision to do it this way was driven partly by politics and partly by social mores.

On the political front it boiled down to the terms of Second Treaty, which, eighteen years ago, had terminated the second Red-Blue war, sometimes called the War in the Woods to distinguish it from the earlier War on the Rocks. The treaty imposed strict limitations on the number of robots that either side could send down to the surface. For that matter, it also limited the number of humans; but the upshot was that, given those limits, human surveyors could gather more useful information about conditions on New Earth than could robots beaming data up to the ring.

On the social front it was a question of Amistics, which was a term that had been coined ages ago by a Moiran anthropologist to talk about the choices that different cultures made as to which technologies they would, and would not, make part of their lives. The word went all the way back to the Amish people of pre-Zero America, who had chosen to use certain modern technologies, such as roller skates, but not others, such as internal combustion engines. All cultures did this, frequently without being consciously aware that they had made collective choices.

To the extent that Blue had a definable culture, it tended to view technological aids with some ambivalence, a state of mind boiled down into the aphorism "Each enhancement is an amputation." This was not so much a definable idea or philosophy as it was a prejudice, operant at a nearly subliminal level. It was traceable to certain parts of the Epic. In many of these, Tavistock Prowse played a role; he was seen as its literal embodiment in the sense that he had actually undergone a series of amputations, and been consumed as food, after throwing in his lot with the Swarm. Blue saw itself—according to cultural critics, *defined* itself—as the inheritors of the traditions of *Endurance*. By process of elimination, then, Red was the culture of the Swarm. A century and a half ago, Red had sealed itself off behind barriers both physical and cryptographic, so not much was known of its culture, but plenty of circumstantial evidence suggested that it had different Amistics from Blue. Specifically, the Reds were enthusiastic about personal technological enhancement.

The upshot, here in the cabin of this flivver, was that the missions just concluded by Kath Two, Beled, and Rhys had no value—in effect, they had never happened—until reports had been filed. And the reports could not simply consist of data dumps and pictures. Surveyors had to write actual prose. And the more judgment and insight were condensed into that prose, the more highly it was thought of by people like Doc and, increasingly, his senior students.

Knowing that, Kath Two had been writing her report since before her glider had touched down on a broad swath of grass a fortnight ago. What remained was some editing and a summary. This ought to have come easily. But half an hour after she pulled the document up on her varp, she found herself gazing at it, unable to focus.

"Beled," she finally said. Distinctly enough for him to hear it, not loud enough to wake up Rhys.

"Working on your report?" he asked.

He could see her, and the rest of the cabin, through the translucent light field of his varp. He might have seen the movements of her hands, indicative of text entry. In any case the question had a bit of an edge to it. Hours earlier, Beled had noted some uncertainty in Kath Two's face. There was no telling, now, how long he'd been observing her through eyes screened by the varp.

"Did you see any Indigens?" she asked him.

He reached up and slid the varp onto the top of his head: a polite gesture.

"I planned my route to avoid a certain RIZ," he said. Registered Indigen Zone, a place listed by name in the Treaty as a district where Sooners—people who had illegally gone to the surface ahead of schedule—were grandfathered in under the politely evasive term

"Indigens" and allowed to live subject to certain restrictions. "I saw it from a distance. They did not see me."

"Of course not," Kath Two said, suppressing a smile.

"Does that answer your question?" Beled asked, knowing that it didn't.

"I think I saw one not in a RIZ," Kath Two said.

This piqued Beled's attention. "Establishing a settlement or—"

"No," Kath Two said firmly. "I'd have mentioned that. I think he, or she, was in scope." Meaning, conducting activities, such as hunting and gathering, within the scope of Second Treaty. "Most likely fishing. But at least two hundred kilometers from the nearest RIZ."

"A long way to carry a dead fish," Beled remarked.

"Yeah," Kath Two said, and felt her face warm slightly. Obvious as it seemed now that Beled had pointed it out, she'd missed that detail.

"Did you investigate further?" Beled asked.

"Unable," Kath Two said. "I saw this person from my glider, on my way out."

"It is not mandatory to explain every last thing in your report," Beled pointed out. "To leave a loose end, under those circumstances, is acceptable. It will give some other surveyor a challenging and welcome task to shoulder."

An idea came to Kath Two. "What if we were shouldering it?"

"Explain."

"Does it seem to you as though there was an unusual concentration of Survey activity in that one zone?"

"Unusual," Beled allowed, after thinking about it for a few moments. "Not without precedent."

"Makes me wonder," Kath Two said, "if some previous surveyor saw what I saw, and triggered a wave of missions in the same area."

"In that case," Beled pointed out, "Survey would have informed us of what it was they were sending us to look for."

That was so sensible, and Beled said it with such simple conviction, that Kath Two nodded and declined to press it any further. But she was thinking, *Unless it is something they don't want us to know.*

The conversation with Beled had been useful in that it had given her a way to proceed, which was simply to type up the Indigen sighting as a loose end, and thus drop it into the lap of whoever read the report. She went to work on that general plan, trying to clarify the fleeting memory in her mind's eye, to sort out objective observations, made in the moment, from judgments and suppositions she'd added later. Which was tricky, since the latter were supposed to be part of her job.

A while later Rhys was awakened by an alarm he'd set on his wrist. He made a sleepy flight to the toilet and back, looking at her in the classic style of the extrovert who wants you to drop whatever you're doing so that you can have a conversation with him. After exchanging a few words with Beled, he settled in to work on his own report, and the cabin was quiet for a while. Later the two men broke out some rations and had a snack, talking of this and that.

Kath Two was snapped out of her work reverie by a mild shift in their tone of voice. Now they were talking about something important. Not in an urgent or concerned way. A glance at the display told her what it was: they were nearing the ring, which meant that they were about to lance through the twenty-kilometer-wide gap between two space habitats. There was no reason that this should be a problem, but it was the sort of feat that focused one's attention and brought a discernible edge to one's voice.

She reached up and found the lever on her varp that activated an opaque screen over the lenses: essentially, a blindfold. Her view of the cabin was now blocked. The only things she could see were those being projected into her eyes by the varp. At the same time she activated an application that gave her the ability to see the flivver's surroundings as if she were floating adrift in space. The same service could have been provided by a bubble of glass on the flivver's hull, but it wouldn't have been as good. It would have exposed the user's head to cosmic radiation, and the contrasty light would have made it difficult to see certain things. The varp, on the other hand, played games with the light's dynamic range so that bright things were less so while dim things were bright enough to see; it gave everything a luminous warm quality that did not exist in reality. It was so far superior to looking at the world directly that many space suits eschewed transparencies altogether and just encased the wearer's head in a radiation-shielded dome with a varp on the inside.

She was now "looking" at an enhanced view of the universe from their current location, which was just inside, but rapidly approaching, the habitat ring.

The ring was spinning past them. It was a little like being on the inside of a carousel watching the horses wheel by, except that instead of horses, these were space habitats as much as thirty kilometers across, and they were moving at three thousand meters per second.

The task was to shoot between two of them without getting hit. By the standards of orbital mechanics it was no great feat, but it looked shockingly dangerous, and as such it was great fun to watch. As Kath Two looked straight ahead, the habitats seemed to be whizzing across their path like the teeth of a buzz saw. But through an apparent miracle the flivver found a gap between two of them.

"Whip dock in three," announced a synthesized voice, and Kath Two's hands moved around to check the straps holding her into her seat.

An immense bullwhip was burgeoning toward them. Its general dimensions were about those of an exceptionally long Old Earth freight train, but instead of boxcars it was made up of many flynks coupled nose-to-tail into a chain.

If Rhys's earlier preparations had gone according to plan—and Kath Two would have heard about it, were that not the case—then, several hours ago, the hundreds of flynks that lived in this whip station had begun to assemble themselves into a chain. When it had reached the desired length—which was a function of the specific mission to be performed—the chain had joined itself nose-to-tail into an endless loop and gone into motion, driven by a simple linear motor in the whip station. It had formed an elongated oval known as an Aitken loop and then devoted some time to tweaking its shape and dialing in its exact velocity. Flynks were simple beasts, consisting mostly of structure: solid aluminum cast into certain shapes. Each flynk had a knuckle amidships, enabling it to bend freely in both directions—in mechanical engineering terms, it was just a heavy-duty universal joint. Fore and aft it had couplers that enabled it to form a strong, rigid connection with other flynks. Somewhere in all of that structure were a few grams of silicon that made it smart, and lines for carrying power and information down the length of the chain.

A few moments ago, word had gone out to one of the flynks that it should decouple from the one behind it. This had happened just as it was emerging from the whip station. At the instant the coupler had disconnected, the system had stopped being an Aitken loop and started being a giant bullwhip. The niksht—a very old mispronunciation of *Knickstelle,* referring to the U-shaped bend at the apex of the loop—had begun to propagate away from the whip station, towing the free end of the whip behind it, accelerating as it went, and rapidly building to thousands of meters per second of velocity. This was the thing Kath Two saw in the VR: the elbow in the whip, coming right at them. The free end was concealed behind it, but she knew that in a few moments it would come whipping around in a huge final burst of acceleration.

All the energy was directed "backward" from the point of view of the bored crew members who were presumably monitoring all of this in the station at the "handle" end of the whip. They were moving a lot faster than the flivver. In order to make physical contact with the approaching craft, they had to reach "back." And "reach" wasn't really the right term; they had to *punch* backward with explosive suddenness to match the flivver's much lower velocity. This was the kind of task that bullwhips were made for.

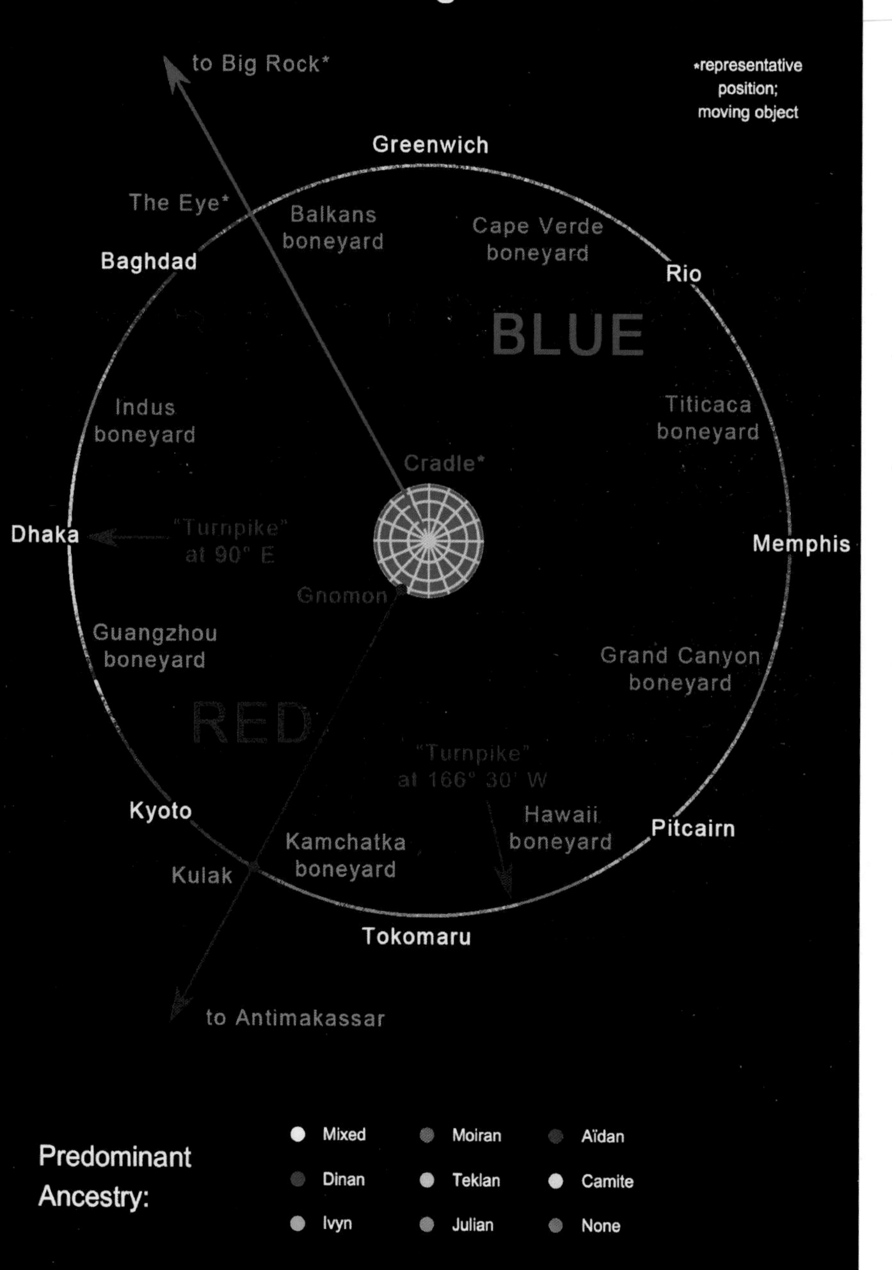
The Habitat Ring circa A+5000
to Big Rock*
*representative position; moving object
Greenwich
The Eye*
Balkans boneyard
Cape Verde boneyard
Baghdad
Rio
BLUE
Indus boneyard
Titicaca boneyard
Cradle*
Dhaka
"Turnpike" at 90° E
Memphis
Gnomon
Guangzhou boneyard
Grand Canyon boneyard
RED
"Turnpike" at 166° 30' W
Kyoto
Hawaii boneyard
Pitcairn
Kamchatka boneyard
Kulak
Tokomaru
to Antimakassar
Predominant Ancestry:
Mixed
Moiran
Aïdan
Dinan
Teklan
Camite
Ivyn
Julian
None

Still, she couldn't help but flinch as the final few flynks snapped around toward them. The perspective on the VR was almost sickening. The eye was confused by the fact that the whip as a whole was moving away from them so rapidly, and yet its uncoiling tip was coming right at them. Any failure in the calculations and it would have either hurtled away from them, leaving them alone and adrift, or else smashed into them at hypersonic closing velocity and destroyed them as surely as a bolide strike during the Epic.

Instead of which the two velocities matched perfectly and the last flynk in the chain was, just for a moment, right there in front of them, much like the hanger she had docked with earlier.

"Coupling," said the voice, unnecessarily since she could hear the mechanical connection being made and then feel the acceleration as the flivver was slapped sideways and then jerked forward by the momentum of the whip. "Brace for stabilization." A polite way of saying that the situation in the whip was a little chaotic in the aftermath of the snap-around. In general they were now being pulled forward with tremendous force, being brought up to a speed to match that of the whip station and all the other objects in the habitat ring. But the physics of the whip led to some side-to-side oscillation, some surges and lapses in the acceleration that could be dampened but not removed by the tiny adjustments of the flynks. "Hebel has toggled," the voice confirmed. "Hebel," like *Knickstelle,* was a term from the German; it was a lever at the base of the whip, anchored to the whip station and capable of flipping freely from one side to the other. It was, in effect, the arm that held the handle and cracked the whip, and shortly after the completion of the first crack—the one that had culminated in successful docking—it had snapped around to the other side of the station and initiated a second crack in the opposite direction. A new niksht had been formed, just at the place where the whip was attached to the hebel, and was beginning to accelerate "forward," accelerating the flivver to the velocity it would need to accomplish the rest of the mission.

The process lasted for about three minutes. The visual cues in her headset gave her mind the context: the buzz saw whirling past them seemed to slow down. Of course it was still moving at the same speed; in truth the flivver was speeding up to match its pace. But, from her point of view, the habitat ring stopped looking like a whirling dervish and began to resolve itself into a series of discrete objects, still rushing past them, but more and more slowly until the whole ring seemed to grind to a halt. And at that moment, something especially huge drifted into view: the Eye, dead in their path.

"Decoupling," the voice announced, and not a moment too soon, since the acceleration had become difficult to tolerate. Had they not broken their connection to the tip of the whip, the gee forces would have rendered them unconscious, then killed them, and finally ripped the flivver to shreds. Flynks were built to survive forces that humans and ordinary spacecraft could not. But the geometry and the timing of the niksht had been programmed so that it would bring them to their desired velocity and release them into their new trajectory just before the crisis that, in an Old Earth bullwhip, would have been signaled by the sharp bang of a sonic boom. Weightlessness returned, unless you counted a bit of corrective jostling from the flivver's thrusters. Kath Two's vision cleared and she swallowed a few times, trying to settle her stomach.

The funny thing was that the entire procedure, from Kath Two's landing her glider in the hanger, to the bolo release, to the just-concluded interaction with the whip, would have looked graceful, even gentle, when viewed from a distance. In order to understand the sheer intensity of the acceleration and the jostling, you had to live through it.

Trying to think about something other than her stomach, she took a good look at the Eye.

Right now it was encircling Akureyri, a big (population 1.1 million), newish (eighty-four years old) habitat constructed in the style known informally as the double barrel, historically known as the

O'Neill Island Three type. It was two large cylinders, parallel to each other, rotating in opposite directions. Each was enshrouded in complexes of mirrors and other infrastructure. The mirrors were aimed at the sun, whose light was bounced through windowed strips on the cylinder walls to illuminate the landscapes within. But it was about six in the evening local time, and so those mirrors were gradually being feathered to simulate twilight. By using the varp to zoom in, Kath Two could have peered through the windows to see the farms, forests, waterways, and habitations inside Akureyri, but she knew generally what it would look like, so she remained zoomed-out for now.

Which she had to, if she was going to take in the Eye. Akureyri, big as it was, was dwarfed by the construct surrounding it. Of this, the most eye-catching part was the Manhattan-on-a-roller-coaster spectacle of the Great Chain, whipping around at terrific speed, completing a full circuit every five minutes.

But that wasn't where they were going. As the Eye became larger and larger in her view, its whirling iris drifted to one side, and it became clear that the flivver's tiny corrective burns had aimed them toward one of those inhabited bits contained within its massive, pitted iron frame: a ring of four score docking ports encircled by a large, glowing yellow letter Q that was universally recognizable as the logo and the badge of Quarantine.

At a glance, two-thirds of the ports in the Q were already occupied by other ships, mostly flivvers of various types plus a couple of liners. The ports were individually numbered with glowing digits, and annotated, in the mixture of Latin and Cyrillic used throughout the ring, as to their purposes:

TRANZIT
IMMIGRAШON
MILITARY
CURVEY
CPEЦ

A ring of green lights surrounding a vacant port—number 65—began to flash. The systems that were controlling the flivver already knew where to go, so this was solely for the benefit of human beings, as well as serving as a backup plan in the rare event that a vehicle needed to be piloted by hand.

Kath Two had seen enough dockings in her time, so she peeled off the varp and held it in her lap through the ensuing series of nudges and jerks, which terminated with the opening of the airlock door.

A yellow-striped tube stretched away into the part of Quarantine set aside for people who, like them, were returning from the surface of Earth. A few meters in, they were confronted by a one-way door, constructed so that only one person at a time could pass through it. Hanging on a rack nearby were a number of hard bracelets, color-coded to indicate that they were intended for Survey personnel, also striped with machine-readable glyphs. Kath Two selected one and ratcheted it around her wrist. After a moment, a red diode began to blink on its back and digits began to count time. She waved it at the door, which unlocked itself and allowed her to pass into the tube beyond.

This part of the Q consisted essentially of plumbing: a snarl of human-sized pipes that drained people away from incoming ships and let them pool in separate reservoirs until they had passed muster. Kath Two, Rhys, and Beled would be inspected visually for invasive species and pathogens, their clothes and equipment sterilized. There would be mandatory showers and scrubbings. Stool and blood samples would be taken and tested. Because they were Survey, however, little interest would be shown in their backgrounds, their politics, their emotional stability, their motivations. Survey personnel had already been vetted for that sort of thing. Depending on how busy the lab facilities were, it could take anywhere from six to twenty-four hours.

THE SUSPICION, FOLLOWED BY THE CERTAINTY, THAT KATH TWO WAS being detained crept up on her. After a few hours, she was given clearance to move freely about the common areas of the Q's no-man's-land: eateries, shops, lounges, and recreational facilities strung around a torus with about half a gee of simulated gravity. This meant that she had passed all the biological tests. But the bracelet continued to blink red. The digits counted up to a day, then a day and a half. She shifted her sleep schedule to Eye time and began to experience jet lag.

The Q was pretty crowded—perhaps that figured into the delay. The Eye had, in the last couple of weeks, swept westward across the oldest, most densely populated regions of the Greenwich segment, headed for the Cape Verde boneyard and the Rio segment beyond. At such a location, close to a boneyard where the habitats were big and new, the Q would expect to see a large volume of "in transit" passengers: emigrants from older and more crowded places bound for big new habitats like Akureyri. It took decades to fully populate one of those things; their population was ramped up gradually as new housing was constructed and the life-supporting ecosystem was cultivated and tuned. In a short while the Eye would reach the Cape Verde boneyard and the census in this place would drop to near zero: just a few workers going to jobs on new habitats, and some patient long-range travelers. But for now the facilities in the no-man's-land were operating at capacity and there were queues for food and drink, especially at places that catered to families. For people often emigrated when they had small children who they thought would benefit from being planted in a clean new place where they could run around.

So Kath Two told herself, for a while, that the delay was purely bureaucratic in nature, a result of too many emigrants and not enough Q staff on hand. But on the second day she noticed Beled in the recreation center, operating a resistance training device at some insane power level only usable by young male Teklans. Later, after he had showered, she caught up with him in a bar and he mentioned that he had seen Rhys headed for the exit with his bracelet flashing green.

"When was this?" she asked.

"Yesterday," Beled said. "Eight hours and twenty minutes after we docked."

A few hours later, Kath Two and Beled vacated their single rooms and moved into a slightly larger double. They began sleeping together without having sex, which was a fairly common behavior pattern for Moiran/Teklan couples who scarcely knew each other. When Beled got an erection, which was fairly often, he would go into the tiny en suite bathroom and masturbate. This way of dealing with it was sufficiently common that for him to have behaved in any other way would have been noteworthy. She knew that she could rely on him to show impeccable discipline, and he knew that this was her expectation, and so it could go on indefinitely until one of them signaled a change.

Unable to sleep, not as proficient as Beled at masturbation, she heaved his massive arm off her chest, a project akin to dragging an unconscious ten-year-old boy to the other side of the bed, and slipped out, looking for a place to kill time until she felt drowsy.

At the cafeteria, waiting in line for chocolate, she found herself standing next to a small, lithe Julian woman in her sixties. The woman had been reading a book, or pretending to. As the wait stretched on she seemed to lose interest. She closed the book, stifled a yawn, and fixed her gaze on Kath Two. "Back from the surface?"

This was obvious from the color of Kath Two's wristband. But Kath Two understood that the woman was just trying to strike up a conversation. "Yes."

"Home for you?" the woman asked, referring to the Eye.

"I'm sort of between homes at the moment. Survey duty makes it hard to settle down."

"Ah, taking a little R & R on the Great Chain. Good for you."

Kath Two understood perfectly well that this woman was a Quarantine agent.

This was how the Q operated: not by interrogating you in a windowless room but by striking up a casual conversation. The purpose of these common areas was to supply a range of venues and opportunities.

It was important not to be seen as dissimulating, so Kath Two said: "I expect some R & R might happen, but really I'm bound for Stromness."

"Ah, visiting a friend at university?"

Was it telling the truth to call Doc a friend? "More of a mentor. A teacher," she said.

"Well, I've heard Stromness is lovely. Never been."

Many, perhaps most, who were probed in this way never even realized that they were talking to a Quarantine agent. That was because most people passed through the Q rarely, if at all; and when they did, they tended to be jumbled together with large groups of travelers in settings where this sort of conversation might easily be mistaken for idle chitchat.

Kath Two was a sufficiently experienced traveler to know exactly what was going on. And the other woman knew that she knew. They would carry on with the charade anyway. Kath Two resisted the temptation to make trouble by asking the Julian where she had come from and where she was going. The woman would no doubt have some plausible story cued up. Obliging her to rattle it off would only waste time.

As the queue crept forward, they came in view of a display panel above the counter, showing a scene from the Epic. The time code in the corner was A+3.139, placing it about a year and a half into the Big Ride. The footage was from an arklet—not *Endurance*—so this was most likely from the Swarm. There was simulated gravity, so the arklet had to be part of a bolo. Kath Two didn't recognize any of the people at first. They were, of course, all rootstock humans, clearly recognizable as not belonging to any of the seven current human races, but close enough that she could still feel what they were feeling. They spoke, like everyone else in the Epic, in the archaic accents of five thousand years ago.

No Eves were currently in the frame. The only Eves in the Swarm, of course, had been Julia and Aïda. So this was probably what they called sidestory, which was to say, video from the Epic that, while it didn't capture the words or the deeds of any of the Eves, was still deemed important enough to have been incorporated into the canon and to show up on playlists in locations like this café. Kath Two had a vague sense that she had seen it before, many years ago, perhaps in school. She had lost track of days and time zones, but she was fairly sure that today was Julsday, and so any Epic scenes being broadcast in a place like this were most likely commemorative of something that Eve Julia had said or done. "Happy Eve Day," she said, as a polite reflex, to the Julian standing next to her.

"Good day to you," the woman returned, which confirmed that today was in fact Julsday.

Kath Two watched the scene long enough to get the gist of it. She was growingly certain that she remembered these people and their situation. The Seven Fat and Seven Thin was a bolo that had consisted of two heptads. One of them had experienced a breakdown in food production because of a contagious blight that had started in one of its arklets and eventually spread to the other six. The result was seven arklets full of starving people, connected by a long cable to seven arklets in which there was plenty to eat. They had worked out a system of sending spacewalkers up their respective cables to the center point where the two paws were latched together. There, care packages from the Seven Fat would be handed over to spacewalkers from the Seven Thin, who would descend back to the afflicted heptad and distribute the food. But seven arklets could not produce food for fourteen. All went hungry, and people in the Seven Thin began to die. The problem was exacerbated by the fact that this bolo had become separated from the main Swarm.

The particular scene now being broadcast was a video conference between the starvelings of the Seven Thin and the only slightly better-fed occupants of the Seven Fat, made more wrenching by the fact that family members and old friends had found themselves separated by that cable. Kath Two was sure she remembered it now. In a few minutes, they would establish radio contact with the White Arklet and bring Eve Julia into the conversation to ask for her advice. She would make a little speech about what they must do. The story would end with the Seven Thin cutting themselves loose from the bolo. They timed it in such a way that the Seven Fat would be flung back in the direction of the main swarm, ensuring their at least temporary survival, while the Seven Thin went hurtling away in the opposite direction. In effect, the doomed ones used themselves as propellant to save the others. The tale was made more complicated, and more poignant, by other details that Kath Two would be subjected to if she stood here watching it long enough. The Seven Thin heptad was one of the few that contained part of the Human Genetic Archive, and so its sacrifice had been part of the seemingly inexorable series of mishaps that had led to the Council of the Seven Eves and the creation of the new human races. And their decision to sacrifice themselves had not been unanimous; it had been preceded by a mutiny, and hand-to-hand fighting from one arklet to the next as a minority of the starvelings had attempted to save themselves by donning space suits and ascending the cable. The man who had fought his way to the control panel and mashed the button that had severed the bolo was named Julius Mwangi. There was a habitat named after him at thirty-eight degrees, zero minutes east, hovering over his birthplace in Kenya. The "zero minutes" part being significant, since habitats lying on meridians were traditionally named after heroes of the Epic.

All of that came back to Kath Two's mind during the time it took the café workers to make her coffee. For, since it had become obvious that she was being interrogated, she thought it best to change her order from chocolate to something with a little more caffeine. "This is on me," she said to the Quarantine agent, since it was traditional to do small favors for strangers on their Eve Day. Had this been Moirsday, someone else might have paid for her coffee.

"Oh, no, I couldn't," the woman said. Which was probably true on a literal level; she could not accept a favor from someone she was interrogating. "But if you would allow me to sit with you . . ."

"Of course," Kath Two said, and waited while the woman's coffee was made. The screen above the counter had cut to a different part of the Epic, consisting of a conversation that had taken place aboard *Endurance* shortly before the Final Burn, in which Dinah and Ivy had talked each other into believing that Julia wasn't as bad as all that. Kath Two had always found it a little cloying. People quoted lines from it all the time. It had served as the basis for political movements and parties that had sought to build stronger alliances between the Julians and other races. As such, its timing was fortuitous. Had Kath Two been of a Julian turn of mind, she'd have wondered whether the whole thing had been staged, the playlist's timing rigged by someone behind the scenes at Quarantine so that she would see it just before sitting down to coffee with this woman. Because that was how Julians were. It was the choice that Eve Julia had made during the Council of the Seven Eves. Her strain, living in relative isolation in their segment of the ring, had intensified it through the selective breeding process known as Caricaturization. Julians had developed huge eyes, sleek ears, and small mouths as part of that; it was the single easiest way to identify one from across the room.

The woman saluted before sitting down. Julians saluted with their left hands, kept off to the side of the face so that the hand never passed through the eyeline. "Ariane," she said. A common Julian name, derived from the rockets launched from Kourou, which Eve Julia had defended by nuking the Venezuelans. "Ariane Casablancova." Meaning that she was the daughter of a woman named Casablanca, after the White House.

Kath Two saluted back. "Kath Amalthova Two." For Kath Two's mother had been named after the asteroid that had sheltered Moira and her lab through the Big Ride.

Ariane sat down across from her, huge eyes fixed impassively on Kath Two's face.

"Look," Kath Two said, "I'm no good at this. I don't belong to any kupol and I don't want to join. Just ask me what is on your mind."

"Just wondering if you saw anything interesting on the surface."

"My whole point in going there is to see interesting things. I hardly see anything that is not interesting."

Ariane just sat expectantly.

"I filed a report," Kath Two said.

"And discussed its contents with Beled Tomov?"

"Yes."

"But not with Rhys Alaskov."

"Rhys was asleep when Beled and I were talking."

"You slept quite a bit as well," Ariane remarked. "Ten hours on the flivver."

"I had been flying a glider all day."

"With frequent naps."

"Every time a Moiran sleeps in a little bit," Kath Two said, "it doesn't mean that we are going epi. Sometimes we are just tired, is all."

"Time will tell. Now you are journeying to have a face-to-face conversation with your mentor," Ariane said. "Or so you think."

"What does that mean?"

"Dr. Hu is not on Stromness. You would know as much if you had coordinated with him. But you didn't. Instead you made an impulsive plan, spur of the moment, to visit a place with which you have good associations. Something's troubling you. You are aware that you might be starting to go epi. You won't discuss it with 'Doc' until you are face-to-face with him, in a place where you feel safe. It must be something you observed on the surface. Something unexpected."

Telling Ariane Casablancova to read Kath Two's report wouldn't help. Probably she had already perused it several times. She wanted to hear the story fresh.

"I might have seen a human," Kath Two said.

"Might?"

"It was a glimpse. From a distance."

"Not another surveyor—or else you wouldn't see anything remarkable in it."

"Surveyors wear bright clothes, for visibility."

"Beled didn't."

"When he was passing near the RIZ, no, of course not. I'm speaking in general."

"Go on."

"This person was wearing the opposite. Sort of like—"

"Like what?"

"You ever see pre-Zero videos with hunters? They used to wear clothes that would make them less visible."

"Camouflage," Ariane said.

"Yeah. I think this person was in camouflage."

"Not a surveyor, then."

"So—military, perhaps?" Kath Two asked. "But the only purpose of military is to fight other military. And I'm pretty sure there's no other military down there. Unless there's been some kind of infraction. But if there'd been an infraction, I'd have been warned of it before I was dropped. Hell, they'd have sent a Thor after me."

"Did it occur to you that it might be a *fresh* infraction? Which you were the first to notice?"

The question kind of hung there. Ariane's implication was clear. If Kath Two had witnessed anything of the sort, she ought to have reported it immediately instead of sleeping for ten hours and then making a harebrained effort to find Doc in a place where he wasn't.

"No," she said. "That's not what this was."

"How do you know?"

"I was making passes over the lake for a long time. I was clearly visible. Anyone who was there for no good reason would have simply hidden in the trees until I was gone. That's not what this person did. They were down near the shore in a place where they could get a clear view of what I was doing. Like—"

"Like what?" Ariane asked.

"Like they were gawking."

After a long silence, Ariane repeated the word, "Gawking."

"Yeah." Until this point, Moira had felt uncomfortable under Ariane's gaze, but now she looked directly into the great penetrating eyes for a while.

"When this person moved," Ariane said, "did you get any sense as to posture and gait?"

"I don't think it was a Neoander," Kath Two said, shaking her head. "*That* I would have reported."

Ariane blinked and said, "The simplest explanation is, of course . . ."

"An Indigen. Which is the possibility I discussed with Beled." She was feeling a little on the defensive now. "But what would one be doing there? So far from the nearest RIZ."

"It is a mystery."

"Yes."

"That explains why you broke profile," Ariane said, nodding.

"I don't even know what 'broke profile' means to you people."

"Did you ever get the sense that you were being watched? Followed?"

Ariane Casablancova had the damnable habit of asking good questions.

"You have to assume, when you're down there, that—"

"That you are not going unnoticed by local megafauna. Of course."

"Over time, hiking solo, trying to be aware of that, it can make you sort of, I don't know—" She didn't want to use the word "paranoid" around a Julian, since it was a racially charged word. Ariane seemed to sense this, and found it ever so slightly amusing. She leaned forward slightly, trying to help Kath Two over the sticky place.

"You develop a heightened awareness. Perhaps, to be safe, you interpret the sounds of the wilderness—"

"In the most conservative possible way, yeah. Like, the morning of my departure I was awakened by patches of light moving around on my tent. I thought for a minute that it might be caused by the movement of a large animal, passing between me and the sun. Then I emerged from the tent and saw that it had just been my imagination, that the light was shining between tree branches that were moving in the wind."

"Interesting! That heightened awareness of things, over a long enough span of time, does seem just like the sort of stimulus that could trigger an epigenetic shift in a Moiran," Ariane said.

"The thought had occurred to me."

"You didn't mention it in your report."

This was the first time Ariane had come out and admitted that she'd read the report, and so it pulled Kath Two up short.

She was distracted by a large Teklan entering the café with a green bracelet on his wrist. But it wasn't Beled. Just another surveyor, recently arrived, perhaps part of the same dragnet.

Obviously Beled had filed a very complete report, including his conversation with Kath Two on the flivver. From another type of person she might have found this an irritating indiscretion, but for a Teklan it was to be expected.

"I didn't mention it in my report," Kath Two said, "because in my judgment it was only my imagination, not a genuine, reportable Survey event."

"If you don't object to my going all juju—" This was a self-deprecating term for Julian-style cognition.

"Go ahead."

"Perhaps your initial impression was correct, and it was, in fact, caused by a large animal—a human—passing between you and the sun. A mistake committed by someone who was watching you furtively. And when he—I'll call him a he—noticed his shadow on your tent, he realized he'd blundered, and withdrew down the slope into the woods, and watched you from there."

"It is entirely possible," Kath Two said. Out of politeness she refrained from adding that it was the kind of thing that could only have been spun from a Julian mind.

"How has your sleep been since then?"

"Very sporadic and jet laggy, which is why I'm here. I think it is possible that I might have started to go epi on the last day, but now that I'm back in civilization my system is confused, and the shift is being aborted." Here, Kath Two might have reached up to feel her own face had she been sitting across the table from a Moiran friend. *Do I look different?* But Ariane would have no way of knowing the answer.

Kath Two added, "I've been sleeping with Beled. I think that is helping pull me back."

"Very well. I hope your adjustment—whether or not it includes becoming Kath Amalthova Three—is a smooth one."

"Am I free to leave?"

"It's not my decision. Your status remains indefinite."

"Afraid I'll blab about it?"

"It's not for me to be afraid about such things. My personal advice? Don't blab about it. But you know your rights. You can't be detained just because you think you might have seen a camouflaged gawker in the middle of nowhere." Ariane seemed to consider her next move before adding, "Otherwise you'd see a lot more Survey people bottled up in this café."

ARIANE WAS RIGHT ABOUT DOC. HE HAD LEFT HIS HOME IN THE misty campus of Stromness—a habitat in the predominantly Ivyn part of the ring, consisting entirely of university—and was en route to Cradle. Along the way he was spending a bit of time on the Great Chain. So when Kath Two finally took the obvious step of getting in touch with him directly, he responded within a few minutes and told her where he could be found.

At about the same time, the diode on Kath Two's wristband turned green, informing her that she was free to leave. She went to the room she'd been sharing with Beled to find that he had already departed. She gathered up her sterilized possessions and went to the exit, where the robot that was the door inspected her wristband. Apparently it liked what it saw, because it unlocked itself and allowed her to pass through. At the same moment the wristband sprang free and went dark. On her way out she tossed it into a bin.

Half an hour's floating along Eye passageways took her to the On Ramp, where she piled onto a capsule along with two dozen other visitors, strapped herself in, and was fired like a bullet down a gun barrel whose muzzle, at just the right moment, synched up with an arrival platform on the Great Chain. One gee of simulated gravity took effect as they were swept up into the rotation of the circular city. Attendants, stationed near the capsule's exit door, helped the new arrivals onto the platform and looked each one in the eye to make sure they were all right. People who weren't accustomed to sudden shifts in gravity were apt to suffer from dizzy spells or worse. Most of the attendants were Camites. This was a considered choice, ratified by many centuries of practice. Even the most hot-blooded Dinan would be willing to admit to one of these unassuming people that he was feeling woozy. The elaborate Dinan code of chivalry obliged them to show special politeness to Camites, whom they identified as weak and childlike.

Kath Two walked with only minor unsteadiness toward the top of a moving stairway that would take her down to the mass transit level. The ceiling above was high and arched, like a grand Old Earth train station, and its nickel-iron fretworks were atwitter with birds, a whole society of them going about its internecine trends and controversies while keeping an eye on the human traffic below. Specialized siwis, wrapped around the struts and girders like pythons around tree branches, moved along at a rate too gradual for the birds to notice, cleaning off their shit. The birds were all the same species, called the grizzled crow: a small corvid, half of whose feathers were devoid of pigment, giving it a salt-and-pepper appearance. This feature had been added by its designers simply as a visual flag so that they could be easily distinguished from rootstock crows. They moved in wheeling gray cyclones through the vaulted space overhead, but they were also comfortable shooting up and down the angled shafts that connected it to the transit level below. As Kath Two walked along the platform, a single one of those birds peeled away from a spiraling and squawking murder and dove toward her. As it hied in closer she became more and more certain that it was homing in on her face. It pulled up just short of colliding with her and, lacking a place to perch, hovered before her in ungainly style, treading air and slipping backward to match her pace. "The grove in the temperate rain forest," it said, or as near as a crow could come to pronouncing those words, and then beat air and took off, rising toward the rafters but then banking hard down the slanted tube that would take it back into the transit. Nor was it the only grizzled crow that was completing such an errand; similar encounters were happening all around her. Perhaps a score of the birds were perched on the safety railing that surrounded the entrance to the moving stair, muttering things that they had heard from humans. One of them, who perhaps had listened to a couple making love, was producing a crow's approximation of an orgasmic moan. Three of them were singing a popular song in unison. One was barking like a dog. A few were trying to cadge food from people who were carrying snacks. One of them just kept repeating "meet me at the train station at dot sixteen," another "I'll be wearing a red scarf."

At the bottom of the moving stair the crows were flying in and out of snug little rookeries that had been built for them at the ends of the tube cars, so that they wouldn't foul the seats. Ten minutes on one of those cars took Kath Two to Aldebrandi Gardens. This was a series of six consecutive blocks that had been constructed as botanical preserves. Each consisted of a rectangular slab of ecosystem covered by a lofty arched glass roof under which simulated Earth landforms had been built. The temperature and humidity of each had been tuned to simulate a different part of Old Earth. Plants and other organisms, sequenced from digital records, had been cultivated here, and supplemented later with birds, insects, and small animals. Creatures fostered and studied here had later been disseminated to factories in other parts of the ring where they'd been propagated in vast numbers and used to seed New Earth.

Starting at the hot end, Kath Two walked through a Southeast Asian jungle so humid that moisture condensed on her face before she could even begin to perspire. No sky was visible beneath its triple canopy, but when she stepped through the next airlock into Chihuahuan desert, she was treated to a direct view up through its ceiling into space, and blasted with sunlight bounced in by a robotic mirror mounted outside. Hanging up there in the center of the Great Chain was a little habitat called Surtsey. For during Kath Two's stay in Quarantine, the Eye had moved on from Akureyri, passed the even larger habitat of Sean Probst at twenty degrees west, and was now entering a sort of boundary zone on the edge of the Cape Verde boneyard. She knew nothing of Surtsey, but it looked like a placeholder habitat, a sort of construction shed that would be used as the basis for something planned a minute or two west of here. Her skin and hair dried out instantly under the sun, and by the time she reached the end of the block, she almost wished she'd stayed below in the tunnels, where she needn't have worried about cactus spines and rattlesnakes.

The next ecosystem was Fynbos, the characteristic environment of the Cape of Good Hope, cooler but no less sunny, a riot of scrappy flowering plants, a favorite of picnickers and birdwatchers from elsewhere in the Great Chain. It was a little too crowded for her taste, and so she marched straight down its length, trying not to be distracted by its many small charms, and entered the next block. This was almost more aquarium than terrarium, being a simulation of Old Earth Louisiana bayou. A plank walkway snaked among its moss-covered trees, carrying her over teeming reptile-infested waters to the airlock at its far end, where she stopped to pull a jacket out of her knapsack and don a pair of gloves.

Eight-hundred-year-old Douglas firs filled the next block from end to end. This one had been engineered to simulate the temperate rain forest of pre-Zero British Columbia, so its roof had been equipped with filters that damped the sun down to a steady silver glow that seemed to come from all directions. The lack of shadows made it seem brighter, in its way, than the unobstructed sunlight in the Chihuahuan biome. Ferns, moss, and epiphytes grew on fallen logs so thickly that they seemed to have been sprayed from a hose. A skein of faint paths ran through it. Kath Two followed one of them to the Kupol Grove: a relatively open space near the center, ringed by particularly enormous trees, where she found Doc, four of his students, his aide, and his robot sitting on moss-covered rocks and logs.

Dr. Hu Noah and most of his students were Ivyn. In Doc's case it was difficult to tell, since extreme old age tended to obscure racial differences. He'd lost his hair long ago, and his skin was blotchy from years spent down on the surface doing research in unfiltered sunlight. Limp skin dangled from his sharp cheekbones like wet laundry from the edge of a rock, and eventually joined into a system of wattles mostly concealed by a scarf wrapped around his neck. That, and other touches meant to keep him comfortable, had been seen to by his nurse, a stocky Camite wearing a knapsack full of medical supplies. Curled at Doc's feet like a sleeping dog was a grabb with a display panel in its back showing live readouts of his vital signs, which it was monitoring through a bundle of wireless connections. A pole projected vertically from its back to about the level of Doc's waist, where it forked to a pair of handlebars. It was a smart cane. When he grabbed the handlebars it would help him stand up. It would then steady his locomotion even on the roughest terrain, adding its six legs to his two.

Doc's students ranged in age from twenty to seventy. Kath Two had never met any of them before. There was nothing unusual in that; the TerReForm was the largest project ever undertaken by the human race, and 99 percent of it still lay in the future. She recognized the oldest one's face from pictures in scientific journals.

She felt awkward. Walking into the clearing and making herself known to these people had required a kind of courage. There was a class system within TerReForm. Doc was at its apex. Survey personnel were not so much at its bottom as on its wild fringes. Not so much looked down upon as looked at askance, seen as not entirely serious.

But they were polite. All except Doc greeted her with the Ivyn variant of the salute, an understated gesture that incorporated a suggestion of a bow. Doc held both of his hands out so that she could take them carefully in hers. He squeezed with surprising strength and she squeezed back.

Then suddenly they were alone. Whether by prearrangement or because the other Ivyns had sensed something, they all withdrew. Even the nurse stepped away and contented herself with a stroll around the clearing, holding her hand up from time to time to check Doc's readouts on a palm-sized device.

"You're coming to Cradle with me," he announced. "There is need of a team."

"A new research project?" she asked.

Doc's eyes closed for a moment in disagreement, then sprang open, gazing at her directly. "A Seven," he corrected himself.

"Hmm. And I'm to be—"

"One of us, yes."

Doc said this as if it were obvious. But it wasn't, not to Kath Two. A Seven—a group consisting of one person from each race—

was usually assembled for some ceremonial purpose, like dedicating a new habitat or signing a treaty. Not Kath Two's thing at all. And even if it had been, she was confused by the suggestion that she was to be in the same Seven as Doc. Because usually, when a Seven was being assembled, some effort was made to have all the members be of like status. And this was decidedly not the case between her and Doc. The gap in age, fame, and eminence was almost too wide to measure.

What could possibly make Kath Two special enough to deserve such an honor?

Her confusion lasted for only a few moments before she saw it, so obvious: it was something to do with what she had seen on the surface.

She saw faint amusement around Doc's eyes as he watched her figuring it all out. This turned to a mildly apprehensive look as he perceived that Kath Two was getting ready to blurt something. And that alone caused her to stifle it. She said nothing. They would talk of it only when Doc felt it was time.

"You've never been to Cradle before," he said.

"That's correct."

"Well, it should be a new kind of adventure for you then."

"I'll try not to look like a tourist."

"Look like whatever you please," he said. "We'll be too busy to worry much about such things."

"When do we—"

"Twelve hours, give or take," he said, and looked over to the Camite. "Is that about right, Memmie?"

Memmie nodded. "Cabins have been booked on the elevator departing at twenty-two thirty."

Kath Two hadn't met Memmie before, but had heard about this person of indeterminate gender who kept Doc alive and looked after many of his affairs. "Memmie" was short for Remembrance, a common Camite name. At the moment Memmie seemed to be presenting as female, with a saronglike wrap around the waist of a coverall that was otherwise utilitarian in the extreme, appearing to consist entirely of cargo pockets. Some neck jewelry and a turban-like head covering completed the ensemble. Her use of the passive voice—"Cabins have been booked"—was racially typical. Memmie, of course, had done the booking, made the other arrangements, and looked after the significant fund transfers needed to book a number of elevator cabins on short notice. But getting her to say that this had been her doing would have been like extracting teeth from her jaw. Some saw it as a becoming habit of humility; others saw it as irritatingly passive-aggressive. Kath Two had no opinion. She had a few free hours on the Great Chain and needed to make the most of them.

"See you there," she said.

"I shall look forward to it," Doc answered.

KATH TWO DESCENDED TO THE TRANSIT LEVEL AT THE END OF THE block and took the tube around the ring to a district of midrise blocks full of stores, markets, kupols, restaurants, and theaters, and spent the day drifting around, looking at things, buying little except for small items of clothing and toiletries she imagined she might need on the next leg of her journey. Square meter for square meter, this was the finest shopping district in the human universe, drawing its stock from every habitat visited by the Eye, attracting the sophisticated and well-heeled natives of the Great Chain as well as tourists from whichever habitats were currently in reach.

She was feeling a kind of vague ambient pressure—enhanced, no doubt, by the advertising that walled her in on all sides—to buy clothes, or try on jewelry, or get a hairstyle that would make her fit in better on Cradle. That was a place for people more important than Kath Two: brisk, poised paragons in uniforms or smart outfits, speed-walking down corridors in murmuring clusters, exchanging glances across lobbies. Kath One had been much more susceptible to those kinds of social influences and would have been emptying her bank account at this moment, trying to silence the little voice in her head telling her she wasn't pretty or stylish enough. But Kath One had died at the age of thirteen and been replaced by Kath Two, whose brain had a rather different set of emotional responses. It wasn't that she was unafraid. Everyone was afraid of something. Kath Two was afraid that she would make the wrong choices, and make a fool and a spectacle of herself, if she tried to dress up to Cradle's standards. Better to lurk, observe, and merge, as she did when flying in a glider.

On her way back down to the tube, she happened to pass by a bookstall, where she picked up a paper copy of one of her favorite history books and downloaded a whole series of novels set on Old Earth. The paper copy was an extravagance, something she would add to her little library the next time she made it to one of her caches. For like a lot of young Moirans, Kath Two didn't even try to establish a fixed home. With a home came a social circle, and perhaps a family. All of which was fine for the people of the other races. But until a Moiran "took a set," such permanent arrangements were unwise, placing husband, children, coworkers, and friends at risk of waking up one day to find that their wife, mother, colleague, or pal had effectively died and been replaced by someone else. So rather than renting apartments, young Moirans opted for storage caches in places they were wont to visit. Sometimes it was a shelf in a friend's closet, sometimes a locker in a Survey or military base, sometimes a commercial niche in a big city with a robot doorkeeper that would ID you. Abandoned caches were legion, their contents forever being sold at auction.

Kath Two was the sort of person whose caches were apt to be crammed with paper books. For her, the electronic books were an insurance policy of sorts. The four-day elevator ride might be nothing more than a prelude to further journeys, some of which might take her to places with little to no bandwidth, and nothing was worse than getting stuck in a situation like that with nothing to read.

Elsewhere on the Great Chain was a block-long historical museum, stacked by era, with one floor for each millennium, beginning with the pre-Zero world on the ground floor and proceeding upward. Of course, very few physical artifacts remained from pre-Zero, so that floor consisted mostly of pictures and reconstructed environments. But the Arkies had been allowed to bring a few possessions into space with them, and some of those had survived the Epic and the ensuing five thousand years. So it was possible to look at actual smartphones and tablets and laptops that had been manufactured on Old Earth. They did not work anymore, but their technical capabilities were described on little placards. And they were impressive compared to what Kath Two and other modern people carried around in their pockets. This ran contrary to most people's intuition, since in other areas the achievements of the modern world—the habitat ring, the Eye, and all the rest—were so vastly greater than what the people of Old Earth had ever accomplished.

It boiled down to Amistics. In the decades before Zero, the Old Earthers had focused their intelligence on the small and the soft, not the big and the hard, and built a civilization that was puny and crumbling where physical infrastructure was concerned, but astonishingly sophisticated when it came to networked communications and software. The density with which they'd been able to pack transistors onto chips still had not been matched by any fabrication plant now in existence. Their devices could hold more data than anything you could buy today. Their ability to communicate through all sorts of wireless schemes was only now being matched—and that only in densely populated, affluent places like the Great Chain.

There was no telling, of course, what was going on in the Red zone between the turnpikes. Signals intelligence shining out into space from their part of the habitat ring suggested that the Aïdans were at least as advanced, in their use of mobile communications, as people here. Because they were also quite good at encryption, there was no way of telling what they were saying to one another. But Blue, for its part, had made a conscious decision not to repeat what was known as Tav's Mistake.

It was unfair, of course, for billions of people to focus blame on one representative of his culture who had died in a bad way five thousand years ago. The Epic, however, tended to have this effect on people's thinking. In the same way that certain people of Old Earth, raised on the Bible, would have referred to masturbation as the Sin of Onan, those of the modern world tended to classify personal virtues and failings in terms of well-known historical figures from the era of the Cloud Ark, the Big Ride, and the first generations on Cleft. Fair or not, Tavistock Prowse would forever be saddled with blame for having allowed his use of high-frequency social media tools to get the better of his higher faculties. The actions that he had taken at the beginning of the White Sky, when he had fired off a scathing blog post about the loss of the Human Genetic Archive, and his highly critical and alarmist coverage of the *Ymir* expedition, had been analyzed to death by subsequent historians. Tav had not realized, or perhaps hadn't considered the implications of the fact, that while writing those blog posts he was being watched and recorded from three different camera angles. This had later made it possible for historians to graph his blink rate, track the wanderings of his eyes around the screen of his laptop, look over his shoulder at the windows that had been open on his screen while he was blogging, and draw up pie charts showing how he had divided his time between playing games, texting friends, browsing Spacebook, watching pornography, eating, drinking, and actually writing his blog. The statistics tended not to paint a very flattering picture. The fact that the blog posts in question had (according to further such analyses) played a seminal role in the Break, and the departure of the Swarm, only focused more obloquy upon the poor man.

Anyone who bothered to learn the history of the developed world in the years just before Zero understood perfectly well that Tavistock Prowse had been squarely in the middle of the normal range, as far as his social media habits and attention span had been concerned. But nevertheless, Blues called it Tav's Mistake. They didn't want to make it again. Any efforts made by modern consumer-goods manufacturers to produce the kinds of devices and apps that had disordered the brain of Tav were met with the same instinctive pushback as Victorian clergy might have directed against the inventor of a masturbation machine. To the extent that Blue's engineers could build electronics of comparable sophistication to those that Tav had used, they tended to put them into devices such as robots. Cleft's initial population had been eight humans and hundreds of robots (thousands, if nats were counted as individuals). Both numbers had expanded since then. Only in the last century had the human population pulled even with that of non-nat robots.

The end result, for a young woman in a bookstall above a tube station on the Great Chain, was that she was dwelling in habitats, and being moved around by machines, far beyond the capabilities of Old Earth. She was being served and looked after by robots that were smarter and more robust than their ancestors—the Grabbs and so on that Eve Dinah had programmed on Izzy. And yet the information storage capacity of her tablet, and its ability to connect, were still limited enough that it made sense for her to download books over a cable while that was easy, and to make room for them in the tablet's storage chips by deleting things she had already read.

That sorted, she rode transit to the Off Ramp, where she climbed into a capsule, facing backward, and felt deceleration push her back into her couch as it was flung off the Great Chain into a tube lined with electromagnetic decelerators.

Back now in the zero gee environment of the Eye's nonrotating frame, she began to navigate its internal companionways, pushing herself along lighted tubes marked with the icon of Cradle: a pair of mountains enclosed within a semicircular dome. This led her, within a few minutes, to a transit station where she and two random strangers climbed into a four-person bubble that presently went into motion and began to whoosh at greater and greater speed down a long and perfectly straight tube. They were traveling from the rim of the great

Eye's iris out to its inner vertex, the one closest to Earth, a distance of some eighty kilometers, and so hand-over-handing their way down a shaft wasn't an option. Kath Two, who had been awake now for something like sixteen hours, felt herself dozing off.

She jerked awake near the end of the trip, convinced that she had heard her name being spoken.

The pod had a video screen on its front bulkhead, and one of the other passengers, to pass the time, had begun playing back a segment of the Epic that must have taken place around twenty years after Zero. This could be guessed from the visible signs of aging on the faces of the surviving Eves, and from the fact that the first generation of their offspring were adolescents. This segment of the Epic told the story of how a personal rift between Eve Dinah and Eve Tekla had been mediated and settled by some of the youngsters, led by Catherine Dinova. It was frequently pointed to as one of the first moments when the children of the Eves had begun to think and take action for themselves. Lines of dialogue from it were quoted frequently in modern-day discussions.

Kath Two wondered, as she always did, whether the people of the Epic would have said and done some of what they had, had they known that, five thousand years later, billions of people would be watching them on video screens, citing them as examples, and quoting them from memory. Over the first few decades on Cleft, the cameras had died one by one. Depending on how you felt about ubiquitous surveillance, the result had either been a new Dark Age and an incalculable loss to history, or a liberation from digital tyranny. Either way, it signaled the end of the Epic: the painstakingly recorded account of everything that the people of the Cloud Ark had done from Zero onward. After that it had all been oral history for about a thousand years, since there had been no paper to write on and no ink to write on it with. Memory devices were scarce and jury-rigged. Every single chip had been used for critical functions such as robots and life support.

A tone sounded, warning the passengers of deceleration, and the pod eased to a stop in the terminal. Even after it had come to rest, however, they experienced a mild sense of gravity. It was too faint to be perceived other than as an annoying tendency for objects not otherwise constrained to drift "downward," where "down" in this part of the Eye meant "toward the Earth." To prevent that drift from getting out of hand, some floors of lightweight decking had been constructed. But the gravity was still so faint that you could fly around by pushing off against anything solid. Kath Two collected her bag, strapped it to her back, and glided out into the terminal. The other travelers from her pod seemed to know where they were going and so she followed them "down" through staggered gaps in those decks. This part of the Eye was bare bones in an almost literal sense; it was where the massive structural limbs that held the whole thing together converged to a sharp point, aimed forever at Earth. The metal was honeycombed with tunnels and cavities engineered for various purposes. The carbon cables that held Cradle suspended above Earth's atmosphere some thirty-six thousand kilometers below diverged here and ran taut through long sheltered passageways all the way to the other end of the Eye, where they came together again and emerged to connect with the Big Rock beyond. The passageways and chambers used by humans were tiny by comparison.

Set into the very point of the Eye was a glass dome, half a dozen meters in diameter. From it you could look straight down the bore of the tether—which was actually a tubular array of sixteen smaller tendons—and see the Earth. From this distance, the planet looked about as big as a person's face seen from across a small table. An Old Earther, seeing it from here, might think at first that nothing had ever changed. It still had the same general look: blue oceans, white icecaps, green-and-brown continents partly obscured by swirling white vortices of weather. Those continents stood in roughly the same places as the old ones, for not even the Hard Rain could make much of a dent in a tectonic plate. But the landforms had been radically resculpted, with many inland seas, and deep indentations in coastlines, created by large impacts. New island chains, frequently arc shaped, had been created by ejecta and by volcanic activity.

The Eye was always above the equator; currently it hovered over a spot about halfway between Africa and South America, whose coasts echoed each other's shape in a way that made their tectonic history obvious even to nonscientists. The low-lying terrain along both coastlines had huge bites taken out of it, frequently with rocky islands jutting out in the centers of the bites: central peaks of big impact craters. Archipelagoes reached out into the Atlantic but trailed off well short of joining the two continents.

The geography of New Earth, though beautiful to look at, made little impression on Kath Two, since she had been studying it her whole life and had spent years tromping around on it. For now, her attention was captured by the giant machines in which the view was framed. Surrounding her, and just visible in her peripheral vision, was another of those ubiquitous tori, spinning around to provide simulated gravity for the staff who lived here with their families, looking after the tether and the elevator terminal. Inward of that were the sixteen orifices where the tether's primary cables were routed into the frame of the Eye. Each of those cables, though it looked solid from a distance, was actually made of sixteen more cables, and so on and so forth down to a few fractal iterations. All of these ran parallel between the Eye and Cradle. Webbing them together was a network of smaller diagonal tendons, arranged so that if one cable broke, neighboring ones would take the force until a robot could be sent out to repair it. Cables broke all the time, because they'd been hit by bolides or simply because they had "aged out," and so if you squinted your eyes and looked closely enough at the tether, you could see that it was alive with robots. Some of these were the size of buildings, and clambered up and down the largest cables simply to act as mother ships for swarms of smaller robots that would actually effect the repairs. This had been going on, to a greater or lesser extent, for many centuries. This end of the cable had beanstalked downward from the Eye while the other had grown in the opposite direction, reaching out away from the habitat ring and from Earth, acting as a counterbalance.

Cradle was much too small to be picked out at this distance. Even if it had been large enough to see, her view of it would have been blocked by the elevator, which was on its final approach, and expected to reach the terminal in about half an hour. It had a general resemblance to an Old Earth wagon wheel, with sixteen spokes reaching inward from its rim to a hotel-sized spherical hub where the people were. Watching it approach produced the mildly alarming illusion that it was going to come crashing through the dome. In that case, two domes would have been destroyed in the collision, since the hub was capped by a dome similar to this one where passengers could relax on couches and gaze up at the view of the approaching Eye and the habitat ring spreading out to either side of it. But of course it slowed down and stopped short of contact. Through the glass, now just a stone's throw away, she could see the new arrivals unbuckling their seat belts, gathering their things, and floating toward the exits. Most of them were wearing military uniforms, or else the dark, well-designed clothing that she associated with comersants and politicos. Not really her crowd. But Doc had invited her, which was all the credentials anyone really needed.

Through the flimsy internal partitions she could hear several dozen arrivals making their way to Quarantine. These were eventually bound either for the Great Chain or the much smaller torus that encircled this end of the tether. Through the dome she could see housekeeping robots, and a few human staff, making their sweep through the hub's lounge. After a few minutes, a green light came on above a door, and she joined a flow of a few dozen departing passengers.

Within minutes she was ensconced in a small private cabin in the elevator's hub, where she would spend the four-day journey to the tether's opposite terminus. A chime warned her when the elevator began to accelerate downward, but it moved at a speed that was extremely modest by the normal standards of space travel, so she felt no need to strap in. She climbed into her bed and slept.

THE ELEVATOR WAS A HOLLOW CYLINDER TEN STORIES HIGH, WITH A glass dome at each end, one aimed up at the Eye and the other aimed down at Earth. The floors beneath those domes were made of glass, so that the light shone through from end to end. The outer walls were windowless and heavily shielded against cosmic radiation, but on the inside, the cabins and lounges had windows onto the atrium. Or at least the more expensive cabins did; Kath Two's was at the periphery, hard up against the outer wall, with no windows other than a tiny porthole onto a ring-shaped corridor. Which was fine with her. At the beginning of the journey they were in near weightlessness, but as the days went on, gravity would increase, reaching one normal gee at Cradle. She could tell when she woke up that she had not slept for long, since gravity was still quite faint, perhaps comparable to what had once existed on the moon.

She wandered up and down the atrium looking for a place where she could sit and read her book. Several bars and restaurants fronted on it, but these were not places for Kath Two, as she could tell just from the look of the people and the prices quoted on the menus. Comfy-looking chairs and couches were distributed around the glass floor of the atrium, and a coffee bar stood along one edge, so she ended up there.

After an hour or so, Beled Tomov turned up and sat in her general vicinity but made no move to interrupt her reading. When she came to a good stopping place, she looked up and happened to notice Ariane Casablancova sitting on the opposite side of the atrium, working on a tablet.

So they had five of the Seven: Doc, Memmie, Ariane, Beled, and Kath Two. The only two missing were the Dinan and, somewhat more problematically, the Aïdan.

Kath Two and Beled ran into Doc and Memmie later when they wordlessly agreed to go to the least expensive of the eateries and get some food. Somewhat uncharacteristically, Doc was not surrounded by students, scholars, and TerReForm bigwigs. He was just sitting at one end of the room carefully eating soup. Memmie was at his elbow, reaching in frequently to tuck his napkin back into his collar. Neither of them reacted when Kath Two and Beled took seats at the same table, but after a few minutes Doc said, "Lieutenant Tomov, it is good to see you again. Greetings," and the two of them exchanged salutes in their respective racial styles.

Lieutenant, obviously, was a military and not a Survey rank, and so this confirmed the unsurprising fact that Beled's relationship to Survey was, at best, ambiguous. Much more interesting was the fact that he and Doc had already met.

"I hope that this assignment will not prove an inconvenience," Doc continued.

"All duty is inconvenient to a greater or lesser degree, or it would not be duty."

"I was thinking more of the advancement of your career, Lieutenant. In your future dossier, this will stand out as a highly anomalous episode. Depending on who is reading that dossier, it might help you or hurt you."

"I don't concern myself with such matters," Beled returned.

"Some would call that unwise, but I tend not to favor the company of such. You, on the other hand, will do nicely."

"May I ask why I was so honored?"

Doc's eyes moved briefly to Kath Two. "Kath here will be worried that it's because she shared an indiscretion with you. Drew you into it. Or perhaps she is a little bit exasperated with you for having passed it on in your report."

Kath Two shook her head no, but did not wish to interrupt Doc. Beled, however, seemed to take it in.

Doc continued. "None of that really counted. You are a known quantity, now, not only to me but also to Kath Two and to Ariane, which is somewhat useful. But even without all of that, you would have been a fine choice. Not everything must be for a reason. Never mind what our Julian friends say."

He had noticed Ariane Casablancova approaching them, somewhat tentatively, with a tray of food. He made an almost subliminal gesture with his eyes toward Memmie, who stood up and fetched an extra chair from an adjoining table. Ariane joined them. Kath Two felt vaguely uncomfortable. A day earlier this woman had held and wielded power over her, had known things about her that would normally have been private matters. What was she to Kath Two now? Presumably an equal member of the Seven.

Ariane had, of course, worked this all out ahead of time, and prepared for it. "Kath Two and Beled," she said, "our first meetings were in a formal bureaucratic setting that now leads to some awkward feelings. I look forward to reacquainting myself with both of you as a colleague."

"Noted," said Beled.

"Thank you," said Kath Two. But if anything she felt even more awkward now. Ariane's little speech had not been delivered warmly. More like she was ticking her way down a checklist. In that vein, she now turned her searchlight eyes toward the other two. "Dr. Hu. Remembrance."

"Doc," Doc said, "and Memmie."

"It is good to make your acquaintances in person."

These formal and somewhat chilly conversational gambits led nowhere, and so after an awkward silence Ariane tucked into her meal.

"Doc," Kath Two said, "may we know what the hell we are doing? What is this Seven for?"

"It looks like a Five to me," Doc said puckishly, somewhat breaking the tension. For Memmie, Ariane, and Beled had all aimed sharp looks at Kath Two, startled by the informal way in which she had just spoken to her old professor. Doc, who clearly didn't care, continued:

"When we are Seven—which will be in a few days, on Cradle—then I will explain it once, to everyone, at the same time."

"Fair enough," Kath Two said. "What should we be doing in the meantime?"

"All of the things you will look back on fondly later when you have not been able to do them for a long time."

It was a lovely thought. Kath Two tried to be duly appreciative of the generous sentiment behind it during the remainder of the journey. But nothing of the sort really happened. She read more than she had intended to of the books she had acquired on the Great Chain. At meals, and in the recreation center, she placed herself in Beled's eye line, just in case he was in the mood. But things were different now. Their time together in the Q had been an ideal setup for a relationship of a casual and temporary nature. It had never gone beyond sleeping in the same bed, but it might have. The knowledge that they would probably never see each other again had made it easy to shack up for a couple of nights and enjoy each other's company in a way that would have posed too many complications had they been working together.

Now they were working together. Beled had wisely pulled back. She understood, and considered a certain amount of sexual frustration an acceptable price to pay for being prudent.

She had two meals with Ariane, and in her spare time she made desultory attempts to learn more about the Julian from network searches. Kath Two assumed that all such search activity was being monitored and logged by someone—possibly someone who was in touch with Ariane through whatever agency Ariane worked for. As time went by, Kath Two was less and less certain that that was actually Quarantine. Or perhaps another way of saying it was that Quarantine's public face—the people who talked to you when you were traveling between space habitats—was only one avatar of something that had to be much bigger and more complicated. In the same way that Survey and military were different things, and yet drawing a sharp line between them could be difficult, so it was with police and Quarantine. And once you broadened the scope to include police, you were talking about other things besides routine law and order work. At some level, intelligence and counterintelligence were under that umbrella. Kath Two had no way of guessing where Ariane fit into that system. Searching the network too avidly for personal details about Ariane Casablancova would have been noticed, and would have been a bad idea. Not searching at all would almost have been more suspicious. So Kath Two searched a little, and found less. Low-level Q officers might be mentioned on the network from time to time, as the result of a police report or a public relations initiative, but there was nothing of the sort for Ariane—assuming that this was even her real name.

A compulsion for privacy was hardly unusual for a Julian living and working in Blue. The Julian part of the ring, centered on the Tokomaru habitat, was the least populous of the eight segments. Ninety-five percent of it lay on the Red side of the turnpike. Only a tiny sprinkling of habitats projected east of Kiribati into the Blue zone, and in those the Julians had been diluted by the more numerous and aggressive Teklans, whose segment lay just on the far side of the Hawaii boneyard. Thus the Julians had maintained enough of a presence in Blue that they could live and work in it without being seen as aliens, or immigrants. Many of them were "dukhos," playing approximately the same role in modern society as priests had done pre-Zero.

The destruction of Old Earth and the reduction of the human population to eight had done for the idea that there was a God, at least in any sense remotely similar to how most pre-Zero believers had conceived of Him. Thousands of years had passed before anyone, even in the most remote outposts of human settlement, had dared to suggest that religion, in anything like its traditional sense, might be or ought to be revived. In its place a new set of thoughtways had grown up under the general heading of "dukh," a Russian word referring to the human spirit. Dukh-based institutions had developed under the general term of "kupol," a word that harked back to the glass bubble that had served as a kind of interfaith chapel and meditation room on *Endurance*. Modern-day kupols all traced their origins back to that structure, which Dubois Harris had called the Woo-Woo Pod. When people nowadays watched scenes from the Epic that took place in it, they were in the backs of their minds thinking of their local kupols and the people who staffed them. A professional member of a kupol's staff was generally called a dukho, a truncation of the Russian word "dukhobor," meaning one who wrestled with spiritual matters. Kupols, like churches of old, were supported by contributions from their members. Some, as on the Great Chain, were richly endowed, magnificent buildings. Others, like the one in the Q, were just quiet rooms where people could go to think or to seek help from what amounted to social workers. Dukhos tended to trace their lineage back to Luisa, who had played a similar role during the Epic, and some of the better-educated ones drew explicit connections between their kupols and the Ethical Culture Society, where Luisa had gone to school in New York. But Luisa, of course, had not produced a race. The dukho profession had ended up being dominated by Julians. The Julian habitat of Astrakhan, which hovered anomalously in the middle of the Dinan segment, had become a sort of hothouse for the production of dukhos of various denominations. Kath Two was able to establish that Ariane had originated from there, but little else. It was fine. There were ample reasons for Ariane to keep to herself and lead a quiet life.

MOST OF THE GIANT NICKEL-IRON MOON CORE FRAGMENT NAMED Cleft had been melted down and reshaped into what was now the Eye. The engineers had not been able to bring themselves, however, to destroy the part of it immediately surrounding the place where *Endurance* had come to rest at the end of the Big Ride, and where the bodies of

Doob, Zeke Petersen, and other heroes of the Epic had been interred directly into iron catacombs. That patch of the asteroid—the deep, shielded declivity where the first several generations of the new human races had lived out their entire lives—had come to be known as Cradle.

Everyone had, of course, seen the chapter from the Epic where Doob had gone out on his last space walk with Eve Dinah, looked up at the walls of iron rising from the valley floor, and foreseen that one day a ceiling of glass would be built over the top, turning the "Vale of the Eves" into a huge greenhouse where children would be able to float about unencumbered by space suits, eating fresh greens from terraced gardens. It was probably the biggest tearjerker in the whole Epic, and a perennial favorite. All of Doob's predictions had, of course, come true. Cradle had ended up supporting a population of several thousand, until later generations had been obliged to push outward.

Cradle's main defect had been a lack of simulated gravity, which had obliged those early generations to construct what amounted to glorified merry-go-rounds on which children could take turns being centrifuged in order to foster bone growth. Subsequent habitats—spinning tori mounted to the walls of the cleft—had actually been more crowded and confined than Izzy itself, and many generations had lived cramped lives in them with only occasional opportunities for R & R in Cradle's sunny open volumes. In time they had learned to make bigger and better habitats, and Cradle had been abandoned for many centuries, an occasional destination for historians or curiosity seekers.

The construction of the Eye had, in effect, cut Cradle and its immediate surroundings loose from Cleft, and it had drifted in a boneyard for a while until the decision had been made to give it a new purpose. The original greenhouse, which was a wreck by that point, had been replaced by a new, bigger, retractable cover. The underside had been planed flat. The canyon walls had been terraced back, making them less steep, and not incidentally creating valuable, buildable real estate. A nickel-iron yoke had been arched over the whole thing so that it could be attached to the bottom end of the thirty-six-thousand-kilometer tether that dangled from the Eye.

The icon in the transit station—two hills enclosed in a bubble—was a simplified depiction of what Cradle actually looked like. Its total inhabitable footprint was a circular zone about two thousand meters in diameter, which put it on about the same scale as downtown Boston or the City of London. This was cleaved by the Vale of the Eves, whose walls had once been nearly vertical. Now this was true only of the bottom-most ten meters or so: a slot that snaked through the bottom of the town like a gully. It became a rust-brown river when there was heavy rain, and so they had maintained an island in the middle of the stream, exactly on the site where *Endurance* had touched down. Once, it had been possible to go there and touch the little nubs of steel where Eve Dinah had welded the ship into place. These, however, had since been protected under glass domes so that they would not rust, or get worn away by tourists' fingers. The ship itself was long gone, of course; the survivors had begun dismantling it almost as soon as they had arrived, and what little they hadn't used was radioactive waste, long since shipped away to carefully tended locations in boneyards.

It was therefore a city constructed on two dizzyingly steep hills that faced each other across a crevasse. A kilometer-long bridge, celebrated for its grace, arched across the gulf between the hills, a plunging wedge of air flocculent with grizzled crows.

It was a city of compounds. Some of these dated back to the early days of its construction, when the bubble had not yet been completed and there had been a need to make smaller inflatable domes over certain areas. Others had been built in imitation of those first ones. Neither the compounds—which, for structural reasons, tended to be circular—nor the overall topography lent themselves to a grid street pattern. Consequently the map was a chaos of switchbacks and meanders and streets that turned suddenly into stairways or tunnels.

Limitations on building height led people to dig down into the underlying metal, rather than building upward, and so most of the city's square footage was hidden. The buildings were like icebergs, larger below than above.

Above grade, stone was a popular building material. Older and less prestigious buildings used the synthetic rock known as moonstone, made from pieces of Earth's former satellite. Newer and nicer buildings were made from marble, granite, or other rock quarried from the surface of the Earth itself. For the one resource that the shattered surface of Earth had been able to produce in abundance, even before it had an atmosphere, had been rocks. The city thus presented a hard face to pedestrians in its narrow streets. Those granted access to compounds would, however, find themselves in fragrant gardens under the shade of trees. Since Cradle was confined to the equator, green things grew there so luxuriantly that they had to be kept in check by hordes of little grabbs with pruning bill hands.

Atop each of the hills was a park. Rising above one of those parks was a roundish, domed building called the Capitol. Rising above the other was a squarish, pillared colonnade called the Change, short for Exchange.

At the time Kath Two and the other passengers arrived, Cradle was dangling two thousand meters above the waters of the Atlantic Ocean, being dragged due west toward where the equator cut across the reshaped coastline of South America. This movement reflected the fact that, thirty-six thousand kilometers above it, the Eye was traversing the habitat ring westward, or CASFON (Clockwise As Seen From Over the North pole). Being nothing more than a weight on the end of a long string, Cradle always followed the movements of the Eye. The city's dome was open, with its baffles raised to reduce the windblast.

It was balmy and humid. This was almost always true on the equator, but altitude and the brisk movement of the air made it pleasant enough. The smell of that air, redolent of salt and iodine and marine life, was proof irrefutable that Kath Two was back in the atmosphere of New Earth.

It was an artificial atmosphere. The human races had bombarded the parched and dead surface of the planet with comet cores for hundreds of years just to bring the sea level up to where they wanted it. Then they had infected that water with organisms genetically engineered to produce the balance of gases needed to support life—and, having done that, to commit suicide, so that their biomass could be used as nutrients for the next wave of atmosphere-building creatures.

According to their measurements, the result was a nearly perfect reproduction of Old Earth's atmosphere. No one who breathed it after a lifetime spent in habitats needed scientific data to back that up. Its smell penetrated to some ancient part of the brain, triggering instincts that must go all the way back to hominid ancestors living on the shores of Africa millions of years ago. As she knew from having traveled to Earth many times, it was a kind of intoxicant. It was the best drug in the universe. It made people want to be on Earth more than anything. It was the reason that Cradle—which was bathed in that air, being dragged through it all the time on the end of its thirty-six-thousand-kilometer string—was the most exclusive community in existence. And it was the reason that Red and Blue had twice gone to war over the right to live on the surface.

Cradle was hung from the end of the tether by a sort of bucket handle that arched high above the middle of the city. The bucket handle was hollow, accommodating a surprisingly ramshackle elevator system that took Kath Two and some other passengers down to a platform embedded in the city's bedrock, or "bedmetal," along its northern limb. From there a ramp took them up into the streets of the city itself.

The tops of the walls all around the exit were white with crow shit. Hundreds of birds were perched where they could view the faces of those emerging into the light and swoop down to deliver messages to ones they had recognized. Other new arrivals stretched their hands out to offer little snacks. A well-dressed Ivyn man, bustling along ahead of Kath Two, quickly attracted a grizzled crow by that strategy. With his other hand he held out a little tablet that, as Kath Two knew, must be showing someone's photograph. "Coffee at the Change, dot seventeen," the man said. The crow gulped the snack down in a move that looked almost like vomiting in reverse, then flapped away screaming the same words into the ether. Other grizzled crows, not hungry or not currently on errands, were keeping up a raucous murmur that, if you listened to it, might give you clues as to what was going on in the equities market or the political world.

At first the new arrivals moved together in a pack, visibly distinct from the ordinary foot traffic of the place, but within a few hundred meters this had dispersed, and Kath Two found herself alone, no different from anyone else.

She knew the general layout from schoolbooks. She had arrived on the north side—Change Hill. Perhaps a native would have known as much just from the attire of the people, the way they walked. These were comersants, working by day in subterranean offices, ascending to the surface for meals, recreation, and other means of enjoying their wealth. Commerce was, of course, spread all about the habitat ring, and the old centers of Greenwich, Rio, Baghdad, et al. had financial hubs that rivaled, and in some ways eclipsed, Change Hill. But nothing could ever compete with this place for prestige. The wealthiest and most powerful financiers, the up-and-coming traders in places like Greenwich, no matter how well they were doing for themselves, were forever haunted by the thought that they might be missing something on Cradle.

Because so much of that activity was taking place below the surface, the streetscape of Change Hill was deceptively quiet, a little like an old Spanish city during siesta. Soon lost, and resigned to the fact that doing so would make her look like a tourist, Kath Two took the piece of paper out of her pocket and reminded herself of the address. She already knew it was on the south side and that she would either have to cross the bridge—which was clearly visible, arcing high above the city—or descend all the way to the floor of the vale and cross the gully at its bottom. The latter tempted her, but she knew that she would want to spend a lot of time there, looking at the place where *Endurance* had touched down and where Eve Dinah had walked with Dubois Harris. That was best saved for later. So she climbed, winding her way through the streets, which were paved with a stone whose reddish-brown color hid the rust stains that streaked down from every exposed bit of bedmetal. She cut across the park beside the Change, where young traders in good clothes, out on snack breaks, were sitting on benches prodding their tablets, or sprawled in clusters on the grass laughing, or playing lawn sports with colored balls.

The bridge's northern end met the park's edge. From far below, the bridge had looked slender and graceful, belying what she now understood was its real bulk. Here it broadened to form a massive connection with Change Hill. Even at its apogee, however, it was broad enough for twenty people to walk abreast. After turning around one last time to admire the marble columns of the Change and to hear the roar of voices within, she faced south and began to ascend. In the early going the bridge was a stairway, but as the arch gradually flattened with height, it turned into a ramp, faced in white marble, broken with occasional landings. She had been informed that the real reason for these was to prevent wheeled objects from going fully out of control. If so that purpose had been artfully concealed by turning them into little sculpture gardens where bridge climbers could pause for refreshment beneath rose-covered bowers.

While not immune to such temptations, Kath Two was at bottom a serious walker who did not like to stop once she had gotten going. She was thinking, reviewing in her mind the journey on the elevator, which had been largely uneventful. This, as she had gradually realized, was a part of its charm and of its exclusivity. It was possible to reach Cradle quickly, if you had enough money to charter, or authority to commandeer, the right vehicles. Most people used the elevator, though. Thus Cradle was separated from the rest of the human world not so much by distance as by time. Spending that much time was a sort of luxury, afforded only to a few. Of course, passengers worked en route—this explained all of those expensive restaurants and bars around the atrium, with their private meeting rooms. But Kath Two hadn't had any real work to do. She had gone for long hours without talking to another human at all, and had done a lot of reading and watching of entertainment on screens. She had slept normally, confirming that any epigenetic shift that might have gotten started last week had been aborted.

All of this just made her want to reach the meeting place so that she could at least have an explanation from Doc, meet the missing Dinan and Aïdan, and get started on whatever it was the Seven was supposed to be doing.

She maintained a brisk pace to the top of the arch but there permitted herself a few minutes' pause. At the apex, the walkway broadened into a scenic overlook affectionately known as Hurricane Heights. The wind was so powerful here that it made her eyes water. She turned her back to it and toddled carefully over to the eastern railing, on the lee side. She blinked her vision clear and allowed herself a few minutes' gawking down into the compounds and the streets and the Vale. The sun was setting behind her. Since they were on the equator it would set quickly. The Vale was already in shadow, but the stone walls of the compounds and the fronts of the buildings were emanating a magical pink-gold glow. Lights were coming on in windows along purple-shaded streets.

It was a real place. Not like the artificial environments of the habitat ring. Some of the larger habitats came close to possessing this quality—the sense that you were in something close to a real planetary environment. But it was always dispelled as soon as you looked up and saw the opposite side of the habitat hanging a few kilometers above your head. Here, you could look up and see endless sky, the stars coming out, the gleaming necklace of the habitat ring rising perpendicularly from the eastern horizon. The thing that made it real was the air, the sheer quantity of it, the endless variety of its movements and its smells. She wished she had a glider so that she could go dancing in it.

ACCORDING TO A LEGEND THAT WAS ALMOST CERTAINLY INCORrect, the overlook where Kath Two was standing—the center of the bridge—was the location where Eve Dinah's demolition charge had exploded after she had made her choice and tossed it into space.

The compromise that Dinah had forced by placing that bomb against the window of the Banana had seemed elegant and straightforward for about as long as it had taken for the bomb to go off.

In one sense, the gaming of the system had begun even before it was thought of, when Eve Julia had pointed out that she would have few babies and Eve Aïda had prophesied that she would have many.

It had not taken long for the other Eves to make similar calculations. As Arkies, picked in the Casting of Lots, Camila and Aïda were younger than the others, with two to three decades of fertility ahead of them. If they decided to become baby factories, and if they were lucky, each of them could conceivably bear as many as twenty children before menopause. Dinah, Ivy, Moira, and Tekla, all in their early thirties, might bear a few each. Roughly speaking, therefore, those four had as much combined childbearing power, if you wanted to think about it that way, as the younger pair of Camila and Aïda.

Julia, as she had pointed out, would be lucky to bear one child before menopause. And she had not needed Doob to explain the exponential math. The Julians were going to be swamped. They were going to be mere curiosities. People in the distant future, coming home from work, would exclaim to their partners, "You'll never guess what I saw today—an honest to god Julian!"

Those were the mathematical rudiments of the new Great Game, and the roots of much of what had happened since then. The preponderance of later historical scholarship suggested that most of the Eves didn't know that they were playing a game until they were a few years into it. Aïda, based on what she had said in her Curse, might have been the exception to that rule. But decisions made about one's children were the most personal decisions that one could make, and no mother of sound mind would have admitted to herself, at the time, that she was playing a sort of game vis-à-vis the other mothers.

In a way it would have been simpler had they gone about it more cold-bloodedly.

Consciously or not, the Seven Eves sorted themselves into Four, Two, and One. The Four were Dinah, Ivy, Tekla, and Moira. The Two were Camila and Aïda. Arithmetic suggested that the descendants of the Four would be about as numerous as those of the Two. Existing friendships and affinities already linked the Four and created an unspoken compact, not articulated until they were long dead, to the effect that their children would embody complementary qualities. Dinans, in a sense, did not have to be complete humans as long as Ivyns were around to do some of the things they weren't as good at. This was a blunt way of saying it, which was why it went unsaid for a long time, but hundreds of years later the descendants of the Four could look back and see that it had always been so. By that time it was so deeply ingrained in their DNA and their cultures that there was no going back.

The Two, by contrast, had no natural affinity with each other, and no existing relationship. Camila and Aïda had not met until shortly before the Council of the Seven Eves. All that they shared—and it wasn't much to go on—was an aversion to Julia. Both of them had, at one point or another, fallen under Julia's spell only to be disappointed by her. In Camila's case the seduction had happened during a White House dinner. For her part, Aïda had been talked by Julia into joining the Swarm, only to end up leading the rebel faction that had deposed and mutilated her. Given the way that had all turned out, it was of course unlikely that Camila, or anyone of sound mind, would consciously align herself with Aïda. And yet the mathematics of the Four and the Two created a kind of gravity, invisibly drawing her that way. The breach that had opened between Camila and Dinah during the Council of the Seven Eves would not be forgotten.

Considered more calmly, Camila's words had a persuasive power that couldn't be denied. It simply *was* the case that their descendants would be living bottled up in confined spaces for many generations to come. As Luisa had demonstrated through her research, and as the people of the Cloud Ark had just finished proving in spectacular fashion, it wasn't a good way for normal, unaltered humans to live. If the survival of the human race depended on rewiring their brains to make them better at such a lifestyle, then perhaps they had best get on with it.

In a way, that decision had been taken out of their hands by Camila, who had made her choice clear, and only needed to work out the details with Moira. She had, in effect, made the first clear move in the great genetic game. And contrary to her own stated principles it was, in a way, the most aggressive move possible: she had let them know that her descendants—who were likely to be quite numerous—would get along just fine in the conditions they would all be facing for the first ten, twenty, or hundred generations. The other six were left to follow her lead or to react against it.

Dinah, Ivy, and Tekla in essence reacted against it, with Moira eventually making another choice; but the historical fact was that Moira's descendants had, more often than not, been part of the bloc of the Four.

Aïda had played the game more overtly. This had basically consisted of waiting the others out to see what they would do, and then making countermoves. The other Eves decided early, and stuck with those decisions. All of Dinah's children—she ended up having five of them—were recognizably of a type. The same was true of Ivy's three, and Tekla's six. Julia only got to choose once. Camila's sixteen offspring varied from one to the next, as she tinkered with her decisions based on behaviors she was observing among her first children. But she had never wavered from the general template that she had laid out during the Council of the Seven Eves.

Aïda's seven children, however, were all different. Exactly what she was thinking was known only to Moira, the Keeper of Secrets, the Mother of Races. For the other Eves told Moira what they wanted in confidence, and she took those confidences to her grave. But it was plain enough—and in any event, it became the accepted version of history—that the first five children of Aïda had been conceived as reactions to what other Eves—all except Moira—were doing.

Aïda's stance toward the others had been well articulated in the Curse. She knew that the other six Eves would always loathe her personally and that this feeling would inevitably be transferred to her offspring. Human nature being what it was, Dinan children, thousands of years from now, would be throwing rocks at Aïdan children on playgrounds and making jokes about cannibalism. They would never be assimilated into the society descended from the Four. Therefore, to the extent that Dinah was making choices about the virtues that her offspring would embody, and thereby making a move in the game, Aïda sought a countermove. Which might consist of conceiving a child that would be like Dinah's, except more so. Or of inventing an anti-Dinan, a type of human uniquely suited to exploiting the weaknesses in the Dinan type.

Thus the first five children of Aïda. She had, however, been unable to employ the same strategy vis-à-vis Moira, for the basic reason that Moira knew exactly what Aïda was doing, down to the specific DNA base pairs that had been altered in her ova. If this were a game, then Eve Moira always had the last move. The failures of her first eight pregnancies had only deepened the mystery. Since she had never articulated her choice, no one really knew what she had done, which made Moirans an enigmatic race, not only to the other races, but to themselves. But it was plainly the case that Moirans were the only race capable of "going epi." Kath Two's genome, like that of every other life-form, was fixed. A copy of it lived in every cell in her body. But which of those genes were being expressed at a given time, and which were lying dormant, was changeable to a degree far beyond what humans were normally capable of. It would have amounted to a kind of superpower, had there been a way to control it. But, certain hoary old legends to the contrary, there wasn't. Kath Two never knew when she might fall asleep for a week and wake up a different person named Kath Three. Sometimes the results were brilliant. Rarely they were fatal. Sometimes they were inconvenient, or downright embarrassing. Most of the latter cases had something to do with what happened, like it or not, when a Moiran fell in love. In any case, this was the choice that Eve Moira had made and the gift she had conferred on her daughter, Cantabrigia. And it was assumed that she had done so because she believed that this degree of plasticity would somehow bring the world back into balance against the choices that Aïda had been making.

Julia, the One, looked to make the best of a bad situation by endowing her offspring with qualities that would make them useful and important in spite of much smaller numbers. She had already expressed, during the Council of the Seven Eves, the idea that there was real value in the ability to envision possible futures. And she had linked it to leadership, or, failing that, to the ability to give useful advice to leaders. When that trait ran out of control and sought dark paths it led to depression, paranoia, and other forms of mental illness. The challenge then was to find a way of combining that trait with a more positive mentality. Julia's research—and she did a lot of research—therefore tended to center on the history of sages, seers, ecstatics, shamans, artists, depressives, and paranoiacs throughout history, and the extent to which those traits could be localized to specific base pairs in their genomes and fostered by acculturation.

Historians had come along much later and developed their own vocabulary for telling the story of the succeeding five thousand years. The first pregnancies were called Gestations. Not counting the numerous miscarriages, there had been thirty-nine of them, distributed among the Seven Eves, before Camila, the last to stop bearing children, had finally gone through menopause. From these, thirty-five viable girls had resulted. Thirty-two had gone on to have children of their own. By then, Eve Moira had figured out how to synthesize Y chromosomes, and so some of the second generation had been male. The result, therefore, had been thirty-two Strains. Each of the seven new races had embodied more than one Strain. The Strains were recognizably different and yet clearly classifiable as belonging to one race or another, somewhat as East Africans differed from West Africans but still looked like Africans to Europeans.

"Correction" was the name given to the phase that had begun after the first round of Gestations, when Eve Moira had fixed errors that had led to several nonviable infants. In a sense, Correction went on continuously all through the first round of Gestations and began to taper off as the daughters of the Eves began to produce second-generation children. It faded into a next stage, Stabilization, which lasted through the following ten generations or so as Y chromosomes were patched up, lingering genetic mistakes were fixed, and members of different Strains began to interbreed to produce hybrids within their own racial groups. During this time the lessons of the black-footed ferret were put to use as various techniques were employed to increase heterozygosity.

In truth a vast library of human genetic sequences was available in digital form, and once they had survived the first few generations in Cradle, and trained hundreds of bright young people to be genetic engineers, they could, in theory, have resequenced the original human race from scratch. This was the sort of thing Eve Moira had done by synthesizing the first artificial Y chromosome. But it was not what they collectively chose to do. That choice was altogether cultural, not scientific. Decisions had been made in the Council of the Seven Eves. Races had been founded that were, by then, several generations old. They had begun to develop their own distinctive cultures. To undo those decisions by reverting to the "rootstock" human race was viewed almost as a kind of auto-genocide. The competition that had developed among the different races rendered it unthinkable. So the genetic records of rootstock humanity were put to work adding a healthy degree of heterozygosity back into the existing races, rather than trying to go backward.

Thus Stabilization, which had continued until about the twelfth generation, by which point even the Julian race had grown large enough to go on propagating through normal means without the need for lab-based adjustments.

Stabilization had blended into Propagation, the next phase generally recognized by historians, which was fairly self-explanatory: the descendants of the Seven Eves had continued to have sex with each other and make more babies. This had occupied much of the first half of the First Millennium and led to a condition of overcrowding so severe that it had made obligatory the formation of separate colonies away from Cradle. For there were other places, perhaps not quite so favored as Cleft, but still well suited for the building of new habitats. They had reached the point, by then, of being able to construct new machines for moving about in space. It was time. Or so insisted the descendants of the Four, who sensed that conditions had become inimical to them in the crowded precincts of Cradle. Camila had been frank about her strategy of making new humans well suited to life in confined spaces. She had succeeded in doing so. And once the early habitats of Cradle had grown crowded, her strategy had begun to look like a good one. Whether it was purely an expression of their own racial mythologies or a biological necessity, the Four had reached out and pioneered new habitats, at first in other locations on Cleft, later on other fragments of Peach Pit. The descendants of Aïda had done likewise, sometimes cohabiting with the Four, more often going it alone.

It wasn't so much that Aïda had done things that couldn't be undone as that she had said things that couldn't be unsaid. In that sense her Curse had real effect. An individual Aïdan of the Second Millennium was the product of a mixed-race culture that was more than a thousand years old. He or she had grown up with persons of all races, loving some and hating others, getting on well, perhaps, with certain Teklans and Moirans while getting into fights with certain Aïdans. In terms of his or her own personal experiences, there was no reason to stick together with others of the same race. But each race did have an ineradicable narrative, by now encoded into a culture that had become ancient. The narrative of the Aïdans was that their Eve had spawned not just one race but a "race of races," a mosaic, as proof that her children could do all that those of the other Eves could, and more. And if you were a descendant of Aïda, clearly endowed with genetic markers that she had chosen for that purpose, then the inexorable force of that narrative would drive you toward colonies populated largely or purely by other Aïdans.

As the Aïdans were less numerous than the descendants of the Four, their Second Millennium colonies had tended to be smaller and more Spartan, leading to a symbiotic relationship with the Camites, who tended to thrive in such environments. Aïdans built colonies but Camites made them work.

In any case, the formation of new colonies and habitats during the Second Millennium had led to a phase that the historians called Isolation: the formation of racially "pure" populations. Isolation led to Caricaturization: selective breeding, pursued consciously in some cases and unconsciously in others, that had the effect over many generations of intensifying racial differences. The example cited most often was a gradual change in eye color among Moirans. Eve Moira's eyes had been hazel: relatively light in color by the standards of black people, but not all that unusual. By the end of the Second Millennium, many Moirans had eyes so pale in color as to appear golden in strong light. On the walls of the Great Chain's fashion stores, blown up to ten times life size, Moiran fashion models still gazed at you through shockingly yellow, catlike eyes. Because pale eyes had been a distinctive characteristic of Eve Moira, it had become thought of as beautiful and desirable, and Moirans with pale eyes had found it easier to mate and reproduce, intensifying the trait over time, to the point of caricature. Kath Two herself, no model, was frequently complimented on the lightness of her eyes, which were closer to green than yellow. But modern, appearance-conscious Moirans were frequently startled when they saw photographs of their Eve with her eyes that were merely greenish-brown.

The shift in Moiran eye color was obvious and easily documented, but the same thing, mutatis mutandis, had happened with scores of other phenotypes among all the races. Selective mating had the power to wreak impressive changes over time, without any artificial meddling. In some cases, though, racial isolates had acquired genetic labs of their own. These had been used for many purposes, usually considered benign. In some cases, they had been used for Enhancement, which meant deliberate genetic manipulation for the purpose of rendering racial characteristics more pronounced—the artificial acceleration of what was happening "naturally" in the way of Caricaturization. Sometimes this led to freaks, monsters, and disasters. But often it worked. And when its results mated within isolated groups, those isolates became more and more pronounced embodiments of their races.

The end result of all this tended to be nonviable populations clearly identifiable as inbred. So, as often as Isolation, Caricaturization, and Enhancement had taken root and run their courses, they had led either to extinction of colonies or to an ameliorative process called Cosmopolitanization, wherein formerly isolated groups had remerged with their long-lost cousins of the same race and bred back in the direction of healthy and sustainable hybridized strains.

Not surprisingly, Cosmopolitanization had flourished as the habitat ring had been formed during the most recent millennium, suddenly creating a vast amount of new living space far more appealing than the cramped, dark tori in which people had been living for the last four thousand years. The isolates, some of whom hadn't been heard from for centuries, some of whom could not even speak Anglisky (as the Russian-inflected English, now shared by essentially all humans, was called), emerged from their holes and recombined with their extended families in a population explosion the likes of which had not been seen since Old Earth's twentieth century. Most of the population of most of the races had thus converged on a set of renormalized racial profiles, while preserving a few extreme tribal isolate strains, variously treasured, feared, or persecuted by others of the same race.

Or at least that was how it was in Blue. Red had exhibited the same general trends among its Aïdan mosaic, its hundreds of millions of Camites, and the roughly 80 percent of Julians who had decided to throw in their lot with Red. The current state of affairs between the turnpikes could only be speculated at, since no communication, other than stray signals intelligence and a propaganda channel that most people ignored, had been received from that part of the habitat ring for almost two hundred years.

FOR A FEW MINUTES THE LAST LIGHT OF THE SUN HAD BEEN STRIKing spires, statues, and carved stonework on the fronts of some fantastic old kupols mounted to the seemingly vertical cliff before her: the flank of Capitol Hill. But then suddenly it was near dark. Kath Two turned, accepting the windblast on her right side, and descended the south limb of the bridge. As much as she loved the power of the air, she felt herself scurrying the last few steps to get down into the shelter of the buildings. Capitol Hill was higher than Change Hill and so, rather than debouching into a park, as it did on its north end, the bridge here stabbed into the flank of the slope. Kath Two was plunged directly into a snarl of streets that were but indifferently illuminated by light spilling from occasional doorways and lamps that the owners of some compounds had decided to mount along the tops of their walls. "The streetscape of Bordeaux draped over the topography of Rio de Janeiro" was how the city had been described by its designer, a Julian/Moiran breed who had been born more than four thousand years after both of those cities had been annihilated.

She had a device in her pocket that knew her exact latlong. Those numbers were, of course, useless in a city that was being dragged through the air on the end of a rope. Her reluctance to pull the thing out and look at it, however, went deeper than that. Being here had plunged her into a sort of reverie none the less compelling for being obviously the product of fantasy: namely, that she was walking around in a city on Old Earth. She didn't want to spoil it until she was well and truly lost. So she let her feet take her through the red stone streets, trying to go uphill as much as she went downhill, using the towers of great old kupols as landmarks, when unsure of herself circling back toward the abutment of the bridge. For she had been told that the meeting place was not far from the bridge. She might have asked for directions, but the temperature had dropped, the glittering arc of the habitat ring had been obscured by high clouds, and it had begun to rain, a hissing curtain of small, warm drops. Pedestrians had all disappeared into wherever it was they knew to go. She'd been warned that Capitol Hill was deserted after dark; this seemed doubly true when a storm was brewing.

Several times she had passed by the front of the same building, or seen it from down the length of a street. For it stood at a place where several ways angled together into a cramped asterisk of wet cobblestones, and so sudden views of it kept jumping into her peripheral vision as she ambled along the nearby alleys. That intersection was there because of a house-sized block of stone that jutted from the hillside and forced all the nearby streets to stretch around it. The stone, as she could guess, was a crumb of the moon's mantle that had become embedded in its iron core. It might have been in there for a billion years, or it might have been a loose bolide that had slammed into red-hot Peach Pit shortly after Zero and gotten stuck in the congealing metal. Cleft and its siblings had many of those. They were usually treated as impurities in the melt. This one had been left in situ, presenting a rugged gray face to the streets that wrapped around it. Atop it, ten meters above street level, someone had constructed a round stone tower. Fanning out behind, like a ship's hull behind its jutting prow, was a triangular building that she could guess had a nice compound in its center.

The third or fourth time Kath Two saw this tower it was from a distance of perhaps a hundred meters. She was gazing at it straight down one of those narrow streets. On its upper story it had a row of arched windows, looking out in all directions. Warm light was shining out of those windows, and she could see people sitting at tables, drinking and talking and eating and reading. All of those activities sounded good to her, and she entertained a hope that it might be some kind of public house—not a private club.

The entrance was not obvious, but she found it around to the right side, where a mousehole had been cut into the metal matrix in which the rock was embedded. The tunnel angled upward and curled around, becoming a spiral stair partly obstructed by rusticles the size of small trees. Actual candles burned in niches. One turn of the helix took her out of the metal and into the stone; two took her to an arch-topped door of real wood, unmarked except for a wrought-metal door knocker in the shape of a bird with a heavy curved beak. Hand-forged feathers of black iron and palladium made it grizzled. Through the door she could feel warmth and hear conversation.

She reached for the knocker, unsure yet whether the place was meant to be public or private. Then suddenly she was conscious of the scrap of paper in her hand. She stretched it out under the light of the nearest candle.

THE CROW'S NEST
SOUTH CRADLE

She pushed the door open and entered. The first thing that came into her view was a semicircular bar of old copper, a row of tap handles, a window behind looking into a busy kitchen. Music came out of a back room, not so loud as to interfere with conversation, but enough to make her nod her head slightly with its beat. She didn't recognize the style, but she knew the type: something that had been cooked up by people isolated in a mining colony or an early habitat, people who knew how to dance.

Tending bar was a healthy-looking Dinan man in his forties. He seemed not to know that he was quite handsome. He was polishing a glass while scanning a piece of paper with handwritten numbers on it—a bar tab. Standing there alone, facing outward at the sweep of windows with its astonishing view of Cradle, he looked like the captain of an Old Earth ship.

A few moments after she had entered—neither so soon as to make her feel conspicuous nor so late as to make her feel neglected—he looked up at her and raised his eyebrows slightly. Or perhaps "eyebrow" was better since, as she now saw, one side of his face had taken serious damage.

"What are you drinking, Kath Amalthova Two?"

THE ORIGINAL NATS HAD BEEN DEVELOPED IN THE WORKSHOPS OF Arjuna Expeditions in Seattle and launched into space shortly before Zero, where they had crawled around on the surface of Amalthea under the eye of Eve Dinah. Later, during the first two years of the Epic, the original design had been modified to work on, and in, ice. Every child knew the story of how such nats had been used, first to bring *Ymir* to rendezvous with Izzy, then to merge those two objects into *Endurance*. As such, nats resonated more strongly in Blue culture than in Red, but they were used on both sides of the turnpikes. Or to be more precise, both cultures used a vast family tree of species and subspecies of nat, all descended from the first Arjuna model and all sharing, to a greater or lesser degree, the code base originally created by programmers like Larz Hoedemaeker and Eve Dinah. The number of different uses to which nats, and swarms thereof, had been put over the millennia was uncountable. They were as ubiquitous and as various as hammers and knives had been pre-Zero.

Like hammers and knives, they could be used for constructive or destructive purposes. In the latter category was a whole taxonomy of nats designed to be projected at high speed out of gunlike devices. Most of these were designed to fold up into a compact form, like a dart or bullet, so that they could be accommodated in magazines, bandoliers, and the like, and fed into the breeches of firing mechanisms.

Only a single gun, in the sense of a traditional pre-Zero firearm, had survived the Hard Rain and found its way to Cleft. This was, of course, the revolver that Julia had removed from Pete Starling's shoulder holster and secreted on her person until the moment when she had attempted to shoot Tekla with it. Camila had interceded, probably saving Tekla's life, and suffered burns that had left her scarred and in pain for the remainder of her days. Later, the same weapon had fallen into the hands of Aïda. She had issued it to a member of her band who had fired the Last Bullet from the Last Gun to kill Steve Lake. The weapon was now in the collection of the historical museum on the Great Chain. Whether and how it was put on public display was a reliable barometer of the state of Red-Blue relations.

Since the metalworking technology needed to make new guns had also been destroyed, and since many generations had passed on Cleft before anyone had even conceived a need for gunlike objects, the entire armaments industry, when it had finally gotten rebooted, had done so from a clean slate. The results owed more to Tasers, several of which had made their way to Cleft, than to traditional firearms. The latter had been designed to project a dumb lump of metal at high speed and been optimized over time to deliver high rates of fire. But spraying dumb lumps of metal around the cramped interior of a space habitat was not a good fit for any use that could be conceived of by the engineers who, hundreds of years after the arrival on Cleft, began to think once again about how to make projectile weapons. During the intervening centuries, violence had generally been a matter of grappling, punching, and the use of hand weapons such as metal rods, with really dangerous stuff like knives and swords used only in a few cases by people who had gone well off the political or psychological rails. The first new projectile weapons were made specifically for use against those. The maximum range was perhaps ten meters, so the projectiles didn't have to travel with high velocity. They had to be smart in the sense that if they missed the target—if they struck anything that was not a human being—they should become as nondestructive as possible. This generally meant that they would deploy what amounted to tiny drag chutes and slow themselves down as quickly as possible, while preparing to fragment against, as opposed to penetrating, whatever they hit. On the other hand, any projectile fortunate enough to reach its target should try to do something useful, which generally meant incapacitating, injuring, or killing it. Clearly, all of these decisions were well above the pay grade of dumb lumps of metal and so nats were used instead. These were not as dense as lead, so they had a low ballistic coefficient and could not travel very far. Again, however, in the context of a space habitat this was a good thing.

After a sort of dark age during which the Cleft colony had lacked the resources needed to advance the art of robotics, and contented themselves with fixing, and making copies of, the original models, new engineering resources had begun going into this branch of technology. The bolder programmers were daring to meddle with code files that had last been checked in by Eve Dinah. Mechanical engineers were figuring out how to reboot ancient CAD software and examine the digital blueprints created by Larz. Their initial efforts were fairly simple, such as making a nat that would automatically throw out a drag chute after it had traveled a certain distance without hitting anything. More effort went into the projectors than the projectiles. Police and military users tended to be Teklans, whose Anglisky contained more Russian loan words than that of other races, and borrowed many characters from the Cyrillic alphabet. "Katapult" was their preferred term for the device that threw the projectile nats. They shortened it to various affectionate terms such as "kat" and "katya." The second half of the word, "pult," seemed to have a connection to "pulya," pronounced with a long U as in "pool," which was the Russian word for "bullet." After a brief, awkward phase of trying to combine the term "nat" with "pulya" in various ways, meaning something like "bullet-robot," they had just settled for "pulya," which was sufficiently precise in a universe that no longer included any actual old-school bullets. Other words from the antediluvian gun world made it through unchanged, such as "shoot" and "shot," but officers giving the command to shoot tended now to say "pul," recalling what skeet and trap shooters had once called out when they wanted a clay pigeon to be thrown.

Use of the term "pulya" without any modification tended to irritate knowledgeable interlocutors in exactly the same way as pre-Zero gun nuts had reacted to laypersons who used the word "bullet." This reflected the fact that pulyas came in an even vaster range of sizes and types than old-school ammo. There were only so many things that could be done with a lump of lead. A far wider range of options lay open to the pulya engineer. An alternative term, "ambot," was also used. This was all context dependent. Grunts, who tended to see these things as necessary burdens to be hauled around in bulk, loaded into kats, unjammed from firing mechanisms, etc., tended to use "pulya," but once the projectile had actually been fired and begun to execute its program, it tended to be called an "ambot." When speaking of bulk supplies, people would say "botmo" in the same way that "ammo" had been used on Old Earth.

The sort of person who needed to be shot at by the authorities because he or she was committing violence, or threatening to, with edged weapons, was unlikely to submit meekly to advances in the technologies used to enforce civil order. Directly they began to develop countermeasures, which, of course, then needed to be surmounted by the engineers in turn. If an ambot, for example, could be fooled into believing that it had missed its target or struck something that was not a human, it could be rendered nearly harmless. Camouflage changed its purpose from fooling the human eye to fooling the electronic brains of ambots. Armor was no longer made to stop extremely fast pieces of lead. Its purpose now was to protect the wearer from the invasive strivings of ambots. Warriors became living, moving fortresses under siege of multiple ambots that often used swarm tactics to find a way inside before their batteries ran down. The old tactical calculus of projectile warfare changed in other ways too. Katapults and botmo that had been captured by the enemy, or that had simply fallen to the floor and been picked up, could be rendered inert and useless by digital means. Some of them would try to find their way back to their masters, and so battle zones in which a lot of botmo had been expended tended to look as though they were infested by army ants as spent ambots attempted to swarm back toward the combatants who had fired them.

In any event, the authorities had enjoyed a monopoly over the production and use of such weapons until sometime in the Second Millennium, when the number of widely separated habitats, and resulting political fragmentation, led to a situation in which the civil authorities from Habitat A might actually have cause to shoot at those of Habitat B. The number of different types of katapults and ambots, and of the defensive measures used against them, exploded. No complete catalog of types had existed for thousands of years. Here and there one might stumble across a museum display in which a few dozen or even a few hundred types of ambots had been rendered inert and mounted to a wall with explanatory plaques beneath them explaining in what millennium they had been invented, by whom, and in which habitat they had been used to prosecute this or that disturbance. But everyone knew implicitly that such displays only included samples that had at random made their way into a particular collector's drawer.

"Disturbance" was used a lot more often than "war," even for relatively large events such as the conflicts that had occurred over the last few centuries between Red and Blue. Because space habitats were so vulnerable, prosecuting an actual war in the sense of a twentieth-century, Old Earth total war was unthinkable. Nuclear weapons had not been reinvented because there was no need for them. A rock thrown across the ring at a space habitat would kill as many people as a hydrogen bomb. The same strategic calculus therefore applied as on Old Earth during and after the Cold War, namely that on no account would Red and Blue risk actual, open war with each other but that many small conflicts could happen in places where they might be passed off, by the majority of the news-reading populace, as too minor to worry about. The only two conflicts that were denoted, in retrospect, as wars were ones that had taken place the old-fashioned way, on the surface of the planet: the War on the Rocks, 4878–4895, and the War in the Woods, 4980–4985.

When Kath Two walked into the Crow's Nest and was greeted by the Dinan with the damaged face, it was 5003, so about twenty years after the high-water mark of the War in the Woods. The Dinan looked to be about forty years old. The scars on his face had been there for a long time.

"One of those," she said, nodding at a nearby tap handle adorned with a handwritten label identifying it as cider.

"Coming right up," he said. "Since I have you at a disadvantage, my name's Ty Lake."

"Short for Tycho or . . ."

"Tyuratam. Bit of a mouthful."

His accent was that of an Indigen. So, from this brief exchange she was able to surmise quite a bit about his history. His parents had probably been Sooners, which was to say, people who had been so eager to escape from the settled life of space habitats that they had found ways of getting down to the surface of New Earth just as soon as the TerReForm had rendered it marginally inhabitable. Doing so was a violation of First Treaty, which had ended the War on the Rocks a few decades earlier, and so it was discouraged. Comings and goings from the bigger and older habitats of the ring were easily monitored by the authorities, and so Sooners tended to depart from liminal zones on the edges of boneyards and near the two turnpikes. On the Blue side, Dinans were strongly overrepresented among Sooners. Teklans tended to be the coplike authorities given responsibility for chasing them down and breaking up their human-smuggling rings, leading to stereotypical depictions in popular culture of Dinans as charismatic pirates and Teklans as humorless straight arrows. Or at least that had been the case until the Sooners' transgressions had led to the War in the Woods, in which the predominantly Teklan armed forces had been obliged to rescue many Dinan adventurers. Depictions nowadays were a little more nuanced and made the older ones seem campy.

Thus Kath Two could reasonably guess that Ty's parents had been Sooners and had established themselves on the surface long enough to have at least one native-born son. The connection back to boneyards meant that Sooners tended to be people with a certain amount of skill in making things, and so many of the early Sooner communities had been soundly constructed on an engineering level even if their political culture had been a little on the rough and ready side. Ty, presumably, had grown up in that environment and found himself, in his late teens or early twenties, embroiled in the War in the Woods. Some ambot of some type—no point in worrying about the details—had found its way through his armor (assuming he was even wearing any) and done damage to his face. This was the sort of thing ambots tended to be good at. In combat it was frequently more useful to disable than to kill, and so ambots fought like chimpanzees, aiming for the face, the hands, and the genitals. Faces were easy to recognize and hard to spoof, so those were a favored target. Ty might have suffered these injuries in many different circumstances, e.g., a Red-on-Blue raid between two rival Sooner communities, but there was something about his posture and his manners that suggested a connection to the military, and so she guessed he had been officially recruited to fight for the Blue side, and suffered his injury in a straight-up battle between organized military formations.

He obviously ran this place. This was clear from the way he was treated by staff and customers alike. In and of itself it wasn't unusual for a retired veteran to open a bar. That was so normal as to border on stereotype. It was a little less easy to explain how such a person could end up in control of this particular bit of real estate, which was probably worth more than some entire space habitats.

The brand name on the tap handle, combined with the fact that it was handwritten, both implied that this beverage had been produced from apples plucked from trees growing in the soil of New Earth. Under the terms of Second Treaty, which had terminated the War in the Woods, the only people allowed to live on the surface and do things like tend orchards were the descendants of Sooners, now renamed Indigens. The fact of this cider's being on tap here proved, or else was a very well-crafted marketing campaign intended to create the impression, that Ty Lake maintained close connections with at least one Indigen community and that he was importing its produce directly from its Registered Indigen Zone, or RIZ. This made it a desirable luxury good, since most food was produced, far more cheaply and reliably, in habitats. Drinking beverages or eating food produced in a RIZ was for wealthy connoisseurs. Perhaps to allay any concerns Kath Two might be having on that score, Ty said, "On the house," as he set the glass on its coaster.

"That is kind of you," Kath Two said, as her eye strayed to the black slate above the bar and noticed a shocking figure quoted in the way of price.

"On the contrary," Ty said. "Normal courtesy for a fellow member of my Seven."

So, Tyuratam Lake was their Dinan.

It made sense, if the Seven was going to be doing anything on the surface, anything that might involve a RIZ.

"You're a bit early," Ty said. "Some of the others are here." He tossed his head back. This looked like one of those bars that went on forever, rambling into annexes and back rooms in a way that no architect would countenance, unless they were a very sly architect indeed. So, she inferred he was making reference to some kind of back room or snuggery that she would never be able to find on her own. "Came up the back way," he added.

"There's a back way?"

"There's always a back way."

"Doc?"

"Showed up half an hour ago."

For the most important living architect of the TerReForm to walk into the front door of a crowded bar on Capitol Hill would be to create all manner of unnecessary distractions. Doc would be recognized. People would want to demonstrate how important they were by walking up to him and introducing, or reintroducing, themselves. It would become tiresome and it would wear him out. People would talk about it, perhaps even to the point of fouling up whatever mission the Seven was being organized for. Of course Doc had used the back way.

"Anyone else?" she asked.

"Besides the nurse? Just the big fella."

So Beled had arrived too. Or so she guessed until several minutes later, when Beled walked in through the same door that Kath Two had used. He looked around the place in a manner that made it obvious he had never been here before.

Quickly he picked out Kath Two's face. He did not react, but moved toward her directly. Kath Two had taken the last available bar stool, but Beled cut through the crowd, which was easy for him since people tended to get out of his way, and stood behind her, close enough that she could feel his warmth on her back. He ordered a popular brand of inexpensive beer from another member of the staff: a breed, probably Camite/Julian, female, somewhat exotic. Ty had drifted away and resumed whatever he'd been doing with the bar tab. Kath Two checked her timepiece and guessed that Ty was getting ready to clock out so that he could take them back to the room where they would have the meeting. As the woman behind the bar handed the beer from her tiny hand into Beled's huge mitt, Kath Two pivoted toward him, tinked her glass against his, and said, "To the Seven."

Beled was busy for a moment thanking the barmaid in somewhat over-formal style, but then nodded and joined Kath Two in a drink. Kath Two explained what she knew of Tyuratam Lake and Beled spent the next several minutes appraising the Dinan from a distance, drawing who knew what conclusions.

Presently Ty finished his paperwork and slipped around the corner of the bar, catching Kath Two's eye as he did so. She could see that for him to extract himself from the society of the Crow's Nest was no insignificant thing, since many knew him and wanted to say hello. But he seemed to have learned a sort of posture and gait that made him look too busy to brook interruption.

Kath Two found it hard to keep up with Ty's meandering course through the various rooms and corridors, and ended up allowing Beled to step in front of her so that he could break trail. Because Beled was much taller and wider than she was, this made it difficult for her to see what was ahead of them. But at length she became conscious of being in a long down-sloping corridor with a stone floor, and stone walls paneled over with wood to make them seem warmer. Various doors led off of it, but one stood at the end, and this Ty opened for them. She saw warm light spilling out, glancing off the polished rock between Beled's legs and the wood paneling around his shoulders.

"Welcome to the Bolt Hole," Ty said.

Kath Two followed Beled into the room and then collided with his backside, bouncing off him and taking a step back. He had come to a dead stop upon entering and dropped into a slight crouch, one foot ahead of the other and pointed straight ahead. Sidling around him, Kath Two followed his gaze, and his toe's azimuth, across the room.

The Bolt Hole was a cozy little place with an oval table just big enough for seven. Doc was seated nearest the door, flanked by Memmie and by his robot. Across from him was Ariane Casablancova. Seated at the far end of the table, facing the door, was the man that Ty must have meant when he had spoken of "the big fella." Because of his position behind the table, all that was visible were his head, shoulders, and arms. The arms seemed long and quite heavily constructed. What really drew attention, though, was the architecture of the big fella's skull. His head looked like the head that a normal person's head would develop into if they kept growing beyond adulthood into some more pronounced phase of development. Thick reddish-brown eyebrows did little to conceal a prominent ridge of bone above the eyes. When Kath Two first saw him he was draining a pint glass, which looked even smaller in his hand than it had in Beled's; but when he set it down to expose the lower half of his clean-shaven face, she saw the set of his jaw, and the size of his teeth, and understood that the seventh member of the Seven was not just any Aïdan but a Neoander.

EVE AÏDA HAD FOUNDED SEVEN STRAINS OVER THE COURSE OF THIRteen separate pregnancies. The failure rate had been so high because the alterations she had demanded from Eve Moira had been so extreme. She had been willing to accept some unsuccessful pregnancies, given that she saw herself as having plenty of time until menopause compared to all the other Eves save Camila. And Camila she did not see as a competitor, given that Camila wanted to raise a race of people who were not inclined to compete with anyone.

The Eves, confined to a small volume of inhabitable space on Cleft for the remainder of their lives, were impoverished in many ways. Of information, however, they had an inexhaustible wealth. Essentially every document that had ever been digitized was available to them, at least until such time as the memory chips on which it was all archived began to fail: a decay that had begun on a small scale but that would take decades to have any serious effect.

Aïda began to research human genetics. To the extent that her genome was the final expression of a long historical process—a dense and cryptic encoding of everything that her ancestors had learned by managing to survive long enough to reproduce—this meant learning about the history of human evolution as well. Her genome, like that of all the other Arkies, had been sequenced and evaluated before she had left Earth. A copy of the report had been provided to her. It contained information as to what parts of the world her ancestors had come from. Much of this was what you would expect for an Italian woman, but there were details she hadn't known, such as some genetic connections to Northern African Jews, to an isolated tribe in the Caucasus, and to the Nordic peoples. Based on certain genetic markers it was also clear that, like many Europeans, she was part Neanderthal.

Later analysis, by historical scholars, of the bread crumb trails left by Aïda in computer logs suggested that she had spent almost as much time studying the genomes of the Four, whom she saw as her direct competitors, as her own. And of the Four, she spent as much time learning about Moira's genome as Dinah's, Tekla's, and Ivy's combined. This was because Moira was of African descent, and Aïda had become fascinated by the idea that Africans carried more genetic diversity within their genomes than non-Africans, as a simple result of the fact that humanity had originated on that continent and spread outward. Non-African races had been founded by isolated groups of adventurers. Breeding among themselves, they had created gene pools that were necessarily limited to what they had brought with them: only a subset of what was to be found in Africa. This idea had been used to explain, for example, why Africa contained both the tallest and the most diminutive people in the world, and why so many top athletes were African. It wasn't because they were naturally better athletes but because the bell-shaped curve of random genetic variation was wider. For every African who was a great athlete there was presumably another who was miserably uncoordinated, but no one paid any notice to the latter. Whether or not this was a valid theory, the fact was that Aïda swallowed it hook, line, and sinker and used it to inform her genetic strategy in the Great Game. And to the extent that the Four bothered to develop counterstrategies, they had to take it into account. The very existence of Moirans, as a race, was a result. Rather than try to follow all of Aïda's machinations in detail, base pair for base pair, Eve Moira had chosen to tinker with those aspects of the genome that controlled epigenetics, making her children into Swiss Army knives.

Tekla had been an easier target, where Aïda was concerned, since she had stated so forthrightly what she considered desirable in a future race. It was easy enough to see that the children of Tekla were going to be strong, disciplined, formidable fighters. And one did not have to be a military genius to understand that fighting, for the foreseeable future—several millennia of being bottled up in space colonies—was going to be up close and personal. To the extent that violence was going to be an ongoing factor in human history, it was going to be a style of violence that relied on size, strength, and toughness. If history was any guide, those best at violence might end up ruling over everyone else. Aïda was not about to see her children dominated by the sons and daughters of Tekla.

She might simply have done what Tekla did, and created versions of herself modified for certain traits associated with athleticism. Instead, having become fascinated by the odd detail in her genetic report, she had embarked on a program to reawaken the Neanderthal DNA that, or so she imagined, had been slumbering in her and her ancestors' nuclei for tens of thousands of years. It was a somewhat insane idea, and in any case she didn't have enough Neanderthal in her to make it feasible, but she did produce a race of people with vaguely Neanderthal-like features, and in later centuries the processes of Caricaturization, Isolation, and Enhancement—which had affected all the races to some extent—had wrought especially pronounced changes on this subrace. Gene sequences taken from the toe of an actual Neanderthal skeleton, found on Old Earth and sequenced before Zero, were put to use. Old Earth paleontology journals had been data-mined for stats on bone length and muscle attachment so that those could be hard-coded into the Neoander wetware. The man sitting at the end of the table was the artificial product of breeding and of genetic engineering, but, had he been sent back in time to prehistoric Europe, he would have been indistinguishable, at least in his outward appearance, from genuine Neanderthals.

The creation of the new race had happened incrementally, over centuries. By the time Neoanders existed it was too late to bother with the trifling ethical question of whether it was really a good thing to have created them. During their slow differentiation from the other races they had developed a history and a culture of their own, of which they were as proud as any other ethnic group.

Not surprisingly, much of that history was about their relationship with Teklans, which was, as foreordained, largely combative. At its most simple-minded and stupidly reductionist bones, the Teklan side of the story was that Neoanders were dangerous ape-men brought into existence by a crazy Eve as a curse upon the other six races. The Neoander side had it that Teklans were what Hitler would have produced if he'd had genetic engineering labs, and that it was a damned good thing that Eve Aïda had had the foresight to produce a countervailing force of earthy, warm, but immensely strong and dangerous protectors.

Much of this combative relationship had become irrelevant as the tactical landscape had become dominated by katapults and ambots, and physical strength had become less important to the outcome of fights. But the old primordial animus remained, and explained why Beled's immediate response, upon entering a room that contained a Neoander, was to make himself ready for hand-to-hand combat.

Doc chose to ignore this. *If he even notices,* Kath Two thought, but she was pretty sure Doc noticed everything. "Beled, Kath, I do not believe you have met Langobard."

It was a fairly common Aïdan name.

"Bard for short," Langobard offered.

"Langobard, may I present Beled Tomov and Kath Amalthova Two."

Bard rose to his full height, which was not all that impressive, while performing the Aïdan version of the salute, which was done with both hands. He then reached out across a seemingly impossible distance with his right, offering to shake. Beled was still reluctant to move, and so Kath Two stepped forward and extended her hand. She had never made physical contact before with a Neoander. Even in Red they had become somewhat scarce, as many of the existing population had moved down to New Earth to become Indigens. In Blue they were rarely seen at all. Langobard took her hand with elaborate delicacy, swallowing it up in a meat paw with fingers the size of baby arms, and giving it the gentlest of squeezes. He was clean-shaven and carefully groomed, wearing a good suit of clothes that actually fit—prompting her to wonder where such a person would find a tailor. He had a slightly bemused look on his face, as if he knew what she was thinking. "Charmed," he said, with a little nod that only emphasized the size and mass of his head. And after she had nodded back, he released her hand, no worse for wear, and stretched it out toward Beled. "Lieutenant Tomov? Pleasure to meet you. What's it going to be? Punch in the face? Handshake? Or a big warm hug?" He swung his hand back while extending the other arm, displaying a wingspan much greater than his height, as though offering to embrace Beled across the table. This, at least, broke the tension enough that Beled finally collected himself into a less minatory posture, saluted, and extended his hand in return. The Teklan's hand gripped the Neoander's just a few centimeters away from Kath Two's face. She could hear the knuckles cracking as they tested each other's strength. Standing on the far side of this spectacle was Ty, watching it with an expression that was not all that easy to read, given that the damaged side of his face was toward her. But she thought she detected a certain level of wry amusement, perhaps a little dampened by awe.

Ty caught Kath Two looking, then shook his head and snorted.

"I hope I didn't overdress," Bard remarked, after he and Beled had finally let go of each other without incident. "I sometimes overcompensate when I come to Cradle."

"Is that often?" Ty asked.

Kath Two understood that Bard's remark had been a conversational gambit and not just a bald assertion. Ty, with the social reflexes of a Dinan bartender, had recognized it as such and was already following up.

"It's actually surprising that you and I have never crossed paths before," Bard said, addressing Ty but watching Kath Two out of the corner of his eye. Only after she had sat down in one of the available chairs did he resume his seat. He picked up the empty glass. "I noted on your drinks list that you cellar some surface produce. Thank you for the beer, by the way."

"You're most welcome," Ty said.

"I have spent most of my life on the surface," Bard explained, "where some members of my clan grow grapes. We produce wine. Our primary market is restaurants in Cradle, though we do ship a few cases up to private cellars on the Great Chain."

"Well then, that's one explanation for our not having met," Ty said.

Kath Two interpreted this to mean *The Crow's Nest generally doesn't stock such high-end wine,* but Bard got a sly look on his face and, after a moment, returned, "Did you have another possible explanation in mind, Ty?"

"Where is your clan's vineyard?" Beled demanded. Then, in a belated attempt to soften it, he added, "If you don't mind."

"Oh, it's not a secret," Bard said. "Antimer. Just near the line of demarcation."

She didn't know much about the place but she could visualize it: a crescent-shaped archipelago in the middle latitudes between the Aleutians and Hawaii. It was the rim of a huge impact crater. Some of the islands were fairly large. The largest of them straddled the antimeridian—180 degrees east or west of Greenwich—which was the origin of the name. But most of the archipelago lay to the east of there, stretching all the way across the longitude of 166 degrees, 30 minutes west. That was the location of one of the two turnpikes that the Aïdans had built across the ring. It was as far west as the Eye could travel, and so it served as a border between Red and Blue. Since it was in the middle of the Pacific, which, notwithstanding the best efforts of the Hard Rain, was still largely an empty expanse of water, there wasn't much of a land border. 166 Thirty did cross through Beringia: the union of Alaska with the easternmost part of Siberia. A land border did, therefore, exist in that place as well as in the somewhat more climatically benign part of Antimer lying a few thousand kilometers due south. This was the "line of demarcation" that Bard had alluded to, carefully omitting mention of on which side of it the vineyard was actually located. The border was fuzzy. There was no need to bother with strict enforcement on a world so thinly populated. The much longer land border at ninety degrees east, above Dhaka, wandered all over the place as it rambled north across the broadest part of Asia, squirming this way and that to circumvent craters, Himalayas, and other complications.

The general picture that Bard had therefore conveyed, in just a few words, was something like this. His "clan"—whatever that meant—of Neoanders had gone down to the surface as soon as it had become livable. They might have been Sooners (which was what Kath Two had been assuming of Tyuratam Lake) but, given their race, it was more probable that they had been military, sent down to Antimer—which was a fairly inviting piece of real estate—to secure it. For most of the Antimer chain lay on the Red side of the line of demarcation and constituted a valuable possession. But it had this troublesome extension onto the other side where Blue could, if it chose, establish a beachhead. From there, military incursions might be made westward in the event that the treaty failed. All of these things had come to pass during the War in the Woods. During the treaty negotiations that had concluded it, Red had made efforts to claim all of Antimer for itself—effectively defining a little eastward excursion in the Line of Demarcation that would rid it of this particular thorn in its side. No agreement had been reached on that item, so it remained in dispute. Had more people been living there, there might have been a demilitarized zone, a no-man's-land, and all the other apparatus of disputed Cold War boundaries. As it was, things were just fuzzy. A tacit agreement was in place not to stir up trouble. But on both sides it was heavily populated with military settlements, and/or Survey installations, just to keep an eye on things. The obvious explanation for a lot of Neoanders living there was that they'd been sent down as a military force and brought their families with them. Upon the expiration of their term of service, they had declined the invitation to return to whatever crowded space habitat had been their place of origin and had dispersed into the countryside, which was said to be a very nice place to live. This was technically illegal but Red authorities had probably looked the other way, figuring that seeding the place with Neoanders could only strengthen their hold on it.

Their Neanderthal heritage had been fabricated out of whole cloth, yet it was taken more or less seriously by everyone—it was a sort of consensual historical hallucination. Aïda and some of her more bloody-minded descendants might have hoped it would instill fear of, or at least respect for, the fighting prowess of this subrace. Some Neoanders reveled in that. Many of them, however, preferred a revisionist view of Neanderthal history that painted them as highly intelligent (their brains were larger than those of "modern" humans), artistically gifted, and essentially peaceful proto-Europeans. Neoanders of a more intellectual bent held seminars about it. More practical-minded ones tried to live it. There was no better place to live it, Kath Two had to admit, than Antimer, which had a temperate European-style climate. And so it was entirely plausible that a group of Neoanders who had been sent down by Red as shock troops would, within a generation or two, end up running vineyards in that fuzzily defined border zone near the line of demarcation and, once the vines had reached maturity, trying to sell wine on the ring. The early market would be high-end connoisseurs and restaurants and so they would need a member of the clan who cleaned up well, had good manners, and knew how to wear clothes, to establish commercial contacts in places like Cradle.

This entire picture, or something close to it, was summoned up in the minds of Kath Two and, presumably, Ty and Beled and the others as soon as the words were spoken. But Ty's remark—*That's one explanation for our not having met*—and Bard's nonanswer—*Did you have another possible explanation in mind?*—were still lodged there awkwardly. Was Ty meaning to question Bard's story? The look on Ariane's face, as she regarded the Neoander, was not what you would call warm. But of course the Julian would be suspicious, would look for other explanations than what lay on the surface.

Ty seemed to have noticed this too; his eyes were jumping back and forth between Ariane and Bard.

Bard looked up at Ty and smiled, his huge upper lip pulling back to expose the row of yellowish enamel boulders planted in his upper jaw. "I'll bet that as our Seven spends time together, Tyuratam and I will have all sorts of opportunities to tell colorful stories about what our families have gotten up to during their decades on the surface."

Which didn't answer the question. But it was charming, and it deflected the issue by making the point that Tyuratam Lake's background, should he choose to discuss it with them, was likely to be at least as complicated as that of Langobard. Perhaps a bit of guilt-tripping there too, implicitly asking them why they were so curious about the Neoander when other members of the Seven might be worthy of some scrutiny too.

Ariane sat back in her chair and pretended to look at her fingernails. She was not the least bit satisfied. Trying for a minute to think like a Julian, Kath Two imagined how it must look to her: a creature selectively bred by crazy people to be capable of killing with his bare hands, who at the same time was extraordinarily crafty in his social interactions.

"I am what I am," Ty said.

"And what is that?" Ariane asked.

"A bartender. Always happy to make new acquaintances." He nodded at Bard. "Or to provide guests with drinks. Anyone thirsty?"

No one admitted to being thirsty.

"For beverages, I meant," Ty added. "I'm sure we are all thirsty for knowledge."

Doc liked that. "Knowledge in general, Tyuratam?"

"Oh, I'd be living on Stromness if I were a knowledge-in-general man," Ty said. "A collector of facts. No, I take a more utilitarian stance."

"Meaning that you would like to know why we are here," Doc said.

Ty seemed to find the question overly blunt, and raised the ridge of scar tissue that had once been a honey-colored eyebrow. "If you'd enjoy saying something about it, I'd enjoy listening," he admitted. "If not, well, I'm willing to come along for the ride—up to a point."

Doc now looked across the table toward Ariane, in a way that made tumblers click inside of Kath Two's head. He was handing control of the meeting to Ariane. It might be going too far to say that she was in charge, but she was probably in communication with whoever was.

"Most of our operations will be on the surface," she said. "You might have inferred as much from the fact that we have gone out of our way to involve Indigens"—she glanced at Ty and Bard—"and Survey personnel." She nodded at Kath Two and at Beled. The last gesture elicited another one of those sardonic snorts from Ty—pointing out, apparently, just how implausible it was that a man fitting the profile of Lieutenant Tomov could possibly be taken seriously as a member of Survey. Ariane gave Ty a cool look, as if to say *Don't start,* then continued: "And I need hardly belabor the longstanding connection with the surface embodied by Doc and Memmie."

Conspicuously absent from the list, now, was Ariane herself, but if she was aware of the omission, she didn't show it. Everyone was left to make what guesses and assumptions they might about how her career—whatever it might be—was connected with the surface.

"Discretion is important," Ariane continued, "which is why we will tend to operate out of Cradle and use atmospheric or surface transportation." Meaning airplanes and things that crawled on the surface of New Earth as opposed to rocket ships, bolos, and Aitken-Kucharski devices like giant whips. "Whenever possible, we will enter and exit Cradle on foot—via the subterranean passages that are afforded by sockets."

"When's the next—" Kath Two started to ask.

"Cayambe," Ariane said. "Two days from now."

"We are going to travel from Cayambe to Beringia on the surface?" Kath Two asked.

Ty and Bard both looked at her curiously.

"I haven't said anything about Beringia," Ariane pointed out.

"But it's obviously where we're going," Kath Two said. "It's where Beled and I—and a lot of other people—were sent on Survey. It's where I saw what I saw, and told Beled about it. This whole thing was precipitated by that, wasn't it?"

"It has been brewing for longer. Years," Ariane said. "But you're not wrong."

"Ty's from that part of the world—I can tell by his accent. Bard is from south of there, on Antimer," Kath Two went on.

"We will head north from the Cayambe Socket, yes," Ariane said.

"North a hell of a long way," Ty pointed out.

"We are not prevented from using air transport," Ariane reminded him.

"If we can get a big enough glider," Kath Two put in, "the mountain wave will take us right up the Andes, the Sierras, and the Cascades in a day or two."

"I am fairly confident," Ariane said, "that we can get a big enough glider."

THE UNDERSURFACE OF CRADLE, ONLY VISIBLE TO PEOPLE STANDING on the ground—more specifically, on the equator—looking up at it, was flat and generally egg-shaped, elongated in the direction of its east-west movement. On closer inspection its mostly smooth surface was interrupted from place to place by small hatches, carefully engineered protrusions, orifices, and other details. These were distributed around that otherwise featureless surface in a way that suggested orderly minds at work, addressing complications posed by the asymmetries of the city above.

In several places along the equator of New Earth, ground had been cleared and flattened, and reinforced concrete pads laid. These had the same size and shape as Cradle's undersurface, and were equipped with their own hatches and orifices matching those on Cradle. Cradle could be neatly set down into one of these sockets whenever the Eye happened to be directly overhead. There it might reside for hours or days, taking on or discharging supplies, and otherwise communing with the surroundings. But it never stayed for long, since it had to follow the movements of the Eye, which always had urgent business elsewhere on the ring.

At such times, a traveler who knew nothing of orbiting tethers and the like, emerging from the woods or cresting some nearby hill, and coming into view of Cradle, would perceive it as a normal, which was to say stationary, city. The bucket handle arching high over its top was a heavy hint that something was a bit odd about it. Other than that, however, it would look, in that context, like a somewhat isolated hill fort.

Some of the more well-established sockets had begun to accumulate suburbs: ring-shaped towns that would come to life whenever Cradle was in residence. Most of them had the feel, and shared the purposes, of military bases, scientific installations, and frontier outposts. It had always been envisioned that many such would be built in time, creating a ring around the equator to match the habitat ring far above it, and that once New Earth was opened for general settlement they would grow into important cities. To visit one now, centuries before its glorious peak, was something of an acquired taste—a little like walking around a building site after foundations have been laid and a few walls framed. Builders, dreamers, and people of imagination enjoyed such places; others saw nothing.

Cayambe and Kenya had been the first two sockets, built in the most likely sites on South America and Africa respectively. Each numbered around ten thousand souls.

Cayambe's namesake was a volcano at the intersection of the Andes and the equator, in what had once been the country of Ecuador. It had, of course, taken a beating during the Hard Rain, and resumed erupting for a while, but had now been dormant for about seven hundred years. In any case the Cayambe Socket had been built well clear of its most active vents, placing the volcano's summit, which was once again snow covered, far enough away that it could be admired from any windows on Cradle that happened to be aimed in the right direction.

The Crow's Nest's tower afforded views in almost all directions, and so Tyuratam Lake, standing behind his bar two days later, polishing a glass with a towel, was able to look up between two tap handles and see the summit glide into view and then seemingly rise upward from the horizon as Cradle was lowered gingerly into its socket. Klaxons sounded all over Cradle and across the earthbound ring city that was now coming into view beyond its windscreens. Out of habit Ty stuffed the towel into the pocket of his trousers, letting it dangle down his leg, and reached out to steady himself against the bar. The underside of Cradle and the matching surface below it had been designed so that a disk of air would be trapped between them during the final meter of the descent, and act as a cushion. This was allowed to escape through a picket fence of vents, aimed upward around the periphery of Cradle, and so final docking was, as usual, signaled by a roar of escaping air and plumes of condensed humidity jetting upward into the blue sky over the Andes. The mildest of lurches caused stored glasses and tableware to clink together in cabinets all over the bar.

The klaxons and the vents went silent at the same time. Through the bar's windows, which Ty had left cracked open, he could hear the customary smattering of applause rising up from the stony streets of Capitol Hill. He checked his timepiece. A few politicians and generals, who had leaned back from their breakfasts to observe the docking and admire the profile of Cayambe Volcano, bent forward again, picked up their forks, and resumed their conversations. Cradle had just become the largest city on New Earth, and was scheduled to remain so for twenty-four hours. Its system of windscreens, built to shield the city from the blast created by its movement through the atmosphere, now seemed more like a barbican, thrown up in some past age to defend an old city, but now merely a historical curiosity and a dividing line between neighborhoods.

Other than keeping a curious eye on all comings and goings

through Cradle's eight gates, Quarantine made no effort to control the mingling of populations. Cradle's visits were so brief that to stop, examine, and question everyone passing between it and the sockets would have rendered the whole visit pointless.

Thanks to this relaxed policy, the time it took for an average pedestrian to get from the nearest of the eight gates to the Crow's Nest was nine minutes. The first customer showed up in seven, breathing somewhat heavily, and requested a beer. Ty did not recognize him, but the next two faces that came in the door, thirty seconds later, were familiar. During the next quarter of an hour, the place filled up with a mixture of regulars (from Cradle and Cayambe alike) and curiosity seekers. Ty's staff, well accustomed to these surges, began to open up back rooms. Extra cooks came up through one of the back entrances and began to make use of *mise en place* that had been prepped the night before.

Everything, in other words, ran smoothly. Which was how Ty liked it. The ability of the Crow's Nest to accommodate a socket surge with no intervention from Ty, other than polishing a glass, was, in a sense, his life's work. He had done every job it was possible to do in this place, from floor mopper on upward, and learned over time to select and delegate the work to others who could do it better. He had advanced, in other words, to higher levels of mental activity while always doing enough of the floor mopping and glass polishing to remain in physical contact with the business of the bar and in human contact with the staff. His real job—the job that the Owners paid him for—was to be an observer of the human condition as it was so richly displayed from day to day within these walls.

He was also a judicious *manipulator* of the human condition in the sense of occasionally throwing people out, telling others to settle down in a manner so smooth and humorous that they didn't know they'd been told, and making certain others feel welcome when they seemed ill at ease. All of that was as fundamental to the operation of a bar as mopping the floor. Others on his staff could do such things almost as well as he. Ty had, in other words, developed the Crow's Nest into a sufficiently healthy and robust organism that it was possible for him to disappear for weeks, sometimes even months, without inflicting serious damage. In some ways, his occasional "vacations" actually did more good than harm, in the sense that when he came back he would commonly find that certain members of the staff had risen to the occasion and become more complete and effective human beings in his absence. He was quite certain that he could walk away from the bar forever now and that it would not really miss him. But he was unlikely to do any such thing because it was literally his home—he lived in an apartment on the court behind it—and because the Owners preferred that he stay. And the Owners were among the very few members of all the human races about whose opinions Tyuratam Lake actually gave a damn. They had pointed out to him that even a year's leave of absence, should he choose to take one, would benefit the Crow's Nest, in the sense that he would return to it with fresh eyes and immediately see how beneficial changes might be made.

But he suspected that the true value of the business, in the eyes of the Owners, was not the return it delivered on capital. That was probably close to zero. They might even be running a huge loss, for all he knew. Every month Ty did the books and boiled all the numbers down to a single sheet of paper that he took to the Bolt Hole and slid across the table to the Owners' representative. They never said much about it. Once a year, a question might be asked about one of the numbers, just as a way of letting him know that they were paying attention. But the Owners really valued the Crow's Nest partly as a cultural institution and partly because it gave them access to the sort of information about the lives, thoughts, and deeds of important persons that could only be had in a bar.

He did not care for elaborate goodbyes, particularly in a professional context where a fussy leave-taking might suggest that his going away was a big deal—implying that the staff might not be up to the job of keeping the business running. And so after a few minutes had passed and he had exchanged looks, words, and jokes with a few leading citizens and well-known characters of Cayambe—just long enough to let it be known that he was here—he pulled the towel from his pocket, wiped his hands, and tossed it into the laundry chute beneath the bar. He lingered for a moment just to satisfy himself that the chute was not jammed. But it never was. Satisfied, he edged around the corner of the bar and walked to a table by the windows where Ariane, Kath Two, and Beled were pushing empty plates away, having just concluded a hearty breakfast. Ty himself had eaten light, an hour ago, as was his habit when he expected to spend a good part of the day airborne. "It'll be taken care of," he remarked, and got perfunctory thank-yous from the Moiran and the Teklan. Ariane gave him what he could only guess was meant to be some kind of penetrating look, and nodded. The busy minds of Julians exhausted Ty and he tried to avoid getting drawn into their labyrinthine ways of thinking. Perhaps this Ariane had used whatever connections she had in the intelligence world to investigate him and the Owners, and was drawing all sorts of conclusions—probably wrong ones—about what motivated him to give the Seven free drinks and meals. For it was obvious to Ty that Ariane worked in intelligence. He had seen many such people during the war and he knew their ways.

By now the others could navigate around the Crow's Nest, but there was an expectation that he would lead the way. This derived partly from the fact that it was, after all, his establishment. But even had they been dropped into some completely random location on the surface they would have looked to him to take point because that, for better or worse, was what Dinans did. Answering to a similar racial expectation, Beled took up the rear. This was partly because his ingrained habits of courtesy and discipline obliged him to say "You first" to all the others, and partly so he would wheel about and engage any foes who might assault the rear of the formation.

Ty moved briskly to reduce the chance that he would be buttonholed by some prematurely drunk member of the Cayambe Chamber of Comersants. Within a few moments they had passed into a section of the bar that had not yet been opened to visitors, and thence proceeded down twisting stairways scarcely wide enough to accommodate Beled's shoulders until they reached the triangular courtyard in the center of the compound. Its tropical flowers were glowing like gems in the hard white light of the Andes. Four small cabs awaited them near the big gate that gave out onto the street. Cradle was almost devoid of four-wheeled vehicles when it was aloft, but whenever it was socketed, the place was invaded within minutes by swarms of whatever rolling stock was skinny enough to negotiate its streets. Some of these moved goods, transshipping them from the Eye to customers on the surface, or importing the produce of New Earth to Cradle. Others carried passengers on errands to the ring city and its hinterlands. One of the cabs was already occupied by Doc and Memmie, as could be inferred by the cases of Doc's support infrastructure strapped to its roof rack and the grabb poised to scuttle after it. Bard had climbed into the second cab and was slouched down low. Neoanders were rare enough to draw notice and arouse curiosity in a manner that Ariane quite clearly did not want. He had been keeping to himself in his private room. Ariane climbed into the cab with him. It went without saying that it would be easiest for all concerned if Beled took up a whole cab by himself, and so he did that. Ty and Kath Two got into the last one.

After Doc and Memmie's cab departed, a few minutes passed before Ariane gave her driver the go-ahead. Ty shifted impatiently in his seat, slightly jostling Kath Two. Cradle-compliant cabs did not have a lot of shoulder room.

"What do you think she's doing?" Kath Two asked. Just making conversation. They both knew perfectly well what she was doing.

"A caravan of four, leaving the Crow's Nest and not coming back—too conspicuous for her taste," Ty said.

"At least there's no question of getting lost," Kath Two remarked. She ducked her head low so that she could peer out the window and get a look at the northern sky beyond the city. The sun shafted in and made her eyes glow, picking out glints of yellow in irises that were mostly green and brown. She didn't have the crazy yellow cat-eyes of some Moirans, but there was a bit of that in her ancestral tree. She knew Ty was looking at her but she didn't let on to being self-conscious, which he approved of. She was looking, of course, at the Aitken loop that was their immediate destination. Assuming that it was still operating—and she'd have reacted differently had it gone down—it was rising up out of a mostly subterranean flynk barn on the town's outskirts, surrounded by hangars and maintenance facilities for aircraft that ranged up and down the length of the Andes.

"You have everything you need?" Ty asked. "It'll be a long day for you."

"It'll go by in no time," Kath Two demurred, "because I'll be busy. It'll be long for *you* because you'll be bored. Did you bring a book?"

"People are my books," Ty said. "But I did bring a couple, in case the people all go to sleep."

It was meant as a light joke but he saw her face snag on it, wondering if he was trying to make a racial crack about Moirans. "An annoying habit that many people seem to have," he added.

Apparently a mere two-cab caravan was not enough to trigger Ariane's anxieties, and so the one carrying Beled and the one carrying Ty and Kath Two departed in tandem and began to work their way through streets crowded with pedestrians. They could have done the first part of it more quickly on foot, but when they passed out through the vehicular gate and into the streets of Cayambe, things opened up quite a bit and they were able to use streets that had been designed specifically for four-wheelers. The place seemed dustier than Ty remembered, or maybe he was just seeing it through visitors' eyes. Cradle sophisticates would see its menagerie of robots as comically oversized and ramshackle, its people as a lot of jumped-up backwoodsmen. Ty's kind of people, in other words. The sort of person whose ancestors had stayed in the habitat ring and played by the rules, patiently awaiting the moment when Doc, or some successor of his, would cut the ribbon on New Earth and allow settlers to flood in, had complicated feelings about Sooners and Indigens. On the one hand they were viewed as sharp operators. Tricksters. At the same time they were isolated bumpkins. Ty had learned early how to play both sides of the image. A stranger from the ring who took you for a wide-eyed rube would spill a lot of information before he came to understand the truth, and one who expected you to play tricks on him would let down his guard at the first show of honesty and plain dealings.

IF YOU TOOK A LARGE NUMBER OF FLYNKS—FLYING, AUTONOMOUS chain links—and joined them together into a long chain, and connected its ends to make it into a continuous loop, and then got the whole loop moving through the air like a train composed of little airplanes, each using its stubby winglets to generate its share of the lift, then you had a thing known as an "aitrain," pronounced the way a resident of Old New York would have said "A train." The concept was old enough that its etymology had been obscured by time. It might have been "air train" with the first r elided, or a contraction of "Aitken train." Sometimes, as here, it was a captive aitrain, passing continuously through a fixed installation on the ground and rising from there to a considerable altitude before reversing direction and plunging back down for another circuit. But aitrains could also fly freely in the air: a technology crazy enough that it had become associated with the Aïdan big-brains known as Jinns, or Ghenis, and tended to be used only by Red.

Presumably at Ariane's behest, they took a circuitous route to the aitrain station, swinging wide around the hangar with the big Q on its roof. The caravan collected itself in an unmarked hangar on the edge of the military zone, which Ty viewed as a classic example of the "not quite Survey and not quite military" style. There were no human personnel, just two copies of a specialized kind of grabb posted at each of the wingtips of a big glider, nominal capacity ten. Adequate room for a Seven, or so Ty thought until he climbed aboard and found it preloaded with mysterious equipment cases.

Kath Two made a slow walk around the glider and then climbed aboard, pulled the door shut, and crawled forward onto the couch where she would spend the journey resting on her belly. Everyone else looked away politely as she got her urine collection system squared away. In front of her was the glass dome, more than a meter in diameter, that served as the aircraft's nose. Beled and Bard took opposite window seats in the back row of the passenger compartment. Doc sat in the front row, on the aisle, where he would have the best view forward over Kath Two's backside and out the dome. Memmie sat in the window seat next to him and Ariane grabbed the seat across the aisle from him. Ty had his pick of a few seats in the midsection. He had noticed Ariane's preference for always sitting next to Doc. Were he a jealous sort, or the kind of person who liked having long conversations with eminent scientists, he'd have resented the way she monopolized him. Instead he just found it kind of interesting, and wondered whether Doc would shoo her off at some point so that he could at long last talk to someone else.

The glider began moving around, presumably because Kath Two had told the grabbs holding its wingtips to take it somewhere. The nose tilted down as they descended a ramp into the flynk barn. This was a noisy warren in which thousands of identical robots were hustling around in a manner that looked chaotic and organized at the same time, much like the impression you'd get staring into a beehive. For an earthbound loop system like this one, the flynks had to be aerodynamic, so their inner skeletons were hidden beneath thin plastic fairings, making them into blunt-nosed cylinders, like large bullets, with a little waist in the midsection to give the universal joint freedom to bend this way and that. Each of these flynks was about half a meter in diameter and two meters long and weighed about twice what a large human weighed. Lying on the floor, they were helpless, and so grabbs moved them around by getting them aimed in the right direction and then rolling them about like barrels, creating a scene that looked a little like a swarm of dung beetles going about their work. The general point of the operation seemed to be to channel the flynks in the direction of troughs where they would naturally line up. This enabled them to couple themselves together into short segments of chain. The troughs had roller bearings that made it easy for chain segments to slide forward and back, like trains in a switching yard, and in this manner chain segments could be added to or subtracted from the aitrain while it was operating. Which was to say, while the system was shooting it straight up into the air at high velocity and sucking it back in on the down leg.

In one of those "easy for machines, inconceivable for humans" operations, a coupler on the glider's nose ended up being snapped to the tail end of a flynk chain that presently got concatenated onto the up leg. Rapidly brought up to speed while still in the confines of the flynk barn, the glider pitched upward sharply as it emerged into the light. It began to rise vertically, drawn behind the chain. Nothing was connected to the glider's tail—the loop had been deliberately severed—and so the system had ceased being an Aitken loop. It was now a vertical bullwhip, accelerating the glider to higher and higher velocity as the *Knickstelle* at its apex propagated skyward. Lying now on his back, staring straight up over Kath Two's shoulders, Ty could see small aerodynamic vanes that had deployed from the fuselage of the flynk ahead of them. These, like all the other vanes on all the other thousands of flynks in the chain, effected tiny adjustments to keep the whip trimmed in just the right configuration. The result, a few moments later, was that the glider came snapping over the top just as its connection to the last flynk was severed. In a few seconds it had been hauled two thousand meters straight up and let go with a velocity of a few hundred kilometers per hour. Meanwhile, every other flynk in the chain had decoupled itself fore and aft, causing the entire chain to disintegrate into a linear cloud of identical fragments, each headed in a different direction. Each flynk, sensing that it was aloft and alone, automatically deployed large tail vanes that turned it from a bullet into a badminton shuttlecock. The flynks rapidly slowed down to their terminal velocity, turned nose down, and began to fall toward the ground. A slight canting of the vanes caused them to begin spinning like maple seeds, further slowing their descent, and in this manner the entire swarm began to descend in the direction of an empty lot adjacent to the flynk barn.

All of which had to be pictured in Ty's mind's eye, since they already had left it far behind. But he had seen it many times, as it was one of the basic operations carried out many times a day at any aitrain port. The same flynks, organized in a different way, might just as easily have effected a high-altitude rendezvous with an orbiting bolo, or collected an aircraft and drawn it back downward to safe haven in the barn.

The first half hour of the flight was a little unsettling to Ty's stomach as Kath Two made a few sudden maneuvers, perhaps because she had sensed good air in one direction or bad in another. People who were accustomed to flight in powered aircraft frequently had trouble adjusting to the unpredictability of gliders, but Ty, who had done it before, understood that Kath Two was just hunting for the right way to inject them into the mountain wave hovering invisibly in the upper atmosphere above the Andes crest. He knew she had found it when the juking and jiving stopped and the back of the seat pressed him forward with palpable acceleration. They were in level, steady flight now, proceeding north at something like three hundred kilometers per hour. Kath Two's task henceforth would be to look far into their future with her lidar-enhanced sensorium and make small adjustments needed to dodge pockets of rough air.

Everyone became somewhat listless and fell to reading books or napping. Sitting a couple of rows behind Ty, occupying most of a pair of seats, was Beled Tomov. He was in an attitude of repose, whitish-blue eyes half closed and unfocused, but aimed generally out the window. He was probably trying to maintain a visual fix on the horizon as a way to stave off motion sickness. In any case he did not look to be in a social mood.

Over a series of meals and drinks since the initial meeting of the Seven, Ty had been able to piece together a vague picture of the mission that Kath Two and Beled had recently completed in Beringia. Apparently, Beled had been trying to maintain some kind of threadbare cover story about being Survey. Fortunately, this had now been dispensed with and Doc was openly addressing him as Lieutenant Tomov.

Military were divided into three broad groups generally known as Button Pushers, Ground Pounders, and Snake Eaters. Beled clearly was no Button Pusher. That was the only branch of the service where Ivyns, and even Camites, were present in any numbers. That narrowed it down to Ground Pounder or Snake Eater. He seemed too elite to be a Ground Pounder: the sort of regular troops who would be deployed in large formations along borders on the surface. Oh, it wasn't out of the question. He might simply have been an unusually big and strong GP. But more likely he was a Snake Eater, which was to say a former GP who had been promoted into one of a few special-purpose branches. Those had informal names too: Queeds (Quarantine Enforcement and Detention), Feelies (Forward Intelligence), and Zerks (a contraction of Berserkers). Queeds had by far the lowest status. They were looked at somewhat askance because of their status as what amounted to riot police, called in to quell domestic disturbances but more often just posted near gates to remind people not to make trouble. Popular estimates of their intelligence and moral fiber were none too generous. Ty could not see why such a person would have been chosen for the Seven, and so he deemed it unlikely. Forward Intelligence was a better fit, and an obvious guess since Ty already knew that Beled had very recently been called back from the surface, where he had been moving about on what sounded like a classic Feely kind of mission. Reference had been made to the fact that Beled had passed near at least one RIZ and observed its inhabitants without himself being seen, which was just the sort of thing Feelies were supposed to be good at. The only thing that prevented Ty from simply pigeonholing Beled as a classic Feely was his physique. Because of that, he must allow for the outside chance that Beled Tomov was a Zerk. But only an outside chance, because, contrary to their image in popular entertainment, Zerks were not all huge and muscular. Most of them looked reasonably normal, if unusually fit. The Zerks were not a single unitary force but a mosaic of small units, each of which was trained and equipped for a special type of activity such as fighting in space suits in zero gee, fighting underwater, being dropped from the sky in pods, or cloak-and-dagger urban shenanigans. Thus far Beled Tomov had not shown any clear signs of such specialization. The steps he was taking to avoid motion sickness suggested that he was not accustomed to airborne work. If Ty had to guess, he'd say that this man had started out as a Ground Pounder, spent a lot of time on the surface in a border zone, distinguished himself, been promoted from the ranks, and ended up in some kind of tiny Zerk unit that specialized in sneaking around on the surface.

The only one showing signs of life was Langobard. This stood to reason, since he had been confined to quarters for a few days. Ty moved back, sat next to him, and asked him about his clan's vineyard in Antimer. It was a wholly reasonable line of inquiry from a Cradle bartender, but both men probably understood that it was just an icebreaker. Bard was more than happy to play along, and talked for a while about the volcanic soil of his homeland, how the TerReForm had converted it, in the last few centuries, from a dead mineral rubble to an ecosystem, and how his grandparents had smuggled grapevines down from various botanical gardens in both Blue and Red and suffered through various misadventures on their way to figuring out that certain soil amendments were needed to make it work. Implicit in that story was that they must have been working with some people who weren't Neoanders. Smuggling unauthorized plant species down to the surface would have been dicey enough, for members of that race, if done entirely within Red. On the Blue side of things, Neoanders would have been absurdly conspicuous, liable to being detained and searched by the Q even when they *weren't* engaged in illegal activity. When Ty pointed that out, Bard said yes while shaking his head no, as if to say, *But of course, what you are saying is obvious.* He went on to explain that his people, stationed for over a decade along a border that was entirely peaceful, had over time established cordial relationships with their opposite numbers on the Blue side of the line, which had begun with swapping supplies to enliven their respective diets and progressed to picnics, athletic competitions, and other ways of relieving the boredom. The Teklans (he reported with a glance toward the slumbering Beled) had been standoffish—but his people had always had good relations with Dinans.

Ty saw no reason to doubt the historical truth of this remark, but he understood that Bard meant it on another level as well: as an overture to Ty, which might lead to friendship. Certainly there were grounds, other than that, for the Dinan and the Neoander to understand each other. Both were Indigens who had found lives in the more sophisticated environment of Cradle but still maintained connections to the surface: connections that were second nature to them, but, in the context of the habitat ring at large, were fantastically unusual.

"Well, that's good," Ty said. "I was raised to be scared to death of your lot."

"Of course you were. How far from the border did you grow up?"

By this, Bard meant the place where 166 Thirty cut across

Beringia: a boundary zone similar to that farther south in Antimer. The west or Red side of it corresponded roughly to what had once been Siberia and the east or Blue side to Alaska. The irony being that the two continents had been rejoined by the Hard Rain but then sundered by an imaginary line.

"Oh, we moved about," Ty said. "Remember, unlike your folk, we lacked a legitimate excuse for being there."

The Neoander's huge, highly expressive features reflected a bit of disappointment that his question hadn't really been answered.

"Too close to the line, and we were at risk of being arrested by the Blues stationed there—or being cooked and eaten by Neoander raiding parties," Ty cracked.

It was one of those jokes that was in such exceedingly poor taste that it could go either way: make Bard an enemy for life, or convince him that Ty really did understand. As a conversational gambit it was somewhat risky. But, on the other hand, Ty was cooped up on a glider with six strangers en route to a mission that hadn't been explained yet. The cargo hold had been preloaded with unmarked cases, some of which obviously contained weapons. At least three of the Seven—Beled, Langobard, and Tyuratam—knew how to use them, and Kath Two's Survey training had included a short course on how to use a kat in a pinch. It was not the time or the place for the sorts of elaborate conversational niceties and courtship dances that might be expected in, say, an old private club on Cradle. More important was to get things sorted in a hurry.

Bard laughed and shook his head. "Why not move farther east then?" he asked. "Get away from those threats altogether."

"Because the early Sooner toeholds weren't really sustainable and we had to trade with Blues for vitamins."

"Under the table, I presume."

"Of course."

"What did you give them in return? Your women?"

It was fair payback for the "cooked and eaten" joke: Bard testing him in return. Ty took it in stride. "They were scared of our women."

"Happy Dinahsday, by the way."

"Is it Dinahsday? I've lost track."

But it didn't matter. Having made a crack about Dinan women, Bard had to pay respect to their Eve.

"No," Ty continued, "to answer your question, it's the same thing that led your ancestors to trade victuals across the line."

"A craving for greater variety in the diet," Bard said. "More powerful in the end than sex."

"Yes. Early on we had nothing more to offer them than fresh vegetables."

"Up there?!"

"Summer days are long—you can grow a lot in a crude plastic greenhouse. Later, as the ecosystem spun up, it was meat from small animals, berries, and a few luxury goods like furs."

A thought occurred to Bard. "And how far would your people range in search for those things?"

He was referring, as Ty understood, to Kath Two's story about the camouflaged Indigen in the trees. For she had by now shared this with the others.

"Not *that* far," Ty said.

IN THE VAST AND ANCIENT UNDERTAKING CALLED THE TERREFORM, Survey was a small department, sometimes viewed as a receptacle for eccentric or troublesome personnel. Its outposts were small and, because they needed to be sited along rapidly changing frontiers, makeshift and temporary. TerReForm bases, by contrast, tended to be much larger and more permanent. As a rule they were sited on islands off the coasts of continents. There was a logical scientific reason for doing it thus, but as Doc himself freely admitted, the real reason was more aesthetic and symbolic. Most of the sophisticated genetic sequencing laboratories, and the staff needed to make them work, were up in the ring, where space was tight but brains were plentiful. TerReForm installations on the surface were of a more practical character, and they sprawled over territory in a way that looked extravagant and unruly to habitat dwellers. They combined the functions of botanical garden, experimental farm, arboretum, zoo, and microbiology lab. Small samples, cuttings, or populations of bugs, plants, or beasts that had been developed and nurtured on the ring were dropped in such places to be propagated and observed before being shipped in quantity to the biomes where they would be allowed to run wild. Placing the bases on islands was a simple method for limiting the spread of plants and animals that had escaped from their assigned habitats. It was very far from being foolproof, but it was simple, easy, and fairly effective: an easy fit, in other words, for the Get It Done school.

The TerReForm base for the Central American isthmus was Magdalena. This was a large island in about the same place as the former Islas Marías. Pre-Zero, this had been an archipelago off the west coast of Mexico, somewhat south of the tip of Baja California. The Hard Rain had reforged it into a single island with a few rocks and reefs scattered around, useful for propagating life that was designed to occupy shallow water and tidal zones. The lack of a moon meant that New Earth's tides were caused entirely by the gravity of the sun, which made them weaker and more closely synchronized with the cycle of night and day. Because tidal zones were thought to have disproportionate importance to the ecosystems of land and sea alike, much TerReForm brainpower had been focused on them, and the low-lying banks of wave-washed rubble around Magdalena had become spawning grounds, not just for fish and birds and crustaceans, but for researchers with advanced degrees. Doc himself had spent ten years of his life here, sloshing through tide pools with buckets and shovels.

Ty would not have thought it possible, but Kath Two got them there with a little bit of daylight to spare, in a single day's flying. Around midday she mumbled something about a noteworthy jet stream perturbation, and the possibility (which to her was apparently quite enticing) of catching a stratospheric wave. To Ty it might as well have been "eye of newt, and toe of frog, wool of bat, and tongue of dog." Her next words, though, had been admirably clear: "Hang on." Drinks were spilled and barf bags reached for all around the cabin. Oxygen masks dropped from the ceiling as the glider shot up through the tropopause, and the fuselage creaked and keened as Kath Two trimmed it to peel energy from some kind of fascinating upper-atmosphere anomaly. Several hours later, when, after another understated warning, she banked it nearly upside down and let it dive toward the faintly wrinkled blue water of the Pacific, they had covered many hundreds of kilometers beyond their original flight plan, and their only real problem was dumping energy so that they could make a landing, as opposed to a crater, on Magdalena. The place had a flynk barn, but the loop wasn't operating at the moment, and anyway there was no reason to attempt a midair rendezvous with a flying chain when a simple airstrip was available nearby. An impressive whine sounded through the airframe as Kath Two turned on a pair of turbines in its belly that took in air through scoops and converted its energy to electrical power that was then stored. The next time the glider took off, the whole system could be run backward, driving the turbines as jets to provide some initial energy boost. It wasn't necessary, but it was a way to slow the glider down, and it was a courtesy for the next pilot. Owing to some low banks of clouds, not much about the last phase of the flight made sense to its passengers, but at length the glider shot out the bottom of that weather system and suddenly Magdalena was below them, lit up on its west side by the last of the setting sun. On the purple skin of the sea, thin arcs of foam materialized as incoming wave fronts sensed the bottom or wrapped around submerged reefs. Doc had moved to a window seat so that he could peer down at his old stomping grounds, and in the suddenly quiet cabin Ty was able to hear him remarking on various installations along the shore. Most of these just looked to Ty like picket lines of pilings and ragged shanties of fishnet and plastic. But as Ty had been explaining to Langobard earlier, his Sooner ancestors had made a living from meaner tech than that, and so he did not think less of the scientists who had built them. The wildlife habitats, arboretums, and gardens tiling Magdalena's western slopes looked a little closer to what a member of the general public might expect from a major TerReForm base, and the buildings clustered at the end of the airstrip were as respectable a town as it was possible to find anywhere on the surface. Ramps, stairs, and a long zigzagging road connected it to a harbor a couple of hundred meters below, where, at a glance, perhaps eight significant vessels, a giant flying boat called an ark, and many smaller boats were moored. They enjoyed a brief panorama of the waterfront before the final bank-around and approach took them out of view behind some hills. After the excitements of the flight, the landing was dull, and Ty suspected that Kath Two had just turned it over to an algorithm. The glider touched down on the single wheel that peeked out from the underside of its fuselage. Before it had slowed to the point where it might teeter sideways, a couple of specialized high-speed grabbs had caught up with it, moving in the somewhat disturbing prancing/scuttling gait that they used at such times, and caught hold of the wingtips. They escorted it to a field of tie-downs off to the side of the airstrip. Kath Two, relieved of responsibility, rolled over onto her back, stretched, and rubbed her eyes. Ty was eager to disembark, but he knew that Doc would be the first out the door. He knew this because he could see a considerable welcoming party walk-jogging toward them.

Ariane was looking at the same thing. Ty did not understand why she would be so secretive on Cradle and in Cayambe, only to land them in the one location on the surface where Doc was most famous. He guessed she had her reasons, worked out in painstaking detail and never to be shared with the likes of Ty. They had to land *somewhere* en route to whatever their final destination was, and perhaps TerReForm was enough of a closed community that the buzz Doc would create by landing here would not extend much beyond Magdalena.

ABOUT TWENTY YEARS AGO—AROUND THE TIME OF HIS HUNDREDTH birthday—Dr. Hu Noah (like all Ivyns, he put his family name first, because it was somehow supposed to be more logical) had made a conscious decision to give up on trying to explain to younger people just how little he had actually changed with age. It didn't really matter that these people were making all sorts of wrong assumptions about how his mind and his body were changing. What mattered to them, he had finally come to realize, was that they believed such things to be true. It was more important to them to believe it than it was for him to explain the facts of the situation, and so he had decided to let them think what they thought and to try to find constructive ways to use it. Sometimes this meant sitting so quietly that they forgot he was there and began speaking of him in the third person, using Remembrance as a sort of interpreter. Sometimes he could astonish by speaking up, making it clear that he had been following the conversation all along. Or he would stand up—an action that was always described later, by witnesses, as "springing to his feet" even though it was nothing of the sort—and begin to move about under his own power, which many who didn't know him well seemed to consider miraculous. Because Remembrance was always by his side, and his grabb was always scuttling along beside him, giving him a sort of universal banister and grab-rail, people assumed he was more unsteady than was really the case. In fact, this support system was nothing more than a simple way of playing the odds. A fall could cripple or kill him; why not have the grabb handy? And Remembrance, though she was assumed by most to be a health care worker, was really more of a general-purpose aide de camp and, to put it crudely, a cowcatcher for turning human obstacles out of his path.

He had had many conversations during his long life. Some were fascinating and stayed with him more than a century later. Others were less so. As a younger man he had tolerated those as part of the cost of doing business—a sort of tax that all people must pay in order to take part in civilized society. When he had turned one hundred, he had decided to stop paying that tax. Henceforth he would engage only in conversations that really interested him—which, with a few exceptions for close friends and family members, meant conversations with a purpose. Remembrance carried in her head a list of all the people whom Doc might actually care to have a conversation with, and knew how to turn the others aside, typically by playing the age card. The list changed slowly over time, and certain people, some of whom were quite important, were occasionally discomfited to find that they were no longer on it. The list had been written down only once, twenty years ago, when Doc and Remembrance had established their relationship. She had committed it to memory and destroyed it. It now existed only in her—not Doc's—head. Perhaps 10 percent of the original names remained. Many of them had died. The others had been crossed off, almost always without any volition from Doc. Remembrance stayed off to one side during his conversations, on the pretext that she might be needed to intervene medically. But what she was really doing was following the dialogue and monitoring Doc for signs, not that his heart was failing or his medication wearing off, but that he was bored. Sometimes, during their first decade together, he had gone so far as to glance in her direction and catch her eye for a moment while his interlocutor wasn't looking, and this had been enough to eliminate that person from the list, but since then it had no longer been necessary. In many cases Remembrance had made what Doc had, at the time, considered to be mistakes in her performance of this duty, but on further consideration he had seen what she had seen quicker, and come to agree with her.

Exceptions had to be made for cases like this one, where they had to work with the five other members of the Seven. Some, but not all, of these might have made their way onto Remembrance's list. He had tried to select people such as Kath Two whom he enjoyed talking to, but the others were strangers to him. Ariane Casablancova showed amusing pretention in sitting next to him whenever she could, acting as a gatekeeper between Doc and the remaining four. She took at face value Remembrance's cover story. Had Remembrance not been a Camite, she might have taken it wrong, seeing it as an usurpation of her prerogatives. But that plus the fact that she had lifetime tenure—a sort of platonic marriage to Doc—made Ariane's behavior at most a source of dry amusement.

The system worked beautifully at times such as this one, when a delegation of senior TerReFormers had gathered outside the door of Doc's glider to belabor him with a welcome. It wasn't that they were insincere, just that their quite genuine desire to greet him was all mixed up with other hopes and needs. One might want to get a photograph with him, but be bashful and tediously indirect about making the request. Another might feel that her life work had been unfairly slighted by her peers and would desire some sign of affirmation from Doc. Yet another might be embroiled in some internal political drama of TerReForm and would hope to gain some currency by being seen on Doc's arm. None of it was wrong or unreasonable, but all of it was a waste of time where he was concerned, just further examples of that tax he didn't want to pay anymore. Knowing this without being told, Remembrance exited the glider first. Doc watched out the window as the delegation huddled around her, leaning in close to hear her quiet voice, and furrowed their brows and made exaggerated nods as she explained to them just how exhausted Doc was. At some point she gestured back toward the glider and all of them looked up in unison and saw Doc's face framed in the window. He made the faintest of waves and they all showed their teeth and saluted him in the various styles of their races: mostly Ivyn and Moiran.

Once that was seen to, Doc "sprang to his feet" with a tug on the handle of his grabb, made his way to the door, stood framed there for a few moments so that they could take their pictures, and then made a great show of descending the stair that had folded down from the vehicle's fuselage. The delegation tracked him across the apron of the airstrip, surrounding him in a great loose cloud but not subjecting him to the tiresome demands of polite social interaction. Ariane was right behind and the remaining four trailed at a distance, completely ignored. Ariane had gotten that right, at least: to the kinds of people who lived here, Doc's arrival on Magdalena was such a sensation that even a Neoander went unnoticed.

After Remembrance had turned aside all invitations and offers of hospitality, he dined in his room with Ariane, who reveled in the attention. Tomorrow things would be different and she would have to begin adjusting. In the darkest part of that adjustment—which for a Julian could get very dark indeed—she would look back on this meal and understand it for what it really was: a gesture of respect from Doc that could not be gainsaid by any of the voices muttering away between her ears.

Doc asked her about her upbringing on Astrakhan, which was a smallish, almost pure Julian habitat at forty-eight degrees six minutes east, near the center of the Dinan part of the ring. This anomaly had come about as the result of a vision—in both the literal and figurative senses of that word—of a Julian man named Tomac, who had raised funds and established it as a quasi-religious outpost very early in the history of the ring. In those days, being three degrees and six minutes away from a capital such as Baghdad made it seem like a remote frontier outpost. Since then, of course, the Dinan segment had filled in around it, crowding it between much larger and more modern habitats. But Astrakhan, with a few modern improvements, continued to support some tens of thousands of souls, and was often alluded to by Julians as evidence that their race, though lacking in numbers, was as well established in Blue as any of the Four. It was frequently visited by scholars in the field of Amistics: the study of the choices made by different cultures as to which technologies they would embrace or spurn. This was because Tomac, who'd had peculiar ideas about everything, had made some unusual and instructive choices as far as that went. The isolation of Astrakhan made it a useful test case. For her part Ariane laughed off many of the quasi-religious aspects of the culture in which she had been raised, but Doc sensed that she was doing so because it was expected of her.

Later, as Remembrance was helping him into bed and getting him tuned up for the night, he told her that tomorrow he would begin getting to know the other four members of the Seven a little better, and that he would politely decline Ariane's assistance in doing so. Ariane would have gloried in the opportunity to furnish Doc with dossiers full of statistics, and hours of personal gossip, about Beled, Kath Two, Tyuratam, and Langobard. But Hu Noah had always felt uncomfortable with such disclosures because they raised the obvious question of what was being disclosed, by the same person, to other curious minds, about Doc.

At five o'clock the next morning, Doc was in the recreation center, walking very slowly on a treadmill, when Beled Tomov came in for his daily workout. Beled's double take was so amusing that even Doc, who had made an art form of appearing not to know what was going on, was hard-pressed not to laugh at the poor fellow's expense. Even Remembrance, sitting nearby and reading, felt it best to interpose her book between her face and Beled's startled gaze for a few moments.

"Lieutenant Tomov," Doc said, "I thought you'd never drag yourself out of bed."

Beled remembered his manners and saluted.

"I hope you won't think me rude if I don't reciprocate," Doc said, and nodded down at the treadmill's handlebars. "I have a death grip on these."

Beled was looking around for Ariane. Doc decided not to make any comment. "Is it your practice to warm up first?" he asked.

"It is not considered necessary," Beled answered.

"Ah, too bad, I was thinking we might go for a stroll together," Doc said, nodding at the empty treadmill next to him.

"That can be done," Beled allowed, "if I may stroll at a different pace."

"Suit yourself!" Doc said. "There is a reason I did not attempt this in the wild."

Within a few minutes the Teklan, now stripped to nothing but a pair of briefs, was running flat-out on the treadmill next to Doc's, his hands blades, his arms scissoring, the soles of his bare feet skimming across the textured belt of the treadmill rather than pounding it. Engineered and bred to be a match for Neoanders, Teklans were at a genetic disadvantage because they were built like modern humans and did not partake of Neanderthal DNA. Bard could sleep in, eat and drink whatever he wanted, and still be as strong as the much larger Teklan. This was all perfectly academic, since no one seriously expected Beled and Bard to get into a fight, but it was a cultural habit of long standing that Teklans measured themselves against Neoanders, and used the comparison to spur themselves to even greater diligence than would have been their habit anyway.

In a calm and level tone of voice, as though he were sitting on a couch sipping tea, Beled said, "I never thanked you for sending me on the mission just completed. I assume it was your doing. But I had no way to reach you. I thank you now."

Doc's eyes strayed to a regularly spaced line of scars wrapping around the small of Beled's back, some forming deep craters in the twin pilasters of muscle bracketing his spine. Bisecting that formation was a long vertical scar running right over the lumbar vertebrae, where surgeons had gone in and done something—Doc didn't know the details—to repair damage to the spinal column and, he supposed, add some hardware or bone grafts.

"It was the least I could do," Doc said. "And given what happened in Tibet, I thought you might be better qualified than most to address certain . . . plausible complications that might arise."

"So we will be operating near the border," Beled replied. His tone said that he had long ago surmised this and only wanted final confirmation.

"We will go where the investigation takes us," Doc said.

This surprised Beled slightly, producing a hiccup in his gait, which he spent a few moments resolving.

"These wanderers," Doc went on, "do not seem to be great respecters of borders, or of anything to do with Treaty, and so I thought it best to construct the Seven of persons of like mind."

"Is it to be Beringia, then? Or Antimer?"

"Probably both. Antimer, of course, is closer—a short hop from Hawaii, which is today's destination. But as the trail is warmer in Beringia, I think we shall go there first."

HAWAII THEY REACHED BEFORE NIGHTFALL, TRAVELING AS PASSENgers on a colossal TerReForm vehicle, not really an airplane and not really a boat, that skimmed over the surface at an altitude of no more than four meters. Ground effect vehicles of this class were called arks. They had been designed to deliver massive quantities of plant and animal biomass, nurtured at big offshore TerReForm bases such as Magdalena, to littoral destinations, where they could be slammed down into their new homes or else transferred to other vehicles for shipment inland. Only ten of them had ever been built and only six remained in service. This one was called *Ark Madiba,* after a Moiran biologist of the Fourth Millennium who had in turn been named in memory of a hero of Old Earth.

If their theme was to travel unobtrusively, then *Ark Madiba* was certainly the vehicle for it, being a cavernous, reeking warren of animal pens, fish tanks, bug boxes, and racked peat pots in which exotic plants were growing in stews of manure. A ship making the same run—five thousand kilometers due west—would have taken several days. Provisions would have been needed to feed the beasts, clean the cages, and water the plants. This howling, hammering monstrosity did it in twelve hours, a span brief enough that just about any living thing could survive it without victuals beyond water and perhaps a bit of a snack. In it, the Seven basically disappeared. As the ark's dozens of turbofans roared into life and it began to chunder across Magdalena's harbor, the noise level rose to the point where they could do nothing but insert the earplugs they'd been issued and distribute themselves around the cargo hold in places where the stink wasn't too bad. Doc and Memmie were given special dispensation to enjoy the journey in a tiny capsule near the cockpit, where members of the flight crew could sleep and recreate during multiday flights. The rest of them just tried to make themselves as comfortable as they could and waited for it to be over.

TerReForm had come late to Hawaii. The place was small, idiosyncratic, far away, and complicated—best left for last, after major continents had been booted up. The Hard Rain had loosened the lid on the geological hot spot that had built the islands, reawakening dormant volcanoes on existing islands while causing a seamount southeast of the Big Island to develop, ahead of schedule, into a Bigger Island. This had merged, a thousand years ago, with the former to make a Bigger Island Yet, most of which was still too hot and toxic for TerReForm to bother with. But there was a cove on its north coast, called Mokupuku after a tiny island that had once stood approximately in the same place, around which things were cool and quiet enough to be worth seeding. There, around sunset, *Ark Madiba* effected a sort of controlled crash landing, skidding to a halt offshore of a small TerReForm installation of the sort that were now scattered all over New Earth.

Such as these were the epicenters of the ecological earthquakes that the human races had, for about three centuries, been unleashing on the surface. Sometimes they got their deliveries straight from the sky, other times, as in this case, from arks dispatched out of the larger surface installations. Older ones were clusters of hemispherical domes because they had been constructed before New Earth even had a breathable atmosphere. Newer ones, like this, had a somewhat more welcoming appearance. But their basic purpose was to work with beasts, bugs, and plants, and so their fragrance and the overall style of their operations lay somewhere on a continuum between farm and zoo, with the odd dash of science lab. None of it would have seemed remarkable, at least on an olfactory level, to the vast majority of human beings who had lived on Old Earth in the millennia leading up to the scientific revolution, but the people who endured that voyage in the cargo hold of the great plane/boat were fortunate that the fuselage wasn't pressurized and that ocean air could therefore filter through it.

The staff were almost all Moirans, with a sprinkling of Camites and one visiting scientist who looked like a Dinan/Ivyn breed. Obvious to Kath Two, and probably to the others as well, was that her kin had slept long and hard after coming to this place, where they were cut off from the rest of their race while continually exposed to the pheromones, smells, calls, and behaviors of those animals and plants. Resulting epigenetic shifts had rendered them well qualified to do this kind of work, to do it all day long, and to live here indefinitely. This truly was the back of beyond—even more isolated than certain boneyard habitats that had become proverbial for remoteness—and the Moirans here all shared a kind of thousand-yard stare that was only intensified by the fact that they were predominantly green-eyed. They moved slowly, they appeared to think slowly, and they were always reacting to stimuli—auditory? olfactory? imaginary?—that Kath Two could not even detect.

The existence of seven distinct human races, as well as various Aïdan subraces, provided modern society with a rich fund of opportunities for socially awkward happenings. The few hours they spent on the beach at Mokupuku, watching the locals unload samples from the vehicle and hose the shit out of it with pressurized seawater, were long ones for Kath Two as she sensed other members of the Seven glancing back and forth between her and these, and wondering how long it would take Kath Two to go that way if she extended her stay. These people had created, and were self-aware and self-proud of having created, an original culture around the place where they lived. Which for all practical purposes was synonymous with the ecosystem that they were installing in it. Not for them scientific detachment. Was it really wise to station Moirans in a place where they could live as closely with epigenetic animal species as medieval Europeans had with their swine and their fowl? Were these animals scientific specimens, livestock, or pets to them? Kath Two watched their uncomfortably familiar interactions with those animals and they watched her watching them. They had woven into their dreadlocks the bright feathers of birds that on Old Earth would have been called exotic: a word that was useless here, since humans had made them, patterning them after the parrots, toucans, and cockatoos of long-extinct jungles on the theory that if colorful plumage had been useful to birds there, it would be useful to them here. "Inotic"? "Anthroötic"? Anyway, they were weird people, and they were lifers in the sense that no conceivable home could be found for them on the ring. Not unless they went back to sleep for a while and tried to roll back the changes that their environment had bent on them. But that was no easy thing. As long as a Moiran kept changing, she could keep changing, but if she stayed one way for too long she would "take a set," as the expression went, and find it hard to change back. These, Kath Two suspected, had definitely taken a set. They were obviously interbreeding with the Camite staff, who in racially characteristic fashion had adapted to the place where they had found themselves and were looking for ways to make it work for the people surrounding them.

There was nothing wrong with that. So people on the ring kept saying, because it was the polite thing to say. Nothing wrong with breeds. But the truth of it was that breeds, like weeds, tended to be found in disturbed areas. A sprinkling was nice, especially in sophisticated places like Chainhattan, but seeing a lot of them in one community was a sign that everyone on the ring knew how to read, even if they knew it was impolite to say what they were thinking. The behaviors that these Moirans had invented around everyday things like the sunrise, mealtime, and the interpretation of dreams had a ritualistic quality that to Ariane was obviously fascinating and to Kath Two was a little mortifying. For the first time in her life she was feeling the stirrings of what was called Old Racism: the survival into modern times of racial attitudes, or reenactments thereof, that had existed on Old Earth, had been altogether snuffed out, and were known only because documentation thereof had survived. On a certain kind of diseased mind they exerted the same magnetic pull as they had pre-Zero, and so among a population of millions on the ring you might find one person who'd spent too much time delving into a five-thousand-year-old web archive and become infected with ideas about pre-Zero blacks that he fancied were applicable to Moirans, and so on. It was purely an intellectual curiosity and not at all a factor in real people's lives: a thing Kath Two had heard of, like rabies or Watergate, and she was fascinated to find it stirring in her own mind here of all places. But that was only a passing notion.

Presently her Survey mind kicked in and subsumed all under the scientific method. Here they were at a TerReForm outpost. Many thousands of these existed. Some were huddles of tents presaging more permanent works. Some, like this one, had been around for decades, others for centuries. Some were now abandoned, having served their purpose, and others had become nuclei of RIZes, campuses for gimmicky schools, prison camps, or scientific foundations. A weird culture, utterly nontransferable to the ring, had formed at this one. If it had happened here, something like it must have happened at others. How many? Was New Earth infested with bizarre cultural outliers centered on TerReForm installations? Could you go to what used to be Uzbekistan and find a miniature colony of Ivyn performance artists, developing their own idiosyncratic lichen-based cuisine on the rim of an impact crater the size of Ireland? To what was left of the Iberian Peninsula and visit a colony of Teklan juggernauts making babies with Julian mystics? How far could this go?

Kath Two felt some relief the next morning when, after a pleasant and uneventful campout on the beach, they got back into *Ark Madiba,* now 90 percent empty, and took off north.

The distance to the south coast of Blue Antimer was half what they had covered the day before. Around midday, when the sun was beating down on the deep eaves and shuttered windows of the military complex above, the ark plowed up the harbor there and settled with a vast sigh into a fresh, sparkling azure chop. A smaller TerReForm post, annexed to the military base, sported a single pier long enough to accommodate an ark. The pilots employed a variety of muttering and whining thrusters to get into its general vicinity. The rest was handled by robot tugs pulling on ropes wrapped around massive bitts. The five humans who'd been sharing the cargo hold moved forward to get out of the way of the local TerReForm staff, who boarded the ark, along with a couple of cargo-loading grabbs, to take charge of what little cargo remained: racks of cages housing large carnivores. It was a mix of canids and felids, with a few big snakes. They'd been stashed in different parts of the hold so that they wouldn't wear themselves out menacing one another. Anyone who was connected with Survey, or, for that matter, who knew anything about the TerReForm at all, would understand what this meant: the ecosystem of Antimer was far more developed than that of Hawaii, and was now producing small fauna and herbivores at a pace that required the introduction of bigger predators to keep them in check.

The harbor was an almost perfectly circular impact crater with only a small outlet to the sea. Most of its circumference was claimed by the military base. From somewhere in that zone, a launch cut across the disk of blue water and came up alongside the ark's cockpit door. The Seven descended to it by means of a folding stairway, and thus passed out of TerReForm jurisdiction without any formalities, or even contact with the local staff. Half an hour later they were eating lunch in a private officers' dining room adjoined to a mess hall, and an hour after that they were aboard an airplane—a conventional, powered military craft—that took off from a runway blasted into the stony shore of the island a few miles away and banked northward after it had gained enough altitude to clear the snowcapped peaks along Antimer's central ridge. From that height the eye was no longer beguiled by the peaks and valleys that, at a smaller scale, made the place seem like an Old Earth mountain range. Here it was possible, for those looking out the windows on the left side of the airplane, to see a thousand kilometers westward. The curvature of the archipelago's spine made it obvious that this was the rim of a huge impact crater, created by a big chunk of moon that had come in on a somewhat northward trajectory and pushed a high arc of seafloor and ejecta up above sea level. To the south, a smaller archipelago, curved the opposite way, hinted at the crater's lower rim. That, however, was not visible from the plane's windows. Instead they all gazed west, tracing the arc of mountains as it grew higher and the land beneath it broadened. Somewhere along the way it was sliced by the invisible line of 166 Thirty. Bard pressed his heavy brow against the window and looked long and thoughtfully at his homeland, seeming to identify hills and bays that he remembered, thinking of vineyards. Then Antimer fell away behind and they flew for some hours over the featureless Pacific.

The water was too deep in these parts for the Hard Rain to have visibly reshaped anything, barring another hyperimpact like the one that had created Antimer, and so the general shape of things was little changed until they verged on the continental shelf, just a hundred kilometers or so south of what had once been Alaska's coastline. In the shallows between that and the foothills of the coastal range—a strip of sea and land between one and two hundred kilometers wide—

visible changes had been wrought. But the coastline was basically where it had always been. More effective than direct bolide strikes in the reshaping of the land had been the disappearance of the glaciers and the endless series of tsunamis that had been funneled into this broad bight over the millennia. The one hurled up by the Antimer impact had overtopped the mountains themselves, cresting over what had formerly been glacier-bound peaks and slamming down far inland to boil dry on the hot rocks. Since the beginning of the Cooling Off, about eleven hundred years ago, and particularly since humans had reconstituted the oceans by dropping comets on the surface, snow had begun falling on those peaks again. But it took a long time for glaciers to form, and it would be millennia more before cracked rivers of old blue ice oozed down the mountain valleys to touch the sea.

When that day came, the settlement of Qayaq would have to move out of the way. It was built on a heap of rubble on the western bank of a cold river that hurtled down out of the mountains, just at the place where it emptied into the Pacific. There was not enough space between sea and snow for an airfield of the size Qayaq required, and so they had constructed one out of the mix of fiber and ice known as pykrete. This floated just offshore, a perfectly flat slab laced with tubes through which refrigerated coolant was circulated to keep it solid—not a difficult task in a place where the temperature of sea and air alike was only a few degrees above freezing. Other than that, nothing was really here. Even the TerReForm presence was minimal, it being easier for TerReForm staff to operate from boats.

The Qayaq airfield had to exist because of the Ashwall. West of here, all the way to 166 Thirty and beyond, the chain of volcanoes formerly known as the Kenai and Alaska Peninsulas and the Aleutian chain were in a nearly continual state of eruption. Any pilot meaning to fly north or south across the sixtieth parallel, in the zone bracketed by 166 Thirty on the west and the Rockies on the east, had to make allowances in the flight plan for the likelihood that their path would abruptly be barred by a plume of volcanic ash hurled into the stratosphere by any of a hundred active volcanoes lying upwind. Airplanes were expensive, even more so than they had been on Old Earth. They were too large to manufacture in the ring and transport down to the surface and so they, and other large productions such as arks and ships, had to be built in factories on the surface. Typically these lay on the outskirts of Cradle sockets. In any case, planes had to be babied, given that high-capacity turbofan engines were extraordinarily difficult to make. Every flight plan had to include a possible emergency landing on the artificial floe of Qayaq, which in turn had to be fully capable of hosting big airplanes. So what had been conceived as an emergency landing site had become something of a hub, where planes tended to land just because it was convenient and predictable. In any case it happened to be the final destination of the military flight on which the Seven had hitched a ride, so they had to get off here anyway.

It was about as warm and welcoming as you would expect of a forward airbase constructed on a slab of ice. A low cloud layer kept it in eternal twilight and converted all colors to shades of gray. Across a strip of water, the town sprawled on its rubble pile like a dead starfish. Beyond that was a black wall that they understood to be the lower slopes of the coastal range, carpeted now with young trees but too obscured by mist and gloom to be identifiable as such. Higher up, just below the cloud ceiling, some of these were dusted with fresh snow, or perhaps just ice condensed directly from the fog. Had those clouds been absent, as they were for a few cumulative weeks out of each year, the Seven would have been able to look up above snow-capped peaks to a sky made black by the Ashwall. One of the big volcanoes on Kenai had been erupting copiously for two weeks.

The temptation to cocoon in a microhotel pod on the slab, to eat hot noodles from a cup and watch videos, was strong. Anything to escape the sense of being trapped between ice and sea below, fog and ash above, the Pacific to the south, and the mountain wall to the north. Instead of which Tyuratam Lake announced that he was going into the city to sample its drinking establishments. He did so in a manner so bluff as to make everyone else feel faintly idiotic for even thinking of doing otherwise. Kath Two, Beled, and Langobard said they were in. Doc demurred on grounds of wanting a nap, and Memmie, as always, stayed with Doc. Ariane seemed peeved and conflicted. The politics of race had been gradually coming into play during the journey from Cradle, and now Ty was pushing harder.

According to a five-thousand-year-old understanding shared by most who were not Aïdans, and some who were, Ty was going to be the leader of the group. This was partly because he was a native Beringian who knew his way around the place, but it was mostly just because he was the Dinan, and being the leader was a thing that Dinans did. Ariane had been organizing things—it was she who had somehow strung together the series of flights that had taken them from Cradle to Qayaq—and in the early going she'd had Doc's ear. It had seemed impossible to talk to Doc without going through her. But since then Doc had made a point of spending time privately with the others, and Ariane, after a day or so of confusion and irritation, had accepted this. The natural constraints of group travel had kept them all together. Now Ty was mounting an unauthorized expedition to the mainland, and Ariane was perhaps torn between the desire for that private cup of noodles and the fear that she would miss something.

She ended up coming with them. They broke open one of the chests of gear that had been with them since Cayambe and found warm clothes. Then they hiked across the ice to some steps that led down to a little port for water taxis, and made the trip—just a few hundred meters—to the shore of Beringia. A rambling stair, carved into the rock by mining robots, took them from the water's edge up to the place where the slope became gentle enough to walk on, and then they found themselves looking down a main street that ran inland for all of about a hundred meters before dead-ending against a vertical wall of rock: a boulder that had been forcibly embedded in the flank of a larger mountain. Even from here they could tell that the boulder was a piece of the moon. Efforts had been made to pep the place up by making use of various light-emitting technologies, which now festooned the fronts of the establishments and bled lurid, saturated colors into the translucent air. It could be inferred from the nature of their advertising that the typical customer was military and lonely.

"I SOMETIMES WONDER," BARD SAID, GRIMACING AT THE TASTE OF the local cider, "whether the Eves, being women, really *got* the connection between the male visual system and sex drive." He was looking sidelong at a naked lady at the opposite end of the room.

Kath Two had little interest in the naked lady, but she had turned her back on the rest of the group, a minute earlier, to watch a disturbance. Now she turned to face Bard. "Well, they were *women*. They had spent their whole lives under that gaze. Everything they'd ever been taught about how to dress, how to carry themselves—"

"Yes," Ariane said. "On, if memory serves, Day 287 of the Epic, we have the 'reality television' conversation in which Ivy talks specifically about the importance of Dinah's persona and its treatment in social media."

"How can you remember shit like that?" Ty asked.

Kath Two gave him a somewhat reproachful look. "How can you *not*? That conversation took place only minutes before your Eve met the love of her life."

Ty thought about it. "First bolo?" His eyes flicked away from the naked lady toward a screen above the bar, where a scene from the Epic had been playing with the sound off: Dinah in a space suit, going out on the exterior of *Endurance* to figure out what was wrong with a misbehaving robot. No one was watching it.

"Yes. First bolo," Kath Two said, slightly mollified.

Bard, for his part, was focusing a little too hard on the tiny bubbles in his cider, the dents and scratches in the surface of the table, the electrical wiring bracketed to the ceiling. It was different for him. Ty and Beled could look all they want—that was, after all, the whole point of the establishment. For a Neoander, however, to stare in that way at a woman—she looked like a Dinan or perhaps a Dinan/Teklan breed—was a different matter. Not as far as the proprietors were concerned. The place was actually run, and presumably owned, by women. But there were other customers who had marked Bard when he had come in and who were devoting almost as much attention to him as to the dancers. Had he not been in the company of a larger than normal Teklan and a middle-aged Dinan man with a certain hard-to-pin-down "don't fuck with me" vibe, there might have been trouble. A few of the other patrons might have joined forces to find out whether the stories about Neoanders were tall tales. As matters stood, the only thing Bard had to worry about was being glared at a lot, and possibly coming down with something because of whatever feral strain of yeast had infected the cider.

The template, and the general set of expectations, for communities of this type had been set beginning around five hundred years after Zero, when Cradle had become sufficiently crowded that there had simply been no choice but to spread outward from it. The first outlying habitats had been only a few kilometers away on Cleft. In fact, nearly all settlement had been confined to Cleft until early in the Second Millennium, when the industrial base had developed to the point where other rocks could be colonized. Many more such communities had been depicted in fictional entertainments than had actually existed. This didn't matter, though. As the almost totally factitious and romanticized Old West had been to American culture of the twentieth century, so those yarns were to the people of the habitat ring. So in the rare cases when actual settlements of that type were constructed *de novo,* as here, they tended to be built so as to meet the expectations of people who their whole lives had been watching fiction serials about their Second Millennium precursors.

Even so, there were some surprises. Not so much the fact that it was female-owned. That wasn't uncommon in the adult entertainment industry, and anyway some selection bias was at work—they had chosen to sit down in this place because it didn't feel as creepy to Kath Two and Ariane as some of the others. More unexpected was the fact that as many as half of the people in there were Indigens. Those who weren't—ones who had come across the water from the ice slab floating offshore—were identifiable by haircut, clothing, and bearing. But their numbers were matched by shaggier and more colorful characters whose professions and reasons for being in Qayaq could only be guessed at. It was safe to assume that many of these had come up the coast from a RIZ about twenty kilometers away to engage in trade or other forms of intercourse. But Qayaq itself was bigger and more crowded than they had expected, suggesting growth in population and commerce exceeding the limits set by Treaty. Sheltered by mountains and hidden most of the time under dense clouds, an illicit city was growing up here. If it was happening here, it was happening elsewhere in the Blue part of the world. Red had to know about it. Cloud cover alone couldn't keep such a place secret. Why did Red not file diplomatic protests, then? Because Red was probably doing the same thing, perhaps on an even larger scale, and Red and Blue had come to a tacit agreement not to make trouble.

How many humans lived on the surface? The official numbers for the Blue part of it were about a million, mostly concentrated around Cradle sockets. Maybe the real numbers were much greater.

When they were finally approached, it was by a young Ivyn man with long hair and a wispy beard. Had he been spotted in the same location five thousand or, for that matter, ten thousand years ago, he would have passed for one whose ancestors had crossed from Asia over the original Beringia and flooded into North and South America. He had the wit to understand that the visitors were looking at him warily but the grit to walk to them anyway. He kept his hands casually down to his sides, palms slightly out, as if he had caught himself in the instant before throwing them up and exclaiming "What the fuck are you people doing here?" He was alert and mildly amused. As he drew closer it became clear that he was taller than he'd seemed at first; they'd been misled by his slight build and his stooped posture.

They might have asked the same question—what the fuck are you doing here?—of this young Ivyn. Judging from his clothes—five-year-old fashions from Chainhattan customized with bits of fur, bone, and animal skin—he was an Indigen with commercial links to Qayaq. Maybe the smartest kid in his RIZ, the child of eccentric Ivyn dreamers, looking for things to do with his brain. He'd been hanging out at the bar with some Dinan chums, but all of them had seemed more embarrassed than stimulated by the nude dancers.

"You guys headed over the mountains?" he asked. He had noted their clothing: brand new, high quality, extremely warm.

It seemed like a simple icebreaker to everyone except Ty, who said, "We don't need a guide," before any of the others could answer.

That set the kid back just a little. "A guide," he repeated, as if Ty had just brought a peculiar but somewhat interesting idea into the conversation. "No, I didn't really take you for people who would hire a guide." Meaning adventurous—and, by Treaty, illegal—tourists from the ring.

This left open the question of what he *did* take them for, and so it was a little awkward until he went on: "If you're going to the other side of the mountains, I could show you something."

"Something special? One of a kind? Something you show to people all the time?" Ty asked.

The kid looked shy. "I have been there twice before. It's interesting."

"Been there with paying customers?" Ty asked. "Because—" but he was interrupted by a hand on his arm from Ariane.

"He called it interesting," she said. "He is not motivated by money."

"Very well," Ty said.

"What is your name?" Ariane asked him.

The kid put up his deflector screens and said, "Einstein."

Silence then. When no one laughed, he stood straighter and drifted closer.

"What makes this thing so interesting?"

"It's a fact," Einstein said.

"I don't understand," Kath Two said. "It's a fact that it's interesting or—" but then she stopped, because she had figured it out. An apostrophe belonged before that word. He meant that it was an artifact. A surviving object from the pre-Zero world.

"I would go see that," Ty allowed.

THEY UNDERSTOOD EINSTEIN A LITTLE BETTER THE NEXT DAY when Kath Two flew all of them over the mountains in a glider and they saw just how difficult it must have been for foot travelers like him to have reached the site of the artifact. It raised the question of how he had ever found it in the first place. "Blind luck after getting hopelessly lost in a whiteout" seemed the most likely answer, but perhaps his people had combed the inland slopes of these mountains in a systematic way.

They were traveling in the same type of glider they had used on the leg from the Cayambe socket to Magdalena. Because it had no engines, it could fly through the Ashwall without mechanical damage, and because it traveled more slowly than a jet, they didn't have to worry quite so much about Kath Two's windshield getting fogged by abrasion from microscopic bits of rock. They *did* have to be somewhat concerned about the fact that she could not see where she was going as they flew through the densest part of the cloud. But she knew the altitudes of the nearby peaks and stayed well above them. Once the view had cleared a little bit, she was able to take advantage of the ash, which worked in the air somewhat like a drop of ink in swirling water, making currents and vortices obvious.

Einstein seemed exotic to the Seven in that he had been born on the surface and had never left it. This was his first journey in an aircraft of any kind. Seeing the mountains from above demanded some mental adjustments, which he made quickly. And in any case he knew the latitude and longitude of the artifact. After they had passed over the crest of the mountains and gotten into clear air, he directed Kath Two toward a high valley slung between the coastal range and a subsidiary crest beyond. Its upper reaches were devoid of life, but farther down the slope, tundra and low scrub were beginning to take hold. That these had been seeded from space was obvious from their regular spacing. Robot pods had fallen out of the sky in precise geometric formations and slammed into the ground in a hexagonal array before breaking open to spill their seed on the ground. Some wag in the bureaucratic bowels of TerReForm had dubbed these things ONANs: Orbital Neo-Agricultural Nacelles. As the years went by and the ecosystem spread out from the ONANs, the hexagonal pattern disappeared into the natural chaos of life. But in a place like this where plants grew slowly it would still be visible centuries from now.

Kath Two made a few passes up and down the length of the valley and identified a stretch of smooth seasonal riverbed, paved with frozen ash-paste, where she thought she could land and take off. The glider's energy storage devices had been charged up the night before and were still at 100 percent. So she made another long orbit to bleed off velocity and then landed while traveling in an uphill direction. She made a gentle touch first, just to verify that the riverbed was in fact frozen solid, then set the glider down decisively. The wingtips dragged at the very end and there was some concern that one of them might strike a protruding rock, but she was able to avoid this and bring the craft to a full stop without damage. Beled and Bard climbed out first, and jogged in opposite directions to the two wingtips. After picking these up off the ground they were able to rotate the glider by walking clockwise in a large circle. Kath Two told them when to stop.

Ty got out and opened a cargo hatch on the side, releasing a couple of siwis that began moving across the ground in their distinctive elbowing style of locomotion, as well as a couple of buckies that began rolling about seeking high ground from which to establish observation posts and communications links. Their main objective now was to get the glider tied down so it wouldn't blow away in a stray gale. The siwis were essentially earth sciences robots, good at digging and tunneling. In a few minutes' time, with a bit of guidance from Doc, they were able to plant anchors in some sturdy-looking boulders flanking the riverbed. Ty and Bard ran ropes from those to the ends of the glider's wings and made it fast while Beled stalked restlessly around the perimeter. Kath Two and Ariane deployed the grabb that Doc used to get about in places like this. It served the same function as a wheelchair, only with legs, so that it could pick its way along terrain where even able-bodied humans would have difficulty making headway. Meanwhile Memmie got him bundled up and ready. Einstein watched it all and asked only a few hundred questions, most of which were cheerfully answered by Doc himself. Einstein would have seen much of this sort of technology on videos in the RIZ, but this was his first direct experience of it.

He knew better than to ask questions about the weapons. Kath Two, Ty, Beled, and Bard all had katapults of different descriptions. They did not arm themselves like soldiers going into war, but more in the precautionary style of Survey personnel venturing into places where large predators or even bad Indigens might be prowling around. Kath Two carried the same type of small katapult that she'd been packing on her recently concluded Survey mission: a sidearm that would use electromagnetic propulsion to hurl one particular kind of ambot toward a large, warm target. Steering itself toward the big infrared blob, the ambot would land on it, like a space probe touching down on an asteroid, and crawl around looking for ways to make it miserable. Any large animal with more than two or three of these things on its body would have other things on its mind than eating Kath Two. Tyuratam Lake had a somewhat older, heavier, and more battered version of a similar weapon. It had two magazines, one of which was exactly the same as Kath Two's. The other presumably housed ambots of a different type, maybe for use against humans. Beled was slung with a considerably bigger two-handed katapult, whose long flexible magazine was draped about him like a bandolier. It was overkill, but it was what he had, and the weight didn't bother him. Langobard, in a style traditional among Red Neoanders, simply had a menagerie of different ambots—perhaps a dozen all told—crawling around on his body, and a katapult strapped to the underside of his forearm, like a splint. When he told it to begin firing, which he would do by means of a control in the palm of his hand, the ambots would get word of it over their network and begin trying to find their way to his elbow so that they could insinuate themselves into the katapult's projection mechanism. It seemed a bit indirect, but it had the advantage that when the ambots had nothing else to do they could patrol Bard's body looking for foreign ambots that had been projected at him by the enemy, and join battle with them.

All of which, while fascinating to Einstein, and indeed to anyone who stopped to think about it, was so routine to the Seven that no one made any mention of it. The behavior of the ambots infesting Bard was somewhat novel and distracting at first to those who'd had little exposure to Red ways, but as they began their trudge down the valley it became clear that the ambots were all executing a program that cashed out in a few repetitive, stereotypical behaviors such as perching on his shoulders or running rings around his midsection. Sometimes a few would make a bid to form a train, but there weren't really enough of them.

During spare moments in the trip from Cradle, Beled and Bard and Ty had sat down together in private rooms, opened up the equipment cases, and made efforts to get the different ambots accustomed to each other, so that the Blue-programmed ones that most of them were using wouldn't identify Bard's more Reddish ammunition as innately hostile, and vice versa. So far it seemed to be working. When the shape of the valley funneled them all together, as when squeezing through a passage between boulders, Bard's ambots seemed to catch the scent of the ones reposing in Beled's snaky bandolier, and would crawl around to that side of Bard's anatomy and aim their sensors in that direction, but it did not seem as though hostilities were about to break out. Since any one communications system was likely to be jammed or hacked by the opposition, your more highly developed ambots communicated with one another in a number of different ways, including sound. Ultrasound was preferred, but all frequencies were used, and so it was occasionally possible to hear Bard's botmo spewing noise as it tried to evaluate, or possibly just to confuse, the Blue botmo all around it. Sometimes it was a hiss and sometimes it was a mathematical tune played too fast for the human ear to process it. In any case, nothing—at least, nothing audible to humans—came back from Beled's, Ty's, or Kath Two's arsenals. Broadly speaking, Blue armaments makers were biased toward the "lots of dumb ambots" philosophy while Red ones went the other way.

On broken terrain, Doc on his grabb made better time than anyone, with the possible exception of Einstein, who was a gifted scrambler. The two of them would surge ahead and then Beled would put on a loping burst and catch up, obeying some kind of instinct to take point. Langobard seemed more inclined to hang back and act as a rear guard, which meant he spent more time in the company of the slower Ariane. Sometimes he simply picked her up and carried her over rough patches. The valley had been flat higher up, but they had to negotiate a steeper transition down to the altitude where vegetation had been seeded by the ONANs. It then became easier going, though they had to find open trails among the dense low shrubs that had taken root in the ashy soil. Their feet and their noses told them that the ground had been preseeded with some kind of microorganism that had presumably been designed to convert volcanic ash—which tended to have toxic stuff like sulfur in it—to a more wholesome kind of soil.

Einstein had played his cards close to his chest until they had deplaned. Since then, he had been providing Doc, and anyone else close enough to eavesdrop, with his own kind of speculative backstory for the thing they were going to visit.

"You'll see when we get there," he said more than once, perhaps betraying some uncertainty as to the correctness of his theory—a word he knew but pronounced to rhyme with "story."

The phrase "I looked it up" was in frequent use by Einstein. He had no idea who Doc was, and just saw him as a very old man who was willing to answer questions. To answer them, but also to ask them in a way that was challenging without being brusque.

"They had these wheeled vehicles—"

"Cars?"

"No, the big box-shaped ones."

"Trucks, or lorries," Doc said.

"My theory is that this 'fact used to be one of those."

"But a minute ago," Doc observed, in the mildest possible tone of complaint, "you were saying it got hurled over the mountains by a tsunami."

"Yeah."

"That would imply that it had been bobbing around somewhere in the ocean."

"That's my theory."

"Would it not have sunk to the bottom? The boxes were not airtight. Sooner or later it would have filled up with water."

"The inside of what used to be the box is all coated with black residue," Einstein offered, also pronouncing that word incorrectly.

"What conclusion do you draw from that?"

"I looked it up, and these trucks were used to carry all kinds of goods. Not just heavy stuff but bags of potato chips, athletic shoes, toys. My theory is that this was one of those. It was near the waterfront when it got hit by one of the earliest tsunamis, a small one that dragged it out into the ocean. And it didn't sink, see, because—"

"Because it was full of bags of potato chips or something," Doc said.

"Right, and it didn't burn, at least not right away, because it was in the water. But then later it got caught up in a really big tsunami, like the one that created Antimer, which heaved it right up over the mountains and slammed it down . . . right over there. We should almost be able to see it."

"Whereupon its contents burned, leaving the black residue," Doc said, gently emphasizing the pronunciation.

"Yeah, and the paint burned off and the tires and all of the other stuff that wasn't steel."

"Would it not then have rusted away, during five thousand years?"

"I looked it up," Einstein said. "The place was very dry. And this truck was probably buried. Yeah, it rusted some. But it was preserved until the Cloudy Century."

Einstein must have looked that up too; the Cloudy Century was roughly 4300–4400, after the oceans had been reinstated but while everything was still quite hot.

"Then, after rivers began flowing again, erosion exposed it. And yeah, the exposed parts are rusted all right. Some parts are of a different metal though."

"Aluminum," Doc said.

But Einstein's discourse was trailing off as he kept looking at the device that was supposed to tell them their latitude and longitude. He was giving every appearance of being lost.

Finally he made a decisive move about fifty meters down-valley, penetrating a bank of tall shrubs. The others followed him. Visibility was poor and so they heard his reaction before seeing the 'fact. "What the—?!"

"What is it?" Ty demanded.

"Someone dug it up!" Einstein exclaimed.

They found themselves standing around the rim of a pit perhaps half a dozen meters in diameter, and the same in depth. Marks in the soil made it obvious that this had been excavated with shovels, and vague footprints proved they had been wielded by humans and not robots. At the deepest part of the excavation, the gray soil had been stained red with rust. But the bottom of the pit was otherwise vacant; whatever had been rusting there was entirely gone. Only a few scraps of hard black plastic, and fragments of steel that had been altogether converted into rust, proved that Einstein hadn't been lying to them all along.

Ty let himself down carefully into the hole, prodded in the wet, rusty mush with his toe, then reached into it and pulled something out. After shaking off lashings of mud, he underhanded it out of the pit to Beled, who picked it out of the air. It was a bent black cylinder.

"The day is not lost," Ty announced. "All of us will get to handle an actual 'fact. That, my friends, is a five-thousand-year-old radiator hose."

A few emotions were competing for the mental energies of the Seven: utter confusion about who had dug this hole, and why. Empathy for the deeply embarrassed Einstein, who had promised them an entire truck. Disappointment that the only things left of it were a rust stain and a radiator hose. A mild sense of alarm at the idea that inexplicable persons with shovels were somewhere about. Swamping all of these, however, like a tsunami cresting over the mountains, was the awareness that they were in the presence of a real artifact from before Zero. As they had established on the flight up here, Doc had seen such things three times in his life, not counting museum exhibits. None of the others had ever seen one at all.

And so they all stood there in silence for several minutes, passing it from hand to hand, thinking about it: the factory where it had been manufactured, the engineers who had designed it, the workers who had assembled the vehicle, the driver who had piloted it around, and the day that the Hard Rain had begun. As it turned out, imagining the fate of seven billion people was far less emotionally affecting than imagining the fate of one.

Beled, after handling the 'fact for a minute and gazing at it inscrutably, handed it off to Kath Two. He withdrew from the edge of the pit and began circling it restlessly. After a minute he called out to the others, but not in a voice of alarm.

About ten meters away, at a break in the slope that afforded a bit of a view down the valley, a sort of totem had been erected: a length of aluminum tubing, white with oxidation, projecting vertically out of the ground to a height about equal to that of a person. At its top, lashed on with a few scraps of copper wire, a circular object: a steel hoop mostly obscured by marred and pitted black stuff, a crossbar through its middle with loose wires dangling from orifices.

"Steering wheel," Ty said. "The plastic coating burned but the steel rim held it together."

"Who put it here?" Ariane asked. She was the last to arrive, and had to insinuate herself among taller members of the Seven in order to get a clear view. As a result she nearly tripped over a long, low mound of disturbed earth. The steering wheel totem had been erected at one end of it.

"Whoever buried the driver," Ty answered.

Doc looked at Einstein. "Were you aware of the existence of human remains?"

Einstein held his hands up. "You have to understand, the truck came down like a dart. Nose first."

"Naturally," Doc said. "All the weight was in the engine block. The box, as we have established, was filled with something light."

"The only part that was sticking out was maybe this much of the bumper, and some of the box." Einstein was holding his hands about a meter apart. "The place where the human was—"

"The cab," Ty said.

"—was deep underground. You have to understand, all this digging—"

"Came as a complete surprise to you. Yes, we understand that," Doc said.

"When were you last here?" Langobard asked.

"Two years ago," Einstein said. "But you have to understand: if someone from my RIZ had gone up here with shovels and dug up a whole truck, I'd have heard about it."

"Where's the incentive?" Ariane asked.

Everyone looked at her.

"As it was—in situ—the truck was priceless. Legally or not, tourists would have paid any amount of money to come and view it. To dig it up makes sense—so that tourists could get a full view of it. But—"

"But instead it has been completely dismantled," Doc said, "and everything of value taken away."

"Of value?! I don't understand what you mean by that word," Ariane said.

"The Diggers were after the engine block," Doc said, as if this would answer her question—which it by no means did. But after a few moments she had a thought.

"Ah," Ariane said, "you think it was looters."

Bard was right with her. "You think," he supposed, "that the engine block is now sitting in a display case in the private gallery of some wealthy collector on Cradle."

"That is not an unreasonable supposition," Doc admitted, in a tone that, however, made it clear that no such idea had actually crossed his mind. "But it strikes me as unusual for looters to go to so much trouble to give a ceremonial burial to the driver."

"If it was not valuable as loot—as a collector's item—then what possible value could the engine block have had?" Kath Two asked.

"It was valuable," Doc said, "as iron. As a several-hundred-kilogram sample of pure metal that could be melted down and cast into other shapes."

"Is there anything in the universe *less* valuable than iron?" Bard scoffed. "We have been living inside of giant chunks of it for five thousand years."

"*We* have," Doc agreed, and with a small movement of his hand caused his grabb-chair to withdraw from the grave site and begin picking its way back toward the excavation. Remembrance threw an unreadable look over her shoulder and followed him.

They reconvened and viewed the pit through fresh eyes. Ty pointed out a place where the gray ash was freckled with tiny red-brown spots, and guessed that someone had worked there with a hacksaw, sprinkling iron sawdust on the ground, and that the tiny flakes had rusted. Slipping the ash between his fingers he produced a few bright sparks of clean metal. Bard found a scarred wedge of dense wood, battered on its fat end with many hammer blows, and guessed it had been used to part the engine block into pieces that could be more easily carried. Beled, continuing to circle the perimeter, came up with a pole of hard wood somewhat more than a meter long, neatly rounded at one end, snapped off sharp at the other. "They broke one of their shovels," he said. Holding the pole before him, he rotated it until he was able to see an inscription that had been stamped into the wood. "Srap Tasmaner," he announced.

"Let me see that," Doc said.

Beled handed it to him. Doc gazed at it for a while without speaking. The longer he looked at this seemingly trivial piece of debris, the more he drew attention to himself, until the others were all standing there silently watching him. His deeply hooded eyes were downcast and it was difficult to tell whether he was focusing all of his mental powers on the thing, or fast asleep.

Finally he rotated the pole until its sharp end was pointed downward, and used it to scratch a letter into the dirt.

C

"You read this, Beled, as a letter S, but as you probably learned in school, it was once used to represent a number of sounds including the one we write as K."

He wrote a K beneath the C.

"The next few letters are familiar and we write them the same way in Anglisky."

CRA
KRA

"You misread the fourth letter as a defective P. A natural mistake since we no longer use the old glyph F, which it resembles. Instead we use the Cyrillic phi."

CRAF
KRAФ

"The next two letters are TS, for which we have a more wieldy one-letter substitute in Anglisky."

CRAFTS
KRAФЦ

"The next three are the same in English and Anglisky."

CRAFTSMAN
KRAФЦMAN

"Craftsman," Beled said, reading the bottom row. "But what of the R at the end?"

CRAFTSMAN®

"When it's enclosed in a little circle, it's not a letter to be pronounced at all, but a sign that this is a sort of commercial trademark. Or I should say 'was.' It was a trademark five thousand years ago, apparently."

About halfway through this lecture on ancient and modern orthography, Ariane had become intensely focused, and for the last part of it had been holding one hand over her mouth. "I have seen its like in the Epic!" she exclaimed through her fingers. "*New Caird*'s landing on *Ymir*. Vyacheslav went out the airlock to clear ice from the docking port. He used a shovel just like this one."

"You are saying—" Kath Two prompted Doc.

"I am saying that this shovel handle is itself a five-thousand-year-old 'fact that could fetch a high price on Cradle," Doc said, lifting it up and brushing the dirt from its broken end. Ariane snapped a picture of it and thumbed at her tablet. "It was thrown away," Doc continued, "because it was of no use to its owners, who knew that they could get wooden poles anywhere in Beringia just by cutting down a tree."

"What sort of people think that iron is valuable and five-thousand-year-old artifacts are garbage?" Kath Two asked. She was interrupted by a faint high-pitched beeping sound that was emanating from all of them at once.

They had all been issued earpieces so that they could communicate if they became separated. Most had removed these and pocketed them, or simply draped them around their necks, but Beled still had his in. He pressed one hand to his ear and held the other in front of him, as if checking a timepiece. But he was actually looking at a small flat screen that was strapped to his wrist. He then pivoted to gaze up the valley in the direction from which they had come, but the view was blocked by foliage and terrain.

"Large animals moving in their vicinity have been detected by the buckies," he said, "and one of them has gone silent."

"Yesterday," Doc said, "when young Einstein here proposed we make a junket into the mountains to have a look at an artifact, I was resistant to the idea at first. I saw it as a mere diversion, of a touristical nature. I gave my assent to the idea because I saw it as an opportunity to carry out a dry run for the procedures we would be using later, when we got started for real. I see now, however, that it is the main event."

THE DIGGERS HAD ERECTED ANOTHER TOTEM NEXT TO THE GLIDER's side door: a circular hoop of bent branches, thrust into the air on a pole made from a debarked sapling about five meters tall. The Seven recognized it as a more naturalistic version of the steering wheel totem that had been placed at the driver's grave. Did it have some meaning to these people? It was difficult, now, not to read it as a glyph symbolizing the Agent's penetration of the moon. But it also looked like the Greek letter phi, which had made its way into the Anglisky alphabet as a substitute for both F and PH. As such it could have been an initial for just about anything—Fire? Fear? Philosophy?

Before they had moved from the site of the dig, Bard, Beled, and Ty had scouted the vicinity, spiraling out from it in larger and larger circles until satisfied that no one was nearby. They had found footprints and other signs that someone had been through very recently—perhaps watching them as they had tried to make sense of the disappearance of the truck.

As they had retraced their steps up the valley, then, they had spied sentinels, perched in places that were meant to be conspicuous, atop boulders and rubble mounds flanking the streambed, leaning on lances whose steel heads gleamed softly in the blue-gray light sifting down out of the overcast sky. Others carried strange-looking contraptions of cables, pulleys, and bent steel, which Beled identified as powerful bows. From this distance it was difficult to say much about their appearance. More than a few were redheads; the men tended to be bearded; they wore clothing that in some cases was out-and-out camouflage, in others was just meant to blend in with natural backgrounds.

When they had passed between the first pair of sentries, Beled, on point, had held up his hand, signaling that they should stop. The obvious concern had been that by going any farther they would begin placing these people to their rear, effectively allowing themselves to be surrounded. But the sentries, apparently understanding this, now began to move up the slope abreast of them, leaving them a clear exit.

Or at least a clear pedestrian exit. By the time the Seven and their young guide came in view of the totem raised above the glider, it had been surrounded by perhaps two dozen Diggers. They had pulled all the equipment cases out of the cargo hatch, laid them out on the ground in neat rows, and begun going through their contents. Some of them were making lists of what they found, taking inventory of what they seemingly thought of as their new property.

"I take it you have never seen or heard of such people, Einstein," Doc said.

"Rumors. But not this many. We just thought they were strays from other RIZes."

"Well, as you can see, they are something else," Doc said. He raised his voice slightly, addressing the whole group. "Now that we've had some time for the shock to wear off, I think you all understand what we are looking at. These people are not descendants of the Seven Eves. They are rootstock. Their ancestors survived the Hard Rain and somehow found a way to live belowground until quite recently. Most likely they are cousins of yours, Tyuratam Lake."

It took Ty a few moments to understand that Doc was alluding to events five thousand years in the past. "By way of Rufus MacQuarie?" he said.

Doc blinked in assent. "Dinah's father, as is well documented in the Epic, went belowground with some like-minded persons. Efforts have been made, during the last century, to find their underground home and learn what became of them. All unavailing."

"Perhaps they didn't wish to be found," Ty said.

"How long have you known of this?" Ariane asked.

"How long have *you* known of it, Ariane?" Doc returned. "Did the unusual orders you were given not fill you with a certain amount of curiosity?"

"Of course! But I never—"

"Many of us have wondered, have speculated. The first solid evidence that I know of emerged about a year ago. Prior to that there were rumors, as Einstein says, but they could be more easily explained by supposing that some renegade Sooners were running around in the boondocks, living as they pleased. Or that they were forward scouts sent by Red to probe Blue territory. Indeed, Survey found examples of both." Doc's eyes strayed toward Beled, who met his gaze. "Red has made surprisingly deep incursions into central Asia, for example. Lieutenant Tomov may bear witness to that, if you can draw him out on the subject. Like many who have fought, he finds it tiresome to converse with ones who haven't."

"So you have been engaged in a systematic investigation for at least a year" was the only thing about all of that that Ariane seemed to find interesting.

"As have you, Ariane. It is just that you didn't know it until now. I myself was not really sure until—" Doc looked over at Memmie, who had taken custody of the shovel handle and fallen into the habit of employing it as a walking staff. Doc got a faintly mischievous look on his face. "Until I held in my hands the Stick of Srap Tasmaner."

"How much do we know about them?" Langobard asked.

"As of this moment," Doc said, "the eight of us know a hundred times as much about these people as all other Spacers put together."

"Spacers?"

Again the mischievous look. "In our discussions—our *entirely hypothetical* discussions—we found ourselves needing some term that we could use to denote the descendants of the Seven Eves—the inhabitants of the ring—as opposed to people like this. We settled on Spacers."

"That makes it sound even more like all of this was foreordained," Ariane said.

Her reproachful tone was getting on all of their nerves. Nonetheless they were surprised when it was Remembrance who said something. Perhaps the Camite felt emboldened by possession of a stick large enough to give the Julian a sound whack or two. More likely she was offended by Ariane's accusatory tone, which hinted that Doc had been less than honest. Planting the Srap Tasmaner for balance on the uneven ground and turning to face Ariane, she said: "Of note here is that we are making first contact with a race of cousins hidden from us for five millennia. Some would find that remarkable."

"And I *do,* Memmie!" Ariane said, after a few moments spent recovering from her shock at being spoken to this way by a Camite. "But in order to handle the situation well I think we need to know the larger context."

"Any well-informed Spacer knows the context," Memmie returned, sweeping her free hand up across the sky. "It is only a certain type of mind that scorns what is known by all and treats secrets as jewels."

After this Ariane seemed to feel that further conversation would not be to her advantage. It was only the ten millionth such conversation that had taken place during the long, fraught, weirdly personal relationship between Julians and Camites, so Ariane knew her cue to shut up and look aggrieved.

There had been very little discussion, as yet, of the possibility of violence. Body language and shared glances among Ty, Bard, and Beled suggested that they had all been thinking about it. Einstein did them the favor of blurting it out: "What do you guys think? Can we take 'em?"

"Yes" was the answer from all three.

"But archery is a concern," Ty added.

"A factor is how much they know about us and our armaments. Have they been scouting us for years?"

Beled aimed the question at Doc, as if he would somehow know. The look on Ariane's face was something like *See, I knew it!* but Doc merely looked amused. "If so," Doc said, "they have rarely if ever seen us use our weapons, and so they are unlikely to know how those work."

"Well, they have taken all of our buckies offline," Beled remarked, with another glance at the screen on his wrist.

"They appear to have retained some knowledge of how technology works," Doc pointed out. "Even if they don't have the ability to manufacture their own buckies, they can recognize them for what they are. So of course they would disable those."

"It is a hostile act," Beled muttered.

"If we let their archers come within range," Ty pointed out, "then they will have us. We should consider *that* a hostile act."

"Then we should not go much farther," Bard said.

"That's what I'm saying," Ty replied.

They had approached now to within about a hundred meters of the glider and had the full attention of the Diggers surrounding it. Four of them had claimed the high places around it, where buckies had been stationed earlier, and two more had clambered up onto the tops of the wings. The strangely orderly looters had ceased their activities and pressed forward to see what was going to happen. At least three of them were children, and there were as many women as men.

"Mixed messages," Bard said, and made a gesture that caused his fellow Spacers to stop where they were.

"Let me have a go at this," Ty said, "if it's true they are related to me." He strode forward several paces beyond Beled, stopped, and then pantomimed drawing back an arrow and shooting it in a high trajectory. He then pointed at the archers.

Immediately one of the Digger men, near the center of the group, turned to face the others and backed several paces away from them, swiveling his head to get a picture of how the formation might look from the Spacers' point of view. He shouted something that, from this distance, could not really be heard above the sound of the wind on the rocks. The archers and the sentinels eventually responded, though not crisply. They clambered down from the high places and, on further exhortation from the leader, set their bows down and backed away from them.

The leader turned to face Ty and held out his hands, palms up.

Ty set his katapult on a nearby rock.

A second man now separated himself from the Digger group and began making his way forward, making reasonable headway but steadying himself on a pair of walking sticks. His head was bald and his beard was gray. When he drew abreast, the leader, who was somewhat younger, began ambling forward, matching the older man's pace.

Doc set his grabb chair into motion. Memmie, out of habit, paced him, but after she had taken several steps forward, he stayed her with a hand gesture. "I will take that, however," he said, and extended his hand toward the stick. She gave it to him and he tucked it under one arm.

Ty waited for Doc to catch up, and then began to advance by his side.

Some of the Diggers seemed keen to follow the action and began to creep forward, touching off internal controversies, and prompting Beled and Bard to move ahead as well. Through a sort of nonverbal negotiation, the two sides arrived at a deal where a total of eight Diggers—the two out in front, plus six more trailing in an echelon behind—ventured out into the open space to match the eight Spacers. Among the Diggers were some warrior types, keeping a close eye on Bard and Beled, but women and a child too. On the Spacer side, Ty and Doc were out front, with Memmie a few paces behind.

Einstein, Ariane, and Kath Two maintained some distance while Bard and Beled, who were conspicuously armed, remained in the deeper background, split out to either side, respecting an unspoken agreement that they would stay out of weapon range as the Diggers' archers were doing.

The two formations drew up within speaking distance, and looked at each other for a spell.

To the Spacers, the Diggers were familiar looking from old videos: they were rootstock humans such as populated the Epic. Genetically they were homogeneous. They were white people with blond or red hair, and eyes that seemed to have gone pale in the darkness of their caves. Their skin was fair by nature, but freckled by exposure to the aboveground sun. They were smaller than rootstock humans, but not so much so that any one of them would have seemed dwarfish on a busy street in the Chain. Except for Teklans and Neoanders, who had occupational reasons for needing to be large, the descendants of the Eves had also lost stature, particularly during the First Millennium. They had been slow to gain it back, even during the Fifth, when by and large they'd had plenty of room to stand up straight. These Diggers—at least the limited sample standing close enough for Ty to evaluate them—did seem uncommonly stocky, however.

For their part, the Diggers had more to gawk at, since it could be guessed from their reactions that they had seen little or nothing of Spacers. Ty looked unremarkable to them. Doc was interesting largely because of his age and his means of getting around. Kath Two, Memmie, and Einstein might have looked strange more because of their coloration than any genetic alterations. Something was definitely odd about Ariane's facial structure. Beled, and particularly Bard, were to them monsters.

After a minute of sizing them up, the older Digger stomped forward a couple of paces and spoke in the pre-Zero English that all

Spacers knew from the Epic: "Cowards who ran away, you are trespassing on a world that is no longer yours to call home. Begone."

"This is going well," Ty remarked to Doc.

"He is putting on a show of strength for the others," Doc said. "Best let him. If you would, please?"

He issued a command that caused his grabb's legs to fold, bringing it as low to the ground as it could go, and extended a hand. Ty took his arm and steadied him as he stepped off the robot and found footing on the ground. He planted the stick with his other hand, then cautiously let go of Ty. Then he advanced a step. All of these actions produced murmurs among the Diggers. Perhaps they had seen Doc initially as some kind of cyborg, but now understood that he was just a very old man. He walked several paces until he found a flat spot that suited him, then planted the stick.

"I may look five thousand years old," he began, "but I am in truth a mere descendant of those you style cowards. Though I daresay you would take a more charitable view if you knew of the deeds that they performed during their long exodus. Do I have the honor of addressing one whose ancestor was Rufus MacQuarie?"

"We are all of that lineage," the old man boomed.

"Then I think I have something that belongs to you," Doc said. Moving deliberately, he pulled the stick out of its purchase on the ground and hefted it up until it lay horizontally across both of his outstretched palms. "Please accept my apologies for having borrowed it without your remit."

Had the Spacers been able to watch all of the Diggers' reactions at once, it would have yielded a bonanza of intelligence about the workings of their minds and of their society. That degree of mind reading was, in general, the sort of task assigned to Julians, so it could be assumed that Ariane's moiling brain and avid senses were running full blast.

The young males seemed divided between a more vindictive

group who wanted the stick of Srap Tasmaner confiscated immediately, and others of a more chivalrous turn of mind.

The group at large comprised a minority who were indignant about Doc's expropriation of their shovel handle, but—more significantly—a majority who felt ashamed at the idea that they would take away an old man's walking stick.

What those two groups had in common was that they took what Doc had said at face value. A smaller inner circle—the old man, the younger leader, and a woman of intermediate age who had stepped forward to confer with them—had the wit to understand that Doc was playing to the crowd, and not actually trying to initiate a conversation about the ownership of a piece of wood.

In other words, the Diggers were, as a whole, reacting much as any other group of humans might have done. Which was interesting and important data in and of itself, since much might have changed during five thousand years in the mines.

The discussion among the three leaders went on at some length and led eventually to an epidemic of head nodding. The old man squared off, sticks planted, his face set in judgment. The younger man and the middle-aged woman advanced toward Ty and Doc respectively. The man came to a halt two paces away from Ty, just out of the range where shaking hands or fisticuffs might become plausible. The woman kept on coming and took the stick out of Doc's outstretched hands. This touched off a wave of fascinated reactions among the Diggers watching at a distance.

In a quiet but clear voice, the woman said, "Old man, you have shamed us with your words and obliged us to answer in kind. No hand shall be laid on you by virtue of your age."

She stepped forward past Doc, sliding her hands together at the blunt end of the shovel handle, and began to whirl it around. Then with a decisive lunge forward she brought it down on the side of Memmie's head.

Memmie collapsed to her knees and then to all fours, her head—

already dribbling blood—sagging almost to the ground, exposing the back of the neck. And that was where the woman drove the sharp end of the stick, ramming it in several inches deep, well into the center of the thorax where it would strike lung or heart or both. Remembrance did not topple but rather deflated, settling gradually to a fetal position on the ground.

The younger man meanwhile launched himself at Ty. It was not clear whether his intention was to inflict damage or merely to restrain him while Remembrance was sacrificed. In any case his foot dislodged a stone as he made his move, creating a sound that gave Ty a bit of warning. He was able to turn so that the attacker rolled around him rather than striking him dead-on. The Digger's downhill movement became a disadvantage, overbalancing him. Hooking the man's ankle and kicking upward, Ty made him fall hard on his face. Both of his feet were projecting up in the air, soles of his moccasins exposed to the sky. Ty hooked a leg through the crook of a knee and then dropped his weight, bending the foot forward; the man's heel would have gone all the way to his buttock had Ty's lower leg not been interposed behind the back of his thigh and his upper calf muscle, where it threatened to rip the man's knee apart. The man scrabbled at the ground and so Ty put more weight on it, the stink of the old moccasin in his nostrils, and felt a preliminary pop inside of the joint. The man screamed and stopped struggling.

All of this happened in the same moments as the woman was killing Remembrance, and so Ty did not really take that in until he had placed the man fully under his control. He was just drawing focus on Memmie and understanding how bad it was when he saw a movement in his peripheral vision and looked over to see Doc telescoping to a seated position on the ground. He had turned around and witnessed the attack on Memmie.

"I want evac. I want evac," Ariane was saying. Ty had no idea to whom she was talking.

Strange high whistling noises came from the sky. Ty looked up and saw a flight of arrows arcing over his head. They passed as well over the heads of Ariane, Kath Two, and Einstein and thunked into the ground or skittered on the rocks at the feet of Beled and Bard, who had been advancing until then.

The woman with the stick had been in a sort of trance, but now drew focus on Ty and saw how it had gone with him and the younger man. Rage flashed over her face. She aimed the sharp bloody end of the stick at Ty and began to run at him.

Ty heaved his full weight onto the younger man's foot and snapped his leg. Then he stood up, getting clear of the screaming and flailing Digger. He had come up with a rock in his hand, which he flung at the woman's face. His aim was off, but still it forced her to falter and dodge, and gave him time to snatch up two more and advance one pace. Two more rocks, one of which struck home on her collarbone, and two more paces. On her back heel she aimed a thrust at him, but she telegraphed it and he parried it easily with his left forearm, snaking the full length of his arm around the shaft so that its bloody tip was trapped against his body. He reached out with his free hand, poked her in the eye with his thumb, grabbed her ear, and wrenched her away from the stick like a discarded wrapper. The older man was coming at him with his sticks a-flailing in both hands, and more formidably, several of the young warrior types were running with lances leveled. Ty walked straight at the old man, knocking his sticks away with controlled strokes of the shovel handle, spun him around so that the man's back was against his chest, brought the handle up across the man's throat, and locked it in place, crooked in his elbow, his hand pressing against the back of the man's bald head. He then began dragging the man backward and downhill toward the remainder of the Seven. For this human shield might work to protect Ty's front, but the boys with the lances were already moving to circle around behind him, and he had to hope that the others would protect his rear.

One of the equipment boxes up by the glider now seemed to

explode. But it was a strange sort of explosion with no flame, and little sound. Rather, the crate seemed to dissociate into a dense, gritty cloud, which became translucent as it spread. A moment later the same thing occurred with a second crate nearby. Both crates ended up lying on their sides, empty.

The Diggers in the vicinity of the glider were all exclaiming in surprise, or just plain screaming. The nature of what was happening was not clear, even to Ty. It was enough to put the lancers into a more cautious frame of mind, as it gave rise to fears that they were being attacked from behind. Their advance faltered and they looked to see what was the matter.

A thin gray layer was skimming over the ground, headed downhill toward them. It looked a little like a spent wave as it washes and foams over a flat beach just before settling into the sand, parting around rocks and recombining in their lee. More like an avalanche, though, in that it gathered speed as it came on. As it rushed past Ty and the old man, parting around their feet, he was able to focus and resolve it as a swarm of ambots of two different types—one type from each of the crates that had emptied themselves. They were all mixed together. Once they chittered past Einstein, Ariane, and Kath Two, they spread out across the flat open slope separating them from Beled and Bard. Those two were split out to the sides, just beyond arrow range. The swarm then forked as all the ambots of one type converged on Beled and all those of the other type made for Bard. The former group—the Blue-pattern ambots—were smaller, leggier, and quicker on broken ground. That swarm gathered itself together into a clicking, glittering, hissing firehose stream and leaped from the ground at Beled. Rather than striking him, though, it washed around him. In the interval of a few moments he was clothed from head to toe in an armor made of overlapping scales, each scale being the beetle-like back of an ambot. They had swarmed over him and locked themselves together. A few strays clambered over the others' backs seeking, and plugging, holes.

Langobard's swarm was a little longer in reaching him. During the final fifty meters or so it became ropy as it passed through a kind of phase transition. Where possible, ambots were copulating, jacking the couplers on their snouts into matching ones in the tails of those ahead of them, forming pairs, then strings of three and four that combined with others, so that by the time the swarm came close to its master it had converged into half a dozen long, whippy ropes, and as many shorter segments. These ambots were basically flynks, more at home flying than crawling. They had some limited ability to fly solo, but were much happier when combined into aerial trains. During their career down the slope they'd picked up a decent amount of energy just by losing altitude, and so in the last few meters they were able to rear up off the ground like cobras and leap into the air, shooting past Langobard but banking into tight turns behind him, curving round, nose seeking tail, until they had formed aitrains: closed loops, fully airborne, flying endless circles around his body, defeating gravity with the modest amount of lift provided by their stubby winglets. He gave them greater speed by the simple expedient of pawing at them from time to time, but they also drew energy from a field being generated by a power plant on his back. Perhaps a third of the flynks had failed to find their way into chains sufficiently long to form aitrains, and so a few shorter segments found his ankles and spiraled up his legs, like snakes climbing trees. There were also some singletons who had not been able to join even a short chain; these found their way to him and climbed as high as they could, competing noisily for perching space on his shoulders. As Bard now moved across space he looked like a combination of Da Vinci's Vitruvian Man, inscribed within a system of circles, and early depictions of the atom, surrounded by an array of circular orbitals. Each aitrain sang a different note as its flynks sawed through the air, the pitch rising as it absorbed energy and built velocity. He and Beled were moving to join forces, both edging closer to the Diggers as their defenses came online. A single exploratory shaft, fired at a high arc by the foremost of the archers, plunged toward Langobard, but was casually flicked out of the way by a momentary deflection of an aitrain.

It was nothing Ty hadn't seen before, but it was nonetheless distracting. Forcing himself to attend to things nearer and more pressing, he saw that a warrior had advanced to Doc, who was lying on his side struggling feebly, and raised his lance as if to strike him dead with a single downward thrust. But he had paused. Perhaps he only intended to create a threat. Perhaps he was gobsmacked by what had just happened with the ambot swarms.

Ty was dragging the old Digger back toward Ariane and Kath Two and Einstein, who had prudently flattened themselves behind a brow in the slope that afforded some minimal protection against direct arrow shots—though none against plunging shafts. The next time he turned around to look downhill, Bard and Beled had vanished, and the only clue as to where they had concealed themselves came from the movements of a few straggler ambots striving to catch up with them. Part of him felt let down that they had not advanced in force and simply destroyed the Diggers. A better part of him understood that they were too smart and too professional for that; they would find cover, hang back, observe, and wait for cooler heads to prevail.

Ariane was darting back down the hill. She picked up Ty's katapult from the rock where he had set it down. Good.

Excited sentries, posted up in the rocks that flanked the valley, were hollering news of Bard's and Beled's movements in the Diggers' oddly biblical phrasings. It sounded as though the Teklan and the Neoander were moving rapidly to high ground.

One of the sentries blurted out a sharp cry and went silent. This distracted all the other Diggers for a few moments.

Ariane ran uphill a little past Ty, dropped to a knee, and pressed the muzzle of Ty's katapult against the back of the neck of the woman who had killed Memmie. This woman had collected herself to a seated position on the ground and had been holding one hand over the eye that Ty had earlier poked.

Ariane's gesture was a curious one, recognizable from pre-Zero filmed entertainment as the sort of thing you would do with the sort of firearm that projected dumb lead bullets at high speed. It made less sense with a katapult. But as nonverbal communication with the Diggers, it worked.

"Three hundred meters downhill of the glider," Ariane was saying, presumably to the same imaginary friend she had addressed a little earlier. Then, to the woman, "Get up. One way or another, your mind is about to get blown."

Ty heard himself let out a little snort of suppressed laughter. Apparently the part of the brain that identified things as funny kept running as a background process even when its contributions were useless. The way Ariane was moving, the things she was saying, were so out of character for her that Ty's higher brain didn't know what to make of it; in the meantime he was chuckling as if watching some sort of comedy sketch.

The woman got her feet under her. Ariane grabbed her by the hood of her parka and pulled her fully upright, then began marching her down the hill with the kat's muzzle pressed against the side of her head. Ty stood there and watched her go by.

"Ariane," he said, "what are you doing?"

"You don't seem to realize," she said, "that this changes everything." She let the katapult drop away from the woman's head for a moment, then swung it up and aimed it at Ty. It gave off the characteristic *whang* of an ambot being shot out of its muzzle and then she put it back against the woman's head.

Ty felt the impact like a punch in the rib cage and recoiled from it instinctively. But even before he could recover from that, the ambot had entrenched itself in his clothes, extruded a couple of needle-sharp probes into his side, and begun jamming his nervous system. Having been hit by these before, he knew that the best he could hope for was to strike the ground with something other than his face, so he released his grip on the shovel handle, and on the old Digger, and went down.

Had he been able to speak, he'd have told Kath Two not to worry about him—to do something about Ariane. But his teeth were banging together too hard to form words, and it was all he could do to keep his breathing muscles working.

The old man staggered away, fell to his knees, and found the shovel handle on the ground right in front of him. He grabbed it with one hand, planted it, grabbed it with the other, and used it to lever himself back up. He advanced on Ty, who was just lying on the ground in spasms. Ty was then aware of a dark shape above him, and looked up to see Kath Two standing over him, facing the old man, raising an arm instinctively to defend herself. The shovel handle struck that arm with a thud and sent Kath Two stumbling away, crying out in pain. The man then raised the pointed end of the stick above Ty.

"Iniquitous mutant!" he cried. Then he added something that was drowned out by the *whang* of a katapult. Kath Two, using her own sidearm, had shot him in the belly from point-blank range. The stick dropped from the man's hands and added to Ty's inventory of minor aches and pains as it came down point first on his chest. The man toppled next to Ty, going down hard and banging his head on a rock.

Suddenly Ty was in the clear, at least neurologically. Einstein, kneeling above him with a bone-handled knife, had pried the ambot off him, and now used the knife's steel pommel to smash it to bits against a rock.

Kath Two was down on one knee moving her damaged arm about in slow motion, her mouth frozen in the O of a suppressed scream.

Ty's gaze was drawn to movement in the clouds above Kath Two's head: a glowing rod levering down out of the sky. Visually it was a near match for what had just happened with the shovel handle, except that in this case the object was kilometers in length and incandescing as if it had just been pulled from the bed of coals at the foundation of a bonfire.

He understood now. He swiveled his head sideways so that he

could look down the slope. In a clear patch a stone's throw away—about three hundred meters downhill of the glider—the ground was glowing ruby red where it was being painted from above by lasers: three bright spots forming an equilateral triangle, and a grainy circle centered in that. The light washed briefly over Ariane's head and shoulders as she shoved her hostage into the middle of the circle.

The glowing stick came straight down on top of them, enveloping them in its hollow end, and then sprang back up into the sky, leaving nothing save a trail of footprints that terminated in the center of a perfectly circular depression in the ground. Around that was a penumbra of vegetation that had been toasted by radiant heat. In the moments before the device was drawn back up through the cloud cover they were able to see the booth that had scooped up Ariane and her hostage, telescoping back up inside the red-hot tube in preparation for its departure from the atmosphere.

THE MECHANISM THAT ARIANE HAD SUMMONED WAS CALLED A Thor. It consisted of a big rock—the head of a god-sized maul—with a very long and lightweight "handle" capable of reaching all the way to the surface even while the "head" was just grazing the upper reaches of the atmosphere. The whole thing spun like a thrown hammer, which was to say that the long handle flailed in a large circle around the head.

At the end of the handle was the capture booth, large enough to accommodate three people if they stood close together. During descent and ascent it was enclosed within an outer shell designed to survive the rigors of passage through the atmosphere. The handle would stride down out of space in the same general style as the hanger bolo that Kath Two and Beled had recently used, except that instead of pausing in the upper atmosphere to collect aircraft, this one would spear all the way down to the surface and grab whatever happened to be standing in the target zone—which it would paint beforehand with lasers so that the passengers would know where to stand. The head of the hammer would subsequently pivot forward into the atmosphere, catch air, and slow down, levering the handle sharply upward and catapulting the payload into a much higher orbit. The head would detach itself and fall downrange as a meteorite. This, of course, made it a single-use device, used only in emergencies, and even then when the need was so extreme that it was considered worth the risk of dropping a bolide on some basically random spot downrange.

So it could be assumed that a fresh crater now decorated the interior of North America somewhere to the east of here, and that Ariane and her captive were en route to a safe haven in the Red segment of the ring. What awaited them there could only be guessed at, but for Ariane it was probably going to be a substantial reward, a medal, and a promotion to some high rank in Red's military intelligence branch.

Doc never spoke another coherent word. Seeing what had happened to Memmie, he had suffered a stroke that had immediately rendered him aphasic. Swelling of the brain killed him an hour later. The Diggers buried him and Memmie together in the place where they had fallen.

The old Digger looked better after a few hours, aside from some symptoms indicative of a concussion. The younger one got his leg splinted. Both were in a murderous frame of mind toward the three remaining captives. But it seemed that the majority of the Diggers were taken aback by what had happened, and were advocating a more level-headed approach to future relations between their tribe and the sort of civilization that could produce things like Ariane's Thor and Beled's and Langobard's weaponized ambot swarms.

As a way of demonstrating their own technological prowess, or perhaps simply to blow off steam, the Diggers detonated a lump of some kind of home-brewed explosive in the open space between the glider and the fresh graves. Evidently this was meant as a warning for Bard and Beled, who were presumed to be watching from nearby cover.

Ty, Einstein, and Kath Two were fitted with hinged collars of bent steel. When these were closed around the neck, loops in the free ends came into alignment so that a chain could be run through them, locking them shut while stringing all the captives together. At one end, the chain was terminated by an ancient padlock that was too large to pass through the loops on Kath Two's collar. The other end was then affixed, by means of a bolt, to a large wooden stake that an especially burly Digger had pounded into the ground with a stone-headed maul that looked like a miniature Thor.

Just uphill of this, and out of the prisoners' reach, other Diggers constructed a little cairn. They topped it with another lump of explosive. They attached wires to the lump for detonation and ran them down to the main Digger camp, which was under the wings of the glider some fifty meters away.

"What just happened?!" Einstein wanted to know, as soon as the Diggers had left them alone. "I mean, that was obviously a Thor. I've heard of them. But . . ." and he threw his hands up in the air.

"Ariane is a mole," Ty said. Then he corrected himself: "*Was* a mole. Now she's probably a hero. A Red hero."

"Red sent the Thor down to, what do you call it, extract her."

"Yeah. Her and, more to the point, a living, breathing biological sample."

Kath Two, at one end of the string, climbed into a sleeping bag and fell asleep. Ty did not expect her to wake up for a long time. He and Einstein moved down-chain as far as they could, to leave her in peace, and squatted on their haunches. The Diggers had left them firewood and kindling. Without discussion, they began laying a fire. It became clear that Einstein had done it before, and so Ty just let him do it. The young Ivyn had very particular ideas about fires.

"Where did you learn how to fight like that?" Einstein asked him. "Are you part Teklan or something?"

"Fighting isn't about knowing how," Ty said. "It's about deciding to."

"Well, I was frozen, man."

"Look, these are times when the decisions that our Eves made five thousand years ago control our actions to a degree that renders us basically helpless. You were meant to stand back and observe and analyze."

"And you were made to be a hero," Einstein said.

"A hero would have saved Memmie."

"But no one could have seen that coming! The way that woman just went crazy on her . . ."

"We'll be asking ourselves that for a long time." Ty sighed and looked over to the encampment where the Diggers were going about life as if nothing had happened. Some of them were roasting kebabs that they had cut from the carcass of a big herbivore killed down in the woods. There were a lot of kids under ten years old, but few teenagers. Half of the women looked pregnant. "Play your role, Einstein. You're the Ivyn in our group now that Doc's gone. What do you see?"

Einstein seemed reluctant to speak, so Ty prompted him: "I see a population explosion."

Einstein snapped into focus and nodded his head.

"You've never heard of these people," Ty went on, "even though your RIZ is just on the other side of these mountains and your people patrol up here all the time."

"Rufus MacQuarie's mine was far to the north," Einstein offered. "These people must have just come out into the open recently."

"Look for the oldest child down there and that probably tells you the date."

"But the atmosphere's been breathable for three hundred years! Why would they wait until now?"

Ty nodded toward the center of the Digger camp: the big bed of coals, the meat roasting over it.

"Food?" Einstein said.

"Food and fuel," Ty confirmed. "They've been down in their hole living on God only knows what—cave tofu or something—since the beginning of the Hard Rain. Every so often maybe they would sample the air outside. When it became breathable they probably went out and had a look around. But it was still a wasteland, not capable of supporting life. It's only in the last few years that TerReForm has seeded that part of Beringia with animals big enough to be worth the effort expended in hunting them. That was the starting gun—the signal for them to come out."

"And to begin having kids as fast as they could, apparently."

"Apparently. Now, Einstein, what does that tell you about gender roles?"

"Well, to begin with, they don't have an Eve, they have an Adam—Rufus—so it could easily be more pat—patree—"

"Patriarchal."

"Thanks. And then if all the women are expected to make lots of babies—"

"That tells you something," Ty said. "Now, here's the big question that is kind of staring us in the face. You're a Digger, okay? You're not stupid. All you have to do is pop your head out of your cave on a clear night and look into the southern sky and you can see the habitat ring. And over time you can see the Eye moving back and forth across it and you can see new habitats lighting up as they are built. You can see bolos coming in low across the sky and TerReForm aircraft flying right overhead and showers of ONANs coming down straight from the ring. And you're no ignorant savage. Your folk have maintained a reasonably advanced engineering culture. Those compound bows. That lump of explosive. So you wouldn't have interpreted all of that as gods or angels or any of that."

"They've known," Einstein said. "From the first—"

"For centuries," Ty said, nodding. "As long as they could breathe outside."

"For that long, they have known that billions of humans were living in the sky," Einstein said. "But they didn't make any attempt to signal."

"More than that. They hid from us!" Ty said. "Efforts were made, you know, to find the MacQuarie mine several decades ago. These people must have made some kind of decision that they didn't want to be found."

"Why would they do that?"

"That's what I am asking. Fear? Anger?"

"The old guy really hates us. 'Cowards who ran away' is what he considers us."

"It's what he *called* us," Ty allowed. "And he called us that really loudly. He wasn't really talking to us, I think."

Einstein nodded. "I see what you mean. He was talking to the people behind him."

"If I'm squatting in my mine shaft eating cave tofu when I know perfectly well that there are lots of humans up in geosync living in better conditions, then I need some kind of powerful incentive to stay in my cave. To conceal my presence."

"Some kind of dukh or I dee—"

"Ideology," Ty said with a nod. "I should have seen all this. God damn me for not seeing it a few minutes quicker."

"Seeing what?"

"That only a mind virus, a shared hallucination, could explain the suddenness of their appearance aboveground."

"Doc didn't see it either," Einstein said. He was only trying to make Ty feel better, but then he looked slightly appalled at himself for having spoken ill of his dead kinsman.

"No," Ty said, "he sure didn't. Now, what have we learned about how these people think?"

"They have, what do you call it, a chip on the shoulder."

Ty nodded. "It was supremely important to the leaders that they put on a show of dominance under the gaze of their flock. Which they did. Then Doc did the thing with the Srap Tasmaner. A gesture of reconciliation but also a way of shaming them for being such complete assholes. Maybe not a bad move when dealing with people who have been acculturated to be more reasonable, to get along with each other."

"People like us. People who have had to coexist in habitats forever."

"But to them it was a challenge to their authority in front of their flock and so they had to make an extreme reaction. To dehumanize us."

"We are the aliens," Einstein said.

"Yes," Ty said. "We are the bug-eyed monsters now."

"And the longer Bard and Beled are out lurking in the darkness—"

"The easier it gets for them to paint us as such," Ty said. "And that's why they have us isolated. The leaders don't want us talking to their flock—letting them see we're only human."

"But hang on a sec," Einstein said. "That means that the leaders must know we are not really bug-eyed monsters."

Ty had no response. Certain aspects of the situation were not really adding up. He considered it as they got the fire going and let themselves be hypnotized by the flames.

After the beginning of the Hard Rain, no fire—in the sense of open burning of solid, carbon-rich fuel—had been constructed by humans—by Spacers, anyway—for 1,735 years. It had taken that long to build a habitat large enough to grow trees, with enough atmosphere to handle the oxygen demand of a fire and to absorb the resulting smoke. Ancient digitized Boy Scout manuals had been consulted. It had worked the first time. The four pyro-pioneers responsible—all Dinans—had stood around it, staring into the flames as Ty was doing now, and probably thinking about all that had happened since the last time humans had smelled woodsmoke.

He and Einstein had not even started in on the topic of Ariane.

She was the worst nightmare of any Julian trying to live an honest life in Blue: someone ostensibly Blue who turns out to be a Red mole. How long had she been insinuating herself into intelligence, working her way up the ranks? Or had she only just decided to switch sides? In either case, she was up in the Red part of the ring now with the woman she had abducted. What must the Diggers make of that? Did they even know that there were two kinds of Spacers?

And what was Red intelligence learning from that woman? Had Ty not watched her murder Remembrance in cold blood, he'd have felt sorry for her.

THREE PERSONS APPROACHED FROM THE MAIN DIGGER CAMP UNDER the glider's wings: a warrior with a steel-headed lance; a middle-aged, prematurely grizzled man with a grim look about him; and another whom Ty took for a boy until they drew closer and he saw that it was a short-haired teenaged girl, even more diminutive than was typical among these people. She carried herself oddly, keeping her head tilted down and turned to one side, looking at the world through the corner of her eye, though this might have been necessitated by the fact that she was following close behind the grizzled man and needed to peek around his rib cage in order to see where she was going. Scampering over obstructions that he took in stride, she seemed to take two steps for his every one. She looked like nothing so much as a squirrel trying to keep pace with a dog.

As they drew within speaking range the graybeard stopped the spearman with a nod, then took another pace forward. The girl faltered. Noting this, the graybeard made a gesture that encouraged her to venture a bit closer. She cringed up against his backside and peered out through his armpit.

"I am Donno," announced the graybeard. "To me you may speak, but no others save the Psych here." Or at least that is what Ty thought he heard.

"I am Tyuratam Lake," Ty said. "And this is Einstein. The woman there is Kath Two; she is unlikely to join the conversation."

"Tyuratam," said the Psych in a husky voice, "a city in Central Asia, close to the Soviet space launch facility of Baikonur in Kazakhstan. Einstein, a theoretical physicist of the early twentieth century, before Zero."

Donno heard the Psych out but did not look at her or make any sign of recognition. His attention was fixed on Ty. The words of the Psych were just a buzzing in his ear. "When Kath Two awakens, you will tell her the rule I have just proclaimed," Donno said, "and see to it that she abides by it."

"I will tell her the rule," Ty said, "and she will keep her own counsel as to abiding by it. Over her I wield no authority. It is not how our society is organized."

Donno looked as though he didn't believe a word of what Ty had just said. "You are Dinan."

So, they knew about the Seven Eves. How had they come by that knowledge? Abducting stragglers, interrogating them? Or had they been in covert contact with some Spacer?

"Yes," Ty said.

"You are the leader of the group."

Ty said nothing. It seemed unlikely to work for him to explain that it was complicated.

"What did you do with Marge?" Donno asked.

"Who is Marge?"

"The woman who was taken up by the thing that reached down out of space."

Ty was tempted to make the irritable point that Donno had just answered his own question. Instead he just stared back, wondering where to begin.

"The other mutant—a Julian?"

"Yes."

"She attacked you with your own weapon. You were surprised."

"Indeed I was, Donno."

"She betrayed you?"

"Yes."

"Is she of the western people?"

To Donno, that would suggest the Spacers living in the part of Beringia west of 166 Thirty.

"Red is what we call them."

Donno nodded as if he'd heard it before. "You are Blue, then."

"Yes, we are Blue. We avoid using Thors."

"Thor: a Germanic deity of immense strength, associated with lightning, armed with a hammer," the Psych said.

"Is your name short for Encyclopedia?" Einstein asked her.

Donno threw Einstein a killing look. Einstein was oblivious to it; he was looking at the girl with fascination and then some.

"Yes," she answered before Donno could stay her by raising his hand. She dodged away as if expecting to be cuffed, then smiled back at Einstein.

Ty had just been rendered almost dizzy by a clear and sharp image from the Epic: a photograph that Rufus had emailed to Dinah shortly before the White Sky, depicting the library that he and his friends had assembled in their underground fastness. Proudly displayed in its center was a row of identically bound volumes called the *Encyclopædia Britannica*.

This girl—the Cyc, not the Psych—had read it. She had physically handled those old books. Or perhaps handwritten copies of them.

"He is Ivyn," Donno said, nodding at Einstein. It wasn't a question. Then, his initial flash of anger having cooled, he took a more careful look at the kid from the RIZ.

"His eyelids look that way because of epicanthic folds," said the Cyc, who had been conducting an unnecessarily close inspection of the Ivyn's face.

"Shut up," Donno told her. Then he turned his attention back to Ty. "The Red Julian—"

"Ariane," Ty said.

"She was a spy within your ranks?"

"So it would seem."

"Interesting. Rufus's library has some novels about such things, in the decades before Zero, but I never thought I would lay eyes on a real mole."

It was an unusually long-winded and revealing statement from Donno, and seemed to invite a witticism about moles and living underground, but Ty thought better of following up in that vein.

"I never thought I would lay eyes on someone like you," he tried.

"All these thousands of years, you've thought we were dead!" Donno said. "Well, you thought wrong."

"Before everything went to hell down there," Ty said, "the old man—"

"Pop Loyd."

"Pop Loyd stated that we were not welcome here."

"He spoke truthfully," Donno said.

"I don't mean to be stupid," Ty said, "but this is important and so I am sure you will agree with me that it is something I need to understand very clearly. Your group—do you have a name for it?"

"The human race," Donno said.

"Very well then, the human race is laying claim to this territory and doesn't wish people like us—descendants of the Seven Eves—to be here at all."

"Not without our remit. That is correct."

"What is the territory you are laying exclusive claim to?"

"I beg your pardon?"

"This valley? This mountain range? All of Beringia?"

"The entire land surface of the planet Earth," Donno said, shaking his head and uttering the words very clearly and slowly. "Your people abandoned it. It's ours."

That was a bit of a conversation stopper, at least where Ty was concerned. Einstein, however, blurted out the inevitable adolescent-Ivyn question: "What about the oceans?"

"You will have to take that up with the Pingers," Donno said.

"Pingers?"

Donno looked at Einstein as if he were some kind of imbecile.

"The sea people," said the Cyc. "They live—" but Donno raised his hand again and she went silent.

So did everyone else. Which was how Donno seemed to prefer it. He now had a few moments' leisure to look about. He nodded toward Kath Two. "Is she sick?"

"No," Ty said. "Her kind sometimes sleep for long periods."

"Moiran, judging from her coloration?"

Ty was dying to know how the Diggers had come by their knowledge, rudimentary as it was, of the Spacers. But this was no time to ask. "Yes," he said.

Donno was now literally counting on his fingers. He got as far as five. "The two fighters?"

Ty nodded. "The big one is Teklan."

"And the ape-man?"

"A subrace of the Aïdans, called a Neoander."

Donno nodded. "We have seen his like in the west." He extended two more fingers. "So in your group was one of each race—and?" He nodded at Einstein. "A spare Ivyn, for when the old one died?"

"A local guide," Ty corrected him. "We were a Seven, yes. That is a grouping that we create on special occasions, when we need a formal delegation." What he said next was guesswork, but he needn't worry about being contradicted at this point. "The old Ivyn who is now dead—Doc, we called him—suspected that you were down here. He came down to investigate, and he did so as part of a Seven. Befitting its importance."

This seemed to throw Donno off balance. Clearly he was not the sort of man who much cared what other people thought. But it had now entered his mind for the first time that the events of some hours ago could be seen in another light: one that was hardly flattering to the Diggers. He could see this but he was hardly receptive to it. "No doubt you see us as a bunch of savages. You do not even view your incursion on our lands as the aggressive act that it was. Coming here with your armed warriors, your glider, your Thor."

"Donno, how many Spacers do you imagine are on the surface of Earth right now?"

"We are not ignorant. We know they are all over what you call Beringia."

"They are all over the world," Ty said.

"This, if it is true, does not change our position," Donno said.

"Your positions are strong and firmly stated," Ty said, after a longish interval during which he simply could not think of anything to say. "May I ask then why it is you have come here to parley with me?"

"Your warriors are taking ours," Donno complained.

"As one who knows something of warriors," Ty said, "you can well imagine how this all looks to them." He closed his hand around the chain and gave it a little shake.

Again, it was the wrong thing to say. The mere suggestion that it might be possible to look at a thing from more than one point of view was infuriating to these people. Ty needed to get that fact through his head.

"I understand that we are in a state of war," Donno said, "and that there are prisoners of war on *both* sides."

"How would you like to proceed, then?"

"Nonviolently," Donno said, "which is more than I can say of some of the others." He nodded across to the other campfire.

"I await your proposal, then," Ty said.

"We await yours," Donno spat back, and turned to stalk away so abruptly that the Cyc had to scamper out of his path. The big galoot with the spear likewise turned to go. The Cyc was a little slower to disengage, however. She stayed where she was, maintaining visual lock on Einstein's epicanthic folds.

"What's your name?" Einstein asked her.

"Sonar Taxlaw!" shouted Donno. "Come!"

"Now you know it," she said. She turned away with some reluctance and scurried down toward the glider. But even after she had rejoined her kin around their campfire, they could see her face, a pale moon aimed in their direction.

"Where to start?" Ty asked.

He was really talking to himself. But it seemed to jar Einstein out of a reverie. Einstein sighed and somehow pulled himself together. " 'We have seen his like in the west.' Donno said that. About Bard."

"Yes, he did."

"I guess the Diggers must have sent some scouts out across 166 Thirty. They would not have been aware that they were crossing a border. See, it is nothing more than an imaginary line."

Ty couldn't help laughing. "Einstein, if we ever get out of this, I'm going to send you to charm school."

"Huh?"

"Etiquette classes for Ivyns. How to talk to people of other races."

"Why?"

"Never mind. I interrupted you. Go ahead."

"Those scouts must then have seen some Red border troops. Neoanders."

"And if you were in their moccasins, what would you think when you first laid eyes on a Neoander?"

"Bug-eyed, no. Monster, yes."

Ty nodded. "With due respect for Bard and his kin, it would have been better if the first Spacers they encountered had been Dinans."

"What of the Neoanders?" Einstein asked.

It took Ty a moment to follow. "Hmm. If they saw the Diggers while the Diggers were seeing them, they'd have reported it."

"Red knew about the Diggers. Maybe a long time ago."

"Knew, or at least suspected," Ty agreed. He could feel parts of his brain relaxing as the mystery dissolved. "They put their intelligence assets to work on it. Ariane started sniffing around for clues. Used her connections to Survey for all they were worth. Pulled strings to get assigned to the Seven. And brought home the prize."

"If you want to think of Marge as a prize," Einstein responded. Searching the boy's face in firelight, Ty couldn't tell whether this was deadpan humor or just more social cluelessness. It didn't matter though.

"The Pingers!" Einstein called out, as if it were obviously the next topic.

"Sonar Taxlaw said they were sea people—before Donno shut her up," Ty said.

"Do you think he beats her?" Einstein asked.

It was such an emotional can of worms that Ty considered it carefully before answering. Once in his life, before the war, he had fallen for a girl as quickly as Einstein had for Sonar Taxlaw. That one brief experience with stupid blind love sufficed to make it possible for him to acknowledge its reality and respect its power.

"I think," he said, "that their society is comfortable with corporal punishment to the point where what keeps people like her in line is the fear of it. Not the reality. I think there's nothing you can do about it and that if you do so much as look sideways at Donno he will kill you. But you can probably get away with small gestures of kindness toward the Cyc—assuming you're ever allowed near her again. If you show her too much favor she will be punished. If you touch her, we're all dead."

"Why?"

"Because this is one of those cultures that is psychotic about female reproductive organs. Now, let's get back to the Pingers. Name mean anything to you?"

"No. You?" said Einstein. Ty's peroration had affected him terribly and reduced him to monosyllables.

"I have a vague recollection," Ty said, "but I would have to look it up to be sure."

"'Sea people' suggests boats," Einstein said. "But—"

“But we’d have noticed those.”

“Maybe it’s a contingent of Diggers that hides in the thick forests along the coast,” Einstein tried.

“Donno claimed all the land, though,” Ty said, “and said the Pingers had jurisdiction over the oceans.”

“So what’s your theory?”

“I don’t have one,” Ty said. He was lying.

This ended the evening’s conversation. They rolled out sleeping bags and bedded down. Ty slept surprisingly well. He woke up once, to the howling of wild canids. The volcanic eruptions that had been making the Ashwall so thick seemed to have abated, for the stars had come out and the habitat ring was now visible in the southern sky, the Eye shining somewhere above the Galápagos. The canids had spied it too, apparently.

He crawled out of his bag to take a leak, then checked on Kath Two. She was shivering, her forehead hot, but not to a point that he considered alarming.

They had taken his timepiece away from him, but he guessed it was about three in the morning—twelve hours, perhaps, since the Thor had touched down. Ariane and Marge would be reaching a Red habitat around now. For according to the inexorable laws of orbital mechanics, transfer time to geosync was always about twelve hours. He wondered if they were going to the Red capital of Kyoto, or to some military habitat, or even to the Kulak, hovering above the Makassar Strait. The booth would be crowded with the two of them in it. He could only speculate on what Marge’s state of mind must have been. The confrontation over the Srap Tasmaner most people would have considered strange, and violent—the stuff of bizarre post-traumatic nightmares. She couldn’t have seen her gunpoint abduction by Julia coming. But all that was perfectly normal compared to what had happened next. It was unlikely Marge had looked into the sky and seen the Thor approaching. All she would have known was that suddenly she was trapped in a small booth with an armed mutant and experiencing powerful gee forces for the first time in her life. A few minutes later she'd have known weightlessness. Probably not how Marge had seen her day shaping up when she had rolled out of the sack this morning. Had Julia begun to interrogate her straightaway? Or played nice with her? Or perhaps just jabbed her with a dose of tranquilizer to tide her over for twelve hours?

To Marge, the Thor just would have been unutterably bizarre. To Ty or any other Spacer, it was clearly an act of war—the most egregious violation of Treaty that he had heard of in twenty years. Though, come to think of it, he'd picked up enigmatic snatches of conversation, exchanged between persons of import in the Crow's Nest, hinting at dark doings in the South Seas. Presumably there was a reason that they—whoever they were—had chosen Beled Tomov as the Teklan member of the Seven. Beled whose back was cratered with scars that could only have resulted from pitched battle with whip-cracking Neoanders. Likewise there was apparently more to Bard than met the eye.

And Ty? He too was a veteran of ground combat with the scars to prove it. But there were many others who might have been chosen in his stead—ones better suited to leading an expedition and making first contact with what to the Spacers was an alien race from another planet. No, Ty had been chosen because of where he worked and who owned it. Very old money was behind the Crow's Nest. And enough of it that its Owners didn't mind losing some every month to keep the place going. It was a kind of eleemosynary institution, created to serve not culture and not dukh, but a thing called the Purpose. And if Ty kept working there for another few decades, perhaps one of the Owners would sit him down one day in the Bolt Hole and deign to tell him what exactly the Purpose was.

With all of that in his mind he somehow slipped back into sleep and did not awaken until the sun was up. The spear carrier came within range and tossed them three ration packets from the glider's stores. Einstein woke up and consumed his as only a teenaged boy was capable of doing. Ty ate at a more measured rate while keeping an eye on Kath Two. She had awakened long enough to remove the lid from her meal and pick at some of the blander offerings. But this led directly to vomiting, dry heaves, and a return to sleep.

They passed the day in a desultory long-range staredown with the Diggers, who grew fewer and more aggrieved as the hours wore on.

"Do you have a theory yet?" Einstein asked him as they were consuming the midday ration-toss.

"About what?"

"The Pingers."

Ty, having naught else to do, let his mouth run. "The girl's name. Sonar. I can think of a weird coincidence related to that."

"Yes?" Einstein was all ears for anything related to Sonar Taxlaw.

"It's a technology they used before Zero. Undersea radar based on sound waves. They would send out pulses of sound called pings."

"You think the Pingers live under the sea?"

"It all fits. Except . . ."

"Except what?"

"Where the hell did they come from?"

"Survivors? Like the Diggers?"

"I don't see how it's possible," Ty said.

None of the scouts who went out looking for Bard and Beled returned. It was beginning to raise the question of who was really holding whom hostage. The ones who'd gone missing had friends, parents, and children who soon became desperate to know what had become of them and began asking awkward questions of those in command. Late in the afternoon, the Diggers were reinforced by a band of some twenty additional warriors coming up the valley, carrying dead animals on long sticks. The Diggers all held a parley around their cookfire. After they had eaten their fill, Donno came up alone, using a short spear as a walking stick or a wizard's staff. The sun had gone down, so Ty heard him before he saw him.

"We carry out an exchange," Donno announced, "and you people get out of here without further casualties."

Is that what you call murdering people? Ty wanted to ask. Instead, he said, "Very well. How would you like to proceed?"

"Well," Donno said, beginning to sputter a bit, "we need to be able to communicate with them! But everyone we send out disappears!"

"Would you like me to do it?"

"Then you'll just run away."

"It is not necessary to talk face-to-face," Ty said.

"You have radios?" Donno asked suspiciously.

Radio. A queer old word. The Diggers had searched them all, made sure they had no communication devices.

"No," Ty said. He leaned back and reached into an open ration pack, took out a piece of bread, tore off a bit of it. Dual sparks, all around, shone in the retinas of grizzled crows. They'd brought a dozen of them on the glider, in modular cages made for traveling. The Diggers had inadvertently released them, and they'd been hanging around the campsite ever since. They knew what Ty was doing and were already jockeying for position, smacking one another with their wings and squawking. Ty held out his hand with the piece of bread on it, and almost before he'd unfurled his fingers the morsel had been pecked out by a crow who was now regarding him intently. "Beled. Bard," he said. The normal procedure was to display a picture of the recipient, but these birds had some ability to recognize names and map them onto faces, and during spare moments on the journey, the Seven had been training them. "Our hosts wish to negotiate an exchange of prisoners."

Ty closed his hand and waved the bird away. It flapped off into the gloom screaming the message. He looked at Donno and enjoyed the consternation on the Digger's face. "We should hear back soon," he said.

Donno turned without a word and strode back to the Digger campfire.

Half an hour passed. It became fully dark. The canids began howling. Ty looked up into the sky expecting to see the habitat ring coming out. So did all the Diggers. But the ring was not the only bright thing in the sky tonight. There was also a meteor shower. A strangely orderly one. It seemed to be headed directly for them.

Donno came running back, accompanied by more spearmen, all in an ugly mood. "Is this an attack force?!" he demanded. "Coming to rescue you?"

"So," Ty said, "you know what those are?"

"The pods you use to fall out of orbit, when you want to land a person quickly. Now, answer my question."

"This is Blue territory," Ty said, then held up a hand to suppress Donno's inevitable protest. "*According to Treaty.* If Blue forces were coming to rescue us, they would simply fly over the mountains from Qayaq—much easier than dropping people forty thousand kilometers from the habitat ring." He was willing himself to maintain eye contact with Donno and to keep his voice as relaxed and conversational as he could manage. The spearmen had fanned out to form a ring around their little camp, aiming the points of their weapons inward. Einstein really didn't like that, and Ty could hear links of chain clicking through the loops on the younger man's collar as he edged closer.

"Who are they, then?" Donno demanded.

"By process of elimination," Ty said, "they are Red."

"But you said you consider this Blue territory!"

"Yes. You might be interested to know," Ty said, "that this makes it a breach of Treaty, and an act of war."

Donno stood gobsmacked. Ty was tempted to say *Welcome to the modern world!* but instead he added, "You might wish to keep this in mind, if you sign a treaty with them."

A grizzled crow landed on the ground nearby, and addressed Ty. "We are coming."

THAT THESE DROP PODS WERE OF MILITARY DESIGN WAS OBVIOUS from the way they came in: fast. Each had a set of vanes, mounted near the top, that sprang out when it was a couple of thousand meters above the surface, slowing its fall. But not until the pod was just a few tens of meters above the ground did its retro-rockets come on: not just one but a circular array of thumb-sized solids that created a cylindrical piston of fire on which the pod eased to a stop, coming to light on a tripod of buglike legs that deployed themselves at the last possible moment and absorbed the shock of contact.

The first thirteen drop pods landed in a nearly perfect circular formation, about a kilometer down the valley. As soon as they touched down they sprang open. Their hatches faced inward. The pod-ring thus presented nothing but armored backshells to any foes outside of it. Any foes inside were in for a bad time.

Seconds later a fourteenth pod landed in the center and a man climbed out. On his signal, the thirteen somersaulted out of their pods and rolled sideways onto their bellies, looking outward into the space beyond, which was now well illuminated by blinding lights shining from the backshells. In actual battle the next procedure would have been to start killing anything they could see, but instead the leader shouted a command that caused all of them to stand up, holster their kats, and dust themselves off. Ten of the thirteen were Neoanders. Three others had the more normal modern-human look. Those, and the one in the middle, were likely B-types, or Betas: the most numerous of the Aïdan subraces.

The peloton—for that was the Aïdan term for a unit of this size—adopted a parade rest position, facing outward and resisting the temptation to watch as four more drop pods landed in the space they had just circumscribed. The occupants of these were a little slower to climb out. It seemed evident that they were civilians who hadn't done it before. While they were doing so, another pod landed, this one outside the circle; it was of a somewhat different design, used to land cargo. The peloton moved forward to form a loose perimeter around this one. The civilians opened it and removed various items: most obviously, a few sections of tubing that they snapped together to form a pole. To the top of this, they affixed a circular hoop, creating a rather more stylish and high-tech version of the circle-on-a-stick totem that the Diggers favored. Below the hoop they tied on a red, fork-tailed streamer, known in Blue vernacular as the Serpent's Tongue, frequently used as a Red emblem in battle or, more usually, athletic competitions. And below that they attached a large white flag.

The performance was so amusing that even Ty, who knew he should be attending to other things, was a little surprised when he noticed that the half-dozen Digger warriors surrounding their little camp were all lying on the ground twitching helplessly. This had occurred so recently that some of their handmade spears were still toppling to the ground. In one of those peculiar, focused insights that comes to one when things are happening very fast, he noticed that the leaf-shaped spearheads had been hand-forged, and wondered idly if the metal had been scavenged from the truck they'd excavated.

Naturally he looked toward the explosive device on the nearby cairn. He saw that the wires had been severed. A hand the size of a dinner plate appeared above the top of the cairn, scooped up the explosive charge, and hurled it into oblivion.

Beled had materialized near the wooden stake, which he was examining in something like wonder. After trying its connection to the end of the chain, he knelt down, gripped it with both hands, and began pulling. Langobard, now that he'd dispensed with the explosive, loped over to join him. Squatting, he scooped away some dirt to get better purchase, and added his strength. Half a meter of the stake suddenly emerged from the ground, causing both men to tumble back. From a semi-reclining position, Bard swatted at it with one hand, as if shooing away an insect, and snapped it off at ground level. Ty, Einstein, and Kath were still chained together, but free to move.

Since Bard was now operating in a more stealthy mode, he was not surrounded by a whining complex of aitrains; rather, he had gotten all of his flynks jacked together into a single long rope that was looped and draped around his torso in a complex pattern that Ty had seen before, and that he supposed had been developed by Neoanders over thousands of years.

Ty reeled the stake fragment in, hand-over-handing the chain through his neck collar, and grabbed it in both hands like a club. He used its free end to scatter the campfire and darken the encampment. Kath, still half in her sleeping bag, was up on all fours, vomiting. Beled strode over to her, scooped one arm under her midsection, hoisted her up, and slung her over his shoulder. He had not really broken stride, and so the other two prisoners were now obliged to go with him. Langobard trailed the group, impulsively snatching up a spear—as a keepsake?

It had not been the most surgical extraction in the history of warfare. It was very far from being the most cack-handed, however. More fighting might have ensued had the main encampment of Diggers not been utterly transfixed by the approach of the Red delegation. Ty was just allowing himself to believe that they'd gotten away clean when he heard a voice from out of the dark, only a few meters away:

"I found this."

Directly the speaker was painted by a crossfire of red lasers from Beled's and Bard's katapults. In the dark it was impossible to see her face, but Ty had already recognized the voice. "Hold your fire," he said.

The Cyc stepped closer. Bard risked illuminating her with a dim light. She was holding the lump of explosive in her hand. It must have rolled down the slope toward the main Digger encampment.

"Sonar Taxlaw," Ty said.

"You remembered!" she exclaimed. Then, apparently as some sort of explanation, she offered: "Volume seventeen."

"Okay, Sonar," Ty said, "you are free to go. Or you can come with us. As much as I would hate to deprive your folk of their knowledge of the last part of the S topics and the beginning of the Ts, I recommend coming with us." He was working out how to explain matters to Sonar without taking all night, but Sonar abruptly said "Okay!" and, in her scurrying way, fell into step with them.

"You can leave that," Ty said, nodding at the lump of explosive.

"A mixture of RDX with beeswax and vegetable oil," Sonar said helpfully. "It will not detonate without—"

"I know," Ty said, "but we don't need it."

Sensing eyes upon him, he looked toward the massive silhouette of Bard. The Neoander's face was in darkness, but Ty could guess that it bore an incredulous expression. "I'll explain later," Ty said.

They walked briskly uphill for several minutes, their view across and down the valley improving as they went. Far below them, the Red delegation had been ascending toward the glider encampment at a stately pace, following in the footsteps that the Seven had made yesterday. Quite clearly, they wanted to be as obvious as possible, and so they were advancing in a pool of brilliant illumination made by portable lanterns, which the members of the peloton were aiming toward the center. The same goal—not seeming to sneak up on the Diggers—might have been achieved simply by waiting a few hours and doing it in daylight. But that was just typical Blue thinking. They were doing it at night for the sheer drama and pageantry of it, this being the sort of thing that Red, by and large, was simply better at than Blue. Ty almost laughed out loud when they got to a place where they could get their first clear look at the approaching spectacle. He was comparing it in his mind to the pitiful show that the Seven had put on yesterday. Of course, the Seven had been surprised, so it wasn't a fair comparison. But the Diggers would not be making allowances for fairness. What they were seeing was probably a lot closer to how their folk, stuck underground, might have been imagining this moment during the last five thousand years. A tall Aïdan with a mane of glossy black hair preceded the rest. He wore some kind of ceremonial robe that streamed in the cold wind draining down the valley and glowed warmly in the light shone on him by the peloton. Advancing with a measured tread, he held the hoop standard in an absurdly dramatic pose with his upper hand reversed so that the thumb was down and the palm faced forward. It was meaningless but it looked great. A few paces behind him walked an older man with gray hair swept back from his high brow and a neatly trimmed beard. His robes were more subdued but, one suspected, really smashing if you could see them up close. A gold chain around his neck supported a medallion on his chest. His right arm was extended to cradle the left hand of none other than Marge the Digger, whom he was escorting up the hill in the manner of a dad giving away the bride. She was wearing what she'd last been seen in, supplemented with a warmer garment thrown over her shoulders like a cape. It kept trying to fall off as she waved her free hand over her head, signaling to her Digger kin that all was well. When they recognized her, they shouted words of greeting and she waved the more vigorously; her cape fell off and was replaced by one of the uniformed Betas.

Even at a distance it was obvious that the standard bearer and the one escorting Marge were Aretaics, which was to say, Aïdans of the first line of descent, presumably conceived as competitors to the children of Eve Dinah. They were tall and long-maned, with magnificent noses and excellent posture.

A few paces behind Marge and the senior Aretaic were a Camite and one of the Betas, walking abreast. They were joined by a pole about two meters long; each of them supported an end in the crooks of her elbows. In the pole's center was a gleaming lump about the size of a person's head, which any Spacer would recognize as a small nickel-iron asteroid, as common in space as dead leaves were on the reforested surface. But rare down here, even after the Hard Rain. Ariane must have told her higher-ups about the truck, what the excavation of its engine block said about the lengths that the Diggers would go to in order to get their hands on a bit of metal, and how grateful they would be for such a gift. Or perhaps Ariane had been broadcasting the entire mission to Kyoto through some covert, encrypted channel. Anyway, it would make a better token of friendship than a busted shovel handle.

Two of the members of the peloton were musicians. At a certain point one of them began to beat a drum that was harnessed to his midsection, and another began to play a melody on a shiny horn. Ty was convinced he'd heard it in the Epic somewhere, but it took Bard to place it.

" 'Bread of Heaven,' " he said. "It's what Rufus and company were singing when they welded themselves in."

"Also known as 'Guide Me, O Thou Great Jehovah,' or in the original Welsh, 'Cwm Rhondda,' " added Sonar Taxlaw.

"*Fuck,* these people are good!" Ty exclaimed.

"How long do you suppose they've been preparing this?" Bard asked.

"They have been way ahead of us for months. Maybe years," Ty said. "But having said that, there's little in what we're seeing that couldn't have been thrown together in a few hours."

"Confirmed," said Beled. He had let Kath gently to the ground, where she now lay in a fetal position curled about his shin. He was looking at the procession through optics. "The ring at the top of the standard? It is an exercise hoop covered in silver tape. The white flag? A bedsheet."

"Do we even need to bother watching how this goes?" Bard asked.

And then he looked to Ty to give the answer. It had not been a rhetorical question. He was awaiting orders.

Beled Tomov looked at him too.

"How is she?" Ty asked. "Pulse, respiration okay?"

"I think it is the usual," Beled said with a nod. Meaning that abrupt hormone shifts in Kath's system were giving her something akin to morning sickness. Her microbiome—the ecosystem of bacteria that lived in her gut and on her skin—had been thrown into disarray, and she was being colonized by any old germs, including ones from the Diggers that had never been exposed to a Moiran body.

"Can you put her on your back or something?"

Beled nodded and dropped to one knee. He had been carrying a pack on his back. He emptied its contents on the ground and began slashing leg holes in its bottom corners so that Kath could just be inserted into it, like an infant into a carrier.

"We can't rule out that our guys will show up in force," Ty said, referring to Blue military. He looked south over the mountains, but didn't see anything coming. Nor would he, of course; anything headed their way from Qayaq would be running dark. "Have you been in touch with them?"

"Yes," Bard said. During this little pause he had been rooting a multitool out of his belt. He approached Ty, who held out the broken stake. Bard got his tool clamped around the head of the bolt and began to twist it out.

Ty nodded wearily. On one level, he had just asked a stupid question. But the Diggers' attack—hell, for that matter, their *existence*—had taken them by surprise, and since then he'd been preoccupied with being a prisoner under conditions so primitive as to verge on slapstick. He ought to have been thinking about the larger picture.

Blue might bomb this whole valley into the Stone Age. But probably not. It was *already* in the Stone Age.

Bard and Beled had gotten a message up to Denali, which was the closest major Teklan military habitat to 166 Thirty. Everyone of consequence in Blue would now be aware that the Diggers existed, that the initial contact had been botched, and that there was a hostage situation. The Thor would have made it clear that Red was a step ahead of them. The descent of those drop pods, a few minutes ago, would have made it clearer. The brilliant pool of light in which the Red delegation moved was as much for the benefit of long-lensed video cameras peering down from orbit as for the Diggers.

It was a fait accompli that Red would make formal contact, in about thirty seconds, with the Diggers, and that it would go a lot better than yesterday. Ariane would have prepped them, told them what to say: Yes, of course we accept your claim to the Earth's surface. Its justice is self-evident. We have plenty of room in orbit. No need for habitations on the planet. Of course, as you've already learned firsthand, you can't trust those people from Blue. We might be persuaded to install a discreet military presence just to keep them from encroaching on your territory. As long as we're there, some cultural exchange programs might be in order. We could offer medicine. Dental care. Technical advice in rebuilding your civilization. How may we be of assistance?

"Blue isn't coming tonight," Ty said. "It would just play into their hands." He nodded down at the procession, which was only a few meters away from making first contact with an equally sized group of Diggers. "But some members of that peloton might come after us. They'd look like heroes if they could march us back into camp in shackles."

"Or carry our heads in on spikes," Bard suggested in a casual tone.

"Shh!" Ty said, with a glance toward the newest member of their band. But the Cyc looked unconcerned.

"Sonar," Ty said, "we are going to have to move. Get away from any patrols those guys might send out, while it's still dark. Can you do that? Move rapidly over rough terrain, in the dark?"

"Sure," Sonar said, a little too blithely for Ty's taste. But before he could press her, she added: "Guess we'll be going north then?"

"Why do you say that?"

"Because the main group is going south. Probably as soon as the sun is up."

"How far south were they thinking of going?" As it was, they were less than a hundred kilometers from the southern coast of Beringia.

"To the sea," Sonar said, as if this were self-evident.

"What's going to happen then?"

The question seemed simple enough, but it led to an outburst of chuckles from Sonar. "They're going to wonder what became of me, that's what!" she said, when she could get her mirth under control.

"They're probably wondering that already," Einstein remarked.

"No, I mean they'll be needing me then!"

"Why?" Einstein asked.

"It's a riddle."

The bolt had been removed now, freeing the end of the chain, which Ty pulled clear of his collar. He opened the thing up and tossed it on the ground. The gesture caught the eye of the Cyc, who probably saw it as a shocking way to treat valuable metal. Ty was now free, holding the massive stake fragment and managing to control a certain natural impulse to bash her head in. This was not a time for riddles.

Einstein got the chain out of his own collar, then carried it in the direction of Kath so that he could help her.

"The purpose of your expedition—before we blundered into your path, that is—was to go to the edge of the water and make contact with the Pingers," Ty ventured.

"Pingers?" Bard asked.

Ty ignored him, maintaining his focus on the Cyc. "You, by virtue of your mastery of volume seventeen of the *Encyclopædia Britannica,* are the closest thing your folk have to an expert on the only technology capable of summoning them."

"Oh, I'm an expert on other topics as well!" Sonar said. "Sophism, South Carolina, Pope Sylvester II . . ."

Ty decided to let the witticisms go by without positive or negative reinforcement. "What were you guys going to say to them?"

"It's they who want to talk to us!" Sonar said. "They left us a message—a cairn on the beach. We are coming to respond."

The ensuing silence lasted a long time: long enough for the final stanza of "Bread of Heaven" to stop reverberating from the mountain walls, long enough for the Aïdan leader's opening greeting—written and pronounced in flawless pre-Zero English—to move through a solid paragraph of awe-inspiringly sycophantic salutations. Long enough for Bard to get the unchained Kath socketed into his backpack.

"We move south," Ty announced. "Bard, you keep pace with the Cyc. If she slows us down, carry her. I'm going to need your radio."

"My what?!" Bard exclaimed.

"An electromagnetic communications device—" Sonar began, but Ty cut her off.

"The thingamajibber you use to talk to Denali. I'm going to tell them we have a second chance."

"A second chance to do what?"

"To make friends with the natives of this planet."

THEY CRESTED A PASS IN THE COASTAL RANGE THE FOLLOWING DAY and began making their way down toward the sea. When the going became easy enough to allow for something like normal conversation, Ty asked, "How many Cycs are there in total?"

Sonar's little head snapped around, like a bird's, to regard him curiously. She would never look you directly in the eye, but she would lurk in your peripheral vision and sneak peeks all day long.

"I know," Ty said. "As many as there are volumes of the *Encyclopædia Britannica*. But I don't know what that number is, because we no longer have copies of it lying around."

"Well, there are the Ten, the Nineteen, and the One," Sonar said.

"The Ten are the Micropædia. Many short articles. The Nineteen are the Macropædia: longer, more in-depth articles. The One is the Propædia, the Outline."

"Which category do you belong to?"

Einstein, walking ahead of them down the slope, wheeled around. "She already told us she was volume seventeen!" Normally good-natured, he was being unusually chippy all of a sudden. He returned his attention to the rocky terrain in front of him, displaying a flushed neck beneath his ponytail.

"Excuse me," Ty said. Then, turning back to the Cyc, he asked, "Is that just luck of the draw? Or—"

"No!"

Of course not.

"The older Cycs started me on smaller books, to evaluate me."

"When? At what age did they start you?"

"When it was decided that I was not a breeder."

Einstein turned around again, this time so suddenly that he lost his footing and fell on his ass. The reaction was so outsized that Ty had to look away from it lest he break out laughing. But this brought Langobard into his line of sight, and the Neoander was in similar trouble. The two men had to stop walking and turn their backs on each other for a few moments just to keep their composure.

"If I can just anticipate some questions that I believe may be uppermost in young Einstein's mind," Langobard said, "would it be untoward of me to inquire what, precisely, makes you 'not a breeder'?"

The Cyc shrugged, staring down the mountain toward the Pacific Ocean as if she had not given the topic very much thought recently. "I know not. Of mean stature? Nothing special to behold? On the spectrum?"

"For context," Ty asked, "how many young women out of ten are designated as breeders?"

"Four, maybe?"

"So being a nonbreeder is more common than being a breeder," Ty said, for Einstein's benefit.

"Of course, now that we have come out of the Hole, and we have more space, more people are breeding," Sonar said. "I speak of how it was ten years ago."

She had earlier told them that she was sixteen. "Okay. So they think they know enough about you at the age of six to make that determination. They start you out on easier books. Then what?"

"If you can read at all, you just start reading the whole Cyc."

"And so that's why you know stuff about radio, and epicanthic folds, and other topics not in volume seventeen."

"Yes. You have to read the whole thing. By ten, they decide whether you are Micropædia or Macropædia quality."

"Is one of those more prestigious than the other?"

"Of course!" Sonar exclaimed, without bothering to say which was which.

"I'll bet the Micropædia is just like memorizing a bunch of trivia," Einstein essayed. Somewhat dangerously, in case he guessed wrong. But love had made him impetuous.

"Yes, you have to be able to hold more in your head to be one of the Nineteen," Sonar said, favoring Einstein with a warm gaze.

"So, did you have to kill the previous Sonar Taxlaw in single combat or something?" Ty asked, and immediately thought better of it, since in general Diggers did not seem to have a well-developed sense of humor. Einstein threw him a mean look.

"No, not in this case," the Cyc said politely, leaving open the question of in what cases the Diggers did actually employ such methods. "My mentor was Ceylon Congreve."

"Now, that is a lovely and distinguished name!" Langobard exclaimed. "Volume three?"

"Four," she said, with a note of surprise in her voice, as if not quite able to believe that someone could not know this.

"Do the original paper copies still exist?" Ty asked.

"Oh, yes," Sonar said, "but we handle them only on ceremonial occasions. We work with handwritten copies."

"Rufus must have squirreled away a lot of paper."

"Tons of it," said the Cyc. "Acid-free, one hundred percent cotton."

During their nighttime escape over the mountains, they'd had little time for such conversations, and so their knowledge of Digger culture was still spotty. Some reasonable guesses could be made simply from the known history of the Hard Rain. The phase known as the Cooling Off had not begun until some thirty-nine hundred years after Zero, when the human races' efforts to police the lunar rubble belt had finally paid off with a sharp falloff in the number of bolides striking the surface. Until then, the Diggers had been obliged to maintain a small, steady population in the space that Rufus had provided. Expansion of the Hole had been limited by the fact that it was a sealed system, with no place to put spoil—the quantities of loose material created by digging. As anyone knew who had ever dug a hole in the ground with a shovel, the size of the dirt pile—the spoil—was always larger than the volume of the hole. They'd been able to dump some spoil down a deep and otherwise useless shaft, but once this had been filled, they'd been unable to expand their living space for as long as the Hard Rain had made a direct connection to the outside too dangerous to be contemplated. So during that phase—well over three thousand years—they had devoted all of their energies to maintaining a community of several hundred people. Hence the rigid controls on breeding. Thanks to their Cycs, they knew everything about contraception, but they had no ability to manufacture things like condoms and pills, so that lore was mostly useless. The limitations on breeding were enforced by moral strictures, by segregation of the sexes, and by surgical sterilization. This, like all of their surgery, was performed without chemical anesthesia once they'd run out of drugs, which occurred fairly soon after Zero.

Apparently they had gotten rather good at acupuncture and at biting down on things.

The reduction in the intensity of the Hard Rain would have been obvious to them on one level, since they could hear the impacts through the walls of the Hole. On another level it was easy to miss, since even dramatic changes spanned generations. But they had kept meticulous records of the frequency and intensity of strikes and so they recognized the downward trend in the late Fourth Millennium. When it was adjudged safe, they drilled an adit—a horizontal tunnel—out the side of the mountain until it broke out of a slope that they guessed was steep enough to have shed ejecta, preventing the buildup of rocky debris that now covered most of Earth's surface to a considerable depth. That much had been true, but the debris at the base of the mountain had piled higher than they had expected—almost high enough to block the opening of their adit. Anyway, it had worked well enough that they had been able to push spoil out of it and thus begin expanding the Hole. The atmosphere was still far from breathable, so they'd been obliged to keep it sealed when they were not actively dumping stuff out of it, to prevent fumes from seeping in and poisoning the atmospheric system that they had looked after so meticulously for nearly four thousand years. This system, it seemed, was similar in principle to those used on space habitats. Carbon dioxide was removed by a combination of chemical scrubbers and green plants. Both of these required energy: the scrubber chemical had to be heated to drive off the CO_2 it had absorbed, and the plants required light. Since they were cut off from the sun, they got their energy geothermally, using works that Rufus and the others of his generation had sunk deep into the roots of the mountain. The maintenance of this system had been the full-time occupation of everyone in the Hole for the entire time they'd been down there. When they had neared the end of their stock of light-emitting diodes they had revived the art of making lightbulbs, consulting the Cyc for particulars, blowing artisanal glass envelopes and winding the filaments by hand. Likewise with many other things they had found themselves in need of.

Ty, not really an expert on technology, made little headway in trying to imagine the particulars. Someone of a more technical bent might have devoted weeks to debriefing Sonar Taxlaw and extracting every last detail about how they had managed to get along with just the stuff available to them underground. More important for present purposes was to get a general understanding of the Diggers' culture, and why they behaved as they did.

The requirement for a steel-spined authoritarian culture was obvious. Any power structure one of whose main goals was to prevent humans from fucking each other at will had to be extremely formidable. Had these people been living in, for example, the agricultural paradise of the Nile Delta, they might have been able to get away with some mazy religious dogma as the basis for that system. But instead they had been trapped within a large machine that would kill them all if allowed to go on the fritz, and so they had been obliged to develop a culture in which engineering became their dukh. Their finite supply of tungsten, stockpiled by wise Rufus, had to be stretched and husbanded so that their descendants thousands of years in the future would be able to manufacture lightbulbs to grow plants to make food and air. And so on and so forth in every particular of how these people lived their daily lives. Thirty people—the Ten, the Nineteen, and the One—were, at any given time, Cycs. Another thirty were toiling as their apprentices. Others played specific roles such as breeder mom, glassblower, acupuncturist, filament winder, potato nurturer, pump fixer. Structurally, culturally, it was very like a Bronze Age theocracy, but without any trace of God or the supernatural.

To that point it was not radically different from the subcultures of many First and Second Millennium space habitats, which—at least for a little while—gave Ty the idea that he could get a quick handle on Digger culture. But that fantasy soon evaporated. Those early Spacers had been living in cramped conditions, yes, and they had been just as dependent upon technology as the Diggers in their Hole. So of course there were some common features in the two cultures. But Spacers had always been able to look outside to see what the situation was, and—at least after a couple of thousand years of hunkering down in especially large rocks—to venture forth and do something about it. Even in their most desperate hours they had always expected to reinherit the Earth. The Diggers' only way of knowing their situation and their fate was to listen to loud noises, tally them on acid-free, 100 percent cotton paper, and, every few years, compare the tally with a similar one made by some ancestor a couple of hundred years previously. For the first four thousand years, hope of a better future must have been seen as sheer folly. Worse than that, as an active betrayal of Digger principles, since people with hopes were apt to become profligate in spending resources and taking risks.

Which all made for a picture of those first four millennia that was as clear as it was bleak. But change would come hard to a society like that one. What was most interesting to Ty was what had begun to go on within that society when they'd punched the spoil adit to the surface and begun to expand their underground domain. Their day-to-day lives would not have changed much, but they'd have had at least the abstract possibility that their civilization might expand, that more people might be able to breed.

All of that had occurred more than a thousand years ago. The Hole had grown to the point where it could support a population of two thousand; then, around 4700 when the atmosphere had become breathable, they'd been able to take it up to ten thousand. All still beneath the surface, however, since there'd been little for them above it.

At some point the Committee—which was what they called their ruling council—must have become aware that vast numbers of humans were living in space and actively prosecuting the TerReForm. They could simply have walked out onto the surface and sent out some kind of an SOS at that point. Instead they had made a positive decision to conceal themselves, to hide their spoil dumps, to shun communication with the Spacers. The central question, then, was why they had made such a choice. Sonar Taxlaw wasn't much help in explaining it. When Ty or the others asked questions, she offered nonresponsive answers that told of a subterranean culture in which such things were never spoken of.

It was clear, however, that having made that decision, the Committee would have to explain it, justify it, and perpetuate it by painting the Spacers as alien mutants, and furthermore by cultivating a finely developed sense of racial grievance against the cowards who had run away and abandoned them. All of which had been on vivid display during the brief and disastrous conversation between Doc and the Digger contingent.

BETWEEN EINSTEIN'S PERSONAL KNOWLEDGE OF THE TERRAIN, GEOgraphical folklore stored in the Cyc's encyclopedic mind, and Beled's digital map, they knew generally where to go at any particular moment. What made it difficult was negotiating obstacles in the terrain and steering clear of large animals. The latter group might, in theory, include Red military patrols, but they had no reason to believe that they were being pursued yet. Why would Red bother? Marching some Blue prisoners back in chains might score them some points with their new Digger friends, but having chased them off into the darkness was nearly as effective. Perhaps more so given the importance to the Diggers of the meme of Spacers as cowards.

Ty considered explaining to the Cyc that if her group of Diggers had turned up on the *west* side of 166 Thirty making the same preposterous territorial claims, Red, instead of approaching them with music and nuggets of space iron, would simply have vaporized them. But burdening the poor girl with that awareness wasn't going to help.

They holed up in a pocket of shelter beneath a leaf of rock about the size of a football field that had been driven like a blade into the southern slope of a coastal mountain. There they consumed a day recovering from their exertions and waiting out a snowstorm, while communicating in short bursts with a transmitter on the Denali habitat. Blue military dropped a pod through the storm. Kath awakened long enough to announce that it had landed just down the slope from them. Bard stomped out there, his huge feet acting like snowshoes, and returned a quarter of an hour later dragging it behind him. He then stood for a few minutes contemplating Kath. Her sickness had abated, but she woke up now only to eat, eliminate, or make delphic pronouncements.

The pod contained food, fuel, ammunition, robots, and equipment for snow travel that stood them in good stead during the next day, as they descended out of the mountains toward the southern coast. Much of this happened under cover of the heavy clouds that almost always blanketed this part of the world, and so if anyone was watching them, it had to be directly—by actually following them around—or with flying robots. But now they had flying robots of their own that could alert them to the presence of both. Since those remained quiet, they felt reasonably certain that they were not being tracked, except by large canids who tended to make their presence obvious by howling a lot. Because of them, the next night was a restless one, and led to an early departure and a final day of hiking that rapidly developed into a pell-mell descent out of the Alpine zone and toward the Pacific.

During their lunch break, they spied a trio of single-person gliders—inflatables like the one Kath Two had taken on her Survey mission—dipping and darting along the coast from the general direction of Qayaq. As these carried Blue markings and were transmitting Blue codes, Beled felt comfortable divulging their position. Minutes later the gliders had touched down in an expanse of heather a few hundred meters below them. Their occupants climbed out, eviscerated their cargo holds, and began to deflate their gliders so that they could be rolled up. Most of that work ended up being done by a Teklan, shorter and more lithe than Beled. This left the other two new arrivals free to approach. One of them was a Camite whose gait and posture were more expressive of male than of female characteristics, and so Ty made a mental note to employ male pronouns until and unless the Camite requested otherwise. He wore one of the utilitarian coveralls employed by Survey personnel, with red cross patches on the chest and shoulder, marking him as a medic. The other was a middle-aged Ivyn dressed in civilian clothes marginally more posh than might be expected in the wilderness of Beringia, but suited to the conditions.

Regarding them from a more sheltered position overlooking the meadow, Ty had mixed feelings. Any assistance was, of course, welcome. He had known better than to expect a thunderous show of force. Blue's high political councils, having been caught badly off guard, and having lost the first round to their Red counterparts, would still be assessing the situation and thinking about their options. For public consumption, they were probably characterizing the Seven as a plain vanilla Survey team that had fallen victim to an ambush. They didn't want to undercut that story now by sending in an undeniably military force.

The name printed on the Camite's uniform was Hope, which probably meant that, like many Camites, he only used one name. Bent under a medical pack, he went directly to Kath. Beled and Bard were descending to the meadow to help the Teklan pack up the gliders.

The Ivyn singled out Ty from a distance and approached him. The family name on his uniform was Esa and he introduced himself as Arjun. The former was an acronym frequently seen in the background of shots in the Epic, standing for "European Space Agency." It had become a common name. Ty considered asking Arjun flat out who he was and what he did for a living that caused him to show up in circumstances like these. But he knew it would get him nowhere. The man would have some bland answer cued up. He was probably some kind of high-powered intelligence analyst with five advanced degrees.

"How's this all playing up on the ring?" Ty asked him. "Do I even want to know?"

The mere question caused Arjun to break eye contact and gaze out over the sea.

"That bad?" Ty prompted him.

"You know the Aretaics," Arjun said.

"They made it into grand opera, eh?"

"That's as good a description as any. I am still coming to grips with it. Of course, we rarely see content from the Red side of the ring."

"Just the propaganda," Ty said.

"Yes, and when we see that, we have a laugh at the overwrought style, the baroque production values, while harboring an inner sense of anxiety that some people within Blue might—"

"Might actually believe their shit?"

"Exactly."

"So Red did broadcast it."

Arjun nodded. "Live, to the whole ring."

"Sorry I missed the show. We bolted before the actual contact. It seemed like as good a time as any."

"That was a fine tactic," Arjun replied, "and saved you a great deal of annoyance."

"How do you mean?"

Arjun turned to look directly at him. "The Diggers," he said, "were as receptive to Red's overtures as they were hostile to yours."

Ty felt something in his chest. The awareness that he had failed, and that people knew it. It was not a feeling to which he was accustomed, and he did not like it. "So," he said, "the Diggers ate it up?"

"They signed an alliance with Red on the spot. Red recognized their claim to the entire land surface of Earth and urged Blue to follow suit."

"Just as a matter of basic human decency," Ty said sourly.

"Of course. The saber-rattling began the next day . . ."

Esa Arjun broke off as he noticed, and focused on, Sonar Taxlaw, who was standing next to Einstein, who was telling her how the gliders worked. Ty had grown used to it; all those two did the whole time they were awake was explain things to each other. But it was new to Arjun.

"She's the . . ." Arjun said, and trailed off. Ty tried to put himself in Arjun's shoes: laying eyes on a rootstock human for the first time in his life, seeing someone who was clearly human and yet not of any identifiable human race, thinking about all that her ancestors had lived through.

"Yeah," Ty said.

Arjun managed to snap out of his reverie and looked back at Ty. "The narrative being put out is that you abducted her."

"Of course."

Einstein said something funny. The Cyc laughed and leaned into him affectionately. His arm found its way around her waist, the hand sliding down to the hip.

"Are those two . . ." Arjun began.

"Fucking? Not yet. But only because we've been on the run."

"The Diggers, from what intelligence we've been able to scrape together, believe in strict gender roles and . . ."

"Not fucking. Yeah. I'll talk to Einstein. Tell him to not fuck her."

"But you didn't . . ."

"Abduct her? No, she just tagged along."

Sensing doubt, or at least curiosity, from the Ivyn, Ty continued: "And more would do the same given the chance. The transition to surface life is putting their culture through a blender. Which is why their leaders are being so reactionary."

Arjun nodded. "And how's your Moiran?"

Ty sighed. "She saw Doc and Memmie die, and suffered a blunt-force trauma to her arm, and was forced to draw her kat, and to use it. As soon as it happened she went into what I'm guessing is a classic POTESH." This was military jargon for post-traumatic epigenetic shift.

"That is confirmed," said Hope, who seemed to have finished an initial scan of Kath's vital signs. "Higher metabolism and hyper-acute senses are observable. Her microbiome is a mess; I'm tuning it up with probiotic supplements that'll be a better fit with her new phenotype. Suggested by the nausea are big hormone shifts. Possibly predictive of some future . . ."

"Testosterone poisoning?" Ty suggested, finishing Hope's thought. Hope responded with a diffident nod of the head.

Ty turned his attention back to Arjun. "So three billion people just learned that the Diggers exist. How are they taking it?"

"Well, obviously it is a sensational bit of news," Arjun said. "People are intensely curious." He turned his head again to study Sonar Taxlaw. "As am I. I admit it."

"Does the general public know how badly the first contact went wrong?" Ty asked.

"None of the identities of your Seven are public knowledge. Certainly no one has the faintest idea that Hu Noah had anything to do with it."

"So Red hasn't been trumpeting that."

"It wouldn't be to Red's advantage, as I see it," Arjun said. "Now that they are allied with the Diggers, they want to make the Diggers out to be sympathetic. Revealing that they killed Hu Noah and his nurse would hardly serve that end."

"So we are just being made out to be some sort of anonymous thug squad. The Diggers chased us off with help from Red. We abducted a hostage as we were running away."

Arjun looked him in the eye. "No intelligent person in Blue believes that, of course."

"But Blue hasn't put out a countervailing narrative yet either."

"It isn't Blue's strong suit." Arjun sighed. "Never has been, right?

We're technocrats. We make decisions like engineers. Which doesn't always line up with what people imagine they want."

"Are you speaking of Blue in general?" Ty asked. "Or Rio in particular?" Using the name of the Ivyn central habitat as synecdoche for its culture.

"Both. A Blue mentality that places us at the top of the decision-making pyramid. There's a reason why the very few Aïdans who have become prominent in Blue have been musicians, actors, artists."

"They're supplying something our culture lacks," Ty said.

"*You* were supposed to supply it," Arjun said. Meaning, as Ty understood, the Dinan race. "And you did, during the heroic age."

Ty could feel a not altogether cheerful smile on his face. "By actually doing things, you mean," he said, "as opposed to pretending to do them in made-up entertainment programs."

"You know what, though? It's *all* entertainment. Real or made up. It's stuff that people watch on screens or varps. Red gets that."

"Well," Ty said, "maybe we can continue the discussion in my bar if we get out of this. But the bottom line for now, if I'm hearing you right, is that, narrative-wise, Red is killing us."

"We have been a little distracted," Arjun said, showing a bit of defensiveness for the first time.

"By what Red did, you mean," Ty said. He was referring to the insertion of the peloton, Marge's glorious return, and the lovey-dovey stuff between their delegation and the Diggers.

Arjun did not out-and-out disagree, but the look on his face was a bit impatient, the smart teacher working with the slow pupil. "More by what they've *been* doing. For a while now."

"Well," Ty said, "as a mere bartender, I wouldn't know about anything other than what is on the news feeds. So tell me. What have they been doing?"

"What do you know about the Kulak?"

"What any civilian lacking a security clearance would know," Ty answered carefully. "People are assumed to be living in the fist part of it."

"Kulak" was Russian for "fist." In this context it denoted an irregular lump of nickel-iron some thirty kilometers across. A hundred and fifty years ago, Red had moved it from the Kamchatka boneyard to a position above the Makassar Strait, where it had orbited ever since. Like a loosely clenched fist, it had a cavity down the middle, a tunnel now presumed to be lined with rotating habitats. Red's answer to the Great Chain.

"Then there's the rigging and spars whatnot surrounding that," Ty went on. For the fist, viewed from a distance, seemed to be tangled in a sparse web of cables, like a seed in a spiderweb. Above and below—to the nadir and zenith sides—these converged on hard points to which the long cables extending down to Earth's surface and up to the counterweight—the Antimakassar—were attached.

Sonar Taxlaw, a few meters away, had been engaged in a public display of affection with Einstein, but withdrew slightly and turned her head to listen.

Ty had grown accustomed to her ways. It was because he had said "spars." That was between Sonar and Taxlaw in the *Encyclopædia Britannica,* and thus belonged to her domain of knowledge. During their hike over the mountains and down the other side, she had turned out to be well informed, at least by troglodyte standards, about space exploration and the sun. So it had been easy to bring her up to speed on the last five thousand years' off-planet developments. She now began to drift toward Ty. Einstein followed her as if his eyes were connected to her butt cheeks with fishhooks.

Oblivious to all this—for he had his back to it—Arjun was regarding him coolly, expecting more. Ty went on: "The part on the surface—their answer to Cradle—we don't know much about. They've been building it under the sea."

"They call it the Gnomon," Arjun informed him. Then he spelled the word out.

"What does it mean?"

"It used to be the thing that stood up in the middle of a sundial, to cast the shadow. Aligned with the Earth's axis."

Ty considered it. "Interesting choice of words."

"It's big, Ty. Much bigger than Cradle. There's a reason they've been building it in the ocean. Partly to hide it from us. And partly because it's too large to construct on terra firma."

"How big are we talking about exactly?"

"There is only so much I'm at liberty to say," Arjun said. Then he drew out a tablet and began tapping at it, pulling up a world map, panning and zooming toward the mess of islands between Southeast Asia and Australia. "But just look at this and tell me what you see." He handed it to Ty.

"Southeast Asia!" exclaimed the Cyc, who had drawn close enough to see all of this over Arjun's shoulder. "Is there anything you would care to know of it? Or of Sulawesi? Or of Sri Lanka?"

The Ivyn regarded her with fascination.

"I don't need to look," Ty said. "I know what's there. The equator runs through all of that and rarely crosses over the land, and Red never stops whining about it."

"Not true! Sumatra . . ." said the Cyc.

"A big island to be sure," Ty said, "but not a continent. Do you remember, Sonar, what I told you about how the Eye works? What Cradle does?"

"Touches the equator," she returned.

"And *only* the equator. Which is great if you control Africa and South America. Which Blue does. But most of Red's territory lies north or south of the line."

Sonar wasn't going to be talked down so easily. "Singapore is close," she said, "and that is connected to Asia."

"The former location of Singapore is *close,* yes. But not *on* the equator. It's one or two degrees north. Cradle can't dock there."

"And that one detail, more than anything else, is what infuriated the Aïdans about the design of the Eye and Cradle," Arjun put in.

Sensing Einstein behind her, the Cyc leaned comfortably back against him and started rattling off facts—her default mode of social interaction. "Aïdans," she said. "The ABC hierarchy. Aretaics, Betas, Camites."

"Camites are a different race," Einstein reminded her.

"Oh yeah. The relationship of the A and the B to the C is more akin to Symbiosis."

Ty and Einstein exchanged a wry look.

Oblivious, Sonar Taxlaw gazed down the hill toward Langobard. "Neoanders. And two more. The smart ones and the crazy ones."

"Jinns and Extats," Einstein said. "They don't get out much."

Arjun's fascination with seeing a rootstock human had given way to impatience. He focused on Ty again. "This is old history, of course," he said, "but never forgotten by some people. Way back when the Eye was being designed—I'm talking a thousand years ago—there were alternative schemes proposed. The one we ended up with was simplest, easiest to build with what people had back then. The Eye, the Big Rock, and a small Cradle with sockets on the equator. Great for access to South America and Africa. Almost useless, however, in the stretch of the equator under the habitats where Aïdans, half of the Camites, and most of the Julians lived."

"What later became Red," Einstein put in, for Sonar Taxlaw's benefit.

"One of the reasons Red later coalesced, and built such a strong counteridentity to Blue, was their sense of grievance over this decision. We should have waited, they said. We could have had something much more useful than Cradle." Arjun zoomed in on Indonesia and dragged out a skinny rectangle, straddling the equator and spanning most of Red's latitudes. "If instead of Cradle we had made something in the shape of a long arc, spanning a greater distance north-south, it might have connected with Asia down here, where Singapore used to be. And here it could touch the northern cape of New Guinea. And New Guinea could be connected to Australia by dropping enough rocks into the shallows between them."

"A long arc. Aligned with the Earth's axis, casting a shadow on the ground," Ty said, nodding. "A Gnomon."

"It would have to be huge!" Einstein exclaimed.

Arjun nodded. "Plans for it were drawn up. Studies commissioned on how it might be constructed, in orbit or on the surface. It was deemed too ambitious. So wiser heads prevailed," said Arjun, "or so it seemed at the time, and we built what we built. We can always make something bigger later, they said. But it didn't turn out that way. Blue forgot about it. Red didn't. Their Jinns put as much effort into thinking about it as our Ivyns put into epigenetics. As soon as they closed the border and put up the two turnpikes, they went to work. What have they been doing that whole time?"

"Smiting the Torres Strait with an unceasing storm of bolides," said Sonar Taxlaw, pointing to the narrows where Australia's northern cape almost poked New Guinea in the belly. "Filling it in. Damming the currents. Making a wall against those that swim in the sea."

Arjun nodded.

Then his head snapped around to focus on the Cyc.

He stared at her intently for a moment, then looked at Ty. "Did you . . ." he began.

"Not a word," Ty said.

"Einstein, did you tell her about Red's illegal terraforming operation here?" And he tapped the same place on the map.

"First I've heard of it," Einstein said.

"Sonar," Arjun said, "how did you know about that?"

"The Pingers told us," Sonar said.

"Who the hell are the Pingers?"

"The people we are going to talk to," Sonar said.

Beled and Bard had been assisting the Teklan. Those three now approached, carrying the glider packs. They set them down and began camouflaging them under such foliage as was available in this place: scrubby brushes that had been socked into the brow of the slope to stabilize it and provide refuge for small animals. Ty got the feeling, from cues in the Teklan's physique and general style of movement, that he was some manner of Snake Eater. When it became evident to the Teklan that the two larger men were better than he was at uprooting plants and moving dirt, this man left them to finish the task and approached. Tucked under his left arm was a container matching the general size and shape of those still used, in Chainhattan, to transport pizza. Dangling from that hand was a roughly cubical equipment case. With his free right hand he exchanged salutes with Ty and identified himself as one Roskos Yur. He then set the two parcels in front of Ty and backed away from them.

"Thank you," Ty said.

"You're welcome, sir."

"Why," Arjun asked, "did you want those? Do you have any idea what it cost to get them here?"

"The Cyc can explain along the way," Ty said.

Arjun held his gaze on Ty for a moment, then glanced away with a diffident nod. Roskos Yur, by contrast, looked hard at him, and wouldn't stop looking. After a few moments of this, Ty felt obliged to meet the Teklan's eye. Now that Ty could scan this man's insignia more carefully, he could see that he was part of a unit stationed at Nunivak: one of the forward Blue outposts, right up against the border. It was a byword for remote and isolated. It made Qayaq seem like a metropolis. Full of Snake Eaters always being sent off on crazy missions.

"That's not really what he's asking, sir," said Roskos Yur. "He's really asking, who the fuck are you?"

"Sergeant Major Yur—" Arjun said, in a tone of protest.

But Yur would not be stopped. "And don't tell us you're a bartender, sir."

"The late Dr. Hu handpicked Mr. Lake for inclusion in the Seven," Arjun pointed out.

"And now he's ramrodding this—" Yur looked about at the group and gave out an incredulous snort. "I don't even know how to describe it. 'Ragtag' makes it sound like more than it is."

"He led them out of a difficult situation," Arjun said.

"A difficult situation for which he's partly responsible, sir," Yur shot back.

"And at the moment he knows more about the Diggers, and the situation on the ground, than anyone. I assume he requested those objects for a reason, which will be explained as we go."

Ty held up a hand. "Sergeant Major Yur doesn't trust me because my allegiance isn't clear to him. Fair enough."

Yur's face softened a little, and his gaze flicked to one side for a moment. Taking advantage of this break in the staredown, Ty turned to face Esa Arjun.

The Ivyn made the tiniest movement that was still recognizable as shaking his head *no*. Once he was certain that Ty had caught it, he looked at Roskos Yur. "Sergeant Major," Arjun said quietly, "there are more things in heaven and earth than are dreamt of in your philosophy."

Yur snorted. "Is that a fancy way of saying it's above my pay grade, sir?"

"Yes."

"I just want to know if it's some kind of fucking dukh shit, sir."

"Oh, is that all?" Ty asked. "Why didn't you say so?"

"No," Arjun said, the tension suddenly gone from his voice. "There's no dukh involved."

"Because that bar he works for—"

"It's not connected with any established kupol."

"Then who the hell is it connected with, sir?" Yur demanded. "I made some inquiries with friends of mine in intel. That bar makes no fucking sense as a business proposition. Its ownership structure is . . . unusual. Connections to Red, I'm told."

"One of the Owners happens to be of part Aïdan ancestry," Ty admitted, "but be careful of making unwarranted assumptions about where his loyalties lie."

"Does this have something to do with the Purpose?" Roskos Yur demanded.

Neither Ty nor Arjun answered. After a few moments of this silence, Yur heaved a sigh, then continued in a more moderate tone: "Never mind. I see it now. It's some kind of Purpose thing. Above my pay grade. You should have just told me." He drew himself up and saluted. "What are my orders, sir?"

"We march to the sea," Ty said, "following the Cyc's directions. And moving as fast as we can. Complicating matters is that our Moiran may have to be carried."

"Actually," said Langobard, who had been loping in their direction and was now in earshot, "we may have to work rather hard to keep up with her." He extended one long arm, pointing down the slope of the meadow.

The first thing they all saw was the huge form of Beled, charging downhill at the near-sprint that, as they all knew, he could maintain for hours. Far ahead of him, then, they saw Kath Amalthova Three, moving even faster.

HOPE'S DRUGS AND PROBIOTICS HAD SETTLED KATHREE'S MOOD A bit and reduced the nausea to the point where she could almost ignore it. This had been resolving on its own, but she was glad of any pharmaceutical assistance she could get; her body had become ravenous and she needed to keep her food down. But the most important drug in her system right now—so important that Hope had strapped a little pump to Kathree's arm, the better to keep dribbling it in—was one designed to home in on her amygdala and put the brakes on any slow neurological train wreck that might be under way there in reaction to the trauma she had seen four days ago. As such it was reaching her brain a few days too late—but apparently it was one of those "better late than never" things. It might help interrupt a vicious cycle in which her brain would keep replaying that little horror movie over and over, deepening the damage a little bit each time. The fact that she'd spent so much time asleep might also be helping her in that regard. Some tangible and biologically measurable benefit might have accrued to her as a result of having spent most of that time physically strapped to Beled, her cheek on his shoulder, all but sucking him into her nostrils. For his part the Teklan had shown no particular reaction to having an indolent, vomit-scented coma patient on his back during the day, and curled up against his belly during the night. The two of them had still never had sex, but she feared now that once she was cleaned up and feeling better she would be on him like a succubus. It was a well-known POTESH symptom, which had produced colorful and legendary results in Moiran communities that had survived collective trauma.

But since having rampant sex with everything that moved wasn't really an option today, she sought other outlets for her surging physical energy. The hike from the meadow down to the sea was longer than it had appeared and she ended up ranging far in front of the others, obliging Beled to push himself hard just to keep her in sight. She could not see him because he was behind her, but she could sense his footfalls through the ground. She could hear his breathing and the faint clicking of the ambots that he carried on his person, and when the wind was from behind she could smell the institutional wipes that he had been using for hygiene, and the detergent that had been used to clean his uniform, the lubricant in his kat, his most recent meal. Her ranging so far out in front of the others was partly a way to burn off a physical energy that threatened to make her crazy but as much an effort to get into a place where she was not taking in an equal amount of sensory data from everyone in the group. One was enough.

She stormed through a hedge of whippy plants that had been seeded in a dune above the beach and broke out onto the wet sand. Waves were breaking half a kilometer out and washing up toward her in fizzing sheets. The smell in her nostrils spoke of an incalculable density of marine life, akin to what she had scented when she had stood on the top of the bridge in Cradle, but much more finely resolved now. This despite the chemically induced suppression of her amygdala. Without Hope's drugs in her system she might have spiraled into a sort of panic attack. As it was she felt her body overheating and looked down at her bare arms as if expecting them to crack open like sausages on a grill. Dropping from a run to a stride, she marched straight down the beach peeling off clothes as she went and depositing them in a ragged career over her footprints. Soon, but not soon enough, the surf was washing her ankles, then her shins. She dropped to her knees and let herself topple forward into an onrushing wave that caught her fall and let her down easy. Naked, she was floating facedown in the water, whose icy cold only made the exposed parts of her skin—buttocks and shoulder blades—feel as if they were under a broiler.

Pressed for a rational explanation of why she was lying facedown in the Pacific, eyes open, gazing at a starfish, she could not have answered. But it was having an effect. Her heart, which had been thumping out of control, dropped to something much closer to a normal rate, and a surprising amount of time passed before she felt obliged to plant her hands and knees in the sand, push herself up on all fours, and suck in a breath of air.

She got her legs under her and squatted, then pivoted so that her back was to the sea. Her legs and buttocks were still submerged, cooling off from the run.

Beled Tomov was standing a few meters away, surf washing around his ankles, breathing heavily, looking as though a dip in the icy Pacific might do him some good. But this was not his intent. He had been ready to pull Kathree out if she had gone too long without breathing.

They looked at each other, Kathree's gaze saying *I would do you right now, right here* and his saying *I know* and hers saying *I know that you know.*

"Did you hear anything?" he asked.

That was unexpected.

"Just now," he explained, "when your head was under."

"You mean, in the water?"

"Yes."

"Like what?"

"You haven't been listening, have you?"

"Are you kidding? I've been listening so hard it's driving me out of my mind."

"To the conversation, I mean."

"No. Everyone talks too loud."

He considered it. Then he turned a little to one side and stretched out one arm, drawing her attention to a rocky headland that interrupted the beach a few hundred meters away. "There," he said.

The thermal spike in her body had finally subsided, so she pulled her clothes back on and they walked along the beach toward the headland: an abrupt, almost artificial-looking rampart of shattered rock, held together by the roots of trees and scrub. It divided the beach like the blade of a shovel.

She did not even know why they had been going to the sea. Was someone going to pick them up there? Was there even a plan? Or had they simply run away until they could run no farther?

"The Diggers believe," Beled said, "in the existence of people who live beneath the sea. The Pingers. Supposedly there have been contacts. At specific places along the coast of Beringia." He nodded in the direction they were going.

"As in face-to-face contacts?"

Beled shrugged: a movement that, given the size of his shoulders, could almost be picked up on a seismograph. "I fancied you might have heard something while your head was under the water," he said. "They use a tech called sonar."

Her disordered brain was a little while putting this all together.

She knew a little about sonar. Survey used it to map the bottoms of lakes and to count fish. "No coincidence that we are traveling with someone of that name?"

Beled nodded. "She has been telling us about them, but much of it sounds more legend than fact."

"Where do they live? Submarines?"

He shrugged again. "No one seems to know. Apparently they are good at holding their breath."

The headland could not be skirted without a boat. They ended up cutting back inland so that they could get past it. This required gaining a couple of hundred meters in altitude and bushwhacking through vegetation that had grown thick on the south-facing slope.

When they reached a place from which they could look down toward the sea, it became obvious that they were on the edge of an impact crater a kilometer or so in diameter. The headland that had blocked their passage down the beach was part of its rim; this curved out into the Pacific, forming one side of a bay. A mirror image of it, as they could now see, formed the opposite side. The bolide that had formed the crater had struck very close to the shore. The central impact peak was a sharp rocky islet just a stone's toss from the beach, precisely centered between the twin headlands. It was easy enough for the eye to fill in the missing shape of the rim. Out in the water between the headlands, it must be slung in a submerged arc. And indeed it was possible to see waves breaking as they tripped over it. On the landward side, the rim blended into the natural slope. The impact had hollowed out a bowl whose steepness now forced Beled and Kathree to make an awkward, skidding descent into the cove below. The beach there was more rocky than sandy, and many of the rocks had the translucency of wave-worn beach glass.

They could hear the remainder of the party on the slope high above, catching up with them.

The middle of the beach—just opposite the sharp little island—

seemed like the natural place to make camp. A little heap of glassy stones had been made there—just big enough to make it clear that this was no natural deposit, but an intentional act. "Their signal," Beled explained. "We should build a fire now." He began ranging along the beach picking up driftwood. Kathree, drawn somehow by the cairn, squatted there to wait for the others. She could hear Sonar Taxlaw chattering as she negotiated the slope above, running circles around the others, whose footfalls and breathing were audible.

"Their history is divided into three Deluges. The First Deluge was of rock and fire. It chased them into the deepest trenches of the sea, where it never fully dried out, even after the rest of the oceans had boiled off. They bred a race capable of living in confined spaces. The Second Deluge was of ice and water."

"The Cloudy Century!" Einstein said.

"Yes, when you dropped comets on them for hundreds of years. They noticed that seas were expanding, growing away from the trenches where they had been holed up, expanding their range. They transformed themselves into a race that could swim in the sea."

"When you say they transformed themselves," asked Arjun, "do you mean genetic engineering or—"

"Selective breeding," Sonar insisted. "If wolves could become poodles in a few thousand years, think what humans could turn into, if there was a need! They began to explore the seafloor. They found a lot of industrial junk that had been washed into the oceans during the Hard Rain and sunk to the bottom. There is nothing of metallurgy that is a mystery to them."

"Which is why you trade with them?" Ty ventured. "Because you are short on metal?"

"And they are short on things we have," Sonar affirmed.

"You said there were three Deluges," Einstein reminded her. "The Third Deluge?"

"Is now," said the Cyc. "A Deluge of life, beginning with microorganisms and culminating with you."

"Meaning, the Spacers," Ty guessed.

"Yes. And the only Spacers they know about are the ones who dropped a lot of rocks into the Torres Strait and built the thing at Makassar."

"How is all of this being imparted to you?" asked Arjun.

"Imparted?"

"Have you, Sonar, actually had face-to-face conversations with Pingers?"

"Me *personally*?!" she asked, sounding amazed and horrified by the very idea. "Oh no, just looked down on them from up here."

"So you lurk up above while more senior members of your clan go down to the beach and talk to the Pingers."

"Talking is difficult. Communication is mostly through the written word. They didn't have paper until we gave them some of ours. We use slates and chalk."

Kathree's eye went to a detail she had noticed a minute ago: an unnatural-looking deposit of flat black rocks half buried in wave-driven sand. As the remainder of the party made their final descent to the water's edge, she used a piece of driftwood to scrape sand and gravel away from these until she could worry one loose. Though it was rough around the edges, it had clearly been shaped by humans: a slab of black rock about as thick as her finger, big enough to hold in the crook of an arm, smooth enough to write on. Scattered in the muck around it she'd seen lumps of calcium carbonate: chalk. Traces of it were still visible on the slates. Not writing but a fragment of a diagram, a map perhaps, and a few numbers.

PROJECTING FROM ONE SIDE OF THE ISLET, JUST BELOW THE TOP OF it, was a snarl of driftwood: the stump of a tree that a storm had torn from the edge of a cliff somewhere along the coast and later hurled up here. As soon as he arrived, Ty dropped his pack, emptied his pockets, and picked up the boxy equipment case that Roskos Yur had delivered in his glider. Holding this up above his head to keep it dry, he waded out to the islet, cursing at the intensity of the cold. At its deepest, the water came up to his waist, with occasional waves clipping him under the chin. He tossed the case up onto the flank of the islet and then clambered up after it.

After gazing curiously at the stump for some moments, he squatted down, gripped it by a couple of protruding roots, and overturned it, causing it to tumble into the surf. He then edged back out of the others' sight line to reveal what had been hidden beneath it: a vertical section of stout steel pipe, about a hand's breadth in diameter, rising to the height of a person's knee, topped with a flat disk of battered steel the size of a dinner plate. The pipe wasn't rooted to the boulder itself. It was part of a longer object that extended out into the sea. The part above the waterline was lashed to spikes that had been driven into crevices in the rock, in a style that they had already learned to recognize as typical Digger improvisation.

Ty's attention strayed to something he had noticed at his feet. He bent down and heaved it up so that all on the beach could see it: a sledgehammer improvised from a length of pipe and a chunk of steel. Then he looked at the Cyc. Looking back at Ty she held her hands out, palms toward the gray sky, as if to say: *See? Just like I said.*

Ty turned away from them, gazing down into the sea before the boulder. After a few moments he turned back around. "How far does it extend?" he shouted.

"The pipe? A few score yards," answered the Cyc. "The crater is as a horn, channeling the sound out into the deep."

She had scarcely finished the sentence before Ty hauled off with the sledgehammer and brought it down with all his might on the steel plate. The result was a blindingly loud metallic ping, drowned out, as it faded, by a scream from Kathree, who sank to her knees in the sand with her hands clamped over her head.

"Better get her out of here," Ty said—she could hear him through her hands. She felt Beled reaching around her from behind, crooking her in one arm below her breasts, heaving her to her feet. Which was welcome on one level. But she was tired of being the one who had to be carried, and so she unwound herself from him, turned her back on the sea, and marched up toward the belt of scrub that marked the limit of the beach. Ty gave her a respectable head start before shouting, "Plug your ears." She did so, and a moment later felt another ping go through her like an icicle jammed into the base of her skull. A moment later came another and another, not in a steady rhythm, but sporadic. And by the time she had climbed up to a place where she could look down over the cove, fingers in her ears, and not suffer pain from each stroke of the hammer, she had made sense of what Ty was doing.

Each of the human races had its own set of cultural traditions that it traced back to its respective Eve. These were propagated from one generation to the next by social rituals, school curricula, and youth groups. Young Teklans learned zero-gravity gymnastics with a martial arts flair, competing on obstacle courses that reproduced specific maneuvers that Tekla had performed during the Epic. Julians competed on debate teams and went on lengthy retreats intended to symbolize their Eve's exile and ordeal in the Swarm. And so on.

Young Dinans learned Morse code. It was used very rarely.

Moirans most certainly *didn't* learn it, and so Kathree had no idea what message Tyuratam Lake was banging out into the deep.

Everyone, of course, had watched the scene in the Epic, at the beginning of the Hard Rain, where Eve Dinah had made her final transmission to Rufus. This had trailed off with many repetitions of the code QRT, which—especially after Dinah had dissolved in sobs, and slowed her transmission speed to a crawl—had a kind of solemn fanfare-like rhythm to it, beginning with *pahm, pahm, pa-pahm*. The letter Q. Kathree recognized that pattern, at least, more frequently than you would expect in normal English sentences. So, Ty was using ancient Q codes to shorten his message. But she hadn't a clue what he was actually saying. He belted it out over and over again, a syncopated phrase of long and short strokes that started to get under her skin after a while. He stopped when Sonar Taxlaw waded out to the rock and assured him that, if the Pingers were about, they would surely have heard the message by now.

"How long now?" he asked. He was shouting over the rush of the surf and because he had probably gone deaf.

"Depends on how far away they are," said Sonar Taxlaw. "Maybe a day. Maybe three."

"Great," Ty said, and looked up to catch the eye of Roskos Yur, who, following a timeless military instinct, pushed his sleeve back to check his timepiece.

Ty unlatched the lid of the box and began to take out pieces of equipment and to peruse instructional brochures. Kathree was too far away to see the details, and in any case it was getting dark. As the sky faded, she could see Ty sitting on the shore of the islet, facing out toward the sea, occasionally flicking on a small light and fussing with equipment. Perched next to him, swaddled in sleeping bags that Einstein had brought out to her, was the Cyc. She wore a bulky pair of headphones, occasionally turning her head toward Ty in an alert birdlike way to make some sort of comment. Esa Arjun paced slowly back and forth on the beach, just out of the waves' reach, passing occasionally near Einstein, who just stood there gazing fretfully at his beloved. Hope had gone to ground in a small tent pitched a few meters higher up, on drier sand; a bluish flicker through its walls suggested he was working with a tablet, maybe trying to learn something about POTESH management.

So much for the lower camp where Hope, Ty, Einstein, Sonar Taxlaw, and Arjun had made themselves at home. Beled had followed Kathree uphill. Langobard and Roskos Yur later followed him. Spreading out, bushwhacking in all directions, they identified a curved brow in the slope: the line of demarcation between the crater's inland edge and the preexisting landscape from which it had been blasted. Above it, the slope was much gentler. Indeed, the first thing one saw upon cresting the rim was a slight drop in altitude. Before them, as they stood with their backs to the sea and their faces to the mountains, was a bog a few hundred meters in extent, with a pine forest rising up on its far side. They backpedaled a few paces and set to work establishing an upper camp just below the summit of the rim. Few words were spoken, but it was obvious that its purpose was to defend the beach if and when Red forces approached. If the foe came straight down out of the mountains, they would have to cross the bog. If they came along the beach, they would have to scale or circumvent a prong of the crater's rim. Either way, they would be clearly visible from this vantage point.

It could be guessed that an ONAN had struck the ground somewhere nearby, several decades ago. Seed-packed siwis had slithered out of it, roaming about, mapping elevations and soil moisture, comparing notes over a mesh network. The collective had noticed the break in the slope leading down to the sea. Following a program drilled into it by some coder up on the ring, it had decided that the coastline might be stabilized here by planting some seeds that would grow up into tough, low, scrubby vegetation. And so it had all come to pass. Siwis that happened to wander away from the beach had found the flat ground beyond the rim and planted it with different species that would thrive in a wet environment. The vegetation had created a bit of a natural dam, holding back water coming down out of the mountains above them. One day it might be a lake, but for now it was a black bog, squishy and knee-deep and screened with grasses and reeds that favored that sort of ground.

Kath Two had not been a fighter. Her weapons training had given her the bare minimum of skill needed to discharge a katapult in the direction of a hungry canid. Kathree didn't know, yet, whether that was one of the things that had shifted. In a sense it did not matter. No matter how good she might turn out to be at combat, she would never be as effective as Beled, Bard, and—judging from appearances—Roskos Yur. She was, however, finding them to be a dull, slow bunch. They failed to notice much that was obvious to her.

And it was clear that they were tired and fading toward sleep. After it had gotten fully dark, Kathree consumed three consecutive full meals from the rations that Roskos Yur had brought with him, then slipped away and climbed a short distance farther up, to the very top of the rim, from which she could look and listen inland.

When she returned, she startled Roskos Yur, whose steady breathing had been audible from a thousand paces away. He'd been asleep, or close to it.

"You should warn me when you are approaching, Kath Two!" he hissed.

"She's dead."

"Kath Three, then."

"No one is coming," she said, "at least not for a few hours."

"Not unless they drop from the sky," he retorted.

Langobard, ever sociable, had approached. "They will not come by air," he said. "If they can take us out quietly, they will do so—and never say a word of it. But to make a full assault? That would clash with the narrative that they are building for the consumption of the people of the ring."

"When are we going to begin writing our own fucking narrative?" Yur said. And there the conversation stalled.

But his question was answered an hour later when Kathree, then the rest of them, discerned a whine and a rumble coming from the direction of the water. Running lights appeared over the horizon, coming from the south over the limit of the world, but then winked out as the pilot made the decision to run dark. It was clear from the sound, and from the way it hugged the water, that this thing was neither an airplane nor a ship but the in-between thing known as an ark. They heard it sough into the water a kilometer away and switch over to the chugging engines it used to maneuver on the surface. It dropped anchor several hundred meters offshore: well away from the land, so as to respect the hair-trigger sensibilities of the Diggers, but close enough that people and gear could be ferried to and fro on small boats. It opened its big rear cargo ramp, allowing the sea to flood its interior and float a collection of small boats and barges that had been packed aboard. On one of these, a small party came ashore. Kathree heard them conversing, mostly with Ty and Arjun, though Einstein as usual found a way to make himself part of the action.

A barge from the ark had been towed into the open water between it and the shore, and anchored. The sounds coming from it spoke of complex mechanical internals. After a few minutes it began to rumble and hum, and a fountain of glittering flynk chain, an upside-down U, grew out of its top and began to extend skyward as its velocity built and its sound sharpened into a steady keening note. Within a few minutes the aitrain had elevated to a height of perhaps a hundred meters and begun to give off a soft light, filling the cove and the beach with enough illumination for people to move about easily and read documents. Kathree could now read the name of the ark, blazoned on its fuselage near the nose: *Darwin*. It must have been sent out from a big TerReForm base—most likely Haida, which served the northern Pacific coast.

The aitrain that they had deployed on the barge was a common enough military device. As such it was probably radiating in other wavelengths besides just visible light. It was a sort of all-in-one communications hub that was interconnecting everything that had line of sight to it, as well as uplinking to Denali and other installations in the ring.

Sleep was now out of the question for Kathree, and so she made her way down the crater to the beach. When she emerged from the brush she discovered Einstein and the Cyc, standing next to each other in a crossfire of lights, facing a camera. To one side, sorting through notes, was a new arrival, a tall Moiran woman with the posture, the self-possession, and the golden eyes of a fashion model. She wore clothing suited for the chilly, damp coast of Beringia. It hung on her slender but strong frame in a way that suggested it had been made for her, probably by a clever designer on the Great Chain.

Kathree didn't have to get any closer to understand what was happening: the tall Moiran woman was producing just what Roskos Yur had asked for. She began by talking directly into a camera for some time, then interviewed Einstein and the Cyc. It was all being beamed live to the ring.

Kathree sat alone on the beach, hugging her knees and watching the woman do what she did and wondering what events in her life had caused her to shift into what she was now, so tall, so lovely, so watchable. She did not have the manner of one who had been born beautiful, which made Kathree suspect that she had come by it through some kind of personal disaster. After she was finished doing her interviews, she shut down the lights and the cameras, approached Esa Arjun, and stood face-to-face with him for a while, just talking. Both of them had put on varps and Kathree got the idea that they were conversing about whatever it was that the devices were projecting into their eyes.

Kathree became certain that Kath Two had seen the woman broadcasting from trouble spots around the ring: habitats where general strikes or civil disorder had gotten out of hand, where Quarantine Enforcement or police had been called in to break things and hurt people.

The mere fact that Kathree was sitting still long enough to make such observations and to string such thoughts together was indicative of a coming crash—the inevitable result of how she had spent most of the day. It was about halfway between midnight and dawn, and Kathree felt herself plummeting toward sleep with the same power and inevitability as *Endurance* diving into her final pass through perigee.

Instead of which she found herself gazing at, and being gazed at by, the tall Moiran woman, who had silently drawn almost to within arm's length of her. Kathree jumped to her feet and nearly fell over.

"Kath Amalthova Three," the woman said, "I am Cantabrigia Barth Five."

Five. Wow. "You must have seen some crazy shit," Kathree said. "I hope for your sake you have taken a set in your current form."

Cantabrigia Five made a tiny movement of her golden eyes, by way of acknowledging the remark, but let it pass without comment. "I am what amounts to the commanding officer here," she said.

It was neither the craziest nor the least crazy thing Kathree had heard lately, so she took it impassively. By outward appearances, Cantabrigia Five was a video journalist. But it made sense that, in a world where no police or military action could be judged successful unless it looked good to ordinary persons watching it on video screens, she was also a general.

Arjun had approached from behind Cantabrigia Five and now took up a position just to one side, peering over her right shoulder. He caught Kathree's eye briefly and nodded.

"Over the wireless," said Cantabrigia Five, "I just now spoke to Sergeant Major Yur and Lieutenant Tomov and Langobard, and gave them *their* instructions. These are *yours.* A small Red military force is approaching. They are still some hours away. We have intelligence that they are being guided this way by two Diggers familiar with the route. When they get here, there may or may not be a fight. If there is, do not enter into it directly. Stay clear of our buckies. Look for the Diggers. If you can prevent them from doing harm, by all means do so. But dead Diggers on a video screen is a thing we cannot afford."

Kathree nodded. "I understand."

Arjun apparently felt that some explanation was required. "We don't know when, or if, the Pingers will show up. So we need to buy time."

"Okay," Kathree said. "What are we hoping to buy it with?"

The look on Arjun's face suggested that the question had been impertinent. But Cantabrigia Five responded by reaching up to remove the varp she had perched atop her head. She swept it off and handed it to Kathree, who arranged it carefully on her own face. The fit was imperfect and so she had to hold it in position with one hand to get the right focus.

"You'll want the sound track," said Cantabrigia Five. "It's just not the same otherwise."

"Sound track?" Kathree said. But a faint shift in the set of Cantabrigia Five's face hinted that some deadpan humor was at work and that she should just play along. Groping along the sides of her head, she found the earbuds and flipped them down into position.

The varp was causing her to see a number of imaginary objects, most of which were grayed and/or blurred—it had figured out that Kathree was not its owner and so it had disabled anything personal or private. Hanging in space between her and Arjun, however, was a softly glowing red token having the apparent size of a table tennis ball, with a dimple in one side. He reached out and gave this a light tap and it flew in her direction. "Be my guest," he said. She caught it in her hand and put her thumb into the dimple, then swooped it around in a big oval in front of her face. This caused a flat screen to make itself visible. She then drew the red ball toward her, sweeping the screen through a third dimension to define a volume about the size of a laundry basket.

Cantabrigia Five hadn't been kidding about the sound track. It was a full orchestra, comprising some instruments that would have been familiar to Mozart and others that had been invented thousands of years after Zero. It, and a large choir, poured a three-dimensional ocean of sound into her ears, performing the Red national anthem. Not the peppy, truncated version heard at sporting events but the symphonic arrangement, calculated to make people sit still and be awed.

A nickel-iron fist seemed to be hanging in the volume of space she had just swept out above the beach. The Kulak. Stout spars jutted from it here and there: anchor points for hair-thin lines of rigging that extended in various directions, seeming to disappear in the vast distance. Moving carefully lest she turn an ankle on a cobble, Kathree circled around it until she could peer down the hole in the center. There, she saw movement: rings of light, each of them similar to the Great Chain, stacked up the interior, each spinning at a different rate, but all protected within the lumpy shell of the asteroid, many kilometers thick. This triggered a programmed camera movement that took her by surprise and obliged her to plant her feet and steady herself by laying a hand on Cantabrigia Five's forearm. The povv, or point of virtual view, took a slow dive down the center of the Kulak, which had now expanded far beyond the basket-sized volume to surround her. She could not control the speed of the movement but she could gaze in all directions and see through the glass roofs of the ring-shaped cities, picking out green fields where youngsters were kicking balls, blue ponds around which lovers strolled hand in hand, bustling high-rise districts, residential utopias, cozy schools, and military bases where Betas and Neoanders practiced martial arts and marksmanship under the billowing red flag.

"Is this all real, or—"

"A mix," said Arjun, "of stuff they've actually built and renderings of what they imagine."

"And has this actually been made public or—"

"Broadcast six hours ago," he said. "It is a huge reveal." Never before had Red divulged any pictures—real or imagined—of the inside of the Kulak.

By now the fly-through had reached the far end, and she could see space opening up around her as the povv exited from the Kulak's maw. The familiar sight of the habitat ring became visible, sweeping around in both directions to enclose the blue Earth in its jeweled embrace. From the system of rigging woven around the iron fist, a cable descended straight to the equator. Slowly at first, then building speed, the povv descended, achieving in a few seconds what would have taken several days in any kind of realistic elevator. Even through a screen of bright clouds Kathree could pick out the complex landforms of Southeast Asia to the north and, to the south, the huge dun slab of Australia, now joined to New Guinea by a lumpy gray-green tendril. The povv chose to zoom down on that first, coming close enough that it became possible to see a road traversing the land bridge. Then it veered and banked onto a northwesterly course, following the green, steaming spine of New Guinea to the cape at its end, where it nearly touched the equator. There, construction was visible: cleared land, buildings, excavations, a hazy web of infrastructure, glimpsed but not lingered on. The povv soared out over a turquoise sea cluttered with landforms she recognized vaguely from having seen them on maps. But after a few moments her eye was drawn to something that was flagrantly unnatural, looking as if it had been drawn in with a ruler and a pencil: the tether from the Kulak, plunging vertically into the ocean between two big islands. These, she realized, had to be Borneo and Sulawesi, and the water between them the Makassar Strait. The povv's movement slowed, then stopped. The symphony and the choir were laboring through a slow crescendo. A change, more felt than seen, came over the display: the programmed camera movement was finished and the varp was now responding once again to Kathree's movements. Like a giantess bestriding the strait, she could move around and look at it from different angles. For a moment nothing really happened. Then her eye picked up turbulence in the sea, around where the tether stabbed into it. The surface was welling up and foaming. The tiny wrinkles of normal surface waves were erased, replaced by vast green whorls and galactic arms of swirling foam. Bending forward she saw angry gulls wheeling about. That detail convinced her that what she was seeing was real—not a rendering. The disturbed region grew north and south, spreading away from the cable—which she knew to be on the equator—without growing east-west. The cable forked, then forked again, becoming a fan that broadened north and south to support the full length of whatever was roiling the strait.

It erupted from the surface first at the equator, then proceeded to rip a gash in the sea that spread up and down the meridian with immense velocity. The object could hardly be observed at first for all the water draining from it, plunging in multiple Niagaras back into the sea and hurling up a storm front of spray that rose higher than the structure itself. But in a minute the Gnomon became visible. Kathree had to back away to get a picture of the whole length of it. She extended her left hand and made a counterclockwise knob-twiddling gesture, reducing the volume of the Kyoto Philharmonic's brass section before the bass trombones and kettledrums imploded her skull.

If the designers of the Gnomon had intended to make the anti-Cradle, they could hardly have done better. It had the long wicked curve of a katana—the better to follow the curvature of the Earth—combined with the translucent delicacy of an insect's exoskeleton. Indeed, it seemed to be unfolding, reshaping itself as it rose into the air, an origami praying mantis molting into a larger body. Its manifold corrugations and arching carapaces spoke of a million Jinns toiling in cubicles for centuries to build the strongest thing they could imagine with minimum weight.

"What's it made of?"

"Carbon and magnesium, mostly," said Arjun. "Two light, strong materials that can be extracted from ocean sediments."

"Is that how they did it?"

"Yes," said Cantabrigia Five.

"Energy intensive," Arjun remarked. "They ran power down the tether to a production facility on the ocean floor."

"They had workers living on the ocean floor?"

"Robots."

"And therein lies an opportunity," said Cantabrigia Five.

The producers of this spectacle had once again seized control of the povv and begun taking Kathree on a forced march up the length of the Gnomon, slowing down to linger on the good bits and zooming past what was repetitive. She got the idea, which was that it had a sort of carriage that could move north-south on a giant rail and connect with the ground along a range of latitudes. That it had its own internal train lines connecting residential pods, military installations, luxury resorts for the whole family, and so much more. It was obviously rendered—stuff that hadn't actually been built yet. Her inability to control what the povv was doing made her a little queasy. She levered the earbuds up, closed her eyes, and carefully pulled the varp away from her face. Then she opened her eyes on reality: the beach, the islet, her two interlocutors. She handed the varp back. "What sort of opportunity?"

"If you are going to make first contact with an intelligent alien race," said Cantabrigia Five, "dropping huge strip-mining robots into their homeland might not be your best move."

Kathree pondered that one for a bit. "Ah," she said.

"Yes."

"So there's a reason they were so keen to make nice with the Diggers."

"Having fucked it up spectacularly with the Pingers. Yes." Cantabrigia Five stared at her for a little while. Her silence and her gaze were impressive, yet Kathree did not feel wholly uncomfortable.

Finally she went on: "Actions taken here today will cast long shadows into the future of New Earth. With more resources here, we might have effected a more elaborate strategy, with less uncertainty. But the mere fact of having had more would have spoiled it."

"HOW DID YOU GUYS COME UP WITH ALL THIS?" TY ASKED.

He was squatting on the islet next to the Cyc, who was still swaddled in sleeping bags, only her hands and head exposed. She was holding an instruction manual, angling it toward the light of the flynk chain. This was still illuminating the cove, but the crew of *Ark Darwin* had dimmed it so that people could sleep. She had to focus intensely to read the words, many of which must be unfamiliar to her. Her lips moved slightly as she parsed unfamiliar Cyrillic characters sprinkled through almost every word. Headphones buried her ears in great donuts of foam. She hadn't heard Ty, didn't know he was looking at her. So he had his fill of looking for a minute. She wasn't his type, and anyway she was very young. But he was beginning to see what Einstein saw in her. Einstein had to know that there was nobody for him on his RIZ, no Indigen girl he could have an interesting conversation with. And yet if he were to somehow find his way to the habitat ring, he'd be looked on by all the smart girls there as a hillbilly.

The device in the box was a portable sonar rig. It was capable of sending out pings, but that wasn't how they were using it. They were using it to listen. Sonar Taxlaw had virtually wrenched it from Ty's grasp and mastered it. The arrival of *Ark Darwin* and the movements of the boats and the barge had caused her no end of annoyance, but with a little encouragement from Ty, she'd begun to see it as an interesting science experiment, a way of understanding what those technologies must sound like to Pingers and other mammals that frequented the deep.

Moving carefully on the steep, glassy surface of the islet, he edged into her peripheral vision and gave her a light tap on the shoulder. He hated to break her out of her reverie, but there were questions he needed answered. She was stunned for a moment, as if she'd just been teleported into this location from a thousand miles away, but rapidly she came around and pulled one of the headphones away from her ear. "Come again?"

"All of this." Ty rested a hand on the battered plate atop the pipe, nodded toward the makeshift sledgehammer. "How did you come up with it? How do the Pingers know that when they want to talk to you they should build a cairn on the beach at such-and-such place?"

"We began sending out scout parties as soon as the atmosphere became breathable," Sonar said.

"That'd be three hundred years ago," Ty said.

"Two hundred and eighty-two."

"Just making the point that this is old history."

"Not that old."

Ty heaved a sigh. "Not within living memory."

"It is not merely an oral tradition, if that's what you're getting at," Sonar said. "We maintain written records."

"On one hundred percent cotton paper. Yes. Go on."

"There was nothing for the scouts to eat, of course. So they could only range as far as they could go with food that they carried on their backs. But in time they discovered edible seaweed and bivalves along the coast."

Ty nodded. "Once TerReForm's engineered algae had done its job of building the atmosphere, it needed to be held in check. TerReForm seeded the coasts with filter feeders and the oceans with krill."

"Those clams were the first meat anyone had eaten in forty-seven hundred years," said the Cyc. "Scout parties that hugged the coast could stay out as long as they wanted, and roam for months or years, eating better than the Diggers who stayed in the Hole."

"Being a scout must have been popular."

"Too popular. Some went rogue, and had to be hunted down and subjected to the discipline of the Committee."

"That sounds . . . unpleasant."

"It was not a good time. A lot of what you see that is bad in our culture started in those years."

"Anyway, the scouts would emerge from the Hole," said Ty, "and make a beeline for the nearest coast."

"Exactly, and this route we have been traveling is like a game trail for us—we know it backwards and forwards. Well, at some point, after discipline had been reestablished, a scout party was exploring the coast a few kilometers from here, making camp up in the trees. One of them looked down and saw a person just walk up out of the sea. This person carried a little shovel like you might use to dig clams, and had a basket, but no clothes. He or she dug some clams and tossed them into the basket and then strolled back down into the ocean and disappeared."

"No scuba gear. No wet suit."

"Correct, just a belt with a knife. Well, word of this got back to the Hole and they talked to a predecessor of mine."

"A previous Sonar Taxlaw, you mean."

"Yes. A scout party went back down to the same place the next year and set up a contraption like this one, except not as good, and used it to send signals out into the deep. Nothing. Years, then decades went by. All they had to go on was the one sighting. Some old Digger who had been on a lot of scouting parties came up with the idea of building a bigger and better noisemaker here—he reckoned that the shape of the crater would act as a horn, channeling the sound outwards. To make a long story short, it worked. Contact was made."

"How recently?"

"About fifty years," Sonar said. "Then it was broken off around the time that you had your war. Five years ago, though, we began to see cairns."

KATHREE WAS AWAKENED MUCH AS KATH TWO HAD BEEN ON THE morning when she had seen the Digger from her glider: by a certainty that something was out there, supported by no real evidence. This time, she was responding to sound: something she'd heard while still asleep, accessible only through a memory that eluded her the harder she reached for it. She rolled over onto her belly, propped herself up on her elbows, aimed her face uphill, closed her eyes, opened her mouth, and froze. For the first few minutes she wasn't trying to hear anything, just taking in the ambient soundscape so that she could detect any noises that did not belong in it. The flynk chain on that barge was still operating, producing a steady note that could be filtered out by the mind's neural circuitry. She was aware that Bard too had suddenly become very quiet, but she didn't know whether he had heard something or was simply following her cue. Kath Two might have been bookish and unobtrusive, but Kathree was the sort of person who kept nearby men on their toes.

She heard it again: the same sound that had probably awakened her in the first place. And this time she knew what it was: hand-forged steel arrowheads clinking faintly in a quiver, like coins in a pocket. The dilemma of the Digger hunter being that those shafts had to be held loosely enough to be fluidly drawn and nocked, but not so loosely that they jangled with each footfall. In measured strides across level ground, their kit might make no noise, but in a breathless predawn descent of an uneven slope, things might work themselves loose. As that aural picture sharpened in her mind, she could sense footfalls too, and hear bodies pushing through brush. The party, she guessed, was more numerous than the jangling quivers.

Another Kath Two memory connected: preparing for Survey work in areas with a lot of Indigens, she had read ancient histories of the American West, where white men had made use of aborigines as scouts and guides.

Langobard was hearing things too now, and had begun knuckle-walking along the little picket line that they had established below the rim of the crater, quietly waking Roskos Yur and Beled Tomov. Kathree followed him, going to each man in turn and saying in a low voice: "Maybe two Diggers with bows and arrows, guiding a small unit of Neoanders."

"How small?" Beled asked.

"Probably not a full peloton. I will guess it is half of the group we observed landing."

"Go and notify Ty," Beled said. "Tell him to turn the light on." And since it was too dark to see anything, he put a hand on the top of her shoulder, just where it curved up toward the neck, and gave the muscle there a pleasurable squeeze. Then he flattened his palm against her shoulder and gave her a firm shove downhill.

A minute later she was down on the beach. Sonar Taxlaw was still sitting out on the islet wearing headphones. Einstein was snoring in a sleeping bag. Ty was sleeping in one of the little pop-up shelters that had been supplied by the people from *Ark Darwin,* which was still anchored offshore, detectable by the slap of waves against its hull. As for Esa Arjun, she nearly collided with him, for he was simply standing there on the beach, robed in a sleeping bag. Odds were fifty-fifty that he was silently meditating, or that he had gotten up to take a piss. Ivyns could be a little funny when their brains got the better of them. Either way—whether he was pissing or thinking—he was temporarily useless, and so she went straight to the shelter and awoke Tyuratam Lake. That took a bit longer than she had been hoping for, which frustrated her greatly since it was now so obvious to her that something was happening up above: she could hear the building whine of the body-orbiting flynk chains that Neoanders employed as both armor and weapons, but could not tell whether this was Langobard getting ready to mount a defense, or the interlopers coming down the hill. The latter she could easily hear now; they had abandoned stealth in favor of haste.

"They're coming," she said. "Two Diggers, some Neoanders."

Ty reached for his katapult, then remembered yet again that it had been taken by Ariane.

"Beled says to turn the light on."

She was expecting him to use some sort of electronic device—the sort of thing the Diggers lumped together under the heading of "radio"—but instead Ty rolled up to a seated position, bolted out of the shelter, and simply walked down the beach, hopping and cursing as his bare feet unerringly found stones. "Turn the light on!" he shouted. He cupped his hands around his mouth. "Hey! Turn the light on!" In this quiet cove, his words were loud as dynamite. Kathree heard some kind of answering shout from the direction of the barge. And from the boulder, a hissing noise. "Shh! Shh!" She thought it was waves surging against the stone until the flynk chain began to glow, illuminating Sonar Taxlaw, who had stood up and turned around to face them. She was shushing them with a finger pressed against her lips. "Shh, be quiet!" she insisted.

"Full blast!" Ty shouted. "All you got."

"They're coming!" said the Cyc. And seeing that no one else cared, she caught the eye of Arjun, who had dropped his robe on the beach like a puddle and was advancing toward her—striding directly into the surf. "We're hurting their ears."

She heard shouting up above: fighters who had dropped all pretense of stealth and were closing for combat. The timbre of their voices was that of Neoanders. Suddenly feeling a desperate need to be up there in the fray, Kathree spun on her heel, getting ready to sprint back up the slope. She nearly collided with Cantabrigia Five.

"You are going back up?"

"I feel like I have to," Kathree said.

"Godspeed. Remember. No damaged Diggers."

Cantabrigia Five pivoted away from her in a manner that made the long skirts of her warm cloak flare beautifully, and gave Kathree a last look at her regal profile, her excellent posture emphasized by close-cropped hair.

As Kathree scrambled back up she reviewed the more detailed instructions that Cantabrigia Five had given her some hours ago: *Stay clear of our buckies.* Those would be camera-carrying buckies, shooting video of whatever was about to happen. They'd be programmed to look for clear, high ground.

Kathree dropped to a low crouch perhaps fifty meters shy of Langobard. She could not see him, but she could hear the flynks careering around him as they whacked into small branches.

Above and to her right, a boulder projected from the slope. It was too hard and too steep to support anything except moss. The pale stone was prominent in the directional light of the big aitrain below. A sapling had found a perch on its top, grappling the rock with a mostly exposed root system, and reaching toward the sky with a few straggly boughs that had been sculpted by the wind from the sea. Near it she saw movement, which she identified as a bucky rolling into position atop the boulder. She could see it, so it could see her. She flattened herself behind a particularly dense knot of shrubs and grass, and used her ears, which was about all she had to go on just now.

Clink, clink. There it was. The sound, again, of those hand-forged Digger arrowheads jostling in their quiver. Drowned out by the building whine of a nearby flynk chain, reconfiguring itself under the command of its owner.

She risked looking up and saw a Neoander coming out into a place from which he had clear air to that bucky on the boulder. It wasn't Bard. It was a Red grunt in military kit. He reached out and closed his right hand on one of the chains flying around him, arresting its movement. At the same time the chain parted on the opposite side of his body and turned into a whip. It lashed out directly at the bucky on the boulder. Its shape and course were visible at first. Then it accelerated through the sound barrier and became invisible, known only by its results: a sonic bang, the complete disintegration of the bucky, and the toppling of the little sapling, cut clean through. The whip slowed as it arced back in the general direction of its owner, and, like a snake in space, reorganized itself into another flying aitrain spinning in the opposite direction from before. Having thus eliminated a robotic sentry on what to him was the left flank, the Neoander drew back toward the center of the action and disappeared from Kathree's view.

Kathree moved toward the boulder. The destruction of one of Cantabrigia Five's video buckies made it a good place for her to be. She was churning headlong toward the base of the rock, wondering how she was going to find her way to the top, when movement above caught her eye. She stopped and looked steeply upward at a Digger who had just emerged onto its crown to claim the vacated high ground. He had come down the slope so impetuously that he nearly overran the top of the boulder. He had to plant a foot just short of disaster and wheel his arms backward to regain his balance. As he did so the arrowheads clinked together in his quiver. Kathree froze and crouched, watching him regain his equilibrium. Had he looked straight down he'd have seen her, but he had eyes only for what was going on to his right: judging from sounds, the beginnings of a confused fight in a cluttered place. The Digger reached back, drew out a single shaft, and nocked it to his steel bow, looking out over the scene of the action below. He was thinking about choosing a target when Kathree's ambot hit him in the shoulder and sent him down twitching.

Shooting the man had been easy. Not in the physical sense—that would have been easy in any case, since he was standing right there, and the ambot was largely self-aiming. It had been *psychologically* easy. Days ago, when she'd been in the worst part of her shift, barely conscious, she'd overheard Ty speaking to Einstein: *Fighting isn't about knowing how. It's about deciding to.* Even in her delirium she had understood that the decision Ty spoke of wasn't an intellectual one. It was an overcoming of the emotional barrier that, in any civilized society, prevented people from doing damage to each other. She knew that because, hours earlier, she had done it. During that shocking initial combat between the Seven and the Diggers, she had stepped in to protect Ty after Ariane had shot him, and the old Digger had struck her on the arm with the Srap Tasmaner, bruising the bone, and something about that intense physical contact had pushed her through the barrier, made it easy to aim her katapult at the man and fire it. Since then, well-meaning members of the group had approached her to offer their sympathies. All they'd wanted to talk about was Doc and Memmie, and what a shock it must have been for Kath to lose them so suddenly. Implicit was that Kath had gone epi because of their deaths. A reasonable-seeming assumption. But wrong. It had happened, rather, in the moment when the old man had attacked her and she had fought back. Doc, at the time, had still been alive, and Memmie, though mortally wounded, had still been breathing. So Kath Two had actually been the first member of the Seven to die.

Anyway, she was now the sort of girl who shot people. Useful to know.

This all happened on what Blue would consider its right flank and Red would call its left. As aboriginal scouts supporting regular forces, the Diggers would stay on the wings or out in front. Which would imply that the other Digger—she was increasingly certain that there were exactly two of them—was likely to be on the opposite flank.

The boulder itself was too steep to climb, but ashy talus had spilled to either side of it, forming loose ramps. She churned up one of these and gained an altitude where she could flatten herself against the slope and peer across the battleground. It was contained within a broad, shallow sump where water finding its way down from the slopes of the coastal range was dammed up against the outer wall of the crater. It was heavily grown over, and so its boggy nature was not evident until one set foot in it. Bard, Beled, and Roskos Yur had moved aggressively forward, made a show of force, then withdrawn to let the Red force get literally bogged down. Acting in Blue's favor were difficulties in communication between, on the one hand, tightly organized, high-tech Red troops and, on the other, aboriginal scouts who only knew about wireless communications because a long line of Cycs named Proboscidea Rubber had memorized the "Radio" entry.

Anyway Kathree was now well forward of her compatriots, off to what they would call the right side of the bog. In order to reach its opposite flank she could try going straight across, but this would bring her directly into the envisioned path of the Red grunts as well as trapping her in the marsh. She could cut back toward the sea and run along the camp where they'd slept last night, but she already knew that most of the buckies were stationed there. Or she could proceed farther inland and run through the pine forest that rose above the uphill side of the bog. That would take her directly across Red's line of advance, which seemed like a bad idea on the face of it. But the Reds were just an isolated hit squad, not the vanguard of a larger force. They did not have lines of communication back to their rear. Once they had put ground behind them, they had no claim to it, no power there. Given that she could move over rough ground faster than even Beled, and given that she could hear the Neoanders a mile away, she liked her chances. So she kept moving uphill, rather than down, staying well off to the flank until she had gained a bit of altitude, then turning her attention inward.

The Red Neoanders were clearly audible. All but one of them were below her, and as she paused and waited, she heard the thudding footfalls of the straggler going by her. They were getting orders from their B, or Beta, as per racial stereotype. To her credit, the B was not hanging back and commanding from the rear; she seemed to be in the thick of things, which placed her downslope just where the going started to get marshy enough to give them second thoughts about the way they were heading. They must have noticed by now that the native scout on their left had disappeared, which might encourage them to steer toward the right. In any case, they were briefly stymied. They were all downhill of Kathree. And they were all facing the other way.

Looking directly across the slope she saw nothing but tall pine-like trees, forming a canopy that had stifled development of undergrowth. It would be easy going. A traversing run would take her rapidly to the opposite side of the field of battle, where she ought to be able to follow the other Digger's trail down to wherever he'd stationed himself and zap him with an ambot before he was able to do anything heroic and stupid.

The bang of a Neoander's flynk whip sounded from below, and she heard someone cry out and a clamor of whanging noises as ambots were projected toward targets.

Feeling suddenly very late, she began to run through the trees, moving openly now. When gaps appeared, she looked down across the bog. The vantage from here was excellent.

Which explained why she nearly collided with a lone man who had stationed himself in one of those clear places, perfectly situated to overlook the bog and the cove below. His only company was a robot: a siwi with a video camera for a head, capable of rising up out of its coils like a cobra from a basket and aiming its lens in any direction. The man was standing with his back to the fight, facing his siwi, which was shooting down the hill. Kathree was quite close to that siwi when she stumbled upon this, and so, when she first took it all in, she understood the setup exactly, just as a billion Red viewers would be doing in a few minutes: in the foreground, the man, framed in rugged rocks and trees that would fill habitat dwellers with that aching need to come down here and colonize the surface. In the near background, the bog where the fighting was under way. Beyond that, the cove nestled between the pincers of wave-beaten rock, the flynk barge with its column of light making the whole scene into day, *Ark Darwin* farther out, rocking slowly on low seas, and the sky adding some light of its own as the dawn approached.

The man wasn't expecting her. She got the impression, somehow, that he'd been rehearsing, going over his lines, clearing his throat, preparing for a performance. So she had a few moments in which to stare at him.

The three incarnations of Kath Amalthova had, in their collective lifespan, only laid eyes on live Aretaics a few times, and then only from a distance. So she had no clear measure of what counted as impressive or handsome among that race. But this one had to be one of the finer specimens. He must be over two full meters in height. His long raven hair was swept back from his forehead to make the most of a high noble brow, a strong prominent nose, large, jet-black, deep-set eyes. A few creases on his face gave him an air of sober maturity.

Five thousand years ago, aristocracy had died, along with almost everything else, and yet the idea of aristocracy—the aspirations that it, at least in an idealized form, drew out of the human psyche—lived on in everything about this man's appearance, his attire, his posture, and the way in which he gazed upon Kathree when he had recovered from his astonishment and understood what was happening. The look on his face said that this unexpected encounter was fascinating, as well as slightly amusing, the sort of twist of fortune that happened from time to time to sophisticated persons, and that, political differences notwithstanding, the two of them might one day discuss the whole affair wryly over a glass of fine red wine from Antimer. Or at least that was the case until Kathree's ambot struck him right in the middle of his forehead.

Sensing movement and hearing the discharge of her katapult, the siwi—which apparently had some rudimentary ability to follow what was interesting—swiveled in her direction, but she stomped at its neck from behind. It gave way beneath the impact of her heel and made a creditable effort to remain standing, but was forced to uncoil itself so as to effect a soft landing on the ground. From there it might have pursued her into the trees, had it been programmed for pursuit. But it was really nothing more than a moderately smart camera platform, and so it stayed where it was, doggedly trying to center the face of the Aretaic in the middle of its frame. Since the Aretaic was rolling and writhing like a man on fire, this gave its algorithms a vigorous workout.

Kathree resumed her headlong run through the trees. She bent her course back toward the sea, entering the final leg of a U-shaped career around the bog. She slowed down. If her conjecture was correct, she must be drawing close to the other Digger. And unlike Bard, Beled, and Roskos Yur, she had nothing to protect her from those steel-headed arrows.

She heard a creaking noise from uphill—behind her. She turned around to see a redheaded, blue-eyed Digger, no more than five meters away, holding an arrow at full draw, aimed right at her. The freshly sharpened edges of its hand-forged steel warhead made bright arcs as they reflected the light from the cove. She had holstered her katapult to leave both hands free for scrambling. She had nothing.

Cantabrigia Five hadn't exactly commanded her to incapacitate both of the Digger scouts. Just to prevent them from doing harm, and to prevent their dead bodies from showing up on video screens around the ring.

"You're making a terrible mistake," she said.

The Digger didn't move, but he did blink slowly. She took it as assent to keep talking. "Those people—the Reds—are only pretending to be your friends so that they can piggyback on your claim to the surface. They want to take it all for themselves."

"And you?" he asked.

"Blue is no better, in some ways."

"Then why should we heed your counsel?"

"You should heed no one's counsel blindly. Neither mine—nor his." She made a little movement of the head toward the Aretaic.

Silence as he considered it.

"Do you know Ceylon Congreve?" she asked.

"Of course."

"Has Ceylon Congreve spoken to you of chess?"

"We do not need a Cyc to tell us of chess," the Digger said. "We play it all the time."

"Then you know that pawns are weak—except for when their position on the board gives them power. Early in the game they are sacrificed freely. Late in the game they may checkmate the king."

She was interrupted by another whipcrack from below, followed by two more in rapid succession. She fought the temptation to turn around and look. The Digger's blue eyes strayed toward the battlefield, took something in, then returned to her. At no time did the arrowhead waver.

Kathree continued: "*You are pawns.* You can't begin to imagine how small and weak you are compared to the forces above. If you allow yourself to be played as such by Red, you will be sacrificed as soon as it suits their purposes. If you play a longer game, though, you can yet grow powerful. As powerful as the other human races."

With a suddenness that made Kathree flinch, the Digger raised his weapon and relaxed the arm that had been drawing the arrow back. He plucked the nock off the string and placed the arrow back in his quiver.

"I take your words with a grain of salt," he said.

"Good."

"But some of what you say confirms suspicions that I have harbored in my breast since the coming of the Red people, and so I have made up my mind to go back and speak to the others of these matters." And then he simply turned his back on Kathree and began hiking back up into the mountains of Beringia.

"I KNOW YOUR STORY, TYURATAM LAKE," SAID CANTABRIGIA FIVE, "OR at least the portions of it that have made their way into official records."

"Half of it, then."

"Be that as it may, I sense how distracting this must be for you." She made the tiniest suggestion of a glance up the slope. Even though her eyes were screened by the lenses of a stylish varp, their golden hue magnified the gesture. "Part of you wishes to join the battle. That's commendable, but I need you—the Purpose needs you—here."

"Fine. You have my attention," Ty said. Inappropriately, irrelevantly, he was wondering how old this woman was. Epigenetic shifts could roll back many of the visible effects of aging. At least one Moiran, Jamaica Hammerhead Twelve, had lived to the age of two hundred. Ty's estimate of Cantabrigia Five's age increased by a decade every time he interacted with her. Currently he was thinking that she might be eighty years old.

"What do you know of the Pingers?" she asked.

"In all honesty, they sound more myth than fact."

"Myth carries more weight anyway, in times like these."

"What do *you* know of them?" Ty demanded.

For once, Cantabrigia Five seemed a little off balance. She looked at him sharply, lifted her varp, rested it on the top of her head.

"I need to know," Ty said, "whether they came out of some Red gene lab."

"Red doesn't even know they exist," said Cantabrigia Five.

"Did we make them?"

"Blue? No, your hypothesis was correct, Ty."

"And how would you know what my hypothesis was?"

Her eyes strayed to the pizza box, which was leaning against a boulder that protruded from the beach. "I know what is in there."

"Thank you," Ty said. He turned away from her and began striding in the direction of a tall young Ivyn, standing on the beach and gazing up nervously toward the sounds of battle. "Einstein! Eyes on me. Time for you to make history."

CRACKING A WHIP MADE OF SMALL ROBOTS JOINED END TO END into a long, flexible chain was neither an especially bad nor an especially good way of engaging a foe in ambot-based combat. Extensive studies conducted within Blue military research labs had concluded that, on average, it was somewhat less effective than the more obvious procedure of just shooting individual ambots out of katapults. A dissenting opinion held that such studies were flawed because they failed to take into account two factors that were important in actual battle: One, the psychological impact on a defender who knew that the attack might literally whip around and come at him from any direction, including around corners or over barricades. Two, the element of skill, which was difficult to measure scientifically; the test subjects wielding those things in the lab were unlikely to have the same knack for it as Neoanders who had grown up using them and who had access to an ancient body of lore—a martial art, in effect—that they were disinclined to share with anyone else. If the whip was allowed to dissociate in midcrack, then its component ambots would be flung toward the target at supersonic velocity, which was as good as could be achieved by shooting the same objects out of a katapult. If it made contact with the target, direct physical damage would be inflicted *and* the ambots that had inflicted it could decouple themselves and carry out their usual programs. And if the whipcrack was off target, the chain could be recovered in full with no waste of ammunition. All the ambots came back for another attempt: something that certainly could not be said of ones that had been fired out of kats.

On Kathree's list, if they ever got out of this, was to sit down over a glass of pinot noir with Langobard and ask him where he had picked up his skills in this department, since, until recently, he had been sustaining a fairly credible cover story about being a peaceful wine merchant in Cradle. She already suspected that he would deflect any such questions by saying that the Antimer Neoanders, like many cultures throughout human history, had a tradition of teaching martial arts to their young ones.

A skeptic might remark that fighting with whips made of little robots might be all well and good in the clean and well-ordered confines of a space habitat or a hollowed-out asteroid, or when dueling in space suits in a vacuum, or in relatively uncluttered places, such as deserts and icecaps on the surface. But in a bog full of dense, head-high vegetation it was simply a mistake. Kathree's ears were taking in vast amounts of data that her brain didn't know what to do with. Someone who had grown up practicing these arts, as Langobard apparently had, might have been able to hear nuances in these repetitive bangs. A crack that landed on its target would sound different from one that dissociated into a burst of flying ambots, which in turn would sound different from one that had whipped back toward the attacker or gotten fouled up in vegetation. Instead of which, all she could tell was that they were fighting down there. By the time she had completed her circuit of the bog and returned to their original line of defense above the cove, they had been fighting for rather a long time, which she interpreted as good news. She was trying to think like Cantabrigia Five, who probably wouldn't worry so much about trivial matters like casualties and the control of the battlefield. More important was the narrative of the battle. And so far what it looked like was that a small Blue group, conducting Treaty-approved survey operations on their side of the Treaty-defined boundary, had been pursued by bloodthirsty Red Neoanders until trapped against the ocean, where they were now putting up a heroic and surprisingly prolonged last-ditch stand to protect a few noncombatants. Kathree didn't wish to be this cynical, for Cantabrigia Five really was a fantastically appealing and charismatic person, but she suspected, at some level, that a Blue fatality or two, up in the bog, and perhaps an on-camera interview with a maimed and bereaved survivor, might be the perfect counter for the propaganda coup that the Aretaics had scored a few days ago.

Thoughts such as those were luxuries she did not afford herself until she had reached a position above the cove, well behind the battle zone. And—no coincidence—also behind the line of camera-carrying buckies recording the heroic rearguard action.

She looked down at the lower camp. A sunrise, in weather like this, was too much to ask for, but the sky was getting brighter all the time, and was now illuminating the beach more effectively than the towering Aitken loop on the barge. Perhaps in response to the sounds of battle, half a dozen or so inflatable boats had emerged from the flooded hull of *Ark Darwin* and begun making their way in, each carrying a few people who appeared to be wearing helmets. Good. But, annoyingly to Kathree, they were maintaining some distance. Sonar Taxlaw was standing on the boulder waving them off. She'd been joined by Einstein, who was doing likewise. That was about to become an intolerably crowded boulder, because Tyuratam Lake was wading out to join them with that pizza box under one arm. He had managed to equip himself with a dry suit, which probably made the experience a good deal more comfortable for him.

Cantabrigia Five and Arjun were on the shore, facing out to sea, as if there were not a pitched battle going on a few hundred meters above them.

Two of the buckies dislodged themselves from their positions above Kathree and began rolling down the slope like wire-frame boulders. At first this seemed uncontrolled, like an avalanche, but then they began to stretch and deform in a way that accommodated the rocky ground rushing beneath them, and slowed to a mincing style of descent. One of them perched on a spot where it could get a clear view of the entire cove and the other picked its way down to the sand, angling for close-ups, apparently. Cantabrigia Five turned toward it and advanced a few steps. Facing squarely into its camera, she began speaking words that Kathree had no hope of hearing at this distance.

Kathree saw all of this while leaning back against the steep pitch of the inner crater wall. Just above her was a line of vegetation that had taken root along its brow, where the ground was level and the sunlight was as plentiful as it would ever get in these parts. It spread for some tens of meters to her left and to her right, walling off the cove from the bog and the high country above.

Some loud grunting noises, and the sound of a lot of little sticks getting damaged, caused her to look sharply to her left just in time to see two large men, locked together, erupt through the wall of brush and tumble out into the open. Since the slope below was steep, they rolled together for several meters down toward the beach before the larger one—Beled—was able to lash out with one foot and plant it downslope, bringing both of them to a stop. At the same time he pushed up with both arms, shoving his opponent—a Neoander—completely off the ground, in a bid to flip him backward and send him tumbling down even farther. But the Neoander seemed to anticipate this and made his much longer arms whip around Beled's torso, scrabbling for purchase on his rib cage.

Perhaps 50 percent of Beled's body was still covered by ambots locked together to form a patchy carapace. The Neoander's right hand came down on a cluster of them that was protecting Beled's armpit, and those obliged their owner by delivering a clearly audible shock into the offending hand. This disrupted whatever grapple the Neoander had been attempting. Still, Beled's gambit had basically failed, and he ended up toppling backward as his opponent's momentum overthrew him. When he understood this he stopped fighting it and bent his knees, turning what might have been an ungainly sprawl into something more like a back somersault that employed the Neoander's stomach as an impact cushion. Kathree heard a snapping noise but was a little slow to understand it as a rib being broken. The Neoander, on his back, involuntarily tried to contract into a fetal position, bringing his head up into Beled's descending fist. The contact between the delicate structures of the modern hand and the massive bone arches of the Neanderthal skull was unequal and there was more cracking, to Beled's disadvantage. Still, the blow gave the Neoander a jolt, which was enough time for Beled finally to draw a knife from a sheath and press it against the other's throat. He kept pressing until the Neoander's head was against the ground.

The fighting—at least that part of it—was over and Kathree was able for the first time to process a full image of Beled's state: bloody, half-naked, spitting teeth, breathing much faster than he ever did when sprinting flat out on a treadmill. Anyway he was alive, and the fight was over for him, unless he chose to neutralize this opponent by cutting his throat. Which seemed inadvisable since he was now under the direct coverage of a bucky with a camera in it. The ancient Teklan-Neoander fights of asteroid mining lore might have ended with throat cutting, but not this one.

Other things happened in the bog that she did not see. Langobard emerged with Roskos Yur slung over his back in a fireman's carry, and began tromping down the slope in some haste, not looking back. Beled, watching, called out a warning to him. In the same instant Kath heard movement from the bog and saw a human silhouette—not a Neoander—vault through the gap that had been torn in it by Beled and his opponent, and begin running after Bard. She was a squat woman with close-cropped hair, in military kit—a classic B. Kathree aimed her katapult at her and fired an ambot, then two more, but all of them somehow missed—the B was evidently wearing some kind of armor that was good at spoofing this particular model, and so she could stand there all day shooting at her and nothing would happen. Still, the B heard the katapult go *whang* and sensed the ambots zipping around her, which was enough to stall her for a moment. She turned toward Kathree. The look on her face suggested that she had not expected to see a female Moiran. As she was taking in this extraordinary spectacle, a fist-sized rock struck her on the downhill side of her head and, to all appearances, killed her.

Kathree looked down the slope to see Beled following through from having thrown the rock. He had transferred his unbloodied knife to his broken hand, and now shifted it back. Nearby was Bard, who had paused in his headlong sprint toward the beach and turned around to see what Beled was throwing rocks at. Blood seemed to be draining out of him.

On second thought, it was draining out of Sergeant Major Yur.

The Neoander that Beled had been restraining rolled up to his feet. Just as rapidly he went down again, and a katapult *whang* traveled up to Kathree's ears. When Langobard turned around, she saw that Roskos Yur, badly mauled but still conscious, had brought his weapon into play with his free hand.

If there were other Red forces to be accounted for, they were either dead, unconscious, or in retreat toward the mountains.

For the first time in what seemed like a while—but had probably been just a few seconds of elapsed time—Kathree directed her attention to what was going on below.

The rubber boats from the ark had made a decision to avoid the middle of the cove. Instead they were splitting to either side to make landfall on the prongs formed by the crater's rim. From there, they could hike around if need be.

A person was walking out of the water.

TY HANDED THE PIZZA BOX UP TO EINSTEIN AND TOLD HIM TO OPEN it and to keep what was inside of it dry and near to hand. The dry suit was doing a fine job of keeping his legs warm and so he decided to remain below, thigh deep in the water next to the islet. His time in the war had left him with distrust, bordering on disgust, with people like Cantabrigia Five who were always thinking about the narrative. But that way of thinking was infectious. He saw the little scene on the islet through the eyes not of Tyuratam Lake, but of a video camera beaming coverage to the ring. And he thought it looked perfect the way it was: the small conical spike of glass, grubby around the waterline with wave-washed sand, supporting two people: Einstein with the pizza box, and, standing next to him with a finger hooked through his belt loop, the Cyc with one headphone on and the other off. In fact he attended so closely to the image that he almost missed the main event. The look on the others' faces told him he had best turn around and look out to sea.

Only the head and shoulders were protruding above the waves. The Pinger was trudging up the sloping floor of the crater as if returning from a casual underwater stroll. He or she breathed loudly and deeply for a little while, apparently reoxygenating, but then settled down to a more normal respiration. Where did they live? Where had this person come from? They must have diving bells, or something, that moved about underwater.

The Pinger was hairless and sleek, and, as soon became evident, lacked external genitalia. So, a woman? But if so it was a woman without breasts; and as far as Ty knew, these were still mammals.

A few paces behind was a roundish object that presently turned out to be supported by a neck, which turned out to be anchored in a sloping pair of shoulders. This one did have breasts. And behind her was yet a third person of the same general description.

As the first one ascended into shallower water, the shape of his body became clearer: round, and, in general, sort of projectile-like. Some part of Ty's brain wanted to identify him as a fat man. And maybe he was fat, in the same way that an otter or a seal is: a thick layer of subcutaneous fat held in beneath taut, rather thick-looking skin. But in no way did he seem flabby or jiggly. His overall style of movement suggested heavy musculature hidden beneath that smooth jacket of, for lack of a better word, blubber. Basically naked, he did have a kind of web harness strapped around his torso, with a sufficient number of odds and ends attached to it to make it clear that he was a technological being. At first the Pingers had seemed black, but as they came out of the water it became clear that their skin was dark gray, and mottled with patches of lighter gray, shading toward blues and greens. Their bellies were of lighter hue than their backs, and the mottling tended to run up their sides.

Ty didn't like to stare. But he couldn't help it. Nothing was visible between their legs save a system of concentric folds within which, Ty assumed, a fairly normal set of genitalia must be hiding. Perhaps just awaiting a suitable invitation to present themselves.

They were drawing close enough now that their faces could be looked at. The underlying skulls probably looked the same as those of rootstock humans. But eyes, ears, and nostrils were guarded by systems of muscled flaps that were always in some amount of motion. Sonar Taxlaw's earlier remark about breeding wolves into poodles had been a bit indelicate. But the analogy held up. These people were to more ordinary humans as bulldogs were to hounds. All the same stuff was there. You just had to look for it a little harder.

Ty turned back to look at Einstein and Sonar. Understandably, they had eyes only for the approaching Pingers. "Einstein," he said. Then, louder: "Einstein!"

Startled, Einstein nearly fell into the water, then focused on Ty.

"Do you want it?" he mouthed, nodding at the rectangle gripped in his hands.

"No," Ty said, "it has to be a child of Ivy."

"Now?"

"Now."

Einstein gripped the thing's bottom corners in his hands and held it up above his head so that the approaching visitors could get a clear view of it.

It was a picture, blown up to about half a meter square. Any Spacer would recognize it as an iconic image from the Epic. It was the last photograph that Ivy's fiancé, Cal Blankenship, had texted to her from the conning tower of his submarine, moments before closing the hatch and diving to escape from the opening salvo of the Hard Rain. The image was dominated by two concentric circles: in the middle distance, the aperture of the open hatch, framing a disk of sky already split in two by the fiery trace of a bolide. Surrounding that, much closer to the camera, the engagement ring that he had just removed from his finger.

The question was whether Cal's descendants would recognize it. The lead Pinger's face unfolded a little, his gray eyes seeming to become larger, his ears blooming from mere slits into something more resembling normal human ears, except smaller and sleeker. He stopped trudging in knee-deep water. The other two drew abreast of him. All three were gazing up at the picture held aloft by the shivering Ivyn. Ty's ears were tickled by high-pitched vocalizations that were almost recognizable as English words. The Pingers were talking to one another, turning their heads to exchange remarks, pointing at the picture, gesticulating broadly. Of course, people who spent a lot of time underwater would become good at talking with their hands.

The female Pinger said something emphatic, getting the attention of the other two. Ty couldn't understand the words, but the tone and the body language were emphatic: "Shut up. Listen. I know what this is."

She held her left hand in front of her body. The palm was elongated. The fingers were stubby and, when she spread them apart, slightly webbed. With her right hand she enclosed the ring finger of the left and pantomimed sliding a ring off. She held the imaginary ring aloft, then brought her left hand up to her face and twitched her index finger once, pretending to take a picture.

KATHREE FELT HERSELF, AS SHE WATCHED ALL OF THIS, SLIDING down the slope on her ass in a semicontrolled manner, almost afraid that she might scare the Pingers away with a sudden movement. Bard had reached the lower camp quicker and laid Sergeant Major Yur out on a sleeping bag, where Hope was attending to him, already hooking up an intravenous tube. Kathree passed by Beled, who was straddling the helpless Red Neoander, putting huge plastic ties on his ankles and wrists.

She made it down to the beach, keeping well clear of Cantabrigia Five, who was speaking into a camera, and Arjun, who was just watching and mumbling into his varp.

Several more Pingers had waded up into the shallows. One of them—a male, strapped with more gear than the others—had approached Ty, and seemed to be trying to communicate with him. Ty was grinning, but he kept cupping a hand around his ear and shaking his head. The Pinger reached out, gently took Ty's wrist, and plucked at the black stuff of his dry suit. Ty responded by mimicking the same gesture on the slick skin of the Pinger's arm. Both of them laughed. The Pinger's teeth were white and they were sharp.

The first three Pingers had come ashore on the islet and were inspecting the photograph, which Einstein was holding now in front of his chest, part invitation and part shield. Sonar Taxlaw, not so encumbered, faced off uncertainly against the female Pinger, who suddenly stepped forward and embraced her.

On the beach, Cantabrigia Five exchanged a satisfied look with Esa Arjun and glanced toward the sky.

Epilogue

"CAL SENT MORE THAN ONE PHOTO TO EVE IVY DURING THE WEEKS leading up to the Hard Rain," said Esa Arjun. "A total of seventeen, including that one." He nodded at the picture. Somewhat the worse for wear, it was leaning against the inner wall of *Ark Darwin*'s fuselage at the end of the table where he and Ty were eating lunch.

He and Ty and Deep. Deep was the Pinger who had approached Ty and befriended him with a nonverbal joke about his dry suit. He was seated a couple of chairs away at the same table. It wasn't really clear whether he thought of himself as part of this conversation.

"Can he understand what I'm saying?" Arjun asked.

"He's getting better. We sound like tuba music to them."

"Is his name really what you say it is?"

"It's the closest I can get to pronouncing it," Ty said, "and he answers to it."

Deep had been tearing into a raw fish filet, served on a platter with some seaweed garnishes. He seemed then to realize that he was being talked about, and tensed up in a way that seemed very human. At a loss for words, he grabbed his cup of cider and raised it to them. They raised theirs in return, and all drank.

"I think he's some kind of technician or scientist," Ty said. "All that stuff in his harness."

"Yes," Arjun said, eyeing the Pinger curiously. "Optics. Electronics. They preserved more technology than the Diggers were able to."

"They had more space," Ty pointed out, "and they could scavenge whatever sank to the bottom." He turned his attention back to Arjun. "Anyway, you were saying about the seventeen photos?"

"Yes. Most of them were of a type referred to, in those days, as selfies. Now, technically, this was a criminal violation of military secrecy. Very strange given that Cal was otherwise so attentive to duty."

"Yes," said Ty, casting his mind back to scenes from the Epic. "I remember Eve Ivy agonizing about that when Eve Julia ordered Cal to nuke Venezuela."

"That's a perfect example. So, this lapse—if that's what it was—has attracted some attention from scholars. All seventeen of the photos were eventually recovered from Ivy's phone. An obscure sub-sub-sub-discipline of historical scholarship grew up around them."

"The kind of thing only Ivyns would care about," said Ty.

"Cloistered in some library on Stromness. Exactly."

Ark Darwin was still riding at anchor outside the cove, and its fuselage was still flooded. This made it a perfect setting for what was happening now: a diplomatic conference between the Pingers and a delegation of important Blue officials who had been pod-dropped, straight from Greenwich, a few hours after the conclusion of the battle above the beach.

Einstein, Sonar Taxlaw, and all the other Blues had evacuated the cove and gone aboard the ark. Beled had been the last to depart; before climbing into the waiting boat, he had freed the captured Neoander and left him enough provisions to keep him in good stead until he could be rescued by his own people. And his own people had shown up in force a few hours later. But according to the deal they themselves had struck with the Diggers, their claim was to the land surface only. And *Ark Darwin* wasn't on the land. So, a growing Red military encampment was spreading around the shore of the cove, facing their Blue counterparts across a few hundred meters of salt water.

The ark's flooded hull was chilly, and obliged the Blue diplomats to dress warmly. Ty, Deep, and Arjun were in a dry space higher up and farther forward, a sort of half-exposed mezzanine where folding tables and chairs had been set up to act as a mess hall for the growing complement of Blue personnel—as well as any Pingers who felt like wading up the ramp. They were eating hot soup and quaffing a funky but quite palatable cider from the northern slope of Antimer.

"Now," said Arjun—enjoying, as only an Ivyn could, the opportunity to wax professorial—"what you must be wondering about these people is—"

"How the hell they survived. With only one submarine."

Arjun nodded. "It turns out that if you look at the work of those scholars I mentioned—the most recent of whom died two centuries ago—there are clues."

"But if the selfies were taken before the Hard Rain even began," Ty protested, "how could there be clues as to what happened after?"

"I mean clues that Cal went out of his way to plant in the background of the photos. Clues intended for Ivy's eyes only. Hints that he had more of a chance than one might imagine."

"Go on." Ty sat back and reached for his cup of cider.

"*We* know all about the Cloud Ark program, because it's where *we* came from. It is our history. We have all of the records in our archives. Well, what Cal was hinting at, with these photos, is that there was another program, perhaps as large, that we never heard about."

"A program to keep people alive under the sea?" Ty asked.

"Exactly. There are, in the background of these photos, detailed bathymetric charts of some of the deepest undersea canyons in the world's oceans. There are documents—binders on a shelf—whose titles suggest that they are about such preparations. Other clues as well—it's all public research, I'll send you the information if you want it."

"Okay," Ty said, just to be cordial. He knew that he would never read those research papers. "But the bottom line is that Deep's people"—he nodded at their tablemate—"didn't survive just because Cal got lucky."

"They have an Epic of their own that, for all we know, might compare to ours," Arjun said.

Sonar and Einstein had been making their way down the food service line and now approached, eyeing the two vacant seats at the table. Arjun took this as his cue to excuse himself. Deep said goodbye to him with a courteous bob of the head. Within moments Ty and his Pinger friend had been joined by the young Ivyn and the Cyc. For a minute or two, the new arrivals did nothing but eat ravenously, the only conversation being Sonar asking the names and origins of the various foods—all new to her—on her tray. Ty handled those inquiries so that Einstein could be left free to stuff his face. After a while this became a source of amusement even to Sonar Taxlaw, who just watched the boy eat, and transferred some of her food to his tray when he began to run low.

"Sometime, you'll have to tell me what it's like," Ty remarked.

"What—" Einstein began, before food got in the way.

"—what's like?" Sonar said, completing his sentence.

"Finding someone so completely. The way you two did."

"That's never happened to you?" Einstein asked. He wasn't being rude. It had simply never occurred to him that he could have had experiences of which Tyuratam Lake knew nothing.

"No. It's never happened to me."

Einstein had begun to approach the point of satiation. He sat back in his chair and cast his gaze over the wreckage of his lunch, looking for any morsels that deserved more attention.

"I have a question for you," he said.

"Fancy that," Ty returned.

"What's the Purpose? People keep mentioning it."

"I wish I knew."

"Very funny, but you know what I'm talking about. Roskos Yur mentioned it. Cantabrigia Five mentioned it. Purpose with a capital P."

"My answer remains the same," Ty said. "No one has ever told me. I have to make guesses, based on what I see from people who act like they know what it is."

"People like the owners of your bar?"

"Evidently."

"And what is your guess?"

Sensing another pair of eyes on him, Ty glanced over toward Deep, who was chewing vigorously, trying to reduce a stubborn wad of seaweed to submission. But he seemed to be following the conversation.

Ty shrugged. "Humans have always—"

He was about to say *deluded themselves* but didn't want to make a poor impression on Deep.

"—preferred to believe that there was a purpose to the universe. Until the moon blew up, they had theories. After Zero, the theories all seemed kind of stupid. Fairy tales for coddled children. No one thought about the big picture for a few thousand years. We were all scrambling to survive. Like ants when their nest has been destroyed. On those rare occasions when we thought about the big picture, it wasn't really that big—Red versus Blue or what have you. There was surprisingly little thinking about the Agent. Where it came from. Whether it was natural or artificial, or even divine."

Einstein, the Cyc, and Deep were all nodding as if to say *Go on, go on!*

But he had nothing to go on with.

"Some people—some Red, some Blue, and some ambiguous folks like the Owners of my bar—maybe even some of those kind of people"—he nodded at Deep—"seem to think they know something."

"Do they?" asked Sonar Taxlaw.

"I have no idea," said Ty. "But from what I've seen, they're not stupid. Even if they are—"

He paused, groping for words.

"Even if they are," Einstein repeated, *"what?!"*

"It's a way—the Purpose is a way—of saying there's something bigger than this crap we've spent the last week of our lives dealing with."

"Red versus Blue crap?"

"Yes. And even though no one is sharing anything with me—*yet*—I like the feeling of that. People who claim they are motivated by the Purpose end up behaving differently—and generally better—than people who serve other masters."

"So it is like believing in God."

"Maybe yes. But without the theology, the scripture, the pigheaded certainty."

Einstein and the Cyc nodded and looked thoughtful. But also, or so it seemed to Ty, a little let down.

"Sorry I didn't have an answer to your question," Ty said.

"What are you going to do next? Now that your Seven is disbanded?" asked Sonar.

"Go back to my bar."

"On Cradle?"

"On Cradle. Once, an astonishing wonder of technological prowess. Now a quaint, outmoded precursor to the vastly superior Gnomon."

"I'd like to see it," Sonar said.

"We have rooms. Apartments where people can stay, around the courtyard in the back."

"They must be expensive."

"They are free," Ty said.

"How do you get one of those free rooms?" Einstein asked.

"Beats me. The Owners hand them out to people who serve the Purpose."

"Very important people, then."

Ty shrugged. "They can't kill you for asking. You're right about the Seven. That's gone. Our Ivyn died. You took his place."

Einstein cackled nervously. "I'm no replacement for Doc!"

"You don't have to replace him. Not in that sense. But look what you did. You made first contact with these guys." He nodded at Deep. "And first contact of another kind with the Diggers."

Both Einstein and Sonar Taxlaw blushed deeply.

"The Cyc came along and replaced Memmie. That's not a traditional Seven. But if we can pry Beled and Kathree apart, and if we can round up a Julian and a Camite who don't hate each other, we'll have ourselves a Nine. The first Nine ever assembled."

Ty was just running his mouth, letting the cider talk. Sonar, however, was taking it all seriously. "But only one of the Aïdan subraces will be represented," she pointed out.

"Bard is plenty."

"You should include the other four," Einstein said.

"That makes thirteen. An unlucky number. And a bit of a crowd, frankly." But the youngsters across the table from him were looking heartrendingly sincere. Ty broke eye contact. "I'll bet I could talk the Owners out of a few free rooms, for such a momentous occasion."

"Are you really going to ask them?!" Sonar exclaimed.

"Nah. As an ancient saying has it, it's easier to ask forgiveness than permission. You are all welcome at the Crow's Nest." Ty looked over at Deep. "Just go easy on the cold baths, man. The plumbing in that place has seen better days, and I'm the only one who knows how to fix it."

Acknowledgments

THE PREMISE OF THIS BOOK CAME TO ME CIRCA 2006, WHEN I WAS working part-time at Blue Origin and became interested in the problem of space debris in low Earth orbit. Researchers in that field had raised concerns over the possibility of a chain reaction smash-up that might create so many fragments of orbiting shrapnel as to render space flight practically impossible. My studies in that area turned out to be of little direct relevance to the company, but the novelist in me scented an idea for a book. During the same period I had also become aware of the immense amount of usable matter present in near-Earth asteroids. Thus by late 2006 I had come up with the basic premise of *Seveneves*. So the first acknowledgment goes to Blue Origin, which was founded circa 2000 by Jeff Bezos under the name Blue Operations LLC and where I had many interesting early conversations with him and other people involved with the company, including Jaime Taaffe, Maria Kaldis, Danny Hillis, George Dyson, and Keith Rosema. It was from Keith that I first heard the idea for the multilayered emergency shelter bubble that appears in this book under the name of Luk. Some of the Baikonur material is very freely adapted from the reminiscences and photographs of George Dyson, Esther Dyson, and Charles Simonyi.

Hugh and Heather Matheson provided background on mining—the industry, the culture, and the lifestyle—which helped me in creating Dinah. If I have stretched truths in my treatment of the MacQuaries' mine in Alaska and their use of ham radio, it is my fault and not theirs. For the record, Hugh recommended that Rufus's operation be situated in the Homestake Mine near Lead, South Dakota, or in the Coeur d'Alene Mining District, Idaho, but I put it in Alaska anyway, to get it farther from the equatorial zone.

Chris Lewicki and the staff of Planetary Resources supplied valuable suggestions during an informal visit that I made to their offices in November 2013. Numerous members of their engineering staff were more than generous with their time on that occasion. (Later Chris mentioned to me that he and other members of the company had been pleasantly surprised to learn that someone was producing science fiction in which the asteroid mining company was, for once, the good guys.)

Marco Kaltofen helped me flesh out the technical details of *Ymir*'s "steampunk" propulsion system and read over the relevant sections of the first draft with a careful eye. Seamus Blackley also supplied useful input during this phase. Having invoked those people's good names, I'll reiterate that if I've taken liberties—accidentally or on purpose—with scientific fact, it should be blamed on me and not on them.

Tola Marts and Tim Lloyd helped sketch out and visualize some of the details of the space hardware described in the book, a project that is still ongoing. Readers may be comforted to know that, thanks to Tola, various aspects of the Eye and the associated tether systems have been designed with appropriate engineering safety factors.

Kris Pister's work on small swarming robots, which I have been following on and off for several years, was formative in the discussion of Nats.

Karen Laur and Aaron Leiby contributed time and effort to envisioning a game based on TerReForm, and though those efforts were stymied by the usual difficulties in obtaining capital, they did help sharpen my thinking about various aspects of the story. As part of a different prospective game project, Tim Miller of Blur Studio, with input from Jascha Little, Zoe Stephenson, Russel Howe, and Jo Balme, came up with ideas and concept art (produced by Chuck Wojtkiewicz, Sean McNally, Tom Zhao, and Joshua Shaw of Blur) for a number of different robots. Ed Allard devoted many hours of his time to prototyping the same game. Again, this work hasn't led to an actual game yet, but it had the side effect of helping me put flesh on the bones of the story. Thanks also to James Gwertzman for introducing me to Ed and for his advice and feedback on this front.

Ben Hawker of Weta Workshop read the manuscript and pointed out that Cradle would be rusty, a detail that had somehow escaped me; hasty last-minute alterations ensued.

Stewart Brand and Ryan Phelan, by dint of their connection with the Long Now Foundation's Revive and Restore Initiative, had much useful background to supply on the genetic challenges associated with reviving species from small breeding populations.

While the first two parts of the story are a tale of straight-up global disaster and hastily improvised technology, I always viewed the third part of it as an opportunity to showcase many of the more positive ideas that have emerged, over the last century, from the global community of people interested in space exploration. Many of the big hardware ideas in the latter part of the book have been kicking around in the literature for decades and will be recognized as old friends by longtime readers of hard science fiction.

Particular recognition and thanks are owed to Rob Hoyt of Tethers Unlimited. Following in the footsteps of the late Robert L. Forward, Rob has worked on a number of ideas in the realm of "big space machines." One of these is the Hoytether, a hugely scaled-up version of which has found its way into this book as the basic design scheme of the tether connecting the Eye to Cradle. Another is the Remora Remover, which, in principle, is the same device as the Lamprey. Rob is also coauthor of a 2000 study on high-altitude rotating tethers, based on early work by Forward and others, that serves as the basis for the glider-to-orbit transfer described in the opening pages of the third part of this book. He deserves credit for all of those contributions as well as thanks for having given the manuscript a close read.

The first phase of Kath Two's journey, from ground to hanger, is inspired by conversations that I have had with Chris Young and Kevin Finke about current trends in the technology of gliders. It is from talking to them, flying with them, and following leads provided by them that I came to understand the fact that the atmosphere contains all the energy we need to fly, and that the only thing preventing us from implementing something like Kath Two's glider is commitment of resources to development of sensors and software—perhaps combined with a few improvements in the treatment of motion sickness.

Arthur Champernowne read an early draft and raised questions about the dynamic stability of the Eye-Cradle tether, which I have, with due respect, elected to ignore completely—but technically sophisticated readers might like to know that it would exhibit all manner of interesting wiggles whose management I have decided to postpone for later work. In the version that Arthur read, the flivver carrying Kath Two made its final insertion to geosynchronous orbit using a plain old-fashioned rocket burn. Arthur objected to that, not on technical but on aesthetic grounds. This finally pushed me over the brink into using an idea I had been carrying around in the back of my head for a while: having the flivver rendezvous with the end of a cracking whip. The scientific literature on this topic, though sparse, dates back to the Victorian era. The earliest technical reference that I have been able to find on the physics of moving chains is a paper by John Aitken during the 1870s, though he attributes some of its content to his friends the Thomson brothers, William (later Lord Kelvin) and James. Aitken's work lay fallow until the 1920s, when it was picked up and used by M. Z. Carriére in a paper about the physics of whips. Subsequent work published by W. Kucharski (1940) and R. Grammel and K. Zoller (1949) filled out the picture. It is an interesting, underexplored topic in classical physics. I talked about it in a sparsely attended lecture at the Oxford Union in June of 2014, and have intentions of publishing more about it, but nothing definite as of this writing (December 2014).

Finally, I would like to express gratitude to my agents, Liz Darhansoff of Darhansoff & Verrill and Richard Green of ICM Partners, and my editor, Jen Brehl, for displaying adaptability as I devoted seven years to trying to figure out just what exactly I wanted to do with this idea.

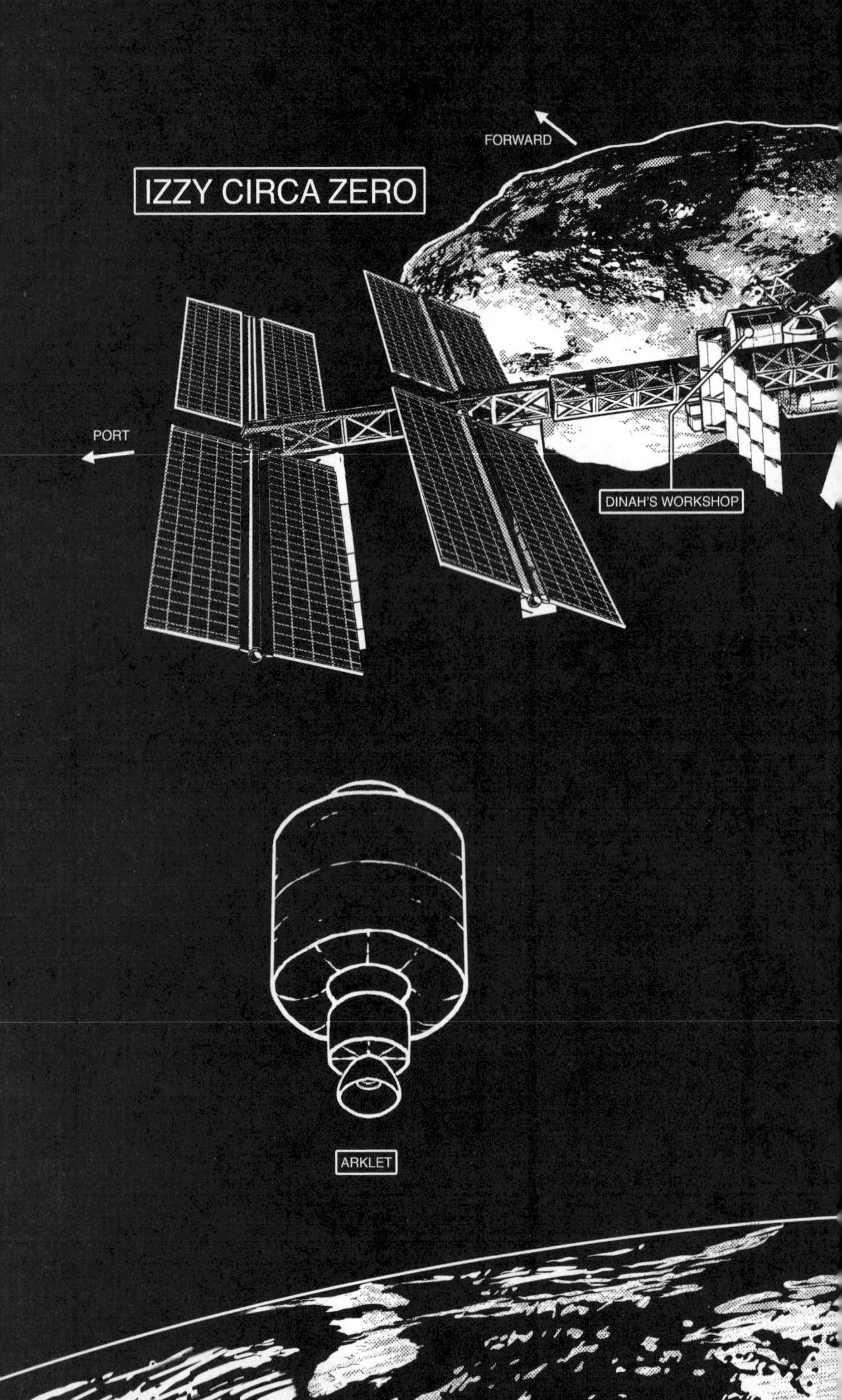

IZZY CIRCA ZERO
FORWARD
PORT
DINAH'S WORKSHOP
ARKLET

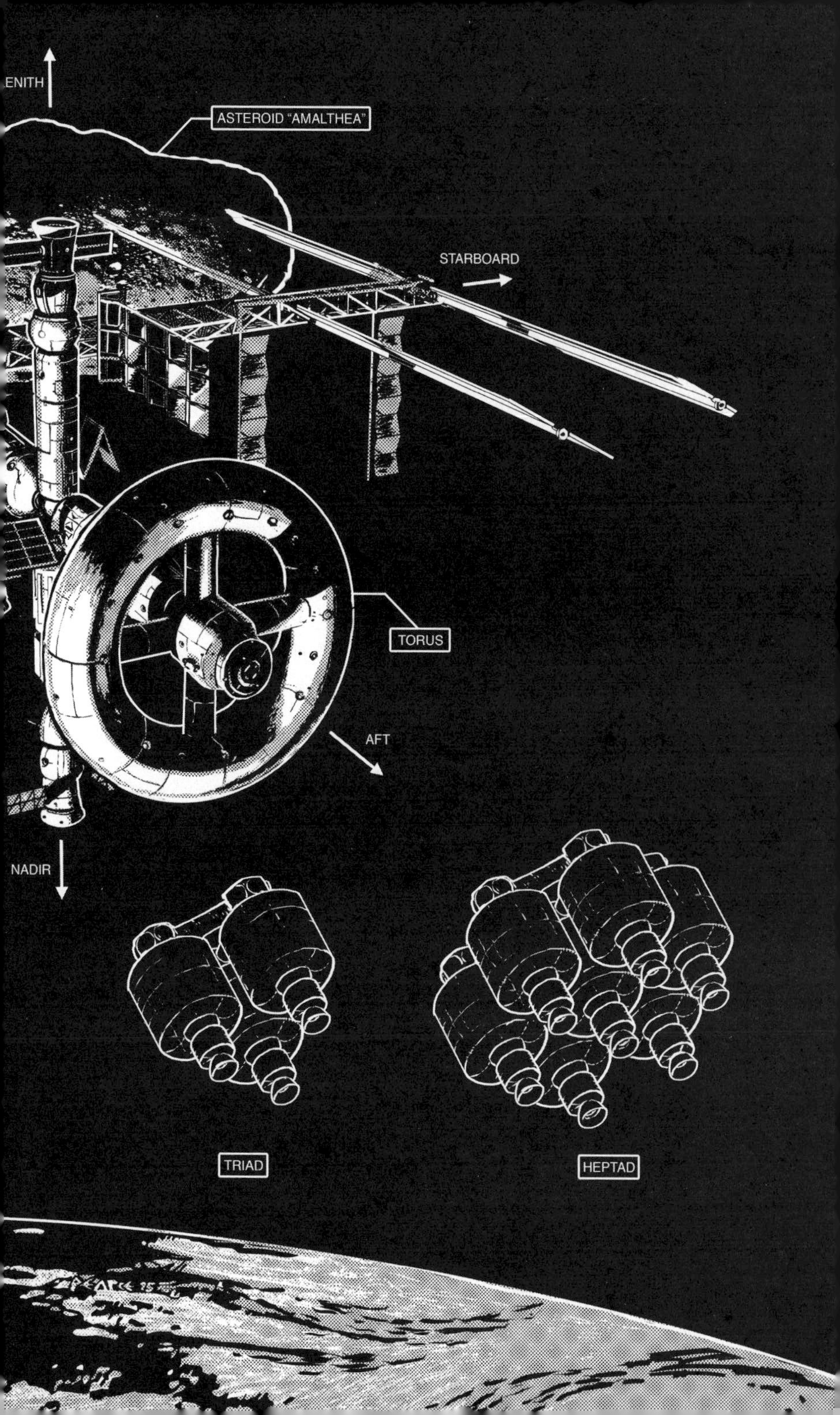
ENITH
ASTEROID "AMALTHEA"
STARBOARD
TORUS
AFT
NADIR
TRIAD
HEPTAD

About the Author

NEAL STEPHENSON is the author of *Reamde, Anathem,* and the three-volume historical epic the Baroque Cycle (*Quicksilver, The Confusion,* and *The System of the World*), as well as *Cryptonomicon, The Diamond Age, Snow Crash,* and *Zodiac*. He lives in Seattle, Washington.